Cirencester
Fosse Way Ca
Stroud Road
Cirencester
GL7 1XA

KT-475-045
cirencester
college
a beacon college

TITUS GROAN

Mervyn Peake was born in 1911 in Kuling, Central Southern China, where his father was a medical missionary. Within a year, the family moved to the Northern city of Tientsin. Peake was educated at Tientsin Grammar School then at Eltham College in South East London. During the Second World War, whilst serving with the army, he established a reputation as a gifted book illustrator with his pictures for *Ride a Cock Horse* (1940), *The Hunting of the Snark* (1941) and *The Rime of the Ancient Mariner* (1943). *Titus Groan* was published in 1946 and was followed, in 1950, by *Gormenghast* and the last time of the Gormenghast saga, *Titus Alone*, was published in 1959. His other works include *Shapes and Sounds* (1941), *Rhymes Without Reason* (1944), *Letters from a Lost Uncle* (1948) and *Mr Pye* (1953) and a play, *The Wit to Woo* (1957). He died in 1968.

Cirencester College, GL7 1XA
Telephone: 01285 640994

350117

C013998708

cirencester
college
a beacon college

BY MERVYN PEAKE

Titus Groan
Gormenghast
Titus Alone

Shapes and Sounds
The Craft of the Lead Pencil
Letters from a Lost Uncle
Mr Pye
Peake's Progress

Poems
Rhymes Without Reason
The Glassblowers
The Rhyme of the Flying Bomb

For children
Captain Slaughterboard Drops Anchor

Mervyn Peake

TITUS GROAN

WITH AN INTRODUCTION BY
Anthony Burgess

Vintage

Random House, 20 Vauxhall Bridge Road,
London SW1V 2SA

Random House Australia (Pty) Limited
20 Alfred Street, Milsons Point, Sydney
New South Wales 2061, Australia

Random House New Zealand Limited
18 Poland Road, Glenfield,
Auckland 10, New Zealand

Random House (Pty) Limited
Isle of Houghton, Je Jubilee Road, Parktown 2193, South Africa

VINTAGE

Published by Vintage 1998

10 9

Copyright © The Estate of Mervyn Peake 1968

This book is sold subject to the condition that it shall not, by way of trade or otherwise, be lent, resold, hired out, or otherwise circulated without the publisher's prior consent in any form of binding or cover other than that in which it is published and without a similar condition including this condition being imposed on the subsequent purchaser

First published in Great Britain by

HAMPSHIRE COUNTY LIBRARY

C013998708	
HJ	02/10/2007
F	£7.99
9780749394929	

The Random House Group Limited Reg. No. 954009

www.randomhouse.co.uk

A CIP catalogue record for this book
is available from the British Library

ISBN 0 7493 9492 7

Papers used by Random House are natural, recyclable products made from wood grown in sustainable forests. The manufacturing processes conform to the environmental regulations of the country of origin

Printed and bound in Great Britain by
Bookmarque Ltd, Croydon, Surrey

Dost thou love picking meat? Or would'st thou see
A man in the clouds, and have him speak to thee?

BUNYAN

CONTENTS

Introduction BY ANTHONY BURGESS	9
THE HALL OF THE BRIGHT CARVINGS	15
THE GREAT KITCHEN	25
SWELTER	31
THE STONE LANES	39
'THE SPY-HOLE'	46
FUCHSIA	51
'TALLOW AND BIRDSEED'	54
A GOLD RING FOR TITUS	58
SEPULCHRAVE	62
PRUNESQUALLOR'S KNEE-CAP	68
THE ATTIC	77
'MRS SLAGG BY MOONLIGHT'	86
KEDA	94
'FIRST BLOOD'	97
'ASSEMBLAGE'	107
'TITUS IS CHRISTENED'	115
MEANS OF ESCAPE	125
'A FIELD OF FLAGSTONES'	128
'OVER THE ROOFSCAPE'	131
'NEAR AND FAR'	136
'DUST AND IVY'	143
'THE BODY BY THE WINDOW'	145
'ULLAGE OF SUNFLOWER'	153
SOAP FOR GREASEPAINT	157
AT THE PRUNESQUALLORS	166
A GIFT OF THE GAB	181
WHILE THE OLD NURSE DOZES	188
FLAY BRINGS A MESSAGE	196
THE LIBRARY	202
IN A LIME-GREEN LIGHT	209
REINTRODUCING THE TWINS	213
'THE FIR-CONES'	223

KEDA AND RANTEL   231
THE ROOM OF ROOTS   244
'INKLINGS OF GLORY'   254
'PREPARATIONS FOR ARSON'   262
THE GROTTO   269
KNIVES IN THE MOON   281
'THE SUN GOES DOWN AGAIN'   285
'MEANWHILE'   293
'THE BURNING'   303
AND HORSES TOOK THEM HOME   319
SWELTER LEAVES HIS CARD   325
THE UN-EARTHING OF BARQUENTINE   329
FIRST REPERCUSSIONS   334
SOURDUST IS BURIED   337
THE TWINS ARE RESTIVE   341
'HALF-LIGHT'   345
A ROOF OF REEDS   348
'FEVER'   353
FAREWELL   357
EARLY ONE MORNING   360
A CHANGE OF COLOUR   369
A BLOODY CHEEKBONE   376
THE TWINS AGAIN   382
THE DARK BREAKFAST   387
THE REVERIES   392
HERE AND THERE   402
PRESAGE   407
IN PREPARATION FOR VIOLENCE   411
BLOOD AT MIDNIGHT   418
GONE   439
THE ROSES WERE STONES   441
'BARQUENTINE AND STEERPIKE'   447
BY GORMENGHAST LAKE   455
COUNTESS GERTRUDE   477
THE APPARITION   478
THE EARLING   484
MR ROTTCODD AGAIN   497

INTRODUCTION

by Anthony Burgess

THE middle and late nineteen-forties saw the appearance of a number of British works of literature which were quick to assume the status of 'classics' — meaning eloquent, authoritative, definitive statements begotten by an epoch but speaking for more than that epoch. All who beguiled the bad days of the end of the war and the start of the peace by reading *Four Quartets, The Unquiet Grave, Brideshead Revisited, The Loved One, Animal Farm* and *Nineteen Eighty-Four*, were aware that these books were only able to say what they did about the human permanencies because of the urgency enforced by the times. They all have in common the concise presentation of a world — Connolly's France, Waugh's alternatives of Catholic order and necropolitan despair, Orwell's two dystopias, Eliot's mystical 'still point' where history is redeemed by eternity. These worlds are built round a separable idea, which may be summed up as man's impotence to be good or happy without cherishing the values the war nearly quelled for ever. One book, however, resisted and still resists the shelling-out of a central sermon or warning. The world created in *Titus Groan* is neither better nor worse than this one: it is merely different. It has absorbed our history, culture and rituals and then stopped dead, refusing to move, self-feeding, self-motivating, self-enclosed. This is the world of Gormenghast.

Titus Groan, the first novel in a trilogy, appeared in 1946. Its author, Mervyn Peake, was then thirty-five. Critical response to the book was very favourable, in some instances ecstatic. Peake continued the fortunes of his hero and the elaboration of his hero's world in *Gormenghast* (1950) and *Titus Alone* (1959). Fine though these sequels are, they could not repeat the impact of the first book: 1946, year of austerity, was very ready for imaginative feasts. But, despite the praise of critics, *Titus Groan* never reached the widest possible public; it was destined to be something of a coterie obsession. Peake makes few appearances in histories of modern fiction, and one can see why. Unlike the vaunted post-war names, he does not seek – in his subject-matter – to probe topical themes like race, class and homosexuality or advance the frontiers of what we call the contemporary consciousness; in technique, he appears to look back rather than forward. His books nourish the private imagination; they do not exemplify the development of an art.

Peake has been praised, but he has also been mistrusted. His prose works are not easily classifiable: they are unique as, say, the books of Peacock or Lovecraft are unique. Moreover, he has too many talents: he is a fine poet and a highly original draughtsman. The Peake style in book illustration is inimitable, and it has been greatly imitated. He has, in his total mastery of the literary as well as the pictorial art, only one peer – Wyndham Lewis. Their aims in both arts could not be more dissimilar, but Peake and Lewis come together in an approach to descriptive writing which owes a great deal to the draughtsman's trade. If their books seem slow-moving, that is because of the immense solidity of their visual contents, the lack of interest in time and the compensatory obsession with filling up space. *Titus Groan* is aggressively three-dimensional. Look at the opening description of Gormenghast, where the term 'a certain ponderous architectural quality' exactly conveys what we are in for. But around the solidity is an extra dimension, one of magic, showing the poet as well as the draughtsman: 'This tower, patched unevenly with black ivy, arose like a mutilated finger from among the fists of knuckled masonry and pointed blasphemously at heaven.'

This sounds like 'Gothic' writing, but the term is inadequate. As we read *Titus Groan*, we seem to be given clues directing us towards the daylight of a literary category, but all the keys change into red herrings. Take the names of the characters, for instance – Nettel ('the octogenarian who lived in the tower above the rusting armoury'); Rottcodd, curator of the Hall of the Bright Carvings; Flay, Swelter, Steerpike, Mrs Slagg, Prunesquallor. These are fitting for a Peacock novel, for Dickens or for a comic children's story. They are farcical, but the mood is not one of easy laughter or even of airy fantasy: the ponderous architectural quality holds everything down, and we have to take the characters very seriously, despite their names. Nor is it appropriate to think in terms of a gallery of glorious eccentrics (a very British concept). Nobody flies away from a centre of normality; everybody belongs to a system built on very rigid rules.

The estate of Gormenghast is sustained by tradition and ritual. Lord Sepulchrave, the father of Titus, is instructed daily by Sourdust, lord of the library, in the acts he must perform. These are laid down in ancient books: 'the exact times; the garments to be worn for each occasion and the symbolic gestures to be used'. The whole ritualistic system is only properly understood by Sourdust – 'the technicalities demanding the devotion of a lifetime, though the sacred spirit of tradition implied by the daily manifestations was understood by all.' This same sacred spirit operates at all levels. Thus, the Great Kitchen is kept clean by eighteen men called the Grey Scrubbers, automata whose calling is predestined and hereditary. But it is out of this kitchen that a revolutionary force emerges – the youth Steerpike who, on his own admission, has 'a disrespectful nature'. He calls the Countess of Groan, that great lady who lives in a sea of white cats, 'the old Bunch of Rags'; he even calls the sun 'the old treacle bun'. Pulling the legs off a stagbeetle, slowly, one by one, he says: 'Equality is the great thing, equality is *everything*.' The worn-out radical arguments sound fresh and sinister in this closed world: 'Don't you think it's wrong if some people have to work all their lives for a little money to exist on while others never do any work and live in luxury?' Steerpike is one of the destroyers. He burns the library, killing its lord and sending Titus's father mad. There is a season of violence and murder. But Gormenghast remains, and the Warden of the Immemorial Rites proclaims Titus its seventy-seventh earl.

The book ends with its titular hero not yet two years old, but there is plenty of time for him: we have finished a mere third of the tripartite epic. And it is as we near the end of *Titus*

Groan that we realize the propriety of applying the term 'epic' in an exact sense. The book is closer to ancient pagan romance than to traditional British fiction. The doomed ritual lord, the emergent hero, the castle, the hall of retainers, the mountain, the lake, the twisted trees, the strange creatures, the violent knives, the dark and the foreboding belong (however qualified by tea, muffins, tobacco and sherry wine) to a prehistoric England. And the magnificence of the language denotes an epic concept.

It is difficult, in post-war English writing, to get away with big rhetorical gestures. Peake manages it because, with him, grandiloquence never means diffuseness; there is no musical emptiness in the most romantic of his descriptions; he is always exact.

The roof of the Twisted Woods reflected the staring circle in a phosphorescent network of branches that undulated in the lower slopes of Gormenghast Mountain .... Every blade of the grass was of consequence, and the few scattered stones held an authority that made their solid, separate marks upon the brain – each one with its own unduplicated shape: each rising brightly from the ink of its own spilling.

Occasionally, as in the book's peroration, he seems to go too far:

Through honeycombs of stone would now be wandering the passions in their clay. There would be tears and there would be strange laughter. Fierce births and deaths beneath umbrageous ceilings ... And there shall be a flame-green daybreak soon. And love itself will cry for insurrection!

But context is everything. The whole book is a gesture only too well aware that it goes too far; there is a certain built-in self-mockery, most evidently proclaimed in the grotesque names and titles. We are asked to accept conventions that it is impossible to take seriously, but within those conventions the blood is genuinely moved or chilled. The husky purr of the Countess, her heavy body decked, thick as foliage, with birds, conveys a shudder authentic enough: 'In Titus it's all centred. Stone and mountain – the Blood and the Observance. Let them touch him.

For every hair that's hurt I'll stop a heart. If grace I have when turbulence is over – so be it; and if not – what then?'

It is a complex book in that it evokes many layers of response: the sophisticated pleasure in consummate artifice, the more naive enjoyment proper to a rather archaic romance, horror which is qualified by disbelief, a kind of 'camp' titillation, self-indulgence in 'Gothic' atmosphere, a genuine aesthetic elation induced by language finely used. It is an intellectual book, in which wit – in the old sense of cerebral play – operates at times when we expect only the nerves to be engaged: 'The Thing scraped the ceiling with its head and moved forward noiselessly in one piece. Having no human possibility of height, it had *no* height. It was not a tall ghost – it was immeasurable; Death walking like an element.' One is always aware of the cool control of the author's intelligence, even in the most romantic flights, maintaining, like an estate generator, the imagined world and excluding the real one. But is the real one totally excluded?

We have to go back to the year of the book's first appearance, the first year after a long and horrifying war, before we can answer that question. The attaching of a calf's skull to dead Sourdust's vertebrae, the cat's claws ripping a 'crimson wedge' from Steerpike's cheek below the right eye, the fight between Flay and Swelter in the Hall of Spiders – these are not gratuitous Gothicisms so much as reflections out of an era of horrors. The burning of hundreds of years of tradition and the madness of an earl deprived of his sustaining props of ritual – these seem to be symbols of the end of true, historical, centuries of order. But it would be dangerous to search too earnestly for the allegorical in *Titus Groan*. It remains essentially a work of the closed imagination, in which a world parallel to our own is presented in almost paranoiac denseness of detail. But the madness is illusory, and control never falters. It is, if you like, a rich wine of fancy chilled by the intellect to just the right temperature. There is no really close relative to it in all our prose literature. It is uniquely brilliant, and we are right to call it a modern classic.

THE HALL OF THE BRIGHT CARVINGS

GORMENGHAST, that is, the main massing of the original stone,
taken by itself would have displayed a certain ponderous architectural quality were it possible to have ignored the circum-
fusion of those mean dwellings that swarmed like an epidemic
around its outer walls. They sprawled over the sloping earth,
each one half way over its neighbour until, held back by the
castle ramparts, the innermost of these hovels laid hold on
the great walls, clamping themselves thereto like limpets to a
rock. These dwellings, by ancient law, were granted this chill
intimacy with the stronghold that loomed above them. Over
their irregular roofs would fall throughout the seasons, the
shadows of time-eaten buttresses, of broken and lofty turrets,
and, most enormous of all, the shadow of the Tower of Flints.
This tower, patched unevenly with black ivy, arose like a mutilated finger from among the fists of knuckled masonry and
pointed blasphemously at heaven. At night the owls made of it
an echoing throat; by day it stood voiceless and cast its long
shadow.

Very little communication passed between the denizens of
these outer quarters and those who lived *within* the walls, save
when, on the first June morning of each year, the entire population of the clay dwellings had sanction to enter the Grounds in
order to display the wooden carvings on which they had been
working during the year. These carvings, blazoned in strange
colour, were generally of animals or figures and were treated in
a highly stylized manner peculiar to themselves. The competi-
tion among them to display the finest object of the year was
bitter and rabid. Their sole passion was directed, once their days
of love had guttered, on the production of this wooden sculpture, and among the muddle of huts at the foot of the outer
wall, existed a score of creative craftsmen whose position as
leading carvers gave them pride of place among the shadows.

At one point *within* the Outer Wall, a few feet from the
earth, the great stones of which the wall itself was constructed,

jutted forward in the form of a massive shelf stretching from east to west for about two hundred to three hundred feet. These protruding stones were painted white, and it was upon this shelf that on the first morning of June the carvings were ranged every year for judgement by the Earl of Groan. Those works judged to be the most consummate, and there were never more than three chosen, were subsequently relegated to the Hall of the Bright Carvings.

Standing immobile throughout the day, these vivid objects, with their fantastic shadows on the wall behind them shifting and elongating hour by hour with the sun's rotation, exuded a kind of darkness for all their colour. The air between them was turgid with contempt and jealousy. The craftsmen stood about like beggars, their families clustered in silent groups. They were uncouth and prematurely aged. All radiance gone.

The carvings that were left unselected were burned the same evening in the courtyard below Lord Groan's western balcony, and it was customary for him to stand there at the time of the burning and to bow his head silently as if in pain, and then as a gong beat thrice from within, the three carvings to escape the flames would be brought forth in the moonlight. They were stood upon the balustrade of the balcony in full view of the crowd below, and the Earl of Groan would call for their authors to come forward. When they had stationed themselves immediately beneath where he was standing, the Earl would throw down to them the traditional scrolls of vellum, which, as the writings upon them verified, permitted these men to walk the battlements above their cantonment at the full moon of each alternate month. On these particular nights, from a window in the southern wall of Gormenghast, an observer might watch the minute moonlit figures whose skill had won for them this honour which they so coveted, moving to and fro along the battlements.

Saving this exception of the day of carvings, and the latitude permitted to the most peerless, there was no other opportunity for those who lived within the walls to know of these 'outer' folk, nor in fact were they of interest to the 'inner' world, being submerged within the shadows of the great walls.

They were all-but forgotten people: the breed that was re-membered with a start, or with the unreality of a recrudescent dream. The day of carvings alone brought them into the sunlight and reawakened the memory of former times. For as far back as even Nettel, the octogenarian who lived in the tower above the rusting armoury, could remember, the ceremony had been held. Innumerable carvings had smouldered to ashes in obedience to the law, but the choicest were still housed in the Hall of the Bright Carvings.

This hall which ran along the top storey of the north wing was presided over by the curator, Rottcodd, who, as no one ever visited the room, slept during most of his life in the hammock he had erected at the far end. For all his dozing, he had never been known to relinquish the feather duster from his grasp; the duster with which he would perform one of the only two regular tasks which appeared to be necessary in that long and silent hall, namely to flick the dust from the Bright Carvings.

As objects of beauty, these works held little interest to him and yet in spite of himself he had become attached in a propinquital way to a few of the carvings. He would be more than thorough when dusting the Emerald Horse. The black-and-olive Head which faced it across the boards and the Piebald Shark were also his especial care. Not that there were any on which the dust was allowed to settle.

Entering at seven o'clock, winter and summer, year in and year out, Rottcodd would disengage himself of his jacket and draw over his head a long grey overall which descended shapelessly to his ankles. With his feather duster tucked beneath his arm, it was his habit to peer sagaciously over his glasses down the length of the hall. His skull was dark and small like a corroded musket bullet and his eyes behind the gleaming of his glasses were the twin miniatures of his head. All three were constantly on the move, as though to make up for the time they spent asleep, the head wobbling in a mechanical way from side to side when Mr Rottcodd walked, and the eyes, as though taking their cue from the parent sphere to which they were attached, peering here, there, and everywhere at nothing in particular. Having peered quickly over his glasses on entering and having repeated the performance along the length of the north wing after enveloping himself in his overall, it was the custom of Rottcodd to relieve his left armpit of the feather duster, and with that weapon raised, to advance towards the first of the carvings on his right hand side, without more ado. Being on the top floor of the north wing, this hall was not in any real sense a hall at all, but was more in the nature of a loft. The only window was at its far end, and opposite the door through which Rottcodd would enter from the upper body of the building. It gave little light. The shutters were invariably lowered. The Hall of the Bright Carvings was illumined night and day by seven great candelabra suspended from the ceiling at intervals of nine feet. The candles were never allowed to fail or even to gutter, Rottcodd himself seeing to their replenishment before retiring at nine o'clock in the evening. There was a stock of white candles in the small dark ante-room beyond the door of the hall, where also were kept ready for use Rottcodd's overall, a huge visitors' book, white with dust, and a step-ladder. There were no chairs or tables, nor indeed any furniture save the hammock at the window end where Mr Rottcodd slept. The boarded floor was white with dust which, so assiduously kept from the carvings, had no alternative resting place and had collected deep and ash-like, accumulating especially in the four corners of the hall.

Having flicked at the first carving on his right, Rottcodd would move mechanically down the long phalanx of colour standing a moment before each carving, his eyes running up and down it and all over it, and his head wobbling knowingly on his neck before he introduced his feather duster. Rottcodd was unmarried. An aloofness and even a nervousness was apparent on first acquaintance and the ladies held a peculiar horror for him. His, then, was an ideal existence, living alone day and night in a long loft. Yet occasionally, for one reason or another, a servant or a member of the household would make an unexpected appearance and startle him with some question appertaining to ritual, and then the dust would settle once more in the hall and on the soul of Mr Rottcodd.

What were his reveries as he lay in his hammock with his

dark bullet head tucked in the crook of his arm? What would he be dreaming of, hour after hour, year after year? It is not easy to feel that any great thoughts haunted his mind nor — in spite of the sculpture whose bright files surged over the dust in narrowing perspective like the highway for an emperor – that Rottcodd made any attempt to avail himself of his isolation, but rather that he was enjoying the solitude for its Own Sake, with, at the back of his mind, the dread of an intruder.

One humid afternoon a visitor *did* arrive to disturb Rottcodd as he lay deeply hammocked, for his siesta was broken sharply by a rattling of the door handle which was apparently performed in lieu of the more popular practice of knocking at the panels. The sound echoed down the long room and then settled into the fine dust on the boarded floor. The sunlight squeezed itself between the thin cracks of the window blind. Even on a hot, stifling, unhealthy afternoon such as this, the blinds were down and the candlelight filled the room with an incongruous radiance. At the sound of the door handle being rattled Rottcodd sat up suddenly. The thin bands of moted light edging their way through the shutters barred his dark head with the brilliance of the outer world. As he lowered himself over the hammock, it wobbled on his shoulders, and his eyes darted up and down the door returning again and again after their rapid and precipitous journeys to the agitations of the door handle. Gripping his feather duster in his right hand, Rottcodd began to advance down the bright avenue, his feet giving rise at each step to little clouds of dust. When he had at last reached the door the handle had ceased to vibrate. Lowering himself suddenly to his knees he placed his right eye at the keyhole, and controlling the oscillation of his head and the vagaries of his left eye (which was for ever trying to dash up and down the vertical surface of the door), he was able by dint of concentration to observe, within three inches of his keyholed eye, an eye which was *not* his, being not only of a different colour to his own iron marble but being, which is more convincing, on the other side of the door. This third eye which was going through the same performance as the one belonging to Rottcodd, belonged to Flay, the taciturn servant of Sepulchrave, Earl of Gormenghast. For

Flay to be four rooms horizontally or one floor vertically away from his lordship was a rare enough thing in the castle. For him to be absent at all from his master's side was abnormal, yet here apparently on this stifling summer afternoon was the eye of Mr Flay at the outer keyhole of the Hall of the Bright Carvings, and presumably the rest of Mr Flay was joined on behind it. On mutual recognition the eyes withdrew simultaneously and the brass doorknob rattled again in the grip of the visitor's hand. Rottcodd turned the key in the lock and the door opened slowly.

Mr Flay appeared to clutter up the doorway as he stood revealed, his arms folded, surveying the smaller man before him in an expressionless way. It did not look as though such a bony face as his could give normal utterance, but rather that instead of sounds, something more brittle, more ancient, something dryer would emerge, something perhaps more in the nature of a splinter or a fragment of stone. Nevertheless, the harsh lips parted. 'It's me,' he said, and took a step forward into the room, his knee joints cracking as he did so. His passage across a room – in fact his passage through life – was accompanied by these cracking sounds, one per step, which might be likened to the breaking of dry twigs.

Rottcodd, seeing that it was indeed he, motioned him to advance by an irritable gesture of the hand and closed the door behind him.

Conversation was never one of Mr Flay's accomplishments and for some time he gazed mirthlessly ahead of him, and then, after what seemed an eternity to Rottcodd he raised a bony hand and scratched himself behind the ear. Then he made his second remark, 'Still here, eh?' he said, his voice forcing its way out of his face.

Rottcodd, feeling presumably that there was little need to answer such a question, shrugged his shoulders and gave his eyes the run of the ceiling.

Mr Flay pulled himself together and continued: 'I said still here, eh, Rottcodd?' He stared bitterly at the carving of the Emerald Horse. 'You're still here, eh?'

'I'm invariably here,' said Rottcodd, lowering his gleaming glasses and running his eyes all over Mr Flay's visage. 'Day in, day out, invariably. Very hot weather. Extremely stifling. Did you want anything?'

'Nothing,' said Flay and he turned towards Rottcodd with something menacing in his attitude. 'I want *nothing*.' He wiped the palms of his hands on his hips where the dark cloth shone like silk.

Rottcodd flicked ash from his shoes with the feather duster and tilted his bullet head. 'Ah,' he said in a non-committal way.

'You say "ah",' said Flay, turning his back on Rottcodd and beginning to walk down the coloured avenue, 'but I tell you, it is more than "ah".'

'Of course,' said Rottcodd. 'Much more, I dare say. But I fail to understand. I am a Curator.' At this he drew his body up to full height and stood on the tips of his toes in the dust.

'A what?' said Flay, straggling above him for he had returned. 'A curator?'

'That is so,' said Rottcodd, shaking his head.

Flay made a hard noise in his throat. To Rottcodd it signified a complete lack of understanding and it annoyed him that the man should invade his province.

'Curator,' said Flay, after a ghastly silence, 'I will tell you something. I know something. Eh?'

'Well?' said Rottcodd.

'I'll tell you,' said Flay. 'But first, what day is it? What month, and what year is it? Answer me.'

Rottcodd was puzzled at this question, but he was becoming a little intrigued. It was so obvious that the bony man had something on his mind, and he replied, 'It is the eighth day of the eighth month, I am uncertain about the year. But why?'

In a voice almost inaudible Flay repeated 'The eighth day of the eighth month'. His eyes were almost transparent as though in a country of ugly hills one were to find among the harsh rocks two sky-reflecting lakes. 'Come here,' he said, 'come closer, Rottcodd, I will tell you. You don't understand Gormenghast, what happens in Gormenghast – the things that happen – no, no. Below you, that's where it all is, under this north wing. What are these things up here? These wooden things? No use now. Keep them, but no use now. Everything is moving.

The castle is moving. Today, first time for years he's alone, his Lordship. Not in my sight.' Flay bit at his knuckle. 'Bedchamber of Ladyship, that's where he is. Lordship is beside himself: won't have me, won't let me in to see the New One. The New One. He's come. He's downstairs. I haven't seen him.' Flay bit at the corresponding knuckle on the other hand as though to balance the sensation. 'No one's been in. Of course not. I'll be next. The birds are lined along the bedrail. Ravens, starlings, all the perishers, and the white rook. There's a kestrel; claws through the pillow. My lady feeds them with crusts. Grain and crusts. Hardly seen her new-born. Heir to Gormenghast. Doesn't look at him. But my lord keeps staring. Seen him through the grating. Needs me. Won't let me in. Are you listening?'

Mr Rottcodd certainly was listening. In the first place he had never heard Mr Flay talk so much in his life before, and in the second place the news that a son had been born at long last to the ancient and historic house of Groan was, after all, an interesting tit-bit for a curator living alone on the upper storey of the desolate north wing. Here was something with which he could occupy his mind for some time to come. It was true, as Mr Flay pointed out, that he, Rottcodd, could not possibly feel the pulse of the castle as he lay in his hammock, for in point of fact Rottcodd had not even suspected that an heir was on its way. His meals came up in a miniature lift through darkness from the servants' quarters many floors below and he slept in the ante-room at night and consequently he was completely cut off from the world and all its happenings. Flay had brought him real news. All the same he disliked being disturbed even when information of this magnitude was brought. What was passing through the bullet-shaped head was a question concerning Mr Flay's entry. Why had Flay, who never in the normal course of events would have raised an eyebrow to acknowledge his presence – why had he now gone to the trouble of climbing to a part of the castle so foreign to him? And to force a conversation on a personality as unexpansive as his own. He ran his eyes over Mr Flay in his own peculiarly rapid way and surprised himself by saying suddenly, 'To what may I attribute your presence, Mr Flay?'

'What?' said Flay, 'what's that?' He looked down on Rott-codd and his eyes became glassy.

In truth Mr Flay had surprised himself. Why, indeed, he thought to himself, had he troubled to tell Rottcodd the news which meant so much to him? Why Rottcodd, of all people? He continued staring at the curator for some while, and the more he stood and pondered the clearer it became to him that the question he had been asked was, to say the very least, un-comfortably pertinent.

The little man in front of him had asked a simple and forth-right question. It had been rather a poser. He took a couple of shambling steps towards Mr Rottcodd and then, forcing his hands into his trouser pockets, turned round very slowly on one heel.

'Ah,' he said at last, 'I see what you mean, Rottcodd – I see what you mean.'

Rottcodd was longing to get back to his hammock and enjoy the luxury of being quite alone again, but his eye travelled even more speedily towards the visitor's face when he heard the remark. Mr Flay had said that he saw what Rottcodd had meant. Had he really? Very interesting. What, by the way, *had* he meant? What precisely was it that Mr Flay had seen? He flecked an imaginary speck of dust from the gilded head of a dryad.

'You are interested in the birth below?' he inquired.

Flay stood for a while as though he had heard nothing, but after a few minutes it became obvious he was thunderstruck. 'Interested!' he cried in a deep, husky voice, 'Interested! The child is a Groan. An authentic male Groan. Challenge to Change! No *Change*, Rottcodd. No Change!'

'Ah,' said Rottcodd. 'I see your point, Mr Flay. But his lord-ship was not dying?'

'No,' said Mr Flay, 'he was not dying, but *teeth lengthen*!' and he strode to the wooden shutters with long, slow heron-like paces, and the dust rose behind him. When it had settled Rott-codd could see his angular parchment-coloured head leaning itself against the lintel of the window.

Mr Flay could not feel entirely satisfied with his answer to

Rottcodd's question covering the reason for his appearance in the Hall of the Bright Carvings. As he stood there by the window the question repeated itself to him again and again. Why Rottcodd? Why on earth Rottcodd? And yet he knew that directly he heard of the birth of the heir, when his dour nature had been stirred so violently that he had found himself itching to communicate his enthusiasm to another being – from that moment Rottcodd had leapt to his mind. Never of a communicative or enthusiastic nature he had found it difficult even under the emotional stress of the advent to inform Rottcodd of the facts. And, as has been remarked, he had surprised even himself not only for having unburdened himself at all, but for having done so in so short a time.

He turned, and saw that the Curator was standing wearily by the Piebald Shark, his small cropped round head moving to and fro like a bird's, and his hands clasped before him with the feather duster between his fingers. He could see that Rottcodd was politely waiting for him to go. Altogether Mr Flay was in a peculiar state of mind. He was surprised at Mr Rottcodd for being so unimpressed at the news, and he was surprised at himself for having brought it. He took from his pocket a vast watch of silver and held it horizontally on the flat of his palm. 'Must go,' he said awkwardly. 'Do you hear me, Rottcodd, I must go?'

'Good of you to call,' said Rottcodd. 'Will you sign your name in the visitors' book as you go out?'

'No! Not a visitor.' Flay brought his shoulders up to his ears. 'Been with lordship thirty-seven years. Sign a *book*,' he added contemptuously, and he spat into a far corner of the room.

'As you wish,' said Mr Rottcodd. 'It was to the section of the visitors' book devoted to the staff that I was referring.'

'No!' said Flay.

As he passed the curator on his way to the door he looked carefully at him as he came abreast, and the question rankled. Why? The castle was filled with the excitement of the nativity. All was alive with conjecture. There was no control. Rumour swept through the stronghold. Everywhere, in passage, archway, cloister, refectory, kitchen, dormitory, and hall it was the same. Why had he chosen the unenthusiastic Rottcodd? And then, in a flash he realized. He must have subconsciously known that the news would be new to no one else; that Rottcodd was virgin soil for his message, Rottcodd the curator who lived alone among the Bright Carvings was the only one on whom he could vent the tidings without jeopardizing his sullen dignity, and to whom although the knowledge would give rise to but little enthusiasm it would at least be new.

Having solved the problem in his mind and having realized in a dullish way that the conclusion was particularly mundane and uninspired, and that there was no question of his soul calling along the corridors and up the stairs to the soul of Rottcodd, Mr Flay in a thin straddling manner moved along the passages of the north wing and down the curve of stone steps that led to the stone quadrangle, feeling the while a curious disillusion, a sense of having suffered a loss of dignity, and a feeling of being thankful that his visit to Rottcodd had been unobserved and that Rottcodd himself was well hidden from the world in the Hall of the Bright Carvings.

THE GREAT KITCHEN

As Flay passed through the servants' archway and descended the twelve steps that led into the main corridor of the kitchen quarters, he became aware of an acute transformation of mood. The solitude of Mr Rottcodd's sanctum, which had been lingering in his mind, was violated. Here among the stone passages were all the symptoms of ribald excitement. Mr Flay hunched his bony shoulders and with his hands in his jacket pockets dragged them to the front so that only the black cloth divided his clenched fists. The material was stretched as though it would split at the small of his back. He stared mirthlessly to right and left and then advanced, his long spidery legs cracking as he shouldered his way through a heaving group of menials. They were guffawing to each other coarsely and one of them, evidently the wit, was contorting his face, as pliable as putty, into shapes that appeared to be independent of the skull, if indeed he had a skull beneath that elastic flesh. Mr Flay pushed past.

The corridor was alive. Clusters of aproned figures mixed and disengaged. Some were singing. Some were arguing and some were draped against the wall, quite silent from exhaustion, their hands dangling from their wrists or flapping stupidly to the beat of some kitchen catch-song. The clamour was pitiless. Technically this was more the spirit which Flay liked to see, or at all events thought to be more appropriate to the occasion. Rottcodd's lack of enthusiasm had shocked him and here, at any rate, the traditional observance of felicity at the birth of an heir to Gormenghast was being observed. But it would have been impossible for him to show any signs of enthusiasm himself when surrounded by it in others. As he moved along the crowded corridor and passed in turn the dark passages that led to the slaughter-house with its stench of fresh blood, the bakeries with their sweet loaves and the stairs that led down to the wine vaults and the underground network of the castle cellars, he felt a certain satisfaction at seeing how many of the roysterers staggered aside to let him pass, for his station as retainer-in-chief to his Lordship was commanding and his sour mouth and the frown that had made a permanent nest upon his jutting forehead were a warning.

It was not often that Flay approved of happiness in others. He saw in happiness the seeds of independence, and in independence the seeds of revolt. But on an occasion such as this it was different, for the spirit of convention was being rigorously adhered to, and in between his ribs Mr Flay experienced twinges of pleasure.

He had come to where, on his left, and halfway along the servants' corridor, the heavy wooden doors of the Great Kitchen stood ajar. Ahead of him, narrowing in dark perspective, for there were no windows, the rest of the corridor stretched silently away. It had no doors on either side and at the far end it was terminated by a wall of flints. This useless passage was, as might be supposed, usually deserted, but Mr Flay noticed that several figures were lying stretched in the shadows. At the same time he was momentarily deafened by a great bellowing and clattering and stamping.

As Mr Flay entered the Great Kitchen the steaming, airless concentration of a ghastly heat struck him. He felt that his body had received a blow. Not only was the normal sickening atmosphere of the kitchen augmented by the sun's rays streaming into the room at various points through the high windows, but, in the riot of the festivities, the fires had been banked dangerously. But Mr Flay realized that it was *right* that this should be as insufferable as it was. He even realized that the four grillers who were forcing joint after joint between the metal doors with their clumsy boots, until the oven began to give under the immoderate strain, were in key with the legitimate temper of the occasion. The fact that they had no idea what they were doing nor why they were doing it was irrelevant. The Countess had given birth; was this a moment for rational behaviour?

The walls of the vast room which were streaming with calid moisture, were built with grey slabs of stone and were the personal concern of a company of eighteen men known as the 'Grey Scrubbers'. It had been their privilege on reaching adolescence to discover that, being the sons of their fathers, their careers had been arranged for them and that stretching ahead of them lay their identical lives consisting of an unimaginative if praiseworthy duty. This was to restore, each morning to the great grey floor and the lofty walls of the kitchen a stainless complexion. On every day of the year from three hours before daybreak until about eleven o'clock, when the scaffolding and ladders became a hindrance to the cooks, the Grey Scrubbers fulfilled their hereditary calling. Through the character of their trade, their arms had become unusually powerful, and when they let their huge hands hang loosely at their sides, there was more than an echo of the simian. Coarse as these men appeared, they were an integral part of the Great Kitchen. Without the Grey Scrubbers something very earthy, very heavy, very real would be missing to any sociologist searching in that steaming room, for the completion of a circle of temperaments, a gamut of the lower human values.

Through daily proximity to the great slabs of stone, the faces of the Grey Scrubbers had become like slabs themselves. There was no expression whatever upon the eighteen faces, unless the lack of expression is in itself an expression. They were simply slabs that the Grey Scrubbers spoke from occasionally, stared from incessantly, heard with, hardly ever. They were traditionally deaf. The eyes were there, small and flat as coins, and the colour of the walls themselves, as though during the long hours of professional staring the grey stone had at last reflected itself indelibly once and for all. Yes, the eyes were there, thirty-six of them and the eighteen noses were there, and the lines of the mouths that resembled the harsh cracks that divided the stone slabs, they were there too. Although nothing physical was missing from any one of their eighteen faces yet it would be impossible to perceive the faintest sign of animation and, even if a basinful of their features had been shaken together and if each feature had been picked out at random and stuck upon some dummy-head of wax at any capricious spot or angle, it would have made no difference, for even the most fantastic, the most ingenious of arrangements could not have tempted into life a design whose component parts were dead. In all, counting the ears, which on occasion may be monstrously expressive, the one hundred and eight features were unable, at the best of times, to muster between them, individually or taken *en masse*, the faintest shadow of anything that might hint at the workings of what lay beneath.

Having watched the excitement developing around them in the Great Kitchen, and being unable to comprehend what it was all about for lack of hearing, they had up to the last hour or two been unable to enter into that festive spirit which had attacked the very heart and bowels of the kitchen staff.

But here and now, on this day of days, cognisant at last of the arrival of the new Lord, the eighteen Grey Scrubbers were lying side by side upon the flagstones beneath a great table, dead drunk to a man. They had done honour to the occasion and were out of the picture, having been rolled under the table one by one like so many barrels of ale, as indeed they were.

Through the clamour of the voices in the Great Kitchen that

rose and fell, that changed tempo, and lingered, until a strident rush or a wheezy slide of sound came to a new pause, only to be shattered by a hideous croak of laughter or a thrilled whisper, or a clearing of some coarse throat – through all this thick and interwoven skein of bedlam, the ponderous snoring of the Grey Scrubbers had continued as a recognizable theme of dolorous persistence.

In favour of the Grey Scrubbers it must be said that it was not until the walls and floor of the kitchen were shining from their exertions that they attacked the bungs as though unweaned. But it was not only they who had succumbed. The same unquestionable proof of loyalty could be observed in no less than forty members of the kitchen, who, like the Grey Scrubbers, recognizing the bottle as the true medium through which to externalize their affection for the family of Groan, were seeing visions and dreaming dreams.

Mr Flay, wiping away with the back of his claw-like hand the perspiration that had already gathered on his brow, allowed his eyes to remain a moment on the inert and foreshortened bodies of the inebriate Grey Scrubbers. Their heads were towards him, and were cropped to a gun-grey stubble. Beneath the table a shadow had roosted, and the rest of their bodies, receding in parallel lines, were soon devoured in the darkness. At first glance he had been reminded of nothing so much as a row of curled-up hedgehogs, and it was some time before he realized that he was regarding a line of prickly skulls. When he had satisfied himself on this point his eyes travelled sourly around the Great Kitchen. Everything was confusion, but behind the flux of the shifting figures and the temporary chaos of overturned mixing tables, of the floor littered with stockpots, basting pans, broken bowls and dishes, and oddments of food, Mr Flay could see the main fixtures in the room and keep them in his mind as a means of reference, for the kitchen swam before his eyes in a clammy mist. Divided by the heavy stone wall in which was situated a hatch of strong timber, was the *garde-manger* with its stacks of cold meat and hanging carcases and on the inside of the wall the spit. On a fixed table running along a length of the wall were huge bowls capable of holding fifty portions. The stock-pots were perpetually simmering, having boiled over, and the floor about them was a mess of sepia fluid and egg-shells that had been floating in the pots for the purpose of clearing the soup. The sawdust that was spread neatly over the floor each morning was by now kicked into heaps and soaked in the splashings of wine. And where scattered about the floor little blobs of fat had been rolled or trodden in, the sawdust stuck to them giving them the appearance of rissoles. Hanging along the dripping walls were rows of sticking knives and steels, boning knives, skinning knives and two-handed cleavers, and beneath them a twelve-foot by nine-foot chopping block, cross-hatched and hollowed by decades of long wounds.

On the other side of the room, to Mr Flay's left, a capacious enormous copper, a row of ovens and a narrow doorway acted as his landmarks. The doors of the ovens were flying wide and acid flames were leaping dangerously, as the fat that had been thrown into the fires bubbled and stank.

Mr Flay was in two minds. He hated what he saw, for of all the rooms in the castle, it was the kitchen he detested most, and for a very real reason; and yet a thrill in his scarecrow body made him aware of how right it all was. He could not, of course, analyse his feelings nor would the idea have occurred to him, but he was so much a part and parcel of Gormenghast that he could instinctively tell when the essence of its tradition was running in a true channel, powerfully and with no deviation.

But the fact that Mr Flay appreciated, as from the profoundest of motives, the vulgarity of the Great Kitchen in no way mitigated his contempt for the figures he saw before him as individuals. As he looked from one to another the satisfaction which he had at first experienced in seeing them collectively gave way to a detestation as he observed them piecemeal.

A prodigious twisted beam, warped into a spiral, floated, or so it seemed in the haze, across the breadth of the Great Kitchen. Here and there along its undersurface, iron hooks were screwed into its grain. Slung over it like sacks half filled with sawdust, so absolutely lifeless they appeared, were two pastry-cooks, an ancient *poissonnier*, a *rôtier* with legs so bandy as to describe a rugged circle, a red-headed *légumier*, and five *sauciers* with their green scarves around their necks. One of them near the far end from where Flay stood twitched a little, but apart from this all was stillness. They were very happy.

Mr Flay took a few paces and the atmosphere closed around him. He had stood by the door unobserved, but now as he came forward a roysterer leaping suddenly into the air caught hold of one of the hooks in the dark beam above them. He was suspended by one arm, a cretinous little man with a face of concentrated impudence. He must have possessed a strength out of all proportions to his size, for with the weight of his body hanging on the end of one arm he yet drew himself up so that his head reached the level of the iron hook. As Mr Flay passed beneath, the dwarf, twisting himself upside down with incredible speed, coiled his legs around the twisted beam and dropping the rest of himself vertically with his face a few inches from that of Mr Flay, grinned at him grotesquely with his head upside down, before Flay could do anything save come to an abrupt halt. The dwarf had then swung himself on to the beam again and was running along it on all fours with an agility more likely to be found in jungles than in kitchens.

A prodigious bellow outvoicing all cacophony caused him to turn his head away from the dwarf. Away to his left in the shade of a supporting pillar he could make out the vague unmistakable shape of what had really been at the back of his brain like a tumour, ever since he had entered the great kitchen.

SWELTER

THE chef of Gormenghast, balancing his body with difficulty upon a cask of wine, was addressing a group of apprentices in their striped and sodden jackets and small white caps. They clasped each other's shoulders for their support. Their adolescent faces steaming with the heat of the adjacent ovens were quite stupefied, and when they laughed or applauded the enormity above them, it was with a crazed and sycophantic fervour.

As Mr Flay approached to within a few yards of the cluster, another roar, such as he had heard a moment or two earlier, rolled into the heat above the wine-barrel.

The young scullions had heard this roar many times before but had never associated it with anything other than anger. At first, consequently, it had frightened them, but they had soon perceived that there was no irritation in its note today.

The chef, as he loomed over them, drunken, arrogant and pedantic, was enjoying himself.

As the apprentices swayed tipsily around the wine cask, their faces catching and losing the light that streamed through a high window, they also, in a delirious fashion – were enjoying themselves. The echoes died from the apparently reasonless bellow of the chief chef and the sagging circle about the barrel stamped its feet feverishly and gave high shrill cries of delight, for they had seen an inane smile evolving from the blur of the huge head above them. Never before had they enjoyed such latitude in the presence of the chef. They struggled to outdo one another in the taking of liberties unheard of hitherto. They vied for favours, screaming his name at the tops of their voices. They tried to catch his eye. They were very tired, very heavy and sick with the drink and the heat, but were living fiercely on their fuddled reserves of nervous energy. All saving one high-shouldered boy, who throughout the scene had preserved a moody silence. He loathed the figure above him and he despised his fellow-apprentices. He leaned against the shadowy side of the pillar, out of the chef's line of vision.

Mr Flay was annoyed, even on such a day, by the scene. Although approving in theory, in practice it seemed to him that the spectacle was unpleasant. He remembered, when he had first come across Swelter, how he and the chef had instantaneously entertained a mutual dislike, and how this antipathy festered. To Swelter it was irksome to see the bony straggly figure of Lord Sepulchrave's first servant in his kitchen at all, the only palliative to this annoyance being the opportunity which it afforded for the display of his superior wit at Mr Flay's expense.

Mr Flay entered Swelter's steaming province for one purpose

only. To prove to himself as much as to others, that he, as Lord Groan's personal attendant, would on no account be intimidated by any member of the staff.

To keep this fact well in front of his own mind, he made a tour of the servants' quarters every so often, never entering the kitchen, however, without a queasiness of stomach, never departing from it without a renewal of spleen.

The long beams of sunlight, which were reflected from the moist walls in a shimmering haze, had pranked the chef's body with blotches of ghost-light. The effect from below was that of a dappled volume of warm vague whiteness and of a grey that dissolved·into swamps of midnight – of a volume that towered and dissolved among the rafters. As occasion merited he supported himself against the stone pillar at his side and as he did so the patches of light shifted across the degraded whiteness of the stretched uniform he wore. When Mr Flay had first eyed him, the cook's head had been entirely in shadow. Upon it the tall cap of office rose coldly, a vague topsail half lost in a fitful sky. In the total effect there was indeed something of the galleon.

One of the blotches of reflected sunlight swayed to and fro across the paunch. This particular pool of light moving in a mesmeric manner backwards and forwards picked out from time to time a long red island of spilt wine. It seemed to leap forward from the mottled cloth when the light fastened upon it in startling contrast to the chiaroscuro and to defy the laws of tone. This ungarnished sign of Swelter's debauche, taking the swollen curve of linen, had somehow, to Mr Flay's surprise, a fascination. For a minute he watched it appear, and disappear to reappear again – a lozenge of crimson, as the body behind it swayed.

Another senseless bout of foot-stamping and screaming broke the spell, and lifting his eyes he scowled about him. Suddenly, for a moment, the memory of Mr Rottcodd in his dusty deserted hall stole into his consciousness and he was shocked to realize how much he had really preferred – to this inferno of time-hallowed revelry – the limp and seemingly disloyal self-sufficiency of the curator. He straddled his way to a vantage point, from where he could see and remain unseen, and from there he noticed that Swelter was steadying himself on his legs and with a huge soft hand making signs to the adolescents below him to hold their voices. Flay noticed how the habitual truculence of his tone and manner had today altered to something mealy, to a conviviality weighted with lead and sugar, a ghastly intimacy more dreadful than his most dreaded rages. His voice came down from the shadows in huge wads of sound, or like the warm, sick notes of some prodigous mouldering bell of felt.

His soft hand had silenced the seething of the apprentices and he allowed his thick voice to drop out of his face.

'Gallstones!' and in the dimness he flung his arms apart so that the buttons of his tunic were torn away, one of them whizzing across the room and stunning a cockroach on the opposite wall. 'Close your ranks and close your ranks and listen mosht attentivesome. Come closer then, my little sea of faces, come ever closer in, my little ones.'

The apprentices edged themselves forward, tripping and treading upon each other's feet, the foremost of them being wedged against the wine-barrel itself.

'Thatsh the way. Thatsh jusht the way,' said Swelter, leering down at them. 'Now we're quite a happly little family. Mosht shelect and advanced.'

He then slid a fat hand through a slit in his white garment of office and removed from a deep pocket a bottle. Plucking out the cork with his lips, that had gripped it with an uncanny muscularity, he poured half a pint down his throat without displacing the cork, for he laid a finger at the mouth of the bottle, so dividing the rush of wine into two separate spurts that shot adroitly into either cheek, and so, making contact at the back of his mouth, down his throat in one dull gurgle to those unmentionable gulches that lay below.

The apprentices screamed and stamped and tore at each other in an access of delight and of admiration.

The chef removed the cork and twisted it around between his thumb and forefinger and satisfying himself that it had remained perfectly dry during the operation, recorked the bottle and returned it through the slit into his pocket.

Again he put up his hand and silence was restored save for the heavy, excited breathing.

'Now tell me thish, my stenching cherubs. Tell me thish and tell me exshtra quickly, who am I? Now tell me exshtra quickly.'

'Swelter,' they cried, 'Swelter, sir! Swelter!'

'Is that *all* you know?' came the voice. 'Is that *all* you know, my little sea of faces? Silence now! and lishen well to me, chief chef of Gormenghast, man and boy forty years, fair and foul, rain or shine, sand and sawdust, hags and stags and all the resht of them done to a turn and spread with sauce of aloes and a dash of prickling pepper.'

'With a dash of prickling pepper,' yelled the apprentices hugging themselves and each other in turn. 'Shall we cook it, sir? We'll do it now, sir, and slosh it in the copper, sir, and stir it up. Oh! what a tasty dish, Sir, Oh! what a tasty dish!'

'Shilence,' roared the chef. 'Silensh, my fairy boys. Silence, my belching angels. Come closer here, come closer with your little creamy faces and I'll tell you who I am.'

The high-shouldered boy, who had taken no part in the excitement, pulled out a small pipe of knotted worm-wood and filled it deliberately. His mouth was quite expressionless, curving neither up nor down, but his eyes were dark and hot with a mature hatred. They were half closed but their eloquence smouldered through the lashes as he watched the figure on the barrel lean forward precariously.

'Now lishen well', continued the voice, 'and I'll tell you exactly who I am and then I'll shing to you a shong and you will know who's shinging to you, my ghastly little ineffectual fillets.'

'A song! A song!' came the shrill chorus.

'Firshtly,' said the chef leaning forward and dropping each confidential word like a cannon ball smeared with syrup. 'Firshtly, I am none other than Abiatha Swelter, which meansh, for you would not know, that I am the shymbol of both excellence and plenty. I am the *father* of exchellence and plenty. Who did I shay I was?'

'Abafer Swelter,' came the scream.

The chef leaned back on his swollen legs and drew the corners of his mouth down until they lost themselves among the shadows of his hot dewlaps.

'Abiatha,' he repeated slowly, stressing the central 'A'. 'Abiatha. What did I shay my name wash?'

'Abiatha,' came the scream again.

'Thatsh right, thatsh right. Abiatha. Are you lishening, my pretty vermin, are you lishening?'

The apprentices gave him to understand that they were listening very hard.

Before the chef continued he applied himself to the bottle once again. This time he held the glass neck between his teeth and tilting his head back until the bottle was vertical, drained it and spat it out over the heads of the fascinated throng. The sound of black glass smashing on the flagstones was drowned in screams of approval.

'Food,' said Swelter, 'is shelestial and drink is mosht entrancing – such flowers of flatulence. Sush gaseous buds. Come closer in, *steal* in, and I will shing. I will lift my sweetest heart into the rafters, and will shing to you a shong. An old shong of great shadness, a most dolorous piece. Come closer in.'

It was impossible for the apprentices to force themselves any closer to the chef, but they struggled and shouted for the song, and turned their glistening faces upwards.

'Oh what a pleasant lot of little joints you are,' said Swelter, peering at them and wiping his hands up and down his fat hips. 'What a very drippy lot of little joints. Oh yesh you are, but *so* underdone. Lishen cocks, I'll twisht your grandma's so shweetly in their graves. We'll make them turn, my dears, we'll make them turn – and what a turn for them, my own, and for the worms that nibble. Where's Steerpike?'

'Steerpike! Steerpike!' yelled the youths, the ones in front twisting their heads and standing upon their toes, the ones in the rear craning forward and peering about them. 'Steerpike! Steerpike! He's somewhere here, sir! Oh there he is sir! There he is sir! Behind the pillar sir!'

'Silence,' bellowed the chef, turning his gourd of a head in the direction of the pointed hands as the high-shouldered boy was pushed forward.

'Here he is, sir! Here he is, sir!'

The boy Steerpike looked impossibly small as he stood beneath the monstrous monument.

'I shall shing to you, Steerpike, to you,' whispered the cook, reeling and supporting himself with one hand against the stone pillar that was glistening with condensed heat, little trickles of moisture moving down its fluted sides. 'To you, the newcomer, the blue mummer and the slug of summer – to you the hideous, and insidious, and appallingly cretinous goat in a house of stenches.'

The apprentices rocked with joy.

'To you, only to you, my core of curdled cat-bile. To you alone, sho hearken diligentiums. Are you sharkening? Are you all lishening for this his how's it goesh. My shong of a hundred yearsh ago, my plaintivly mosht melancholic shong.'

Swelter seemed to forget he was about to sing, and after wiping the sweat from his hands on the head of a youth below him, peered for Steerpike again.

'And why to you, my ray of addled sunshine? Why to you aslone? Shtaking it for granted, my dear little Steerpike – taking it for more than for mosht granted, that you, a creature of lesh consequence than stoat's-blood, are sho far removal'd from anything approaching nature – yet tell me, more rather, don't tell me why your ears which musht originally have been deshigned for fly-papers, are, for shome reason butter known to yourself, kept imodeshtly unfurled. What do you proposhe to do next in thish batter? You move here and there on your little measly legs. I have sheen you at it. You breathe all over my kitchen. You look at thingsh with your insholent animal eyes. I've sheen you doing it. I have sheen you look at me. Your looking at me now. Shteerpike, my impatient love-bird, what doesh it all mean, and why should I shing for you?'

Swelter leaned back and seemed to be considering his own question a moment as he wiped his forehead with the sleeve of his forearm. But he waited for no reply and flung his pendulent arms out sideways and somewhere on the orbit of an immense arc something or other gave way.

Steerpike was not drunk. As he stood below Mr Swelter, he had nothing but contempt for the man who had but yesterday struck him across the head. He could do nothing, however, except stay where he was, prodded and nudged from behind by the excited minions, and wait.

The voice recurred from above. 'It is a shong, my Steerpike, to an imaginawary monshter, jusht like yourshelf if only you were a twifle bigger and more monshtrous shtill. It is a shong to a hard-hearted monshter sho lishen mosht shfixedly, my pretty wart. Closher, closher! Can't you come a little closher to a dirgeous mashterpeesh?'

The wine was beginning to redouble its subversive activity in the chef's brain. He was now supporting himself almost the whole of the while against the sweating pillar and was sagging hideously.

Steerpike stared up at him from under his high bony brow. The cook's eyes were protruding like bloodshot bubbles. One arm hung, a dead-weight, down the fluted surface of the support. The enormous area of the face had fallen loose. It glistened like a jelly.

A hole appeared in the face. Out of it came a voice that had suddenly become weaker.

'I am Shwelter,' it repeated, 'the great chef Abiatha Shwelter, scook to hish Lordshipsh, boardshipsh and all shorts of ships that shail on shlippery sheas. Abiafa Shwelter, man and boy and girls and ribbonsh, lots of kittensh, forty year of cold and shunny, where'sh the money, thick and hairy, I'm a fairy! I'm a shongshter! Lishen well, lishen well!'

Mr Swelter lowered his head downwards over his wine-raddled breast without moving his shoulders and made an effort to see whether his audience was sufficiently keyed up for his opening chords. But he could make out nothing below him saving the 'little sea of faces' which he had alluded to, but the little sea had now become practically obliterated from him by a swimming mist.

'Are you lishening?'

'Yes, yes! The song, the song!'

Swelter lowered his head yet again into the hot spindrift and then held up his right hand weakly. He made one feeble effort to heave himself away from the pillar and to deliver his verses at a more imposing angle, but, incapable of mustering the strength he sank back, and then, as a vast inane smile opened up the lower half of his face, and as Mr Flay watched him, his hard little mouth twisted downwards, the chef began gradually to curl in upon himself, as though folding himself up for death. The kitchen had become as silent as a hot tomb. At last, through the silence, a weak gurgling sound began to percolate but whether it was the first verse of the long awaited poem, none could tell for the chef, like a galleon, lurched in his anchorage. The great ship's canvas sagged and crumpled and then suddenly an enormousness foundered and sank. There was a sound of something spreading as an area of seven flagstones became hidden from view beneath a catalyptic mass of wine-drenched blubber.

THE STONE LANES

MR FLAY'S gorge had risen steadily and, as the dreadful minutes passed, he had been filled with a revulsion so consuming that but for the fact that the chef was surrounded by the youths he would have attacked the drunkard. As it was he bared his sand-coloured teeth, and fixed his eyes for a last moment on the cook with an expression of unbelievable menace. He had turned his head away at last and spat, and then brushing aside whoever stood in his path, had made his way with great skeleton strides, to a narrow doorway in the wall opposite that through which he had entered. By the time Swelter's monologue was dragging to its crapulous close, Mr Flay was pacing onwards, every step taking him another five feet further from the reek and horror of the Great Kitchen.

His black suit, patched on the elbows and near the collar with a greasy sepia-coloured cloth, fitted him badly but belonged to him as inevitably as the head of a tortoise emerging from its shell or the vulture's from a rubble of feathers belong to that reptile or that bird. His head, parchment-coloured and bony, was indigenous to that greasy fabric. It stuck out from the top window of its high black building as though it had known no other residence.

While Mr Flay was pacing along the passages to that part of the castle where Lord Sepulchrave had been left alone for the first time for many weeks, the curator, sleeping peacefully in the Hall of the Bright Carvings, snored beneath the venetian blind. The hammock was still swinging a little, a very little, from the movement caused by Mr Rottcodd's depositing himself therein directly he had turned the key on Mr Flay. The sun burned through t.1e shutters, made bands of gold around the pedestals that supported the sculpture and laid its tiger stripes across the dusty floor boarding.

The sunlight, as Mr Flay strolled on, still had one finger through the kitchen window, lighting the perspiring stone pillar which was now relieved of its office of supporting the chef for the soak had fallen from the wine-barrel a moment after the disappearance of Mr Flay and lay stretched at the foot of his rostrum.

Around him lay scattered a few small flattened lumps of meat, coated with sawdust. There was a strong smell of burning fat, but apart from the prone bulk of the chef, the Grey Scrubbers under the table, and the gentlemen who were suspended from the beam, there was no one left in the huge, hot, empty hall. Every man and boy who had been able to move his legs had made his way to cooler quarters.

Steerpike had viewed with a mixture of amazement, relief and malignant amusement the dramatic cessation of Mr Swelter's oratory. For a few moments he had gazed at the wine-spattered form of his overlord spread below him, then glancing around and finding that he was alone he had made for the door through which Mr Flay had passed and was soon racing down the passages turning left and right as he ran in a mad effort to reach the fresh air.

He had never before been through that particular door, but

he imagined that he would soon find his way into the open and to some spot where he could be on his own. Turning this way and that he found that he was lost in a labyrinth of stone corridors, lit here and there by candles sunk in their own wax

and placed in niches in the walls. In desperation he put his hands to his head as he ran, when suddenly, as he rounded the curve, of a wall a figure passed rapidly across the passage before him, neither looking to right or left.

As soon as Mr Flay—for it was his lordship's servant on his way to the residential apartments – as soon as he had passed from sight, Steerpike peered around the corner and followed, keeping as much as possible in step to hide the sound of his own feet. This was almost impossible, as Mr Flay's spider-like gait besides being particularly long of stride, had, like the slow-march, a time-lag before the ultimate descent of the foot. However, young Steerpike, feeling that here at any rate was his one chance of escaping from these endless corridors, followed as best he could in the hope that Mr Flay would eventually turn into some cool quadrangle or open space where get-away could be effected. At times, when the candles were thirty or forty feet apart, Mr Flay would be lost to view and only the sound of his feet on the flagstones would guide his follower. Then slowly, as his erratic shape approached the next guttering aura he would begin by degrees to become a silhouette, until immediately before the candle he would for a moment appear like an inky scarecrow, a mantis of pitch-black cardboard worked with strings. Then the progression of the lighting would be reversed and for a moment immediately after passing the flame Steerpike would see him quite clearly as a lit object against the depths of the still-to-be-trodden avenues of stone. The grease at those moments shone from the threadbare cloth across his shoulders, the twin vertical muscles of his neck rose out of the tattered collar nakedly and sharply. As he moved forward the light would dim upon his back and Steerpike would lose him, only hearing the cracking of his knee-joints and his feet striking the stones, until the ensuing candle carved him anew. Practically exhausted, first by the unendurable atmosphere of the Great Kitchen and now with this seemingly endless journey, the boy, for he was barely seventeen, sank suddenly to the ground with exhaustion, striking the flags with a thud, his boots dragging harshly on the stone. The noise brought Flay to a sudden halt and he turned himself slowly about, drawing his shoulders up to his ears as he did so. 'What's that?' he croaked, peering into the darkness behind him.

There was no answer. Mr Flay began to retrace his steps, his head forward, his eyes peering. As he proceeded he came into the light of one of the candles in the wall. He approached it, still keeping his small eyes directed into the darkness beyond, and wrenched the candle, with a great substratum of ancient tallow with it, from the wall and with this to help him he soon came across the boy in the centre of the corridor several yards further on.

He bent forward and lowered the great lump of lambent wax within a few inches of Steerpike, who had fallen face downwards and peered at the immobile huddle of limbs. The sound of his footsteps and the cracking of his knee-joints had given place to an absolute silence. He drew back his teeth and straightened himself a little. Then he turned the boy over with his foot. This roused Steerpike from his faintness and he raised himself weakly on one elbow.

'Where am I?' he said in a whisper. 'Where am I?'

'One of Swelter's little rats', thought Flay to himself, taking no notice of the question. 'One of Swelter's, eh? One of his striped rats.' 'Get up', said Mr Flay aloud. 'What you doing here?' and he put the candle close to the boy's face.

'I don't know where I am', said young Steerpike. 'I'm lost here. Lost. Give me daylight.'

'What you doing here, I said ... what you doing here?' said Flay. 'I don't want Swelter's boys here. Curse them!'

'I don't *want* to be here. Give me daylight and I'll go away. Far away.'

'Away? Where?'

Steerpike had recovered control of his mind, although he still felt hot and desperately tired. He had noticed the sneer in Mr Flay's voice as he had said 'I don't want Swelter's boys here,' and so, at Mr Flay's question 'Away where?' Steerpike answered quickly, 'Oh anywhere, anywhere from that dreadful Mr Swelter.'

Flay peered at him for a moment or two, opening his mouth several times to speak, only to close it again.

'New?' said Flay looking expressionlessly through the boy.

'Me?' said young Steerpike.

'*You*,' said Flay, still looking clean through the top of the boy's head, 'New?'

'Seventeen years old, sir,' said young Steerpike, 'but new to that kitchen.'

'When?' said Flay, who left out most of every sentence.

43

Steerpike, who seemed able to interpret this sort of short-hand talk, answered.

'Last month. I want to leave that dreadful Swelter,' he added, replaying his only possible card and glancing up at the candle-lit head.

'Lost, were you?' said Flay after a pause, but with perhaps less darkness in his tone. 'Lost in the Stone Lanes, were you? One of Swelter's little rats, lost in the Stone Lanes, eh?' and Mr Flay raised his gaunt shoulders again.

'Swelter fell like a log,' said Steerpike.

'Quite right,' said Flay, 'doing honours. What have you done?'

'Done, sir?' said Steerpike, 'when?'

'What Happiness?' said Flay, looking like a death's-head. The candle was beginning to fail. 'How much Happiness?'

'I haven't any happiness,' said Steerpike.

'What! no Great Happiness? Rebellion. Is it rebellion?'

'No, except against Mr Swelter.'

'Swelter! Swelter! Leave his name in its fat and grease. Don't talk of that name in the Stone Lanes. Swelter, always Swelter! Hold your tongue. Take this candle. Lead the way. Put it in the niche. Rebellion is it? Lead the way, left, left, right, keep to the left, now right ... I'll teach you to be unhappy when a Groan is born ... keep on ... straight on ...'

Young Steerpike obeyed these instructions from the shadows behind him.

'A Groan is born', said Steerpike with an inflection of voice which might be interpreted as a question or a statement.

'Born,' said Flay. 'And you mope in the Lanes. With me, Swelter's boy. Show you what it means. A male Groan. New, eh? Seventeen? Ugh! Never understand. Never. Turn right and left again – again ... through the arch. Ugh! A new body under the old stones – one of Swelter's, too ... don't like him, eh?'

'No, sir.'

'H'm,' said Flay. 'Wait here.'

Steerpike waited as he was told and Mr Flay, drawing a bunch of keys from his pocket and selecting one with great care as though he were dealing with objects of rarity inserted it into the lock of an invisible door, for the blackness was profound. Steerpike heard the iron grinding in the lock.

'Here!' said Flay out of the darkness. 'Where's that Swelter boy? Come here.'

Steerpike moved forward towards the voice, feeling with his hands along the wall of a low arch. Suddenly he found himself next to the dank smelling garments of Mr Flay and he put forward his hand and held Lord Groan's servant by a loose portion of the long jacket. Mr Flay brought down his bony hand suddenly over the boy's arm, knocking it away and a t'ck, t'ck, t'ck, sounded in the tall creature's throat, warning him against any further attempts at intimacy.

'Cat room,' said Flay, putting his hand to the iron knob of the door.

'Oh,' said Steerpike, thinking hard and repeating 'Cat room' to fill in time, for he saw no reason for the remark. The only interpretation he could give to the ejaculation was that Flay was referring to him as a cat and asking to be given more room. Yet there had been no irritation in the voice.

'Cat room,' said Flay again, ruminatively, and turned the iron door-knob. He opened the door slowly and Steerpike, peering past him, found no longer any need for an explanation.

A room was filled with the late sunbeams. Steerpike stood quite still, a twinge of pleasure running through his body. He grinned. A carpet filled the floor with blue pasture. Thereon were seated in a hundred decorative attitudes, or stood immobile like carvings, or walked superbly across their sapphire setting, inter-weaving with each other like a living arabesque, a swarm of snow-white cats.

As Mr Flay passed down the centre of the room, Steerpike could not but notice the contrast between the dark rambling figure with his ungainly movements and the monotonous cracking of his knees, the contrast between this and the superb elegance and silence of the white cats. They took not the slightest notice of either Mr Flay or of himself save for the sudden cessation of their purring. When they had stood in the darkness, and before Mr Flay had removed the bunch of keys from his pocket, Steerpike had imagined he had heard a heavy, deep throbbing, a monotonous sea-like drumming of sound, and he now knew that it must have been the pullulation of the tribe.

As they passed through a carved archway at the far end of the room and had closed the door behind them he heard the vibration of their throats, for now that the white cats were once more alone it was revived, and the deep unhurried purring was like the voice of an ocean in the throat of a shell.

'THE SPY-HOLE'

'WHOSE are they?' asked Steerpike. They were climbing stone stairs. The wall on their right was draped with hideous papers that were peeling off and showed rotting surfaces of chill plaster behind. A mingling of many weird colours enlivened this nether surface, dark patches of which had a submarine and incredible beauty. In another dryer area, where a great sail of paper hung away from the wall, the plaster had cracked into a network of intricate fissures varying in depth and resembling a bird's-eye view, or map of some fabulous delta. A thousand imaginary journeys might be made along the banks of these rivers of an unexplored world.

Steerpike repeated his question, 'Whose are they?' he said.

'Whose what?' said Flay, stopping on the stairs and turning round. 'Still here are you? Still following me?'

'You suggested that I should,' said Steerpike.

'Ch! Ch!' said Flay, 'what d'you want, Swelter's boy?'

'Nauseating Swelter,' said Steerpike between his teeth but with one eye on Mr Flay, 'vile Swelter.'

There was a pause during which Steerpike tapped the iron banisters with his thumb-nail.

'Name?' said Mr Flay.

'My name?' asked Steerpike.

'Your name, yes, your name. I know what *my* name is.' Mr Flay put a knuckly hand on the banisters preparatory to mounting the stairs again, but waited, frowning over his shoulder, for the reply.

'Steerpike sir,' said the boy.

'Queerpike, eh? eh?' said Flay.

'No, Steerpike.'

'What?'

'Steerpike. Steerpike.'

'What for?' said Flay.

'I beg your pardon?'

'What for, eh? Two Squeertikes, two of you. Twice over. What for? One's enough for a Swelter's boy.'

The youth felt it would be useless to clear up the problem of his name. He concentrated his dark eyes on the gawky figure above him for a few moments and shrugged his shoulders imperceptibly. Then he spoke again, showing no sign of irritation.

'Whose cats were those, sir? May I ask?'

'Cats?' said Flay, 'who said cats?'

'The white cats,' said Steerpike. 'All the white cats in the Cat room. Who do they belong to?'

Mr Flay held up a finger. 'My Lady's,' he said. His hard voice seemed a part of this cold narrow stairway of stone and iron. 'They belong to my Lady. Lady's white cats they are. Swelter's boy. All hers.'

Steerpike pricked his ears up, 'Where does she live?' he said. 'Are we close to where she lives?'

For answer Mr Flay shot his head forward out of his collar and croaked, 'Silence! you kitchen thing. Hold your tongue you greasy fork. Talk too much', and he straddled up the stairs, passing two landings in his ascent, and then at the third he turned sharply to his left and entered an octagonal apartment where full-length portraits in huge dusty gold frames stared from seven of the eight walls. Steerpike followed him in.

Mr Flay had been longer away from his lordship than he had intended or thought right and it was on his mind that the earl might be needing him. Directly he entered the octagonal room he approached one of the portraits at the far end and pushing the suspended frame a little to one side, revealed a small round hole in the panelling the size of a farthing. He placed his eye to this hole and Steerpike watched the wrinkles of his parchment-coloured skin gather below the protruding bone at the base of the skull, for Mr Flay both had to stoop and then to raise his head in order to apply his eye at the necessary angle. What Mr Flay saw was what he had expected to see.

From his vantage point he was able to get a clear view of three doors in a corridor, the central one belonging to the chamber of her ladyship, the seventy-sixth Countess of Groan. It was stained black and had painted upon it an enormous white cat. The wall of the landing was covered with pictures of birds and there were three engravings of cacti in bloom. This door was shut, but as Mr Flay watched the doors on either side were being constantly opened and closed and figures moved quickly in and out or up and down the landing, or conversed with many gesticulations or stood with their chins in the curled palms of their hands as though in profound meditation.

'Here', said Flay without turning round.

Steerpike was immediately at Flay's elbow. 'Yes?' he said.

'Cat door's hers', said Flay removing his eye, and then, stretching his arms out he spread his long fingers to their tips and yawned cavernously.

Young Steerpike glued his eye to the hole, keeping the heavy gold frame from swinging back with his shoulder. All at once he found himself contemplating a narrow-chested man with a shock of grey hair and glasses which magnified his eyes so that they filled the lenses up to their gold rims, when the central door opened, and a dark figure stole forth, closing the door behind him quietly, and with an air of the deepest dejection. Steerpike watched him turn his eyes to the shock-headed man, who inclined his body forward clasping his hands before him. No notice was taken of this by the other, who began to pace up and down the landing, his dark cloak clasped around him and trailing on the floor at his heels. Each time he passed the doctor, for such it was, that gentleman inclined his body, but as before there was no response, until suddenly, stopping immediately before the physician in attendance, he drew from his cape a slender rod of silver mounted at the end with a rough globe of black jade that burned around its edges with emerald fire. With this unusual weapon the mournful figure beat sadly at the doctor's chest as though to inquire whether there was anyone at home. The doctor coughed. The silver and jade implement was pointed to the floor, and Steerpike was amazed to see the doctor, after hitching his exquisitely creased trousers to a few inches above his ankle, squat down. His great vague eyes swam about beneath the magnifying lenses like a pair of jellyfish seen through a fathom of water. His dark grey hair was brushed out over his eyes like thatch. For all the indignity of his position it was with a great sense of style that he became seated following with his eyes the gentleman who had begun to walk around him slowly. Eventually the figure with the silver rod came to a halt.

'Prunesquallor', he said.

'My Lord?' said the doctor, inclining his grey hayrick to the left.

'Satisfactory, Prunesquallor?'

The doctor placed the tips of his fingers together. 'I am exceptionally gratified my lord, exceptionally. Indeed I am. Very, very much so; ha, ha, ha. Very, very much so.'

'Professionally you mean, I imagine?' said Lord Sepulchrave, for as Steerpike had begun to realize to his amazement, the tragic-looking man was none other than the seventy-sixth Earl of Groan and the owner of, as Steerpike put it to himself, the whole caboodle, bricks, guns and glory.

'Professionally ...' queried the doctor to himself, '... what does he mean?' Aloud he said, 'professionally, my lord, I am unspeakably satisfied, ha, ha, ha, ha, and socially, that is to say, er, as a gesture, ha, ha, I am over-awed. I am a proud fellow, my lord, ha, ha, ha, ha, a very proud fellow.'

The laugh of doctor Prunesquallor was part of his conversation and quite alarming when heard for the first time. It appeared to be out of control as though it were a part of his voice, a top-storey of his vocal range that only came into its own when the doctor laughed. There was something about it of wind whistling through high rafters and there was a good deal of the horse's whinny, with a touch of the curlew. When giving vent to it, the doctor's mouth would be practically immobile like the door of a cabinet left ajar. Between the laughs he would speak very rapidly, which made the sudden stillness of his beautifully shaven jaws at the time of laughter all the more extraordinary. The laugh was not necessarily connected with humour at all. It was simply a part of his conversation.

'Technically, I am so satisfied as to be unbearable even to myself, ha, ha, ha, he, he, ha. Oh very, very satisfactory it all was. Very much so.'

'I am glad', said his lordship, gazing down at him for a moment. 'Did you notice anything?' (Lord Sepulchrave glanced up and down the corridor.) 'Strange? Anything unusual about him?'

'Unusual?' said Prunesquallor. 'Did you say unusual, my lord?'

'I did', said Lord Sepulchrave, biting his lower lip. 'Anything wrong with him? You need not be afraid to speak out.'

Again his lordship glanced up and down the landing but there was no one to be seen.

'Structurally, a sound child, sound as a bell, tinkle, tinkle, structurally, ha, ha, ha,' said the doctor.

'Damn the structure!' said Lord Groan.

'I am at a loss, my lord, ha, ha. Completely at a loss, sir. If not structurally, then how, my lord?'

'His face', said the earl. 'Didn't you see his face?'

Here the doctor frowned profoundly to himself and rubbed his chin with his hand. Out of the corner of his eyes he looked up to find his lordship scrutinizing him. 'Ah!' he said lamely, 'the face. The face of his little lordship. Aha!'

'Did you notice it, I say?' continued Lord Groan. 'Speak man!'

'I noticed his face, sir. Oh yes, definitely I noticed it.' This time the doctor did not laugh but drew a deep breath from his narrow chest.

'Did you or did you not think it was strange? Did you or did you not?'

'Speaking professionally,' said Doctor Prunesquallor, 'I should say the face was irregular.'

'Do you mean it's ugly?' said Lord Groan.

'It is unnatural', said Prunesquallor.

'What is the difference, man', said Lord Groan.

'Sir?' questioned the doctor.

'I asked if it was ugly, sir, and you answer that it is unnatural. Why must you hedge?'

'Sir!' said Prunesquallor, but as he gave no colour to the utterance, very little could be made of it.

'When I say "ugly" have the goodness to use the word. Do you understand?' Lord Groan spoke quietly.

'I comprehend, sir. I comprehend.'

'Is the boy hideous,' persisted Lord Groan as though he wished to thrash the matter out. 'Have you ever delivered a more hideous child? Be honest.'

'Never', said the doctor. 'Never, ha, ha, ha, ha. Never. And never a boy with such – er, ha, ha, ha, never a boy with such extraordinary eyes.'

'Eyes?' said Lord Groan, 'what's wrong with them?'

'Wrong?' cried Prunesquallor. 'Did you say "wrong" your lordship? Have you not seen them?'

'No, quick, man. Hurry yourself. What is it? What is the matter with my son's eyes?'

'They are violet.'

FUCHSIA

As his lordship stared at the doctor another figure appeared, a girl of about fifteen with long, rather wild black hair. She was gauche in movement and in a sense, ugly of face, but with how small a twist might she not suddenly have become beautiful. Her sullen mouth was full and rich – her eyes smouldered.

A yellow scarf hung loosely around her neck. Her shapeless dress was a flaming red.

For all the straightness of her back she walked with a slouch.

'Come here', said Lord Groan as she was about to pass him and the doctor.

'Yes father', she said huskily.

'Where have you been for the last fortnight, Fuchsia?'

'Oh, here and there, father', she said, staring at her shoes.

She tossed her long hair and it flapped down her back like a pirate's flag. She stood in about as awkward a manner as could be conceived. Utterly un-feminine – no man could have invented it.

'Here and there?' echoed her father in a weary voice. 'What does "here and there" mean? You've been in hiding. Where, girl?'

' 'N the libr'y and 'n the armoury, 'n walking about a lot', said Lady Fuchsia, and her sullen eyes narrowed. 'I just heard silly rumours about mother. They said I've got a brother – idiots! idiots! I hate them. I haven't, have I? Have I?'

'A little brother', broke in Doctor Prunesquallor. 'Yes, ha, ha, ha, ha, ha, ha, ha, a minute, infinitesimal, microscopic addition to the famous line is now behind this bedroom door. Ha, ha, ha, ha, ha, ha, he, he, he! Oh yes! Ha, ha! Oh yes indeed! Very much so.'

'No!' said Fuchsia so loudly that the doctor coughed crisply and his lordship took a step forward with his eyebrows drawn together and a sad curl at the corner of his mouth.

'It's not true!' shouted Fuchsia, turning from them and twirling a great lock of black hair round and round her wrist. 'I don't believe it! Let me go! Let me go!'

As no one was touching her, her cry was unnecessary and she turned and ran with strange bounds along the corridor that led from the landing. Before she was lost to view, Steerpike could hear her voice shouting from the distance, 'Oh how I hate! hate! hate! How I *hate* people! Oh how I *hate* people!'

All this while Mr Flay had been gazing out of a narrow window in the octagonal room and was preoccupied with certain matters relating to how he could best let Lord Groan know that he, Flay, his servant for over forty years, disapproved of having been put aside as it were at the one moment when a son had been born – at the one moment when he, Flay, would have been invaluable as an ally. Mr Flay was rather hurt about the whole business, and he very much wanted Lord Groan to know this, and yet at the same time it was very difficult to think of a way in which he could tactfully communicate his chagrin to a man quite as sullen as himself. Mr Flay bit his nails sourly. He had been at the window for a much longer time than he had intended and he turned with his shoulders raised, an attitude typical of him and saw young Steerpike, whose presence he had forgotten. He strode over to the boy and catching him by his coat-tails jerked him backwards into the centre of the room. The great picture swung back across the spy-hole.

'Now,' he said, 'back! You've seen her door, Swelter's boy.'

Steerpike, who had been lost in the world beyond the oak partition, was dazed, and took a moment to come to.

'Back to that loathsome chef?' he cried at last, 'oh no! couldn't!'

'Too busy to have you here', said Flay, 'too busy, can't wait.'

'He's ugly', said Steerpike fiercely.

'Who?' said Flay. 'Don't stop here talking.'

'Oh so ugly, he is. Lord Groan said so. The doctor said so. Ugh! So hideous.'

'Who's hideous, you kitchen thing', said Flay, jerking his head forward grotesquely.

'Who?' said Steerpike. 'The baby. The new baby. They both said so. Most terrible he is.'

'What's this?' cried Flay. 'What's these lies all about? Who've you heard talking? Who've you been listening to? I'll tear your little ears off, you snippet thing! Where've you been? Come here!'

Steerpike, who had determined to escape from the Great Kitchen, was now bent on finding an occupation among those apartments where he might pry into the affairs of those above him.

'If I go back to Swelter I'll tell him and all of them what I heard his lordship say and then ...'

'Come here!' said Flay between his teeth, 'come here or I'll break your bones. Been agaping, have you? I'll fix you.' Flay propelled Steerpike through the entrance at a great pace and halted halfway down a narrow passage before a door. This he unlocked with one of his many keys and thrusting Steerpike inside turned it upon the boy.

'TALLOW AND BIRDSEED'

LIKE a vast spider suspended by a metal chord, a candelabrum presided over the room nine feet above the floor boards. From its sweeping arms of iron, long stalactites of wax lowered their pale spilths drip by drip, drip by drip. A rough table with a drawer half open, which appeared to be full of birdseed, was in such a position below the iron spider that a cone of tallow was mounting by degrees at one corner into a lambent pyramid the size of a hat.

The room was untidy to the extent of being a shambles. Everything had the appearance of being put aside for the moment. Even the bed was at an angle, slanting away from the wall and crying out to be pushed back flush against the red wallpaper. As the candles guttered or flared, so the shadows moved from side to side, or up and down the wall, and with those movements behind the bed there swayed the shadows of four birds. Between them vacillated an enormous head. This umbrage was cast by her ladyship, the seventy-sixth Countess of Groan. She was propped against several pillows and a black shawl was draped around her shoulders. Her hair, a very dark red colour of great lustre, appeared to have been left suddenly while being woven into a knotted structure on the top of her head. Thick coils still fell about her shoulders, or clustered upon the pillows like burning snakes.

Her eyes were of the pale green that is common among cats. They were large eyes, yet seemed, in proportion to the pale area of her face, to be small. The nose was big enough to appear so in spite of the expanse that surrounded it. The effect which she produced was one of bulk, although only her head, neck, shoulders and arms could be seen above the bedclothes.

A magpie moving sideways up and down her left forearm, which lay supine upon the bedclothes, pecked intermittently at a heap of grain which lay in the palm of her hand. On her shoulders sat a stonechat, and a huge raven which was asleep. The bed-rail boasted two starlings, a missel-thrush and a small owl. Every now and then a bird would appear between the bars of a small high window which let in less than no light. The ivy had climbed through it from the outside and had begun to send its tendrils down the inner wall itself and over the crimson wallpaper. Although this ivy had choked out what little light might have trickled into the room, it was not strong enough to prevent the birds from finding a way through and from visiting Lady Gertrude at any hour of night or day.

'That's enough, that's enough, that's enough!' said the Countess in a deep husky voice, to the magpie. 'That's enough for you today, my dear.' The magpie jumped a few inches into the air and landed again on her wrist and shook his feathers; his long tail tapped on the eiderdown.

Lady Groan flung what remained of the grain across the room and the stonechat hopping from the bed-rail to her head, took off again from that rabous landing ground with a flutter, circled twice around the room steering during his second circuit through the stalactites of shining wax, and landed on the floor beside the grain.

The Countess of Groan dug her elbows into the pillows behind her, which had become flattened and uncomfortable and levered her bulk up with her strong, heavy arms. Then she relaxed again, and spread out her arms to left and right along the bedrail behind her and her hands drooped from the wrists at either extremity, overhanging the edges of the bed. The line of her mouth was neither sad nor amused, as she gazed abstractedly at the pyramid of wax that was mounting upon the table. She watched each slow drip as it descended upon the blunt apex of the mound, move sluggishly down the uneven side and solidify into a long pulpy petal.

Whether the Countess was thinking deeply or was lost in vacant reverie it would have been impossible to guess. She reclined hugely and motionlessly, her arms extended along the iron rail, when suddenly a great fluttering and scrambling broke into the wax-smelling silence of the room and turning her eyes to the ivy-filled window, fourteen feet from the ground, the Countess without moving her head, could see the leaves part and the white head and shoulders of an albino rook emerge guiltily.

'Ah-ha,' she said slowly, as though she had come to a conclusion, 'so it is you, is it? So it is the truant back again. Where has he been? What has he been doing? What trees has he been sitting in? What clouds has he been flying through? What a boy he is! What a bunch of feathered whiteness. What a bunch of wickedness!'

The rook had been sitting fringed on all sides with the ivy leaves, with his head now on one side, now on the other; listening or appearing to listen with great interest and a certain show of embarrassment, for from the movement that showed itself in the ivy leaves from time to time, the white rook was evidently shifting from foot to foot.

'Three weeks it is,' continued the Countess, 'three weeks I've been without him; I wasn't good enough for *him*, oh no, not for Master Chalk, and here he is back again, wants to be forgiven! Oh yes! Wants a great treeful of forgiveness, for his heavy old beak and months of absolution for his plumage.'

Then the Countess hoisted herself up in bed again, twisted a strand of her dark hair round a long forefinger, and with her face directed at the doorway, but her eyes still on the bird, said as though to herself and almost inaudibly, 'Come on then.' The ivy rustled again, and before that sound was over the bed itself vibrated with the sudden arrival of the white rook.

He stood on the foot-rail, his claws curled around it, and stared at Lady Groan. After a moment or two of stillness the white rook moved his feet up and down on the rail in a treading motion and then, flopping on to the bedclothes at her ladyship's feet, twisted his head around and pecked at his own tail, the feathers of his neck standing out as he did so, crisply like a ruff. The pecking over he made his way over the undulating terrain of the bed, until within a few inches of her ladyship's face, when he tilted his big head in a characteristic manner and cawed.

'So you beg my pardon, do you?' said Lady Groan, 'and you think that's the end of it? No more questions about where you've been or where you've flown these three long weeks? So that's it, is it, Master Chalk? You want me to forgive you for old sakes' sake? Come here with your old beak and rub it on my arm. Come along my whitest one, come along, then. Come along.' The raven on Lady Groan's shoulder awoke from his sleep and raised his ethiopian wing an inch or two, sleepily. Then his eyes focused upon the rook in a hard stare. He sat there wide awake, a lock of dark red hair between his feet. The small owl as though to take the place of the raven fell asleep. One of the starlings turned about in three slow paces and faced the wall. The missel-thrush made no motion, and as a candle guttered, a ghoul of shadow from under a tall cupboard dislodged itself and moved across the floorboards, climbed the bed, and crawled half way across the eiderdown before it returned by the same route, to curl up and roost beneath the cupboard again.

Lady Groan's gaze had returned to the mounting pyramid of tallow. Her pale eyes would either concentrate upon an object in a remorseless way or would appear to be without sight, vacant, with the merest suggestion of something childish. It was in this abstracted manner that she gazed through the pale pyramid, while her hands, as though working on their own account, moved gently over the breast, head and throat of the white rook.

For some time there was complete silence in the room and it was with something of a shock that a rapping at the panels of her bedroom door awakened Lady Groan from her reverie.

Her eyes now took on the concentrated, loveless, cat-like look.

The birds coming to life at once, flapped simultaneously to the end rail of the bed, where they stood balancing in a long uneven line, each one on the alert, their heads turned towards the door.

'Who's that?' said Lady Groan heavily.

'It's me, my lady,' cried a quavering voice.

'Who's that hitting my door?'

'It's me with his lordship,' replied the voice.

'What?' shouted Lady Groan. 'What d'you want? What are you hitting my door for?'

Whoever it was raised her voice nervously and cried, 'Nannie Slagg, it is. It's me, my lady; Nannie Slagg.'

'What d'you want?' repeated her ladyship, settling herself more comfortably.

'I've brought his Lordship for you to see', shouted Nannie Slagg, a little less nervously.

'Oh, you have, have you? You've brought his lordship. So you want to come in, do you? With his lordship.' There was a moment's silence. 'What for? What have you brought him to me for?'

'For you to see, if you please, my lady,' replied Nannie Slagg. 'He's had his bath.'

Lady Groan relaxed still further into the pillows. 'Oh, you mean the *new* one, do you?' she muttered.

'Can I come in?' cried Nannie Slagg.

'Hurry up then! Hurry up then! Stop scratching at my door. What are you waiting for?'

A rattling at the door handle froze the birds along the iron bed-rail and as the door opened they were all at once in the air, and were forcing their way, one after another through the bitter leaves of the small window.

A GOLD RING FOR TITUS

NANNIE SLAGG entered, bearing in her arms the heir to the miles of rambling stone and mortar; to the Tower of Flints and the stagnant moat; to the angular mountains and the lime-green river where twelve years later he would be angling for the hideous fishes of his inheritance.

She carried the child towards the bed and turned the little face to the mother, who gazed right through it and said:

'Where's that doctor? Where's Prunesquallor? Put the child down and open the door.'

Mrs Slagg obeyed, and as her back was turned Lady Groan bent forward and peered at the child. The little eyes were glazed with sleep and the candlelight played upon the bald head, moulding the structure of the skull with shifting shade.

'H'm', said Lady Groan, 'what d'you want me to do with him?'

Nannie Slagg, who was very grey and old, with red rims around her eyes and whose intelligence was limited, gazed vacantly at her ladyship.

'He's had his bath,' she said. 'He's just had his bath, bless his little lordship's heart.'

'What about it?' said Lady Groan.

The old nurse picked the baby up dexterously and began to rock him gently by way of an answer.

'Is Prunesquallor there?' repeated Lady Groan.

'Down', whispered Nannie, pointing a little wrinkled finger at the floor, 'd-downstairs; oh yes, I think he is still downstairs taking punch in the Coldroom. Oh dear, yes, bless the little thing.'

Her last remark presumably referred to Titus and not to Doctor Prunesquallor. Lady Groan raised herself in bed and looking fiercely at the open door, bellowed in the deepest and loudest voice, 'SQUALLOR!'

The word echoed along the corridors and down the stairs, and creeping under the door and along the black rug in the Coldroom, just managed, after climbing the doctor's body, to find its way into both his ears simultaneously, in a peremptory if modified condition. Modified though it was, it brought doctor Prunesquallor to his feet at once. His fish eyes swam all round his glasses before finishing at the top, where they gave him an expression of fantastic martyrdom. Running his long, exquisitely formed fingers through his mop of grey hair, he drained his glass of punch at a draught and started for the door, flicking small globules of the drink from his waistcoat.

Before he had reached her room he had begun a rehearsal of the conversation he expected, his insufferable laughter punctuating every other sentence whatever its gist.

'My lady,' he said, when he had reached her door and was showing the Countess and Mrs Slagg nothing except his head around the door-post in a decapitated manner, before entering. 'My lady, ha, ha, he he. I heard your voice downstairs as I er – was –'

'Tippling,' said Lady Groan.

'Ha, ha – how very right you are, how very very right you are, ha, ha, ha, he, as I was, as you so graphically put it, ha, ha, tippling. Down it came, ha, ha – down it came.'

'What came?' interrupted the Countess loudly.

'Your voice,' said Prunesquallor, raising his right hand and deliberately placing the tips of his thumb and little finger together, 'your voice located me in the Coldroom. Oh yes, it did!'

The Countess stared at him heavily and then dug her elbows into the pillow.

Mrs Slagg had rocked the baby to sleep.

Doctor Prunesquallor was running a long tapering forefinger up and down a stalactite of wax and smiling horribly.

'I called you', said the Countess, 'to tell you, Prunesquallor, that tomorrow I get up.'

'Oh, he, ha, ha, oh ha, ha, my ladyship, oh, ha, ha, my lady-ship – *tomorrow*?'

'Tomorrow,' said the Countess, 'why not?'

'Professionally speaking –' began Doctor Prunesquallor.

'Why not?' repeated the Countess interrupting him.

'Ha, ha, most abnormal, most unusual, ha, ha, ha, most unique, so *very soon*.'

'So you would docket me, would you, Prunesquallor? I thought you would; I guessed it. I get up tomorrow – tomorrow *at dawn*.'

Doctor Prunesquallor shrugged his narrow shoulders and raised his eyes. Then placing the tips of his fingers together and addressing the dark ceiling above him, 'I *advise*, but never order', he said, in a tone which implied that he could have done any amount of ordering had he thought it necessary. 'Ha ha, ha, oh no! I only advise.'

'Rubbish', said the Countess.

'I do not think so', replied Prunesquallor, still gazing upwards. 'Ha, ha, ha, ha, oh no! not at all.' As he finished speaking his eyes for a second travelled downwards at great speed and took in the image of the Countess in bed and then even more rapidly swam up the glasses. What he had seen disquieted him, for he had found in her expression such a concentration of distaste that as he deflected his gaze away from her he found that his feet were moving backwards one after the other and that he was at the door before he knew that he had decided what to do. Bowing quickly he withdrew his body from the bedroom.

'Isn't he sweet, oh isn't he the sweetest drop of sugar that ever was?' said Mrs Slagg.

'Who?' shouted the Countess so loudly that a string of tallow wavered in the shifting light.

The baby awoke at the sound and moaned, and Nannie Slagg retreated.

'His little lordship,' she whimpered weakly, 'his pretty little lordship.'

'Slagg,' said the Countess, 'go away! I would like to see the boy when he is six. Find a wet nurse from the Outer Dwellings. Make him green dresses from the velvet curtains. Take this gold ring of mine. Fix a chain to it. Let him wear it around his wry little neck. Call him Titus. Go away and leave the door six inches open.'

The Countess put her hand under the pillow and drew forth a small reed, placed it in her vast mouth and gave it breath. Two long sweet notes sang out through the dark air. At the sound, Mrs Slagg, grabbing the gold ring from the bedclothes, where the Countess had thrown it, hurried as fast as her old legs could carry her from the room as though a werewolf were at her heels. Lady Groan was leaning forward in bed, her eyes were like a child's; wide, sweet and excited. They were fixed upon the door. Her hands were gripping the edges of her pillow. She became rigid.

In the distance, a vibration was becoming louder and louder until the volume seemed to have filled the chamber itself, when suddenly there slid through the narrow opening of the door and moved into the fumid atmosphere of the room an undulation of whiteness, so that, within a breath, there was no shadow in all the room that was not blanched with cats.

SEPULCHRAVE

EVERY morning of the year, between the hours of nine and ten, he may be found, seated in the Stone Hall. It is there, at the long table that he takes his breakfast. The table is raised upon a dais, and from where he sits he can gaze down the length of the grey refectory. On either side and running the entire length, great pillars prop the painted ceiling where cherubs pursue each other across a waste of flaking sky. There must be about a thousand of them all told, interweaving among the clouds, their fat limbs for ever on the move and yet never moving, for they are imperfectly articulated. The colours, once garish, have faded and peeled away and the ceiling is now a very subtle shade of grey and lichen green, old rose and silver.

Lord Sepulchrave may have noticed the cherubs long ago. Probably when a child he had attempted more than once to count them, as his father had done, and as young Titus in his turn will try to do; but however that might be, Lord Groan had not cast up his eyes to the old welkin for many years. Nor did he ever stare about him now. How could he *love* this place? He was a part of it. He could not imagine a world outside it; and the idea of loving Gormenghast would have shocked him. To have asked him of his feelings for his hereditary home would be like asking a man what his feelings were towards his own hand or his own throat. But his lordship remembered the cherubs in the ceiling. His great grandfather had painted them with the help of an enthusiastic servant who had fallen seventy feet from the scaffolding and had been killed instantly. But it seemed that Lord Sepulchrave found his only interest in these days among the volumes in his library and in a knob of jade on his silver rod, which he would scrutinize for hours on end.

Arriving, as was his consistent habit, at exactly nine o'clock every morning, he would enter the long hall and move with a most melancholy air between rows of long tables, where servants of every grade would be awaiting him, standing at their places, their heads bowed.

Mounting the dais he would move around to the far side of

the table where hung a heavy brass bell. He would strike it. The servants sitting down at once, would begin their meal of bread, rice wine and cake.

Lord Groan's menu was otherwise. As he sat, this morning, in his high-backed chair he saw before him – through a haze of melancholia that filmed his brain and sickened his heart, robbing it of power and his limbs of health – he saw before him a snow-white tablecloth. It was set for two. The silver shone and the napkins were folded into the shapes of peacocks and were perched decoratively on the two plates. There was a delicious scent of bread, sweet and wholesome. There were eggs painted in gay colours, toast piled up pagoda-wise, tier upon tier and each as frail as a dead leaf; and fish with their tails in their mouths lay coiled in sea-blue saucers. There was coffee in an urn shaped like a lion, the spout protruding from that animal's silver jaws. There were all varieties of coloured fruits that looked strangely tropical in that dark hall. There were honeys and jams, jellies, nuts and spices and the ancestral breakfast plate was spread out to the greatest advantage amid the golden cutlery of the Groans. In the centre of the table was a small tin bowl of dandelions and nettles.

Lord Sepulchrave sat silently. He did not seem to notice the delicacies spread before him, nor when for a moment or two at a time his head was raised, did he appear to see the long cold dining-hall nor the servants at their tables. To his right, at the adjacent corner of the board, was arranged the cutlery and earthenware crockery that implied the imminent arrival of his lordship's breakfast companion. Lord Groan, his eyes upon the jade knob of the rod which he was twisting slowly upon its ferrule, again rang the brass bell and a door opened in the wall behind him. Sourdust entered with great books under his arm. He was arrayed in crimson sacking. His beard was knotted and the hairs that composed it were black and white. His face was very lined, as though it had been made of brown paper that had been crunched by some savage hand before being hastily smoothed out and spread over the tissues. His eyes were deepset and almost lost in the shadows cast by his fine brow, which for all its wrinkles, retained a sweeping breadth of bone.

The old man seated himself at the end of the table, and stacked the four volumes beside a porcelain decanter, and raising his sunken eyes to Lord Groan, murmured these words in a weak and shaking voice and yet with a certain dignity as though it were not simply a case of having to get through the ritual, but that it was now, as always, well worth getting through.

'I, Sourdust, lord of the library, personal adviser to your lordship, nonagenarian, and student of the Groan lore, proffer to your lordship the salutations of a dark morning, robed as I am in rags, student as I am of the tomes, and nonagenarian as I happen to be in the matter of years.'

This was delivered in one breath and then he coughed unpleasantly several times, his hand at his chest.

Lord Groan propped his chin on the knuckles of his hands that were cupping the jade knob. His face was very long and was olive coloured. The eyes were large, and of an eloquence, withdrawn. His nostrils were mobile and sensitive. His mouth, a narrow line. On his head was the iron crown of the Groans that fastens with a strap under the chin. It had four prongs that were shaped like arrow heads. Between these barbs small chains hung in loops. The prerogative of precedent on his side, he was wrapped in his dark grey dressing-gown.

He did not seem to have heard Sourdust's salutations, but focusing his eyes for the first time upon the table, he broke a corner off a piece of toast, and placed it mechanically in his mouth. This he muzzled in his cheek for the major part of the meal. The fish became cold on the plate. Sourdust had helped himself to one of them, a slice of water-melon and a fire-green egg, but all else lost its freshness or its heat upon the ritualistic table.

Below in the long basement of the hall the clattering of the knives had ceased. The rice wine had been passed up and down the table, and the jugs were empty. They were waiting for the sign to go about their duties.

Sourdust, having wiped his old mouth with the napkin, turned his eyes to his lordship, who was now leaning back in the chair and sipping at a glass of black tea, his eyes un-focused as usual.

The Librarian was watching the left eyebrow of his lordship. It was twenty-one minutes to ten by the clock at the far end of the hall. Lord Groan appeared to be looking through this clock. Three-quarters of a minute went by, it was ten seconds – five seconds – three seconds – one second – to twenty to ten. It was twenty minutes to ten. Lord Groan's left eyebrow rose up his forehead mechanically and stayed suspended beneath three wrinkles. Then it slowly lowered itself. At the movement, Sourdust arose and stamped upon the ground with an old thin leg. The crimson sacking about his body shook as he did so and his beard of black and white knots swung madly to and fro.

The tables were at once emptied and within half a minute the last of the retainers had vanished from the hall, and the servants' door at the far end had been closed and bolted.

Sourdust re-seated himself, panting a little and coughing in an ugly way. Then he leaned across the table and scratched the white cloth in front of Lord Groan with a fork.

His lordship turned his black and liquid eyes towards the old librarian and adviser. 'Well?' he said, in a far-away voice, 'what is it, Sourdust?'

'It is the ninth day of the month', said Sourdust.

'Ah', said his lordship.

There was a period of silence, Sourdust making use of the interim by re-knotting several tassels of his beard.

'The ninth', repeated his lordship.

'The ninth', muttered Sourdust.

'A heavy day,' mused his lordship, 'very heavy.'

Sourdust, bending his deep-set eyes upon his master, echoed him: 'A heavy day, the ninth ... always a heavy day.'

A great tear rolled down Sourdust's cheek threading its way over the crumpled surface. The eyes were too deeply set in their sockets of shadow to be seen. By not so much as the faintest sign or movement had Sourdust suggested that he was in a state of emotional stress. Nor was he, ever, save that at moments of reflection upon matters connected with the traditions of the Castle, it so happened that great tears emerged from the shadows beneath his brow. He fingered the great tomes beside his plate. His lordship, as though making the resolve after long deliberation, leaned forward, placed his rod on the table and adjusted his iron crown. Then, supporting his long olive chin with his hands, he turned his head to the old man: 'Proceed', he whispered.

Sourdust gathered the sacking about himself in a quick shaky way, and getting to his feet moved round to the back of his own chair which he pushed a few inches closer to the table, and squeezing between the table and the chair he re-seated himself carefully and was apparently more comfortable than before. Then with great deliberation, bending his corrugated brow upon each in turn he pushed the varied assortment of dishes, cruets, glasses, cutlery and by now tepid delicacies away from before him, clearing a semi-circle of white cloth. Only then did he remove the three tomes from beside his elbow. He opened them one after the other by balancing them carefully on their vellum spines and allowing them to break open at pages indicated by embroidered book-markers.

The left hand pages were headed with the date and in the first of the three books this was followed by a list of the activities to be performed hour by hour during the day by his lordship. The exact times; the garments to be worn for each occasion and the symbolic gestures to be used. Diagrams facing the left hand page gave particulars of the routes by which his lordship should approach the various scenes of operation. The diagrams were hand tinted.

The second tome was full of blank pages and was entirely symbolic, while the third was a mass of cross references. If, for instance, his lordship, Sepulchrave, the present Earl of Groan, had been three inches shorter, the costumes, gestures and even the routes would have differed from the ones described in the first tome, and from the enormous library, another volume would have had to have been chosen which would have applied. Had he been of a fair skin, or had he been heavier than he was, had his eyes been green, blue or brown instead of black, then, automatically another set of archaic regulations would have appeared this morning on the breakfast table. This complex system was understood in its entirety only by Sourdust – the technicalities demanding the devotion of a lifetime, though the sacred spirit of tradition implied by the daily manifestations was understood by all.

For the next twenty minutes Sourdust instructed his lordship in the less obvious details of the day's work that lay ahead, in a high cracked old voice, the cross-hatching of the skin at the corners of his mouth twitching between the sentences. His lordship nodded silently. Occasionally the routes marked down for the 'ninth' in the diagrams of the first tome are obsolete, as for instance, where at 2.37 in the afternoon Lord Groan was to have moved down the iron stairway in the grey vestibule that led to the pool of carp. That stairway had been warped and twisted out of shape seventy years ago when the vestibule had been razed to the ground in the great fire. An alternative route had to be planned. A plan approaching as far as possible to the spirit of the original conception, and taking the same amount of time. Sourdust scored the new route shakily on the tablecloth with the point of a fork. His lordship nodded.

The day's duties being clear, and with only a minute to run before ten, Sourdust relaxed in his chair and dribbled into his black-and-white beard. Every few seconds he glanced at the clock.

A long sigh came from his lordship. For a moment a light appeared in his eyes and then dulled. The line of his mouth seemed for a moment to have softened.

'Sourdust,' he said, 'have you heard about my son?'

Sourdust, with his eyes on the clock, had not heard his lordship's question. He was making noises in his throat and chest, his mouth working at the corners.

Lord Groan looked at him quickly and his face whitened under the olive. Taking a spoon he bent it into three-quarters of a circle.

The door opened suddenly in the wall behind the dais and Flay entered.

'T's time', he said, when he reached the table.

Lord Sepulchrave rose and moved to the door.

Flay nodded sullenly at the man in crimson sacking, and after filling his pockets with peaches followed his lordship between the pillars of the Stone Hall.

PRUNESQUALLOR'S KNEE-CAP

FUCHSIA'S bedroom was stacked at its four corners with her discarded toys, books and lengths of coloured cloth. It lay in the centre of the western wing and upon the second floor. A walnut bed monopolized the inner wall in which stood the doorway. The two triangular windows in the opposite wall gave upon the battlements where the master sculptors from the mud huts moved in silhouette across the sunset at the full moon of alternate months. Beyond the battlements the flat pastures spread and beyond the pastures were the Twisted Woods of thorn that climbed the ever steepening sides of Gormenghast mountain.

Fuchsia had covered the walls of her room with impetuous drawings in charcoal. There had been no attempt to create a design of any kind upon the coral plaster at either end of the bedroom. The drawings had been done at many an odd moment of loathing or excitement and although lacking in subtlety or proportion were filled with an extraordinary energy. These violent devices gave the two walls of her bedroom such an appearance of riot that the huddled heaps of toys and books in the four corners looked, by comparison, compact.

The attic, her kingdom, could be approached only through this bed-chamber. The door of the spiral staircase that ascended into the darkness was immediately behind the bedstead, so that to open this door which resembled the door of a cupboard, the bed had to be pulled forward into the room.

Fuchsia never failed to return the bed to its position as a precaution against her sanctum being invaded. It was unnecessary, for no one saving Mrs Slagg ever entered her bedroom and the old nurse in any case could never have manoeuvred herself up the hundred or so narrow, darkened steps that gave eventually on the attic, which since the earliest days Fuchsia could remember had been for her a world undesecrate.

Through succeeding generations a portion of the lumber of Gormenghast had found its way into this zone of moted half-light, this warm, breathless, timeless region where the great rafters moved across the air, clouded with moths. Where the dust was like pollen and lay softly on all things.

The attic was composed of two main galleries and a cock loft, the second gallery leading at right angles from the first after a descent of three rickety steps. At its far end a wooden ladder rose to a balcony resembling a narrow verandah. At the left extremity of this balcony a doorway, with its door hanging mutely by one hinge, led to the third of the three rooms that composed the attic. This was the loft which was for Fuchsia a very secret place, a kind of pagan chapel, an eyrie, a citadel, a kingdom never mentioned, for that would have been a breach of faith – a kind of blasphemy.

On the day of her brother's birth, while the castle beneath her, reaching in room below room, gallery below gallery, down, down to the very cellars, was alive with rumour, Fuchsia, like Rottcodd, in his Hall of the Bright Carvings was unaware of the excitement that filled it.

She had pulled at the long black pigtail of a chord which hung from the ceiling in one corner of her bedroom and had set a bell jangling in the remote apartment which Mrs Slagg had inhabited for two decades.

The sunlight was streaming through the eastern turrets and was lighting the Carvers' Battlement and touching the sides of the mountain beyond. As the sun rose, thorn tree after thorn tree on Gormenghast mountain emerged in the pale light and became a spectre, one following another, now here, now there, over the huge mass until the whole shape was flattened into a radiant jagged triangle against the darkness. Seven clouds like a group of naked cherubs or sucking-pigs, floated their plump pink bodies across a sky of slate. Fuchsia watched them through her window sullenly. Then she thrust her lower lip forward. Her hands were on her hips. Her bare feet were quite still on the floorboards.

'Seven', she said, scowling at each. 'There's seven of them. One, two, three, four, five, six, seven. Seven clouds.'

She drew a yellow shawl more tightly around her shoulders for she was shivering in her nightdress, and pulled the pigtail again for Mrs Slagg. Rummaging in a drawer, she found a stick of black chalk and approaching an area of wall that was comparatively vacant she chalked a vicious 7 and drew a circle round it with the word 'CLOWDS' written beneath in heavy, uncompromising letters.

As Fuchsia turned away from the wall she took an awkward shuffling step towards the bed. Her jet black hair hung loosely across her shoulders. Her eyes, that were always smouldering, were fixed on the door. Thus she remained with one foot forward as the door knob turned and Mrs Slagg entered.

Seeing her, Fuchsia continued her walk from where she had left off, but instead of going towards the bed, she approached Mrs Slagg with five strides, and putting her arms quickly around the old woman's neck, kissed her savagely, broke away, and then beckoning her to the window, pointed towards the sky. Mrs Slagg peered along Fuchsia's outstretched arm and finger and inquired what there was to look at.

'Fat clouds', said Fuchsia. 'There's seven of them.'

The old woman screwed up her eyes and peered once more but only for a moment. Then she made a little noise which seemed to indicate that she was not impressed.

'Why seven?' said Fuchsia. 'Seven is for something. What's seven for? One for a glorious golden grave – two for a terrible torch of tin; three for a hundred hollow horses; four for a knight with a spur of speargrass; five for a fish with fortunate fins, six – I've forgotten six, and seven – what's seven for? Eight for a frog with eyes like marbles, nine, what's nine? Nine for a – nine, nine – ten for a tower of turbulent toast – but what is seven. What is seven?'

Fuchsia stamped her foot and peered into the poor old nurse's face.

Nannie Slagg made little noises in her throat which was her way of filling in time and then said, 'Would you like some hot milk, my precious? Tell me now because I'm busy, and must feed your mother's white cats, dear. Just because I'm of the energetic system, my dearheart, they give me everything to do. What did you ring for? Quickly, quickly my caution. What did you ring for?'

Fuchsia bit her big red lower lip, tossed a mop of midnight

from her brow and gazed out of the window, her hands grasping her elbows behind her. Very stiff she had become and angular.

'I want a big breakfast', said Fuchsia at last. 'I want a lot to eat, I'm going to think today.'

Nannie Slagg was scrutinizing a wart on her left forearm.

'You don't know where I'm going, but I'm going somewhere where I can think.'

'Yes, dear', said the old nurse.

'I want hot milk and eggs and lots of toast done only on one side'. Fuchsia frowned as she paused; 'and I want a bag of apples to take along with me for the whole of the day, for I get hungry when I think.'

'Yes, dear', said Mrs Slagg again, pulling a loose thread from the hem of Fuchsia's skirt. 'Put some more on the fire, my caution, and I'll bring your breakfast and make your bed for you, though I'm not very well.'

Fuchsia descended suddenly upon her old nurse again and kissing her cheek, released her from the room, closing the door on her retreating figure with a crash that echoed down the gloomy corridors.

As soon as the door had closed, Fuchsia leaped at her bed and diving between the blankets head first, wriggled her way to the far end, where from all appearances, she became engaged in a life and death struggle with some ambushed monster. The heavings of the bedclothes ended as suddenly as they had begun and she emerged with a pair of long woollen stockings which she must have kicked off during the night. Sitting on her pillows she began pulling them on in a series of heaves, twisting with difficulty, at a very late stage, the heel of each from the front to the back.

'I won't see anybody today,' she said to herself – 'no, not anybody at all. I will go to my secret room and think things over.' She smiled a smile to herself. It was sly but it was so childishly sly that it was lovable. Her lips, big and well-formed and extraordinarily mature, curled up like plump petals and showed between them her white teeth.

As soon as she had smiled her face altered again, and the

petulant expression peregrine to her features took control. Her black eyebrows were drawn together.

Her dressing became interrupted between the addition of each garment by dance movements of her own invention. There was nothing elegant in these attitudes into which she flung herself, standing sometimes for a dozen of seconds at a time in some extraordinary position of balance. Her eyes would become glazed like her mother's and an expression of abstract calm would for an instant defy the natural concentration of her face. Finally her blood-red dress, absolutely shapeless, was pulled over her head. It fitted nowhere except where a green cord was knotted at her waist. She appeared rather to inhabit, than to wear her clothes.

Meanwhile Mrs Slagg had not only prepared the breakfast for Fuchsia in her own little room, but was on the way back with the loaded tray shaking in her hands. As she turned a corner of the corridor she was brought to a clattering standstill by the sudden appearance of Doctor Prunesquallor, who also halting with great suddenness, avoided a collision.

'Well, well, well, well, well, ha, ha, ha, if it isn't dear Mrs Slagg, ha, ha, ha, how very very, very dramatic', said the doctor, his long hands clasped before him at his chin, his high-pitched laugh creaking along the timber ceiling of the passage. His spectacles held in either lens the minute reflection of Nannie Slagg.

The old nurse had never really approved of Doctor Prunesquallor. It was true that he belonged to Gormenghast as much as the Tower itself. He was no intruder, but somehow, in Mrs Slagg's eyes he was definitely wrong. He was not her idea of a doctor in the first place, although she could never have argued why. Nor could she pin her dislike down to any other cause. Nannie Slagg found it very difficult to marshal her thoughts at the best of times, but when they became tied up with her emotions she became quite helpless. What she felt but had never analysed was that Doctor Prunesquallor rather played down to her and even in an obtuse way made fun of her. She had never thought this, but her bones knew of it.

She gazed up at the shock-headed man before her and wondered why he never brushed his hair, and then she felt guilty for allowing herself such thoughts about a gentleman and her tray shook and her eyes wavered a little.

'Ha, ha, ha, ha, ha, my dear Mrs Slagg, let me take your tray, ha, ha, until you have tasted the fruits of discourse and told me what you have been up to for the last month or more. Why have I not seen you, Nannie Slagg? Why have my ears not heard your footfall on the stairs, and your voice at nightfall, calling ... calling ...?'

'Her ladyship don't want me any more, sir', said Nannie Slagg, looking up at the doctor reproachfully. 'I am kept in the west wing now, sir.'

'So that's it, is it?' said Doctor Prunesquallor, removing the loaded tray from Nannie Slagg and lowering both it and himself at the same time to the floor of the long passage. He sat there on his heels with the tray at his side and peered up at the old lady, who gazed in a frightened way at his eye swimming hugely beneath his magnifying spectacles.

'You are *kept* in the west wing? So that's it?' Doctor Prunesquallor with his forefinger and thumb stroked his chin in a profound manner and frowned magnificently. 'It is the word "kept", my dear Mrs Slagg, that galls me. Are you an animal, Mrs Slagg? I repeat are you an animal?' As he said this he rose halfway to his feet and with his neck stretched forward repeated his question a third time.

Poor Nannie Slagg was too frightened to be able to give her answer to the query.

The doctor sank back on his heels.

'I will answer my own question, Mrs Slagg. I have known you for some time. For, shall we say, a decade? It is true we have never plumbed the depths of sorcery together nor argued the meaning of existence – but it is enough for me to say that I have known you for a considerable time, and that you are *no animal*. No animal *whatsoever*. Sit upon my knee.'

Nannie Slagg, terrified at this suggestion, raised her little bony hands to her mouth and raised her shoulders to her ears. Then she gave one frightened look down the passage and was about to make a run for it when she was gripped about the knees, not unkindly, but firmly and without knowing how she got there found herself sitting upon the high bony knee-cap of the squatting doctor.

'You are *not* an animal', repeated Prunesquallor, 'are you?'

The old nurse turned her wrinkled face to the doctor and shook her head in little jerks.

'Of course you're not. Ha, ha, ha, ha, ha, of course you're not. Tell me what you *are*?'

Nannie's fist again came to her mouth and the frightened look in her eyes reappeared.

'I'm ... I'm an old woman', she said.

'You're a very unique old woman', said the doctor, 'and if I am not mistaken, you will very soon prove to be an exceptionally invaluable old woman. Oh yes, ha, ha, ha, oh yes, a very invaluable old woman indeed.' (There was a pause.) 'How long is it since you saw her ladyship, the Countess? It must be a very long time.'

'It is, it is', said Nannie Slagg, 'a very long time. Months and months and months.'

'As I thought', said the doctor. 'Ha, ha, ha, as I very much thought. Then you can have no idea of why you will be indispensable?'

'Oh no, sir!' said Nannie Slagg, looking at the breakfast tray whose load was fast becoming cold.

'Do you like babies, my very dear Mrs Slagg?' asked the doctor, shifting the poor woman on to his other acutely bended knee joint and stretching out his former leg as though to ease it. 'Are you fond of the little creatures, taken by and large?'

'Babies?' said Mrs Slagg in the most animated tone that she had so far used. 'I could eat the little darlings, sir, I could eat them up!'

'Quite,' said Doctor Prunesquallor, 'quite so, my good woman. You could eat them up. That will be unnecessary. In fact it would be positively injurious, my dear Mrs Slagg, and especially under the circumstances about which I must now enlighten you. A child will be placed in your keeping. Do not devour him Nannie Slagg. It is for you to bring him up, that is true, but there will be no need for you to swallow

74

him first. You would be, ha, ha, ha, ha – swallowing a Groan.'

This news filtered by degrees through Nannie Slagg's brain and all at once her eyes looked very wide indeed.

'No, oh no, sir!'

'Yes, oh yes, sir!' replied the physician. 'Although the Countess has of late banished you from her presence, yet, Nannie Slagg, you will of necessity be restored, ha, ha, ha, be restored to a very important state. Sometime today, if I am not mistaken, my wide-eyed Nannie Slagg, I shall be delivering a brand new Groan. Do you remember when I delivered the Countess of Lady Fuchsia?'

Nannie Slagg began to shake all over and a tear ran down her cheek as she clasped her hands between her knees, very nearly overbalancing from her precarious perch.

'I can remember every little thing sir – every little thing. Who would have thought?'

'Exactly,' interrupted Doctor Prunesquallor. 'Who would have thought. But I must be going, ha, ha, ha, I must dislodge you, Nannie Slagg, from my patella – but tell me, did you know nothing of her ladyship's condition?'

'Oh, sir,' said the old lady, biting her knuckle and shifting her gaze. 'Nothing! nothing! No one ever tells me anything.'

'Yet all the duties will devolve on you', said Doctor Prunesquallor. 'Though you will doubtless enjoy yourself. There is no doubt at all about that. Is there?'

'Oh, sir, another baby, after all this time! Oh, I could smack him already.'

'Him?' queried the doctor. 'Ha, ha, ha, you are very sure of the gender, my dear Mrs Slagg.'

'Oh yes, sir, it's a him, sir. Oh, what a blessing that it is. They will let me have him, sir? They will let me won't they?'

'They have no choice', said the doctor somewhat too briskly for a gentleman and he smiled a wide inane smile, his thin nose pointing straight at Mrs Slagg. His grey hayrick of hair removed itself from the wall. 'What of my Fuchsia? Has she an inkling?'

'Oh, no, not an inkling. Not an inkling, sir, bless her. She hardly ever leaves her room except at night, sir. She don't know nothing, sir, and never talks to no one but me.'

The doctor, removing Nannie Slagg from his knee, rose to his feet. 'The rest of Gormenghast talks of nothing else, but the western wing is in darkness. Very, very, very strange. The child's nurse and the child's sister are in darkness, ha, ha, ha. But not for long, not for long. By all that's enlightened, very much not so!'

'Sir?' queried Nannie Slagg as the doctor was about to move away.

'What?' said Doctor Prunesquallor, scrutinizing his finger nails. 'What is it my dear Mrs Slagg? Be quick.'

'Er – how is she, sir? How is her ladyship?'

'Tough as behemoth', said Prunesquallor, and was around the corner in an instant, and Nannie Slagg, with her mouth and eyes wide open, could, as she lifted up the cold tray, hear his feet in a far passage tapping an elegant tattoo as he moved like a bird towards the bedroom of the Countess of Groan.

As Mrs Slagg knocked at Fuchsia's door, her heart was beating very fast. It was always a long time before she realized the import of whatever she were told, and it was only now that the full measure of what the doctor had divulged was having its effect. To be again, after all these years, the nurse of an heir to the house of Groan – to be able to bathe the helpless limbs, to iron out the little garments and to select the wet nurse from the outer dwellings! To have complete authority in anything connected with the care of the precious mite – all this was now weighing with a great load of painful pride across her heart that was beating rapidly.

So overpowered was she by this emotion that she had knocked twice before she noticed that there was a note pinned upon the outside of the door. Peering at it she at last made out what Fuchsia had scrawled in her invariable charcoal.

Can't wait until the doomsday – you're so SLOW!

Mrs Slagg tried the door handle although she knew that the door would be locked. Leaving the tray and the apples on the mat outside she retreated to her own room where she might indulge herself in halcyon glimpses of the future. Life, it seemed, was not over for her.

THE ATTIC

MEANWHILE Fuchsia had, after waiting impatiently for her breakfast, gone to a cupboard where she kept an emergency supply of eatables – half an old seed cake and some dandelion wine. There was also a box of dates which Flay had purloined and brought up for her several weeks before, and two wrinkled pears. These she wrapped in a piece of cloth. Next she lit a candle and placed it on the floor near the wall, then hollowing her strong young back she laid hold of the foot-rail of her bed and dragged it back sufficiently for her to squeeze herself between the rail and the wall and to unlatch the cupboard door. Stretching over the head-rail she grasped her bundle of food and then picked up the candle from near her feet, and ducking her head crept through the narrow opening and found herself at the lowermost steps of the flight that led upwards in dark spirals. Closing the door behind her, she dragged a bolt into position and the tremors which she always experienced at this moment of locking herself in, took hold of her and for a moment she shook from head to foot.

Then, with her candle lighting her face and the three sliding steps before her as she climbed, she ascended into her region.

As Fuchsia climbed into the winding darkness her body was impregnated and made faint by a qualm as of green April. Her heart beat painfully.

This is a love that equals in its power the love of man for woman and reaches inwards as deeply. It is the love of a man or of a woman for their world. For the world of their centre where their lives burn genuinely and with a free flame.

The love of the diver for his world of wavering light. His world of pearls and tendrils and his breath at his breast. Born as a plunger into the deeps he is at one with every swarm of lime-green fish, with every coloured sponge. As he holds himself to the ocean's faery floor, one hand clasped to a bedded whale's rib, he is complete and infinite. Pulse, power and universe sway in his body. He is in love.

The love of the painter standing alone and staring, staring at the great coloured surface he is making. Standing with him in the room the rearing canvas stares back with tentative shapes halted in their growth, moving in a new rhythm from floor to ceiling. The twisted tubes, the fresh paint squeezed and smeared across the dry upon his palette. The dust beneath the easel. The paint has edged along the brushes' handles. The white light in a northern sky is silent. The window gapes as he inhales his world. His world: a rented room, and turpentine. He moves towards his half-born. He is in love.

The rich soil crumbles through the yeoman's fingers. As the pearl diver murmurs, 'I am home' as he moves dimly in strange water-lights, and as the painter mutters, 'I am me' on his lone raft of floorboards, so the slow landsman on his acre'd marl – says with dark Fuchsia on her twisting staircase, 'I am home.'

It was this feeling of belonging to the winding stair and the attic which Fuchsia experienced as she ran her right hand along the wooden wall as she climbed and encountered after some time the loose board which she expected. She knew that only eighteen steps remained and that after two more turns in the staircase the indescribable grey-gold filtering glow of the attic would greet her.

Reaching the top-most step she stooped and leaned over a three-foot swing door, like the door of a byre, unfastened the latch and entered the first of the three sections of the attic.

An infiltration of the morning's sun gave the various objects a certain vague structure but in no way dispelled the darkness. Here and there a thin beam of light threaded the warm brooding dusk and was filled with slowly moving motes like an attenuate firmament of stars revolving in grave order.

One of these narrow beams lit Fuchsia's forehead and shoulder, and another plucked a note of crimson from her dress. To her right was an enormous crumbling organ. Its pipes were broken and the keyboard shattered. Across its front the labour of a decade of grey spiders had woven their webs into a shawl of lace. It needed but the ghost of an infanta to arise from the dust to gather it about her head and shoulders as the most fabulous of all mantillas.

In the gloom Fuchsia's eyes could barely be seen for the light upon her forehead sank deeper shadows, by contrast, through her face. But they were calm. The excitement that had wakened within them on the stairway had given place to this strange calm. She stood at the stairhead almost another being.

This room was the darkest. In the summer the light seemed to penetrate through the fissures in the warped wood and through the dislodged portions of stone slating in a less direct way than was the case in the larger room or gallery to its right. The third, the smallest attic, with its steps leading upwards from the gallery with the banistered verandah was the best lit, for it boasted a window with shutters which, when opened, gave upon a panorama of roof-tops, towers and battlements that lay in a great half-circle below. Between high bastions might be seen, hundreds of feet beneath, a portion of quadrangle where-in, were a figure to move across, he would appear no taller than a thimble.

Fuchsia took three paces forward in the first of the attics and then paused a moment to re-tie a string above her knee. Over her head vague rafters loomed and while she straightened her-self she noticed them and unconsciously loved them. This was the lumber room. Though very long and lofty it looked rela-tively smaller than it was, for the fantastic piles of every imaginable kind of thing, from the great organ to the lost and painted head of a broken toy lion that must one day have been the plaything of one of Fuchsia's ancestors, spread from every wall until only an avenue was left to the adjacent room. This high, narrow avenue wound down the centre of the first attic before suddenly turning at a sharp angle to the right. The fact that this room was filled with lumber did not mean that she ignored it and used it only as a place of transit. Oh no, for it was here that many long afternoons had been spent as she crawled deep into the recesses and found for herself many a strange cavern among the incongruous relics of the past. She knew of ways through the centre of what appeared to be hills of furniture, boxes, musical instruments and toys, kites, pic-tures, bamboo armour and helmets, flags and relics of every kind, as an Indian knows his green and secret trail. Within reach of her hand the hide and head of a skinned baboon hung dustily over a broken drum that rose beyond above the dim ranges of this attic medley. Huge and impregnable they looked in the warm still half-light, but Fuchsia, had she wished to, could have disappeared awkwardly but very suddenly into these fantastic mountains, reached their centre and lain down upon an ancient couch with a picture book at her elbow and been entirely lost to view within a few moments.

This morning, she was bound for the third of her rooms and moved forward through the canyon, ducking beneath the stuffed leg of a giraffe that caught a thread of the moted sunlight and which, propped across Fuchsia's path, made a kind of low lintel immediately before the passage curved away to the right. As Fuchsia rounded this bend she saw what she expected to see. Twelve feet away were the wooden steps which led down to the second attic. The rafters above the steps were warped into a sagging curve so that it was not possible to obtain more than a restricted view of the room beyond. But the area of empty floor that was visible gave an indication of the whole. She descended the steps. There was a ripping away of clouds; a sky, a desert, a forsaken shore spread through her.

As she stepped forward on the empty board, it was for her like walking into space. Space, such as the condors have shrill inklings of, and the cock-eagle glimpses through his blood.

Silence was there with a loud rhythm. The halls, towers, the rooms of Gormenghast were of another planet. Fuchsia caught at a thick lock of her hair and dragged her own head back as her heart beat loudly and, tingling from head to foot little diamonds appeared at the inner corners of her eyes.

With what characters she had filled this lost stage of emptiness! It was here that she would see the people of her imagination, the fierce figures of her making, as they strolled from corner to corner, brooded like monsters or flew through the air like seraphs with burning wings, or danced, or fought, or laughed, or cried. This was her attic of make-believe, where she would watch her mind's companions advancing or retreating across the dusty floor.

Gripping her eatables tightly in their cloth, her feet echoing dully, she walked onwards towards the fixed ladder that led to the balcony at the far end. She climbed the ladder, both feet coming together on each rung for it was difficult for her to climb with the bottle and her food for the day tucked under her arm. There was no one to see her strong ~traight back and shoulders and the gauche, indecorous movements of her legs as she climbed in her crimson dress; nor the length of her tangled and inky hair. Half-way up she was able to lift her bundle above her head and push it on to the balcony, and then to swarm after it and find herself standing with the great stage below her as empty as an unremembered heart.

As she looked down, her hands on the wooden banister that ran along the attic verandah, she knew that at a call she could set in motion the five main figures of her making. Those whom she had so often watched below her, almost as though they were really there. At first it had not been easy to understand them nor to tell them what to do. But now it would be easy, at any rate for them to enact the scenes that she had watched them so often perform. Munster, who would crawl along the rafters and drop chuckling into the middle of the floor in a cloud of dust and then bow to Fuchsia before turning and searching for his barrel of bright gold. Or the Rain Man, who moved always with his head lowered and his hands clasped behind him and who had but to lift his eyelid to quell the tiger that followed him on a chain.

These and the dramas in which they took part were now latent in the room below her, but Fuchsia passed the high-backed chair where she would sit at the verendah edge, pulled back the door carefully on its one hinge, and entered into the third of the three rooms.

She put her bundle upon a table in one corner, went to the window and pushed open the two shutters. Her stocking was half-way down her leg again and she knotted the string more firmly round her thigh. It was often her habit in this room to think aloud to herself. To argue with herself. Looking down from her little window upon the roofs of the castle and its adjacent buildings she tasted the pleasure of her isolation. 'I am alone', she said, her chin in her hands and her elbows on the sill. 'I am quite alone, like I enjoy it. Now I can think for there's no one to provoke me here. Not in my room. No one to tell me what I ought to do because I'm a Lady. Oh no. I do just what I like here. Fuchsia is quite alright here. None of them knows where I go to. Flay doesn't know. Father doesn't know. Mother doesn't know. None of them knows. Even Nannie doesn't know. Only I know. I know where I go. I go here. This is where I go. Up the stairs and into my lumber room. Through my lumber room and into my acting room. All across my acting room and up the ladder and on to my verandah. Through the door and into my secret attic. And here it is I am. I am here now. I have been here lots of times but that is in the past. That is over, but now I'm here it's in the present. This is the present. I'm looking on the roofs of the present and I'm leaning on the present window-sill and later on when I'm older I will lean on this window-sill again. Over and over again.

'Now I'll make myself comfortable and eat my breakfast', she continued to herself, but as she turned away her quick eyes noticed in the corner of one of the diminished quadrangles far below her an unusually large gathering of what she could just make out to be servants from the kitchen quarters. She was so used to the panorama below her being deserted at that hour in the morning, the menials being at their multifarious duties about the castle that she turned suddenly back to the window and stared down with a sense of suspicion and almost of fear. What was it that quickened her to a sense of something irreparable having been done? To an outsider there would have been nothing untoward or extraordinary in the fact that a group had gathered hundreds of feet below in the corner of a sunny stone quadrangle, but Fuchsia born and bred to the iron ritual of Gormenghast knew that something unprecedented was afoot. She stared, and as she stared the group grew. It was enough to throw Fuchsia out of her mood and to make her uneasy and angry.

'Something has happened,' she said, 'something no one's told me of. They haven't told me. I don't like them. I don't like any of them. What are they all doing like a lot of ants down there? Why aren't they working like they should be?' She turned around and faced her little room.

Everything was changed, she picked up one of the pears and bit a piece out of it abstractedly. She had looked forward to a morning of rumination and perhaps a play or two in the empty attic before she climbed down the stairs again to demand a big tea from Mrs Slagg. There was something portentous in the group far below her. Her day was disrupted.

She looked around at the walls of her room. They were hung with pictures once chosen as her favourites from among the scores that she had unearthed in the lumber room. One wall was filled with a great mountain scene where a road like a snake winding around and around the most impressive of crags was filled with two armies, one in yellow and the other, the invading force battling up from below, in purple. Lit as it were by torch-light the whole scene was a constant source of wonder to Fuchsia, yet this morning she gazed at it blankly. The other walls were less imposingly arranged, fifteen pictures being distributed among the three. The head of a jaguar; a portrait of the twenty-second Earl of Groan with pure white hair and a face the colour of smoke as a result of immoderate tattooing, and a group of children in pink and white muslin dresses playing with a viper were among the works which pleased her most. Hundreds of very dull heads and full-length portraits of her ancestors had been left in the lumber room. What Fuchsia wanted from a picture was something unexpected. It was as though she enjoyed the artist telling her something quite fresh and new. Something she had never thought of before.

A great writhing root, long since dragged from the woods of Gormenghast mountain, stood in the centre of the room. It had been polished to a rare gloss, its every wrinkle gleaming. Fuchsia flung herself down on the most imposing article in the room, a couch of faded splendour and suavity of contour in which the angles of Fuchsia's body as she lay in a half sprawl were thrown out with uncompromising severity. Her eyes which, since she had entered the attic, had taken on the calm expression so alien to her, were now smouldering again. They moved about the room as though they were seeking in vain a resting place, but neither the fantastic root, nor the ingenious patterns in the carpet below her had the power to hold them.

'Everything's wrong. Everything. Everything', said Fuchsia. Again she went to the window and peered down at the group in the quadrangle. By now it had grown until it filled all that was visible of the stone square. Through a flying buttress to the left of her she could command a view of four distant alleys in a poor district of Gormenghast. These alley-ways were pranked with little knots of folk, and Fuchsia believed that she could hear the far sound of their voices rising through the air. It was not that Fuchsia felt any particular interest in 'occasions' or festivities which might cause excitement below, but that this morning she felt acutely aware that something in which she would become involved was taking place.

On the table lay a big coloured book of verses and pictures. It was always ready for her to open and devour. Fuchsia would turn over the pages and read the verses aloud in a deep dramatic voice. This morning she leaned forward and turned over the pages listlessly. As she came upon a great favourite she paused and read it through slowly, but her thoughts were elsewhere.

THE FRIVOLOUS CAKE

A freckled and frivolous cake there was
　　That sailed on a pointless sea,
Or any lugubrious lake there was
　　In a manner emphatic and free.
How jointlessly, and how jointlessly
　　The frivolous cake sailed by
On the waves of the ocean that pointlessly
　　Threw fish to the lilac sky.

Oh, plenty and plenty of hake there was
　　Of a glory beyond compare,
And every conceivable make there was
　　Was tossed through the lilac air.

Up the smooth billows and over the crests
　　Of the cumbersome combers flew
The frivolous cake with a knife in the wake
　　Of herself and her curranty crew,
Like a swordfish grim it would bounce and skim

(This dinner knife fierce and blue),
And the frivolous cake was filled to the brim
  With the fun of her curranty crew.

Oh, plenty and plenty of hake there was
  Of a glory beyond compare –
And every conceivable make there was
  Was tossed through the lilac air.

Around the shores of the Elegant Isles
  Where the cat-fish bask and purr
And lick their paws with adhesive smiles
  And wriggle their fins of fur,
They fly and fly 'neath the lilac sky –
  The frivolous cake, and the knife
Who winketh his glamorous indigo eye
  In the wake of his future wife.

The crumbs blow free down the pointless sea
  To the beat of a cakey heart
And the sensitive steel of the knife can feel
  That love is a race apart.
In the speed of the lingering light are blown
  The crumbs to the hake above,
And the tropical air vibrates to the drone
  Of a cake in the throes of love.

She ended the final verse with a rush, taking in nothing at all of its meaning. As she ended the last line mechanically, she found herself getting to her feet and making for the door. Her bundle was left behind, open, but, save for the pear, untouched on the table. She found herself on the balcony and lowering herself down the ladder was in the empty attic and within a few moments had reached the head of the stairs in the lumber room. As she descended the spiral staircase her thoughts were turning over and over.

'What have they done? What have they done?' And it was in a precipitous mood that she entered her room and ran to the corner where, catching hold of the pigtail bell-rope she pulled it as though to wrench it from the ceiling.

Within a few moments Mrs Slagg came running up to the door, her slippered feet scraping along unevenly on the floorboards. Fuchsia opened the door to her and as soon as the poor old head appeared around the panels, she shouted at it, 'What's happening Nannie, what's happening down there? Tell me at once, Nannie, or I won't love you. Tell me, tell me.'

'Quiet, my caution, quiet', said Mrs Slagg. 'What's all the bother, my conscience! oh my poor heart. You'll be the death of me.'

'You must tell me, Nannie. Now! now! or I'll hit you,' said Fuchsia.

From so small a beginning of suspicion Fuchsia's fears had grown until now, convinced by a mounting intuition, she was almost on the point of striking her old nurse, whom she loved so desperately. Nannie Slagg took hold of Fuchsia's hand between eight old fingers and squeezed it.

'A little brother for you, my pretty. Now *there's* a surprise to quieten you; a little *brother*. Just like you, my ugly darling – born in the lapsury.'

'No!' shouted Fuchsia, the blood rushing to her cheek. 'No! no! I won't have it. Oh no, no, no! I won't! I won't! It *mustn't* be, it *mustn't* be!' And Fuchsia flinging herself to the floor burst into a passion of tears.

'MRS SLAGG BY MOONLIGHT'

THESE then, Lord Sepulchrave, the Countess Gertrude, Fuchsia their eldest child, Doctor Prunesquallor, Mr Rottcodd, Flay, Swelter, Nannie Slagg, Steerpike and Sourdust, have been discovered at their pursuits on the day of the advent, and have perhaps indicated the atmosphere into which it was the lot of Titus to be born.

For his first few years of life, Titus was to be left to the care of Nannie Slagg, who bore this prodigious responsibility proudly upon her thin little sloping shoulders. During the first half of this early period only two major ceremonies befell the child and of these Titus was happily unaware, namely the christening, which took place twelve days after his birth, and a ceremonial breakfast on his first birthday. Needless to say, to Mrs Slagg, every day presented a series of major happenings, so entirely was she involved in the practicalities of his upbringing.

She made her way along the narrow stone path between the acacia trees on this memorable nativity evening and downhill to the gate in the castle wall which led into the heart of the mud dwellings. As she hurried along, the sun was setting behind Gormenghast mountain in a swamp of saffron light and her shadow hurried alongside between the acacia trees. It was seldom that she ventured out of doors and it was with quite a flutter that she had opened with difficulty the heavy lid of a chest in her room and extricated, from beneath a knoll of camphor, her best hat. It was very black indeed, but by way of relief it had upon its high crown a brittle bunch of glass grapes. Four or five of them had been broken but this was not very noticeable.

Nannie Slagg had lifted the hat up to her shoulder level and peered at it obliquely before puffing at the glass grapes to remove any possible dust. Seeing that she had dulled them with her breath she lifted up her petticoat and doubling up over her hat she gave a quick little polish to each fruit in turn.

Then she had approached the door of her room almost furtively and placed her ear at the panel. She had heard nothing, but whenever she found herself doing anything unorthodox, no matter how necessary, she would feel very guilty inside and look around her with her red rimmed eyes opened wide and her head shaking a little, or if alone in a room, as at the moment, she would run to the door and listen.

When she felt quite certain that there was no one there she would open the door very quickly and stare out into the empty passage and then go to her task again with renewed confidence. This time, the putting on of her best hat at nine o'clock at night with the idea of sallying forth from the castle, down the long drive and then northwards along the acacia avenue, had been enough to send her to her own doorway as though she suspected someone might be there, someone who was listening to her thoughts. Tiptoeing back to her bed she had added fourteen inches to her stature by climbing into her velvet hat. Then she had left the room, and the stairs had seemed frighteningly empty to her as she descended the two flights.

Remembering, as she turned through the main doorway of the west wing, that the Countess herself had given her the orders to pursue this unusual mission, she had felt a little stronger, but whatever factual authority, it was something much deeper that had worried her, something based upon the unspoken and iron-bound tradition of the place. It had made her feel she was doing wrong. However, a wet nurse had to be found for the infant and the immediate logic of this had jostled her forward. As she had left her own room she had picked up a pair of black woollen gloves. It was a soft, warm, summer evening but Nannie Slagg felt stronger in her gloves.

The acacia trees, silhouetted on her right, cut patterns against the mountain and on her left glowed dimly with a sort of subterranean light. Her path was striped like the dim hide of a zebra from the shadows of the acacia trunks. Mrs Slagg, a midget figure beneath the rearing and overhanging of the aisle of dark foliage, awakened small echoes in the neighbouring rocks as she had moved, for her heels beat a quick uneven measure on the stone path.

This avenue lasted for some considerable distance, and when at last the old nurse found herself at its northern end she was welcomed by the cold light of the rising moon. The outer wall of Gormenghast had suddenly reared above her. She passed through an archway.

Mrs Slagg knew that about this hour the Dwellers would be at their supper. As she pattered onwards the memory of a very similar occasion worked its way into her consciousness: The time when she had been delegated to make a similar choice for Fuchsia. That time it had also been in the evening although an hour or so earlier. The weather had been gusty and she remembered how her voice had failed to carry in the wind, and how they had all misunderstood her and had imagined that Lord Groan had died.

Only three times since that day had she been to this part of the Dwellers' province, and on those occasions it had been to take Fuchsia for the long walks that at one time she had so insisted upon, rain or shine.

Mrs Slagg's days of long walks were over, but she had on one of those occasions passed the mud huts when the Dwellers were having their last meal. She knew that the Dwellers always had their supper in the open, at tables that reached in four long rows over the drab, grey-coloured dust. In this dust, she remembered, a few cactus trees were alone able to take root.

Following the gradual decline of a scarred green that sloped from the arch in the wall and petered out into the dust upon which the hovels were built, she saw suddenly, on raising her eyes from the path, one of these cactus trees.

Fifteen years is a difficult depth of time for an old woman's memory to plumb – more difficult than the waters of her childhood, but when Mrs Slagg saw the cactus tree she remembered clearly and in detail how she had stopped and stared at the great scarred monster on the day of Fuchsia's birth.

Here it was again, its flaking bole dividing into four uprights like the arms of a huge grey candlestick studded with thorns, each one as large and brutal as the horn of a rhinoceros. No flaming flower relieved its black achromatism although that tree had been known long ago to burst open with a three-hour glory. Beyond this tree the ground rose into a little dreary hill, and it was only when she had climbed this hill that Mrs Slagg saw before her the Dwellers at their long tables. Behind them the clay huts were huddled together in a grey swarm, spreading to the foot of the wall. Four or five cacti grew between and reared over the supper tables.

The cacti were similar both in size and in the way they split into high uncouth prongs to the one which Mrs Slagg first saw, and as she approached, were edged with the hot afterglow of the sun.

At the line of tables nearest the outer wall were ranged the elderly, the grandparents, the infirm. To their left, were the married women and their children whom they were tending.

The remaining two tables were filled with men and boys. The girls from the age of twelve to twenty-three had their meals in a low mud building on their own, a few of them being delegated to wait each day upon the ancients at their tables immediately under the battlements.

Beyond, the land dipped into a dry shallow valley which held the dwellings, so that as she came forward step by step the figures at the tables had for their background the rough roofs of mud, the walls of their huts being hidden by the contour of the ground. It was a dreary prospect. From the lush shadows of the acacia drive Mrs Slagg had suddenly broken in upon an arid world. She saw the rough sections of white jarl root and their bowls of sloe wine standing before them. The long tubular jarl root which they dug each day from a wood in the vicinity, stood upon the tables every evening, sliced up into scores of narrow cylinders. This, she remembered, was their traditional diet.

Noting the white roots spreading away in perspective, each piece with its shadow, she remembered with a flutter that her social status was very much in advance of that held by these poor mud-hut dwellers. It was true that they made pretty carvings, but they were not *within* the walls of Gormenghast, and Nannie Slagg, as she approached the nearest table, pulled on her gloves more tightly still and worked them up around her fingers, pursing her little wrinkled mouth.

The Dwellers had seen her immediately her hat had appeared above the dry brow of the hill, and every head had been turned, and every eye focused upon her. The mothers had paused, some of them with spoons halfway to their children's mouths.

It was unusual for them to have the 'Castles', as they termed any who came from within the walls, approach them at their meals. They stared without moving and without speaking.

Mrs Slagg had stopped. The moonlight flared on the glass grapes.

A very old man like a prophet arose and approached her. When he reached her he stood silently until an elderly woman who had waited until he halted, was helped to her feet and, following his example, had reached Mrs Slagg and stood silently by the old man's side. Thereupon two magnificent urchins of five or six years of age had been sent forward from the table of mothers. These two, when they reached Mrs Slagg stood quietly and then, lifting their arms in imitation of their elders and, placing their wrists together cupped their hands and bowed their heads.

They remained in this attitude for a few moments until the old man lifted his shaggy head and parted the long rough line of his mouth.

'Gormenghast', he said, and his voice was like the noise of boulders rolling through far valleys, and as he had said 'Gormenghast' the intonation was such as implied reverence. This was the greeting of the Dwellers to any who were of the Castle and once that word had been spoken the person to whom it was addressed replied – 'The Bright Carvers'. Conversation could then proceed. This response, deaf as the Dwellers were to any flattery, holding themselves to be the supreme judges of their work and indifferent to the outside interest, was in its way a palliative in the sense that it put them where they felt in their bones they belonged – on a spiritual if not a worldly or hereditary level. It introduced a certain concord at the outset. It was a master stroke of judgement, a tower of tact, in the seventeenth Earl of Groan, when hundreds of years before he had introduced this tenet into the ritual of the Castle.

Very, very far from bright were the Carvers themselves. They were uniformly dressed in dark grey cloth, tied about the waist with tough thongs which were stripped from the outer surface of the jarl root, whose inner hard white flesh they ate. Nothing was bright about their appearance, save one thing. The light in the eyes of the younger children. Indeed, in the youths and maidens also up to the age of nineteen and sometimes twenty. These young Dwellers were in such contrast to their elders, even to those in their mid-twenties, that it was difficult to imagine that they were of the same stock. The tragic reason was that after they had come to their physical maturity of form their loveliness crumbled away and they became withered as flowers after their few fresh hours of brilliance and strength.

No one looked middle aged. The mothers were, save for the few who had borne their children in their late teens, as ancient in appearance as their own parents.

And yet they did not die as might be imagined, any earlier than is normal. On the contrary, from the long line of ancient faces at the three tables nearest the great wall, it might be imagined that their longevity was abnormal.

Only their children's had radiance, their eyes, the sheen on their hair, and in another way, their movements and their voices. Bright with a kind of *unnatural* brightness. It was not the wholesome lustre of a free flame, but of the hectic radiance that sheet-lightning gives suddenly to limbs of trees at midnight; of sudden flares in the darkness, of a fragment that is lit by torchlight into a spectre.

Even this unnatural emanation died in these youths and girls when they had reached their nineteenth year; along with the beauty of their features, this radiance vanished too. Only *within* the bodies of the adult Dwellers was there a kind of light, or if not light, at least hotness – the hotness of creative restlessness. These were the Bright Carvers.

Mrs Slagg hoisted her little claw of a hand very high in the air. The four who were lined in front of her had taken less formal stances, the children peering up at her with their slim, dusty arms around each others' shoulders.

'I have come', she said in a voice which, thin as a curlew, carried along the tables, 'I have come – although it is so late – to tell you a wonderful thing.' She readjusted her hat and felt as she did so, with great pleasure, the shining volume of the glass grapes.

The old man turned to the tables and his voice rolled out along them. 'She has come to tell us a wonderful thing', and the old woman followed him up like a distorted echo and screamed, 'A wonderful thing.'

'Yes, yes, it is wonderful news for you,' the old nurse continued. 'You will all be very proud, I am quite sure.'

Mrs Slagg, now she had started was rather enjoying herself. She clasped her gloved hands together more tightly whenever she felt a qualm of nervousness.

'We are all proud. All of us. The Castle', (she said this in a rather vain way) 'is very very satisfied and when I tell you what has happened, then, you'll be happy as well; oh yes, I am sure you will. Because I know you are *dependent* on the castle.'

Mrs Slagg was never very tactful. 'You have some food thrown down to you from the battlements every morning, don't you?' She had pursed her mouth and stopped a moment for breath.

A young man lifted his thick black eyebrows and spat.

'So you are very much thought of by the Castle. Every day you are thought of, aren't you? And that's why you'll be so happy when I tell you the wonderful thing that I'm going to tell you.'

Mrs Slagg smiled to herself for a moment, but suddenly felt a little nervous in spite of her superior knowledge and had glanced quickly, like a bird, from one face to another. She had bridled up her wispy head and had peered as sternly as she could at a small boy who answered her with a flashing smile. His hair was clustered over his shoulders. Between his teeth as he grinned glistened a white nugget of jarl root.

She shifted her gaze and clapped her hands together sharply two or three times as though for silence, although there was no noise at all. Then she suddenly felt she wanted to be back in the castle and in her own little room and she said before she knew it, 'A new little Groan has been born, a little boy. A little boy of the Blood. I am in charge, of course, and I want a wet nurse for him *at once*. I must have one *at once* to come back with me. There now! I've told you everything.'

The old women had turned to one another and had then walked away to their huts. They returned with little cakes and bottles of sloe wine. Meanwhile the men formed a large circle and repeated the name Gormenghast seventy-seven times. While Mrs Slagg waited and watched the children who had been set playing, a woman had come forward. She told Mrs Slagg that her child had died a few hours after he had been born some days ago but that she was strong enough and would come. She was, perhaps, twenty, and was well-built, but the tragic disintegration

of her beauty had begun although her eyes still had the afterglow upon them. She fetched a basket and did not seem to expect any sort of refusal to her offer. And Nannie Slagg was
about to ask a few questions, as she felt would be correct, but
the Dweller, packing the sloe wine and cakes into a basket, had
taken Mrs Slagg quietly by the arm and the old nurse found
herself to be making for the Great Wall. She glanced up at
the young woman beside her and wondered whether she had
chosen correctly, and then, realizing that she hadn't chosen
at all, she half stopped and glanced back nervously over her
shoulder.

KEDA

THE cactus trees stood hueless between the long tables. The
Dwellers were all in their places again. Mrs Slagg ceased to
interest them. There were no shadows save immediately below every object. The moon was overhead. It was a picture
painted on silver. Mrs Slagg's companion had waited with her
quietly. There was a kind of strength in the way she walked
and in the way she kept silent. With the dark cloth hanging to
her ankles and caught in at her waist with the thong of jarl
root; with her bare legs and feet and her head still holding the
sunset of her darkened day, she was in strange contrast to little
Nannie Slagg, with her quick jerky walk, her dark satin dress,
her black gloves, and her monumental hat of glass grapes. Before they descended the dry knoll towards the archway in the
wall, a sudden guttural cry as of someone being strangled, froze
the old woman's blood and she clutched at the strong arm
beside her and clung to it like a child. Then she peered towards
the tables. They were too far for her to see clearly with her
weak eyes, but she thought she could make out figures standing
and there seemed to be someone crouching like a creature about
to spring.

Mrs Slagg's companion appeared, after glancing casually in
the direction of the sound, to take no more notice of the inci-

dent, but keeping a firmer grip this time on the old lady, propelled her forward towards the stone gate.

'It is nothing', was the sole reply which Mrs Slagg received and by the time the two were in the acacia avenue her blood had quietened.

When they were turning from the long drive into the doorway of Gormenghast through which Nannie had stepped out into the evening air so surreptitiously an hour or so before, she glanced up at her companion and shrugging her shoulders a little, contrived to take on an expression of mock importance.

'Your name? Your name?' she said.

'Keda.'

'Well, Keda, dear, if you will follow me, I will take you to the little boy. I'll show you him myself. He is by the window in *my* room.' Nannie's voice suddenly took on a confidential, almost pathetic note. 'I haven't a very big room', she said, 'but I've always had the same one, I don't like any of the other ones,' she added rather untruthfully, 'I'm nearer Lady Fuchsia.'

'Perhaps I shall see her', said the girl, after a pause.

Nannie suddenly stopped on the stairs. 'I don't *know* about that,' she said, 'oh no, I'm not *sure* about that. She is very strange. I never know what she's going to do next.'

'To do?' said Keda. 'How do you mean?'

'About little Titus.' Nannie's eyes began to wander. 'No, I don't know what she'll do. She's such a terror – the naughtiest terror in the castle – she can be.'

'Why are you frightened?' said Keda.

'I know she'll hate him. She likes to be the only one, you know. She likes to dream that she's the queen and that when the rest are dead there'll be no one who can order her to do anything. She said, dear, that she'd burn down the whole place, burn down Gormenghast when she was the ruler and she'd live on her own, and I said she was wicked, and she said that everyone was – everyone and everything except rivers, clouds, and some rabbits. She makes me frightened sometimes.'

They climbed up remaining steps, along a passageway and up the remaining flight to the second floor in silence.

When they had come to the room Mrs Slagg placed her finger

at her lips and gave a smile which it would be impossible to describe. It was a mixture of the cunning and the maudlin. Then turning the handle very carefully she opened the door by degrees and putting her high hat of glass grapes through the narrow opening by way of a vanguard, followed it stealthily with all that remained of her.

Keda entered the room. Her bare feet made no noise on the floor. When Mrs Slagg reached the cradle she put her fingers to her mouth and peered over it as though into the deepest recesses of an undiscovered world. There he was. The infant Titus. His eyes were open but he was quite still. The puckered-up face of the newly-born child, old as the world, wise as the roots of trees. Sin was there and goodness, love, pity and horror, and even beauty for his eyes were pure violet. Earth's passions, earth's griefs, earth's incongruous, ridiculous humours – dormant, yet visible in the wry pippin of a face.

Nannie Slagg bending over him waggled a crooked finger before his eyes. 'My little sugar,' she tittered. 'How *could* you? how *could* you?'

Mrs Slagg turned round to Keda with a new look in her face. 'Do you think I should have left him?' she said. 'When I went to fetch you. Do you think I should have left him?'

Keda stared down at Titus. Tears were in her eyes as she watched the child. Then she turned to the window. She could see the great wall that held in Gormenghast. The wall that cut her own people away, as though to keep out a plague; the walls that barred from her view the stretches of arid earth beyond the mud huts where her child had so recently been buried.

To come within the walls was itself something of an excitement to those of the mud huts and something which in the normal course of events was reserved for the day of the Bright Carvings, but to be within the castle itself was something unique. Yet Keda did not seem impressed and had not troubled to ask Mrs Slagg any questions nor even so much as glance about her. Poor Mrs Slagg felt this was something of an impertinence but did not know whether or not she ought to say something about it.

But Titus had stolen the limelight and Keda's indifference was soon forgotten, for he was beginning to cry, and his crying grew and grew in spite of Mrs Slagg's dangling a necklace in front of his screwed up eyes and an attempt at singing a lullaby from her half-forgotten store. She had him over her shoulder, but his shrill cries rose in volume. Keda's eyes were still upon the wall, but of a sudden, breaking herself away from the window, she moved up behind Nannie Slagg and, as she did so, parted the dark brown material from her throat and freeing her left breast, took the child from the shoulders of the old woman. Within a few moments the little face was pressed against her and struggles and sobs were over. Then as she turned and sat at the window a calm came upon her as from her very centre, the milk of her body and the riches of her frustrated love welled up and succoured the infant creature in her keeping.

'FIRST BLOOD'

TITUS, under the care of Nannie Slagg and Keda, developed hourly in the western wing. His weird little head had changed shape, from day to day as the heads of infants do, and at last settled to its own proportion. It was both long and of a bulk that promised to develop into something approaching the unique.

His violet eyes made up, in the opinion of Mrs Slagg, for any strangeness in the shape of his head and features which were, after all, nothing extraordinary for a member of his family.

Even from the very first there was something lovable about Titus. It is true that his thin crying could be almost unbearable, and Mrs Slagg, who insisted upon having the whole charge of him between his meals, was driven at times to a kind of fluttering despair.

On the fourth day the preparations for his christening were well in hand.

This ceremony was always held in the afternoon of the twelfth day, in a pleasant open room on the ground level, which, with its bay windows, gave upon the cedar trees and shaven lawns that sloped away to the Gormenghast terraces where the Countess walked at dawn with her snow-white cats.

The room was perhaps the most homely and at the same time the most elegant in the castle. There were no shadows lurking in the corners. The whole feeling was of quiet and pleasing distinction, and when the afternoon sun lit up the lawns beyond the bay windows into a green-gold carpet, the room with its cooler tints became a place to linger in. It was seldom used.

The Countess never entered it, preferring those parts of the castle where the lights and the shadows were on the move and where there was no such clarity. Lord Sepulchrave was known to walk up and down its length on rare occasions and to stop and stare at the cedars on the lawn as he passed the window, and then to leave the room again for a month or two until the next whim moved him.

Nannie Slagg had on a few occasions sat there, furtively knitting with her paper bag of wool on the long refectory table in the centre, and the high back of the carved chair towering over her. Around her the spaciousness of the temperate room. The tables with their vases of garden flowers, plucked by Pentecost, the head gardener. But for the most part the room was left empty week after week, saving for an hour in the morning of each day when Pentecost would arrange the flowers. Deserted as the room was, Pentecost would never permit a day to pass in which he had not changed the water in the vases and refilled them again with taste and artistry, for he had been born in the mud huts and had in his marrow the love and understanding of colour that was the hall-mark of the Bright Carvers.

On the morning of the christening he had been out to cut the flowers for the room. The towers of Gormenghast rose into the morning mists and blocked away a commotion of raw cloud in the eastern sky. As he stood for a moment on the lawns he looked up at the enormous piles of masonry and could vaguely discern among the shadows the corroded carvings and broken heads of grey stone.

The lawns beneath the west wall where he stood were black with dew, but where, at the foot of one of the seven cedars, a grazing shaft of sun fell in a little pool of light, the wet grass blazed with diamonds of every colour. The dawn air was cold, and he drew more closely about him the leather cape which he wore over his head like a monk. It was strong and supple and had been stained and darkened by many storms and by the dripping of the rain from moss-gloved trees. From a cord hanging at his side hung his gardening knife.

Above the turrets, like a wing ripped from the body of an eagle, a solitary cloud moved northwards through the awakening air quilled with blood.

Above Pentecost the cedars, like great charcoal drawings, suddenly began to expose their structure, the layers of flat foliage rising tier above tier, their edges ribbed with sunrise.

Pentecost turned his back upon the castle and made his way through the cedars, leaving in his wake upon the glittering blotches of the dew, black imprints of feet that turned inwards. As he walked it seemed that he was moving into the earth. Each stride was a gesture, a probing. It was a kind of downward, inward search, as though he knew that what was important for him, what he really understood and cared for, was below him, beneath his slowly moving feet. It was in the earth – it was the earth.

Pentecost, with his leather cowl, was not of impressive dimensions, and his walk, although filled with meaning, had nevertheless something ridiculous about it. His legs were too short in proportion to his body, but his head, ancient and lined, was nobly formed and majestic with its big-boned, wrinkled brow and straight nose.

Of flowers he had a knowledge beyond that of the botanist, or the artist, being moved by the growth rather than the fulfilment, the organic surge that found its climax in the gold or the blue rather than in the colours, the patterns or anything visible.

As the mother who would not love the child the less were its face to be mutilated, so was he with flowers. To all growing things he brought this knowledge and love, but to the apple tree he gave himself up wholly.

Upon the northern slope of a low hill that dropped gradually to a stream, his orchard trees arose clearly, each one to Pentecost a personality in its own right.

On August days Fuchsia from her window in the attic could see him far below standing at times upon a short ladder, and sometimes when the boughs were low enough, upon the grass, his long body and little legs foreshortened and his cowl over his fine head hiding his features; and diminutive as he appeared from that immense height, she could make out that he was polishing the apples into a mirror-like gloss as they hung from the boughs, bending forward to breathe upon them and then with silk cloth rubbing them until she could see the glint upon their crimson skins – even from the height of her eirie in the shadowy loft.

Then he would move away from the tree that he had burnished and pace around it slowly, enjoying the varied grouping of its apples and the twisted stem of the supporting bole.

Pentecost spent some time in the walled-in garden, where he cut the flowers for the christening room. He moved from one part to another until he knew and could visualize the vases filled in the room and had decided upon the colour for the day.

The sun was by now clear of the mists and like a bright plate in the sky, rose as though drawn up by an invisible string. In the Christening Room there was still no light, but Pentecost entered by the bay-window, a dark mis-proportioned figure with the flowers smouldering in his arms.

Meanwhile the castle was either awaking or awakened. Lord Sepulchrave was having his breakfast with Sourdust in the refectory. Mrs Slagg was pushing and prodding at a heap of blankets beneath which Fuchsia lay curled up in darkness. Swelter was having a glass of wine in bed, which one of the apprentices had brought him, and was only half awake, his huge bulk wrinkled in upon itself in a ghastly manner. Flay was muttering to himself as he walked up and down an endless grey passage, his knee joints, like a clock, ticking off his every step. Rottcodd was dusting the third of the carvings, and sending up little clouds with his feet as he moved; and Doctor Prunesquallor was singing to himself in his morning bath. The walls of the bathroom were hung with anatomical diagrams painted on long scrolls. Even in his bath he was wearing his glasses and as he peered over the side to recover a piece of scented soap, he sang to his external oblique as though it were his love.

Steerpike was looking at himself in a mirror and examining an insipid moustache, and Keda in her room in the northern wing was watching the sunlight as it moved across the Twisted Woods.

Lord Titus Groan, innocent that the breaking day heralded the hour of his christening, was fast asleep. His head was lolling over on one side and his face was nearly obscured by the pillow, one of his little fists rammed in his mouth. He wore a yellow silk nightdress, covered with blue stars, and the light through the half-drawn blinds crept over his face.

The morning moved on. There was a great deal of coming and going. Nannie was practically insane with excitement and without Keda's silent help would have been incapable of coping with the situation.

The christening dress had to be ironed, the christening rings and the little jewelled crown to be procured from the iron case in the armoury, and only Shrattle had the key and he was stone deaf.

The bath and dressing of Titus had to be especially perfect, and with everything to do the hours slipped away all too quickly for Mrs·Slagg and it was two o'clock in the afternoon before she knew where she was.

Keda had found Shrattle at last and had persuaded him by ingenious signs that there was a christening that afternoon and that the crown was necessary and that she would return it as soon as the ceremony was over, and had in fact smoothed over, or solved all the difficulties that made Nannie Slagg wring her hands together and shake her old head in despair.

The afternoon was perfect. The great cedars basked magnificently in the still air. The lawns had been cut and were like dull emerald glass. The carvings upon the walls that had been engulfed in the night and had faltered through the dawn were now chiselled and free in the brightness.

The Christening Room itself looked cool and clear and unperturbed. With space and dignity it awaited the entrance of the characters. The flowers in their vases were incredibly gracious. Pentecost had chosen lavender as the dominant note for the room, but here and there a white flower spoke coolly to a white flower across the green carpet spaces and one gold orchid was echoed by another.

Great activity might have been observed in many of the rooms of Gormenghast as the hour of three approached, but the cool room waited in a serene silence. The only life in the room lay in the throats of the flowers.

Suddenly the door opened and Flay came in. He was wearing his long black moth-eaten suit, but there had been some attempt on his part at getting rid of the major stains and clipping the more ragged edges of cuff and trouser into straight raw lines. Over and above these improvements he wore around his neck a heavy chain of brass. In one hand he balanced, on a tray, a bowl of water. The negative dignity of the room threw him out in relief as a positive scarecrow. Of this he was quite unconscious. He had been helping to dress Lord Sepulchrave, and had made a rapid journey with the christening bowl as his lordship stood polishing his nails at the window of his bedroom, his toilet completed. The filling of the bowl and placing it on the central table in the cool room was his only duty, until the actual ceremony took place. Putting the bowl down unceremoniously on the table he scratched the back of his head and then drove his hands deep into his trouser pockets. It was some time since he was last in the Cool Room. It was not a room that he cared for. To his mind it was not a part of Gormenghast at all. With a gesture of defiance he shot his chin forward like a piece of machinery and began to pace around the room glancing malevolently at the flowers, when he heard a voice beyond the door, a thick, murderously unctuous voice.

'Woah, back there, woah! back there; watch your feet, my little rats' eyes! To the *side*. To the *side*, or I'll fillet you! Stand still! stand *still*! Merciful flesh that I should have to deal with puts!'

The door knob moved and then the door began to open and Flay's physical opposite began to appear around the opening.

For some time, so it seemed to Flay, taut areas of cloth evolved in a great arc and then at last above them a head around the panels and the eyes embedded in that head concentrated their gaze upon Mr Flay.

Flay stiffened – if it is possible for something already as stiff as a piece of teak to stiffen still further – and he lowered his head to the level of his clavicles and brought his shoulders up like a vulture. His arms were absolutely straight from the high shoulders to where the fists were clenched in his trouser pockets.

Swelter, as soon as he saw who it was, stopped dead, and across his face little billows of flesh ran swiftly here and there until, as though they had determined to adhere to the same impulse, they swept up into both oceans of soft cheek, leaving between them a vacuum, a gaping segment like a slice cut from a melon. It was horrible. It was as though nature had lost control. As though the smile, as a concept, as a manifestation of pleasure, had been a mistake, for here on the face of Swelter the idea had been abused.

A voice came out of the face: 'Well, well, well,' it said, 'may I be boiled to a frazzle if it isn't Mr Flee. The one and only Flee. Well, well, well. Here before me in the Cool Room. Dived through the keyhole, I do believe. Oh, my adorable lights and liver, if it isn't the Flee itself.'

The line of Mr Flay's mouth, always thin and hard, became even thinner as though scored with a needle. His eyes looked up and down the white mountain, crowned with its snowy, high cloth hat of office, for even the slovenly Swelter had dressed himself up for the occasion.

Although Mr Flay had avoided the cook whenever possible, an occasional accidental meeting such as today's was unavoidable, and from their chance meetings in the past Mr Flay had learned that the huge house of flesh before him, whatever its faults, had certainly a gift for sarcasm beyond the limits of his own taciturn nature. It had therefore been Mr Flay's practice, whenever possible, to ignore the chef as one ignores a cesspool by the side of a road, and although his pride was wounded by Swelter's mis-pronunciation of his name and the reference to his thinness, Flay held his spiky passions in control, merely striding to the doorway after his examination of the other's bulk and spitting out of the bay window as though to clear his whole system of something noxious. Silent though he had learned by experience to be, each galling word from Swelter did not fail to add to the growing core of hatred that burned beneath his ribs.

Swelter, as Mr Flay spat, had leaned back in his traces as though in mock alarm, his head folded back on his shoulders, and with an expression of comic concentration, had gazed alternately at Mr Flay and then out of the window several times. 'Well, well, well,' he said in his most provoking voice that seemed to seep out of dough – 'well, well, well – your accomplishments will never end. Baste me! Never. One lives and learns. By the little eel I skinned last Friday night, one lives and one learns.' Wheeling round he presented his back to Mr Flay and bellowed, 'Advance and make it sprightly! Advance the triumvirate, the little creatures who have wound themselves around my heart. Advance and be recognized.'

Into the room filed three boys of about twelve years of age. They each carried a large tray stacked with delicacies.

'Mr Flee, I will introduce you,' said Swelter, as the boys approached, glueing their frightened eyes on their precarious cargoes. 'Mr Flee – Master Springers – Master Springers – Mr Flee. Mr Flee – Master Wrattle, Master Wrattle – Mr Flee. Mr Flee – Master Spurter, Master Spurter – Mr Flee. Flee – Springers – Flee – Wrattle – Flee – Spurter – Flee!'

This was brought out with such a mixture of eloquence and impertinence that it was too much for Mr Flay. That he, the first servant of Gormenghast – Lord Sepulchrave's confidant – should be introduced to Swelter's ten-a-penny kitchen boys was trying him too hard, and as he suddenly strode past the chef towards the door (for he was in any event due back with his lordship), he pulled the chain over his head and slashed the heavy brass links across the face of his taunter. Before Swelter had recovered, Mr Flay was well on his way along the passages. The chef's face had suffered a transformation. All the vast *media* of his head became, as clay becomes under the hand of the modeller, bent to the externalization of a passion. Upon it, written in letters of pulp, was spelt the word *revenge*. The eyes had almost instantly ceased to blaze and had become like little pieces of glass.

The three boys had spread the delicacies upon the table, and, leaving in the centre the simple christening bowl, they now cowered in the bay window, longing in their hearts to run, to run as they had never run before, out into the sunshine and across the lawns and over streams and fields until they were far, far away from the white presence with the hectic red marks of the chain-links across its face.

The chef, with his hatred so riveted upon the person of Flay, had forgotten them and did not vent his spleen upon them. His was not the hatred that rises suddenly like a storm and as suddenly abates. It was, once the initial shock of anger and pain was over, a calculated thing that grew in a bloodless way. The fact that three minions had seen their dreaded overlord suffer an indignity was nothing to Swelter at this moment, for he could see the situation in proportion and in it these children had no part.

Without a word he walked to the centre of the room. His fat hands rearranged a few of the dishes nimbly upon the table. Then he advanced to a mirror that hung above a vase of flowers and examined his wounds critically. They hurt him. Catching sight of the three boys as he shifted his head in order to peer again more closely at himself, for he was only able to see portions of his face at one and the same time, he signalled to them to be gone. He followed shortly afterwards and made his way to his room above the bakeries.

By this time the hour was practically at hand for the gathering and from their various apartments the persons concerned were sallying forth. Each one with his or her particular stride. His or her particular eyes, nose, mouth, hair, thoughts and feelings. Self-contained, carrying their whole selves with them as they moved, as a vessel that holds its own distinctive wine, bitter or sweet. These seven closed their doors behind them, terrifyingly *themselves*, as they set out for the Cool Room.

There were, in the Castle, two ladies, who, though very seldom encountered, were of the Groan blood, and so, when it came to a family ceremony such as this, were of course invited. They were their ladyships Cora and Clarice, sisters-in-law to Gertrude, sisters of Sepulchrave, and twins in their own right. They lived in a set of rooms in the southern wing and shared with each other an all-absorbing passion for brooding upon an irony of fate which decreed that they should have no say in the affairs of Gormenghast. These two along with the others were on their way to the Cool Room.

Tradition playing its remorseless part had forced Swelter and Flay to return to the Cool Room to await the first arrival, but luckily someone was there before them – Sourdust, in his sacking garment. He stood behind the table, his book open before him. In front of him the bowl of water, around which the examples of Swelter's art sat, perched on golden salvers and goblets that twinkled in the reflected sunlight.

Swelter, who had managed to conceal the welts on his face by an admixture of flour and white honey, took up his place to the left of the ancient librarian, over whom he towered as a galleon above a tooth of rock. Around his neck he also wore a ceremonial chain similar to that of Flay, who appeared a few moments later. He stalked across the room without glancing at the chef, and stood upon the other side of Sourdust, balancing from the artist's point of view if not the rationalist's, the components of the picture.

All was ready. The participants in the ceremony would be arriving one by one, the less important entering first, until the penultimate entrance of the Countess harbingered a necessary piece of walking furniture, Nannie Slagg, who would be carrying in her arms a shawl-full of destiny – the Future of the Blood Line. A tiny weight that was Gormenghast, a Groan of the strict lineage – Titus, the Seventy-Seventh.

'ASSEMBLAGE'

FIRST to arrive was the outsider – the commoner – who through his service to the family was honoured by a certain artificial equality of status, liable at any moment to be undermined – Doctor Prunesquallor.

He entered fluttering his perfect hands, and, mincing to the table, rubbed them together at the level of his chin in a quick, animated way as his eyes travelled over the spread that lay before him.

'My very dear Swelter, ha, ha, may I offer you my congratulations, ha, ha, as a doctor who knows something of stomachs, my dear Swelter, something indeed of stomachs? Not only of stomachs but of palates, of tongues, and of the membrane, my dear man, that covers the roof of the mouth, and not only of the membrane that covers the roof of the mouth but of the sensitized nerve endings that I can positively assure you are tingling, my dear and very excellent Swelter, at the very thought of coming into contact with these delicious-looking oddments that you've no doubt tossed off at an odd moment, ha, ha, very, very likely I should say, oh yes, very, very likely.'

Doctor Prunesquallor smiled and exhibited two brand new rows of gravestones between his lips, and darting his beautiful white hand forward with the little finger crooked to a right angle, he lifted a small emerald cake with a blob of cream atop of it, as neatly off the top of a plate of such trifles as though he were at home in his dissecting room and were removing some organ from a frog. But before he had got it to his mouth, a hissing note stopped him short. It came from Sourdust, and it caused the doctor to replace the green cake on the top of the pile even more swiftly than he had removed it. He had forgotten for the moment, or had pretended to forget, what a stickler for etiquette old Sourdust was. Until the Countess herself was in the room no eating could begin.

'Ha, ha, ha, ha, very very right and proper Mr Sourdust, very right and proper indeed', said the doctor, winking at Swelter. The magnified appearance of his eyes gave this familiarity a peculiar unpleasantness. 'Very, very right indeed. But that's what this man Swelter does to one, with his irresistible little lumps of paradise – ha, ha, he makes one quite barbarian he does, don't you Swelter? You barbarize one, ha, ha, don't you? You positively barbarize one.'

Swelter, who was in no mood for this sort of badinage, and in any case preferred to hold the floor if there was to be any eloquence, merely gave a mirthless twitch to his mouth and continued to stare out of the window. Sourdust was running his finger along a line in his book which he was re-reading, and Flay was a wooden effigy.

Nothing, however, seemed to be able to keep the mercury out of Doctor Prunesquallor, and after looking quickly from face to face, he examined his finger nails, one by one, with a ridiculous interest; and then turning suddenly from his task as he completed the scrutiny of the tenth nail, he skipped to the window, a performance grotesquely incongruous in one of his years, and leaning in an over-elegant posture against the window frame, he made that peculiarly effeminate gesture of the left hand that he was so fond of, the placing of the tips of thumb and index finger together, and thus forming an O, while the remaining three fingers were strained back and curled into letter C's of dwindling sizes. His left elbow, bent acutely, brought his hand about a foot away from him and on a level with the flower in his buttonhole. His narrow chest, like a black tube, for he was dressed in a cloth of death's colour, gave forth a series of those irritating laughs that can only be symbolized by 'ha, ha, ha,' but whose pitch scraped at the inner wall of the skull.

'Cedars', said Doctor Prunesquallor, squinting at the trees before him with his head tilted and his eyes half closed, 'are excellent trees. Very, very excellent. I positively enjoy cedars, but do cedars positively enjoy me? Ha, ha – do they, my dear Mr Flay, do they? – or is this rather above you, my man, is my philosophy a trifle above you? For if I enjoy a cedar but a cedar does not, ha, ha, enjoy me, then surely I am at once in a position of compromise, being, as it were, ignored by the vegetable world, which would think twice, mark you, my dear fellow, would think twice about ignoring a cartload of mulch, ha, ha, or to put it in another way....'

But here Doctor Prunesquallor's reflections were interrupted by the first of the family arrivals, the twin sisters, their ladyships Cora and Clarice. They opened the door very slowly and peered around it before advancing. It had been several months since they had ventured from their apartments and they were suspicious of everyone and of everything.

Doctor Prunesquallor advanced at once from the window. 'Your ladyships will forgive me, ha, ha, the presumption of receiving you into what is, ha, ha, after all more your own room than mine, ha, ha, ha, but which is nevertheless, I have reason to suspect, a little strange to you if I may be so extraordinarily flagrant; so ludicrously indiscreet, in fact . . .'

'It's the doctor, my dear', the lady Cora whispered flatly to her twin sister, interrupting Prunesquallor.

Lady Clarice merely stared at the thin gentleman in question until anyone but the doctor would have turned and fled.

'I know it is,' she said at last. 'What's wrong with his eyes?'

'He's got some disease of course, I suppose. Didn't you know?' replied Lady Cora.

She and her sister were dressed in purple, with gold buckles at their throats by way of brooches, and another gold buckle each at the end of hatpins which they wore through their grey hair in order apparently to match their brooches. Their faces, identical to the point of indecency, were quite expressionless, as though they were the preliminary lay-outs for faces and were waiting for sentience to be injected.

'What are you doing here?' said Cora, staring remorselessly.

Doctor Prunesquallor bent forward towards her and showed her his teeth. Then he clasped his hands together. 'I am privileged', he said, 'very, very much so, oh yes, very, very much.'

'Why?' said Lady Clarice. Her voice was so perfect a replica of her sister's as might lead one to suppose that her vocal cords had been snipped from the same line of gut in those obscure regions where such creatures are compounded.

The sisters were now standing, one on either side of the doctor, and they stared up at him with an emptiness of expression that caused him to turn his eyes hurriedly to the ceiling, for he had switched them from one to the other for respite from either, but had found no relief. The white ceiling by contrast teemed with interest and he kept his eyes on it.

'Your ladyships,' he said, 'can it be that you are ignorant of the part I play in the social life of Gormenghast? I say the social life, but who, ha, ha, ha, who could gainsay me if I boast that it is more than the *social* life, ha, ha, ha, and is, my very dear ladyships, positively the organic life of the castle that I foster, and control, ha, ha, in the sense that, trained as I undoubtedly am in the science of this, that, and the other, ha, ha, ha, in connection with the whole anomatical caboodle from head to foot. I, as part of my work here, deliver the new generations to the old – the sinless to the sinful, ha, ha, ha, the stainless to the tarnished – oh dear me, the white to the black, the healthy to the diseased. And this ceremony today, my very dear ladyships, is a result of my professional adroitness, ha, ha, ha, on the occasion of a brand new Groan.'

'What did you say?' said Lady Clarice, who had been staring at him the whole time without moving a muscle.

Doctor Prunesquallor closed his eyes and kept them closed for a very long time. Then opening them he took a pace forward and breathed in as much as his narrow chest would allow. Then turning suddenly he wagged his finger at the two in purple.

'Your ladyships', he said. 'You must *listen*, you will never get on in life unless you *listen*.'

'Get *on* in life?' said Lady Cora at once, 'get *on* in life. I like that. What chance have we, when Gertrude has what we ought to have?'

'Yes, yes,' said the other, like a continuation of her sister's voice in another part of the room. 'We ought to have what she has.'

'And what is *that*, my very dear ladyships?' queried Doctor Prunesquallor, tilting his head at them.

'Power', they replied blankly and both together, as though they had rehearsed the scene. The utter tonelessness of their voices contrasted so incongruously with the gist of the subject that even Doctor Prunesquallor was for a moment taken aback and loosened his stiff white collar around his throat with his forefinger.

'It's power we want', lady Clarice repeated. 'We'd like to have that.'

'Yes, it's that we want,' echoed Cora, 'lots of power. Then we could make people do things', said the voice.

'But Gertrude has all the power', came the echo, 'which we ought to have but which we haven't got.'

Then they stared at Swelter, Sourdust and Flay in turn.

'*They* have to be here, I suppose?' said Cora, pointing at them before returning her gaze to Doctor Prunesquallor, who had reverted to examining the ceiling. But before he could reply the door opened and Fuchsia came in, dressed in white.

Twelve days had elapsed since she had discovered that she was no longer the only child. She had steadily refused to see her brother and today for the first time she would be obliged to be with him. Her first anguish, inexplicable to herself, had dulled to a grudging acceptance. For what reason she did not know, but her grief had been very real. She did not know what it was that she resented.

Mrs Slagg had had no time to help Fuchsia to look presentable, only telling her to comb her hair and to put her white dress on at the *last* minute so that it should not be creased, and then to appear in the Cool Room at two minutes past three.

The sunlight on the lawns and the flowers in the vases and the room itself had seemed pleasant auguries for the afternoon before the entrance of the two servants, and the unfortunate incident that occurred. This violence had set a bitter keynote to the ensuing hours.

Fuchsia came in with her eyes red from crying. She curtseyed awkwardly to her mother's cousins and then sat down in a far corner, but she was almost at once forced to regain her feet, for her father, followed closely by the Countess, entered and walked slowly to the centre of the room.

Without a word of warning Sourdust rapped his knuckles on the table and cried out with his old voice: 'All are gathered save only him, for whom this gathering is gathered. All are here save only he for whom we all are here. Form now before the table of his baptism in the array of waiting, while I pronounce the entrance of Life's enterer and of the Groan inheritor, of Gormenghast's untarnished child-shaped mirror.'

Sourdust coughed in a very ill way and put his hand to his chest. He glanced down at the book and ran his finger along a new line. Then he tottered around the table, his knotted grey-and-white beard swinging a little from side to side, and ushered the five into a semi-circle around the table, with their backs to the window. In the centre were the Countess and Lord Sepul-chrave, Fuchsia was to her father's left and Doctor Prune-squallor on the right of Lady Groan, but a little behind the semi-circle. The twin sisters were separated, one standing at either extremity of the arc. Flay and Swelter had retreated a few paces backwards and stood quite still. Flay bit at his knuckles.

Sourdust returned to his position behind the table which he held alone, and was relatively more impressive now that the crag of Flay and the mound of Swelter no longer dwarfed him. He lifted his voice again, but it was hard for him to speak, for there were tears in his throat and the magnitude of his office weighed heavily on him. As a savant in the Groan lore he knew himself to be spiritually responsible for the correct procedure. Moments such as this were the highlights in the ritualistic cycle of his life.

'Suns and the changing of the seasonal moons; the leaves from trees that cannot keep their leaves, and the fish from olive waters have their voices!'

His hands were held before him as though in prayer, and his wrinkled head was startlingly apparent in the clear light of the room. His voice grew stronger.

'Stones have their voices and the quills of birds; the anger of the thorns, the wounded spirits, the antlers, ribs that curve, bread, tears and needles. Blunt boulders and the silence of cold marshes – these have their voices – the insurgent clouds, the cockerel and the worm.'

Sourdust bent down over his book and found the place with his finger and then turned the page.

'Voices that grind at night from lungs of granite. Lungs of blue air and the white lungs of rivers. All voices haunt all moments of all days; all voices fill the crannies of all regions. Voices that he shall hear when he has listened, and when his ear is tuned to Gormenghast; whose voice is endlessness of endlessness. This is the ancient sound that he must follow. The voice of stones heaped up into grey towers, until he dies across the Groan's death-turret. And banners are ripped down from wall and buttress and he is carried to the Tower of Towers and laid among the moulderings of his fathers.'

'How much more is there?' said the Countess. She had been listening less attentively than the occasion merited and was feeding with crumbs from a pocket in her dress a grey bird on her shoulder.

Sourdust looked up from his book at Lady Groan's question. His eyes grew misty for he was pained by the irritation in her voice.

'The ancient word of the twelfth lord is complete, your lady-ship', he said, his eyes on the book.

'Good', said Lady Groan. 'What now?'

'We turn about, I think, and look out on the garden', said Clarice vaguely, 'don't we, Cora? You remember just before baby Fuchsia was carried in, we all turned round and looked at the garden through the window. I'm sure we did – long ago.'

'Where have you been since then?' said Lady Groan, suddenly addressing her sisters-in-law and staring at them one after the other. Her dark-red hair was beginning to come loose over her neck, and the bird had scarred with its feet the soft inky-black pile of her velvet dress so that it looked ragged and grey at her shoulder.

'We've been in the south wing all the time, Gertrude', replied Cora.

'That's where we've been', said Clarice. 'In the south wing all the time.'

Lady Groan emptied a look of love across her left shoulder, and the grey bird that stood there with its head beneath its wing moved three quick steps nearer to her throat. Then she turned her eyes upon her sisters-in-law: 'Doing what?' she said.

'Thinking', said the twins together, 'that's what we've been doing – thinking a lot.'

A high uncontrolled laugh broke out from slightly behind the Countess. Doctor Prunesquallor had disgraced himself. It was no time for him to emphasize his presence. He was there on sufferance, but a violent rapping on the table saved him and all attention was turned to Sourdust.

'Your lordship', said Sourdust slowly, 'as the seventy-sixth Earl of Groan and Lord of Gormenghast, it is written in the laws that you do now proceed to the doorway of the Christening Room and call for your son along the empty passage.'

Lord Sepulchrave, who up to this moment, had, like his daughter beside him, remained perfectly still and silent, his melancholy eyes fixed upon the dirty vest of his servant Flay which he could just see over the table, turned towards the door, and on reaching it, coughed to clear his throat.

The Countess followed with her eyes, but her expression was too vague to understand. The twins followed him with their faces – two areas of identical flesh. Fuchsia was sucking her knuckles and seemed to be the only one in the room uninterested in the progress of her father. Flay and Swelter had their eyes fixed upon him, for although their thoughts were still engaged with the violence of half an hour earlier, they were so much a part of the Groan ritual that they followed his lordship's every movement with a kind of surly fascination.

Sourdust, in his anxiety to witness a perfect piece of traditional procedure, was twisting his black-and-white beard into what must surely have been inextricable knots. He leaned forward over the christening bowl, his hands on the refectory table.

Meanwhile, hiding behind a turn in the passage, Nannie Slagg, with Titus in her arms, was being soothed by Keda as she waited for her call.

'Now, now be quiet, Mrs Slagg, be quiet and it will be over soon', said Keda to the little shaking thing that was dressed up in the shiniest of dark-green satin and upon whose head the grape hat arose in magnificent misproportion to her tiny face.

'Be quiet, indeed', said Nannie Slagg in a thin animated voice.

'If you only knew what it means to be in such a position of honour – oh, my poor heart! You would not dare to try to make me quiet indeed! I have never heard such ignorance. Why is he so long? Isn't it time for him to call me? And the precious thing so quiet and good and ready to cry any minute – oh, my poor heart! Why is he so long? Brush my dress again.'

Keda, who had been commanded to bring a soft brush with her, would have been brushing Nannie's satin dress for practically the whole morning had the old nurse had her way. She was now instructed by an irritable gesture of Mrs Slagg's hand to brush her anew and to soothe the old woman she complied with a few strokes.

Titus watched Keda's face with his violet eyes, his grotesque little features modified by the dull light at the corner of the passage. There was the history of man in his face. A fragment from the enormous rock of mankind. A leaf from the forest of man's passion and man's knowledge and man's pain. That was the ancientness of Titus.

Nannie's head was old with lines and sunken skin, with the red rims of her eyes and the puckers of her mouth. A vacant anatomical ancientry.

Keda's oldness was the work of fate, alchemy. An occult agedness. A transparent darkness. A broken and mysterious grove. A tragedy, a glory, a decay.

These three sere beings at the shadowy corner waited on. Nannie was sixty-nine, Keda was twenty-two, Titus was twelve days old.

Lord Sepulchrave had cleared his throat. Then he called:
'My Son.'

'TITUS IS CHRISTENED'

HIS voice moved down the corridor and turned about the stone corner, and when he first heard the sound of Mrs Slagg's excited footsteps he continued with that part of the procedure which Sourdust had recited to him over their breakfast for the last three mornings.

115

Ideally, the length of time which it took him to complete the speech should have coincided with the time it took Nannie Slagg to reach the door of the Cool Room from the darkened corner.

'Inheritor of the powers I hold,' came his brooding voice from the doorway, 'continuer of the blood-stock of the stones, freshet of the unending river, approach me now. I, a mere link in the dynastic chain, adjure you to advance, as a white bird on iron skies through walls of solemn cloud. Approach now to the bowl, where, named and fêted, you shall be consecrate in Gormenghast. Child! Welcome!'

Unfortunately Nannie, having tripped over a loose flagstone, was ten feet away at the word 'Welcome' and Sourdust, upon whose massive forehead a few beads of perspiration had suddenly appeared, felt the three long seconds pass with a ghastly slowness before she appeared at the door of the room. Immediately before she had left the corner Keda had placed the little iron crown gently on the infant's head to Nannie's satisfaction, and the two of them as they appeared before the assembly made up for their three seconds' tardiness by a preposterous quality that was in perfect harmony with the situation.

Sourdust felt satisfied as he saw them, and their delay that had rankled was forgotten. He approached Mrs Slagg carrying his great book with him, and when he had reached them he opened the volume so that it fell apart in two equal halves and then, extending it forward towards Nannie Slagg, he said:

'It is written, and the writing is adhered to, that between these pages where the flax is grey with wisdom, the first-born male-child of the House of Groan shall be lowered and laid lengthways, his head directed to the christening bowl, and that the pages that are heavy with words shall be bent in and over him, so that he is engulfed in the sere Text encircled with the Profound, and is as one with the inviolable Law.'

Nannie Slagg, an inane expression of importance on her face, lowered Titus within the obtuse V shape of the half-opened book so that the crown of his head just overlapped the spine of the volume at Sourdust's end and his feet at Mrs Slagg's.

Then Lord Sepulchrave folded the two pages over the helpless body and joined the tube of thick parchment at its centre with a safety-pin.

Resting upon the spine of the volume, his minute feet protruding from one end of the paper trunk and the iron spikes of the little crown protruding from the other, he was, to Sourdust, the very quintessential of traditional propriety. So much so that as he carried the loaded book towards the refectory table his eyes became so blurred with tears of satisfaction, that it was difficult for him to make his way between the small tables that lay in his path, and the two vases of flowers that stood so still and clear in the cool air of the room were each in his eyes a fume of lilac, and a blurr of snow.

He could not rub his eyes, and free his vision, for his hands were occupied, so he waited until they were at last clear of the moisture that filmed them.

Fuchsia, in spite of knowing that she should remain where she was, had joined Nannie Slagg. She had been irritated by an attempt that Clarice had made to nudge her in a furtive way whenever she thought that no one was watching.

'You never come to see me although you're a relation, but that's because I don't want you to come and never ask you', her aunt had said, and had then peered round to see whether she was being watched, and noticing that Gertrude was in a kind of enormous trance, she continued:

'You see, my poor child, I and my sister Cora are a good deal older than you and we both had convulsions when we were about your age. You may have noticed that our left arms are rather stiff and our left legs, too. That's not our fault.'

Her sister's voice came from the other side of the semi-circle of figures in a hoarse flat whisper, as though it was trying to reach the ears of Fuchsia without making contact with the row of ears that lay between. 'Not our fault at all', she said, 'not a bit our fault. Not any of it.'

'The epileptic fits, my poor child', continued Cora, after nodding at her sister's interruption, 'have left us practically starved all down the right side. Practically starved. We had these fits you see.'

'When we were about your age', came the empty echo.

'Yes, just about your age,' said Cora, 'and being practically starved all down the right side we have to do our embroidered tapestries with one hand.'

'Only one hand', said Clarice. 'It's very clever of us. But no one sees us.'

She leaned forward as she wedged in this remark, forcing it upon Fuchsia as though the whole future of Gormenghast hung upon it.

Fuchsia fiddled and wound her hair round her fingers savagely.

'Don't do that', said Cora. 'Your hair is too black. Don't do that.'

'Much too black', came the flat echo.

'Especially when your dress is so white.'

Cora bent forward from her hips so that her face was within a foot of Fuchsia's. Then with only her eyes turned away, but her face broadside on to her niece, 'We don't *like* your mother', she said.

Fuchsia was startled. Then she heard the same voice from the other side, 'That's true,' said the voice, 'we don't.'

Fuchsia turned suddenly, swinging her inky bulk of hair. Cora had disobeyed all the rules and unable to be so far from the conversation had moved like a sleep-walker round the back of the group, keeping an eye on the black-velvet mass of the Countess.

But she was doomed to disappointment, for as soon as she arrived, Fuchsia, glancing around wildly, caught sight of Mrs Slagg and she mooched away from her cousins and watched the ceremony at the table where Sourdust held her brother in the leaves of the book. As soon as Nannie was unburdened of Titus Fuchsia went to her side, and held her thin green-satin arm. Sourdust had reached the table with Lord Sepulchrave behind him. He re-instated himself. But his pleasure at the way things were proceeding was suddenly disrupted when his eyes, having cleared themselves of the haze, encountered no ceremonial curve of the select, but a room of scattered individuals. He was shocked. The only persons in alignment were the Countess, who through no sense of obedience, but rather from a kind of coma, was in the same position in which she had first anchored herself, and her husband who had returned to her side. Sourdust hobbled round the table with the tome-full. Cora and Clarice were standing close together, their bodies facing each other but their heads staring in Fuchsia's direction. Mrs Slagg and Fuchsia were together and Prunesquallor, on tip-toe, was peering at the stamen of a white flower in a vase through a magnifying lens he had whipped from his pocket. There was no need for him to be on tip-toe for it was neither a tall table nor a tall vase nor indeed a tall flower. But the attitude which pleased him most when peering at flowers was one in which the body was bent over the petals in an elegant curve.

Sourdust was shocked. His mouth worked at the corners. His old, fissured face became a fantastic area of cross-hatching and his weak eyes grew desperate. Attempting to lower the heavy volume to the table before the christening bowl where a space had been left for it, his fingers grew numb and lost their grip on the leather and the book slid from his hands, Titus slipping through the pages to the ground and tearing as he did so a corner from the leaf in which he had lain sheathed, for his little hand had clutched at it as he had fallen. This was his first recorded act of blasphemy. He had violated the Book of Baptism. The metal crown fell from his head. Nannie Slagg clutched Fuchsia's arm, and then with a scream of 'Oh my poor heart!' stumbled to where the baby lay crying piteously on the floor.

Sourdust was trying to tear the sacking of his clothes and moaning with impotence as he strained with his old fingers. He was in torture. Doctor Prunesquallor's white knuckles had travelled to his mouth with amazing speed, and he stood swaying a little. He had turned a moment later to Lady Groan.

'They resemble rubber, your ladyship, ha, ha, ha, ha. Just a core of india-rubber, with an elastic centre. Oh yes, they are. Very, very much so. Resilience is no word for it. Ha, ha, ha, absolutely no word for it – oh dear me, no. Every ounce, a bounce, ha, ha, ha! Every ounce, a bounce.'

'What are you talking about man!' said the Countess.

'I was referring to your child, who has just fallen on the floor.'

'Fallen?' queried the Countess in a gruff voice. 'Where?'

'To earth, your ladyship, ha, ha, ha. Fallen positively to earth. Earth, that is, with a veneer or two of stone, wood and carpet, in between its barbaric self and his minute lordship whom you can no doubt hear screaming.'

'So that's what it is,' said Lady Groan, from whose mouth, which was shaped as though she were whistling, the grey bird was picking a morsel of dry cake.

'Yes', said Cora on her right, who had run up to her directly the baby had fallen and was staring up at her sister-in-law's face. 'Yes, that's what it is.'

Clarice, who had appeared on the other side in a reverse of her sister's position, confirmed her sister's interpretation, 'that's just what it is.'

Then they both peered around the edge of the Countess and caught each other's eyes knowingly.

When the grey bird had removed the piece of cake from her ladyship's big pursed-up mouth it fluttered from her shoulder to perch upon her crooked finger where it clung as still as a carving, while she, leaving the twins (who, as though her departure had left a vacuum between them came together at once to fill it) proceeded to the site of the tragedy. There she saw Sourdust recovering his dignity, but shaking in his crimson sacking while he did so. Her husband, who knew that it was no situation for a man to deal with, stood aside from the scene, but looked nervously at his son. He was biting the ferrule of his jade-headed rod and his sad eyes moved here and there but constantly returned to the crying crownless infant in the nurse's arms.

The Countess took Titus from Mrs Slagg and walked to the bay window.

Fuchsia, watching her mother, felt in spite of herself a quickening of something akin to pity for the little burden she carried. Almost a qualm of nearness, of fondness, for since she had seen her brother tear at the leaves that encased him, she had known that there was another being in the room for whom the whole fustian of Gormenghast was a thing to flee from. She had imagined in a hot blurr of jealousy that her brother would be a beautiful baby, but when she saw him and found that he was anything but beautiful, she warmed to him, her smouldering eyes taking on, for a second, something of that look which her mother kept exclusively for her birds and the white cats.

The Countess held Titus up into the sunlight of the window and examined his face, making noises in her cheek to the grey bird as she did so. Then she turned him around and examined the back of his head for some considerable time.

'Bring the crown', she said.

Doctor Prunesquallor came up with his elbows raised and the fingers of both hands splayed out, the metal crown poised between them. His eyes rolled behind his lenses.

'Shall I crown him in the sunlight? ha, he, ha. Positively crown him', he said, and showed the Countess the same series of uncompromising teeth that he had honoured Cora with several minutes before.

Titus had stopped crying and in his mother's prodigious arms looked unbelievably tiny. He had not been hurt, but frightened by his fall. Only a sob or two survived and shook him every few seconds.

'Put it on his head,' said the Countess. Doctor Prunesquallor bent forward from the hips in a straight oblique line. His legs looked so thin in their black casing that when a small breath of wind blew from the garden it seemed that the material was blown inwards beyond that part where his shin bones should have been. He lowered the crown upon the little white potato of a head.

'Sourdust', she said without turning round, 'come here.'

Sourdust lifted his head. He had recovered the book from the floor and was fitting the torn piece of paper into position on the corner of the torn page, and smoothing it out shakily with his forefinger.

'Come along, come along now!' said the Countess.

He came around the corner of the table and stood before her.

'We'll go for a walk, Sourdust, on the lawn and then you can finish the christening. Hold yourself still, man', she said. 'Stop rattling.'

Sourdust bowed, and feeling that to interrupt a christening of the direct heir in this way was sacrilege, followed her out of the window, while she called out over her shoulder, 'all of you! all of you! servants as well!'

They all came out and each choosing their parallel shades of the mown grass that converged in the distance in perfectly straight lines of green, walked abreast and silently thus, up and down, for forty minutes.

They took their pace from the slowest of them, which was Sourdust. The cedars spread over them from the northern side as they began their journey. Their figures dwindling as they moved away on the striped emerald of the shaven lawn. Like toys; detachable, painted toys, they moved each one on his mown stripe.

Lord Sepulchrave walked with slow strides, his head bowed. Fuchsia mouched. Doctor Prunesquallor minced. The twins propelled themselves forward vacantly. Flay spidered his path. Swelter wallowed his.

All the time the Countess held Titus in her arms and whistled varying notes that brought through gilded air strange fowl to her from unrecorded forests.

When at last they had re-gathered in the Cool Room, Sourdust was more composed, although tired from the walk.

Signalling them to their stations he placed his hands upon the torn volume with a qualm and addressed the semi-circle before him.

Titus had been replaced in the Book and Sourdust lowered him carefully to the table.

'I place thee, Child-Inheritor,' he said, continuing from where he had been interrupted by the age of his fingers, 'Child-Inheritor of the rivers, of the Tower of Flints and the dark recesses beneath cold stairways and the sunny summer lawns. Child-Inheritor of the spring breezes that blow in from the jarl forests and of the autumn misery in petal, scale, and wing. Winter's white brilliance on a thousand turrets and summer's torpor among walls that crumble – listen. Listen with the humility of princes and understand with the understanding of the ants. Listen, Child-Inheritor, and wonder. Digest what I now say.'

Sourdust then handed Titus over the table to his mother, and cupping his hand, dipped it in the christening bowl. Then, his hand and wrist dripping, he let the water trickle through his fingers and on to the baby's head where the crown left, between its prongs, an oval area of bone-forced skin.

'Your name is TITUS', said Sourdust very simply, 'TITUS the seventy-seventh Earl of Groan and Lord of Gormenghast. I do adjure you hold each cold stone sacred that clings to these, your grey ancestral walls. I do adjure you hold the dark soil sacred that nourishes your high leaf-burdened trees. I do adjure you hold the tenets sacred that ramify the creeds of Gormenghast. I dedicate you to your father's castle. Titus, be true.'

Titus was handed back to Sourdust, who passed him to Nannie Slagg. The room was delicious with the cool scent of flowers. As Sourdust gave the sign, after a few minutes of meditation, that feeding might begin, Swelter came forward balancing four plates of delicacies on each of his forearms and with a plate in either hand went the rounds. Then he poured out glasses of wine, while Flay followed Lord Sepulchrave around like a shadow. None of the company attempted to make conversation, but stood silently eating or drinking in different parts of the room, or stood at the bay window, munching or sipping as they stared across the spreading lawns. Only the twins sat in a corner of the room and made signs to Swelter when they had finished what was on their plates. The afternoon would be for them the theme for excited reminiscence for many a long day. Lord Sepulchrave touched nothing as the delicacies were passed round, and when Swelter approached him with a salver of toasted larks, Flay motioned him away peremptorily, and noticing as he did so the evil expression in the chef's pig-like eyes, he drew his bony shoulders up to his ears.

As the time moved on Sourdust began to grow more and more conscious of his responsibilities as the master of ritual, and eventually, having registered the time by the sun, which was split in half by the slim branch of a maple, he clapped his hands and shambled towards the door.

It was then for the assembled company to gather in the

centre of the room and for one after another to pass Sourdust and Mrs Slagg, who, with Titus on her lap, was to be stationed at his side.

These positions were duly taken up, and the first to walk forward to the door was Lord Sepulchrave, who lifted his melancholy head in the air, and, as he passed his son spoke the one word 'Titus' in a solemn, abstracted voice. The Countess shambled after him voluminously and bellowed 'TITUS' at the wrinkled infant.

Each in turn followed: the twins confusing each other in their efforts to get the first word in, the doctor brandishing his teeth at the word 'Titus' as though it were the signal for some romantic advance of sabred cavalry. Fuchsia felt embarrassed and stared at the prongs of her little brother's crown.

At last they had all passed by, delivering with their own peculiar intonations the final word 'Titus' as they reared their heads up, and Mrs Slagg was left alone, for even Sourdust had left her and followed in the wake of Mr Flay.

Now that she was left by herself in the Cool Room Mrs Slagg stared about her nervously at the emptiness and at the sunlight pouring through the great bay window.

Suddenly she began to cry with fatigue and excitement and from the shock she had received when the Countess had bellowed at his little lordship and herself. A shrunken, pathetic creature she looked in the high chair with the crowned doll in her arms. Her green satin gleamed mockingly in the afternoon light. 'Oh, my weak heart,' she sobbed, the tears crawling down the dry, pear-skin wrinkles of her miniature face – 'my poor, poor heart – as though it were a crime to love him.' She pressed the baby's face against her wet cheek. Her eyes were clenched and the moisture clung to her lashes, and as her lips quivered, Fuchsia stole back and knelt down, putting her strong arms around her old nurse and her brother.

Mrs Slagg opened her bloodshot eyes and leaned forward, the three of them coming together into a compact volume of sympathy.

'I *love* you –', whispered Fuchsia, lifting her sullen eyes. 'I love you, I love you', then turning her head to the door –

'you've made her cry', she shouted, as though addressing the string of figures who had so recently passed through – 'you've made her cry, you beasts!'

MEANS OF ESCAPE

MR FLAY was possessed by two major vexations. The first of these lay in the feud which had arisen between himself and the mountain of pale meat; the feud that had flared up and fructified in his assault upon the chef. He avoided even more scrupulously than before any corridor, quadrangle or cloister where the unmistakable proportions of his enemy might have loomed in sight. As he performed his duties, Mr Flay was perpetually aware that his enemy was in the castle and was haunted by the realization that some devilish plot was being devised, momently, in that dropsical head – some infernal hatching, in a word – *revenge*. What opportunities the chef would find or make, Flay could not imagine, but he was constantly on the alert and was for ever turning over in his dark skull any possibilities that occurred to him. If Flay was not actually frightened he was at least apprehensive to a point this side of fear.

The second of his two anxieties hinged upon the disappearance of Steerpike. Fourteen days ago he had locked the urchin up and had returned twelve hours later with a jug of water and a dish of potatoes only to find the room empty. Since then there had been no sign of him, and Mr Flay, although uninterested in the boy for his own sake, was nevertheless disturbed by so phenomenal a disappearance and also by the fact that he had been one of Swelter's kitchen hands and might, were he to return to the foetid regions from which he had strayed, disclose the fact they had met, and probably, in a garbled version of the affair, put it to the chef that he had been lured away from his province and incarcerated for some sinister reason of his own invention. Not only this, for Mr Flay remembered how the boy had overheard the remarks which Lord Groan had made about his son, remarks which would be detrimental to the dignity of

Gormenghast if they were to be noised abroad to the riff-raff of the castle. It would not do if at the very beginning of the new Lord Groan's career it were common knowledge that the child was ugly, and that Lord Sepulchrave was distressed about it. What could be done to ensure the boy's silence Flay had not yet determined, but it was obvious that to find him was the prime necessity. He had, during his off moments, searched room after room, balcony after balcony, and had found no clue as to his whereabouts.

At night as he lay before his master's door he would twitch and awake and then sit bolt upright on the cold floor-boards. At first the face of Swelter would appear before his eyes, huge and indistinct, with those beady eyes in their folds of flesh, cold and remorseless. He would shoot his hard, cropped head forward, and wipe the sweat from his palms upon his clothes. Then, as the foul phantom dissolved in the darkness, his mind would lure him into the empty room where he had last seen Steerpike and in his imagination he would make a circuit of the walls, feeling the panels with his hands and come at last to the window, where he would stare down the hundreds of feet of sheer wall to the yard below.

Straightening out his legs again his knee joints would crack in the darkness as he stretched himself out, the iron-tasting key between his teeth.

●

What had actually happened in the Octagonal Room and the subsequent events that befell Steerpike are as follows:

When the boy heard the key turn in the lock he half-ran to the door and glued his eye to the keyhole and watched the seat of Mr Flay's trousers receding down the passage. He had heard him turn a corner, and then a door was shut in the distance with a far bang, and thereafter there had been silence. Most people would have tried the handle of the door. The instinct, however irrational, would have been too strong; the first impulse of one who wishes to escape. Steerpike looked at the knob of the door for a moment. He had heard the key turn. He did not disobey the simple logic of his mind. He turned from the only door in the room and, leaning out of the window, glanced at the drop below.

His body gave the appearance of being malformed, but it would be difficult to say exactly what gave it this gibbous quality. Limb by limb it appeared that he was sound enough, but the sum of these several members accrued to an unexpectedly twisted total. His face was pale like clay and save for his eyes, masklike. These eyes were set very close together, and were small, dark red, and of startling concentration.

The striped kitchen tunic which he wore fitted him tightly. On the back of his head was pushed a small white skull cap.

As he gazed downward quietly at the precipitous drop he pursed his mouth and his eyes roved quickly over the quadrangle below him. Then suddenly he left the window and with his peculiar half-run, half-walk, he hurried around the room, as though it were necessary for him to have his limbs moving concurrently with his brain. Then he returned to the window. Everywhere was stillness. The afternoon light was beginning to wane in the sky although the picture of turrets and rooftops enclosed by the window frame was still warmly tinted. He took one last comprehensive glance over his shoulder at the walls and ceiling of the prison room, and then, clasping his hands behind his back, returned his attention to the casement.

This time, leaning precariously out over the sill and with his face to the sky, he scrutinized the rough stones of the wall *above* the lintel and noticed that after twenty feet they ended at a sloping roof of slates. This roof terminated in a long horizontal spine like a buttress, which, in turn, led in great sweeping curves towards the main rooftops of Gormenghast. The twenty feet above him, although seeming at first to be unscalable, were, he noticed, precarious only for the first twelve feet, where only an occasional jutting of irregular stone offered dizzy purchase. Above this height a gaunt, half-dead creeper that was matted greyly over the slates, lowered a hairy arm which, unless it snapped at his weight, would prove comparatively easy climbing.

Steerpike reflected that once astride the cornice he could,

with relatively little difficulty, make his way over the whole outer shell of central Gormenghast.

Again he fastened his gaze upon the first dozen feet of vertical stone, choosing and scrutinizing the grips that he would use. His survey left him uneasy. It would be unpleasant. The more he searched the wall with his intense eyes the less he liked the prospect, but he could see that it *was* feasible if he concentrated every thought and fibre upon the attempt. He hoisted himself back into the room that had suddenly added an atmosphere of safety to its silence. Two courses were open to him. He could either wait and, in due course presumably Flay would reappear and would, he suspected, attempt to return him to the kitchens – or he could make the hazardous trial.

Suddenly, sitting on the floor, he removed his boots and tied them by their laces about his neck. Then he rammed his socks into his pockets and stood up. Standing on tiptoe in the middle of the room he splayed his toes out and felt them tingle with awareness, and then he pulled his fingers sideways cruelly, awakening his hands. There was nothing to wait for. He knelt on the windowsill and then, turning around, slowly raised himself to his feet and stood outside the window, the hollow twilight at his shoulder-blades.

'A FIELD OF FLAGSTONES'

HE refused to allow himself to think of the sickening drop and glued his eyes upon the first of the grips. His left hand clasped the lintel as he felt out with his right foot and curled his toes around a rough corner of stone. Almost at once he began to sweat. His fingers crept up and found a cranny he had scrutinized at leisure. Biting his underlip until it bled freely over his chin, he moved his left knee up the surface of the wall. It took him perhaps seventeen minutes by the clock, but by the time of his beating heart he was all evening upon the swaying wall. At moments he would make up his mind to have done with the whole thing, life and all, and to drop back into space, where his straining and sickness would end. At other moments, as he clung desperately, working his way upwards in a sick haze, he found himself repeating a line or two from some long forgotten rhyme.

His fingers were almost dead and his hands and knees shaking wildly when he found that his face was being tickled by the ragged fibres that hung upon the end of the dead creeper. Gripping it with his right hand, his toes lost purchase and for a moment or two he swung over the empty air. But his hands could bring into play unused muscles and although his arms were cracking he scraped his way up the remaining fifteen feet, the thick, brittle wood holding true, small pieces only breaking away from the sides. As soon as he had edged himself over the guttering, he lay, face downwards, weak and shaking fantastically. He lay there for an hour. Then, as he raised his head and found himself in an empty world of roof tops, he smiled. It was a young smile, a smile in keeping with his seventeen years, that suddenly transformed the emptiness of the lower part of his face and as suddenly disappeared; from where he lay at an angle along the sun-warmed slates, only sections of this new rooftop world were visible and the vastness of the failing sky. He raised himself upon his elbows, and suddenly noticed that where his feet had been prized against the guttering, the support was on the point of giving way. The corroded metal was all that lay between the weight of his body as he lay slanting steeply on the slates and the long drop to the quadrangle. Without a moment's delay he began to edge his way up the incline, levering with his bare feet, his shoulder blades rubbing the moss-patched roof.

Although his limbs felt much stronger after their rest he retched as he moved up the slate incline. The slope was longer than it had appeared from below. Indeed, all the various roof structures – parapet, turret and cornice – proved themselves to be of greater dimensions than he had anticipated.

Steerpike, when he had reached the spine of the roof, sat astride it and regained his breath for the second time. He was surrounded by lakes of fading daylight.

He could see how the ridge on which he sat led in a wide

curve to where in the west it was broken by the first of four towers. Beyond them the sweep of roof continued to complete a half circle far to his right. This was ended by a high lateral wall. Stone steps led from the ridge to the top of the wall, from which might be approached, along a cat-walk, an area the size of a field, surrounding which, though at a lower level, were the heavy, rotting structures of adjacent roofs and towers, and between these could be seen other roofs far away, and other towers.

Steerpike's eyes, following the rooftops, came at last to the parapet surrounding this area. He could not, of course, from where he was guess at the stone sky-field itself, lying as it did a league away and well above his eye level, but as the main massing of Gormenghast arose to the west, he began to crawl in that direction along the sweep of the ridge.

It was over an hour before Steerpike came to where only the surrounding parapet obstructed his view of the stone sky-field. As he climbed this parapet with tired, tenacious limbs he was unaware that only a few seconds of time and a few blocks of vertical stone divided him from seeing what had not been seen for over four hundred years. Scrabbling one knee over the topmost stones he heaved himself over the rough wall. When he lifted his head wearily to see what his next obstacle might be, he saw before him, spreading over an area of four square acres, a desert of grey stone slabs. The parapet on which he was now sitting bolt upright surrounded the whole area, and swinging his legs over he dropped the four odd feet to the ground. As he dropped and then leaned back to support himself against the wall, a crane arose at a far corner of the stone field and, with a slow beating of its wings, drifted over the distant battlements and dropped out of sight. The sun was beginning to set in a violet haze and the stone field, save for the tiny figure of Steerpike, spread out emptily, the cold slabs catching the prevailing tint of the sky. Between the slabs there was dark moss and the long coarse necks of seeding grasses. Steerpike's greedy eyes had devoured the arena. What use could it be put to? Since his escape this surely was the strongest card for the pack that he intended to collect. Why, or how, or when he would use his hoarded scraps of knowledge he could not tell. That was for the future. Now he knew only that by risking his life he had come across an enormous quadrangle as secret as it was naked, as hidden as it was open to the wrath or tenderness of the elements. As he gave at the knees and collapsed into a half-sleeping, half-fainting huddle by the wall, the stone field wavered in a purple blush, and the sun withdrew.

'OVER THE ROOFSCAPE'

THE darkness came down over the castle and the Twisted Woods and over Gormenghast Mountain. The long tables of the Dwellers were hidden in the thickness of a starless night. The cactus trees and the acacias where Nannie Slagg had walked, and the ancient thorn in the servants' quadrangle were as one in their shrouding. Darkness over the four wings of Gormenghast. Darkness lying against the glass doors of the Christening Room and pressing its impalpable body through the ivy leaves of Lady Groan's choked window. Pressing itself against the walls, hiding them to all save touch alone; hiding them and hiding everything; swallowing everything in its insatiable omnipresence. Darkness over the stone sky-field where clouds moved through it invisibly. Darkness over Steerpike, who slept, woke and slept fitfully and then woke again – with only his scanty clothing, suitable more to the stifling atmosphere of the kitchens than to this nakedness of night air. Shivering he stared out into a wall of night, relieved by not so much as one faint star. Then he remembered his pipe. A little tobacco was left in a tin box in his hip pocket.

He filled the bowl in the darkness, ramming it down with his thin, grimed forefinger, and with difficulty lit the strong coarse tobacco. Unable to see the smoke as it left the bowl of the pipe and drifted out of his mouth, yet the glow of the leaf and the increasing warmth of the bowl were of comfort. He wrapped both his thin hands around it and with his knees drawn up to his chin, tasted the hot weed on his tongue as the long minutes dragged by. When the pipe was at last finished he found himself too wide awake to sleep, and too cold, and he conceived the idea of making a blind circuit of the stone field, keeping one hand upon the low wall at his side until he had returned to where he now stood. Taking his cap off his head he laid it on

the parapet and began to feel his way along to the right, his hand rubbing the rough stone surface just below the level of his shoulder. At first he began to count his steps so that on his return he might while away a portion more of the night by working out the area of the quadrangle, but he had soon lost count in the labours of his slow progress.

As far as he could remember there were no obstacles to be

expected nor any break in the parapet, but his memories of the climb and his first view of the sky-field were jumbled up together, and he could not in the inky darkness rely on his memory. Therefore he felt for every step, sometimes certain that he was about to be impeded by a wall or a break in the stone flags, and he would stop and move forward inch by inch only to find that his intuition had been wrong and that the monotonous, endless, even course of his dark circuit was empty before him. Long before he was halfway along the first of the four sides, he was feeling for his cap on the balustrade, only to remember that he had not yet reached the first corner.

He seemed to have been walking for hours when he felt his hand stopped, as though it had been struck, by the sudden right angle of the parapet. Three times more he would have to experience the sudden change of direction in the darkness, and then he would, as he groped forward, find his cap.

Feeling desperate at the stretch of time since he had started his sightless journey he became what seemed to him in the darkness to be almost reckless in his pace, stepping forward jerkily foot by foot. Once or twice, along the second wall, he stopped and leaned over the parapet. A wind was beginning to blow and he hugged himself.

As he neared unknowingly the third corner a kind of weight seemed to lift from the air, and although he could see nothing, the atmosphere about him appeared thinner and he stopped as though his eyes had been partially relieved of a bandage. He stopped, leaned against the wall, and stared above him. Blackness was there, but it was not the opaque blackness he had known.

Then he felt, rather than saw, above him a movement of volumes. Nothing could be discerned, but that there were forces that travelled across the darkness he could not doubt; and then suddenly, as though another layer of stifling cloth had been dragged from before his eyes, Steerpike made out above him the enormous, indistinct shapes of clouds following one another in grave order as though bound on some portentous mission.

It was not, as Steerpike at first suspected, the hint of dawn. Long as the time had seemed to him since he clambered over the parapet, it was still an hour before the new day. Within a few moments he saw for himself that his hopes were ill founded, for as he watched, the vague clouds began to thin as they moved overhead, and between them yet others, beyond, gave way in their turn to even more distant regions. The three distances of cloud moved over, the nearest – the blackest – moving the fastest. The stone field was still invisible, but Steerpike could make out his hand before his face.

Then came the crumbling away of a grey veil from the face of the night, and beyond the furthermost film of the terraced clouds there burst of a sudden a swarm of burning crystals, and, afloat in their centre, a splinter of curved fire.

Noting the angle of the moon and judging the time, to his own annoyance, to be hours earlier than he had hoped, Steerpike, glancing above him, could not help but notice how it seemed as though the clouds had ceased to move, and how, instead, the cluster of the stars and the thin moon had been set in motion and were skidding obliquely across the sky.

Swiftly they ran, those bright marvels, and, like the clouds, with a purpose most immediate. Here and there over the wide world of tattered sky, points of fire broke free and ran, until the last dark tag of cloud had slid away from the firmament and all at once the high, swift beauty of the floating suns ceased in their surging and a night of stationary stars shone down upon the ghostly field of flags.

Now that heaven was alive with yellow stones it was possible for Steerpike to continue his walk without fear, and he stumbled along preferring to complete his detour than to make his way across the flags to his cloth cap. When he reached his starting point he crammed the cap on his head, for anything was precious in those hours that might mitigate the cold. By now he was fatigued beyond the point of endurance.

The ordeal of the last twelve to fifteen hours had sapped his strength. The stifling inferno of Swelter's drunken province, the horror of the Stone Lanes where he had fainted and had been found by Flay, and then the nightmare of his climb up the wall and the slate roof, and thence by the less perilous but by no means easy stages to the great stone field where he now stood, and where when he had arrived he had swooned for the second time that day: all this had taken its toll. Now, even the cold could not keep him awake and he lay down suddenly, and with his head upon his folded arms, slept until he was awakened by a hammering of hunger in his stomach and by the sun shining strongly in the morning sky.

*

But for the aching of his limbs, which gave him painful proof of the reality of what he had endured, the trials of the day before, had about them, the unreality of a dream. This morning as he stood up in the sunlight it was as though he found himself transplanted into a new day, almost a new life in a new world. Only his hunger prevented him from leaning contentedly over the warming parapet and, with a hundred towers below him, planning for himself an incredible future.

The hours ahead held no promise of relaxation. Yesterday had exhausted him, yet the day that he was now entering upon was to prove itself equally rigorous, and though no part of the climbing entailed would be as desperate as the worst of yesterday's adventures, his hunger and faintness augured for the hours ahead a nightmare in sunshine.

Within the first hour from the time when he had awakened, he had descended a long sloping roof, after dropping nine feet from the parapet, and had then come upon a small, winding stone staircase which led him across a gap between two high walls to where a cluster of conical roofs forced him to make a long and hazardous circuit. Arriving at last at the opposite side of the cluster, faint and dizzy with fatigue and emptiness and with the heat of the strengthening sun, he saw spread out before him in mountainous façades a crumbling panorama, a roofscape of Gormenghast, its crags and its stark walls of cliff pocked with nameless windows. Steerpike for a moment lost heart, finding himself in a region as barren as the moon, and he became suddenly desperate in his weakness, and falling on his knees retched violently.

His sparse tow-coloured hair was plastered over his big forehead as though with glue, and was darkened to sepia. His mouth was drawn down very slightly at the corners. Any change in his masklike features was more than noticeable in him. As he knelt he swayed. Then he very deliberately sat himself down on his haunches and, pushing back some of the sticky hair from his brow so that it stuck out from his head in a stiff dank manner, rested his chin on his folded arms and then, very slowly, moved his eyes across the craggy canvas spread below him, with the same methodical thoroughness that he had shown when scanning the wall above the window of the prison room.

Famished as he was, he never for a moment faltered in his scrutiny, although it was an hour later when having covered every angle, every surface, he relaxed and released his eyes from the panorama, and after shutting them for a while fixed them again upon a certain window that he had found several minutes earlier in a distant precipice of grey stone.

'NEAR AND FAR'

WHO can say how long the eye of the vulture or the lynx requires to grasp the totality of a landscape, or whether in a comprehensive instant the seemingly inexhaustible confusion of detail falls upon their eyes in an ordered and intelligible series of distances and shapes, where the last detail is perceived in relation to the corporate mass?

It may be that the hawk sees nothing but those grassy uplands, and among the coarse grasses, more plainly than the field itself, the rabbit or the rat, and that the landscape in its entirety is never seen, but only those areas lit, as it were with a torch, where the quarry slinks, the surrounding regions thickening into cloud and darkness on the yellow eyes.

Whether the scouring, sexless eye of the bird or beast of prey disperses and sees all or concentrates and evades all saving that for which it searches, it is certain that the less powerful eye of the human cannot grasp, even after a life of training, a scene in its entirety. No eye may see dispassionately. There is no comprehension at a glance. Only the recognition of damsel, horse or fly and the assumption of damsel, horse or fly; and so with dreams and beyond, for what haunts the heart will, when it is found, leap foremost, blinding the eye and leaving the main of Life in darkness.

When Steerpike began his scrutiny the roofscape was neither more nor less than a conglomeration of stone structures spreading to right and left and away from him. It was a mist of masonry. As he peered, taking each structure individually, he found that he was a spectator of a stationary gathering of stone personalities. During the hour of his concentration he had seen, growing from three-quarters the way up a sheer, windowless face of otherwise arid wall, a tree that curved out and upwards, dividing and subdividing until a labyrinth of twigs gave to its contour a blur of sunlit smoke. The tree was dead, but having grown from the south side of the wall it was shielded from the violence of the winds, and, judging by the harmonious fanlike beauty of its shape, it had not suffered the loss of a single sapless limb. Upon the lit wall its perfect shadow lay as though engraved with superhuman skill. Brittle and dry, and so old that its first tendril must surely have begun to thrust itself forth before the wall itself had been completed, yet this tree had the grace of a young girl, and it was the intricate lace-like shadow upon the wall that Steerpike had seen first. He had been baffled until all at once the old tree itself, whose brightness melted into the bright wall behind it, materialized.

Upon the main stem that grew out laterally from the wall, Steerpike had seen two figures walking. They appeared about the size of those stub ends of pencil that are thrown away as too awkward to hold. He guessed them to be women for as far as he could judge they were wearing identical dresses of purple, and at first sight it appeared that they were taking their lives in their hands as they trod that horizontal stem above a drop of several hundred feet, but by the relative sizes of the figures and the tree trunk it was obvious that they were as safe as though they had been walking along a bridge.

He had watched them reach a point where the branch divided into three and where as he shaded his eyes he could see them seat themselves upon chairs and face one another across a table.

One of them lifted her elbow in the position of one pouring out tea. The other had then arisen and hurried back along the main stem until she had reached the face of wall into which she suddenly disappeared; and Steerpike, straining his eyes, could make out an irregularity in the stonework and presumed that there must have been a window or doorway immediately above where the tree grew from the wall. Shutting his eyes to rest them, it was a minute before he could locate the tree again, lost as it was among a score of roofs and very far away; but when he did find it he saw that there were two figures once again seated at the table. Beneath them swam the pellucid volumes of the morning air. Above them spread the withered elegance of the dead tree, and to their left its lace-like shadow.

Steerpike had seen at a glance that it would be impossible for him to reach the tree or the window and his eyes had continued their endless searching.

He had seen a tower with a stone hollow in its summit. This shallow basin sloped down from the copestones that surrounded the tower and was half filled with rainwater. In this circle of water whose glittering had caught his eye, for to him it appeared about the size of a coin, he could see that something white was swimming. As far as he could guess it was a horse. As he watched he noticed that there was something swimming by its side, something smaller, which must have been the foal, white like its parent. Around the rim of the tower stood swarms of crows, which he had identified only when one of them, having flapped away from the rest, grew from the size of a gnat to that of a black moth as it circled and approached him before turning in its flight and gliding without the least tremor of its outspread wings back to the stone basin, where it landed with a flutter among its kind.

He had seen, thirty feet below him and frighteningly close, after his eyes had accustomed themselves to the minutiae of distances a head suddenly appear at the base of what was more like a vertical black gash in the sunny wall than a window. It had no window-frame, no curtains, no window-sill. It was as though it waited for twelve stone blocks to fill it in, one above the other. Between Steerpike and this wall was a gap of eighteen to twenty feet. As Steerpike saw the head appear he lowered himself gradually behind an adjacent turret so as not to attract attention and watched it with one eye around the masonry.

It was a long head.

It was a wedge, a sliver, a grotesque slice in which it seemed the features had been forced to stake their claims, and it appeared that they had done so in a great hurry and with no attempt to form any kind of symmetrical pattern for their mutual advantage. The nose had evidently been the first upon the scene and had spread itself down the entire length of the wedge, beginning among the grey stubble of the hair and ending among the grey stubble of the beard, and spreading on both sides with a ruthless disregard for the eyes and mouth which found precarious purchase. The mouth was forced by the lie of the terrain left to it, to slant at an angle which gave to its right-hand side an expression of grim amusement and to its left, which dipped downwards across the chin, a remorseless twist. It was forced by not only the unfriendly monopoly of the nose, but also by the tapering character of the head to be a short mouth; but it was obvious by its very nature that, under normal conditions, it would have covered twice the area. The eyes in whose expression might be read the unending grudge they bore against the nose were as small as marbles and peered out between the grey grass of the hair.

This head, set at a long incline upon a neck as wry as a turtle's cut across the narrow vertical black strip of the window.

Steerpike watched it turn upon the neck slowly. It would not have surprised him if it had dropped off, so toylike was its angle.

As he watched, fascinated, the mouth opened and a voice as strange and deep as the echo of a lugubrious ocean stole out into the morning. Never was a face so belied by its voice.

The accent was of so weird a lilt that at first Steerpike could not recognize more than one sentence in three, but he had quickly attuned himself to the original cadence and as the words fell into place Steerpike realized that he was staring at a poet.

For some time after the long head had emptied itself of a slow, ruminative soliloquy it stared motionlessly into the sky. Then it turned as though it were scanning the dark interior of whatever sort of room it was that lay behind that narrow window.

In the strong light and shade the protruding vertebrae of his neck, as he twisted his head, stood out like little solid parchment-covered knobs. All at once the head was facing the warm sunlight again, and the eyes travelled rapidly in every direction before they came to rest. One hand propped up the stubbly peg of a chin. The other, hanging listlessly over the rough sill-less edge of the aperture swung sideways slowly to the simple rhythm of the verses he then delivered.

> Linger now with me, thou Beauty,
>   On the sharp archaic shore.
> Surely 'tis a wastrel's duty
>   And the gods could ask no more.
> If you lingerest when I linger,
>   If thou tread'st the stones I tread,
> Thou wilt stay my spirit's hunger
>   And dispel the dreams I dread.
>
> Come thou, love, my own, my only,
>   Through the battlements of Groan;
> Lingering becomes so lonely
>   When one lingers on one's own.
>
> I have lingered in the cloisters
>   Of the Northern Wing at night,
> As the sky unclasped its oysters
>   On the midnight pearls of light.
> For the long remorseless shadows
>   Chilled me with exquisite fear.
> I have lingered in cold meadows
>   Through a month of rain, my dear.
>
> Come, my Love, my sweet, my Only,
>   Through the parapets of Groan.
> Lingering can be very lonely
>   When one lingers on one's own.

In dark alcoves I have lingered
    Conscious of dead dynasties.
I have lingered in blue cellars
    And in hollow trunks of trees.
Many a traveller through moonlight
    Passing by a winding stair
Or a cold and crumbling archway
    Has been shocked to see me there.

I have longed for thee, my Only,
    Hark ! the footsteps of the Groan !
Lingering is so very lonely
    When one lingers all alone.

Will you come with me, and linger ?
    And discourse with me of those
Secret things the mystic finger
    Points to, but will not disclose ?
When I'm all alone, my glory,
    Always fades, because I find
Being lonely drives the splendour
    Of my vision from my mind.

Come, oh, come, my own ! my Only !
    Through the Gormenghast of Groan.
Lingering has become so lonely
    As I linger all alone !

Steerpike, after the end of the second verse ceased to pay any
attention to the words, for he conceived the idea, now that he
realized that the dreadful head was no index to the character,
of making his presence known to the poet, and of craving from
him at least some food and water if not more. As the voice
swayed on he realized that to appear suddenly would be a great
shock to the poet, who was so obviously under the impression
that he was alone. Yet what else was there to do? To make
some sort of preparatory noise of warning before he showed
himself occurred to him, and when the last chorus had ended he
coughed gently. The effect was electric. The face reverted instantaneously to the soulless and grotesque mask which Steerpike had first seen and which during the recitation had been

transformed by a sort of inner beauty. It had coloured, the parchment of the dry skin reddening from the neck upwards like a piece of blotting-paper whose corner has been dipped into red ink.

Out of the black window Steerpike saw, as a result of his cough, the small gimlety eyes peer coldly from a crimson wedge.

He raised himself and bowed to the face across the gully.

One moment it was there, but the next, before he could open his mouth, it was gone. In the place of the poet's face was, suddenly, an inconceivable commotion. Every sort of object suddenly began to appear at the window, starting at the base and working up like an idiotic growth, climbing erratically as one thing after another was crammed between the walls.

Feverishly the tower of objects grew to the top of the window, hemmed in on both sides by the coarse stones. Steerpike could not see the hands that raised the mad assortment so rapidly. He could only see that out of the darkness object after object was scrammed one upon the other, each one lit by the sun as it took its place in the fantastic pagoda. Many toppled over, and fell, during the hectic filling of the frame. A dark gold carpet slipped and floated down the abyss, the pattern upon its back showing plainly until it drifted into the last few fathoms of shadow. Three heavy books fell together, their pages fluttering, and an old high-backed chair, which the boy heard faintly as it crashed far below.

Steerpike had dug his nails into the palms of his hands partly from self-reproach for his failure, and partly to keep himself from relaxing in his roofscape scrutiny in spite of his disappointment. He turned his head from the near object and continued to comb the roofs and the walls and the towers.

He had seen away to his right a dome covered with black moss. He had seen the high façade of a wall that had been painted in green-and-black checks. It was faded and partly overgrown with clinging weeds and had cracked from top to bottom in a gigantic saw-toothed curve.

He had seen smoke pouring through a hole between the slabs of a long terrace. He had seen the favourite nesting grounds of the storks and a wall that was emerald with lizards.

ALL this while he had been searching for one thing and one thing only '- a means of entering the castle. He had made a hundred imaginary journeys, taking into account his own weakness, but one after another they had led to blank unscalable walls and to the edges of the roofs. Window after window he took as his objective and attempted to trace his progress only to find that he was thwarted. It was not until the end of the hour approached that a journey he was unravelling in his eye culminated with his entry at a high window in the Western Wing. He went over the whole journey again, from where he sat, to the tiny window in the far wall and realized that it could be done, if luck was on his side and if his strength lasted.

It was now two o'clock in the afternoon and the sun was merciless. He removed his jacket and, leaving it behind him, set forth shakily.

The next three hours made him repent that he had ever left the kitchens. Had it been possible for him to have suddenly been conjured back to Swelter's enormous side he would have accepted the offer in his weakness. As the light began to wane, twenty-four hours after he had lain above the prison room on the sloping roof of slates, he came to the foot of that high wall, near the summit of which was the window he had seen three hours previously. There he rested. He was about midway between the ground two hundred feet below him and the window. He had been accurate in his observation when he had guessed that the face of the wall was covered over its entire area with a thick, ancient growth of ivy. As he sat against the wall, his back against the enormous hairy stem of the creeper as thick as the bole of a tree, the ivy leaves hung far out and over him and, turning his head upwards, he found that he was gazing into a profound and dusty labyrinth. He knew that he would have to climb through darkness, so thick was the skein of the coarse, monotonous foliage; but the limbs of the straggling weed were thick and strong, so that he could rest at times in his climb and lean heavily upon them. Knowing that with every minute that passed his weakness was growing, he did not wait longer than to regain his breath, and then, with a twist of his mouth he forced himself as close as he could to the wall, and engulfed in the dust-smelling darkness of the ivy he began, yet again, to climb.

For how long Steerpike clambered upwards in the acrid darkness, for how long he breathed in the rotten, dry, dust-filled air, is of no consequence compared to the endlessness of the nightmare in his brain. That was the reality, and all he knew, as he neared the window, was that he had been among black leaves for as far back as he could recall – that the ivy stem was dry and coarse and hairy to hold, and that the bitter leaves exuded a pungent and insidious smell.

At times he could see glimpses of the hot evening reflected through the leaves, but for the most part he struggled up in darkness, his knees and knuckles bleeding and his arms weary beyond weariness from the forcing back of the fibrous growth and from tearing the tendrils from his face and clothing.

He could not know that he was nearing the window. Distance, even more than time, had ceased to have any meaning for him, but all at once he found that the leaves were thinning and that blotches of light lay pranked about him. He remembered having observed from below how the ivy had appeared to be less profuse and to lie closer to the wall as it neared the window. The hirsute branches were less dependable now and several had snapped at his weight, so that he was forced to keep to one of the main stems that clung dustily to the wall. Only a foot or two in depth, the ivy lay at his back partially shielding him from the sun. A moment later and he was alone in the sunshine. It was difficult for his fingers to find purchase. Fighting to wedge them between the clinging branches and the wall he moved, inch by inch, upwards. It seemed to him that all his life he had been climbing. All his life he had been ill and tortured. All his life he had been terrified, and red shapes rolled. Hammers were beating and the sweat poured into his eyes.

The questionable gods who had lowered for him from the roof above the prison room that branch of creeper when he was in similar peril were with him again, for as he felt upwards his hand struck a protruding layer of stone. It was the base of a rough window-sill. Steerpike sobbed and forced his body upwards and loosing his hands for a moment from the creeper, he flung his hands over the sill. There he hung, his arms outstretched stiffly before him like a wooden figure, his legs dangling. Then, wriggling feebly, he rolled himself at length over the stone slab, overbalanced, and in a whirl of blackness fell with a crash upon the boarded floor of Fuchsia's secret attic.

'THE BODY BY THE WINDOW'

ON the afternoon following her brother's birth, Fuchsia stood silently at the window of her bedroom. She was crying, the tears following one another down her flushed cheeks as she stared through a smarting film at Gormenghast Mountain. Mrs Slagg, unable to comprehend, made abortive efforts to console her. This time there had been no mutual hugging and weeping, and Mrs Slagg's eyes were filled with a querulous, defeated expression. She clasped her little wrinkled hands together.

'What is it, then, my caution dear? What is it, my own ugliness? Tell me! Tell me at once. Tell your old Nannie about your little sorrows. Oh, my poor heart! you must tell me all about it. Come, inkling, come.'

But Fuchsia might as well have been carved from dark marble. Only her tears moved.

At last the old lady pattered out of the room, saying she would bring in a currant cake for her caution, that no one ever answered her, and that her back was aching.

Fuchsia heard the tapping of her feet in the corridor. Within a moment she was racing along the passage after her old nurse, whom she hugged violently before running back and floundering with a whirl of her blood-red dress down long flights of stairs and through a series of gloomy halls, until she found herself in the open, and beyond the shadows of the castle walls. She ran on in the evening sunshine. At last, after skirting Pentecost's orchard and climbing to the edge of a small pine wood she stopped running and in a quick, stumbling manner forced a path through a low decline of ferns to where a lake lay motionless. There were no swans. There were no wild waders. From the reflected trees there came no cries from birds.

Fuchsia fell at full length and began to chew at the grass in front of her. Her eyes as they gazed upon the lake were still inflamed.

'I hate things! I hate all things! I hate and hate every single tiniest thing. I hate the *world*', said Fuchsia aloud, raising herself on her elbows, her face to the sky.

'I shall live *alone*. Always alone. In a house, or in a tree.'

Fuchsia started to chew at a fresh grass blade.

'Someone will come then, if I live alone. Someone from another kind of world – a new world – not from this world, but someone who is *different*, and he will fall in love with me at once because I live alone and aren't like the other beastly things in this world, and he'll enjoy having me because of my pride.'

Another flood of tears came with a rush. . . .

'He will be tall, taller than Mr Flay, and strong like a lion and with yellow hair like a lion's, only more curly; and he will have big, strong feet because mine are big, too, but won't look so big if his are bigger; and he will be cleverer than the Doctor, and he'll wear a long black cape so that my clothes will look brighter still; and he will say: "Lady Fuchsia", and I shall say: "What is it?" '

She sat up and wiped her nose on the back of her hand.

The lake darkened, and while she sat and stared at the motionless water, Steerpike was beginning his climb of the ivy.

Mrs Slagg was telling her troubles to Keda and trying to preserve the dignity which she thought she ought to show as the head nurse of the direct and only heir to Gormenghast, and at the same time longing to unburden herself in a more natural way. Flay was polishing an ornate helmet which Lord Groan had to wear, that evening being the first after the advent, and Swelter was whetting a long meat-knife on a grindstone. He was doubled over it like a crammed bolster, and was evidently taking great pains to bring the blade to an uncommonly keen edge.

The grindstone, dwarfed ridiculously by the white mass above it, wheeled to the working of a foot-treadle. As the steel whisked obliquely across the flat of the whirling stone, the harsh, sandy whistling of the sound apparently gave pleasure to Mr Swelter, for a wodge of flesh kept shifting its position on his face.

As Fuchsia got to her feet and began to push her way up the hill of ferns, Steerpike was forty feet from her window and clawing away at the dry, dirty bunches of old sparrows' nests that were blocking his upward climb.

When Fuchsia reached the castle she made straight for her room, and when she had closed the door behind her, drew a bolt across it and going to an old cardboard box in a corner found, after some rummaging, a piece of soft charcoal. She approached a space on the wall and stood staring at the plaster. Then she drew a heart and around it she wrote: *I am Fuchsia. I must always be. I am me. Don't be frightened. Wait and see.*

Then she felt a great yearning for her picture-book with the poems. She lit a candle and, pulling back her bed, crept through the stairway door and began to climb spirally upwards to her dim sanctum.

It was not very often that she climbed to the attic in the late afternoon, and the darkness of the front room as she entered stopped her on the last stair for a moment. Her candle as she passed through the narrow gully illumined fitfully the weird assortment that comprised its walls, and when she came to the emptiness of her acting room she moved forward slowly, treading in the pale aura of light cast by the candle-flame.

In her third especial attic she knew that she had left, some weeks before, a supply of red-and-green wax tapers that she had unearthed, put aside, and forgotten. She had rediscovered them. Three of these would light the room up beautifully for she wanted the window to be shut. She climbed the ladder to the balcony, pushed open the door with one hinge and entered, with a gush of dark love.

Her long coloured candles were by the door and she lit one of them immediately from the little white one in her hand.

Turning to place it on the table, her heart stopped beating, for she found that she was staring across the room at a body lying huddled beneath her window.

*

Steerpike had lain in a dead faint for some considerable time when consciousness began to seep through him. Twilight had fallen over Gormenghast. Out of the blackness of his brain far shapes that surrounded him in the room had begun to approach him growing in definition and in bulk as they did so until they became recognizable.

For several minutes he lay there. The comparative coolness of the room and the stillness of his body at length restored in his mind a state of inquiry. He could not remember the room, as was natural, nor could he remember how he had arrived there. He only knew that his throat was parched and beneath his belt a tiger was clawing in his stomach. For a long time he stared at a drunken and grotesque shape that arose from the centre of the floor. Had he been awakened from sleep to see it looming up before him it would no doubt have startled him considerably, but recovering from his faint, he was drained of apprehension; he was only weak. It would have been strange for him to have recognized in the dim light of the twilit room Fuchsia's fantastic Root from the Twisted Woods.

His eyes travelled away from it at length and noticed the darkened pictures on the walls, but the light was too dim for him to be able to discern what they contained.

His eyes moved here and there, recovering their strength; but his body lay inert, until at length he raised himself upon one elbow.

Above him was a table, and with an effort he struggled on to his knees and, gripping its edge raised himself by degrees. The room began to swim before his eyes and the pictures on the walls dwindled away to the size of stamps and swayed wildly across the walls. His hands were not his hands as he gripped the table edge. They were another's hands in which he could vaguely, and in an occult way, feel the shadows of sentiency. But the fingers held on, independently of his brain or body, and he waited until his eyes cleared and he saw below him the stale oddments of food that Fuchsia had brought up to the attic on the morning of the previous day.

They were littered on the table, each object remorseless in its actuality.

The nebulous incoherence of things had changed in his brain, as he stared down upon the still-life group on the table, to a frightening *proximity*.

Two wrinkled pears; half a seed cake; nine dates in a battered white cardboard box, and a jug of dandelion wine. Beside these a large hand-painted book that lay open where a few verses were opposed by a picture in purple and grey. It was to Steerpike in his unusual physical state as though that picture were the world, and that he, in some shadowy adjacent province, were glimpsing the reality.

He was the ghost, the purple-and-grey page was truth and actual fact.

Below him stood three men. They were dressed in grey, and purple flowers were in their dark confused locks. The landscape beyond them was desolate and was filled with old metal bridges, and they stood before it together upon the melancholy brow of a small hill. Their hands were exquisitely shaped and their bare feet also, and it seemed that they were listening to a strange music, for their eyes gazed out beyond the page and beyond the reach of Steerpike, and on and on beyond the hill of Gormenghast and the Twisted Woods.

Equally real to the boy at that moment were the grey-black simple letters that made up the words and the meaning of the verses on the opposite side of the page. The uncompromising visual starkness of all that lay on the table had for a moment caused him to forget his hunger, and although uninterested in poetry or pictures, Steerpike, in spite of himself, read with a curiously slow and deliberate concentration upon the white page of the three old men in their grey and purple world.

> Simple, seldom and sad
> We are;
> Alone on the Halibut Hills
> Afar,

With sweet mad Expressions
   Of old
Strangely beautiful,
  So we're told
By the Creatures that Move
  In the sky
  And Die
On the night when the Dead Trees
  Prance and Cry.

Sensitive, seldom, and sad –
Sensitive, seldom, and sad –

Simple, seldom and sad
  Are we
When we take our path
  To the purple sea –
With mad, sweet Expressions
   Of Yore,
Strangely beautiful,
  Yea, and More
On the Night of all Nights
  When the sky
  Streams by
In rags, while the Dead Trees
  Prance and Cry.

Sensitive, seldom, and sad –
Sensitive, seldom, and sad.

*

Steerpike noticed small thumb-marks on the margin of the page. They were as important to him as the poems or the picture. Everything was equally important because all had become so real now where all had been so blurred. His hand as it lay on the table was now his own. He had forgotten at once what the words had meant, but the script was there, black and rounded.

He put out his hand and secured one of the wrinkled pears. Lifting it to his mouth he noticed that a bite had already been taken from its side.

Making use of the miniature and fluted precipice of hard,

white discoloured flesh, where Fuchsia's teeth had left their parallel grooves, he bit greedily, his top teeth severing the wrinkled skin of the pear, and the teeth of his lower jaw entering the pale cliff about halfway up its face; they met in the secret and dark centre of the fruit – in that abactinal region where, since the petals of the pear flower had been scattered in some far June breeze, a stealthy and profound maturing had progressed by day and night.

As he bit, for the second time, into the fruit his weakness filled him again as with a thin atmosphere, and he carefully lowered himself face down over the table until he had recovered strength to continue his clandestine meal. As he lifted his head, he noticed the long couch with its elegant lines. Taking hold of the seed cake in one hand and the jug of dandelion wine in the other, after tipping the dates out of their cardboard box into his pocket, he felt his way along the edge of the table and stumbled across the few paces that divided him from the couch, where he seated himself suddenly and put his dusty feet up, one after the other, upon the wine-red leather of the upholstery.

He had supposed the jug to contain water, for he had not looked inside when he lifted it and felt its weight in his wrist, and when he tasted the wine on his tongue he sat up with a sudden revival of strength, as though the very thought of it had resuscitated him. Indeed, the wine worked wonders with him, and within a few minutes, with the cake, the dates and the rest of the second pear to support its tonic properties, Steerpike was revived, and getting to his feet he shuffled around the room in his own peculiar way. Drawing his lips back from his closed teeth, he whistled in a thin, penetrating, tuneless manner, breaking off every now and then as his eyes rested with more than a casual glance on some picture or another.

The light was fading very rapidly, and he was about to try the handle of the door to see whether, dark as it was, he could find a still more comfortable room in which to spend the night before he finally stretched himself on the long couch, when he heard the distinct sound of a footstep.

With a hand still outstretched towards the door, he stood motionless for a moment, and then his head inclined itself to the left as he listened. There was no doubt that someone was moving either in the next room or in the next room but one.

Moving one step nearer to the door as silently as a ghost, he turned the handle and drew it back the merest fraction, but sufficiently for him to place one eye at the aperture and to command a view of something which made him suck at his breath.

There was no reason why, because the room he had been in for the last hour or more was small, he should have presumed that the door out of it would lead to an apartment of roughly the same size. But when on peering through the chink between the door and the lintel he saw how mistaken had been his intuition regarding the size of the room beyond, he received a shock second only to that of seeing the figure that was approaching him.

Nor was it only the *size*. It was perhaps even more of a shock to realize that he had been *above* the adjacent room. Through the gloom he watched the figure of a girl, holding in her hand a lighted candle that lit the bodice of her dress to crimson. The floor across which she walked slowly but firmly appeared to stretch endlessly behind her and to her right and to her left. That she was below him and that within a few feet a balcony divided him from her, as she approached, was so unexpected that a sense of unreality such as he had experienced during his recovery from his faint again pervaded him. But the sound of her footsteps was very real and the light of the candle flame upon her lower lip awoke him to the actuality. Even in his predicament he could not help wondering where he had seen her before. A sudden movement of the shadows on her face had awakened a memory. Thoughts moved swiftly through his mind. No doubt there were steps leading up to the balcony. She would enter the room in which he stood. She walked with certainty. She did not hesitate. She was unafraid. These must be her rooms, he had entered. Why was she here at this hour? Who was she? He closed the door softly.

Where had he seen that red dress before? Where? Where? Very recently. The crimson. He heard her climbing the stairs. He glanced around the room. There was no hiding place. As his

eyes moved he saw the Book on the table. Her book. He saw a
few crumbs where the seed cake had been standing on the
cloth. He half ran on tip-toe to the window and glanced down.
The emptiness of the dark air falling to the tops of towers
sickened him as memories of his climb were reawakened. He
turned away. Even as he heard her feet on the balcony he was
saying: 'Where? Where? Where did I see the red dress?' and
as the feet stopped at the door he remembered, and at the same
moment dropped softly to his hands and knees beneath the
window. Then, huddling himself into an awkward position, and
with one arm outstretched limply, he closed his eyes in emula-
tion of the faint from which he had not so long ago recovered.

He had seen her through the circular spyhole in the wall of
the Octagonal Room. She was the Lady Fuchsia Groan, the
daughter of Gormenghast. His thoughts pursued each other
through his head. She had been distraught. She had been enraged
that a brother had been born for her; she had escaped down
the passage from her father. There could be no sympathy *there*.
She was, like her father, ill at ease. She was opening the door.
The air wavered in the candlelight. Steerpike, watching from
between his lashes, saw the air grow yet brighter as she lit two
long candles. He heard her turn upon her heel and take a pace
forward and then there was an absolute silence.

He lay motionless, his head thrown back upon the carpet and
twisted slightly on his neck.

It seemed that the girl was as motionless as he, and in the
protracted and deathly stillness he could hear a heart beating. It
was not his own.

'ULLAGE OF SUNFLOWER'

FOR the first few moments Fuchsia had remained inert, her
spirit dead to what she saw before her. As with those who on
hearing of the death of their lover are numb to the agony that
must later wrack them, so she for those first few moments stood
incomprehensive and stared with empty eyes.

Then, indeed, was her mind split into differing passions, the paramount being agony that her secret had been discovered – her casket of wonder rifled – her soul, it seemed, thrown naked to a world that could never understand.

Behind this passion lay a fear. And behind her fear was curiosity – curiosity as to who the figure was. Whether he was recovering or dying; how he had got there, and a long way behind the practical question of what she should do. As she stood there it was as though within her a bonfire had been lighted. It grew until it reached the zenith of its power and died away, but undestroyable among the ashes lay the ache of a wound for which there was no balm.

She moved a little nearer in a slow, suspicious way, holding the candle stiffly at arms length. A blob of the hot wax fell across her wrist and she started as though she had been struck. Another two cautious paces brought her to the side of the figure and she bent down and peered at the tilted face. The light lay upon the large forehead and the cheekbones and throat. As she watched, her heart beating, she noticed a movement in the stretched gullet. He was alive. The melting wax was hurting her hand as it ran down the coloured side of the candle. A candlestick was kept behind the couch on a rickety shelf and she raised herself from her stooping with the idea of finding it, and began to retreat from Steerpike. Not daring to take her eyes off him, she placed one leg behind the other with a grotesque deliberation and so moved backwards. Before reaching the wall, however, the calf of her leg came into unexpected contact with the edge of the couch, and she sat down very suddenly upon it as though she had been tapped behind the knees. The candle shook in her hand and the light flickered across the face of the figure on the floor. Although it seemed to her that the head started a little at the noise she had made, she put it down to the fickle play of the light upon his features, but peered at him for a long time nevertheless to convince herself. Eventually she curled her legs under her on the couch and raised herself to her knees and, reaching her free hand out behind her, she felt her fingers grip the shelf and after some fumbling close upon the iron candlestick.

She forced the candle at once into one of the three iron arms and, getting up, placed it on the table by her book.

It had come into her mind that some effort might be made to reinvigorate the crumpled thing. She approached it again. Horrible as the thought was, that if she were the means of a recovery she would be compelled to talk to a stranger in *her* room, yet the idea of him lying there indefinitely, and perhaps dying there, was even more appalling.

Forgetting for a moment her fear, she knelt loudly on the floor beside him and shook him by the shoulder, her lower lip sticking out plumply and her black hair falling across her cheeks. She stopped to scrape some tallow from her fingers and then continued shaking him. Steerpike let himself be pushed about and remained perfectly limp; he had decided to delay his recovery.

Fuchsia suddenly remembered that when she had seen her Aunt Cora faint, a very long time ago, in the central hall of the East Wing, her father had ordered a servant in attendance to get a glass of water, and that when they had been unable to get the drink down the poor white creature's throat, they had thrown it in her face and she had recovered immediately.

Fuchsia looked about her to see whether she had any water in the room. Steerpike had left the jug of dandelion wine by the side of the couch, but it was out of her range of vision and she had forgotten it. As her eyes travelled around her room they came at last to rest upon an old vase of semi-opaque dark-blue glass, which a week or so ago Fuchsia had filled with water, for she had found among the wild grass and the nettles near the moat, a tall, heavy-necked sunflower with an enormous Ethiopian eye of seeds and petals as big as her hand and as yellow as even she could wish for. But its long, rough neck had been broken and its head hung in a deadweight of fire among the tares. She had feverishly bitten through those fibres that she could not tear apart where the neck was fractured and had run all the way with her wounded treasure through the castle and up the flights of stairs and into her room, and then up again, around and around as she climbed the spiral staircase, and had found the dark-blue glass vase and filled it with water and then, quite exhausted, had lowered the dry, hairy neck into the depths of the vase and, sitting upon the couch, had stared at it and said to herself aloud :

'Sunflower who's broken, I found you, so drink some water up, and then you won't die – not so quickly, anyway. If you do, I'll bury you, anyway. I'll dig a long grave and bury you. Pentecost will give me a spade. If you don't die, you can stay. I'm going now,' she had finished by saying, and had gone to her room below and had found her nurse, but had made no mention of her sunflower.

It had died. Indeed she had only changed the water once, and with its petals decaying it still leaned stiffly out of the blue glass vase.

Directly Fuchsia saw it she thought of the water in the vase. She had filled it full of clear white water. That it might have evaporated never entered her head. Such things were not part of her world of knowledge.

Steerpike's vision, for he would peer cunningly through his eyelashes whenever occasion favoured, was obtruded by the table and he could not see what the Lady Fuchsia was doing. He heard her approaching and kept his eyelids together, thinking it was just about time for him to groan, and begin to recover, for he was feeling cramped, when he realized that she was bending directly over him.

Fuchsia had removed the sunflower and laid it on the floor, noticing at the same time an unpleasant and sickly smell. There was something pungent in it, something disgusting. Tipping the vase suddenly upside down, she was amazed to see, instead of a rush of refreshing water, a sluggish and stenching trickle of slime descend like a green soup over the upturned face of the youth.

She had tipped something wet over the face of someone who was ill and that to Fuchsia was the whole principle, so she was not surprised when she found that its cogency was immediate.

Steerpike, indeed, had received a nasty shock. The stench of the stagnant slime filled his nostrils. He spluttered and spat the slough from his mouth, and rubbing his sleeve across his face smeared it more thinly but more evenly and completely than before. Only his dark-red concentrated eyes stared out from the filthy green mask, unpolluted.

SOAP FOR GREASEPAINT

FUCHSIA squatted back on her heels in surprise as he sat bolt upright and glared at her. She could not hear what he muttered through his teeth. His dignity had been impaired, or perhaps not so much his dignity as his vanity. Passions he most certainly had, but he was more wily than passionate, and so even at this moment, with the sudden wrath and shock within him, he yet held himself in check and his brain overpowered his anger, and he smiled hideously through the putrid scum. He got to his feet painfully.

His hands were the dull sepia-red of dry blood for he had been bruised and cut in his long hours of climbing. His clothes were torn; his hair dishevelled and matted with dust and twigs and filth from his climb in the ivy.

Standing as straight as he could, he inclined himself slightly towards Fuchsia, who had risen at the same time.

'The Lady Fuchsia Groan,' said Steerpike, as he bowed.

Fuchsia stared at him and clenched her hands at her sides. She stood stiffly, her toes were turned slightly inwards towards each other, and she leaned a little forwards as her eyes took in the bedraggled creature in front of her. He was not much bigger than she was, but much more clever; she could see that at once.

Now that he had recovered, her mind was filled with horror at the idea of this alien at large in her room.

Suddenly, before she had known what she was doing, before she had decided to speak, before she knew of what to speak, her voice escaped from her hoarsely:

'What do you want? Oh, what do you want? This is *my* room. *My* room.'

Fuchsia clasped her hands at the curve of her breasts in the attitude of prayer. But she was not praying. Her nails were digging into the flesh of either hand. Her eyes were wide open.

'Go away,' she said. 'Go away from my room.' And then her whole mood changed as her feelings arose-like a tempest.

'I hate you!' she shouted, and stamped her foot upon the ground. 'I hate you for coming here. I hate you in my room.' She seized the table edge with both her hands behind her and rattled it on its legs.

Steerpike watched her carefully.

His mind had been working away behind his high forehead. Unimaginative himself he could recognize imagination in her: he had come upon one whose whole nature was the contradiction of his own. He knew that behind her simplicity was something he could never have. Something he despised as impractical. Something which would never carry her to power nor riches, but would retard her progress and keep her apart in a world of her own make-believe. To win her favour he must talk in her own language.

As she stood breathless beside the table and as he saw her cast her eyes about the room as though to find a weapon, he struck an attitude, raising one hand, and in an even, flat, hard voice that contrasted, even to Fuchsia in her agony, with her own passionate outcry said:

'Today I saw a great pavement among the clouds made of grey stones, bigger than a meadow. No one goes there. Only a heron.

'Today I saw a tree growing out of a high wall, and people walking on it far above the ground. Today I saw a poet look out of a narrow window. But the stone field that is lost in the clouds is what you'd like best. Nobody goes there. It's a good place to play games and to' (he took the plunge cunningly) '– and to *dream* of things.' Without stopping, for he felt that it would be hazardous to stop:

'I saw today,' he said, 'a horse swimming in the top of a tower: I saw a million towers today. I saw clouds last night. I was cold. I was colder than ice. I have had no food. I have had no sleep.' He curled his lip in an effort at a smile. 'And then you pour green filth on me,' he said.

'And now I'm here where you hate me being. I'm here because there was nowhere else to go. I have seen so much. I have been out all night. I have escaped' (he whispered the word dramatically) 'and, best of all, I found the field in the clouds, the field of stones.'

He stopped for breath and lowered his hand from its posturing and peered at Fuchsia.

She was leaning against the table, her hands gripping its sides. It may have been the darkness that deceived him, but to his immense satisfaction he imagined she was staring *through* him.

Realizing that if this were so, and his words were beginning to work upon her imagination, he must proceed without a pause sweeping her thoughts along, allowing her only to think of what he was saying. He was clever enough to know what would appeal to her. Her crimson dress was enough for him to go on. She was romantic. She was a simpleton; a dreaming girl of fifteen years.

'Lady Fuchsia,' he said, and clenched his hand at his forehead, 'I come for sanctuary. I am a rebel. I am at your service as a dreamer and a man of action. I have climbed for hours, and am hungry and thirsty. I stood on the field of stones and longed to fly into the clouds, but I could only feel the pain in my feet.'

'Go away,' said Fuchsia in a distant voice. 'Go away from me.' But Steerpike was not to be stopped, for he noticed that her violence had died and he was tenacious as a ferret.

'Where can I go to?' he said. 'I would go this instant if I knew where to escape to? I have already been lost for hours in long corridors. Give me first some water so that I can wash this horrible slime from my face, and give me a little time to rest and then I will go, far away, and I will never come again, but will live alone in the stone sky-field where the herons build.'

Fuchsia's voice was so vague and distant that it appeared to Steerpike that she had not been listening, but she said slowly: 'Where is it? Who are you?'

Steerpike answered immediately.

'My name is Steerpike,' he said, leaning back against the window in the darkness, 'but I cannot tell you now where the field of stones lies all cold in the clouds. No, I couldn't tell you that – not yet.'

'Who are you?' said Fuchsia again. 'Who are you in my room?'

'I have told you,' he said. 'I am Steerpike. I have climbed to your lovely room. I like your pictures on the walls and your book and your horrible root.'

'My root is beautiful. Beautiful!' shouted Fuchsia. 'Do not talk about my things. I hate you for talking about my things. Don't look at them.' She ran to the twisted and candle-lit root of smooth wood in the wavering darkness and stood between it and the window where he was.

Steerpike took out his little pipe from his pocket and sucked the stem. She was a strange fish, he thought, and needed carefully selected bait.

'How did you get to my room?' said Fuchsia huskily.

'I climbed,' said Steerpike. 'I climbed up the ivy to your room. I have been climbing all day.'

'Go away from the window,' said Fuchsia. 'Go away to the door.'

Steerpike, surprised, obeyed her. But his hands were in his pockets. He felt more sure of his ground.

Fuchsia moved gauchely to the window taking up the candle as she passed the table, and peering over the sill, held the shaking flame above the abyss. The drop, which she remembered so well by daylight, looked even more terrifying now.

She turned towards the room. 'You must be a good climber,' she said sullenly but with a touch of admiration in her voice which Steerpike did not fail to detect.

'I am,' said Steerpike. 'But I can't bear my face like this any longer. Let me have some water. Let me wash my face, your Ladyship; and then if I can't stay here, tell me where I can go and sleep. I haven't had a cat's nap. I am tired; but the stone field haunts me. I must go there again after I've rested.'

There was a silence.

'You've got kitchen clothes on,' said Fuchsia flatly.

'Yes,' said Steerpike. 'But I'm going to change them. It's the kitchen I escaped from. I detested it. I want to be free. I shall never go back.'

'Are you an *adventurer*?' said Fuchsia, who, although she did not think he looked like one, had been more than impressed by his climb and by the flow of his words.

'I am,' said Steerpike. 'That's just what I am. But at the moment I want some water and soap.'

There was no water in the attic, but the idea of taking him down to her bedroom where he could wash and then go away for food, rankled in her, for he would pass through her other attic rooms. Then she realized that he had, in any event, to leave her sanctum and, saving for a return climb down the ivy the only path lay through the attics and down the spiral staircase to her bedroom. Added to this was the thought that if she took him down now he would see very little of her rooms in the darkness, whereas tomorrow her attic would be exposed.

'Lady Fuchsia,' said Steerpike, 'what work is there that I can do? Will you introduce me to someone who can employ me? I am not a kitchen lackey, my Ladyship, I am a man of purpose. Hide me tonight, Lady Fuchsia, and let me meet someone tomorrow who may employ me. All I want is one interview. My brains will do the rest.'

Fuchsia stared at him, open mouthed. Then she thrust her full lower lip forward and said:

'What's the awful smell?'

'It's the filthy dregs you drowned me in,' said Steerpike. 'It's my face you're smelling.'

'Oh,' said Fuchsia. She took up the candle again. 'You'd better follow.'

Steerpike did so, out of the door, along the balcony, and then down the ladder. Fuchsia did not think of helping him in the ill-lit darkness, though she heard him stumble. Steerpike kept as close to her as he could and the little patch of faint candlelight on the floor which preceded her, but as she threaded her way dexterously between the oddments that lay banked up in the first attic, he was more than once struck across the face, by a hanging rope of spiked seashells, by the giraffe's leg which Fuchsia ducked beneath, and once he was brought to a gasping halt by the brass hilt of a sword.

When he had reached the head of the spiral staircase Fuchsia was already halfway down and he wound after her, cursing.

After a long time he felt the close air of the staircase lighten about him and a few moments later he had come to the last of the descending circles and had stepped down into a bedroom. Fuchsia lit a lamp on the wall. The blinds were not drawn and the black night filled up the triangles of her window.

She was pouring from a jug the water which Steerpike so urgently needed. The smell was beginning to affect him, for as he had stepped down into the room he had retched incontinently, with his thin, bony hands at his stomach.

At the gurgling sound of the water as it slopped into the bowl on Fuchsia's washstand he drew a deep breath through his teeth. Fuchsia, hearing his foot descend upon the boards of her room, turned, jug in hand, and as she did so she overflooded the bowl with a rush of water which in the lamplight made bright pools on the dark ground. 'Water,' she said, 'if you want it.'

Steerpike advanced rapidly to the basin and plucked off his coat and vest, and stood beside Fuchsia in the darkness very thin, very bunched at the shoulders, and with an extraordinary perkiness in the poise of his body.

'What about soap?' said Steerpike, lowering his arms into the basin. The water was cold, and he shivered. His shoulder blades stood out sharply from his back as he bent over and shrugged his shoulders together. 'I can't get this muck off without soap and a scrubbing-brush, your Ladyship.'

'There's some things in that drawer,' said Fuchsia slowly. 'Hurry up and finish, and then go away. You're not in your own room. You're in my room where no one's allowed to come, only my old nurse. So hurry up and go away.'

'I will,' said Steerpike, opening the drawer and rummaging among the contents until he had found a piece of soap. 'But don't forget you promised to introduce me to someone who might employ me.'

'I didn't,' said Fuchsia. 'How do you dare to tell such lies to me? How do you dare!'

Then came Steerpike's stroke of genius. He saw that there was no object in pressing his falsehood any further and, making a bold move into the unknown he leapt with great agility away from the basin, his face now thick in lather. Wiping away the white froth from his lips, he channelled a huge dark mouth with his forefinger and posturing in the attitude of a clown listening he remained immobile for seven long seconds with his hand to his ear. Where the idea had come from he did not know, but he had felt since he first met Fuchsia that if anything were to win her favour it was something tinged with the theatre, the bizarre, and yet something quite simple and guileless, and it was this that Steerpike found difficult. Fuchsia stared hard. She forgot to hate him. She did not see him. She saw a clown, a living limb of nonsense. She saw something she loved as she loved her root, her giraffe leg, her crimson dress.

'Good!' she shouted, clenching her hands. 'Good! good! good! good!' All at once she was on her bed, landing upon both her knees at once. Her hands clasped the footrail.

A snake writhed suddenly under the ribs of Steerpike. He had succeeded. What he doubted for the moment was whether he could live up to the standard he had set himself.

He saw, out of the corner of his eye, which like the rest of his face was practically smothered in soap-suds, the dim shape of Lady Fuchsia looming a little above him on the bed. It was up to him. He didn't know much about clowns, but he knew that they did irrational things very seriously, and it had occurred to him that Fuchsia would enjoy them. Steerpike had an unusual gift. It was to understand a subject without appreciating it. He was almost entirely cerebral in his approach. But this could not easily be perceived; so shrewdly, so surely he seemed to enter into the heart of whatever he wished, in his words or his deeds, to mimic.

From the ludicrous listening posture he straightened himself slowly, and with his toes turned outwards extravagantly he ran a few steps towards a corner of Fuchsia's room, and then stopped to listen again, his hand at his ear. Continuing his run he reached the corner and picked up, after several efforts at getting his hand to reach as far down as the floor, a piece of green cloth which he hobbled back with, his feet as before turned out so far as to produce between them a continuous line.

Fuchsia, in a transport, watched him, the knuckles of her right hand in her mouth, as he began a thorough examination of the bed rail immediately below her. Every now and then he would find something very wrong with the iron surface of the rail and would rub it vigorously with his rag, stand back from it for a longer view, with his head on one side, the dark of the soapless mouth drooping at each corner in anguish, and then polish the spot again, breathing upon it and rubbing it with an inhuman concentration of purpose. All the time he was thinking, 'What a fool I am, but it will work.' He could not sink himself. He was not the artist. He was the exact imitation of one.

All at once he removed with his forefinger a plump sud of soap from the centre of his forehead, leaving a rough, dark circle of skin where it had been, and tapped his frothy finger along the footrail three times at equal intervals, leaving about a third of the soap behind at each tap. Waddling up and down at the end of the bed, he examined each of these blobs in turn and, as though trying to decide which was the most imposing specimen, removed one after the other until, with only the central sud remaining, he came to a halt before it, and then, kicking away one of his feet in an extraordinarily nimble way, he landed himself flat on his face in a posture of obedience.

Fuchsia was too thrilled to speak. She only stared, happy beyond happiness. Steerpike got to his feet and grinned at her, the lamplight glinting upon his uneven teeth. He went at once to the basin and renewed his ablutions more vigorously than ever.

While Fuchsia knelt on her bed and Steerpike rubbed his head and face with an ancient and grubby towel, there came a knock upon the door and Nannie Slagg's voice piped out thinly:

'Is my conscience there? Is my sweet piece of trouble there? Are you there, my dear heart, then? Are you there?'

'No, Nannie, no, I'm not! Not now. Go away and come back again soon, and I'll be here,' shouted Fuchsia thickly, scrambling to the door. And then with her mouth to the keyhole: 'What d'you want? What d'you want?'

'Oh, my poor heart! what's the matter, then? What's the matter, then? What is it, my conscience?'

'Nothing, Nannie. Nothing. What d'you want?' said Fuchsia, breathing hard.

Nannie was used to Fuchsia's sudden and strange changes of mood; so after a pause in which Fuchsia could hear her sucking her wrinkled lower lip, the old nurse answered:

'It's the Doctor, dear. He says he's got a present for you, my baby. He wants you to go to his house, my only, and I'm to take you.'

Fuchsia, hearing a 'Tck! tck!' behind her, turned and saw a very clean-looking Steerpike gesturing to her. He nodded his head rapidly and jerked his thumb at the door, and then, with his index and longest finger strutting along the washstand, indicated, as far as she could read, that she should accept the offer to walk to the Doctor's with Nannie Slagg.

'All right!' shouted Fuchsia, 'but I'll come to *your* room. Go there and wait.'

'Hurry, then, my love!' wailed the thin, perplexed voice from the passage. 'Don't keep him waiting.'

As Mrs Slagg's feet receded, Fuchsia shouted: 'What's he giving me?'

But the old nurse was beyond earshot.

Steerpike was dusting his clothes as well as he could. He had brushed his sparse hair and it looked like dank grass as it lay flatly over his big forehead.

'Can I come, too?' he said.

Fuchsia turned her eyes to him quickly.

'Why?' she said at last.

'I have a reason,' said Steerpike. 'You can't keep me here all night, anyway, can you?'

This argument seemed good to Fuchsia and. 'Oh, yes, you can come, too,' she said at once. 'But what about Nannie,' she added slowly. 'What about my nurse?'

'Leave her to me,' said Steerpike. 'Leave her to me.'

Fuchsia hated him suddenly and deeply for saying this, but she made no answer.

'Come on, then,' she said. 'Don't stay in my room any more.

What are you waiting for?' And unbolting the door she led the way, Steerpike following her like a shadow to Mrs Slagg's bedroom.

AT THE PRUNESQUALLORS

MRS Slagg was so agitated at the sight of an outlandish youth in the company of her Fuchsia that it was several minutes before she had recovered sufficiently to listen to anything in the way of an explanation. Her eyes would dart to and fro from Fuchsia to the features of the intruder. She stood for so long a time, plucking nervously at her lower lip, that Fuchsia realized it was useless to continue with her explanation and was wondering what to do next when Steerpike's voice broke in.

'Madam,' he said, addressing Mrs Slagg, 'my name is Steerpike, and I ask you to forgive my sudden appearance at the door of your room.' And he bowed very low indeed, his eyes squinting up through his eyebrows as he did so.

Mrs Slagg took three uncertain steps towards Fuchsia and clutched her arm. 'What is he saying? What is he saying? Oh, my poor heart, who is he, then? What has he done to you, my only?'

'He's coming, too,' said Fuchsia, by way of an answer. 'Wants to see Dr Prune as well. What's his present? What's he giving me a present for? Come on. Let's go to his house. I'm tired. Be quick, I want to go to bed.'

Mrs Slagg suddenly became very active when Fuchsia mentioned her tiredness and started for the door, holding the girl by her forearm. 'You'll be into your bed in no time. I'll put you there myself and tuck you in, and turn your lamp out for you as I always did, my wickedness, and you can go to sleep until I wake you, my only, and can give you breakfast by the fire; so don't you mind, my tired thing. Only a few minutes with the Doctor – only a few minutes.'

They passed through the door, Mrs Slagg peering suspiciously around Fuchsia's arm at the quick movements of the high-shouldered boy.

Without another word between them they began to descend several flights of stairs until they reached a hall where armour hung coldly upon the walls and the corners were stacked with old weapons that were as rich with rust as a hedge of winter beech. It was no place to linger in, for a chill cut upwards from the stone floor and cold beads of moisture stood like sweat upon the tarnished surface of iron and steel.

Steerpike arched his nostrils at the dank air and his eyes travelled swiftly over the medley of corroding trophies, of hanging panoplies, smouldering with rust; and the stack of small arms, and noted a slim length of steel whose far end seemed to be embedded in some sort of tube, but it was impossible to make it out clearly in the dim light. A sword-stick leapt to his mind, and his acquisitive instincts were sharpened at the thought. There was no time, however, for him to rummage among the heaps of metal at the moment, for he was conscious of the old woman's eyes upon him, and he followed her and Fuchsia out of the hall vowing to himself that at the first opportunity he would visit the chill place again.

The door by which they made their exit lay opposite the flight that led down to the centre of the unhealthy hall. On passing through it they found themselves at the beginning of an ill-lit corridor, the walls of which were covered with small prints in faded colours. A few of them were in frames, but of these only a small proportion had their glass unbroken. Nannie and Fuchsia, being familiar with the corridor, had no thought for its desolate condition nor for the mellowed prints that depicted in elaborate but unimaginative detail the more obviously pictorial aspects of Gormenghast. Steerpike rubbed his sleeve across one or two as he followed, removing a quantity of dust, and glanced at them critically, for it was unlike him to let any kind of information slip from him unawares.

This corridor ended abruptly at a heavy doorway, which Fuchsia opened with an effort, letting in upon the passage a less oppressive darkness for it was late evening, and beyond the door a flock of clouds were moving swiftly across a slate-coloured sky in which one star rode alone.

'Oh, my poor heart, how late it's getting!' said Nannie,

peering anxiously at the sky, and confiding her thoughts to Fuchsia in such a surreptitious way that it might be supposed she was anxious that the firmament should not overhear her. 'How late it *is* getting, my only, and I must be back with your Mother very soon. I must take her something to drink, the poor huge thing. Oh, no, we mustn't be long!'

Before them was a large courtyard and at the opposite corner was a three-storied building attached to the main bulk of the castle by a flying buttress. By day it stood out strangely from the ubiquitous grey stone of Gormenghast, for it was built with a hard red sandstone from a quarry that had never since been located.

Fuchsia was very tired. The day had been overcharged with happenings. Now, as the last of the daylight surrendered in the west, she was still awake and beginning, not ending, another experience.

Mrs Slagg was clasping her arm, and as they approached the main doorway, she stopped suddenly and, as was her usual habit when flustered, brought her hand up to her mouth and pulled at her little lower lip, her old watery eyes peering weakly at Fuchsia. She was about to say something, when the sound of footsteps caused her and her two companions to turn and to stare at a figure approaching in the darkness. A faint sound as of something brittle being broken over and over again accompanied his progress towards them.

'Who is it?' said Mrs Slagg. 'Who is it, my only? Oh, how dark it is!'

'It's only Flay,' said Fuchsia. 'Come on. I'm tired.' But they were hailed from the gloom.

'Who?' cried the hard, awkward voice. Mr Flay's idiom, if at times unintelligible, was anything but prolix.

'What do you want, Mr Flay?' shouted Nannie, much to her own and to Fuchsia's surprise.

'Slagg?' queried the hard voice again. 'Wanted,' it added.

'Who's wanted?' Nannie shrilled back, for she felt that Mr Flay was always too brusque with her.

'Who's with you?' barked Flay, who was now within a few yards. 'Three just now.'

Fuchsia, who had long ago acquired the knack of interpreting the ejaculations of her father's servant, turned her head around at once and was both surprised and relieved to find that Steerpike had disappeared. And yet, was there a tinge of disappointment as well? She put out her arm and pressed the old nurse against her side.

'Three just now,' repeated Flay, who had come up.

Mrs Slagg had also noticed that the boy was missing. 'Where is he?' she queried. 'Where's the ugly youth?'

Fuchsia shook her head glumly and then turned suddenly on Flay, whose limbs seemed to straggle away into the night. Her weariness made her irritable and now she vented her pent-up emotion upon the dour servant.

'Go away! go away!' she sobbed. 'Who wants you here, you stupid, spiky thing? Who wants you – shouting out "Who's there?" and thinking yourself so important when you're only an old thin thing? Go away to my father where you belong, but leave us alone.' And Fuchsia, bursting into a great exhausted cry, ran up to the emaciated Flay and, throwing her arms about his waist, drenched his waistcoat in her tears.

His hands hung at his sides, for it would not have been right for him to touch the Lady Fuchsia however benevolent his motive, for he was, after all, only a servant although a most important one.

'Please go now,' said Fuchsia at last, backing away from him.

'Ladyship,' said the servant, after scratching the back of his head, 'Lordship wants her.' He jerked his head at the old nurse.

'Me?' cried Nannie Slagg, who had been sucking her teeth.

'You,' said Flay.

'Oh, my poor heart! When? When does he want me? Oh, my dear body! What can he want?'

'Wants you tomorrow,' replied Flay and, turning about, began to walk away and was soon lost to sight, and a short time afterwards even the sound of his knee joints was out of hearing.

They did not wait any longer, but walked as swiftly as they could to the main door of the house of sandstone, and Fuchsia gave a heavy rap with a door knocker, rubbing with her sleeve at the moisture in her eyes.

As they waited they could hear the sound of a violin.

Fuchsia knocked at the door again, and a few seconds later the music ceased and footsteps approached and stopped. A bolt was drawn back, the door opened upon a strong light, and the Doctor waved them in. Then he closed the door behind them, but not before a thin youth had squeezed himself past the door-post and into the hall where he stood between Fuchsia and Mrs Slagg.

'Well! well! well! well!' said the Doctor, flicking a hair from the sleeve of his coat, and flashing his teeth. 'So you have brought a friend with you, my dear little Ladyship, so you have brought a friend with you – or' (and he raised his eyebrows) 'haven't you?'

For the second time Mrs Slagg and Fuchsia turned about to discover the object of the Doctor's inquiry, and found that Steerpike was immediately behind them.

He bowed, and with his eye on the Doctor. 'At your service,' he said.

'Ha, ha, ha! but I don't want *anyone* at my service,' said Dr Prunesquallor, folding his long white hands around each other as though they were silk scarves. 'I'd rather have somebody "in" my service perhaps. But not *at* it. Oh, no. I wouldn't have any service left if every young gentleman who arrived through my door was suddenly *at* it. It would soon be in shreds. Ha, ha, ha! absolutely in shreds.'

'He's come,' said Fuchsia in her slow voice, 'because he wants to work because he's clever, so I brought him.'

'Indeed,' said Prunesquallor. 'I have always been fascinated by those who want to work, ha ha. Most absorbing to observe them. Ha, ha, ha! most absorbing and uncanny. Walk along, dear ladies, walk along. My very dear Mrs Slagg, you look a hundred years younger every day. This way, this way. Mind the corner of that chair, my very dear Mrs Slagg, and oh! my dear woman, you *must* look where you're going, by all that's circumspect, you really must. Now, just allow me to open this door and then we can make ourselves comfortable. Ha, ha, ha! that's right, Fuchsia, my dear, prop her up! prop her up!'

So saying, and shepherding them in front of him and at the

same time rolling his magnified eyes all over Steerpike's extra-ordinary costume, the Doctor at last arrived within his own room and closed the door behind himself sharply with a click. Mrs Slagg was ushered into a chair with soft wine-coloured up-holstery, where she looked particularly minute, and Fuchsia into another of the same pattern. Steerpike was waved to a high-backed piece of oak, and the Doctor himself set about bringing bottles and glasses from a cupboard let into the wall.

'What is it to be? What is it to be? Fuchsia, my dear child! what do you fancy?'

'I don't want anything, thank you,' said Fuchsia. 'I feel like going to sleep, Dr Prune.'

'Aha! aha! A little stimulant, perhaps. Something to sharpen your faculties, my dear. Something to tide you over until – ha, ha, ha! you are snug within your little bed. What do you think? what do you think?'

'I don't know,' said Fuchsia.

'Aha! but *I* do. *I* do,' said the Doctor, and whinnied like a horse; then, pulling back his sleeves so that his wrists were bare, he advanced like some sort of fastidious bird towards the door, where he pulled a cord in the wall. Lowering his sleeves again neatly over his cuffs, he waited, on tip-toe, until he heard a sound without, at which he flung open the door, uncovering, as it were, a swarthy-skinned creature in white livery whose hand was raised as though to knock upon the panels. Before the Doctor had said a word Nannie leaned forward in her chair. Her legs, unable to reach the floor, were dangling helplessly.

'It's elderberry wine that you love best, isn't it?' she queried in a nervous, penetrating whisper to Fuchsia. 'Tell the Doctor that. Tell him that, at once. You don't want any stimulant, do you?'

The Doctor tilted his head slightly at the sound but did not turn, merely raising his forefinger in front of the servant's eyes and wagging it, and his thin, rasping voice gave an order, for a powder to be mixed and for a bottle of elderberry wine to be procured. He closed the door, and, dancing up to Fuchsia,

'Relax, my dear, relax,' he said. 'Let your limbs wander wherever they like, ha, ha, ha, as long as they do not stray *too* far, ha, ha, ha! as long as they don't stray *too* far. Think of each of them in turn until they're all as limp as jellyfish, and you'll be ready to run to the Twisted Woods and back before you know where you are.'

He smiled and his teeth flashed. His mop of grey hair glistened like twine in the strong lamplight. 'And what for you, Mrs Slagg? What for Fuchsia's Nannie? A little port?'

Mrs Slagg ran her tongue between her wrinkled lips and nodded as her fingers went to her mouth on which a silly little smile hovered. She watched the Doctor's every movement as he filled up the wineglass and brought it over to her.

She bowed in an old-fashioned way from her hips as she took the glass, her legs pointing out stiffly in front of her for she had edged herself further back in the chair and might as well have been sitting on a bed.

Then all at once the Doctor was back at Fuchsia's chair, and bending over her. His hands, wrapped about each other in a characteristic manner, were knotted beneath his chin.

'I've got something for you, my dear; did your nurse tell you?' His eyes rolled to the side of his glasses giving him an expression of fantastic roguery which on his face would have been, for one who had never met him, to say the least, unsettling.

Fuchsia bent forward, her hands on the red bolster-like arms of the chair.

'Yes, Dr Prune. What is it, thank you, what is it?'

'Aha! ha, ha, ha, ha! Aha, ha, ha! It is something for you to wear, ha, ha! If you like it and if it's not too heavy. I don't want to fracture your cervical vertebrae, my little lady. Oh no, by all that's most healthy I wouldn't care to do that; but I'll trust you to be careful. You will, won't you? Ha, ha.'

'Yes, yes, I will,' said Fuchsia.

He bent even closer to Fuchsia. 'Your baby brother has hurt you. *I* know, ha, ha. *I* know,' the Doctor whispered, and the sound edged between his rows of big teeth, very faintly, but not so faintly as to escape Steerpike's hearing. 'I have a stone for your bosom, my dear child, for I saw the diamonds within your tearducts when you ran from your mother's door. These, if they come again, must be balanced by a heavier if less brilliant stone, lying upon your bosom.'

Prunesquallor's eyes remained quite still for a moment. His hands were still clasped at his chin.

Fuchsia stared. 'Thank you, Dr Prune,' she said at last.

The physician relaxed and straightened himself. 'Ha, ha, ha! Ha, ha, ha!' he trilled, and then bent forward to whisper again. 'So I have decided to give you a stone from another land.'

He put his hand into his pocket, but kept it there as he glanced over his shoulder.

'Who is your friend of the fiery eyes, my Fuchsia? Do you know him well?'

Fuchsia shook her head and stuck her lower lip out as though with instinctive distaste.

The Doctor winked at her, his magnified right eye closing enormously. 'A little later, perhaps,' said Prunesquallor, opening his eyelid again like some sort of sea creature, 'when the night is a little further advanced, a little longer in the molar, ha, ha, ha!' He straightened himself. 'When the world has swung through space a further hundred miles or so, ha, ha! then – ah, yes, ... then –' and for the second time he looked knowing and winked. Then he swung round upon his heel.

'And now,' he said, 'what will you have? And what, in the name of hosiery, are you wearing?'

Steerpike got to his feet. 'I am wearing what I am forced to wear until clothes can be found which are more appropriate,' he said. 'These rags, although an official uniform, are as absurd upon me as they are insulting. Sir,' he continued, 'you asked me what I would take. Brandy, I thank you, sir, Brandy.' Mrs Slagg, staring her poor old eyes practically out of their hot sockets, peered at the Doctor as the speech ended, to hear what he could possibly say after so many words. Fuchsia had not been listening. Something to wear, he had said. Something to lie heavily on her bosom. A stone. Tired as she was she was all excitement to know what it could be. Dr Prunesquallor had always been kind to her, if rather above her, but he had never given her a present before. What colour would the heavy stone be? What would it be? What would it be?

The Doctor was for a moment nonplussed at the youth's self-assurance, but he did not show it. He simply smiled like a crocodile. 'Am I mistaken, dear boy, or is that a kitchen jacket you're wearing?'

'Not only is this a kitchen jacket, but these are kitchen trousers and kitchen socks and kitchen shoes and everything is kitchen about me, sir, except myself, if you don't mind me saying so, Doctor.'

'And what', said Prunesquallor, placing the tips of his fingers together, 'are you? Beneath your foetid jacket, which I must say looks amazingly unhygienic even for Swelter's kitchen. What *are* you? Are you a problem case, my dear boy, or are you a clear-cut young gentleman with no ideas at all, ha, ha, ha?'

'With your permission, Doctor, I am neither. I have plenty of ideas, though at the moment plenty of problems, too.'

'Is that so?' said the Doctor. 'Is that so? How very unique! Have your brandy first, and perhaps some of them will fade gently away upon the fumes of that very excellent narcotic. Ha, ha, ha! Fade gently and imperceptibly away ...' And he fluttered his long fingers in the air.

At this moment a knock upon the door panels caused the Doctor to cry out in his extraordinary falsetto:

'Make entry! Come along, come along, my dear fellow! Make entry! What in the name of all that's rapid are you waiting for?'

The door opened and the servant entered, balancing a tray upon which stood a bottle of elderberry wine and a small white cardboard box. He deposited the bottle and the box upon the table and retired. There was something sullen about his manner. The bottle had been placed upon the table with perhaps too casual a movement. The door had clicked behind him with rather too sharp a report. Steerpike noticed this, and when he saw the Doctor's gaze return to his face, he raised his eyebrows quizzically and shrugged his shoulders the merest fraction.

Prunesquallor brought a brandy bottle to the table in the centre of the room, but first poured out a glass of elderberry wine which he gave to Fuchsia with a bow.

'Drink, my Fuchsia dear,' he said. 'Drink to all those things that you love best. *I* know. *I* know,' he added with his hands folded at his chin again. 'Drink to everything that's bright and glossy. Drink to the Coloured Things.'

Fuchsia nodded her head unsmilingly at the toast and took a gulp. She looked up at the Doctor very seriously. 'It's nice,' she said. 'I like elderberry wine. Do you like your drink, Nannie?'

Mrs Slagg very nearly spilt her port over the arm of the chair when she heard herself addressed. She nodded her head violently.

'And now for the brandy,' said the Doctor. 'The brandy for Master . . . Master . . .'

'Steerpike,' said the youth. 'My name is Steerpike, sir.'

'Steerpike of the Many Problems,' said the Doctor. 'What did you say they were? My memory is so very untrustworthy. It's as fickle as a fox. Ask me to name the third lateral bloodvessel from the extremity of my index finger that runs east to west when I lie on my face at sundown, or the percentage of chalk to be found in the knuckles of an average spinster in her fifty-seventh year, ha, ha, ha! – or even ask me, my dear boy, to give details of the pulse rate of frogs two minutes before they die of scabies – these things are no tax upon my memory, ha, ha, ha! but ask me to remember exactly what you said your problems were, a minute ago, and you will find that my memory has forsaken me utterly. Now why is that, my dear Master Steerpike, why is that?'

'Because I never mentioned them,' said Steerpike.

'That accounts for it,' said Prunesquallor. 'That, no doubt, accounts for it.'

'I think so, sir,' said Steerpike.

'But you *have* problems,' said the Doctor.

Steerpike took the glass of brandy which the Doctor had poured out.

'My problems are varied,' he said. 'The most immediate is to impress you with my potentialities. To be able to make such an unorthodox remark is in itself a sign of some originality. I am not indispensable to you at the moment, sir, because you have never made use of my services; but after a week's employment under your roof, sir, I could become so. I would be invaluable.

I am purposely precipitous in my remarks. Either you reject me here and now or you have already at the back of your mind a desire to know me further. I am seventeen, sir. Do I sound like seventeen? Do I act like seventeen? I am clever enough to know I am clever. You will forgive my undiplomatic approach, sir, because you are a gentleman of imagination. That then, sir, is my immediate problem. To impress you with my talent, which would be put to your service in any and every form.' Steerpike raised his glass. 'To you, sir, if you will allow my presumption.'

The Doctor all this while had had his glass of cognac raised, but it had remained motionless an inch from his lips, until now, as Steerpike ended and took a sip at his brandy, he sat down suddenly in a chair beside the table and set down his own glass untasted.

'Well, well, well, well,' he said at last. 'Well, well, well, well, well! By all that's intriguing this is really the quintessential. What maladdress, by all that's impudent! What an enormity of surface! What a very rare frenzy indeed!' And he began to whinny, gently at first, but after a little while his high-pitched laughter increased in volume and in *tempo*, and within a few minutes he was helpless with the shrill gale of his own merriment. How so great a quantity of breath and noise managed to come from lungs that must have been, in that tube of a chest, wedged uncomfortably close together, it is difficult to imagine. Keeping, even at the height of his paroxysms, an extraordinary theatrical elegance, he rocked to and fro in his chair, helpless for the best part of nine minutes after which with difficulty he drew breath thinly through his teeth with a noise like the whistling of steam; and eventually, still shaking a little, he was able to focus his eyes upon the source of his enjoyment.

'Well, Prodigy, my dear boy! you have done me a lot of good. My lungs have needed something like that for a long time.'

'I have done something for you already, then,' said Steerpike with the clever imitation of a smile on his face. During the major part of the Doctor's helplessness he had been taking stock of the room and had poured himself out another glass of brandy. He had noted the *objets d'art*, the expensive carpets and mirrors, and the bookcase of calf-bound volumes. He had poured out some more port for Mrs Slagg and had ventured to wink at Fuchsia, who had stared emptily back, and he had turned the wink into an affection of his eye.

He had examined the labels on the bottles and their year of vintage. He had noticed that the table was of walnut and that the ring upon the Doctor's right hand was in the form of a silver serpent holding between his gaping jaw a nugget of red gold. At first the Doctor's laughter had caused him a shock, and a certain mortification, but he was soon his cold, calculating self, with his ordered mind like a bureau with tabulated shelves and pigeon-holes of reference, and he knew that at all costs he must be pleasant. He had taken a risky turning in playing such a boastful card, and at the moment it could not be proved either a failure or a success; but this he did know, that to be able to take risks was the keynote of the successful man.

Prunesquallor, when his strength and muscular control were restored sufficiently, sipped at his cognac in what seemed a delicate manner, but Steerpike was surprised to see that he had soon emptied the glass.

This seemed to do the Doctor a lot of good. He stared at the youth.

'You *do* interest me, I must admit that much, Master Steerpike,' he said. 'Oh yes, I'll go that far, ha, ha, ha! You interest me, or rather you tantalize me in a pleasant sort of way. But whether I want to have you hanging around my house is, as you with your enormous brain will readily admit, quite a different kettle of fish.'

'I don't hang about, sir. It is one of those things I never do.'

Fuchsia's voice came slowly across the room.

'You hung about in my room,' she said. And then, bending forward, she looked up at the Doctor with an almost imploring expression. 'He *climbed* there,' she said. 'He's clever.' Then she leaned back in her chair. 'I am tired; and he saw my own room that nobody ever saw before he saw it, and it is worrying me. Oh, Dr Prune.'

There was a pause.

'He climbed there,' she said again.

'I had to go somewhere,' said Steerpike. 'I didn't know it was your room. How could I have known? I am sorry, your Lady-ship.'

She did not answer.

Prunesquallor had looked from one to the other.

'Aha! aha! Take a little of this powder, Fuchsia dear,' he said, bringing across to her the white cardboard box. He removed the lid and tilted a little into her glass which he filled again with elderberry wine. 'You won't taste anything at all, my dear girl; just sip it up and you will feel as strong as a mountain tiger, ha, ha! Mrs Slagg, you will take this box away with you. Four times a day, with whatever the dear child happens to be drinking. It is tasteless. It is harmless, and it is extremely efficacious. Do not forget, my good woman, will you? She needs something and this is the very something she needs, ha, ha, ha! this is the very something!'

Nannie received the box on which was written 'Fuchsia. One teaspoonful to be taken 4 times a day.'

'Master Steerpike,' said the Doctor, 'is that the reason you wanted to see me, to beard me in my den, and to melt my heart like tallow upon my own hearth-rug?' He tilted his head at the youth.

'That is so, sir,' said Steerpike. 'With Lady Fuchsia's permission I accompanied her. I said to her: "Just let me see the Doctor, and put my case to him, and I am confident he will be impressed".'

There was a pause. Then in a confidential voice Steerpike added: 'In my less ambitious moments it is as a research scientist that I see myself, sir, and in my still less ambitious, as a dispenser.'

'What knowledge of chemicals have you, if I may venture to remark?' said the Doctor.

'Under your initial guidance my powers would develop as rapidly as you could wish,' said Steerpike.

'You are a clever little monster,' said the Doctor, tossing off another cognac and placing the glass upon the table with a click. 'A diabolically clever little monster.'

'That is what I hoped you would realize, Doctor,' said Steerpike. 'But haven't all ambitious people something of the monstrous about them? You, sir, for instance, if you will forgive me, are a little bit monstrous.'

'But, my poor youth,' said Prunesquallor, beginning to pace the room, 'there is not the minutest molecule of ambition in my anatomy, monstrous though it may appear to you, ha, ha, ha!'

His laughter had not the spontaneous, uncontrollable quality that it usually possessed.

'But, sir,' said Steerpike, 'there *has* been.'

'And why do you think so?'

'Because of this room. Because of the exquisite furnishings you possess; because of your calf-bound books; your glassware; your violin. You could not have collected together such things without ambition.'

'That is not ambition, my poor confused boy,' said the Doctor: 'it is a union between those erstwhile incompatibles, ha, ha, ha! – taste and a hereditary income.'

'Is not taste a cultivated luxury?' said Steerpike.

'But yes,' said the Doctor. 'But yes. One has the potentialities for taste; on finding this out about oneself, ha, ha! – after a little self-probing, it is a cultivated thing, as you remark.'

'Which needs assiduous concentration and diligence, no doubt,' said the youth.

'But yes; but yes,' answered the Doctor smiling, with a note in his voice that suggested it was only common politeness in him to keep amused.

'Surely such diligence is the same thing as ambitiousness. Ambitiousness to perfect your taste. That is what I mean by "ambition", Doctor, I believe you have it. I do not mean ambition for success, for "success" is a meaningless word – the successful, so I hear, being very often, to themselves, failures of the first water.'

'You interest me,' said Prunesquallor. 'I would like to speak to Lady Fuchsia alone. We haven't been paying very much attention to her, I am afraid. We have deserted her. She is alone in a desert of her own. Only watch her.'

Fuchsia's eyes were shut as she leaned back in the chair, her knees curled up under her.

'While I speak with her you will be so very, very good as to leave the room. There's a chair in the hall, Master Steerpike. Thank you, dear youth. It would be a handsome gesture.'

Steerpike disappeared at once, taking his brandy with him.

Prunesquallor looked at the old woman and the girl. Mrs Slagg, with her little mouth wide open, was fast asleep. Fuchsia had opened her eyes at the sound of the door shutting behind Steerpike.

The Doctor immediately beckoned her to approach. She came to him at once, her eyes wide.

'I've waited so long, Dr Prune,' she said. 'Can I have my stone now?'

'This very moment,' said the Doctor. 'This very second. You will not know very much about the nature of this stone, but you will treasure it more than anyone I could possibly think of. Fuchsia dear, you were so distraught as you ran like a wild pony away from your father and me; so distraught with your black mane and your big hungry eyes – that I said to myself: "It's for Fuchsia", although ponies don't usually care much about such things, ha, ha, ha! But you will, won't you?'

The Doctor took from his pocket a small pouch of softest leather.

'Take it out yourself,' he said. 'Draw it out with this slender chain.'

Fuchsia took the pouch from the Doctor's hand and from it drew forth into the lamplight a ruby like a lump of anger.

It burned in her palm.

She did not know what to do. She did not wonder what she ought to say. There was nothing at all to say. Dr Prunesquallor knew something of what she felt. At last, clutching the solid fire between her fingers, she shook Nannie Slagg, who screamed a little as she awoke. Fuchsia got to her feet and dragged her to the door. A moment before the Doctor opened it for them, Fuchsia turned her face up to his and parted her lips in a smile of such dark, sweet loveliness, so subtly blended with her brooding strangeness, that the Doctor's hand clenched the handle of the door. He had never seen her look like this before. He had always thought of her as an ugly girl of whom he was strangely fond. But now, what was it he had seen? She was no longer a small girl for all her slowness of speech and almost irritating simplicity.

In the hall they passed the figure of Steerpike sitting comfortably on the floor beneath a large carved clock. They did not speak, and when they parted with the Doctor Nannie said: 'Thank you' in a sleepy voice and bowed slightly, one of her hands in Fuchsia's. Fuchsia's fingers clenched the blood-red stone and the Doctor only said: 'Good-bye, and take care, my dears, take care. Happy dreams. Happy dreams,' before he closed the door.

A GIFT OF THE GAB

As he returned through the hall his mind was so engrossed with his new vision of Fuchsia that he had forgotten Steerpike and was startled at the sound of steps behind him. A moment or two earlier Steerpike had himself been startled by footsteps descending the staircase immediately above where he had been sitting in the shadowy, tiger stripes of the bannisters.

He moved swiftly up to the Doctor. 'I am afraid I am still here,' he said, and then glanced over his shoulder following the Doctor's eyes. Steerpike turned and saw, descending the last three steps of the staircase, a lady whose similarity to Dr Prunesquallor was unmistakable, but whose whole deportment was more rigid. She, also, suffered from faulty eyesight, but in her case the glasses were darkly tinted so that it was impossible to tell at whom she was looking save by the general direction of the head, which was no sure indication.

The lady approached them. 'Who is this?' she said directing her face at Steerpike.

'This,' said her brother, 'is none other than Master Steerpike, who was brought to see me on account of his talents. He is anxious for me to make use of his brain, ha, ha! – not, as you might suppose, as a floating specimen in one of my jam jars, ha, ha, ha! but in its functional capacity as a vortex of dazzling thought.'

'Did he go upstairs just now?' said Miss Irma Prunesquallor. 'I said did he go upstairs just now?'

The tall lady had the habit of speaking at great speed and of repeating her questions irritably before there had been a moment's pause in which they might be answered. Prunesquallor had in moments of whimsy often amused himself by trying to wedge an answer to her less complex queries between the initial question and its sharp echo.

'Upstairs, my dear?' repeated her brother.

'I said "upstairs", I think,' said Irma Prunesquallor sharply. 'I think I said "upstairs". Have you, or he, or anyone been upstairs a quarter of an hour ago? Have you? Have you?'

'Surely not! surely not!' said the Doctor. 'We have all been downstairs, I think. Don't you?' he said, turning to Steerpike.

'I do,' said Steerpike. The Doctor began to like the way the youth answered quietly and neatly.

Irma Prunesquallor drew herself together. Her long tightly fitting black dress gave peculiar emphasis to such major bone formations as the iliac crest, and indeed the entire pelvis; the shoulder blades, and in certain angles, as she stood in the lamplight, to the ribs themselves. Her neck was long and the Prunesquallors' head sat upon it surrounded by the same grey thatch-like hair as that adopted by her brother, but in her case knotted in a low bun at the neck.

'The servant is out. OUT,' she said. 'It is his evening out. Isn't it? Isn't it?'

She seemed to be addressing Steerpike, so he answered: 'I have no knowledge of the arrangements you have made, madam. But he was in the Doctor's room a few minutes ago, so I expect it was he whom you heard outside your door.'

'Who said I heard anything outside my door?' said Irma Prunesquallor, a trifle less rapidly than usual. 'Who?'

'Were you not within your room, madam?'

'What of it? what of it?'

'I gathered from what you said that you thought that there was someone walking about upstairs,' answered Steerpike obliquely; 'and if, as you say, you were *inside* your room, then you must have heard the footsteps *outside* your room. That is what I attempted to make clear, madam.'

'You seem to know too much about it. Don't you? don't you?' She bent forward and her opaque-looking glasses stared flatly at Steerpike.

'I know nothing, madam,' said Steerpike.

'What, Irma dear, *is* all this? What in the name of all that's circuitous *is* all this?'

'I heard feet. That is all. Feet,' said his sister; and then, after a pause she added with renewed emphasis: 'Feet.'

'Irma, my dear sister,' said Prunesquallor, 'I have two things to say. Firstly, why in the name of discomfort are we hanging around in the hall and probably dying of a draught that as far as I am concerned runs up my right trouser leg and sets my gluteous maximus twitching; and secondly, what is wrong, when you boil the matter down – with feet? I have always found mine singularly useful, especially for walking with. In fact, ha, ha, ha, one might almost imagine that they had been designed for that very purpose.'

'As usual', said his sister, 'you are drunk with your own levity. You have a brain, Alfred. I have never denied it. Never. But it is undermined by your insufferable levity. I tell you that someone has been prowling about upstairs and you take no notice. There has been no one to prowl. Do you not see the point?'

'I heard something, too,' said Steerpike, breaking in. 'I was sitting in the hall where the Doctor suggested I should remain while he decided in what capacity he would employ me, when I heard what sounded like footsteps upstairs. I crept to the top of the stairs silently, but there was no one there, so I returned.'

Steerpike, thinking the upstairs to be empty, had in reality been making a rough survey of the first floor, until he heard what must have been Irma moving to the door of her room, at which sound he had slid down the bannisters.

'You hear what he says,' said the lady, following her brother with a stiff irritation in every line of her progress. 'You hear what he says.'

'Very much so!' said the Doctor. 'Very much so, indeed. Most indigestible.'

Steerpike moved a chair up for Irma Prunesquallor with such a show of consideration for her comfort and such adroitness that she stared at him and her hard mouth relaxed at one corner.

'Steerpike,' she said, wrinkling her black dress above her hips as she reclined a little into her chair.

'I am at your service, madam,' said Steerpike. 'What may I do for you?'

'What on earth are you wearing? What are you wearing, boy?'

'It is with great regret that at my introduction to you I should be in clothes that so belie my fastidious nature, madam,' he said. 'If you will advise me where I may procure the cloth I will endeavour to have myself fitted tomorrow. Standing beside you, madam, in your exquisite gown of darkness –'

' "Gown of darkness" is good,' interrupted Prunesquallor, raising his hand to his head, where he spread his snow-white fingers across his brow. ' "Gown of darkness". A phrase, ha, ha! Definitely a phrase.'

'You have broken in, Alfred!' said his sister. 'Haven't you? haven't you? I will have a suit cut for you tomorrow, Steerpike,' she continued. 'You will be here, I suppose? Where are you sleeping? Is he sleeping here? Where do you live? Where does he live, Alfred? What have you arranged? Nothing, I expect. Have you done anything? Have you? have you?'

'What sort of thing, Irma, my dear? What sort of thing are you referring to? I have done all sorts of things. I have removed a gallstone the size of a potato. I have played delicately upon my violin while a rainbow shone through the dispensary window; I have plunged so deeply into the poets of grief that save for my foresight in attaching fish-hooks to my clothes I might never again have been drawn earthwards, ha, ha! from those excruciating depths!'

Irma could tell exactly when her brother would veer off into soliloquy and had developed the power to pay no attention at all to what he said. The footsteps upstairs seemed forgotten. She watched Steerpike as he poured her out a glass of port with a gallantry quite remarkable in its technical perfection of movement and timing.

'You wish to be employed. Is that it? Is that it?' she said.

'It is my ardent desire to be in your service,' he said.

'Why? Tell me why,' said Miss Prunesquallor.

'I endeavour to keep my mind in an equipoise between the intuitive, and rational reasoning, madam,' he said. 'But with you I cannot, for my intuitive desire to be of service overshadows my reasons, though they are many. I can only say I feel a desire to fulfil myself by finding employment under your roof. And so,' he added, turning up the corners of his mouth in a quizzical smile, 'that is the reason *why* I cannot exactly say *why*.'

'Mixed up with this metaphysical impulse, this fulfilment that you speak of so smoothly,' said the Doctor, 'is no doubt a desire to snatch the first opportunity of getting away from Swelter and the unpleasant duties which you have no doubt had to perform. Is that not so?'

'It is,' said Steerpike.

This forthright answer so pleased the Doctor that he got up from his chair and, smiling toothily, poured himself yet another glass. What pleased him especially was the mixture of cunning and honesty which he did not yet perceive to be a still deeper strata of Steerpike's cleverness.

Prunesquallor and his sister both felt a certain delight in making the acquaintance of a young gentleman with brains, however twisted those brains might be. It was true that in Gormenghast there were several cultivated persons, but they very seldom came in contact with them these days. The Countess was no conversationalist. The Earl was usually too depressed to be drawn upon subjects which had he so wished he could have discussed at length and with a dreamy penetration. The twin sisters could never have kept to the point of any conversation.

There were many others apart from the servants with whom Prunesquallor came into almost daily contact in the course of his social or professional duties, but seeing them overmuch had dulled his interest in their conversation and he was agreeably surprised to find that Steerpike, although very young, had a talent for words and a ready mind. Miss Prunesquallor saw less of people than her brother. She was pleased by the reference to her dress and was flattered by the manner in which he saw to her comforts. To be sure, he was rather a small creature. His clothes, of course, she would see to. His eyes at first she found rather monkey-like in their closeness and concentration, but as she got used to them she found there was something exciting in the way they looked at her. It made her feel he realized she was not only a lady, but a woman.

Her own brain was sharp and quick, but unlike her brother's it was superficial, and she instinctively recognized in the youth a streak of cleverness akin to her own, although stronger. She had passed the age when a husband might be looked for. Had any man ever gazed at her in this light, the coincidence of his also having the courage to broach such a subject would have been too much to credit. Irma Prunesquallor had never met such a person, her admirers confining themselves to purely verbal approach.

As it happened Miss Prunesquallor, before her thoughts were interrupted by the sound of Steerpike's feet padding past her bedroom door, had been in a state of dejection. Most people have periods of retrospection in which their thoughts are centred upon the less attractive elements in their past. Irma Prunesquallor was no exception, but today there had been something wild about her dejection. After readjusting her glasses irritably upon the bridge of her nose, she had wrung her hands before sitting at her mirror. She ignored the fact that her neck was too long, that her mouth was thin and hard, that her nose was far too sharp, and that her eyes were quite hidden, and concentrated on the profusion of coarse grey hair which swept back from her brow in one wave to where, low down on her neck, it gathered itself into a great hard knot – and on the quality of her skin, which was, indeed, unblemished. These two things alone in her eyes made her an object destined for admiration. And yet, what admiration had she received? Who was there to admire her or to compliment her upon her soft and peerless skin and on her sweep of hair?

Steerpike's gallantry had for a moment taken the chill off her heart.

By now all three of them were seated. The Doctor had drunk rather more than he would have ever prescribed to a patient. His arms were moving freely whenever he spoke and he seemed to enjoy watching his fingers as they emphasized, in dumb show, whatever he happened to be talking about.

Even his sister had felt the effect of more than her usual quota of port. Whenever Steerpike spoke she nodded her head sharply as though in total agreement.

'Alfred,' she said. 'Alfred, I'm speaking to you. Can you hear me? Can you? Can you?'

'Very distinctly, Irma, my very dear, dear sister. Your voice is ringing in my middle ear. In fact, it's ringing in both of them. Right in the very middle of them both, or rather, in both their very middles. What is it, flesh of my flesh?'

'We shall dress him in pale grey,' she said.

'Who, blood of my blood?' cried Prunesquallor. 'Who is to be apparisoned in the hue of doves?'

'Who? How can you say "Who?"! This youth, Alfred, this youth. He is taking Pellet's place. I am discharging Pellet tomorrow. He has always been too slow and clumsy. Don't you think so? Don't you think so?'

'I am far beyond thinking, bone of my bone. Far, far beyond thinking. I hand over the reins to you, Irma. Mount and begone. The world awaits you.'

Steerpike saw that the time was ripe.

'I am confident I shall give satisfaction, dear lady,' he said. 'My reward will be to see you, perhaps, once more, perhaps twice more, if you will allow me, in this dark gown that so becomes you. The slight stain which I noticed upon the hem I will remove tomorrow, with your permission. Madam,' he said, with that startling simplicity with which he interlarded his remarks, 'where can I sleep?'

Rising to her feet stiffly, but with more self-conscious dignity than she had found it necessary to assume for some while past, she motioned him to follow her with a singularly wooden gesture, and led the way through the door.

Somewhere in the vaults of her bosom a tiny imprisoned bird had begun to sing.

'Are you going forever and a day?' shouted the Doctor from his chair in which he was spread out like a length of rope. 'Am I to be marooned forever, ha, ha, ha! for evermore and evermore?'

'For tonight, yes,' replied his sister's voice. 'Mister Steerpike will see you in the morning.'

The Doctor yawned with a final flash of his teeth, and fell fast asleep.

Miss Prunesquallor led Steerpike to the door of a room on the second floor. Steerpike noticed that it was simple, spacious and comfortable.

'I will have you called in the morning, after which I will instruct you in your duties. Do you hear me? Do you hear me?'

'With great pleasure, madam.'

Her passage to the door was more stilted than ever, for she had not for a very long while made such an effort to walk attractively. The black silk of her dress gleamed in the candlelight and rustled at the knees. She turned her head at the door and Steerpike bowed, keeping his head down until the door was closed and she had gone.

Moving quickly to the window he opened it. Across the courtyard the mountainous outline of Gormenghast Castle rose darkly into the night. The cool air fanned his big protruding forehead. His face remained like a mask, but deep down in his stomach he grinned.

WHILE THE OLD NURSE DOZES

FOR the time being Steerpike must be left at the Prunesquallors, where in the somewhat elastic capacity of odd-job man, medical assistant, lady's help and conversationalist, he managed to wedge himself firmly into the structure of the household. His ingratiating manner had, day by day, a more insidious effect, until he was looked upon as part of the *ménage*, being an alien only with the cook who, as an old retainer, felt no love for an upstart and treated him with undisguised suspicion.

The Doctor found him extremely quick to learn and within a few weeks Steerpike was in control of all the dispensary work. Indeed, the chemicals and drugs had a strong fascination for the youth and he would often be found compiling mixtures of his own invention.

Of the compromising and tragic circumstances that were the outcome of all this, is not yet time to speak.

Within the castle the time-honoured rituals were performed daily. The excitement following upon the birth of Titus had in some degree subsided. The Countess, against the warnings of her medical adviser was, as she had declared she would be, up and about. She was, it is true, very weak at first, but so violent was her irritation at not being able to greet the dawn as was her habit, accompanied by a white tide of cats, that she defied the lassitude of her body.

She had heard the cats crying to her from the lawn sixty feet below her room as she lay in bed those three mornings after little Titus had been delivered, and lying there hugely in her candlelit room she had yearned to be with them, and beads of sweat had stood out upon her skin as in her agony she hankered for strength.

Had not her birds been with her, the frustration of her spirit must surely have done her more than the physical harm of getting up. The constantly changing population of her feathered children were the solace of those few days that seemed to her like months.

The white rook was the most constant in his re-appearances at the ivy-choked window, although up to the moment of her confinement he had been the most fickle of visitors.

In her deep voice she would hold converse with him for an hour at a time, referring to him as 'Master Chalk' or her 'wicked one'. All her companions came. Sometimes the room was alive with song. Sometimes, feeling the need to exercise their pinions in the sky, a crowd of them would follow one another through the window of ivy, around which in the shadowy air as they waited their turn to scramble through, a dozen birds at a time would hover, fall and rise, rattling their many-coloured wings.

Thus it might be that from time to time she would be almost deserted. On one occasion only a stonechat and a bedraggled owl were with her.

Now she was strong enough to walk and watch them circling in the sky or to sit in her arbour at the end of the long lawn, and with the sunlight smouldering in the dark red hair and lying wanly over the area of her face and neck, watch the multiform and snow-white convolutions of her malkins.

Mrs Slagg had found herself becoming more and more dependent upon Keda's help. She did not like to admit this to herself. There was something so still about Keda which she could not understand. Every now and again she made an effort to impress the girl with an authority which she did not possess, keeping on the alert to try and find some fault in her. This was so obvious and pathetic that it did not annoy the girl from the Mud Dwellings. She knew that an hour or so afterwards when Mrs Slagg felt that her position was once again established, the old nurse would run up to her, nearly in tears for some petty reason or other and bury her shaking head in Keda's side.

Fond as Keda had become of Titus whom she had suckled and cared for tenderly, she had begun to realize that she must return to the Mud Dwellings. She had left them suddenly as a being who, feeling that Providence has called him, leaves the old life suddenly for the new. But now she realized that she had made a mistake and knew that she would be false to remain any longer in the castle than was necessary for the child. Not so much a mistake as a crime against her conscience, for it was with a very real reason that she had accompanied Mrs Slagg at such short notice.

Day after day from the window in the small room she had been given next to Mrs Slagg's she gazed to where the high surrounding wall of the castle grounds hid from her sight the Dwellings that she had known since her infancy, and where during the last year her passions had been so cruelly stirred.

Her baby, whom she had buried so recently, had been the son of an old carver of matchless reputation among the Dwellers. The marriage had been forced upon her by the iron laws.

Those sculptors who were unanimously classed as pre-eminent were, after the fiftieth year, allowed to choose a bride from among the damsels, and against their choice no shadow of objection could be raised. This immemorial custom had left Keda no option but to become the wife of this man, who, though a sour and uncouth old creature, burned with a vitality that defied his years.

From the morning until the light failed him he would be with his carvings. He would peer at it from all angles, or crouch grotesquely at some distance, his eyes narrowed in the sunlight. Then, stealing up upon it, it would seem that he was preparing to strike like a beast attacking its paralysed quarry; but on reaching the wooden form he would run his great hand over the surfaces as a lover will fondle the breasts of his mistress.

Within three months from the time when he and Keda had performed the marriage ceremony, standing alone upon the marriage hill, to the south of the Twisted Woods, while an ancient voice called to them through the half-lit distances, their hands joined, her feet upon his – within the three months that followed he had died. Suddenly letting the chisel and the hammer fall to the ground, his hands had clutched at his heart, his lips had drawn themselves away from his teeth, and he had crumpled up, his energy passing out of him and leaving only the old dry sack of his body. Keda was alone. She had not loved him but had admired him and the passion that consumed him as an artist. Once more she was free save that, on the day that he died, she felt within her the movement of another life than her own and now, nearly a year later, her firstborn was lying near the father, lifeless, in the dry earth.

The dreadful and premature age that descended so suddenly upon the faces of the Dwellers had not yet completely fallen over her features. It was as though it was so close upon her that the beauty of her face cried out against it, defying it, as a stag at bay turns upon the hounds with a pride of stance and a shaking of antlers.

A hectic beauty came upon the maidens of the Mud buildings a month or so before the ravages to which they were predestined attacked them. From infancy until this tragic interim of beauty their loveliness was of a strange innocence, a crystal-like tranquillity that held no prescience of the future. When in this clearness the dark seeds began to root and smoke was mixed with the flame, then, as with Keda now, a thorny splendour struck outward from their features.

One warm afternoon, sitting in Mrs Slagg's room with Titus at her breast, she turned to the old nurse and said quietly: 'At the end of the month I shall return to my home. Titus is strong and well and he will be able to do without me.'

Nannie, whose head had been nodding a little, for she was always either dropping off for a nap or waking up from one, opened her eyes when Keda's words had soaked into her brain. Then she sat up very suddenly and in a frightened voice called out: 'No! no! you mustn't go. You mustn't! You mustn't! Oh, Keda, you know how old I am.' And she ran across the room to hold Keda's arm. Then for the sake of her dignity: 'I've told you not to call him Titus,' she cried in a rush. ' "Lord Titus" or "his Lordship," is what you *should* say.' And then, as though with relief, she fell back upon her trouble. 'Oh, you can't go! you can't go!'

'I must go,' said Keda. 'There are reasons why I must go.'

'Why? why? why?' Nannie cried out through the tears that were beginning to run jerkily down her foolish wrinkled face. 'Why must you go?' Then she stamped a tiny slippered foot that made very little noise. 'You must answer me! You must! Why are you going away from me?' Then, clenching her hands – 'I'll tell the Countess,' she said, 'I'll tell her.'

Keda took no notice at all, but lifted Titus from one shoulder to another where his crying ceased.

'He will be safe in your care,' said Keda. 'You must find another helper when he grows older for he will be too much for you.'

'But they won't be like you,' shrilled Nannie Slagg, as though she were abusing Keda for her suitability. 'They won't be like *you*. They'll bully me. Some of them bully old women when they are like me. Oh, my weak heart! my poor weak heart! what can I do?'

'Come,' said Keda. 'It is not as difficult as that.'

'It *is*. It *is*!' cried Mrs Slagg, renewing her authority. 'It's worse than that, much worse. Everyone deserts me, because I'm old.'

'You must find someone you can trust. I will try and help you,' said Keda.

'*Will* you? *will* you?' cried Nannie, bringing her fingers up to her mouth and staring at Keda through the red rims of her eyelids. 'Oh, *will* you? They make me do everything. Fuchsia's mother leaves everything to me. She has hardly seen his little Lordship, has she? Has she?'

'No,' said Keda. 'Not once. But he is happy.'

She lifted the infant away from her and laid him between the blankets in his cot, where after a spell of whimpering he sucked contentedly at his fist.

Nannie Slagg suddenly gripped Keda's arm again. 'You haven't told me why; you haven't told me why,' she said. 'I want to know why you're going away from me. You never tell me anything. Never. I suppose I'm not worth telling. I suppose you think I don't matter. Why don't you tell me things? Oh, my poor heart, I suppose I'm too old to be told anything.'

'I will tell you why I have to go,' said Keda. 'Sit down and listen.' Nannie sat upon a low chair and clasped her wrinkled hands together. 'Tell me everything,' she said.

Why Keda broke the long silence that was so much a part of her nature she could not afterwards imagine, feeling only that in talking to one who would hardly understand her she was virtually talking to herself. There had come to her a sense of relief in unburdening her heart.

Keda sat upon Mrs Slagg's bed near the wall. She sat very upright and her hands lay in her lap. For a moment or two she gazed out of the window at a cloud that had meandered lazily into view. Then she turned to the old woman.

'When I returned with you on that first evening,' said Keda quietly, 'I was troubled. I was troubled and I am still unhappy because of love. I feared my future; and my past was sorrow, and in my present you had need of me and I had need of refuge, so I came.' She paused.

'Two men from our Mud Dwellings loved me. They loved me

too much and too violently.' Her eyes returned to Nannie Slagg, but they hardly saw her, nor noticed that her withered lips were pursed and her head tilted like a sparrow's. She continued quietly:

'My husband had died. He was a Bright Carver, and died struggling. I would sit down in the long shadows by our dwelling and watch a dryad's head from day to day finding its hidden outline. To me it seemed he carved the child of leaves. He would not rest, but fight; and stare – and stare. Always he would stare, cutting the wood away to give his dryad breath. One evening when I felt my unborn moving within me my husband's heart stopped beating and his weapons fell. I ran to him and knelt beside his body. His chisel lay in the dust. Above us his unfinished dryad gazed over the Twisted Woods, an acorn between its teeth.

'They buried him, my rough husband, in the long sandy valley, the valley of graves where we are always buried. The two dark men who loved and love me carried his body for me and they lowered it into the sandy hollow that they had scooped. A hundred men were there and a hundred women; for he had been the rarest of the carvers. The sand was heaped upon him and there was only another dusty mound among the mounds of the Valley and all was very silent. They held me in their eyes while he was buried – the two who love me. And I could not think of him whom we were mourning. I could not think of death. Only of life. I could not think of stillness, only of movement. I could not understand the burying, nor that life could cease to be. It was all a dream. I was alive, *alive*, and two men watched me standing. They stood beyond the grave, on the other side. I saw only their shadows for I dared not lift up my eyes to show my gladness. But I knew that they were watching me and I knew that I was young. They were strong men, their faces still unbroken by the cruel bane we suffer. They were strong and young. While yet my husband lived I had not seen them. Though one brought white flowers from the Twisted Woods and one a dim stone from the Gormen Mountain, yet I saw nothing of them, for I knew temptation.

'That was long ago. All is changed. My baby has been buried

and my lovers are filled with hatred for one another. When you came for me I was in torment. From day to day their jealousy had grown until, to save the shedding of blood, I came to the castle. Oh, long ago with you, that dreadful night.'

She stopped and moved a lock of hair back from her forehead. She did not look at Mrs Slagg, who blinked her eyes as Keda paused and nodded her head wisely.

'Where are they now? How many, many times have I dreamed of them! How many, many times have I, into my pillow, cried: "Rantel!" whom I first saw gathering the Root, his coarse hair in his eyes ... cried "Braigon!" who stood brooding in the grove. Yet not with all of me am I in love. Too much of my own quietness is with me. I am not drowned with them in Love's unkindness. I am unable to do aught but watch them, and fear them and the hunger in their eyes. The rapture that possessed me by the grave has passed. I am tired now, with a love I do not quite possess. Tired with the hatreds I have woken. Tired that I am the cause and have no power. My beauty will soon leave me, soon, soon, and peace will come. But ah! too soon.'

Keda raised her hand and wiped away the slow tears from her cheeks. 'I must have love,' she whispered.

Startled at her own outburst she stood up beside the bed rigidly. Then her eyes turned to the nurse. Keda had been so much alone in her reverie that it seemed natural to her to find that the old woman was asleep. She moved to the window. The afternoon light lay over the towers. In the straggling ivy beneath her a bird rustled. From far below a voice cried faintly to some unseen figure and stillness settled again. She breathed deeply, and leaned forward into the light. Her hands grasped the frame of the window on her either side and her eyes from wandering across the towers were drawn inexorably to that high encircling wall that hid from her the houses of her people, her childhood, and the substance of her passion.

FLAY BRINGS A MESSAGE

AUTUMN returned to Gormenghast like a dark spirit re-entering its stronghold. Its breath could be felt in forgotten corridors, – Gormenghast had itself *become* autumn. Even the denizens of this fastness were its shadows.

The crumbling castle, looming among the mists, exhaled the season, and every cold stone breathed it out. The tortured trees by the dark lake burned and dripped, and their leaves snatched by the wind were whirled in wild circles through the towers. The clouds mouldered as they lay coiled, or shifted themselves uneasily upon the stone skyfield, sending up wreaths that drifted through the turrets and swarmed up the hidden walls.

From high in the Tower of Flints the owls inviolate in their stone galleries cried inhumanly, or falling into the windy darkness set sail on muffled courses for their hunting grounds. Fuchsia was less and less to be found in the castle. As, with every day that passed, the weather became increasingly menacing, so she seemed to protract the long walks that had now become her chief pleasure. She had captured anew the excitement that had once filled her when with Mrs Slagg, several years before, she had insisted on dragging her nurse on circuitous marches which had seemed to the old lady both hazardous and unnecessary. But Fuchsia neither needed nor wanted a companion now.

Revisiting those wilder parts of the environs that she had almost forgotten, she experienced both exaltation and loneliness. This mixture of the sweet and bitter became necessary to her, as her attic had been necessary. She watched with frowning eyes the colour changing on the trees and loaded her pockets with long golden leaves and fire-coloured ferns and, indeed, with every kind of object which she found among the woods and rocky places. Her room became filled with stones of curious shapes that had appealed to her, fungi resembling hands or plates: queer-shaped flints and contorted branches; and Mrs Slagg, knowing it would be fruitless to reproach her, gazed each evening, with her fingers clutching her lower lip, at

Fuchsia emptying her pockets of fresh treasures and at the ever-growing hoard that had begun to make the room a tortuous place to move about in.

Among Fuchsia's hieroglyphics on the wall great leaves had begun to take residence, pinned or pasted between her drawings, and areas of the floor were piled with trophies.

'Haven't you got enough, dear?' said Nannie, as Fuchsia entered late one evening and deposited a moss-covered boulder on her bed. Tiny fronds of fern emerged here and there from the moss, and white flowers the size of gnats.

Fuchsia had not heard Nannie's question, so the little old creature advanced to the side of the bed.

'You've got enough now, haven't you, my caution? Oh, yes, yes, I think so. Quite enough for your room now, dear. How dirty you are, my ... Oh, my poor heart, how unappetising you are.'

Fuchsia tossed back her dripping hair from her eyes and neck, so that it hung in a heavy clump like black seaweed over the collar of her cape. Then after undoing a button at her throat with a desperate struggle, and letting the corded velvet fall to her feet, she pushed it under her bed with her foot. Then she seemed to see Mrs Slagg for the first time. Bending forward she kissed her savagely on the forehead and the rain dripped from her on to the nurse's clothes.

'Oh, you dirty thoughtless thing! you naughty nuisance. Oh, my poor heart, how could you?' said Mrs Slagg, suddenly losing her temper and stamping her foot. 'All over my black satin, you dirty thing. You nasty wet thing. Oh, my poor dress! Why can't you stay in when the weather is muddy and blowy? You always were unkind to me! Always, always.'

'That's not true,' said Fuchsia, clenching her hands.

The poor old nurse began to cry.

'Well, *is* it, *is* it?' said Fuchsia.

'I don't know. I don't know at all,' said Nannie. 'Everyone's unkind to me; how should I know?'

'Then I'm going away', said Fuchsia.

Nannie gulped and jerked her head up. 'Going away?' she cried in a querulous voice. 'No, no! you mustn't go away.' And then with an inquisitive look struggling with the fear in her eyes, 'Where to?' she said. 'Where could you go to, dear?'

'I'd go far away from here – to another kind of land', said Fuchsia, 'where people who didn't know that I was the Lady Fuchsia would be surprised when I told them that I *was*; and they would treat me better and be more polite and do some homage sometimes. But I wouldn't stop bringing home my leaves and shining pebbles and fugnesses from the woods, whatever they thought'.

'You'd go away from me?' said Nannie in such a melancholy voice that Fuchsia held her in her strong arms.

'Don't cry,' she said. 'It isn't any good.'

Nannie turned her eyes up again and this time they were filled with the love she felt for her 'child'. But even in the weakness of her compassion she felt that she should preserve her station and repeated: '*Must* you go into the dirty water, my own one, and tear your clothes just like you've always done, caution dear? Aren't you big enough to go out only on nice days?'

'I like the autumn weather,' said Fuchsia very slowly. 'So that's why I go out to look at it.'

'Can't you see it from out of your window, precious?' said Mrs Slagg. 'Then you would keep warm at the same time, though what there is to stare at I don't know; but there, I'm only a silly old thing.'

'I know what I want to do, so don't you think about it any more', said Fuchsia. 'I'm finding things out.'

'You're a wilful thing,' said Mrs Slagg a little peevishly, 'but I know much more than you think about all sorts of things. I do; yes, I do; but I'll get you your tea at once. And you can have it by the fire, and I will bring the little boy in because he ought to be awake by now. Oh dear! there is so much to do. Oh, my weak heart, I wonder how long I will last.'

Her eyes, following Fuchsia's, turned to the boulder around which a wet mark was spreading on the patchwork quilt.

'You're the dirtiest terror in the world,' she said. 'What's that stone for? What is it *for*, dear? What's the *use* of it? You never listen. Never. Nor grow any older like I told you to. There's no one to help me now. Keda's gone, and I do everything.'

Mrs Slagg wiped her eyes with the back of her hand. 'Change your wet clothes or I won't bring you anything, and your dirty wet shoes at once!' ... Mrs Slagg fumbled at the door-handle, opened the door and shuffled away down the corridor, one hand clasped at her chest.

Fuchsia removed her shoes without untying the laces by treading on the heels and working her feet loose. Mrs Slagg had made up a glowing fire and Fuchsia, pulling off her dress, rubbed her wet hair with it. Then, wrapping a warm blanket about her, she fell back into a low armchair that had been drawn up to the fire and, sinking into its familiar softness, gazed absently at the leaping flames with half-closed eyes.

When Mrs Slagg returned with a tray of tea and toasted scones, currant bread, butter and eggs and a jar of honey, she found Fuchsia asleep.

Placing the tray on the hearth she tiptoed to the door and disappeared, to return within the minute with Titus in her arms. He was dressed in a white garment which accentuated what warmth of colour there was in his face. At birth he had been practically bald, but now, though it was only two months later, he was blessed with a mop of hair as dark as his sister's.

Mrs Slagg sat down with Titus in a chair opposite Fuchsia and peered weakly at the girl, wondering whether to wake her at once or whether to let her finish her sleep and then to make another pot of tea. 'But the scones will be cold, too', she said to herself. 'Oh, how tiresome she is.' But her problem was solved by a loud single knuckle-rap at the door, which caused her to start violently and clutch Titus to her shoulder, and Fuchsia to wake from her doze.

'Who is it?' cried Mrs Slagg. 'Who is it?'

'Flay', said the voice of Lord Sepulchrave's servant. The door opened a few inches and a bony face looked in from near the top of the door.

'Well?' said Nannie, jerking her head about. 'Well? Well? What is it?'

Fuchsia turned her head and her eyes moved up the fissure between the door and the wall until they came at last to settle on the cadaverous features.

'Why don't you come inside?' she said.

'No invitation', said Flay flatly. He came forward, his knees cracking at each step. His eyes shifted from Fuchsia to Mrs Slagg and from Mrs Slagg to Titus, and then to the loaded tea-tray by the fire, on which they lingered before they returned to Fuchsia wrapped in her blanket. When he saw she was still looking at him his right hand raised itself like a bunch of blunt talons and began to scratch at a prominent lump of bone at the back of his head.

'Message from his Lordship, my Lady', he said; and then his eyes returned to the tea-tray.

'Does he want me?' said Fuchsia.

'Lord Titus', said Flay, his eyes retaining upon their lenses the pot of tea, toasted scones, currant bread, butter, eggs and a jar of honey.

'He wants little Titus, did you say?' cried Mrs Slagg, trying to make her feet reach the ground.

Flay gave a mechanical nod. 'Got to meet me, quadrangle-arch, half-past eight', added Flay, wiping his hands on his clothes.

'He wants my little Lordship', whispered the old nurse to Fuchsia, who although her first antipathy to her brother had worn off had not acquired the same excited devotion which Nannie lavished upon the infant. 'He wants my little wonder.'

'Why not?' said Flay and then relapsed into his habitual silence after adding: 'Nine o'clock – library.'

'Oh, my poor heart, he ought to be in bed by then', gulped the nurse; and clutched Titus even closer to her.

Fuchsia had been looking at the tea-tray as well.

'Flay,' she said, 'do you want to eat anything?'

By way of reply the spidery servant made his way at once across the room to a chair which he had kept in the corner of his eye, and returned with it to seat himself between the two. Then he took out a tarnished watch, scowled at it as though it were his mortal enemy, and returned it to a secret recess among his greasy black clothes.

Nannie edged herself out of the chair and found a cushion for Titus to lie on in front of the fire, and then began to pour out the tea. Another cup was found for Flay, and then for a long while the three of them sat silently munching or sipping, and reaching down to the floor for whatever they needed but making no effort to look after each other. The firelight danced in the room, and the warmth was welcome, for outside or in the corridors the wet earthy draughts of the season struck to the marrow.

Flay took out his watch again and, wiping his mouth with the back of his hand, arose to his feet. As he did so, he upset a plate at the side of his chair and it fell and broke on the floor. At the sound he started and clutched the back of the chair and his hand shook. Titus screwed his face up at the noise as though about to cry, but changed his mind.

Fuchsia was surprised at so obvious a sign of agitation in Flay whom she had known since her childhood and on whom she had never before noticed any sign of nerves.

'Why are you shaking?' she said. 'You never used to shake.'

Flay pulled himself together and then sat down suddenly again, and turned his expressionless face to Fuchsia. 'It's the night,' he said tonelessly. 'No sleep, Lady Fuchsia.' And he gave a ghastly mirthless laugh like something rusty being scraped by a knife.

Suddenly he had regained his feet again and was standing by the door. He opened it very gradually and peered through the aperture before he began to disappear inch by inch, and the door clicked finally upon him.

'Nine o'clock', said Nannie tremulously. 'What does your father want with my little Lordship at nine o'clock? Oh, my poor heart, what does he want him for?'

But Fuchsia, tired out from her long day among the dripping woods was once more fast asleep, the red firelight flickering to and fro across her lolling head.

THE LIBRARY

THE library of Gormenghast was situated in the castle's Eastern wing which protruded like a narrow peninsula for a distance out of all proportion to the grey hinterland of buildings from which it grew. It was from about midway along this attenuated East wing that the Tower of Flints arose in scarred and lofty sovereignty over all the towers of Gormenghast.

At one time this Tower had formed the termination of the Eastern wing, but succeeding generations had added to it. On its further side the additions had begun a tradition and had created the precedent for Experiment, for many an ancestor of Lord Groan had given way to an architectural whim and made an incongruous addition. Some of these additions had not even continued the Easterly direction in which the original wing had started, for at several points the buildings veered off into curves or shot out at right angles before returning to continue the main trend of stone.

Most of these buildings had about them the rough-hewn and oppressive weight of masonry that characterized the main volume of Gormenghast, although they varied considerably in every other way, one having at its summit an enormous stone carving of a lion's head, which held between its jaws the limp corpse of a man on whose body was chiselled the words: '*He was an enemy of Groan*'; alongside this structure was a rectangular area of some length entirely filled with pillars set so closely together that it was difficult for a man to squeeze between them. Over them, at the height of about forty feet, was a perfectly flat roof of stone slabs blanketed with ivy. This structure could never have served any practical purpose, the closely packed forest of pillars with which it was entirely filled being of service only as an excellent place in which to enjoy a fantastic game of hide-and-seek.

There were many examples of an eccentric notion translated into architecture in the spine of buildings that spread eastwards over the undulating ground between the heavy walls of conifer, but for the most part they were built for some especial purpose, as a pavilion for entertainments, or as an observatory, or a museum. Some in the form of halls with galleries round three sides had been intended for concerts or dancing. One had obviously been an aviary, for though derelict, the branches that had long ago been fastened across the high central hall of the building were still hanging by rusty chains, and about the floor were strewn the broken remains of drinking cups for the birds; wire netting, red with rust, straggled across the floor among rank weeds that had taken root.

Except for the library, the eastern wing, from the Tower of Flints onwards, was now but a procession of forgotten and desolate relics, an Ichabod of masonry that filed silently along an avenue of dreary pine whose needles hid the sky.

The library stood between a building with a grey dome and one with a façade that had once been plastered. Most of the plaster had fallen away, but scraps had remained scattered over the surface, sticking to the stones. Patches of faded colour showed that a fresco had once covered the entire face of the building. Neither doors nor windows broke the stone surface. On one of the larger pieces of plaster that had braved a hundred storms and still clung to the stone, it was possible to make out the lower part of a face, but nothing else was recognizable among the fragments.

The library, though a lower building than these two to which it was joined at either end, was of a far greater length than either. The track that ran alongside the eastern wing, now in the forest and now within a few feet of the kaleidoscopic walls shadowed by the branches of the evergreens, ended as it curved suddenly inwards towards the carved door. Here it ceased among the nettles at the top of the three deep steps that led down to the less imposing of the two entrances to the library, but the one through which Lord Sepulchrave always entered his realm. It was not possible for him to visit his library as often as he wished, for the calls made upon him by the endless ceremonials which were his exacting duty to perform robbed him for many hours each day of his only pleasure – books.

Despite his duties, it was Lord Sepulchrave's habit to resort each evening, however late the hour, to his retreat and to remain there until the small hours of the following day.

The evening on which he sent Flay to have Titus brought to him found Lord Sepulchrave free at seven in the evening, and sitting in the corner of his library, sunk in a deep reverie.

The room was lit by a chandelier whose light, unable to reach the extremities of the room lit only the spines of those volumes on the central shelves of the long walls. A stone gallery ran round the library at about fifteen feet above the floor, and the books that lined the walls of the main hall fifteen feet below were continued upon the high shelves of the gallery.

In the middle of the room, immediately under the light, stood a long table. It was carved from a single piece of the blackest marble, which reflected upon its surface three of the rarest volumes in his Lordship's collection.

Upon his knees, drawn up together, was balanced a book of his grandfather's essays, but it had remained unopened. His arms lay limply at his side, and his head rested against the velvet of the chair back. He was dressed in the grey habit which it was his custom to wear in the library. From full sleeves his sensitive hands emerged with the shadowy transparency of alabaster. For an hour he had remained thus; the deepest melancholy manifested itself in every line of his body.

The library appeared to spread outwards from him as from a core. His dejection infected the air about him and diffused its illness upon every side. All things in the long room absorbed his melancholia. The shadowing galleries brooded with slow anguish; the books receding into the deep corners, tier upon tier, seemed each a separate tragic note in a monumental fugue of volumes.

It was only on those occasions now, when the ritual of Gormenghast dictated, that he saw the Countess. They had never found in each other's company a sympathy of mind or body, and their marriage, necessary as it was from the lineal standpoint, had never been happy. In spite of his intellect, which he knew to be far and away above hers, he felt and was suspicious of the heavy, forceful vitality of his wife, not so much a physical vitality as a blind passion for aspects of life in which he could find no cause for interest. Their love had been passionless, and save for the knowledge that a male heir to the house of Groan was imperative, they would have gladly forgone their embarrassing yet fertile union. During her pregnancy he had only seen her at long intervals. No doubt the unsatisfactory marriage had added to his native depression, but compared with the dull forest of his inherent melancholy it was but a tree from a foreign region that had been transplanted and absorbed.

It was never this estrangement that grieved him, nor anything tangible but a constant and indigenous sorrow.

Of companions with whom he could talk upon the level of his own thought there were few, and of these only one gave him any satisfaction, the Poet. On occasion he would visit that long, wedge-headed man and find in the abstract language with which they communicated their dizzy stratas of conjecture a temporary stir of interest. But in the Poet there was an element of the idealist, a certain enthusiasm which was a source of irritation to Lord Sepulchrave, so that they met only at long intervals.

The many duties, which to another might have become irksome and appeared fatuous, were to his Lordship a relief and a relative escape from himself. He knew that he was past all hope a victim of chronic melancholia, and were he to have had each day to himself he would have had to resort constantly to those drugs that even now were undermining his constitution.

This evening, as he sat silently in the velvet-backed chair, his mind had turned to many subjects like a black craft, that though it steers through many waters has always beneath it a deathly image reflected among the waves. Philosophers and the poetry of Death – the meaning of the stars and the nature of these dreams that haunted him when in those chloral hours before the dawn the laudanum built for him within his skull a tallow-coloured world of ghastly beauty.

He had brooded long and was about to take a candle that stood ready on a table at his elbow and search for a book more in keeping with his mood than were the essays on his knee, when he felt the presence of another thought that had been tempering his former cogitations, but which now stood boldly in his mind. It had begun to make itself felt as something that clouded and disturbed the clarity of his reflections when he had pondered on the purpose and significance of tradition and ancestry, and now with the thought detached from its erudite encumbrances he watched it advance across his brain and appear naked, as when he had first seen his son, Titus.

His depression did not lift; it only moved a little to one side. He rose to his feet and, moving without a sound, replaced the book in a shelf of essays. He returned as silently to the table.

'Where are you?' he said.

Flay appeared at once from the darkness of one of the corners.

'What hour is it?'

Flay brought out his heavy watch. 'Eight, your Lordship.'

Lord Sepulchrave, with his head hanging forward on his breast, walked up and down the length of the library for a few minutes. Flay watched him as he moved, until his master stopped opposite his servant.

'I wish to have my son brought to me by his nurse. I shall expect them at nine. You will conduct them through the woods. You may go.'

Flay turned and, accompanied by the reports of his knee-joints, disappeared into the shadows of the room. Pulling back the curtain from before the door at the far end, he unlatched the heavy oak and climbed the three steps into the night. Above him the great branches of the pines rubbed against one another and grated in his ears. The sky was overcast and had he not made this same journey through the darkness a thousand times he must surely have lost himself in the night. To his right he could sense the spine of the Western Wing although he could not see it. He walked on and in his mind he said: 'Why now? Had the summer to see his son in. Thought he'd forgotten him. Should have seen the child long ago. What's the game? Heir to Gormenghast to come through woods on cold night. Wrong. Dangerous. Catch a cold. But Lordship knows. He knows. I am only his servant. First servant. No one else *that*. Chose me; ME, Flay, because he trusts me. Well may he trust me. Ha, ha, ha! And why? they wonder. Ha ha! Silent as a corpse. That's why.'

As he neared the Tower of Flints the trees thinned and a few stars appeared in the blackness above him. By the time the body of the castle was reached only half the sky was hidden by the night clouds and he could make out vague shapes in the darkness. Suddenly he stopped, his heart attacking his ribs, and drew up his shoulders to his ears; but a moment later he realized that the vague obese patch of blackness a few feet from him was a shrub of clipped box and not that figure of evil who now obsessed him.

He straddled onwards, and came at last to an entrance beneath the sweep of an archway. Why he did not enter it at once and climb the stairs to find Nannie Slagg he did not know. That he could see through the archway and across the darkness of the servants' quadrangle a dim light in a high window of one of the kitchen buildings was in itself nothing unusual. There was generally a light showing somewhere in the kitchen quarters although most of the staff would have resorted to their underground dormitories by that time of night. An apprentice given some fatigue duty to perform after his normal hours might be scrubbing a floor, or an especial dish for the morrow might necessitate a few cooks working late into the evening.

Tonight, however, a dull greenish light from a small window held his eye, and before he realized that he was even intrigued, he found that his feet had forestalled his brain and were carrying him across the quadrangle.

On his way across he stopped twice to tell himself that it was a pointless excursion and that he was in any case feeling extremely cold; but he went on nevertheless with an illogical and inquisitive itch overriding his better judgement.

He could not tell which room it was that gave forth this square, greenish, glow. There was something unhealthy about its colour. No one was about in the quadrangle; there were no other footsteps but his own. The window was too high for even him to peer into, although he could easily reach it with his hands. Once again he said to himself: 'What are you doing? Wasting your time. Told by Lordship to fetch Nannie Slagg and child. Why are you here? What are you doing?'

But again his thin body had anticipated him and he had

begun to roll away an empty cask from against the cloister walls.

In the darkness it was no easy matter to steer the barrel and to keep it balanced upon the tilted rim as he rolled it towards the square of light; but he managed with very little sound to bring it eventually immediately under the window.

He straightened his back and turned his face up to the light that escaped like a kind of gas and hovered about the window in the haze of the autumn night.

He had lifted his right foot onto the barrel, but realized that to raise himself into the centre of the window would cause his face to catch the light from the room. Why, he did not know, but the curiosity which he had felt beneath the low arch was now so intense, that after lowering his foot and pulling the barrel to the right of the small window, he scrambled upon it with a haste that startled him. His arms were outstretched on either side along the viewless walls and his fingers, spread out like the ribs of a bone fan, began to sweat as he moved his head gradually to the left. He could already see through the glass (in spite of a sweep of old cobwebs, like a fly-filled hammock) the smooth stone walls of the room beneath him; but he had still to move his head further into the light in order to obtain a clear view of the floor of the room.

The light that seeped in a dull haze through the window dragged out as from a black canvas the main bone formation of Mr Flay's head, leaving the eye sockets, the hair, an area beneath the nose and lower lip, and everything that lay beneath the chin, as part of the night itself. It was a mask that hung in the darkness.

Mr Flay moved it upwards inch by inch until he saw what he had by some prophetic qualm known all along that it was his destiny to see. In the room below him the air was filled with an intensification of that ghastly green which he had noticed from across the quadrangle. The lamp that hung from the centre of the room by a chain was enclosed in a bowl of lime-green glass. The ghoulish light which it spewed forth gave to every object in the room a theatrical significance.

But Flay had no eyes for the few scattered objects in the nightmare below him, but only for an enormous and sinister *presence*, the sight of which had caused him to sicken and sway upon the cask and to remove his head from the window while he cooled his brow on the cold stones of the wall.

IN A LIME-GREEN LIGHT

EVEN in his nausea he could not help wondering what it was that Abiatha Swelter was doing. He raised his head from the wall and brought it by degrees to its former position.

This time Flay was surprised to find that the room appeared empty, but, with a start at its dreadful nearness, he found that the chef was sitting on a bench against the wall and immediately below him. It was not easy to see him clearly through the filth and cobwebs of the window, but the great pasty dome of his head surrounded by the lamp-tinted whiteness of his swollen clothes, seemed, when Flay located them, almost at arm's length. This proximity injected into Mr Flay's bones a sensation of exquisite horror. He stood fascinated at the pulpy baldness of the chef's cranium and as he stared a portion of its pale plush contracted in a spasm, dislodging an October fly. Nothing else moved. Mr Flay's eyes shifted for a moment and he saw a grindstone against the wall opposite. Beside it was a wooden stool. To his right, he saw two boxes placed about four feet apart. On either side of these wooden boxes two chalk lines ran roughly parallel to each other, and passed laterally along the room below Mr Flay. Nearing the left hand wall of the room they turned to the right, keeping the same space between them, but in their new direction they could not proceed for more than a few feet before being obstructed by the wall. At this point something had been written between them in chalk, and an arrow pointed towards the wall. The writing was hard to read, but after a moment Flay deciphered it as: '*To the Ninth stairs.*' This reading of the chalk came as a shock to Mr Flay, if only for the reason that the Ninth stairs were those by which Lord Sepulchrave's bedroom was reached from the floor below. His eyes returned swiftly to the rough globe of a head beneath him, but there was still no movement except perhaps the slight vibration of the chef's breathing.

Flay turned his eyes again to the right where the two boxes were standing, and he now realized that they represented either a door or an entrance of some sort from which led this chalked passageway before it turned to the right in the direction of the Ninth stairs. But it was upon a long sack which had at first failed to attract his attention that he now focused his eyes. It lay as though curled up immediately between and a little in advance of the two boxes. As he scrutinized it, something terrified him, something nameless, and which he had not yet had time to comprehend, but something from which he recoiled.

A movement below him plucked his eyes from the sack and a huge shape arose. It moved across the room, the whiteness of the enveloping clothes tinctured by the lime-green lamp above. It sat beside the grindstone. It held in its hand what seemed, in proportion to its bulk, a small weapon, but which was in reality a two-handed cleaver.

Swelter's feet began to move the treadles of the grindstone, and it began to spin in its circles. He spat upon it rapidly three or four times in succession, and with a quick movement slid the already razor-keen edge of the cleaver across the whirr of the stone. Doubling himself over the grindstone he peered at the shivering edge of the blade, and every now and then lifted it to his ear as though to listen for a thin and singing note to take flight from the unspeakable sharpness of the steel.

Then again he bent to his task and continued whetting the blade for several minutes before listening once more to the invisible edge. Flay began to lose contact with the reality of what he saw and his brain to drift into a dream, when he found that the chef was drawing himself upwards and travelling to that part of the wall where the chalk lines ended and where the arrow pointed to the Ninth staircase. Then he removed his shoes, and lifted his face for the first time so that Mr Flay could see the expression that seeped from it. His eyes were metallic and murderous, but the mouth hung open in a wide, fatuous smile.

Then followed what appeared to Flay an extraordinary dance, a grotesque ritual of the legs, and it was some time before he realized, as the cook advanced by slow, elaborate steps between the chalk lines, that he was practising tip-toeing with absolute silence. 'What's he practising that for?' thought Flay, watching the intense and painful concentration with which Swelter moved forward step by step, the cleaver shining in his right hand. Flay glanced again at the chalk arrow. 'He's come from the ninth staircase: he's turned left down the worn passage. There's no rooms right or left in the worn passage. I ought to know. *He's approaching the Room.*' In the darkness Flay turned as white as death.

The two boxes could represent only one thing – the doorposts of Lord Sepulchrave's bedroom. And the sack . . .

He watched the chef approach the symbol of himself asleep outside his master's room, curled up as he always was. By now the tardiness of the approach was unendingly slow. The feet in their thick soles would descend an inch at a time, and as they touched the ground the figure cocked his head of lard upon one side and his eyes rolled upwards as he listened for his own footfall. When within three feet of the sack the chef raised the cleaver in both hands and with his legs wide apart to give him a broader area of balance, edged his feet forward, one after the other, in little, noiseless shiftings. He had now judged the distance between himself and the sleeping emblem of his hate. Flay shut his eyes as he saw the cleaver rise in the air above the cumulous shoulder and the steel flared in the green light.

When he opened his eyes again, Abiatha Swelter was no longer by the sack, which appeared to be exactly as he had last seen it. He was at the chalk arrow again and was creeping forward as before. The horror that had filled Flay was aggravated by a question that had entered his mind. How did Swelter know that he slept with his chin at his knees? How did Swelter know his head always pointed to the east? Had he been observed during his sleeping hours? Flay pressed his face to the window for the last time. The dreadful repetition of the same murderous tip-toeing journey towards the sack, struck such a blow at the very centre of his nervous control that his knees gave way and he sank to his haunches on the barrel and wiped the back of his hand across his forehead. Suddenly his only thought was of escape – of escape from a region of the castle that could house such a fiend; to escape from that window of green light; and, scrambling from the cask, he stumbled into the mist-filled darkness and, never turning his head again to the scene of horror, made tracks for the archway from whence he had deviated so portentously from his course.

Once within the building he made directly for the main stairs and with gigantic paces climbed like a mantis to the floor in which Nannie Slagg's room was situated. It was some time before he came to her door, for the west wing in which she lived was on the opposite side of the building and necessitated a *détour* through many halls and corridors.

She was not in her room, and so he went at once to Lady Fuchsia's, where, as he had surmised, he found her sitting by the fire with little of the deference which he felt she should display in front of his Lordship's daughter.

It was when he had knocked at the door of the room with the knuckly single rap, that he had wakened Fuchsia from her sleep and startled the old nurse. Before he had knocked on the panels he had stood several minutes recovering his composure as best he could. In his mind emerged the picture of himself striking Swelter across the face with the chain, long ago as it seemed to him now in the Cool room. For a moment he started sweating again and he wiped his hands down his sides before he entered. His throat felt very dry, and even before noticing Lady Fuchsia and the nurse he had seen the tray. That was what he wanted. Something to drink.

He left the room with a steadier step and, saying that he would await Mrs Slagg and Titus under the archway and escort her to the library, he left them.

REINTRODUCING THE TWINS

AT the same moment that Flay was leaving Fuchsia's bedroom, Steerpike was pushing back his chair from the supper table at the Prunesquallor's, where he had enjoyed, along with the Doctor and his sister Irma, a very tender chicken, a salad and a flask of red wine; and now, the black coffee awaiting them on a little table by the fire, they were preparing to take up warmer and more permanent stations. Steerpike was the first to rise and he sidled around the table in time to remove the chair from behind Miss Prunesquallor and to assist her to her feet. She was perfectly able to take care of herself, in fact she had been doing it for years, but she leaned on his arm as she slowly assumed the vertical.

She was swathed to her ankles in maroon-coloured lace. That her gowns should cling to her as though they were an extra layer of skin was to her a salient point, in spite of the fact that of all people it was for her to hide those angular outcrops of bone with which Nature had endowed her and which in the case of the majority of women are modified by a considerate layer of fat.

Her hair was drawn back from her brow with an even finer regard for symmetry than on the night when Steerpike had first seen her, and the knot of grey twine which formed a culmination as hard as a boulder, a long way down the back of her neck, had not a single hair out of place.

The Doctor had himself noticed that she was spending more and more time upon her toilette, although it had at all times proved one of her most absorbing occupations; a paradox to the Doctor's mind which delighted him, for his sister was, even in his fraternal eyes, cruelly laden with the family features. As she approached her chair to the left of the fire, Steerpike removed his hand from her elbow, and, shifting back the Doctor's chair with his foot while Prunesquallor was drawing the blinds, pulled forward the sofa into a more favourable position in front of the fire.

'They don't meet – I said "They don't *meet*",' said Irma Prunesquallor, pouring out the coffee.

How she could see anything at all, let alone whether they met or not, through her dark glasses was a mystery.

Dr Prunesquallor, already on his way back to his chair, on the padded arms of which his coffee was balancing, stopped and folded his hands at his chin.

'To what are you alluding, my dear? Are you speaking of a brace of spirits? ha ha ha! – twin souls searching for consummation, each in the other? Ha ha! ha ha ha! Or are you making reference to matters more terrestrial? Enlighten me, my love.'

'Nonsense', said his sister. 'Look at the curtains. I said: "Look at the curtains".'

Dr Prunesquallor swung about.

'To me', he said, 'they look exactly like curtains. In fact, they *are* curtains. Both of them. A curtain on the left, my love, and a curtain on the right. Ha ha! I'm absolutely certain they are!'

Irma, hoping that Steerpike was looking at her, laid down her coffee-cup.

'What happens in the *middle*, I said; what happens right down the *middle*?' Her pointed nose warmed, for she sensed victory.

'There is a great yearning one for the other. A fissure of impalpable night divides them. Irma, my dear sister, there is a lacuna.'

'Then *kill* it', said Irma, and sank back into her chair. She glanced at Steerpike, but he had apparently taken no notice of the conversation and she was disappointed. He was leaning back into one corner of the couch, his legs crossed, his hands curled around the coffee-cup as though to feel its warmth, and his eyes were peering into the fire. He was evidently far away.

When the Doctor had joined the curtains together with great deliberation and stood back to assure himself that the Night was satisfactorily excluded from the room, he seated himself, but no sooner had he done so than there was a jangling at the door-bell which continued until the cook had scraped the pastry from his hands, removed his apron and made his way to the front door.

Two female voices were speaking at the same time.

'Only for a moment, only for a moment', they said. 'Just passing – On our way home – Only for a moment – Tell him we won't stay – No, of course not; we won't stay. Of course not. Oh no – Yes, yes. Just a twinkling – only a twinkling.'

But for the fact that it would have been impossible for one voice to wedge so many words into so short a space of time and to speak so many of them simultaneously, it would have been difficult to believe that it was not the voice of a single individual, so continuous and uniform appeared the flat colour of the sound.

Prunesquallor cast up his hands to the ceiling and behind the convex lenses of his spectacles his eyes revolved in their orbits.

The voices that Steerpike now heard in the passage were unfamiliar to his quick ear. Since he had been with the Prunesquallors he had taken advantage of all his spare time and had, he thought, run to earth all the main figures of Gormenghast. There were few secrets hidden from him, for he had that scavenger like faculty of acquiring unashamedly and from an infinite variety of sources, snatches of knowledge which he kept neatly at the back of his brain and used to his own advantage as opportunity offered.

When the twins, Cora and Clarice, entered the room together, he wondered whether the red wine had gone to his head. He had neither seen them before nor anything like them. They were dressed in their inevitable purple.

Dr Prunesquallor bowed elegantly. 'Your Ladyships,' he said, 'we are more than honoured. We are really very much more than honoured, ha ha ha!' He whinnied his appreciation. 'Come right along, my dear ladies, come right the way in. Irma, my dear, we have been doubly lucky in our privileges. Why "doubly" you say to yourself, why "doubly"? Because, O sister, they have *both* come, ha ha ha! Very much so, very much so.'

Prunesquallor, who knew from experience that only a fraction of what anyone said ever entered the brains of the twins, permitted himself a good deal of latitude in his conversation.

mixing with a certain sycophancy remarks for his own amusement which could never have been made to persons more astute than the twins.

Irma had come forward, her iliac crest reflecting a streak of light.

'Very charmed, your Ladyships; I said "very, very charmed".' She attempted to curtsey, but her dress was too tight.

'You know my sister, of course, of course, of course. Will you have coffee? Of course you will, and a little wine? Naturally – or what would you prefer?'

But both the Doctor and his sister found that the Ladies Cora and Clarice had not been paying the slightest attention but had been staring at Steerpike more in the manner of a wall staring at a man than a man staring at a wall.

Steerpike in a well-cut uniform of black cloth, advanced to the sisters and bowed. 'Your Ladyships,' he said, 'I am delighted to have the honour of being beneath the same roof. It is an intimacy that I shall never forget.' And then, as though he were ending a letter – 'I am your very humble servant', he added.

Clarice turned herself to Cora, but kept her eyes on Steerpike.

'He says he's glad he's under the same roof as us', she said.

'Under the same roof', echoed Cora. 'He's very glad of it.'

'Why?' said Clarice emptily. 'What difference does it make about the roof?'

'It couldn't make any difference whatever the roof's like', said her sister.

'I like roofs,' said Clarice; 'they are something I like more than most things because they are on top of the houses they cover, and Cora and I like being over the tops of things because we love power, and that's why we are both fond of roofs.'

'That's why', Cora continued. 'That's the reason. Anything that's on top of something else is what we like, unless it is someone we don't like who's on top of something we are pleased with like ourselves. We're not allowed to be on top, except that our own room is high, oh, so high up in the castle wall, with our Tree – our own Tree that grows from the wall, that is so much more important than anything Gertrude has.'

'Oh yes,' said Clarice; 'she hasn't anything as important as that. But she steals our birds.'

She turned her expressionless eyes to Cora, who met them as though she were her sister's reflection. It may be that between them they recognized shades of expression in each other's faces, but it is certain that no one else, however keen his eyesight, could have detected the slightest change in the muscles that presumably governed the lack of expressions of their faces. Evidently this reference to stolen birds was the reason why they came nearer to each other so that their shoulders touched. It was obvious that their sorrow was conjoined.

Dr Prunesquallor had, during all this, been trying to shepherd them into the chairs by the fire, but to no avail. They had no thought for others when their minds were occupied. The room, the persons around them ceased to exist. They had only enough room for one thought at a time.

But now that there was a sudden lull the Doctor, reinforced this time by Irma, managed to shift the twins by means of a mixture of deference and force and to get them established by the fire. Steerpike, who had vanished from the room, now returned with another pot of coffee and two more cups. It was this sort of thing that pleased Irma, and she tilted her head on its neck and turned up the corners of her mouth into something approaching the coy.

But when the coffee was passed to the twins they did not want it. One, taking her cue from the other, decided that she, or the other one, or possibly both, or neither, did not want it.

Would they have anything to drink? Cognac, sherry, brandy, a liqueur, cherry wine . . .?

They shook their heads profoundly.

'We only came for a moment', said Cora.

'Because we were passing', said Clarice. 'That's the only reason.'

But although they refused on those grounds to indulge in a drink of any sort, yet they gave no indication of being in a hurry to go, nor had they for a long time anything to say, but were quite content to sit and stare at Steerpike.

But after a long interval, halfway through which the Doctor

and his sister had given up all attempts to make conversation, Cora turned her face to Steerpike.

'Boy,' she said, 'what are you here for?'

'Yes,' echoed Clarice, 'that's what we want to know.'

'I want', said Steerpike, choosing his words, 'only your gracious patronage, your Ladyships. Only your favour.'

The twins turned their faces towards each other and then at the same moment they returned them to Steerpike.

'Say that again', said Cora.

'All of it', said Clarice.

'Only your gracious patronage, your Ladyships. Only your favour. That is what I want.'

'Well, we'll give it you', said Clarice. But for the first time the sisters were at variance for a moment.

'Not yet,' said Cora. 'It's too soon for that.'

'Much too soon,' agreed Clarice. 'It's not time yet to give him any favour at all. What's his name?'

This was addressed to Steerpike.

'His name is Steerpike', was the youth's reply.

Clarice leaned forward in her chair and whispered to Cora across the hearthrug: 'His name is Steerpike.'

'Why not?' said her sister flatly. 'It will do.'

Steerpike was, of course, alive with ideas and projects. These two half-witted women were a gift. That they should be the sisters of Lord Sepulchrave was of tremendous strategic value. They would prove an advance on the Prunesquallors, if not intellectually at any rate socially, and that at the moment was what mattered. And in any case, the lower the mentality of his employers the more scope for his own projects.

That one of them had said his name 'Steerpike' would 'do' had interested him. Did it imply that they wished to see more of him? That would simplify matters considerably.

His old trick of shameless flattery seemed to him the best line to take at this critical stage. Later on, he would see. But it was another remark that had appealed to his opportunist sense even more keenly, and that was the reference to Lady Groan.

These ridiculous twins had apparently a grievance, and the object of it was the Countess. This when examined further might lead in many directions. Steerpike was beginning to enjoy himself in his own dry, bloodless way.

Suddenly as in a flash he remembered two tiny figures the size of halma players, dressed in the same crude purple. Directly he had seen them enter the room an echo was awakened somewhere in his subconscious, and although he had put it aside as irrelevant to the present requirements, it now came back with redoubled force and he recalled where he had seen the two minute replicas of the twins.

He had seen them across a great space of air and across a distance of towers and high walls. He had seen them upon the lateral trunk of a dead tree in the summer, a tree that grew out at right angles from a high and windowless wall.

Now he realized why they had said 'Our Tree that grows from the wall that is so much more important than anything Gertrude has.' But then Clarice had added: 'But she steals our birds.' What did that imply? He had, of course, often watched the Countess from points of vantage with her birds or her white cats. That was something he must investigate further. Nothing must be let fall from his mind unless it were first turned to and fro and proved to be useless.

Steerpike bent forward, the tips of his fingers together. 'Your Ladyships,' he said, 'are you enamoured of the feathered tribe? – Their beaks, their feathers, and the way they fly?'

'What?' said Cora.

'Are you in love with birds, your Ladyships?' repeated Steerpike, more simply.

'What?' said Clarice.

Steerpike hugged himself inside. If they could be as stupid as this, he could surely do anything he liked with them.

'Birds,' he said more loudly; 'do you like them?'

'What birds?' said Cora. 'What do you want to know for?'

'We weren't talking about birds,' said Clarice unexpectedly. 'We hate them.'

'They're such silly things', Cora ended.

'Silly and stupid; we hate them', said Clarice.

'*Avis, avis,* you are undone, undone!' came Prunesquallor's voice. 'Your day is over. Oh, ye hordes of heaven! the treetops shall be emptied of their chorus and only clouds ride over the blue heaven.'

Prunesquallor leaned forward and tapped Irma on the knee.

'Pretty pleasing,' he said, and showed her all his brilliant teeth together. 'What did *you* think, my riotous one?'

'Nonsense!' said Irma, who was sitting on the couch with Steerpike. Feeling that as the hostess she had so far this evening had very little opportunity of exhibiting what she, and she alone felt was her outstanding talent in that direction, she bent her dark glasses upon Cora and then upon Clarice and tried to speak to both of them at once.

'Birds,' she said, with something arch in her voice and manner, 'birds *depend* – don't you think, my dear Ladyships – I said birds *depend* a lot upon their eggs. Do you not agree with me? I said do you not agree with me?'

'We're going now', said Cora, getting up.

'Yes, we've been here too long. Much too long. We've got a lot of sewing to do. We sew beautifully, both of us.'

'I am sure you do,' said Steerpike. 'May I have the privilege of appreciating your craft at some future date when it is convenient for you?'

'We do embroidery as well', said Cora, who had risen and had approached Steerpike.

Clarice came up to her sister's side and they both looked at him. 'We do a lot of needlework, but nobody sees it. Nobody is interested in us, you see. We only have two servants. We used –'

'That's all,' said Cora. 'We used to have hundreds when we were younger. Our father gave us hundreds of servants. We were of great – of great –'

'Consequence,' volunteered her sister. 'Yes, that's exactly what it was that we were. Sepulchrave was always so dreamy and miserable, but he did play with us sometimes; so we did what we liked. But now he doesn't ever want to see us.'

'He thinks he's so wise,' said Cora.

'But he's no cleverer than we are.'

'He's not as clever', said Clarice.

'Nor is Gertrude', they said almost at the same moment.

'She stole your birds, didn't she?' said Steerpike, winking at Prunesquallor.

'How did you know?' they said, advancing on him a step further.

'Everyone knows, your Ladyships. Everyone in the castle knows', replied Steerpike, winking this time at Irma.

The twins held hands at once and drew close together. What Steerpike had said had sunk in and was making a serious impression on them. They had thought it was only a private grievance, that Gertrude had lured away their birds from the Room of Roots which they had taken so long preparing. But everyone knew! Everyone knew!

They turned to leave the room, and the Doctor opened his eyes, for he had almost fallen asleep with one elbow on the central table and his hand propping his head. He arose to his feet but could do nothing more elegant than to crook a finger, for he was too tired. His sister stood beside him creaking a little, and it was Steerpike who opened the door for them and offered to accompany them to their room. As they passed through the hall he removed his cape from a hook. Flinging it over his shoulders with a flourish he buttoned it at the neck. The cloak accentuated the highness of his shoulders, and as he drew its folds about him, the spareness of his body.

The aunts seemed to accept the fact that he was leaving the house with them, although they had not replied when he had asked their permission to escort them to their rooms.

With an extraordinary gallantry he shepherded them across the quadrangle.

'Everybody knows, you said.' Cora's voice was so empty of feeling and yet so plaintive that it must have awakened a sympathetic response in anyone with a more kindly heart than Steerpike's.

'That's what you said', repeated Clarice.

'But what can we do? We can't do anything to show what we could do if only we had the power we haven't got,' said Clarice lucidly. 'We used to have hundreds of servants.'

'You shall have them back,' said Steerpike. 'You shall have them all back. New ones. Better ones. Obedient ones. I shall arrange it. They shall work for you, *through* me. Your floor of the castle shall be alive again. You shall be supreme. Give me the administration to handle, your Ladyships, and I will have them dancing to your tune – whatever it is – they'll dance to it.'

'But what about Gertrude?'

'Yes, what about Gertrude', came their flat voices.

'Leave everything to me. I will secure your rights for you. You are Lady Cora and Lady Clarice, Lady Clarice and Lady Cora. You must not forget that. No one must be allowed to forget it.'

'Yes, that's what must happen', said Cora.

'Everyone must think of who we are', said Clarice.

'And never stop thinking about it', said Cora.

'Or we will use our power', said Clarice.

'Meanwhile, I will take you to your rooms, dear ladies. You must trust me. You must not tell anyone what we've said. Do you both understand?'

'And we'll get our birds back from Gertrude.'

Steerpike took them by the elbows as they climbed the stairs.

'Lady Cora,' he said, 'you must try to concentrate on what I am saying to you. If you pay attention to me I will restore you to your places of eminence in Gormenghast from which Lady Gertrude has dethroned you.'

'Yes.'

'Yes.'

The voices showed no animation, but Steerpike realized that only by *what* they said, not by *how* they said it, could he judge whether their brains reacted to his probing.

He also knew when to stop. In the fine art of deceit and personal advancement as in any other calling this is the hallmark of the master. He knew that when he reached their door he would itch to get inside and to see what sort of appointments they had and what on earth they meant by their Room of Roots. But he also knew to a nicety the time to slacken rein. Such creatures as the aunts for all their slowness of intellect had within them the Groan blood which might at any moment, were a false step to be made, flare up and undo a month of strategy. So Steerpike left them at the door of their apartments and bowed almost to the ground. Then as he retired along the oak passage, and was turning a corner to the left he glanced back at the door where he had left the twins. They were still looking after him, as motionless as a pair of waxen images.

He would not visit them tomorrow, for it would do them good to spend a day of apprehension and of silly discussion between themselves. In the evening they would begin to get nervous and need consoling, but he would not knock at the door until the following morning. Meanwhile he would pick up as much information as he could about them and their tendencies.

Instead of crossing over to the Doctor's house when he had reached the quadrangle he decided he would take a stroll across the lawns and perhaps around by the terraces to the moat, for the sky had emptied itself of cloud and was glittering fiercely with a hundred thousand stars.

'THE FIR-CONES'

THE wind had dropped, but the air was bitterly cold and Steerpike was glad of his cape. He had turned the collar up and it stood stiffly above the level of his ears. He seemed to be bound for somewhere in particular, and was not simply out for a nocturnal stroll. That peculiar half-walking, half-running gait was always with him. It appeared that he was eternally upon some secret mission, as indeed from his own viewpoint he generally was.

He passed into deep shadows beneath the arch, and then as though he were a portion of that inky darkness that had awakened and disengaged itself from the main body, he reappeared beyond the archway in the half light.

For a long time he kept close to the castle walls, moving eastwards continually. His first project of making a *détour* by way of the lawns and the terraces where the Countess walked before breakfast had been put aside, for now that he had started walking he felt an enjoyment in moving alone, absolutely alone, under the starlight. The Prunesquallors would not wait up for him. He had his own key to the front door and, as on previous nights, after late wanderings he would pour himself out a nightcap and perhaps enjoy some of the Doctor's tobacco in his little stubby pipe before he retired.

Or he might, as he had so often done before during the night, resort to the dispensary and amuse himself by compounding potions with lethal possibilities. It was always to the shelf of poisons that he turned at once when he entered and to the dangerous powders.

He had filled four small glass tubes with the most virulent of these concoctions, and had removed them to his own room. He had soon absorbed all that the Doctor, whose knowledge was considerable, had divulged on the subject. Under his initial guidance he had, from poisonous weeds found in the vicinity, distilled a number of original and death-dealing pastes. To the Doctor these experiments were academically amusing.

Or on retiring to the Prunesquallors he might take down one of the Doctor's many books and read, for these days a passion to accumulate knowledge of any and every kind consumed him; but only as a means to an end. He must know all things, for only so might he have, when situations arose in the future, a full pack of cards to play from. He imagined to himself occasions when the conversation of one from whom he foresaw advancement might turn to astronomy, metaphysics, history, chemistry, or literature, and he realized that to be able to drop into the argument a lucid and exact thought, an opinion based on what might *appear* to be a life-time study, would instantaneously gain more for him than an hour of beating about the bush and waiting until the conversation turned upon what lay within his scope of experience.

He foresaw himself in control of men. He had, along with his faculty for making swift and bold decisions, an unending patience. As he read in the evenings after the Doctor and Irma had retired for the night, he would polish the long, narrow steel of the swordstick blade which he had glimpsed and which he had, a week later, retrieved from the pile of ancient weapons in the chill hall. When he had first drawn it from the pile it had been badly tarnished, but with the skilful industry and patience with

224

which he applied himself to whatever he undertook, it had now become a slim length of white steel. He had after an hour's hunting found the hollow stick which was screwed into the innocent-looking hilt by a single turn of the wrist.

Whether on his return he would apply himself to the steel of his swordstick, and to the book on heraldry which he had nearly completed, or whether in the dispensary he would grind in the mortar, with the red oil, that feathery green powder with which he was experimenting, or whether he would be too tired to do anything but empty a glass of cognac and climb the stairs to his bedroom, he did not know, nor, for that matter, was he looking so short a way ahead. He was turning over in his mind as he walked briskly onwards not only every remark which he could remember the twins having let fall during the evening, but the trend of the questions which he proposed to put to them on the evening of the day after tomorrow.

With his mind working like an efficient machine, he thought out probable moves and parries, although he knew that in any dealings with the aunts the illogical condition of their brains made any surmise or scheming on his part extraordinarily difficult. He was working with a low-grade material, but one which contained an element which natures more elevated lack – the incalculable.

By now he had reached the most eastern corner of the central body of the castle. Away to his left he could distinguish the high walls of the west wing as they emerged from the ivy-blackened, sunset-facing precipice of masonry that shut off the northern halls of Gormenghast from the evening's light. The Tower of Flints could only be recognized as a narrow section of the sky the shape of a long black ruler standing upon its end, the sky about it was crowded with the stars.

It occurred to him as he saw the Tower that he had never investigated the buildings which were, he had heard, continued on its further side. It was too late now for such an expedition and he was thinking of making a wide circle on the withered lawns which made good walking at this corner of the castle, when he saw a dim light approaching him. Glancing about, he saw within a few yards the black shapes of stunted bushes.

Behind one of these he squatted and watched the light, which he recognized now as a lantern, coming nearer and nearer. It seemed that the figure would pass within a few feet of him, and peering over his shoulder to see in what direction the lantern was moving, he realized that he was immediately between the light and the Tower of Flints. What on earth could anyone want at the Tower of Flints on a cold night? Steerpike was intrigued. He dragged his cape well over himself so that only his eyes were exposed to the night air. Then, remaining as still as a crouching cat, he listened to the feet approaching.

As yet the body of whoever it was that carried the lantern had not detached itself from the darkness, but Steerpike, listening intently, heard now not only the long footsteps but the regular sound of a dry stick being broken. 'Flay', said Steerpike to himself. But what was that other noise? Between the regular sounds of the paces and the click of the knee joints a third, a quicker, less positive sound, came to his ears.

Almost at the same moment as he recognized it to be the pattering of tiny feet, he saw, emerging from the night, the unmistakable silhouettes of Flay and Mrs Slagg.

Soon the crunching of Flay's footsteps appeared to be almost on top of him, and Steerpike, motionless as the shrub he crouched beneath, saw the straggling height of Lord Sepulchrave's servant hastily pass above him, and as he did so a cry broke out. A tremor ran down Steerpike's spine, for if there was anything that worried him it was the supernatural. The cry, it seemed, was that of some bird, perhaps of a seagull, but was so close as to disprove that explanation. There were no birds about that night nor, indeed, were they ever to be heard at that hour, and it was with some relief that he heard Nannie Slagg whisper nervously in the darkness:

'There, there, my only.... It won't be long, my little Lordship dear ... it won't be long now. Oh, my poor heart! why must it be at night?' She seemed to raise her head from the little burden she carried and to gaze up at the lofty figure who strode mechanically beside her; but there was no answer.

'Things become interesting,' said Steerpike to himself. 'Lordships, Flays and Slaggs, all heading for the Tower of Flints.'

When they were almost swallowed into the darkness, Steerpike rose to his feet and flexed his cape-shrouded legs to get the stiffness from them, and then, keeping the sound of Mr Flay's knees safely within earshot, he followed them silently.

*

Poor Mrs Slagg was utterly exhausted by the time they arrived at the library, for she had consistently refused to allow Flay to carry Titus, for he had, much against his better judgement, offered to do so when he saw how she was continually stumbling over the irregularities of the ground, and when, among the conifers how she caught her feet in the pine roots and ground creepers.

The cold air had thoroughly wakened Titus, and although he did not cry it was obvious that he was disconcerted by this unusual adventure in the dark. When Flay knocked at the door and they entered the library, he began to whimper and struggle in the nurse's arms.

Flay retired to the darkness of his corner, where there was presumably some chair for him to sit on. All he said was: 'I've brought them, Lordship.' He usually left out the 'your' as being unnecessary for him as Lord Sepulchrave's primary attendant.

'So I see,' said the Earl of Groan, advancing down the room, 'I have disturbed you, nurse, have I not? It is cold outside. I have just been out to get these for him.'

He led Nannie to the far side of the table. On the carpet in the lamplight lay scattered a score of fir cones, each one with its wooden petals undercut with the cast shadow of the petal above it.

Mrs Slagg turned her tired face to Lord Sepulchrave. For once she said the right thing. 'Are they for his little Lordship, sir?' she queried. 'Oh, he will love them, won't you, my only?'

'Put him among them. I want to talk to you,' said the Earl. 'Sit down.'

Mrs Slagg looked around for a chair and seeing none turned her eyes pathetically towards his Lordship, who was now pointing at the floor in a tired way. Titus, whom she had placed

227

amongst the cones, was alternately turning them over in his fingers and sucking them.

'It's all right, I've washed them in rainwater,' said Lord Groan. 'Sit on the floor, nurse, sit on the floor.' Without waiting, he himself sat upon the edge of the table, his feet crossed before him, his hands upon the marble surface at his side.

'Firstly', he said, 'I have had you come this way to tell you that I have decided upon a family gathering here in a week's time. I want you to inform those concerned. They will be surprised. That does not matter. They will come. You will tell the Countess. You will tell Fuchsia. You will also inform their Ladyships Cora and Clarice.'

Steerpike, who had opened the door inch by inch, had crept up a stairway he had found immediately to his left. He had shut the door quietly behind him and tiptoed up to a stone gallery which ran around the building. Conveniently for him it was in the darkest shadow, and as he leaned against the bookshelves which lined the walls and watched the proceedings below, he rubbed the palms of his hands together silently.

He wondered where Flay had got to, for as far as he could see there was no other way out save by the main doorway, which was barred and bolted. It seemed to him that he must, like himself, be standing or sitting quietly in the shadows, and not knowing in what part of the building that might be, he kept absolute silence.

'At eight o'clock in the evening, I shall be awaiting him and them, for you must tell them I have in my mind a breakfast that shall be in honour of my son.'

As he said these words, in his rich, melancholy voice, poor Mrs Slagg, unable to bear the insufferable depression of his spirit, began to clutch her wrinkled hands together. Even Titus seemed to sense the sadness which flowed through the slow, precise words of his father. He forgot the fir cones and began to cry.

'You will bring my son Titus in his christening robes and will have with you the crown of the direct heir to Gormenghast. Without Titus the castle would have no future when I am gone. As his nurse, I must ask you to remember to instil into his veins, from the very first, a love for his birthplace and his

228

heritage, and a respect for all of the written and unwritten laws of the place of his fathers.

'I will speak to them, much against my own peace of spirit: I will speak to them of this and of much more that is in my mind. At the Breakfast, of which the details will be discussed on this same evening of next week, he shall be honoured and toasted. It shall be held in the Refectory.'

'But he is only two months old, the little thing,' broke in Nannie in a tear-choked voice. 'There is no time to lose, nevertheless,' answered the Earl. 'And now, my poor old woman, why are you crying so bitterly? It is autumn. The leaves are falling from the trees like burning tears – the wind howls. Why must you mimic them?'

Her old eyes gazed at him and were filmed. Her mouth quivered. 'I am so tired, sir,' she said.

'Then lie down, good woman, lie down,' said Lord Sepulchrave. 'It has been a long walk for you. Lie down.'

Mrs Slagg found no comfort in lying upon her back on the huge library floor with the Earl of Groan talking to her from above in phrases that meant nothing to her.

She gathered Titus to her side and stared at the ceiling, her tears running into her dry mouth. Titus was very cold and had begun to shiver.

'Now, let me see my son,' said his Lordship slowly. 'My son Titus. Is it true that he is ugly?'

Nannie scrambled to her feet and lifted Titus in her arms.

'He is not ugly, your Lordship,' she said, her voice quavering. 'My little one is lovely.'

'Let me see him. Hold him up, nurse; hold him up to the light. Ah! that is better. He has improved,' said Lord Sepulchrave. 'How old is he?'

'Nearly three months,' said Nannie Slagg. 'Oh, my weak heart! he is nearly three months old.'

'Well, well, good woman, that is all. I have talked too much tonight. That is all that I wanted – to see my son, and to tell you to inform the Family of my desire to have them here at eight o'clock today week. The Prunesquallors had better come as well. I will inform Sourdust myself. Do you understand?'

'Yes, sir,' said Nannie, already making for the door. 'I will tell them, sir. Oh, my poor heart, how tired I am!'

'Flay!' said Lord Sepulchrave, 'take the nurse back to her room. You need not return tonight. I shall have left in four hours' time. Have my room prepared and the lanthorn on my bedside table. You may go.'

Flay, who had emerged into the lamplight, nodded his head, relit the wick of the lamp, and then followed Nannie Slagg out of the door and up the steps to the starlight. This time he took no heed of her expostulations, but taking Titus from her, placed him carefully into one of his capacious jacket pockets, and then, lifting the tiny struggling woman in his arms, marched solemnly through the woods to the castle.

Steerpike followed, deep in thought, and did not even trouble to keep them in sight.

Lord Sepulchrave, lighting a candle, climbed the staircase by the door and, moving along the wooden balcony, came at last to a shelf of dusty volumes. He blew the grey pollen from the vellum spine of one which he tilted forward from the rest with his index finger and then, turning over a page or two, near the beginning, made his way around the balcony again and down the stairs.

When he had reached his seat he leaned back and his head fell forward on his chest. The book was still in his hand. His sorrowful eyes wandered about the room from under the proud bone of his brow, until they fell at last upon the scattered fir cones.

A sudden uncontrollable gust of anger seized him. He had been childish in gathering them. Titus had not in any case derived any amusement from them.

It is strange that even in men of much learning and wisdom there can be an element of the infantile. It may be that it was not the cones themselves that angered him, but that they acted in some way as a reminder of his failures. He flung the book from him, and then immediately retrieved it, smoothing its sides with his shaking hands. He was too proud and too melancholy to unbend and be the father of the boy in anything but fact; he would not cease to isolate himself. He had done more than he expected himself to do. At the breakfast which he had envisaged he would toast the heir to Gormenghast. He would drink to the Future, to Titus, his only son. That was all.

He sat back again in the chair, but he could not read.

KEDA AND RANTEL

WHEN Keda came back to her people the cacti were dripping with the rain. The wind was westerly, and above the blurred outline of the Twisted Woods the sky was choked with crumpled rags. Keda stood for a moment and watched the dark rulers of the rain slanting steadily from the ragged edge of the clouds to the ragged edge of the woods. Behind the opaque formations the sun was hidden as it sank, so that but little light was reflected from the empty sky above her.

This was the darkness she knew of. She breathed it in. It was the late autumn darkness of her memories. There was here no taint of those shadows which had oppressed her spirit within the walls of Gormenghast. Here, once again an Outer dweller, she stretched her arms above her head in her liberation.

'I am free,' she said. 'I am home again.' But directly she had said these words she knew that it was not so. She was home, yes, among the dwellings where she was born. Here beside her, like an ancient friend, stood the gaunt cactus, but of the friends of her childhood who were left? Who was there to whom she could go? She did not ask for someone in whom she could confide. She only wished that she might go unhesitatingly to one who would ask no questions, and to whom she need not speak.

Who was there? And against this question arose the answer which she feared: There were the two men.

Suddenly the fear that had swept her died and her heart leapt with inexplicable joy and as the clouds above her in the sky had rolled away from their zenith, those that had choked her heart broke apart and left her with an earthless elation and a courage that she could not understand. She walked on in the gathering dusk and, passing by the empty tables and benches

231

that shone unnaturally in the darkness with the film of the rain still upon them, she came at last to the periphery of the mud dwellings.

It seemed at first as though the narrow lanes were deserted. The mud dwellings, rising usually to a height of about eight feet, faced each other across dark lanes like gullies, and all but met overhead. At this hour in the lanes it would have been pitch dark if it had not been for the dwellers' custom of hanging lamps above the doors of all their houses, and lighting them at sunset.

Keda had turned several corners before she came upon the first sign of life. A dwarf dog, of that ubiquitous breed that was so often to be seen slinking along the mud lanes, ran past Keda on little mangy legs, hugging the wall as he ran. She smiled a little. Since childhood she had been taught to despise these scavenging and stunted curs, but as she watched it slink past her she did not despise it, but in the sudden gladness that had filled her heart she knew of it only as a part of her own being, her all-embracing love and harmony. The dog-urchin had stopped a few yards after passing her and was sitting up on its mangy haunches and scratching with one of its hind legs at an itch beneath its ear. Keda felt her heart was breaking with a love so universal that it drew into its fiery atmosphere all things because they *were*; the evil, the good, the rich, the poor, the ugly, the beautiful, and the scratching of this little yellowish hound.

She knew these lanes so well that the darkness did not hinder her progress. The desertion of the mud lanes was, she knew, natural to that hour of evening when the majority of the dwellers would be huddled over their root fires. It was for this reason that she had left the castle so late on her homeward journey. There was a custom among the dwellers that when passing each other at night they should move their heads into the light of the nearest door-lamp and then, as soon as they had observed one another, continue upon their journeys. There was no need for them to show any expression; the chances were that the mutual recognition of friends would be infrequent. The rivalry between the families and the various schools of carving was relentless and bitter, and it would often happen that enemies would find each other's features in this way within a few feet of their own, lit by these hanging lamps; but this custom was rigorously observed – to stare for a moment and pass on.

It had been Keda's hope that she would be able to reach her house, the house which was hers through the death of her old husband, without having to move into the lamplight and be recognized by a passing Dweller, but now she did not mind. It seemed to her that the beauty that filled her was keener than the edge of a sword and as sure a protection against calumny and gossip, the jealousies and underground hatreds which she had once feared.

What was it that had come over her? she wondered. A recklessness alien to the whole quietness of her nature startled but fascinated her. This, the very moment which she had anticipated would fill her with anxiety – when the problems, to escape which she had taken refuge in the castle, would lower themselves over her like an impenetrable fog and frighten her – was now an evening of leaves and flame, a night of ripples.

She walked on. From behind the rough wooden doors of many of the dwellings she could hear the heavy voices of those within. She now came to the long lane that led directly up to the sheer outer wall of Gormenghast. This lane was a little broader than most, being about nine feet wide and broadening at times to almost twelve. It was the highway of the Dwellers, and the daily rendezvous for groups of the Bright Carvers. Old women and men would sit at the doors, or hobble on their errands, and the children play in the dust in the shifting shadow of the great Wall that edged by degrees along the street until by evening it had swallowed the long highway and the lamps were lit. Upon the flat roof of many of the dwellings a carving would be placed, and on evenings of sunset the easterly line of those wooden forms would smoulder and burn and the westerly line against the light in the sky would stand in jet-black silhouette, showing the sweeping outlines and the harsh angles which the Dwellers delighted in contrasting.

These carvings were now lost in the upper darkness above the door lamps, and Keda, remembering them as she walked, peered in vain for a glimpse of them against the sky.

Her home did not lie in this highway but at the corner of a little mud square where only the most venerable and revered of the Bright Carvers were permitted to settle. In the centre of this square stood the pride of the mud dwellers – a carving, some fourteen feet high, which had been hewn several hundred years before. It was the only one of that carver's works which the dwellers possessed although several pieces from his hand were within the castle walls, in the Hall of the Bright Carvings. There were diverse opinions as to who he may have been, but that he was the finest of all the carvers was never disputed. This work, which was repainted each year in its original colours, was of a horse and rider. Hugely stylized and very simple, the bulk of rhythmic wood dominated the dark square. The horse was of the purest grey and its neck was flung backwards in a converse arch so that its head faced the sky, and the coils of its white mane were gathered like frozen foam about the nape of its strained neck and over the knees of the rider, who sat draped in a black cape. On this cape were painted dark crimson stars. He was very upright, but his arms and hands, in contrast to the vitality of the grey and muscular neck of the horse, hung limply at his sides. His head was very sharply cut with the chisel and was as white as the mane, only the lips and the hair relieving the deathlike mask, the former a pale coral and the latter a dark chestnut brown. Rebellious children were sometimes brought by their mothers to see this sinister figure and were threatened with his disfavour should they continue in their wrong-doing. This carving had a terror for them, but to their parents it was a work of extraordinary vitality and beauty of form, and with a richness of mysterious mood the power of which in a work was one of their criteria of excellence.

This carving had come into Keda's mind as she approached that turning from the highway which led to the mud square, when she heard the sound of feet behind her. Ahead, the road lay silent, the door lamps lighting faintly small areas of the earth below them, but giving no intimation of any passing figure. Away to the left, beyond the mud square, the sudden barking of a dog sounded in her ears, and she became conscious of her own footsteps as she listened to those that were over-taking her.

She was within a few yards of one of the door lamps and knowing that were she to pass it before the approaching figure had done so, then both she and the unknown man would have to walk together in the darkness until the next lamp was reached, when the ritual of scanning each other's features would be observed, Keda slackened her pace, so that the observance might be more rapidly disposed of and the follower, whoever he was, might proceed on his way.

She stopped as she came to the light, nor in doing so and waiting was there anything unusual, for such was the not in-frequent habit of those who were nearing the lamps and was, in fact, considered an act of politeness. She moved through the glow of the lamp so that on turning about the rays would illumine her face, and the approaching figure would then both see her and be seen the more easily.

In passing under the lamp the light wavered on her dark brown hair lighting its highest strands almost to the colour of barley, and her body, though full and rounded, was upright and lithe, and this evening, under the impact of her new emotion had in it a buoyancy, an excitement, that through the eyes attacked the one who followed.

The evening was electric and unreal, and yet perhaps, thought Keda, this *is* reality and my past life has been a meaningless dream. She knew that the footsteps in the darkness which were now only a few yards away were a part of an evening she would not forget and which she seemed to have enacted long ago, or had foreseen. She knew that when the footsteps ceased and she turned to face the one who followed she would find that he was Rantel, the more fiery, the more awkward of the two who loved her.

She turned and he was standing there.

For a long time they stood. About them the impenetrable blackness of the night shut them in as though they were in a confined space, like a hall, with the lamp overhead.

She smiled, her mature, compassionate lips hardly parting. Her eyes moved over his face – over the dark mop of his hair, his powerful jutting brow, and the shadows of his eyes that stared as though fixed in their sockets, at her own. She saw his high cheekbones and the sides of his face that tapered to his chin. His mouth was drawn finely and his shoulders were powerful. Her breast rose and fell, and she was both weak and strong. She could feel the blood flowing within her and she felt that she must die or break forth into leaves and flowers. It was not passion that she felt: not the passion of the body, though that was there, but rather an exultation, a reaching for life, for the whole of the life of which she was capable, and in that life which she but dimly divined was centred love, the love for a man. She was not in love with Rantel: she was in love with what he meant to her as someone she *could* love.

He moved forward in the light so that his face was darkened to her and only the top of his ruffled hair shone like wire.

'Keda,' he whispered.

She took his hand. 'I have come back.'

He felt her nearness; he held her shoulders in his hands.

'You have come back,' he said as though repeating a lesson. 'Ah, Keda – is this you? You went away. Every night I have watched for you.' His hands shook on her shoulders. 'You went away,' he said.

'You have followed me?' said Keda. 'Why did you not speak to me by the rocks?'

'I wanted to', he said, 'but I could not.'

'Oh, why not?'

'We will move from the lamp and then I will tell you,' he said at last. 'Where are we going?'

'Where? To where should I go but to where I lived – to my house?'

They walked slowly. 'I will tell you,' he said suddenly. 'I followed you to know where you would go. When I knew it was not to Braigon I overtook you.'

'To Braigon?' she said. 'Oh Rantel, you are still as unhappy.'

'I cannot alter, Keda; I cannot change.'

They had reached the square.

'We have come here for nothing,' said Rantel, coming to a halt in the darkness. 'For nothing, do you hear me, Keda? I must tell you now. Oh, it is bitterness to tell you.'

Nothing that he might say could stop a voice within her that kept crying: '*I* am with you, Keda! I am *life*! I am *life*! Oh, Keda, Keda, *I* am with you!' But her voice asked him as though something separate from her real self were speaking:

'Why have we come for nothing?'

'I followed you and then I let you continue here with me, but your house, Keda, where your husband carved, has been taken from you. You can do nothing. When you left us the Ancients met, the Old Carvers, and they have given your house to one who is of their company, for they say that now that your husband is dead you are not worthy to live in the Square of the Black Rider.'

'And my husband's carvings,' said Keda, 'what has become of them?'

While she waited for him to answer she heard his breathing quicken and could dimly see him dragging his forearm over his brow.

'I will tell you,' he said. 'O fire! why was I so slow – so *slow*! While I was watching for you, watching from the rocks, as I have done every night since you left, Braigon broke into your house and found the Ancients dividing up your own carvings among themselves. "She will not come back," they said of you. "She is worthless. The carvings will be left untended", they said, "and the grain-worm will attack them." But Braigon drew his knife and sent them into a room below the stairs and made twelve journeys and carried the carvings to his own house, where he has hidden them, he says, until you come.

'Keda, Keda, what can *I* do for you? Oh Keda, what can *I* do?'

'Hold me close to you,' she said. 'Where is that music?'

In the silence they could hear the voice of an instrument.

'Keda . . .'

His arms were about her body and his face was deep in her hair.

She could hear the beating of his heart, for her head was lying close to him. The music had suddenly ended and silence, as unbroken as the darkness about them, returned.

Rantel spoke at last. 'I will not live until I take you, Keda. Then I will live. I am a Sculptor. I will create a glory out of wood. I will hack for you a symbol of my love. It will curve in flight. It will leap. It shall be of crimson and have hands as tender as flowers and feet that merge into the roughness of earth, for it shall be its body that leaps. And it shall have eyes that see all things and be violet like the edge of the spring lightning, and upon the breast I shall carve your name – Keda, Keda, Keda – three times, for I am ill with love.'

She put up her hand and her cool fingers felt the bones of his brow and his high cheekbones, and came to his mouth where they touched his lips.

After a little while Rantel said softly: 'You have been crying?'

'With joy,' she said.

'Keda . . .'

'Yes . . .'

'Can you bear cruel news?'

'Nothing can pain me any more,' said Keda. 'I am no longer the one you knew. I am alive.'

'The law that forced you in your marriage, Keda, may bind you again. There is another. I have been told he has been waiting for you, Keda, waiting for you to return. But I could slay him, Keda, if you wish.' His body toughened in her arms and his voice grew harsher. 'Shall I slay him?'

'You shall not speak of death,' said Keda. 'He shall not have me. Take me with you to your house.' Keda heard her own voice sounding like that of another woman, it was so different and clear. 'Take me with you – he will not take me after we have loved. They have my house, where else should I sleep to-night but with you? For I am happy for the first time. All things are clear to me. The right and the wrong, the true and the untrue. I have lost my fear. Are you afraid?'

'I am not afraid!' cried Rantel into the darkness, 'if we love one another.'

'I love all, all,' said Keda. 'Let us not talk.'

Dazed, he took her with him away from the square, and threading their way through the less frequented lanes found themselves at last at the door of a dwelling at the base of the castle wall.

The room they entered was cold, but within a minute Rantel had sent the light from an open fire on the earth dancing across the walls. On the mud floor was the usual grass matting common to all the dwellings.

'Our youth will pass from us soon,' said Keda. 'But we are young this moment and tonight we are together. The bane of our people will fall on us, next year or the year after, but now – NOW, Rantel; it is NOW that fills us. How quickly you have made the fire! Oh, Rantel, how beautifully you have made it! Hold me again.'

As he held her there was a tapping at the window; they did not move, but only listened as it increased until the coarse slab of glass sunk in the mud walls vibrated with an incessant drumming. The increasing volume of the sudden rain was joined by the first howls of a young wind.

The hours moved on. On the low wooden boards, Rantel and Keda lay in the warmth of the fire, defenceless before each other's love.

•

When Keda wakened she lay for some while motionless. Rantel's arm was flung over her body and his hand was at her breast like a child's. Lifting his arm she moved slowly from him, lowered his hand again softly to the floor. Then she rose and walked to the door. And as she took the first steps, there flashed through her the joyous realization that the mood of invulnerability before the world was still with her. She unlatched the door and flung it open. She had known that the outer wall of Gormenghast would face her as she did so. Its rough base within a stone's throw would rise like a sheer cliff. And there it was, but there was more. Ever since she could remember anything the face of the outer wall had been like the symbol of endlessness, of changelessness, of power, of austerity and of protection. She had known it in so many moods. Baked to dusty whiteness, and alive with basking lizards, she could remember how it flaked in the sun. She had seen it flowering with the tiny pink and blue creeper flowers that spread like fields of coloured smoke in April across acres of its temperate surface. She had seen its every protruding ledge of stone, its

every jutting irregularity furred with frost, or hanging with icicles. She had seen the snow sitting plumply on those juttings, so that in the darkness when the wall had vanished into the night these patches of snow had seemed to her like huge stars suspended.

And now this sunlit morning of late autumn gave to it a mood which she responded to. But as she watched its sunny surface sparkling after a night of heavy rain, she saw at the same moment a man sitting at its base, his shadow on the wall behind him. He was whittling at a branch in his hand. But although it was Braigon who sat there and who lifted his eyes as she opened the door, she did not cry in alarm or feel afraid or ashamed, but only looked at him quietly, happily, and saw him as a figure beneath a sparkling wall, a man whittling at a branch; someone she had longed to see again.

He did not get to his feet, so she walked over to him and sat down at his side. His head was massive and his body also; squarely built, he gave the impression of compact energy and strength. His hair covered his head closely with tangled curls.

'How long have you been here, Braigon, sitting in the sun carving?'

'Not long.'

'Why did you come?'

'To see you.'

'How did you know that I had come back?'

'Because I could carve no more.'

'You stopped carving?' said Keda.

'I could not see what I was doing. I could only see your face where my carving had been.'

Keda gave vent to a sigh of such tremulous depth that she clasped her hands at her breast with the pain that it engendered.

'And so you came here?'

'I did not come at once. I knew that Rantel would find you as you left the gate in the Outer Wall, for he hides each night among the rocks waiting for you. I knew that he would be with you. But this morning I came here to ask him where he had found you a dwelling for the night, and where you were, for I knew your house had been taken from you by the law of the Mud Square. But when I arrived here an hour ago I saw the ghost of your face on the door, and you were happy; so I waited here. You are happy, Keda?'

'Yes,' she said.

'You were afraid in the castle to come back; but now you are here you are not afraid. I can see what it is,' he said. 'You have found that you are in love. Do you love him?'

'I do not know. I do not understand. I am walking on air, Braigon. I cannot tell whether I love him or no, or whether it is

241

the world I love so much and the air and the rain last night, and the passions that opened like flowers from their tight buds. Oh, Braigon, I do not know. If I love Rantel, then I love you also. As I watch you now, your hand at your forehead and your lips moving such a little, it is you I love. I love the way you have not wept with anger and torn yourself to shreds to find me here. The way you have sat here all by yourself, oh Braigon, whittling a branch, and waiting, unafraid and understanding everything, I do not know how, for I have not told you of what has transformed me, suddenly?'

She leaned back against the wall and the morning sun lay whitely upon her face. 'Have I changed so much?' she said.

'You have broken free,' he said.

'Braigon,' she cried, 'it is you – it is *you* whom I love.' And she clenched her hands together. 'I am in pain because of you and him, but my pain makes me happy. I must tell you the truth, Braigon. I am in love with all things – pain and all things, because I can now watch them from above, for something has happened and I am clear – clear. But I love you, Braigon, more than all things. It is *you* I love.'

He turned the branch over in his hand as though he had not heard, and then he turned to her.

His heavy head had been reclining upon the wall and now he turned it slightly towards her, his eyes half closed.

'Keda,' he said, 'I will meet you tonight. The grass hollow where the Twisted Woods descend. Do you remember?'

'I will meet you there,' she said. While she spoke the air became shrill between their heads and the steel point of a long knife struck the stones between them and snapped with the impact.

Rantel stood before them, he was shaking.

'I have another knife,' he said in a whisper which they could only just hear. 'It is a little longer. It will be sharper by this evening when I meet you at the hollow. There is a full moon tonight. Keda! Oh Keda! Have you forgotten?'

Braigon got to his feet. He had moved only to place himself before Keda's body. She had closed her eyes and she was quite expressionless.

'I cannot help it,' she said, 'I cannot help it. I am happy.'

Braigon stood immediately before his rival. He spoke over his shoulder, but kept his eyes on his enemy.

'He is right,' he said. 'I shall meet him at sunset. One of us will come back to you.'

Then Keda raised her hands to her head. 'No, no, no, no!' she cried. But she knew that it must be so, and became calm, leaning back against the wall, her head bowed and the locks of her hair falling over her face.

The two men left her, for they knew that they could never be with her that unhappy day. They must prepare their weapons. Rantel re-entered his hut and a few moments later returned with a cape drawn about him. He approached Keda.

'I do not understand your love,' he said.

She looked up and saw his head upright upon his neck. His hair was like a bush of blackness.

She did not answer. She only saw his strength and his high theekbones and fiery eyes. She only saw his youth.

'I am the cause,' she said. 'It is I who should die. And I *will* die,' she said quickly. 'Before very long – but now, now what is it? I cannot enter into fear or hate, or even agony and death. Forgive me. Forgive me.'

She turned and held his hand with the dagger in it.

'I do not know. I do not understand,' she said. 'I do not think that we have any power.'

She released his hand and he moved away along the base of the high wall until it curved to the right and she lost him.

Braigon was already gone. Her eyes clouded.

'Keda,' she said to herself, 'Keda, this is tragedy.' But as her words hung emptily in the morning air, she clenched her hands for she could feel no anguish and the bright bird that had filled her breast was still singing . . . was still singing.

THE ROOM OF ROOTS

'THAT'S quite enough for today,' said Lady Cora, laying down her embroidery on a table beside her chair.

'But you've only sewn three stitches, Cora,' said Lady Clarice, drawing out a thread to arm's length.

Cora turned her eyes suspiciously. 'You have been watching me,' she said. 'Haven't you?'

'It wasn't private,' replied her sister. 'Sewing isn't private.' She tossed her head.

Cora was not convinced and sat rubbing her knees together, sullenly.

'And now I've finished as well,' said Clarice, breaking the silence. 'Half a petal, and quite enough, too, for a day like this. Is it tea time?'

'Why do you always want to know the time?' said Cora. "Is it breakfast time, Cora?" ... "Is it dinner time, Cora?" ... "Is it tea time, Cora?" – on and on and on. You know that it doesn't make any difference *what* the time is.'

'It does if you're hungry,' said Clarice.

'No, it doesn't. Nothing matters very much; even if you're hungry.'

'Yes, it does,' her sister contested. 'I *know* it does.'

'Clarice Groan,' said Cora sternly, rising from her chair, 'you know *too* much.'

Clarice did not answer, but bit her thin, loose lower lip.

'We usually go on much longer with our sewing, don't we, Cora?' she said at last. 'We sometimes go on for hours and hours, and we nearly always talk a lot, but we haven't today, have we, Cora?'

'No,' said Cora.

'Why haven't we?'

'I don't know. Because we haven't needed to, I suppose, you silly thing.'

Clarice got up from her chair and smoothed her purple satin, and then looked archly at her sister. '*I* know why we haven't been talking,' she said.

'Oh no, you don't.'

'Yes, I do,' said Clarice. '*I* know.'

Cora sniffed, and after walking to a long mirror in the wall with a swishing of her skirts, she readjusted a pin in her hair. When she felt she had been silent long enough:

'Oh no, you don't,' she said, and peered at her sister in the mirror over the reflection of her own shoulder. Had she not had forty-nine years in which to get accustomed to the phenomenon she must surely have been frightened to behold in the glass, next to her own face, another, smaller, it is true, for her sister was some distance behind her, but of such startling similarity.

She saw her sister's mouth opening in the mirror.

'I *do*,' came the voice from behind her, 'because I know what *you've* been thinking. It's easy.'

'You *think* you do,' said Cora, 'but I know you *don't*, because I know exactly what you've been thinking all day that I've been thinking and that's why.'

The logic of this answer made no lasting impression upon Clarice, for although it silenced her for a moment she continued: 'Shall I tell you what you've been brooding on?' she asked.

'You can if you like, I suppose. *I* don't mind. What, then? I might as well incline my ear. Go on.'

'I don't know that I want to now,' said Clarice. 'I think I'll keep it to myself, although it's *obvious*.' Clarice gave great emphasis to this word 'obvious'. 'Isn't it tea time yet? Shall I ring the bell, Cora? What a pity it's too windy for the tree.'

'You were thinking of that Steerpike boy,' said Cora, who had sidled up to her sister and was staring at her from very close quarters. She felt she had rather turned the tables on poor Clarice by her sudden renewal of the subject.

'So were you,' said Clarice. 'I knew that long ago. Didn't you?'

'Yes, I did,' said Cora. 'Very long ago. Now we both know.'

A freshly burning fire flung their shadows disrespectfully to and fro across the ceiling and over the walls where samples of their embroidery were hung. The room was a fair size, some thirty feet by twenty. Opposite the entrance from the corridor

245

was a small door. This gave upon the Room of Roots, in the shape of a half circle. On either side of this smaller opening were two large windows with diamond panes of thick glass, and on the two end walls of the room, in one of which was the small fireplace, were narrow doorways, one leading to the kitchen and the rooms of the two servants, and the other to the dining-room and the dark yellow bedroom of the twins.

'He said he would exalt us,' said Clarice. 'You heard him, didn't you?'

'I'm not deaf,' said Cora.

'He said we weren't being honoured enough and we must remember who we are. We're Lady Clarice and Cora Groan; that's who we are.'

'Cora and Clarice', her sister corrected her, 'of Gormenghast.'

'But no one is awed when they see us. He said he'd make them be.'

'Make them be what, dear?' Cora had begun to unbend now that she found their thoughts had been identical.

'Make them be awed,' said Clarice. 'That's what they ought to be. Oughtn't they, Cora?'

'Yes; but they won't do it.'

'No. That's what it is,' said Clarice, 'although I tried this morning.'

'What, dear?' said Cora.

'I tried this morning, though,' repeated Clarice.

'Tried what?' asked Cora in a rather patronizing voice.

'You know when I said "I'll go for a saunter"?'

'Yes.' Cora sat down and produced a minute but heavily scented handkerchief from her flat bosom. 'What about it?'

'I didn't go to the bathroom at all.' Clarice sat down suddenly and stiffly. 'I took some ink instead – *black* ink.'

'What for?'

'I won't tell you yet, for the time isn't ripe,' said Clarice importantly; and her nostrils quivered like a mustang's. 'I took the black ink, and I poured it into a jug. There was lots of it. Then I said to myself, what you tell me such a lot, and what I tell you as well, which is that Gertrude is no better than us – in

246

fact, she's not as good because she hasn't got a speck of Groan blood in her veins like we have, but only the common sort that's no use. So I took the ink and I knew what I would do. I didn't tell you because you might have told me not to, and I don't know why I'm telling you now because you may think I was wrong to do it; but it's all over now so it doesn't matter what you think, dear, does it?'

'I don't know yet,' said Cora rather peevishly.

'Well, I knew that Gertrude had to be in the Central Hall to receive the seven most hideous beggars of the Outer Dwellings and pour a lot of oil on them at nine o'clock; so I went through the door of the Central Hall at nine o'clock with my jug full of ink, and I walked up to her at nine o'clock, but it was not what I wanted because she had a black dress on.'

'What do you mean?' said Cora.

'Well, I was going to pour the ink all over her dress.'

'That would be good, very good,' said Cora. 'Did you?'

'Yes,' said Clarice, 'but it didn't show because her dress was black, and she didn't see me pouring it, anyway, because she was talking to a starling.'

'One of our birds,' said Cora.

'Yes,' said Clarice. 'One of the stolen birds. But the others saw me. They had their mouths open. They saw my decision. But Gertrude didn't, so my decision was no use. I hadn't anything else to do and I felt frightened, so I ran all the way back; and now I think I'll wash out the jug.'

She got up to put her idea into operation when there was a discreet tapping at their door. Visitors were very few and far between and they were too excited for a moment to say 'Come in.'

Cora was the first to open her mouth and her blank voice was raised more loudly than she had intended:

'Come in.'

Clarice was at her side. Their shoulders touched. Their heads were thrust forward as though they were peering out of a window.

The door opened and Steerpike entered, an elegant stick with a shiny metal handle under his arm. Now that he had renovated and polished the pilfered sword-stick to his satisfaction, he carried it about with him wherever he went. He was dressed in his habitual black and had acquired a gold chain which he wore about his neck. His meagre quota of sandy-coloured hair was darkened with grease, and had been brushed down over his pale forehead in a wide curve.

When he had closed the door behind him he tucked his stick smartly under his arm and bowed.

'Your Ladyships,' he said, 'my unwarranted intrusion upon your privacy, with but the summary knock at the panels of your door as my mediator, must be considered the acme of impertinence were it not that I come upon a serious errand.'

'Who's died?' said Cora.

'Is it Gertrude?' echoed Clarice.

'No one has died,' said Steerpike, approaching them. 'I will tell you the facts in a few minutes; but first, my dear Ladyships, I would be most honoured if I were permitted to appreciate your embroideries. Will you allow me to see them?' He looked at them both in turn inquiringly.

'He said something about them before; at the Prunesquallors' it was,' whispered Clarice to her sister. 'He said he wanted to see them before. Our embroideries.'

Clarice had a firm belief that as long as she whispered, no matter how loudly, no one would hear a word of what she said, except her sister.

'I heard him,' said her sister. 'I'm not blind, am I?'

'Which do you want to see first?' said Clarice. 'Our needlework or the Room of Roots or the Tree?'

'If I am not mistaken', said Steerpike by way of an answer, 'the creations of your needle are upon the walls around us, and having seen them, as it were, in a flash, I have no choice but to say that I would first of all prefer to examine them more closely, and then if I may, I would be delighted to visit your Room of Roots.'

'"Creations of our needle", he said,' whispered Clarice in her loud, flat manner that filled the room.

'Naturally,' said her sister, and shrugged her shoulders again, and turning her face to Steerpike gave to the right-hand corner of her inexpressive mouth a slight twitch upwards, which although it was as mirthless as the curve between the lips of a dead haddock, was taken by Steerpike to imply that she and he were above making such *obvious* comments.

'Before I begin,' said Steerpike, placing his innocent-looking swordstick on a table, 'may I inquire out of my innocence why you ladies were put to the inconvenience of bidding me to enter your room? Surely your footman has forgotten himself. Why was he not at the door to inquire who wished to see you and to give you particulars before you allowed yourselves to be invaded? Forgive my curiosity, my dear Ladyships, but where was your footman? Would you wish me to speak to him?'

The sisters stared at each other and then at the youth. At last Clarice said:

'We haven't got a footman.'

Steerpike, who had turned away for this very purpose, wheeled about, and then took a step backwards as though struck.

'No footman!' he said, and directed his gaze at Cora.

She shook her head. 'Only an old lady who smells,' she said. 'No footman at all.'

Steerpike walked to the table and, leaning his hands upon it, gazed into space.

'Their Ladyships Cora and Clarice Groan of Gormenghast have no footman – have no one save an old lady who smells. Where are their servants? Where are their retinues, their swarms of attendants?' And then in a voice little above a whisper: 'This must be seen to. This must end.' With a clicking of his tongue he straightened his back. 'And now', he continued in a livelier voice, 'the needlework is waiting.'

What Steerpike had said, as they toured the walls, began to re-fertilize those seeds of revolt which he had sown at the Prunesquallors'. He watched them out of the corner of his eyes as he flattered their handiwork, and he could see that although it was a great pleasure for them to show their craft, yet their minds were continually returning to the question he had raised. 'We do it all with our left hands, don't we, Cora?' Clarice said.

as she pointed to an ugly green-and-red rabbit of intricate needlework.

'Yes,' said Cora, 'it takes a long time because it's all done like that – with our left hands. Our right arms are starved, you know', she said, turning to Steerpike. 'They're quite, quite starved.'

'Indeed, your Ladyship,' said Steerpike. 'How is that?'

'Not only our left arms,' Clarice broke in, 'but all down our left-hand sides and our right-hand legs, too. That's why they're rather stiff. It was the epileptic fits which we had. That's what did it and that's what makes our needlework all the more clever.'

'And beautiful,' said Cora.

'I cannot but agree,' said Steerpike.

'But nobody sees them,' said Clarice. 'We are left alone. Nobody wants our advice on anything. Gertrude doesn't take any notice of us, nor does Sepulchrave. You know what we ought to have, don't you, Cora?'

'Yes,' said her sister, 'I know.'

'What, then?' said Clarice. 'Tell me. Tell me.'

'Power,' said Cora.

'That's right. Power. That's the very thing we want.' Clarice turned her eyes to Steerpike. Then she smoothed the shiny purple of her dress.

'I rather liked them,' she said.

Steerpike, wondering where on earth her thoughts had taken her, tilted his head on one side as though reflecting upon the truth in her remark, when Cora's voice (like the body of a plaice translated into sound) asked:

'You rather liked what?'

'My convulsions,' said Clarice earnestly. 'When my left arm became starved for the first time. You remember, Cora, don't you? When we had our first fits? I rather liked them.'

Cora rustled up to her and raised a forefinger in front of her sister's face. 'Clarice Groan,' she said, 'we finished talking about that long ago. We're talking about Power now. Why can't you follow what we're talking about? You are always losing your place. I've noticed that.'

'What about the Room of Roots?' asked Steerpike with affected gaiety. 'Why is it called the Room of Roots? I am most intrigued.'

'Don't you *know*?' came their voices.

'He doesn't know,' said Clarice. 'You see how we've been forgotten. He didn't know about our Room of Roots.'

Steerpike was not kept long in ignorance. He followed the two purple ninepins through the door, and after passing down a short passage, Cora opened a massive door at the far end whose hinges could have done with a gill of oil apiece, and followed by her sister entered the Room of Roots. Steerpike in his turn stepped over the threshold and his curiosity was more than assuaged.

If the name of the room was unusual there was no doubt about its being apt. It was certainly a room of roots. Not of a few simple, separate formations, but of a thousand branching, writhing, coiling, intertwining, diverging, converging, interlacing limbs whose origin even Steerpike's quick eyes were unable for some time to discover.

He found eventually that the thickening stems converged at a tall, narrow aperture on the far side of the room, through the upper half of which the sky was pouring a grey, amorphous light. It seemed at first as though it would be impossible to stir at all in this convoluting meshwork, but Steerpike was amazed to see that the twins were moving about freely in the labyrinth. Years of experience had taught them the possible approaches to the window. They had already reached it and were looking out into the evening. Steerpike made an attempt at following them, but was soon inextricably lost in the writhing maze. Wherever he turned he was faced with a network of weird arms that rose and fell, dipped and clawed, motionless yet alive with serpentine rhythms.

Yet the roots were dead. Once the room must have been filled with earth, but now, suspended for the most part in the higher reaches of the chamber, the thread-like extremities clawed impotently in the air. Nor was it enough that Steerpike should find a room so incongruously monopolized, but that every one of these twisting terminals should be *hand-painted* was even more astonishing. The various main limbs and their wooden tributaries, even down to the minutest rivulet of root, were painted in their own especial colours, so that it appeared as though seven coloured boles had forced their leafless branches through the window, yellow, red and green, violet and pale blue, coral pink and orange. The concentration of effort needed for the execution of this work must have been considerable, let alone the almost superhuman difficulties and vexations that must have resulted from the efforts to establish, among the labyrinthic entanglements of the finer roots, which tendril belonged to which branch, which branch to which limb, and which limb to which trunk, for only after discovering its source could its correct colour be applied.

The idea had been that the birds on entering should choose those roots whose colours most nearly approximated to their own plumage, or if they had preferred it to nest among roots whose hue was complementary to their own.

The work had taken the sisters well over three years, and yet when all had been completed the project for which all this work had been designed had proved to be empty, the Room of Roots a failure, their hopes frozen. From this mortification the twins had never fully recovered. It is true that the room, as a room, gave them pleasure, but that the birds never approached it, let alone settled and nested there, was a festering sore at the back of what minds they had.

Against this nagging disappointment was the positive pride which they felt in having a room of roots at all. And not only the Roots but logically enough the Tree whose branches had once drawn sustenance into its highest twigs, and, long ago, burst forth each April with its emerald jets. It was this Tree that was their chief source of satisfaction, giving them some sense of that distinction which they were now denied.

They turned their eyes from its branches and looked around for Steerpike. He was still not unravelled. 'Can you assist me, my dear Ladyships?' he called, peering through a skein of purple fibres.

'Why don't you come to this window?' said Clarice.

'He can't find the way,' said Cora.

252

'Can't he? I don't see why not,' said Clarice.

'Because he can't,' said Cora. 'Go and show him.'

'All right. But he must be very stupid,' said Clarice, walking through the dense walls of roots which seemed to open up before her and close again behind her back. When she reached Steerpike, she walked past him and it was only by practically treading on her heels that he was able to thread his way towards the window. At the window there was a little more space, for the seven stems which wedged their way through its lower half protruded some four feet into the room before beginning to divide and subdivide. Alongside the window there were steps that led up to a small platform which rested on the thick horizontal stems.

'Look outside', said Cora directly Steerpike arrived, 'and you'll see It.'

Steerpike climbed the few steps and saw the main trunk of the tree floating out horizontally into space and then running up to a great height, and as he saw it he recognized it as the tree he had studied from the roof tops, half a mile away near the stone sky-field.

He saw how, what had then seemed a perilous balancing act on the part of the distant figures, was in reality a safe enough exercise, for the bole was conveniently flat on its upper surface. When it reached that point where it began to ascend and branch out, the wooden highway spread into an area that could easily have accommodated ten or twelve people standing in a close group.

'Definitely a *tree*,' he said. 'I am all in favour of it. Has it been dead as long as you can remember it?'

'Of course,' said Clarice.

'We're not as old as *that*,' said Cora, and as this was the first joke she had made for over a year, she tried to smile, but her facial muscles had become, through long neglect, unusable.

'Not so old as what?' said Clarice.

'You don't understand,' said Cora. 'You are much slower than I am. I've noticed that.'

'I WANT some tea,' said Clarice; and leading the way she performed the miraculous journey through the room once more, Steerpike at her heels like a shadow and Cora taking an alternative path.

Once more in the comparatively sane living room where the tapers had been lit by the old woman, they sat before the fire and Steerpike asked if he might smoke. Cora and Clarice after glancing at each other nodded slowly, and Steerpike filled his pipe and lit it with a small red coal.

Clarice had pulled at a bell-rope that hung by the wall, and now as they sat in a semi-circle about the blaze, Steerpike in the centre chair, a door opened to their right and an old dark-skinned lady, with very short legs and bushy eyebrows, entered the room.

'Tea, I suppose,' she said in a subterranean voice that seemed to have worked its way up from somewhere in the room beneath them. She then caught sight of Steerpike and wiped her unpleasant nose with the back of her hand before retiring and closing the door behind her like an explosion. The embroideries flapped outwards in the draught this occasioned, and sank again limply against the walls.

'This is too much,' said Steerpike. 'How can you bear it?'

'Bear what?' said Clarice.

'Do you mean, your Ladyships, that you have become used to being treated in this offhand and insolent manner? Do you not mind whether your natural and hereditary dignities are flouted and abused – when an old commoner slams the doors upon you and speaks to you as though you were on her own degraded level? How can the Groan blood that courses so proudly and in such an undiluted stream, through your veins, remain so quiet? Why in its purple wrath is it not boiling at this moment?' He paused a moment and leant further forward.

'Your birds have been stolen by Gertrude, the wife of your brother. Your labour of love among the roots, which but for that woman would now be bearing fruit, is a fiasco. Even your

Tree is forgotten. I had not *heard* of it. Why had I not heard of it? Because you and all you possess have been put aside, forgotten, neglected. There are few enough of your noble and ancient family in Gormenghast to carry on the immemorial rites, and yet you two who could uphold them more scrupulously than any, are slighted at every turn.'

The twins were staring at him very hard. As he paused they turned their eyes to one another. His words, though sometimes a little too swift for them, communicated nevertheless their subversive gist. Here, from the mouth of a stranger, their old sores and grievances were being aired and formulated.

The old lady with the short legs returned with a tray which she set before them with a minimum of deference. Then inelegantly waddling away, she turned at the door and stared again at their visitor, wiping, as before, the back of her large hand across her nose.

When she had finally disappeared, Steerpike leaned forward and, turning to Cora and Clarice in turn, and fixing them with close and concentrated eyes, he said:

'Do you believe in honour? Your Ladyships, answer me, do you believe in honour?'

They nodded mechanically.

'Do you believe that injustice should dominate the castle?'

They shook their heads.

'Do you believe it should go unchecked – that it should flourish without just retribution?'

Clarice, who had rather lost track of the last question waited until she saw Cora shaking her head before she followed suit.

'In other words,' said Steerpike, 'you think that something must be *done*. Something to crush this tyranny.'

They nodded their heads again, and Clarice could not help feeling a little satisfied that she had so far made no mistake with her shakes and nods.

'Have you any ideas?' said Steerpike. 'Have you any plans to suggest?'

They shook their heads at once.

'In that case,' said Steerpike, stretching his legs out before him and crossing his ankles, 'may I make a suggestion, your Ladyships?'

Again, most flatteringly, he faced each one in turn to obtain her consent. One after the other they nodded heavily, sitting bolt upright in their chairs.

Meanwhile, the tea and the scones were getting cold, but they had all three forgotten them.

Steerpike got up and stood with his back to the fire so that he might observe them both at the same time.

'Your gracious Ladyships,' he began, 'I have received information which is of the highest moment. It is information which hinges upon the unsavoury topic with which we have been forced to deal. I beg your undivided concentration; but I will first of all ask you a question: who has the undisputed control over Gormenghast? Who is it who, having this authority, makes no use of it but allows the great traditions of the castle to drift, forgetting that even his own sisters are of his blood and lineage and are entitled to homage and – shall I say it? – yes, to adulation, too? Who is that man?'

'Gertrude,' they replied. 'Come, come,' said Steerpike, raising his eyebrows, 'who is it who forgets even his own sisters? Who is it, your Ladyships?'

'Sepulchrave,' said Cora.

'Sepulchrave,' echoed Clarice.

They had become agitated and excited by now although they did not show it, and had lost control over what little circumspection they had ever possessed. Every word that Steerpike uttered they swallowed whole.

'Lord Sepulchrave,' said Steerpike. After a pause, he continued. 'If it were not that you were his sisters, and of the Family, how could I dare to speak in this way of the Lord of Gormenghast? But it is my duty to be honest. Lady Gertrude has slighted you, but who could make amends? Who has the final power but your brother? In my efforts to re-establish you, and to make this South Wing once again alive with your servants, it must be remembered that it is your selfish brother who must be reckoned with.'

'He *is* selfish, you know,' said Clarice.

'Of course he is,' said Cora. 'Thoroughly selfish. What shall we do? Tell us! Tell us!'

'In all battles, whether of wits or of war,' said Steerpike, 'the first thing to do is to take the initiative and to strike hard.'

'Yes,' said Cora, who had reached the edge of the chair and was stroking her smooth heliotrope knees in quick, continual movements which Clarice emulated.

'One must choose *where* to strike,' said Steerpike, 'and it is obvious that to strike at the most vulnerable nerve centre of the opponent is the shrewdest preliminary measure. But there must be no half-heartedness. It is all or nothing.'

'All or nothing,' echoed Clarice.

'And now you must tell me, dear ladies, what is your brother's main interest?'

They went on smoothing their knees.

'Is it not literature?' said Steerpike. 'Is he not a great lover of books?'

They nodded.

'He's very clever,' said Cora.

'But he reads it all in books,' said Clarice.

'Exactly.' Steerpike followed quickly upon this. 'Then if he lost his books, he would be all but defeated. If the centre of his life were destroyed he would be but a shell. As I see it, your Ladyships, it is at his library that our first thrust must be directed. You must have your rights,' he added hotly. 'It is only fair that you should have your rights.' He took a dramatic step towards the Lady Cora Groan; he raised his voice: 'My Lady Cora Groan, do you not agree?'

Cora, who had been sitting on the extreme edge of her chair in her excitement, now rose and nodded her head so violently as to throw her hair into confusion.

Clarice, on being asked, followed her sister's example, and Steerpike relit his pipe from the fire and leaned against the mantelpiece for a few moments, sending out wreaths of smoke from between his thin lips.

'You have helped me a great deal, your Ladyships,' he said at last, drawing at his stubby pipe and watching a smoke-ring float to the ceiling. 'You are prepared, I am sure, for the sake of your own honour, to assist me further in my struggle for your deliverance.' He understood from the movements of their perched bodies that they agreed that this was so.

'The question that arises in that case', said Steerpike, 'is how are we to dispose of your brother's books and thereby bring home to him his responsibilities? What do you feel is the obvious method of destroying a library full of books? Have you been to his library lately, your Ladyships?'

They shook their heads.

'How would you proceed, Lady Cora? What method would you use to destroy a hundred thousand books?'

Steerpike removed his pipe from his lips and gazed intently at her.

'I'd burn them,' said Cora.

This was exactly what Steerpike had wanted her to say; but he shook his head. 'That would be difficult. What could we burn it with?'

'With fire,' said Clarice.

'But how would we start the fire, Lady Clarice?' said Steerpike pretending to look perplexed.

'Straw,' said Cora.

'That is a possibility,' said Steerpike, stroking his chin. 'I wonder if your idea would work swiftly enough. Do you think it would?'

'Yes, yes!' said Clarice. 'Straw is lovely to burn.'

'But would it catch the books', persisted Steerpike, 'all on its own? There would have to be a great deal of it. Would it be quick enough?'

'What's the hurry?' said Cora.

'It must be done swiftly,' said Steerpike, 'otherwise the flames might be put out by busybodies.'

'I love fires,' said Clarice.

'But we oughtn't to burn down Sepulchrave's library, ought we?'

Steerpike had expected, sooner or later, that one of them would feel conscience-stricken and he had retained his trump card.

'Lady Cora,' he said, 'sometimes one has to do things which

are unpalatable. When great issues are involved one can't toy with the situation in silk gloves. No. We are making history and we must be stalwart. Do you recall how when I first came in I told you that I had received information? You do? Well, I will now divulge what has come to my ears. Keep calm and steady; remember who you are. I shall look after your interests, have no fear, but at this moment sit down, will you, and attend?

'You tell me you have been treated badly for this and for that, but only listen now to the latest scandal that is being repeated below stairs. "*They* aren't being asked," everyone is saying. "*They* haven't been asked." '

'Asked what?' said Clarice.

'Or where?' said Cora.

'To the Great Gathering which your brother is calling. At this Great Gathering the details for a party for the New Heir to Gormenghast, your nephew Titus, will be discussed. Everyone of importance is going. Even the Prunesquallors are going. It is the first time for many years that your brother has become so worldly as to call the members of his family together. He has, it is said, many things which he wishes to talk of in connexion with Titus, and in my opinion this Great Gathering in a week's time will be of prime importance. No one knows exactly what Lord Sepulchrave has in mind, but the general idea is that preparations must be begun even now for a party on his son's first Birthday.

'Whether you will even be invited to that Party I would not like to say, but judging from the remarks I have heard about how you two have been thrust aside and forgotten like old shoes, I should say it was very unlikely.

'You see,' said Steerpike, 'I have not been idle. I have been listening and taking stock of the situation, and one day my labours will prove themselves to have been justified – when I see you, my dear Ladyships, sitting at either end of a table of distinguished guests, and when I hear the glasses clinking and the rounds of applause that greet your every remark I shall congratulate myself that I had long ago enough imagination and ruthless realism to proceed with the dangerous work of raising you to the level to which you belong.

'Why should you not have been invited to the party? Why? Why? Who are you to be spurned thus and derided by the lowest menials in Swelter's kitchen?'

Steerpike paused and saw that his words had produced a great effect. Clarice had gone over to Cora's chair where now they both sat bolt upright and very close together.

'When you suggested so perspicaciously just now that the solution to this insufferable state of affairs lay in the destruction of your brother's cumbersome library, I felt that you were right and that only through a brave action of that kind might you be able to lift up your heads once more and feel the slur removed from your escutcheon. That idea of yours spelt genius. I appeal to your Ladyships to do what you feel to be consistent with your honour and your pride. You are not old, your Ladyships, oh no, you are not old. But are you young? I should like to feel that what years you have left will be filled with glamorous days and romantic nights. Shall it be so? Shall we take the step towards justice? Yes or no, my dear ladies, yes or no.'

They got up together. 'Yes,' they said, 'we want Power back.'

'We want our servants back and justice back and everything back,' Cora said slowly, a counterpoint of intense excitement weaving through the flat foreground of her voice.

'And romantic nights,' said Clarice. 'I'd like that. Yes, yes. Burn! Burn,' she continued loudly, her flat bosom beginning to heave up and down like a machine. 'Burn! burn! burn!'

'When?' said Cora. 'When can we burn it up?'

Steerpike held up his hand to quieten them. But they took no notice, only leaning forward, holding each other's hands and crying in their dreadful emotionless voices:

'Burn! Burn! Burn! Burn! Burn!' until they had exhausted themselves.

Steerpike had not flinched under this ordeal. He now realized more completely than before why they were ostracized from the normal activities of the castle. He had known they were slow, but he had not known that they could behave like this.

He changed his tone.

'Sit down!' he rapped out. 'Both of you. Sit down!'

They complied at once, and although they were taken aback

260

at the peremptory nature of his order, he could see that he now had complete control over them, and though his inclination was to show his authority and to taste for the first time the sinister delights of his power, yet he spoke to them gently – for, first of all, the library must be burned for a reason of his own. After that, with such a dreadful hold over them, he could relax for a time and enjoy a delicious dictatorship in the South Wing.

'In six days' time, your Ladyships,' he said, fingering his gold chain – 'on the evening before the Great Gathering to which you have not been invited – the library will be empty and you may burn it to the ground. I shall prepare the incendiaries and will school you in all the details later; but on the great night itself when you see me give the signal you will set fire at once to the fuel and will make your way immediately to this room.'

'Can't we watch it burn?' said Cora.

'Yes,' said Clarice, 'can't we?'

'From your Tree,' said Steerpike. 'Do you want to be found out?'

'No!' they said. 'No! No!'

'Then you can watch it from your Tree and be quite safe. I will remain in the woods so that I can see that nothing goes wrong. Do you understand?'

'Yes,' they said. 'Then we'll have Power, won't we?'

The unconscious irony of this caused Steerpike's lip to lift, but he said:

'Your Ladyships will then have Power.' And approaching them in turn he kissed the tips of their fingers. Picking up his sword-stick from the table he walked swiftly to the door, where he bowed.

Before he opened it he said: 'We are the only ones who know. The only ones who will ever know, aren't we?'

'Yes,' they said. 'Only us.'

'I will return within a day or two,' said Steerpike, 'and give you the details. Your honour must be saved.'

He did not say good night, but opened the door and disappeared into the darkness.

'PREPARATIONS FOR ARSON'

On one excuse or another Steerpike absented himself from the Prunesquallors' during the major part of the next two days. Although he accomplished many things during this short period, the three stealthy expeditions which he made to the library were the core of his activities. The difficulty lay in crossing, unobserved, the open ground to the conifer wood. Once in the wood and among the pines there was less danger. He realized how fatal it might prove to be seen in the neighbourhood of the library, so shortly before the burning. On the first of the reconnaissances, after waiting in the shadows of the Southern wing before scudding across the overgrown gardens to the fields that bordered the conifers, he gathered the information which he needed. He had managed after an hour's patient concentration to work the lock of the library door with a piece of wire, and then he had entered the silent room, to investigate the structure of the building. There was a remoteness about the deserted room. Shadowy and sinister though it was by night, it was free of the vacancy which haunted its daylight hours. Steerpike felt the insistent silence of the place as he moved to and fro, glancing over his high shoulder more than once as he took note of the possibilities for conflagration.

His survey was exhaustive, and when he finally left the building he appreciated to a nicety the nature of the problem. Lengths of oil-soaked material would have to be procured and laid behind the books where they could stretch unobserved from one end of the room to the other. After leading around the library they could be taken up the stairs and along the balcony. To lay these twisted lengths (no easy matter to procure without awakening speculation) was patiently a job for those hours of the early morning, after Lord Sepulchrave had left for the castle. He had staggered, on his second visit, under an enormous bundle of rags and a tin of oil to the pine wood at midnight, and had occupied himself during the hours while he waited for Lord Sepulchrave to leave the building in knotting together the odd assortment of pilfered cloth into lengths of not less than forty feet.

When at last he saw his Lordship leave the side door and heard his slow, melancholy footsteps die away on the pathway leading to the Tower of Flints, he rose and stretched himself.

Much to his annoyance the probing of the lock occupied even more time than on the last occasion, and it was four o'clock in the morning before he pushed the door open before him.

Luckily, the dark autumn mornings were on his side, and he had a clear three hours. He had noticed that from without no light could be observed and he lit the lamp in the centre of the room.

Steerpike was nothing if not systematic, and two hours later, taking a tour of the library, he was well satisfied. Not a trace of his handiwork could be seen save only where four extremities of the cloth hung limply beside the main, unused, door of the building. These strips were the terminals of the four lengths that circumscribed the library and balcony and would be dealt with.

The only thing that caused him a moment's reflection was the faint smell of the oil in which he had soaked the tightly twisted cloth.

He now concentrated his attention upon the four strips and twining them together into a single cord, he knotted it at its end. Somehow or other this cord must find its way through the door to the outside world. He had on his last visit eventually arrived at the only solution apart from that of chiselling a way through the solid wall and the oak that formed the backs of the bookshelves. This was obviously too laborious. The alternative, which he had decided on, was to bore a neat hole through the door immediately under the large handle in the shadow of which it would be invisible save to scrutiny. Luckily for him there was a reading-stand in the form of a carven upright with three short, bulbous legs. This upright supported a tilted surface the size of a very small table. This piece stood unused in front of the main door. By moving it a fraction to the right, the twisted cord of cloth was lost in darkness and although its discovery was not impossible, both this risk and that of the faint aroma of oil being noticed, were justifiable.

He had brought the necessary tools with him and although the oak was tough had bored his way through it within half an hour. He wriggled the cord through the hole and swept up the sawdust that had gathered on the floor

By this time he was really tired, but he took another walk about the library before turning down the lamp and leaving by the side door. Once in the open he bore to his right, and skirting the adjacent wall, arrived at the main door of the building. As this entrance had not been used for many years, the steps that led to it were invisible beneath a cold sea of nettles and giant weeds. He waded his way through them and saw the loose end of the cord hanging through the raw hole he had chiselled. It glimmered whitely and was hooked like a dead finger. Opening the blade of a small sharp knife he cut through the twisted cloth so that only about two inches protruded, and to prevent this stub end slipping back through the hole, drove a small nail through the cloth with the butt of his knife.

His work for the night now seemed to be complete and, only stopping to hide the can of oil in the wood, he retraced his steps to the Prunesquallors', where climbing at once to his room he curled up in bed, dressed as he was, and incontinently fell asleep.

The third of his expeditions to the library, the second during the daylight, was on other business. As might be supposed, the childishness of burning down Lord Sepulchrave's sanctum did not appeal to him. In a way it appalled him. Not through any prickings of conscience, but because destruction in any form annoyed him. That is, the destruction of anything inanimate that was well constructed. For living creatures he had not this same concern, but in a well-made object, whatever its nature, a sword or a watch or a book, he felt an excited interest. He enjoyed a thing that was cleverly conceived and skilfully wrought, and this notion, of destroying so many beautifully bound and printed volumes, had angered him against himself, and it was only when his plot had so ripened that he could neither retract nor resist it, that he went forward with a single mind. That it should be the Twins who would actually set light to the building with their own hands was, of course, the lynch-pin of the manoeuvre. The advantages to himself which would accrue from being the only witness to the act were too absorbing for him to ponder at this juncture.

The aunts would, of course, not realize that they were setting fire to a library filled with people: nor that it would be the night of the Great Gathering to which, as Steerpike had told them, they were not to be invited. The youth had waylaid Nannie Slagg on her way to the aunts and had inquired whether he could save her feet by delivering her message to them. At first she had been disinclined to divulge the nature of her mission, but when she at last furbished him with what he had already suspected, he promised he would inform them at once of the Gathering, and, after a pretence of going in their direction, he had returned to the Prunesquallors' in time for his midday meal. It was on the following morning that he told the Twins that they had *not* been invited.

Once Cora and Clarice had ignited the cord at the main door of the library and the fire was beginning to blossom, it would be up to him to be as active as an eel on a line.

It seemed to Steerpike that to save two generations of the House of Groan from death by fire should stand him in very good stead, and moreover, his headquarters would be well established in the South Wing with their Ladyships Cora and Clarice who after such an episode would, if only through fear of their guilt being uncovered, eat out of his hand.

The question of how the fire started would follow close upon the rescue. On this he would have as little knowledge as anyone, only having seen the glow in the sky as he was walking along the South Wing for exercise. The Prunesquallors would bear out that it was his habit to take a stroll at sundown. The twins would be back in their room before news of the burning could ever reach the castle.

Steerpike's third visit to the library was to plan how the rescues were to be effected. One of the first things was, of course, to turn and remove the key from the door when the party had entered the building, and as Lord Sepulchrave had the convenient habit of leaving it in the lock until he removed it on retiring in the small hours, there should be no difficulty about this. That such questions as 'Who turned the key?' and 'how did it disappear?' would be asked at a later date was inevitable, but with a well-rehearsed alibi for himself and the twins, and with the Prunesquallors' cognizance of his having gone out for a stroll on that particular evening, he felt sure the suspicion would no more centre upon himself than on anyone else. Such minor problems as might arise in the future could be dealt with in the future.

This was of more immediate consequence: How was he to rescue the family of Groan in a manner reasonably free of danger to himself and yet sufficiently dramatic to cause the maximum admiration and indebtedness?

His survey of the building had shown him that he had no wide range of choice – in fact, that apart from forcing one of the doors open by some apparently superhuman effort at the last moment, or by smashing an opening in the large skylight in the roof through which it would be both too difficult and dangerous to rescue the prisoners, the remaining possibility lay in the only window, fifteen feet from the ground.

Once he had decided on this window as his focus he turned over in his mind alternative methods of rescue. It must appear, above all else, that the deliverance was the result of a sponta-neous decision, translated at once into action. It did not matter so much if he were suspected, although he did not imagine that he *would* be; what mattered was that nothing could later be proved as *prearranged*.

The window, about four feet square, was above the main door and was heavily glazed. The difficulty naturally centred on how the prisoners were to reach the window from the inside, and how Steerpike was to scale the outer wall in order to smash the pane and show himself.

Obviously he must not be armed with anything which he would not normally be carrying. Whatever he used to force an entrance must be something he had picked up on the spur of the moment outside the library or among the pines. A ladder, for instance, would at once arouse suspicions, and yet some-thing of that nature was needed. It occurred to him that a small tree was the obvious solution, and he began to search for one of the approximate length, already felled, for many of the pines which were cleared for the erection of the library and adjacent buildings were still to be seen lying half buried in the thick needle-covered ground. It did not take him long to come upon an almost perfect specimen of what he wanted. It was about twelve to fifteen feet long, and most of its lateral branches were broken off close to the bole, leaving stumps varying from three inches to a foot in length. 'Here', said Steerpike to himself, 'is *the* thing.'

It was less easy for him to find another, but eventually he discovered some distance from the library what he was searching for. It lay in a dank hollow of ferns. Dragging it to the library wall, he propped both the pines upright against the main door and under the only window. Wiping the sweat from his bulging forehead he began to climb them, stamping off those branches that would be too weak to support Lady Groan, who would be the heaviest of the prisoners. Dragging them away from the wall, when he had completed these minor adjustments, and feeling satisfied that his 'ladders' were now both serviceable yet *natural*, he left them at the edge of the trees where a number of felled pines were littered, and next cast about for something with which he could smash the window. At the base of the adjacent building, a number of moss-covered lumps of masonry had fallen away from the walls. He carried several of these to within a few yards of the 'ladders.' Were there any question of his being suspected later, and if questions were raised as to how he came across the ladders and the piece of masonry so conveniently, he could point to the heap of half-hidden stones and the litter of trees. Steerpike closed his eyes and attempted to visualize the scene. He could see himself making frantic efforts to open the doors, rattling the handles and banging the panels. He could hear himself shouting 'Is there anybody in there?' and the muffled cries from within. Perhaps he would yell: 'Where's the key? Where's the key?' or a few gallant encouragements, such as 'I'll get you out somehow.' Then he would leap to the main door and beating on it a few times, deliver a few more yells before dragging up the 'ladders', for the fire by that time should be going very well. Or perhaps he would do none of these things, simply appearing to them like the answer to a prayer, in the nick of time. He grinned.

The only reason why he could not spare himself both time and energy by propping the 'ladders' against the wall after the last guest had entered the library was that the Twins would see them as they performed their task. It was imperative that they should not suspect the library to be inhabited, let alone gain an inkling of Steerpike's preparations.

On this, the last occasion of his three visits to the library, he once again worked the lock of the side door and overhauled his handiwork. Lord Sepulchrave had been there on the previous night as usual, but apparently had suspected nothing. The tall bookstand was as he had left it, obstructing a view of and throwing a deep shadow over the handle of the main door from beneath which the twisted cloth stretched like a tight rope across the two foot span to the end of the long bookshelves. He could now detect no smell of oil, and although that meant that it was evaporating, he knew that it would still be more inflammable than the dry cloth.

Before he left he selected half a dozen volumes from the less conspicuous shelves, which he hid in the pine wood on his return journey, and which he collected on the following night from their rainproof nest of needles in the decayed bole of a dead larch. Three of the volumes had vellum bindings and were exquisitely chased with gold, and the others were of equally rare craftsmanship, and it was with annoyance, on returning to the Prunesquallors' that night that he found it necessary to fashion for them their neat jackets of brown paper and to obliterate the Groan crest on the fly-leaves.

It was only when these nefarious doings were satisfactorily completed that Steerpike visited the aunts for the second time and re-primed them in their very simple rôles as arsonists. He had decided that rather than tell the Prunesquallors that he was going out for a stroll he would say instead that he was paying a visit to the aunts, and then with them to prove his alibi (for somehow or other they must be got to and from the library without the knowledge of their short-legged servant); their story and that of the Doctor's would coincide.

He had made them repeat a dozen or so times: 'We've been indoors *all* the time. We've been indoors *all* the time,' until they were themselves as convinced of it as though they were reliving the Future!

THE GROTTO

IT happened on the day of Steerpike's second daylight visit to the Library. He was on his return journey and had reached the edge of the pine woods and was awaiting an opportunity to run unobserved across the open ground, when, away to his left, he saw a figure moving in the direction of Gormenghast Mountain.

The invigorating air, coupled with his recognition of the distant figure, prompted him to change his course, and with quick, birdlike steps he moved rapidly along the edge of the wood. In the rough landscape away to his left, the tiny figure in its crimson dress sang out against the sombre background like a ruby on a slate. The midsummer sun, and how much less this autumn light, had no power to mitigate the dreary character of the region that surrounded Gormenghast. It was like a continuation of the castle, rough and shadowy, and though vast and often windswept, oppressive too, with a kind of raw weight.

Ahead lay Gormenghast Mountain in all its permanence, a sinister thing as though drawn out of the earth by sorcery as a curse on all who viewed it. Although its base appeared to struggle from a blanket of trees within a few miles of the castle, it was in reality a day's journey on horseback. Clouds were generally to be seen clustering about its summit even on the finest days when the sky was elsewhere empty, and it was common to see the storms raging across its heights and the sheets of dark rain slanting mistily over the blurred crown and obscuring half the mountain's hideous body, while, at the same time, sunlight was playing across the landscape all about it and even on its own lower slopes. Today, however, not even a single cloud hung above the peak, and when Fuchsia had looked out of her bedroom window after her midday meal she had stared at the Mountain and said: 'Where are the clouds?'

'What clouds?' said the old nurse, who was standing behind her, rocking Titus in her arms. 'What is it, my caution?'

'There's nearly always clouds on top of the Mountain,' said Fuchsia.

'Aren't there any, dear?' 'No,' said Fuchsia. 'Why aren't there?'

Fuchsia realized that Mrs Slagg knew virtually nothing, but the long custom of asking her questions was a hard one to break down. This realization that grown-ups did not necessarily know any more than children was something against which she had fought. She wanted Mrs Slagg to remain the wise recipient of all her troubles and the comforter that she had always seemed, but Fuchsia was growing up and she was now realizing how weak and ineffectual was her old guardian. Not that she was losing her loyalty or affection. She would have defended the wrinkled midget to her last breath if necessary; but she was isolated within herself with no one to whom she could run with that unquestioning confidence – that outpouring of her newest enthusiasms – her sudden terrors – her projects – her stories.

'I think I'll go out', she said, 'for a walk.'

'Again?' said Mrs Slagg, stopping for a moment the rocking of her arms. 'You go out such a lot now, don't you? Why are you always going away from me?'

'It's not from you,' said Fuchsia; 'it's because I want to walk and think. It isn't going away from you. You know it isn't.'

'I don't know anything,' said Nannie Slagg, her face puckered up, 'But I know you never went out all the summer, did you dear? And now that it is so tempersome and cold you are always going out into the nastiness and getting wet or frozen every day. Oh, my poor heart. Why? Why every day?'

Fuchsia pushed her hands into the depths of the big pockets of her red dress.

It was true she had deserted her attic for the dreary moors and the rocky tracts of country about Gormenghast. Why was this? Had she suddenly outgrown her attic that had once been all in all to her? Oh no; she had not outgrown it, but something had changed ever since that dreadful night when she saw Steerpike lying by the window in the darkness. It was no longer inviolate

– secret – mysterious. It was no longer another world, but a part of the castle. Its magnetism had weakened – its silent, shadowy drama had died and she could no longer bear to revisit it. When last she had ventured up the spiral stairs and entered the musty and familiar atmosphere, Fuchsia had experienced a pang of such sharp nostalgia for what it had once been to her that she had turned from the swaying motes that filled the air and the shadowy shapes of all that she had known as her friends; the cobwebbed organ, the crazy avenue of a hundred loves – turned away, and stumbled down the dark staircase with a sense of such desolation as seemed would never lift. Her eyes grew dim as she remembered these things; her hands clenched in her deep pockets.

'Yes,' she said, 'I have been out a lot. Do you get lonely? If you do, you needn't, because you know I love you, don't you? You *know* that, don't you?

She thrust her lower lip forward and frowned at Mrs Slagg, but this was only to keep her tears back, for nowadays Fuchsia had so lonely a feeling that tears were never far distant. Never having had either positive cruelty or kindness shown to her by her parents, but only an indifference, she was not conscious of what it was that she missed – affection.

It had always been so and she had compensated herself by weaving stories of her own Future, or by lavishing her own love upon such things as the objects in her attics, or more recently upon what she found or saw among the woods and wastelands.

'You know that, don't you?' Fuchsia repeated.

Nannie rocked Titus more vigorously than was necessary and by the pursing of her lips indicated that his Lordship was asleep and that she was speaking too loudly.

Then Fuchsia came up to her old nurse and stared at her brother. The feeling of aversion for him had disappeared, and though as yet the lilac-eyed creature had not affected her with any sensation of sisterly love, nevertheless she had got used to his presence in the Castle and would sometimes play with him solemnly for half an hour or so at a time.

Nannie's eyes followed Fuchsia's.

'His little Lordship,' she said, wagging her head, 'it's his little Lordship.'

'Why do you love him?'

'Why do I love him! oh, my poor, weak heart! Why do I love him, stupid? How could you say such a thing?' cried Nannie Slagg. 'Oh my little Lordship *thing*. How could I *help* it – the innocent notion that he is! The very next of Gormenghast, aren't you, my only? The very next of all. What did your cruel sister say, then, what did she say?

'He must go to his cot now, for his sleep, he must, and to dream his golden dreams.'

'Did you talk to me like that when I was a baby,' asked Fuchsia.

'Of course I did,' said Mrs Slagg. 'Don't be silly. Oh, the ignorance of you! Are you going to tidy your room for me now?'

She hobbled to the door with her precious bundle. Every day she asked this same question, but never waited for an answer, knowing that whatever it was, it was *she* who would have to make some sort of order out of the chaos.

Fuchsia again turned to the window and stared at the Mountain whose shape down to the least outcrop had long since scored its outline in her mind.

Between the castle and Gormenghast Mountain the land was desolate, for the main part empty wasteland, with large areas of swamp where undisturbed among the reedy tracts the waders moved. Curlews and peewits sent their thin cries along the wind. Moorhens reared their young and paddled blackly in and out of the rushes. To the east of Gormenghast Mountain, but detached from the trees at its base, spread the undulating darkness of the Twisted Woods. To the west the unkempt acres, broken here and there with low stunted trees bent by the winds into the shape of hunchbacks.

Between this dreary province and the pine wood that surrounded the West Wing of the castle, a dark, shelving plateau rose to a height of about a hundred to two hundred feet – an irregular tableland of greeny-black rock, broken and scarred and empty. It was beyond these cold escarpments that the river wound its way about the base of the Mountain and fed the swamps where the wild fowl lived.

Fuchsia could see three short stretches of the river from her window. This afternoon the central portion and that to its right were black with the reflection of the Mountain, and the third, away to the west beyond the rocky plateau, was a shadowy white strip that neither glanced nor sparkled, but, mirroring the opaque sky, lay lifeless and inert, like a dead arm.

Fuchsia left the window abruptly and closing the door after her with a crash, ran all the way down the stairs, almost falling as she slipped clumsily on the last flight, before threading a maze of corridors to emerge panting in the chilly sunlight.

Breathing in the sharp air she gulped and clenched her hands together until her nails bit at her palms. Then she began to walk. She had been walking for over an hour when she heard footsteps behind her and, turning, saw Steerpike. She had not seen him since the night at the Prunesquallors' and never as clearly as now, as he approached her through the naked autumn. He stopped when he noticed that he was observed and called:

'Lady Fuchsia! May I join you?'

Behind him she saw something which by contrast with the alien, incalculable figure before her, was close and real. It was something which she understood, something which she could never do without, or be without, for it seemed as though it were her own self, her own body, at which she gazed and which lay so intimately upon the skyline. Gormenghast. The long, notched outline of her home. It was now his background. It was a screen of walls and towers pocked with windows. He stood against it, an intruder, imposing himself so vividly, so solidly, against her world, his head overtopping the loftiest of its towers.

'What do you want?' she said.

A breeze had lifted from beyond the Twisted Woods and her dress was blown across her so that down her right side it clung to her showing the strength of her young body and thighs.

'Lady Fuchsia!' shouted Steerpike across the strengthening wind. 'I'll tell you.' He took a few quick paces towards her and reached the sloping rock on which she stood. 'I want you to explain this region to me – the marshes and Gormenghast Mountain. Nobody has ever told me about it. You know the country – you understand it,' (he filled his lungs again) 'and though I love the district I'm very ignorant.' He had almost reached her. 'Can I share your walks, occasionally? Would you consider the idea? Are you returning?' Fuchsia had moved away. 'If so, may I accompany you back?'

'That's not what you've come to ask me,' said Fuchsia slowly. She was beginning to shake in the cold wind.

'Yes, it is,' said Steerpike, 'it is just what I've come to ask you. And whether you will tell me about Nature.'

'I don't know anything about Nature,' said Fuchsia, beginning to walk down the sloping rock. 'I don't understand it. I only look at it. Who told you I knew about it? Who makes up these things?'

'No one,' said Steerpike. 'I thought you must know and understand what you love so much. I've seen you very often returning to the castle laden with the things you have discovered. And also, you *look* as though you understand.'

'I *do*?' said Fuchsia, surprised. 'No, I can't do. I don't understand wise things at all.'

'Your knowledge is intuitive,' said the youth. 'You have no need of book learning and such like. You only have to gaze at a thing to *know* it. The wind is getting stronger, your Ladyship, and colder. We had better return.'

Steerpike turned up his high collar, and gaining her permission to accompany her back to the castle, he began with her the descent of the grey rocks. Before they were halfway down, the rain was falling and the autumn sunlight had given way to a fast, tattered sky.

'Tread carefully, Lady Fuchsia,' said Steerpike suddenly; and Fuchsia stopped and stared quickly over her shoulder at him as though she had forgotten he was there. She opened her mouth as though to speak when a far rattle of thunder reverberated among the rocks and she turned her head to the sky. A black cloud was approaching and from its pendulous body the rain fell in a mass of darkness.

Soon it would be above them and Fuchsia's thoughts leapt backwards through the years to a certain afternoon when, as today, she had been caught in a sudden rainstorm. She had been with her mother on one of those rare occasions, still rarer now, when the Countess for some reason or other decided to take her daughter for a walk. Those occasional outings had been silent affairs, and Fuchsia could remember how she had longed to be free of the presence that moved at her side and above her, and yet she recalled how she had envied her huge mother when the wild birds came to her at her long, shrill, sweet whistle and settled upon her head and arms and shoulders. But what she chiefly remembered was how, on that day, when the storm broke above them, her mother instead of turning back to the castle, continued onwards towards these same layers of dark rock which she and Steerpike were now descending. Her mother had turned down a rough, narrow gully and had disappeared behind a high slab of dislodged stone that was leaning against a face of rock. Fuchsia had followed. But instead of finding her mother sheltering from the downpour against the cliff and behind the slab, to her surprise she found herself confronted with the entrance to a grotto. She had peered inside, and there, deep in its chilly throat, was her mother sitting upon the ground and leaning against the sloping wall, very still and silent and enormous.

They had waited there until the storm had tired of its own anger and a slow rain descended like remorse from the sky. No word had passed between them, and Fuchsia, as she remembered the grotto, felt a shiver run through her body. But she turned to Steerpike. 'Follow me, if you want to,' she said. 'I know a cave.'

The rain was by now thronging across the escarpment, and she began to run over the slippery grey rock surfaces with Steerpike at her heels.

As she began the short, steep descent she turned for an instant to see whether Steerpike had kept pace with her, and as she turned, her feet slipped away from under her on the slithery surface of an oblique slab, and she came crashing to the ground, striking the side of her face, her shoulders and shin with a force that for the moment stunned her. But only for a moment. As she made an effort to rise and felt the pain growing at her cheekbone, Steerpike was beside her. He had been some twelve yards away as she fell, but he slithered like a snake among the rocks and was kneeling beside her almost immediately. He saw at once that the wound upon her face was superficial. He felt her shoulder and shinbone with his thin fingers and found them sound. He removed his cape, covered her and glanced down the gully. The rain swam over his face and thrashed on the rocks. At the base of the steep decline he could see, looming vaguely through the downpour, a huge propped rock, and he guessed that it was towards this that Fuchsia had been running, for the gully ended within forty feet in a high, unscalable wall of granite.

Fuchsia was trying to sit up, but the pain in her shoulder had drained her of strength.

'Lie still!' shouted Steerpike through the screen of rain that divided them. Then he pointed to the propped rock.

'Is that where we were going?' he asked.

'There's a cave behind it,' she whispered. 'Help me up. I can get there all right.'

'Oh no,' said Steerpike. He knelt down beside her, and then with great care he lifted her inch by inch from the rocks. His wiry muscles toughened in his slim arms, and along his spine, as by degrees he raised her to the level of his chest, getting to his feet as he did so. Then, step by tentative step over the splashing boulders he approached the cave. A hundred rain-thrashed pools had collected among the rocks.

Fuchsia had made no remonstrance, knowing that she could never have made this difficult descent; but as she felt his arms around her and the proximity of his body, something deep within her tried to hide itself. Through the thick, tousled strands of her drenched hair she could see his sharp, pale, crafty face, his powerful dark-red eyes focused upon the rocks below them, his high protruding forehead, his cheekbones glistening, his mouth an emotionless line.

This was Steerpike. He was holding her; she was in his arms; in his power. His hard arms and fingers were taking the weight at her thighs and shoulders. She could feel his muscles like bars of metal. This was the figure whom she had found in her attic, and who had climbed up the sheer and enormous wall. He had said that he had found a stone sky-field. He had said that she understood Nature. He wanted to learn from her. How could he with his wonderful long sentences learn anything from her? She must be careful. He was clever. But there was nothing wrong in being clever. Dr Prune was clever and she liked him. She wished she was clever herself.

He was edging between the wall of rock and the slanting slab, and suddenly they were in the dim light of the grotto. The floor was dry and the thunder of the rain beyond the entrance seemed to come from another world.

Steerpike lowered her carefully to the ground and propped her against a flat, slanting portion of the wall. Then he pulled off his shirt and began, after wringing as much moisture from it as he could, to tear it into long narrow pieces. She watched him, fascinated in spite of the pain she was suffering. It was like watching someone from another world who was worked by another kind of machinery, by something smoother, colder, harder, swifter. Her heart rebelled against the bloodlessness of his precision, but she had begun to watch him with a grudging admiration for a quality so alien to her own temperament.

The grotto was about fifteen feet in depth, the roof dipping to the earth, so that in only the first nine feet from the entrance was it possible to stand upright. Close to the arching roof, areas of the rock-face were broken and fretted into dim convolutions of stone, and a fanciful eye could with a little difficulty beguile any length of time by finding among the inter-woven patterns an inexhaustible army of ghoulish or seraphic heads according to the temper of the moment.

The recesses of the grotto were in deep darkness, but it was easy enough for Fuchsia and Steerpike to see each other in the dull light near the shielded entrance.

Steerpike had torn his shirt into neat strips and had knelt down beside Fuchsia and bandaged her head and staunched the bleeding which, especially from her leg, where the injury was not so deep, was difficult to check. Her upper arm was less easy, and it was necessary for her to allow Steerpike to bare her shoulder before he could wash it clean.

She watched him as he carefully dabbed the wound. The sudden pain and shock had changed to a raw aching and she bit her lip to stop her tears. In the half light she saw his eyes smouldering in the shadowy whiteness of his face. Above the waist he was naked. What was it that made his shoulders look deformed? They were high, but were sound, though like the rest of his body, strangely taut and contracted. His chest was narrow and firm.

He removed a swab of cloth from her shoulder slowly and peered to see whether the blood would continue to flow.

'Keep still,' he said. 'Keep your arm as still as you can. How's the pain?'

'I'm all right,' said Fuchsia.

'Don't be heroic,' he said, sitting back on his heels. 'We're not playing a game. I want to know *exactly* how much you're in pain – not whether you are brave or not. I know that already. Which hurts you most?'

'My leg,' said Fuchsia. 'It makes me want to be ill. And I'm cold. Now you know.'

Their eyes met in the half light.

Steerpike straightened himself. 'I'm going to leave you,' he said. 'Otherwise the cold will gnaw you to bits. I can't get you back to the castle alone. I'll fetch the Prune and a stretcher. You'll be all right here. I'll go now, at once. We'll be back within half an hour. I can move when I want to.'

'Steerpike,' said Fuchsia.

He knelt down at once. 'What is it?' he said, speaking very softly.

'You've done quite a lot to help,' she said.

'Nothing much,' he replied. His hand was close to hers.

The silence which followed became ludicrous and he got to his feet.

'Mustn't stay.' He had sensed the beginning of something less frigid. He would leave things as they were. 'You'll be shaking like a leaf if I don't hurry. Keep absolutely still.'

He laid his coat over her and then walked the few paces to the opening.

Fuchsia watched his hunched yet slender outline as he stood for a moment before plunging into the rain-swept gully. Then he had gone, and she remained quite still, as he had told her, and listened to the pounding of the rain.

Steerpike's boast as to his fleetness was not an idle one. With incredible agility he leapt from boulder to boulder until he had reached the head of the gully and from there, down the long slopes of the escarpment, he sped like a Dervish. But he was not reckless. Every one of his steps was a calculated result of a decision taken at a swifter speed than his feet could travel.

At length the rocks were left behind and the castle emerged through a dull blanket.

His entrance into the Prunesquallors' was dramatic. Irma, who had never before seen any male skin other than that which protrudes beyond the collar and the cuffs, gave a piercing cry and fell into her brother's arms only to recover at once and to dash from the room in a typhoon of black silk. Prunesquallor and Steerpike could hear the stair rods rattling as she whirled her way up the staircase and the crashing of her bedroom door set the pictures swaying on the walls of all the downstairs rooms.

Dr Prunesquallor had circled around Steerpike with his head drawn back so that his cervical vertebrae rested against the rear wall of his high collar, and a plumbless abysm yawned between his Adam's apple and his pearl stud. With his head bridled backwards thus, somewhat in the position of a cobra about to strike, and with his eyebrows raised quizzically, he was yet able at the same time to flash both tiers of his startling teeth which caught and reflected the lamplight with an unnatural brilliancy.

He was in an ecstasy of astonishment. The spectacle of a half-nude, dripping Steerpike both repelled and delighted him. Every now and again Steerpike and the Doctor could hear an extraordinary moaning from the floor above.

When, however, the Doctor heard the cause of the boy's appearance, he was at once on the move. It had not taken

Steerpike long to explain what had happened. Within a few moments the Doctor had packed up a small bag and rung for the cook to fetch both a stretcher and a couple of young men as bearers.

Meanwhile, Steerpike had dived into another suit and run across to Mrs Slagg in the castle, whom he instructed to replenish the fire and to have Fuchsia's bed ready and some hot drink brewing, leaving her in a state of querulous collapse, which was not remedied by his tickling her rudely in the ribs as he skipped past her to the door.

Coming into the quadrangle he caught sight of the Doctor as he was emerging from his garden gate with the two men and the stretcher. Prunesquallor was holding his umbrella over a bundle of rugs under which he had placed his medical bag.

When he had caught them up, he gave them their directions saying that he would run on ahead, but would reappear on the escarpment to direct them in the final stage of their journey. Tucking one of the blankets under his cape he disappeared into the thinning rain. As he ran on alone, he made jumps into the air. Life was amusing. So amusing. Even the rain had played into his hand and made the rock slippery. Everything, he thought to himself, can be of use. Everything. And he clicked his fingers as he ran grinning through the rain.

•

When Fuchsia awoke in her bed and saw the firelight flickering on the ceiling and Nannie Slagg sitting beside her, she said:
'Where is Steerpike?'
'Who, my precious? Oh, my poor pretty one!' And Mrs Slagg fidgeted with Fuchsia's hand which she had been holding for over an hour. 'What is it you need, my only? What is it, my caution dear? Oh, my poor heart, you've nearly killed me, dear. Very nearly. Yes, very nearly, then. There, there. Stay still, and the Doctor will be here again soon. Oh, my poor, weak heart!' The tears were streaming down her little, old terrified face.
'Nannie,' said Fuchsia, 'where's Steerpike?'
'That horrid boy?' asked Nannie. 'What about him, precious?

You don't want to see him, do you? Oh no, you couldn't want that boy. What is it, my only? Do you want to see him?'

'Oh, no! no!' said Fuchsia. 'I don't want to. I feel so tired. Are you there?'

'What is it, my only?'

'Nothing; nothing. I wonder where he is.'

KNIVES IN THE MOON

THE moon slid inexorably into its zenith, the shadows shrivelling to the feet of all that cast them, and as Rantel approached the hollow at the hem of the Twisted Woods he was treading in a pool of his own midnight.

The roof of the Twisted Woods reflected the staring circle in a phosphorescent network of branches that undulated to the lower slopes of Gormenghast Mountain. Rising from the ground and circumscribing this baleful canopy the wood was walled with impenetrable shadow. Nothing of what supported the chilly haze of the topmost branches was discernible – only a winding façade of blackness.

The crags of the mountain were ruthless in the moon; cold deadly, and shining. Distance had no meaning. The tangled glittering of the forest roof rolled away, but its furthermost reaches were brought suddenly nearer in a bound by the terrifying effect of proximity in the mountain that they swarmed. The mountain was neither far away nor was it close at hand. It arose starkly, enormously, across the lens of the eye. The hollow itself was a cup of light. Every blade of the grass was of consequence, and the few scattered stones held an authority that made their solid, separate marks upon the brain – each one with its own unduplicated shape: each rising brightly from the ink of its own spilling.

When Rantel had come to the verge of the chosen hollow he stood still. His head and body were a mosaic of black and ghastly silver as he gazed into the basin of grass below him. His cloak was drawn tightly about his spare body and the rhythmic

folds of the drapery held the moonlight along their upper ridges. He was sculpted, but his head moved suddenly at a sound, and lifting his eyes he saw Braigon arise from beyond the rim across the hollow.

They descended together, and when they had come to the level ground they unfastened their cloaks, removed their heavy shoes and stripped themselves naked. Rantel flung his clothes away to the sloping grass Braigon folded his coarse garments and laid them across a boulder. He saw that Rantel was feeling the edge of his blade which danced in the moonlight like a splinter of glass.

They said nothing. They tested the slippery grass with their naked feet.

Then they turned to one another. Braigon eased his fingers around the short bone hilt. Neither could see the expression in the other's face for their features were lost in the shadows of their brows and only their tangled hair held the light. They crouched and began to move, the distance closing between them, the muscles winding across their backs.

With Keda for hearts' reason, they circled, they closed, they feinted, their blades parrying the thrusts of the knife by sudden cross movements of their forearms.

When Rantel carved it was onslaught. It was as though the wood were his enemy. He fought it with rasp and chisel, hacking its flesh away until the shape that he held in his mind began to surrender to his violence. It was in this way that he fought. Body and brain were fused into one impulse – to kill the man who crouched before him. Not even Keda was in his mind now.

His eyes embraced the slightest movement of the other's body, of his moving feet, of his leaping knife. He saw that around Braigon's left arm a line of blood was winding from a gash in the shoulder. Rantel had the longer reach, but swiftly as his knife shot forward to the throat or breast, Braigon's forearm would swing across behind it and smack his arm away from its target. Then at the impact Rantel would spin out of range, and again they would circle and close in upon one another, their shoulders and arms gleaming in the unearthly brilliance.

As Braigon fought he wondered where Keda was. He wondered whether there could ever be happiness for her after himself or Rantel had been killed; whether she could forget that she was the wife of a murderer: whether to fight were not to escape from some limpid truth. Keda came vividly before his eyes, and yet his body worked with mechanical brilliance, warding off the savage blade and attacking his assailant with a series of quick thrusts, drawing blood from Rantel's side.

As the figure moved before him he followed the muscles as

they wove beneath the skin. He was not only fighting with an assailant who was awaiting for that split second in which to strike him dead, but he was stabbing at a masterpiece – at sculpture that leapt and heaved, at a marvel of inky shadow and silver light. A great wave of nausea surged through him and his knife felt putrid in his hand. His body went on fighting.

The grass was blotched with the impression of their feet. They had scattered and crushed the dew and a dark irregular patch filled the centre of the hollow showing where their game with death had led them. Even this bruised darkness of crushed grass was pale in comparison with the intensity of their shadows which, moving as they moved, sliding beneath them, springing when they sprang, were never still.

Their hair was sticking to the sweat on their brows. The wounds in their bodies were weakening them, but neither could afford to pause.

About them the stillness of the pale night was complete. The moonlight lay like rime along the ridges of the distant castle. The reedy marshlands far to the east lay inert – a region of gauze. Their bodies were raddled now with the blood from many wounds. The merciless light gleamed on the wet, warm streams that slid ceaselessly over their tired flesh. A haze of ghostly weakness was filling their nakedness and they were fighting like characters in a dream.

●

Keda's trance had fallen from her in a sudden brutal moment and she had started to run towards the Twisted Woods. Through the great phosphorescent night, cloakless, her hair unfastening as she climbed, she came at last to the incline that led to the lip of the hollow. Her pain mounted as she ran. The strange, unworldly strength had died in her, the glory was gone – only an agony of fear was with her now.

As she climbed to the ridge of the hollow she could hear – so small a sound in the enormous night – the panting of the men, and her heart for a moment lifted, for they were alive.

With a bound she reached the brow of the slope and saw

them crouching and moving in moonlight below her. The cry in her throat was choked as she saw the blood upon them, and she sank to her knees.

Braigon had seen her and his tired arms rang with a sudden strength. With a flash of his left arm he whirled Rantel's daggered hand away, and springing after him as swiftly as though he were a part of his foe, he plunged his knife into the shadowy breast.

As he struck he withdrew the dagger, and as Rantel sank to the ground, Braigon flung his weapon away.

He did not turn to Keda. He stood motionless, his hands at his head. Keda could feel no grief. The corners of her mouth lifted. The time for horror was not yet. This was not *real* – yet. She saw Rantel raise himself upon his left arm. He groped for his dagger and felt it beside him in the dew. His life was pouring from the wound in his breast. Keda watched him as, summoning into his right arm what strength remained in his whole body, he sent the dagger running through the air with a sudden awkward movement of his arm. It found its mark in a statue's throat. Braigon's arms fell to his sides like dead weights. He tottered forward, swayed for a little, the bone hilt at his gullet, and then collapsed lifeless across the body of his destroyer.

'THE SUN GOES DOWN AGAIN'

'EQUALITY', said Steerpike, 'is the thing. It is the only true and central premise from which constructive ideas can radiate freely and be operated without prejudice. Absolute equality of status. Equality of wealth. Equality of power.'

He tapped at a stone that lay among the wet leaves with his swordstick and sent it scurrying through the undergrowth.

He had waylaid Fuchsia with a great show of surprise in the pine woods as she was returning from an evening among the trees. It was the last evening before the fateful day of the burning. There would be no time tomorrow for any dallying of this kind. His plans were laid and the details completed. The

Twins were rehearsed in their rôles and Steerpike was reasonably satisfied that he could rely on them. This evening, after having enjoyed a long bath at the Prunesquallors', he had spent more time than usual dressing himself. He had plastered his sparse tow-coloured hair over his bulging forehead with unusual care, viewing himself as he did so from every angle in the three mirrors he had erected on a table by the window.

As he left the house, he spun the slim swordstick through his fingers. It circled in his hand like the spokes of a wheel. Should he, or should he not pay a quick call on the Twins? On the one hand he must not excite them, for it was as though they had been primed for an examination and might suddenly forget everything they had been taught. On the other hand, if he made no direct reference to tomorrow's enterprise but encouraged them obliquely it might keep them going through the night. It was essential that they should have a good night's sleep. He did not want them sitting bolt upright on the edge of their beds all night staring at each other, with their eyes and mouths wide open.

He decided to pay a very short visit and then to take a stroll to the woods, where he thought he might find Fuchsia, for she had made a habit of lying for hours beneath a certain pine in what she fondly imagined was a secret glade.

Steerpike decided he would see them for a few moments, and at once he moved rapidly across the quadrangle. A fitful light was breaking through the clouds, and the arches circumscribing the quadrangle cast pale shadows that weakened or intensified as the clouds stole across the sun. Steerpike shuddered as he entered the sunless castle.

When he came to the door of the aunts' apartments he knocked, and entered at once. There was a fire burning in the grate and he walked towards it, noticing as he did so the twin heads of Cora and Clarice twisted on their long powdered necks. Their eyes were staring at him over the embroidered back of their couch, which had been pulled up to the fire. They followed him with their heads, their necks unwinding as he took up a position before them with his back to the fire, his legs astride, his hands behind him.

'My dears,' he said, fixing them in turn with his magnetic eyes; 'my *dears*, how are you? But what need is there to ask? You both look radiant. Lady Clarice, I have seldom seen you look lovelier; and your sister refuses to let you have it all your own way. You refuse utterly, Lady Cora, don't you? You are about as bridal as I ever remember you. It is a delight to be with you again.' The twins stared at him and wriggled, but no expression appeared in their faces.

After a long silence during which Steerpike had been warming his hands at the blaze Cora said, 'Do you mean that I'm glorious?'

'That's not what he said,' came Clarice's flat voice.

'Glorious', said Steerpike, 'is a dictionary word. We are all imprisoned by the dictionary. We choose out of that vast, paper-walled prison our convicts, the little black printed words, when in truth we need fresh sounds to utter, new enfranchised noises which would produce a new effect. In dead and shackled language, my dears, you *are* glorious, but oh, to give vent to a brand new sound that might convince you of what I really think of you, as you sit there in your purple splendour, side by side! But no, it is impossible. Life is too fleet for onomatopoeia. Dead words defy me. I can make no sound, dear ladies, that is apt.'

'You could try,' said Clarice. 'We aren't busy.'

She smoothed the shining fabric of her dress with her long, lifeless fingers.

'Impossible,' replied the youth, rubbing his chin. 'Quite impossible. Only believe in my admiration for your beauty that will one day be recognized by the whole castle. Meanwhile, preserve all dignity and silent power in your twin bosoms.'

'Yes, yes,' said Cora, 'we'll preserve it. We'll preserve it in our bosoms, won't we, Clarice? Our silent power.'

'Yes, all the power we've got,' said Clarice. 'But we haven't got much.'

'It is coming to you,' said Steerpike. 'It is on its way. You are of the blood; who else but you should wield the sceptre? But alone you cannot succeed. For years you have smarted from the insults you have been forced to endure. Ah, how patiently, you have smarted! How patiently! Those days have gone. Who is it that can help you?' He took a pace towards them and bent forward. 'Who is it that can restore you: and who will set you on your glittering thrones?'

The aunts put their arms about one another so that their faces were cheek to cheek, and from this doublehead they gazed up at Steerpike with a row of four equidistant eyes. There was no reason why there should not have been forty, or four hundred of them. It so happened that only four had been removed from a dead and endless frieze whose inexhaustible and repetitive theme was forever, eyes, eyes, eyes.

'Stand up,' said Steerpike. He had raised his voice.

They got to their feet awkwardly and stood before him evil. A sense of power filled Steerpike with an acute enjoyment.

'Take a step forward,' he said.

They did so, still holding one another.

Steerpike watched them for some time, his shoulders hunched against the mantelpiece. 'You heard me speak,' he said. 'You heard my question. Who is it that will raise you to your thrones?'

'Thrones,' said Cora in a whisper; 'our thrones.'

'Golden ones,' said Clarice. 'That is what we want.'

'That is what you shall have. Golden thrones for Lady Cora and Lady Clarice. Who will give them to you?'

He stretched forward his hands and, holding each of them firmly by an elbow, brought them forward in one piece to within a foot of himself. He had never gone so far before, but he could see that they were clay in his hands and the familiarity was safe. The dreadful proximity of the identical faces caused him to draw his own head back.

'Who will give you the thrones, the glory and the power?' he said. 'Who?'

Their mouths opened together. 'You,' they said. 'It's *you* who'll give them to us. Steerpike will give them to us.'

Then Clarice craned her head forward from beside her sister's and she whispered as though she were telling Steerpike a secret for the first time.

'We're burning Sepulchrave's books up,' she said, 'the whole of his silly library. We're doing it – Cora and I. Everything is ready.'

'Yes,' said Steerpike. 'Everything is ready.'

Clarice's head regained its normal position immediately above her neck, where it balanced itself, a dead thing, on a column, but Cora's came forward as though to take the place of its counterpart and to keep the machinery working. In the same flat whisper she continued from where her sister had left off:

'All we do is to do what we've been told to do.' Her head came forward another two inches. 'There isn't anything difficult. It's easy to do. We go to the big door and then we find two little pieces of cloth sticking through from the inside, and then –'

'We set them on fire!' broke in her sister in so loud a voice that Steerpike closed his eyes. Then with a profound emptiness: 'We'll do it *now*,' said Clarice. 'It's easy.'

'Now?' said Steerpike. 'Oh no, not now. We decided it should be tomorrow, didn't we? Tomorrow evening.'

'I want to do it *now*,' said Clarice. 'Don't you, Cora?'

'No,' said Cora.

Clarice bit solemnly at her knuckles. 'You're frightened,' she said; 'frightened of a little bit of fire. You ought to have more pride than that, Cora. I have, although I'm gently manured.'

'Mannered, you mean,' said her sister. 'You *stupid*. How ignorant you are. With our blood, too. I am ashamed of our likenesses and always will be, so *there*!'

Steerpike brushed an elegant green vase from the mantel with his elbow, which had the effect he had anticipated. The four eyes moved towards the fragments on the floor – the thread of their dialogue was as shattered as the vase.

'A sign!' he muttered in a low, vibrant voice. 'A portent! A symbol! The circle is complete. An angel has spoken.'

The twins stared open-mouthed.

'Do you see the broken porcelain, dear ladies?' he said. 'Do you *see* it?'

They nodded.

'What else is that but the *Régime*, broken for ever – the bullydom of Gertrude – the stony heart of Sepulchrave – the ignorance, malice and brutality of the House of Groan as it now stands – smashed for ever? It is a signal that your hour is at hand. Give praise, my dears; you shall come unto your splendour.'

'When?' said Cora. 'Will it be soon?'

'What about tonight?' said Clarice. She raised her flat voice to its second floor, where there was more ventilation. 'What about tonight?'

'There is a little matter to be settled first,' said Steerpike. 'One little job to be done. Very simple; very, very simple; but it needs clever people to do it.' He struck a match.

In the four lenses of the four flat eyes, the four reflections of a single flame, danced – danced.

'Fire!' they said. 'We know all about it. All, all, all.'

'Oh, then, to bed,' said the youth, speaking rapidly. 'To bed, to bed, to bed.'

Clarice lifted a limp hand like a slab of putty to her breast and scratched herself abstractedly. 'All right,' she said. 'Good night.' And as she moved towards the bedroom door she began to unfasten her dress.

'I'm going too,' said Cora. 'Good night.' She also, as she retired, could be seen unclasping and unhooking herself. Before the door closed behind her she was half unravelled of imperial purple.

Steerpike filled his pocket with nuts from a china bowl and letting himself out of the room began the descent to the quadrangle. He had had no intention of broaching the subject of the burning, but the aunts had happily proved less excitable than he had anticipated and his confidence in their playing their elementary rôles effectively on the following evening was strengthened.

As he descended the stone stairs he filled his pipe, and on coming into the mild evening light, his tobacco smouldering in the bowl, he felt in an amiable mood, and spinning his swordstick he made for the pine woods, humming to himself as he went.

He had found Fuchsia, and had built up some kind of conversation, although he always found it more difficult to speak to her than to anyone else. First he inquired with a certain sincerity whether she had recovered from the shock. Her cheek was inflamed, and she limped badly from the severe pain in her leg. The Doctor had bandaged her up carefully and had left instructions with Nannie that she must not go out for several days, but she had slipped away when her nurse was out of the room, leaving a scribble on the wall to the effect that she loved her; but as the creature never looked at the wall the message was abortive.

By the time they had come to the edge of the woods Steerpike was talking airily of any subject that came into his head, mainly for the purpose of building up in her mind a picture of himself as someone profoundly brilliant, but also for the enjoyment of talking for its own sake, for he was in a sprightly mood.

She limped beside him as they passed through the outermost trees and into the light of the sinking sun. Steerpike paused to remove a stag-beetle from where it clung to the soft bark of a pine.

Fuchsia went on slowly, wishing she were alone.

'There should be no rich, no poor, no strong, no weak,' said Steerpike, methodically pulling the legs off the stag-beetle, one by one, as he spoke. 'Equality is the great thing, equality is *everything*.' He flung the mutilated insect away. 'Do you agree, Lady Fuchsia?' he said.

'I don't know anything about it, and I don't care much,' said Fuchsia.

'But don't you think it's wrong if some people have nothing to eat and others have so much they throw most of it away? Don't you think it's wrong if some people have to work all their lives for a little money to exist on while others never do any work and live in luxury? Don't you think brave men should be recognized and rewarded, and not just treated the same as cowards? The men who climb mountains, or dive under the sea, or explore jungles full of fever, or save people from fires?'

'I don't know,' said Fuchsia again. 'Things ought to be fair, I suppose. But I don't know anything about it.'

'Yes, you do,' said Steerpike. 'When you say "Things ought to be fair" it is exactly what I mean. Things *ought* to be fair. Why aren't they fair? Because of greed and cruelty and lust for power. All that sort of thing must be stopped.'

'Well, why don't you stop it, then?' said Fuchsia in a distant voice. She was watching the sun's blood on the Tower of Flints, and a cloud like a drenched swab, descending, inch by inch, behind the blackening tower.

'I am going to,' said Steerpike with such an air of simple confidence that Fuchsia turned her eyes to him.

'You're going to stop cruelty?' she asked. 'And greediness, and all those things? I don't think you could. You're very clever, but, oh no, you couldn't do anything like that.'

Steerpike was taken aback for a moment by this reply. He had meant his remark to stand on its own – a limpid statement of fact – something that he imagined Fuchsia might often turn over in her mind and cogitate upon.

'It's nearly gone,' said Fuchsia as Steerpike was wondering how to reassert himself. 'Nearly gone.'

'What's nearly gone?' He followed her eyes to where the circle of the sun was notched with turrets. 'Oh, you mean the old treacle bun,' he said. 'Yes, it will get cold very quickly now.'

'Treacle bun?' said Fuchsia. 'Is that what you call it?' She stopped walking. 'I don't think you ought to call it that. It's not respectful.' She gazed. As the death-throes weakened in the sky, she watched with big, perplexed eyes. Then she smiled for the first time. 'Do you give names to other things like that?'

'Sometimes,' said Steerpike. 'I have a disrespectful nature.'

'Do you give people names?'

'I have done.'

'Have you got one for me?'

Steerpike sucked the end of his swordstick and raised his straw-coloured eyebrows. 'I don't think I have,' he said. 'I usually think of you as Lady Fuchsia.'

'Do you call my mother anything?'

'Your mother? Yes.'

'What do you call my mother?'

'I call her the old Bunch of Rags,' said Steerpike.

Fuchsia's eyes opened wide and she stood still again. 'Go away,' she said.

'That's not very fair,' said Steerpike. 'After all, you *asked* me.'

'What do you call my father, then? But I don't want to know. I think you're cruel,' said Fuchsia breathlessly, 'you who said you'd stop cruelty altogether. Tell me some more names. Are they *all* unkind – and funny?'

'Some other time,' said Steerpike, who had begun to feel chilly. 'The cold won't do your injuries any good. You shouldn't be out walking at all. Prunesquallor thinks you're in bed. He sounded very worried about you.'

They walked on in silence, and by the time they had reached the castle night had descended.

'MEANWHILE'

THE morning of the next day opened drearily, the sun appearing only after protracted periods of half-light, and then only as a pale paper disc, more like the moon than itself, as, for a few moments at a time it floated across some corridor of cloud. Slow, lack-lustre veils descended with almost imperceptible motion over Gormenghast, blurring its countless windows, as with a dripping smoke. The mountain appeared and disappeared a score of times during the morning as the drifts obscured it or lifted from its sides. As the day advanced the gauzes thinned, and it was in the late afternoon that the clouds finally dispersed to leave in their place an expanse of translucence, that stain, chill and secret, in the throat of a lily, a sky so peerless, that as Fuchsia stared into its glacid depths she began unwittingly to break and re-break the flower-stem in her hands.

When she turned her head away it was to find Mrs Slagg watching her with such a piteous expression that Fuchsia put her arms about her old nurse and hugged her less tenderly than was her wish, for she hurt the wrinkled midget as she squeezed.

Nannie gasped for breath, her body bruised from the excess

of Fuchsia's burst of affection, and a gust of temper shook her as she climbed excitedly onto the seat of a chair.

'How *dare* you! How *dare* you!' she gasped at last after shaking and wriggling a miniature fist all around Fuchsia's surprised face. 'How *dare* you bully me and hurt me and crush me into so much pain, you wicked thing, you vicious, naughty thing! *You*, whom I've always done everything for. *You*, whom I washed and brushed and dressed and spoiled and cooked for since you were the size of a slipper. You ... you ...' The old woman began to cry, her body shaking underneath her black dress like some sort of jerking toy. She let go of the rail of the chair, crushed her fists into her tearful, bloodshot eyes, and, forgetting where she was, was about to run to the door, when Fuchsia jumped forward and caught her from falling. Fuchsia carried her to the bed and laid her down.

'Did I hurt you very much?'

Her old nurse, lying on the coverlet like a withered doll in black satin, pursed her lips together and waited until Fuchsia, seating herself on the side of the bed, had placed one of her hands within range. Then her fingers crept forward, inch by inch, over the eiderdown, and with a sudden grimace of concentrated naughtiness she smacked Fuchsia's hand as hard as she was able. Relaxing against the pillow after this puny revenge, she peered at Fuchsia, a triumphant gleam in her watery eyes.

Fuchsia, hardly noticing the malicious little blow, leant over and suffered herself to be hugged for a few moments.

'Now you must start getting dressed,' said Nannie Slagg. 'You must be getting ready for your father's Gathering, mustn't you? It's always one thing or another. "Do this. Do that." And my heart in the state it is. Where will it all end? And what will you wear today? What dress will look the noblest for the wicked, tempestable thing?'

'You're coming, too, aren't you?' Fuchsia said.

'Why, what a *thing* you are,' squeaked Nannie Slagg, climbing down over the edge of the bed. 'Fancy such an ignorous question! I am taking his little LORDSHIP, you big stupid!'

'What! is Titus going, too?'

'Oh, your *ignorance*,' said Nannie. ' "Is Titus going, *too*?" she says.' Mrs Slagg smiled pityingly. 'Poor, poor, wicked thing! what a querail!' The old woman gave forth a series of pathetically unconvincing laughs and then put her hands on Fuchsia's knees excitedly. 'Of *course* he's going,' she said. 'The Gathering is *for* him. It's about his Birthday Breakfast.'

'Who else is going, Nannie?'

Her old nurse began to count on her fingers.

'Well, there's your father,' she began, placing the tips of her forefingers together and raising her eyes to the ceiling. 'First of all there's him, your father. . . .'

*

As she spoke Lord Sepulchrave was returning to his room after performing the bi-annual ritual of opening the iron cupboard in the armoury, and, with the traditional dagger which Sourdust had brought for the occasion, of scratching on the metal back of the cupboard another half moon, which, added to the long line of similar half moons, made the seven hundred and thirty-seventh to be scored into the iron. According to the temperaments of the deceased Earls of Gormenghast the half moons were executed with precision or with carelessness. It was not certain what significance the ceremony held, for unfortunately the records were lost, but the formality was no less sacred for being unintelligible.

Old Sourdust had closed the iron door of the ugly, empty cupboard with great care, turning the key in the lock, and but for the fact that while inserting the key a few strands of his beard had gone in with it and been turned and caught, he would have felt the keen professional pleasure that all ritual gave him. It was in vain for him to pull, for not only was he held fast, but the pain to his chin brought tears to his eyes. To bring the key out and the hairs of his beard with it would ruin the ceremony, for it was laid down that the key must remain in the lock for twenty-three hours, a retainer in yellow being posted to guard the cupboard for that period. The only thing to do was to sever the strands with the knife, and this is eventually what the old man did, after which he set fire to the grey tufts of his alienated hairs that protruded from the keyhole like a fringe around the key. These flamed a little, and when the sizzling had ceased Sourdust turned apologetically to find that his Lordship had gone.

When Lord Sepulchrave reached his bedroom he found Flay laying out the black costume that he habitually wore. The Earl had it in his mind to dress more elaborately this evening. There had been a slight but perceptible lifting of his spirit ever since he had conceived this Breakfast for his son. He had become aware of a dim pleasure in having a son. Titus had been born during one of his blackest moods, and although he was still shrouded in melancholia, his introspection had, during the last few days, become tempered by a growing interest in his heir, not as a personality, but as the symbol of the Future. He had some vague presentiment that his own tenure was drawing to a close and it gave him both pleasure when he remembered his son, and a sense of stability amid the miasma of his waking dreams.

Now that he knew he had a son he realized how great had been the unspoken nightmare which had lurked in his mind. The terror that with *him* the line of Groan should perish. That he had failed the castle of his forebears, and that rotting in his sepulchre the future generations would point at his, the last of the long line of discoloured monuments and whisper: 'He was the last. He had no son.'

As Flay helped him dress, neither of them speaking a word, Lord Sepulchrave thought of all this, and fastening a jewelled pin at his collar he sighed, and within the doomed and dark sea-murmur of that sigh was the plashing sound of a less mournful billow. And then, as he gazed absently past himself in the mirror at Flay, another comber of far pleasure followed the first, for his books came suddenly before his eyes, row upon row of volumes, row upon priceless row of calf-bound Thought, of philosophy and fiction, of travel and fantasy; the stern and the ornate, the moods of gold or green, of sepia, rose, or black; the picaresque, the arabesque, the scientific – the essays, the poetry and the drama.

All this, he felt, he would now re-enter. He could inhabit the

world of words, with, at the back of his melancholy, a solace
he had not known before.

*

'Then *next*,' said Mrs Slagg, counting on her fingers, 'there's
your mother, of course. Your father and your mother – that
makes Two.'

*

Lady Gertrude had not thought of changing her dress. Nor had
it occurred to her to prepare for the gathering.

She was seated in her bedroom. Her feet were planted widely
apart as though for all time. Her elbows weighed on her knees,
from between which the draperies of her skirt sagged in heavy
U-shaped folds. In her hands was a paper-covered book, with
a coffee-stain across its cover and with as many dogs' ears as it
had pages. She was reading aloud in a deep voice that rose above
the steady drone of a hundred cats. They filled the room. Whiter
than the tallow that hung from the candelabra or lay broken on
the table of birdseed. Whiter than the pillows on the bed. They
sat everywhere. The counterpane was hidden with them. The
table, the cupboards, the couch, all was luxuriant with harvest,
white as death, but the richest crop was all about her feet where
a cluster of white faces stared up into her own. Every luminous,
slit-pupilled eye was upon her. The only movement lay in the
vibration in their throats. The voice of the Countess moved on
like a laden ship upon a purring tide.

As she came to the end of every right-hand page and was turning it over her eyes would move around the room with an expression of the deepest tenderness, her pupils filling with the
minute white reflections of her cats.

Then her eyes would turn again to the printed page. Her
enormous face had about it the wonderment of a child as she
read. She was re-living the story, the old story which she had so
often read to them.

'And the door closed, and the latch clicked, but the prince
with stars for his eyes and a new-moon for his mouth didn't
mind, for he was young and strong, and though he wasn't

handsome, he had heard lots of doors close and click before this one, and didn't feel at all frightened. But he would have been if he had known who had closed the door. It was the Dwarf with brass teeth, who was more dreadful than the most spotted of all things, and whose ears were fixed on backwards.

'Now when the prince had finished brushing his hair . . .'

•

While the Countess was turning the page Mrs Slagg was ticking off the third and fourth fingers of her left hand.

'Dr Prunesquallor and Miss Irma will come as well, dear: they always come to nearly everything – don't they, though I can't see *why* – they aren't ancestral. But they always come. Oh, my poor conscience! it's always I who have to bear with them, and do everything, and I'll have to go in a moment, my caution, to remind your mother, and she'll shout at me and make me so nervous; but I'll have to go for she won't remember, but that's just how it *always* happens. And the Doctor and Miss Irma make another two people, and that makes four altogether.' Mrs Slagg gasped for breath. 'I don't like Dr Prunesquallor, my baby; I don't like his proud habits,' said Nannie. 'He makes me feel so silly and small when I'm not. But he's always asked, even when his vain and ugly sister isn't; but she's been asked this time so they'll both be there, and you must stay next to me, won't you? Won't you? Because I've got his little Lordship to care for. Oh, my dear heart! I'm not well – I'm not; I'm *not*. And nobody cares – not even you.' Her wrinkled hand gripped at Fuchsia's. 'You will look after me?'

'Yes,' said Fuchsia. 'But I like the Doctor.'

Fuchsia lifted up the end of her mattress and burrowed beneath the feather-filled weight until she found a small box. She turned her back on her nurse for a moment and fastened something around her neck, and when she turned again Mrs Slagg saw the solid fire of a great ruby hung beneath her throat.

'You must wear it *today*!' Mrs Slagg almost screamed. 'Today, today, you naughty thing, when everyone's there. You will look as pretty as a flowering lamb, my big, untidy thing.'

'No, Nannie, I won't wear it like that. Not when it's a day

like today. I shall wear it only when I'm alone or when I meet a man who reverences me.'

*

The Doctor, meanwhile, lay in a state of perfect contentment in a hot bath filled with blue crystals. The bath was veined marble and was long enough to allow the Doctor to lie at full length. Only his quill-like face emerged above the perfumed surface of the water. His hair was filled with winking lather-bubbles; and his eyes were indescribably .roguish. His face and neck were bright pink as though direct from a celluloid factory.

At the far end of the bath one of his feet emerged from the depths. He watched it quizzically with his head cocked so far upon one side that his left ear filled with water. 'Sweet foot,' he cried. 'Five toes to boot and what-not in the beetroot shoot!' He raised himself and shook the hot water gaily from his ear and began swishing the water on either side of his body,

The eyes closed and the mouth opened and all the teeth were there shining through the steam. Taking a great breath, or rather, a deep breath, for his chest was too narrow. for a great one, and with a smile of dreadful bliss irradiating his pink face, the Doctor emitted a whinny of so piercing a quality, that Irma, seated at her boudoir table, shot to her feet, scattering hairpins across the carpet. She had been at her toilet for the last three hours, excluding the preliminary hour and a half spent in her bath – and now, as she swished her way to the bed-room door, a frown disturbing the powder on her brow, she had, in common with her brother, more the appearance of having been plucked or peeled, than of cleanliness, though *clean* she was, scrupulously clean, in the sense of a rasher of bacon.

'What on earth is the matter with you; I said, what on earth is the matter with you, Bernard?' she shouted through the bathroom keyhole.

'Is that you my love? Is that you?' her brother's voice came thinly from behind the door.

'Who *else* would it be; I said, who *else* would it be,' she yelled

299

back, bending herself into a stiff satin right angle in order to get her mouth to the keyhole.

'Ha, ha, ha, ha, ha,' came her brother's shrill, unbearable laughter. 'Who else indeed? Well, well, let us think, let us *think*. It might be the moon-goddess, but that's improbable, ha, ha ha; or it might be a sword swallower approaching me in my professional capacity, ha, ha, that is *less* improbable – in fact, my dear tap-root, have you by any chance been swallowing swords for years on end without ever telling me, ha, ha? Or haven't you?' His voice rose: 'Years on end, and swords on end – where will it. end, if our ears unbend – what shall I spend on a wrinkled friend in a pair of tights like a bunch of lights?'

Irma who had been straining her ears cried out at last in her irritation: 'I suppose you know you'll be late – I said: "I suppose you –"'

'A merry plague upon you, O blood of my blood,' the shrill voice broke in. 'What is Time, O sister of similar features, that you speak of it so subserviently? Are we to be the slaves of the sun, that second-hand, overrated knob of gilt, or of his sister, that fatuous circle of silver paper? A curse upon their ridiculous dictatorship! What say you, Irma, my Irma, wrapped in rumour, Irma, of the incandescent tumour?' he trilled happily. And his sister rose rustling to her full height, arching her nostrils as she did so, as though they itched with pedigree. Her brother annoyed her, and as she seated herself again before the mirror in. her boudoir she made noises like a lady as she applied the powder-puff for the hundredth time to her spotless length of neck.

•

'Sourdust will be there, too,' said Mrs Slagg, 'because he knows all about things. He knows what order you do things in, precious, and when you must *start* doing them, and when you ought to *stop*.'

'Is that everyone?' asked Fuchsia.

'Don't hurry me,' replied the old nurse, pursing her lips into a prune of wrinkles. 'Can't you wait a minute? Yes, that makes five, and you make six, and his little Lordship makes seven . . .'

'And you make eight,' said Fuchsia. 'So you make the most.'

'Make the most what, my caution?'

'It doesn't matter,' said Fuchsia.

*

While, in various parts of the Castle, these eight persons were getting ready for the Gathering the twins were sitting bolt upright on the couch watching Steerpike drawing the cork out of a slim, dusty bottle. He held it securely between his feet and bending over with the corkscrew firmly embedded was easing the cork from the long black cormorant throat.

Having unwound the corkscrew and placed the undamaged cork on the mantelpiece, he emptied a little of the wine into a glass and tasted it with a critical expression on his pale face.

The aunts leaned forward, their hands on their knees, watching every movement.

Steerpike took one of the Doctor's silk handkerchiefs from his pocket and wiped his mouth. Then he held the wineglass up to the light for a long time and studied its translucence.

'What's wrong with it?' said Clarice slowly.

'Is it poisoned?' said Cora.

'Who poisoned it?' echoed Clarice.

'Gertrude,' said Cora. 'She'd kill us if she could.'

'But she can't,' said Clarice.

'And that's why we're going to be powerful.'

'And proud,' added Clarice.

'Yes, because of today.'

'Because of *today*.'

They joined their hands.

'It is a good vintage, your Ladyship. A very adequate vintage. I selected it myself. You will, I know, appreciate it fully. It is not poisoned, my dear women. Gertrude, though she has poisoned your lives, has not, as it so happens, poisoned this particular bottle of wine. May I pour you out a glassful each, and we will drink a toast to the business of the day?'

'Yes, yes,' said Cora. 'Do it now.'

Steerpike filled their glasses.

'Stand up,' he said.

The purple twins arose together, and as Steerpike was about to propose the toast, his right hand holding the glass on the level of his chin and his left hand in his pocket, Cora's flat voice broke in:

'Let's drink it on our Tree,' she said. 'It's lovely outside. On our Tree.'

Clarice turned to her sister with her mouth open. Her eyes were as expressionless as mushrooms.

'That's what we'll do,' she said.

Steerpike, instead of being annoyed, was amused at the idea. After all, this was an important day for him. He had worked hard to get all in readiness and he knew that his future hung upon the smooth working of his plan, and although he would not congratulate himself until the library was in ashes, he felt that it was up to him and the aunts to relax for a few minutes before the work that lay ahead.

To drink a toast to the Day upon the boughs of the dead Tree appealed to his sense of the dramatic, the appropriate and the ridiculous.

A few minutes later the three of them had passed through the Room of Roots, filed along the horizontal stem and sat down at the table.

As they sat, Steerpike in the middle and the twins at either side, the evening air was motionless beneath them and around. The aunts had apparently no fear of the dizzy drop. They never thought of it. Steerpike, although he was enjoying the situation to the full, nevertheless averted his eyes as far as possible from the sickening space below him. He decided to deal gently with the bottle. On the wooden table their three glasses glowed in the warm light. Thirty feet away the sunny south wall towered above and fell below them featureless from its base to its summit save for the lateral offshoot of this dead tree, halfway up its surface, on which they sat, and the exquisitely pencilled shadows of its branches.

'Firstly, dear Ladyships,' said Steerpike, rising to his feet and fixing his eyes upon the shadow of a coiling bough, 'firstly I propose a health to you. To your steadfast purpose and the faith you have in your own destinies. To your courage. Your intelligence. Your beauty. He raised his glass. 'I drink,' he said, and took a sip.

Clarice began to drink at the same moment, but Cora nudged her elbow. 'Not yet,' she said.

'Next I must propose a toast to the future. Primarily to the Immediate Future. To the task we have resolved to carry through today. To its success. And also to the Great Days that will result from it. The days of your reinstatement. The days of your Power and Glory. Ladies, to the Future!'

Cora, Clarice and Steerpike lifted their elbows to drink. The warm air hung about them, and as Cora's raised elbow struck her sister's and jogged the wineglass from her hand, and as it rolled from the table to the tree and from the tree out into the hollow air, the western sunlight caught it as it fell, glittering, through the void.

'THE BURNING'

ALTHOUGH it was Lord Sepulchrave who had summoned the Gathering, it was to Sourdust that the party turned when they had all arrived in the library, for his encyclopaedic knowledge of ritual gave authority to whatever proceedings were to follow. He stood by the marble table and, as the oldest, and in his opinion, the wisest person present, had about him a quite understandable air of his own importance. To wear rich and becoming apparel no doubt engenders a sense of well-being in the wearer, but to be draped, as was Sourdust, in a sacrosanct habit of crimson rags is to be in a world above such consideration as the price and fit of clothes and to experience a sense of propriety that no wealth could buy. Sourdust knew that were he to demand it the wardrobes of Gormenghast would be flung open to him. He did not want it. His mottled beard of alternate black and white hairs was freshly knotted. The crumpled parchment of his ancestral face glimmered in the evening light that swam through the high window.

Flay had managed to find five chairs, which he placed in a

line before the table. Nannie, with Titus on her lap, took up the central position. On her right Lord Sepulchrave and on her left the Countess Gertrude sat in attitudes peculiar to them, the former with his right elbow on the arm of the chair and his chin lost in the palm of his hand, and the Countess obliterating the furniture she sat in. On her right sat the Doctor, his long legs crossed and a footling smile of anticipation on his face. At the other end of the row his sister sat with her pelvis at least a foot to the rear of an excited perpendicular – her thorax, neck and head. Fuchsia, for whom, much to her relief, no chair was to be found, stood behind them, her hands behind her back. Between her fingers a small green handkerchief was being twisted round and round. She watched the ancient Sourdust take a step forward and wondered what it must feel like to be so old and wrinkled. 'I wonder if I'll ever be as old as that,' she thought; 'an old wrinkled woman, older than my mother, older than Nannie Slagg even.' She gazed at the black mass of her mother's back. 'Who is there anyway who isn't old? There isn't anybody. Only that boy who hasn't any lineage. I wouldn't mind much, but he's different from me and too clever for me. And even he's not young. Not like I'd like my friends to be.'

Her eyes moved along the line of heads. One after the other: old heads that didn't understand.

Her eyes rested at last on Irma.

'She hasn't any lineage, either,' said Fuchsia to herself, 'and her neck is much too clean and it's the longest and thinnest and funniest I've ever seen. I wonder if she's really a white giraffe all the time, and pretending she isn't.' Fuchsia's mind flew to the stuffed giraffe's leg in the attic. 'Perhaps it belongs to *her*,' she thought. And the idea so appealed to Fuchsia that she lost control of herself and spluttered.

Sourdust, who was about to begin and had raised his old hand for the purpose, started and peered across at her. Mrs Slagg clutched Titus a little tighter and listened very hard for anything further. Lord Sepulchrave did not move his body an inch, but opened one eye slowly. Lady Gertrude, as though Fuchsia's splutter had been a signal, shouted to Flay, who was behind the library door:

'Open the door and let that bird in! What are you waiting for, man?' Then she whistled with a peculiar ventriloquism, and a wood warbler sped, undulating through the long, dark hollow of library air, to land on her finger.

Irma simply twitched but was too refined to look round, and it was left to the Doctor to make contact with Fuchsia by means of an exquisitely timed wink with his left eye behind its convex lens, like an oyster shutting and opening itself beneath a pool of water.

Sourdust, disturbed by this unseemly interjection and also by the presence of the wood warbler, which kept distracting his eye by running up and down Lady Gertrude's arm, lifted his head again, fingering a running bowline in his beard.

His hoarse and quavering voice wandered through the library like something lost.

The long shelves surrounded them, tier upon tier, circum-scribing their world with a wall of other worlds imprisoned yet breathing among the network of a million commas, semi-colons, full stops, hyphens and every other sort of printed symbol.

'We are gathered together', said Sourdust, 'in this ancient library at the instigation of Sepulchrave, 76th Earl to the house of Gormenghast and lord of those tracts of country that stretch on every hand, in the North to the wastelands, in the South to the grey salt marshes, in the East to the quicksands and the tideless sea, and in the West to knuckles of endless rock.'

This was delivered in one weak, monotonous stream. Sour-dust coughed for some time and then, regaining his breath, continued mechanically: 'We are gathered on this seventeenth day of October to give ear to his Lordship. These nights the moon is in the ascendant and the river is full of fish. The owls in the Tower of Flints seek their prey as heretofore and it is appro-priate that his Lordship should, on the seventeenth day of an autumn month, bring forward the matter that is in his mind. The sacred duties which he has never wavered to perform are over for the hour. It is appropriate that it should be now – now, at the sixth hour of the daylight clock.

'I as master of Ritual, as Guardian of the Documents and as

Confidant to the Family, am able to say that for his Lordship to speak to you in no way contravenes the tenets of Gormenghast.

'But, your Lordship, and your revered Ladyship,' said Sourdust in his old sing-song, 'it is no secret to those here gathered that it is towards the child who now occupies pride of place, it is towards Lord Titus that our thoughts will converge this afternoon. That is no secret.'

Sourdust gave vent to a dreadful chesty cough. 'It is to Lord Titus,' he said, gazing mistily at the child and then, raising his voice, 'it is to Lord Titus,' he repeated irritably.

Nannie suddenly realized that the old man was making signs at her, and understood that she was to lift the infant up in the air as though he were a specimen, or something to be auctioned. She lifted him, but no one looked at the exhibit except Prunesquallor, who nearly engulfed Nannie, baby and all with a smile so devouring, so dental, as to cause Nannie to raise her shoulder against it and to snatch Titus back to her little flat chest.

'I will turn my back on you and strike the table four times,' said Sourdust. 'Slagg will bring the child to the table and Lord Sepulchrave will –' here he suffered a more violent fit of coughing than ever, and at the same moment Irma's neck quivered a little and she in her own way followed suit with five little ladylike barks. She turned her head apologetically in the direction of the Countess and wrinkled her forehead in self-deprecation. She could see that the Countess had taken no notice of her mute apology. She arched her nostrils. It had not crossed her mind there was a smell in the room other than the prevalent smell of musty leather: it was just that her nostrils with their hypersensitive nerve-endings were acting on their own accord.

Sourdust took some time to recover from his bout, but eventually he straightened himself and repeated:

'Slagg will bring the child to the table, and Lord Sepulchrave will graciously advance, following his menial, and on arriving at a point immediately behind me will touch the back of my neck with the forefinger of his left hand.

'At this signal I and Slagg will retire, and Slagg, having left the infant on the table, Lord Sepulchrave will pass behind the table and stand facing us across its surface.'

'Are you hungry, my little love? Is there no grain inside you? Is that it? Is that it?'

The voice came forth so suddenly and heavily and so closely upon the quavering accents of Sourdust that everyone felt for the first few moments that the remark was addressed to them personally; but on turning their heads they could see that the Countess was addressing herself exclusively to the wood warbler. Whether the warbler made any reply was never ascertained for not only was Irma seized with a new and less ladylike bout of short dry coughs, but her brother and Nannie Slagg, joining her, filled the room with noise.

The bird rose into the air, startled, and Lord Sepulchrave stopped on his passage to the table and turned irritably to the line of noisy figures; but as he did so a faint smell of smoke making itself perceptible for the first time caused him to raise his head and sniff the air in a slow, melancholy way. At the same time Fuchsia felt a roughness in her throat. She glanced about the room and wrinkled her nose, for smoke though still invisible was infiltrating steadily through the library.

Prunesquallor had risen from beside the Countess and with his white hands wound about each other and with his mouth twisted into a quizzical line he permitted his eyes to move rapidly around the room. His head was cocked on one side.

'What's the matter, man?' asked the Countess heavily from immediately below him. She was still seated.

'The matter?' queried the Doctor, smiling more emphatically but still keeping his eyes on the move. 'It is a case of atmosphere, as far as I can dare to judge at such very, very short notice, your Ladyship, as far as I *dare* to judge, ha, ha, ha! It is a case of thickening atmosphere, ha, ha!'

'Smoke,' said the Countess heavily and bluntly. 'What is the matter with smoke? Haven't you ever smelt it before?'

'Many and many a time, your Ladyship,' answered the Doctor. 'But never, if I may say so, never in *here*.'

The Countess grunted to herself and settled deeper into the chair.

'There never *is* smoke in here,' said Lord Sepulchrave. He turned his head to the door and raised his voice a little:

'Flay.'

The long servant emerged out of the shadows like a spider.

'Open the door,' said Lord Sepulchrave sharply; and as the spider turned and began its return journey his Lordship took a step towards old Sourdust, who was by now doubled over the table in a paroxysm of coughing. His Lordship taking one of Sourdust's elbows beckoned to Fuchsia, who came across the room and supported the old man on the other side, and the three of them began to make their way to the door in Flay's wake.

Lady Groan simply sat like a mountain and watched the little bird.

Dr Prunesquallor was wiping his eyes, his thick glasses pushed for the moment above his eyebrows. But he was very much on the alert and as soon as his spectacles were again in place he grinned at everyone in turn. His eye lingered for a moment on his sister Irma, who was systematically tearing an expensively embroidered cream-coloured silk handkerchief into small pieces. Behind the dark lenses of her glasses her eyes were hidden from view, but to judge from the thin, wet, drooping line of her mouth and the twitching of the skin on her pointed nose it might be safely assumed that they were making contact with, and covering the inner side of, the lenses of her spectacles with the moisture with which the smoke had filmed them.

The Doctor placed the tips of his fingers and thumbs together and then, separating the tapering extremities of the index fingers, he watched them for a few seconds as they gyrated around one another. Then his eyes turned to the far end of the room where he could see the Earl and his daughter, with the old man between them, approaching the library door. Someone, presumably Flay, seemed to be making a great deal of noise in wrestling with the heavy iron door-handle.

The smoke was spreading, and the Doctor, wondering why in the devil's name the door had not been thrown open, began to peer about the room in an effort to locate the source of the ever-thickening wreaths. As he took a step past Nannie Slagg he saw that she was standing by the table from whose marble surface she had plucked Titus. She was holding him very closely to herself and had wrapped him in layers of cloth which had completely hidden him from view. A sound of muffled crying could be heard coming from the bundle. Nannie's little wrinkled mouth was hanging open. Her streaming eyes were redder than usual with the stinging smoke. But she stood quite still.

'My very dear good woman,' said Dr Prunesquallor, turning on his heel as he was about to float past her, 'my very dear Slagg, convey his minute Lordship to the door that for some reason that is too subtle for me to appreciate remains shut. Why, in the name of Ventilation, *I* don't know. But it *does*. It remains shut. Take him nevertheless, my dear Slagg, to the aforesaid door and place his infinitesimal head at the keyhole (surely *THAT'S* still open!), and even if you cannot squeeze the child right through it you can at least give his Lordship's lungs something to get on with.'

Nannie Slagg was never very good at interpreting the Doctor's long sentences, especially when coming through a haze of smoke, and all that she could gather was that she should attempt to squeeze her tiny Lordship through the keyhole. Clutching the baby even tighter in her thin arms, 'No! no! no!' she cried, retreating from the doctor.

Dr Prunesquallor rolled his eyes at the Countess. She was apparently aware of the state of the room at last and was gathering together great swathes of drapery in a slow, deliberate manner preparatory to rising to her feet.

The rattling at the library door became more violent, but the indigenous shadows and the smoke combined to make it impossible to see what was going on.

'Slagg,' said the Doctor, advancing on her, 'go to the door immediately, like the intelligent woman you are!'

'No! no!' shrieked the midget, in so silly a voice that Doctor Prunesquallor after taking a handkerchief from his pocket lifted her from her feet and tucked her under his arm. The handkerchief enveloping Nannie Slagg's waist prevented the nurse's garments from coming in contact with the Doctor's clothes. Her legs, like black twigs blown in the wind, gesticulated for a few moments and then were still.

Before they had reached the door, however, they were met by Lord Sepulchrave, who emerged darkly from the smoke. 'The door has been locked from the outside,' he whispered between fits of coughing.

'Locked?' queried Prunesquallor. 'Locked, your Lordship? By all that's perfidious! This is becoming intriguing. Most intriguing. Perhaps a bit too intriguing. What do you think, Fuchsia, my dear little lady? Eh? ha, ha! Well, well, we must become positively cerebral, mustn't we? By all that's enlightened we really must! Can it be smashed?' He turned to Lord Sepulchrave. 'Can we breach it, your Lordship, battery and assault and all that delicious sort of thing?'

'Too thick, Prunesquallor, said Lord Sepulchrave: 'four-inch oak.'

He spoke slowly in strange contrast to Prunesquallor's rapid, ejaculatory chirping.

Sourdust had been propped near the door, where he sat cough-ing as though to shake his old body to bits.

'No key for the other door,' continued Lord Sepulchrave slowly. 'It is never used. What about the window?' For the first time a look of alarm appeared on his ascetic face. He walked quickly to the nearest bookshelves and ran his fingers along the spines of calf. Then he turned with a quickness unusual for him. 'Where is the smoke thickest?'

'I've been searching for its origin, your Lordship,' came Prune-squallor's voice out of the haze. 'It's everywhere so thick that it's very difficult to say. By all the pits of darkness it most damnably is. But I'm looking, ha, ha! I'm looking.' He trilled for a moment like a bird. Then his voice came again. 'Fuchsia, dear!' he shouted. 'Are you all right?'

'Yes!' Fuchsia had to swallow hard before she could shout back, for she was very frightened, 'Yes, Dr Prune.'

'Slagg!' shouted the Doctor, 'keep Titus near the keyhole. See that she does, Fuchsia.'

'Yes,' whispered Fuchsia; and went in search of Mrs Slagg.

It was just then that an uncontrolled scream rang through the room.

Irma, who had been tearing her cream-coloured handkerchief, now found that she had ripped it into such minute particles that with nothing left to tear, and with her hands in forced idleness, she could control herself no longer. Her knuckles had tried to stifle the cry, but her terror had grown too strong for such expedients, and at the final moment she forgot all she had learnt about decorum and about how to be a lady, and clenching her hands at her thighs she had stood on tip-toe and screamed from her swanlike throat with an effect calculated to freeze the blood of a macaw.

An enormous figure had loomed out of the smoke a few feet from Lord Sepulchrave, and as he watched the vague head take shape and recognized it as that belonging to the top half of his wife's body, his limbs had stiffened, for Irma's scream had rung out simultaneously with the appearance of the head, the untoward proximity of which conjoined with the scream giving ventriloquistic horror to the moment. Added to the frightfulness of a head and a voice, attacking his ear and eye simultaneously though from different distances, was the dreadful conception of Gertrude losing control in that way and giving vent to a scream of such a shrill pitch as to be incompatible with the slack 'cello string that reverberated so heavily in her throat. He knew at once that it was *not* Gertrude who had screamed, but the very idea that it might have been, filled him with sickness, and there raced through his mind the thought that for all his wife's uncompromising, loveless weight of character it would be a grim and evil thing were she to change.

The flat blur of his wife's head turned itself towards the scream upon a blurred neck, and he could see the vast wavering profile begin to move away from him, inch by inch, and steer into the thickness beyond, charting its course by the shrill shooting-star of Irma's cry.

Lord Sepulchrave gripped his hands together convulsively until his knuckles were bloodless and their ten staring crests wavered whitely through the smoke which lay between his hands and his head.

The blood began to beat a tattoo at his temples, and upon his high white brow a few big beads gathered.

He was biting at his lower lip, and his eyebrows were drawn down over his eyes as though he were cogitating upon some academic problem. He knew that no one could see him, for by now the smoke was all but opaque, but he was watching himself. He could see that the position of his arms, and the whole attitude of his body was exaggerated and stiffened. He discovered that his fingers were splayed out in a histrionic gesture of alarm. It was for him to control his members before he could hope to organize the activities in the smoke-filled room. And so he watched and waited for the moment to assert himself, and as he watched he found himself struggling. There was blood on his tongue. He had bitten his wrist. His hands were now grappling with one another and it seemed an eternity before the fingers ceased their deadly, interlocked and fratricidal strangling. Yet his panic could have taken no longer than a few moments, for the echo of Irma's scream was still in his ears when he began to loosen his hands.

Meanwhile Prunesquallor had reached his sister's side and had found her bridling her body up in preparation for another scream. Prunesquallor, as urbane as ever, had nevertheless something in his fish-like eyes that might almost be described as determination. One glance at his sister was sufficient to make him realize that to attempt to reason with her would be about as fruitful as to try to christianize a vulture. She was on tiptoe and her lungs were expanded when he struck her across her long white face with his long white hand, the pent breath from her lungs issuing from her mouth, ears and nostrils. There was something of shingle in the sound – of shingle dragged seawards on a dark night.

Dragging her across the room swiftly, her heels scraping the floor, he found a chair, after probing around in the smoke with his delicate feet, and sat his sister in it.

'Irma!' he shouted into her ear, 'my humiliating and entirely unfortunate old string of whitewash, sit where you are! Alfred will do the rest. Can you hear me? Be good now! blood of my blood, be good now, damn you!'

Irma sat quite still as though dead, save for a look of profound wonder in her eyes.

Prunesquallor was on the point of making another effort to locate the origin of the smoke when he heard Fuchsia's voice high above the coughing that by now was a constant background of noise in the library.

'Dr Prune! Dr Prune! quickly! Quickly, Dr Prune!'

The Doctor pulled down his cuffs smartly over his wrists, tried to square his shoulders, but met with no success, and then began to pick his way, half running, half walking, towards the door where Fuchsia, Mrs Slagg and Titus had been last seen. When he judged he was about half way to the door and was clear of the furniture, Prunesquallor began to accelerate his speed. This he did by increasing not only the length of his stride but the height also, so that he was, as it were, prancing through the air, when he was brought to a sudden ruthless halt by a collision with something that felt like an enormous bolster on end.

When he had drawn his face away from the tallow-smelling draperies that seemed to hang about him like curtains, he stretched out his hand tentatively and shuddered to feel it come in contact with large fingers.

''Squallor?' came the enormous voice. 'Is that 'Squallor?' The mouth of the Countess was opening and shutting within an inch of his left ear.

The Doctor gesticulated eloquently, but his artistry was wasted in the smoke.

'It *is*. Or rather,' he continued, speaking even more rapidly than usual – 'it is *Prunesquallor*, which is, if I may say so, more strictly correct, ha, ha, ha! even in the dark.'

'Where's Fuchsia?' said the Countess. Prunesquallor found that his shoulder was being gripped.

'By the door,' said the Doctor, longing to free himself from the weight of her Ladyship's hand, and wondering, even in the middle of the coughing and the darkness, what on earth the material that fitted around his shoulders so elegantly would look like when the Countess had finished with it. 'I was on the point of finding her when we met, ha, ha! met, as it were, so palpably, so inevitably.'

'Quiet, man! quiet!' said Lady Gertrude, loosening her grasp.

'Find her for me. Bring her here – and smash a window, Squallor, smash a window.'

The Doctor was gone from her in a flash and when he judged himself to be a few feet from the door – 'Are you there, Fuchsia?' he trilled.

Fuchsia was just below him, and he was startled to hear her voice come up jerkily through the smoke.

'She's ill. Very ill. Quick, Dr Prune, quick! Do something for her.' The Doctor felt his knees being clutched. 'She's down here, Dr Prune. I'm holding her.'

Prunesquallor hitched up his trousers and knelt down at once.

There seemed to be more vibration in the atmosphere in this part of the room, more than could be accounted for by any modicum of air that might have been entering through the keyhole. The coughing was dreadful to hear; Fuchsia's was heavy and breathless; but the thin, weak, and ceaseless coughing of Mrs Slagg gave the Doctor the more concern. He felt for the old nurse and found her in Fuchsia's lap. Slipping his hand across her little chicken-bosom he found that her heart was the merest flutter. To his left in the darkness there was a mouldy smell, and then the driest series of brick-dust coughs he had ever heard revealed the proximity of Flay, who was fanning the air mechanically with a large book he had clawed out of a near-by shelf. The fissure left in the row of hidden books had filled immediately with the coiling smoke – a tall, narrow niche of choking darkness, a ghastly gap in a row of leather wisdom teeth.

'Flay,' said the Doctor, 'can you hear me, Flay? Where's the largest window in the room, my man? Quickly now, where is it?'

'North wall,' said Flay. 'High up.'

'Go and shatter it at once. At once.'

'No balcony there,' said Flay. 'Can't reach.'

'Don't argue! Use what you've got in that head of yours. You know the room. Find a missile, my good Flay – find a missile, and break a window. Some oxygen for Mrs Slagg. Don't you think so? By all the zephyrs, yes! Go and help him, Fuchsia. Find where the window is and break it, even if you have to throw Irma at it, ha, ha, ha! And don't be alarmed. Smoke, you know, is only smoke: it's not composed of crocodiles, oh dear no, nothing so tropical. Hurry now. Break the window somehow and let the evening pour itself in – and I will see to dear Mrs Slagg and Titus, ha, ha, ha! Oh dear, yes!'

Flay gripped Fuchsia's arm, and they moved away into the darkness.

Prunesquallor did what he could to help Mrs Slagg, more by way of assuring her that it would be over in a brace of shakes than through anything scientific. He saw that Titus was able to breathe although wrapped up very tightly. Then he sat back on his heels and turned his head, for an idea had struck him.

'Fuchsia!' he shouted, 'find your father and ask him to sling his jade-cane at the window.'

Lord Sepulchrave, who had just fought down another panic, and had nearly bitten his lower lip in half, spoke in a wonderfully controlled voice immediately after the Doctor had finished piping his message.

'Where are you, Flay?' he said.

'I'm here,' said Flay from a few feet behind him.

'Come to the table.'

Flay and Fuchsia moved to the table, feeling for it with their hands.

'Are you at the table?'

'Yes, Father,' said Fuchsia, 'we're both here.'

'Is that you, Fuchsia?' said a new voice. It was the Countess.

'Yes,' said Fuchsia. 'Are you all right?'

'Have you seen the warbler?' answered her mother. 'Have you seen him?'

'No,' said Fuchsia. The smoke was stinging her eyes and the darkness was terror. Like her father, she had choked a score of cries in her throat.

Prunesquallor's voice rang out again from the far end of the room: 'Damn the warbler and all its feathered friends! Have you got the missiles, Flay?'

'Come here,' you 'Squallor,' began the Countess; but she could not continue, for her lungs had filled with black wreaths.

For a few moments there was no one in the room who was capable of speaking and their breathing was becoming momently more difficult. At last Sepulchrave's voice could be distinguished.

'On the table,' he whispered – 'paper-weight – brass – on the table. Quick – Flay – Fuchsia – feel for it. Have you found it? – Paper-weight – brass.'

Fuchsia's hands came across the heavy object almost at once, and as they did so the room was lit up with a tongue of flame that sprang into the air among the books on the right of the unused door. It died almost at once, withdrawing itself like the tongue of an adder, but a moment later it shot forth again and climbed in a crimson spiral, curling from left to right as it licked its way across the gilded and studded spines of Sepulchrave's volumes. This time it did not die away, but gripped the leather with its myriad flickering tentacles while the names of the books shone out in ephemeral glory. They were never forgotten by Fuchsia, those first few vivid titles that seemed to be advertising their own deaths.

For a few moments there was a deadly silence, and then, with a hoarse cry, Flay began to run towards the shelves on the left of the main door. The firelight had lit up a bundle on the floor, and it was not until Flay had picked it up and had carried it to the table that the others were reminded with horror of the forgotten octogenarian – for the bundle was Sourdust. For some time it was difficult for the Doctor to decide whether he were alive or not.

While Prunesquallor was attempting to revive the old man's breathing as he lay in his crimson rags upon the marble table, Sepulchrave, Fuchsia and Flay took up positions beneath the window, which could be seen with ever growing clarity. Sepulchrave was the first to fling the brass paper-weight, but his effort was pitiable, final proof (if any were needed) that he was no man of action, and that his life had not been mis-spent among his books. Flay was the next to try his skill. Although having the advantage of his height, he was no more successful than his Lordship, on account of a superabundance of calcium deposit in his elbow joints.

While this was going on, Fuchsia had began to climb up the bookshelves, which reached upwards to within about five feet of the window. As she climbed laboriously, her eyes streaming and her heart beating wildly, she scooped the books to the ground in order to find purchase for her hands and feet. It was a difficult climb, the ascent being vertical and the polished shelves too slippery to grip with any certainty.

The Countess had climbed to the balcony, where she had found the wood-warbler fluttering wildly in a dark corner. Plucking out a strand of her dark-red hair she had bound the bird's wings carefully to its sides, and then after laying its pulsing breast against her cheek, had slipped it between her own neck and the neck of her dress, and allowed it to slide into the capacious midnight regions of her bosom, where it lay quiescent between great breasts, thinking, no doubt, when it had recovered from the terror of the flames, that here, if anywhere, was the nest of nests, softer than moss, inviolate, and warm with drowsy blood.

When Prunesquallor had ascertained beyond doubt that Sourdust was dead, he lifted one of the loose ends of crimson sacking that straggled across the marble table from the ancient shoulders and laid it across the old man's eyes.

Then he peered over his shoulders at the flames. They had spread in area and now covered about a quarter of the east wall. The heat was fast becoming insufferable. His next glance was directed to the door that had so mysteriously become locked, and he saw that Nannie Slagg, with Titus in her arms, was crouching immediately before the keyhole, the only possible place for them. If the only window could be broken and some form of erection constructed below it, it was just possible that they could climb out in time, though how, in heaven's name, they were to descend on the far side was another matter. A rope, perhaps. But where was a rope to be found – and for that matter what could the erection be constructed with?

Prunesquallor peered around the room in an effort to catch sight of anything that might be used. He noticed that Irma was full length on the floor, and twitching like a section of conger-eel that has been chopped off but which still has ideas of its own. Her beautiful, tightly fitting skirt had become rucked up around her thighs. Her manicured nails were scratching convulsively at the floor boards. 'Let her twitch,' he said to himself quickly. 'We can deal with her later, poor thing.' Then he turned his eyes again to Fuchsia, who was by now very near the top of the bookcase and was reaching down precariously for her father's rod with the knob of black jade.

'Keep steady, my Fuchsia-child.'

Fuchsia dimly heard the Doctor's voice come up to her from below. For a moment everything swam before her eyes, and her right hand which gripped the slippery shelf was shaking. Slowly her eyes cleared. It was not easy for her to swing the rod with her left hand, but she drew her arm back stiffly preparatory to swinging at the window with a single rigid movement.

The Countess, leaning over the balcony, watched her as she coughed heavily, and shifting her gaze between her seismic bouts whistled through her teeth to the bird in her bosom, pulling the neck of her dress forward with a forefinger as she did so.

Sepulchrave was gazing upwards at his daughter half way up the wall among the books that danced in the crimson light. His hands were fighting each other again, but his delicate chin was jutting forward, and there was mixed with the melancholy of his eyes not more of panic than would be considered reasonable in any normal man under similar conditions. His home of books was on fire. His life was threatened, and he stood quite still. His sensitive mind had ceased to function, for it had played so long in a world of abstract philosophies that this other world of practical and sudden action had deranged its structure. The ritual which his body had had to perform for fifty years had been no preparation for the unexpected. He watched Fuchsia with a dream-like fascination, while his locked hands fought on.

Flay and Prunesquallor stood immediately below Fuchsia, for

she had been swaying above them. Now, with her arm extended and ready to strike they moved a little to the right in order to escape any glass that might fly inwards.

As Fuchsia began to swing her arm at the high window she focused her eyes upon it and found herself staring at a face – a face framed with darkness within a few feet of her own. It sweated firelight, the crimson shadows shifting across it as the flames leapt in the room below. Only the eyes repelled the lurid air. Close-set as nostrils they were not so much eyes as narrow tunnels through which the Night was pouring.

AND HORSES TOOK THEM HOME

As Fuchsia recognized the head of Steerpike the rod fell from her outstretched arm, her weakened hand loosed its grasp upon the shelf and she fell backwards into space, the dark hair of her head reaching below her as she fell, her body curving backwards as though she had been struck.

The Doctor and Flay, leaping forward, half caught her. A moment later and the glass above them came splintering into the room, and Steerpike's voice from overhead cried:

'Hold your horses! I'm letting down a ladder. Don't panic there. Don't panic!'

Every eye was turned from Fuchsia to the window, but Prunesquallor as he had heard the glass break above him had shielded the girl by swinging her behind him. It had fallen all about them, one large piece skimming the Doctor's head and splintering on the floor at his feet. The only one to sustain any injury was Flay, who had a small piece of flesh nicked from his wrist.

'Hang on there!' continued Steerpike in an animated voice which sounded singularly unrehearsed. 'Don't stand so near, I'm going to crack some more glass out.'

The company below the window drew back and watched him strike off the jagged corners of glass from the sides of the window with a piece of flint. The room behind them was now well ablaze, and the sweat was pouring from their upturned faces, their clothes scorching dangerously, and their flesh smarting with the intense heat.

Steerpike, on the outside of the wall, standing on the short protruding branches of the pine-ladder began to struggle with the other length of pine which he had propped beside him. This was no easy job, and the muscles of his arms and back were strained almost to failing point as he levered the long pole upwards and over his shoulder by degrees, keeping his balance all the while with the greatest difficulty. As well as he could judge the library ought by now to be in perfect condition for a really theatrical piece of rescue work. Slowly but surely he edged and eased the pole across his shoulder and through the broken window. It was not only a heavy and dangerous feat, standing as he was, balanced upon the stubby six-inch off-shoots of pine and hauling the resinous thing over his shoulder, but what added to his difficulty was these lateral stubs themselves which caught in his clothes and on the window ledge at each attempt he made to slide the long monster through the opening and down into the bright library.

At last both difficulties were overcome and the gathering on the inner side of the wall below the window found the fifteen-foot bole of a pine edging its way through the smoky air above them, swaying over their heads and then landing with a crash at their feet. Steerpike had held fast to the upper end of the pole and it would have been possible for one of the lighter members of the party to have climbed it at once, but Prunesquallor moved the base of the tree a little to the left and swivelled it until the most powerful of the stubby, lateral 'rungs' were more conveniently situated.

Steerpike's head and shoulders now appeared fully in view through the broken window. He peered into the crimson smoke. 'Nice work,' he said to himself, and then shouted, 'Glad I found you! I'm just coming!'

Nothing could have gone more deliciously according to plan. But there was no time to waste. No time to crow. He could see that the floor-boards had caught and there was a snake of fire slithering its way beneath the table.

Steerpike lifted his voice. 'The Heir of Gormenghast!' he shouted. 'Where is Lord Titus? Where is Lord Titus?'

Prunesquallor had already reached Mrs Slagg, who had collapsed over the child, and he lifted them both together in his arms and ran swiftly back to the ladder. The Countess was there; they were all there at the foot of the pine; all except Sourdust, whose sacking had begun to smoulder. Fuchsia had dragged Irma across the floor by her heels and she lay as though she had been washed ashore by a tempest. Steerpike had crawled through the window and was a third of the way down the bole. Prunesquallor, climbing to the third rung, was able to pass Titus to the youth, who retreated through the window backwards and was down the outer ladder in a flash.

He left the infant among the ferns under the library wall and swarmed up the ladder for the old nurse. The tiny, limp midget was almost as easy to deal with as Titus, and Prunesquallor passed her through the window as though he were handling a doll.

Steerpike laid her next to Titus, and was suddenly back at the window. It was obvious that Irma was the next on the list, but it was with her that the difficulties began. The moment she was touched she began to thrash about with her arms and legs. Thirty years of repression were finding vent. She was no longer a lady. She could never be a lady again. Her pure white feet were indeed composed of clay and now with all the advantages of a long throat she renewed her screaming, but it was weaker than before, for the smoke which had coiled around her vocal cords had taken their edge away, and they were now more in the nature of wool than gut. Something had to be done with her, and quickly. Steerpike swarmed down the top half of the pole and dropped to the library floor. Then, at his suggestion, he and the Doctor began to strip away lengths of her dress with which they bound her arms and legs, stuffing the remainder in her mouth. Together, with the help of Flay and Fuchsia, they heaved the writhing Irma by degrees up the ladder, until Steerpike, climbing through the window, was able to drag her through into the night air. Once through, she was treated with still less decorum, and her descent of the wall was abrupt, the boy with the high shoulders merely seeing to it that she should not break more bones than was necessary. In point of fact she broke none, her peerless flesh sustaining only a few purple bruises.

Steerpike had now three figures in a row among the cold ferns. While he was swarming back, Fuchsia was saying, 'No, I don't want to. You go now. Please, you go now.'

'Silence, you child,' answered the Countess. 'Don't waste time. As I tell you, girl! as I tell you! At once.'

'No, Mother, no —'

'Fuchsia dear,' said Prunesquallor, 'you will be out in a brace of shakes and ladders! ha, ha, ha! It will save time, gipsy! Hurry now.'

'Don't stand there gauping, girl!'

Fuchsia glanced at the Doctor. How unlike himself he looked, the sweat pouring from his forehead and running between his eyes.

'Up you go! up you go,' said Prunesquallor.

Fuchsia turned to the ladder and after missing her foothold once or twice disappeared above them.

'Good girl!' shouted the Doctor. 'Find your Nannie Slagg! Now, then, now, then, your Ladyship, up you go.'

The Countess began to climb, and although the sound of the wooden stubs being broken on either side of the pole accompanied her, yet her progress towards the window held a prodigious inevitability in every step she took and in every heave of her body. Like something far larger than life, her dark dress shot with the red of the fire, she ploughed her way upwards to the window. There was no one on the other side to help her, for Steerpike was in the library, and yet for all the contortions of her great frame, for all the ungainliness of her egress, a slow dignity pervaded her which gave even to the penultimate view – that of her rear disappearing hugely into the night – a feeling rather of the awesome than the ludicrous.

There remained only Lord Sepulchrave, Prunesquallor, Flay and Steerpike.

Prunesquallor and Steerpike turned to Sepulchrave quickly in order to motion him to follow his wife, but he had disappeared.

There was not a moment to lose. The flames were crackling around them. Mixed with the smell of the smoke was the smell of burning leather. There were few places where he could be, unless he had walked into the flames. They found him in an alcove a few feet from the ladder, a recess still hidden to some extent from the enveloping heat. He was smoothing the backs of a set of the Martrovian dramatists bound in gold fibre and there was a smile upon his face that sent a sick pang through the bodies of the three who found him. Even Steerpike watched that smile uneasily from beneath his sandy eyebrows. Saliva was beginning to dribble from the corner of his Lordship's sensitive mouth as the corners curved upwards and the teeth were bared. It was the smile one sees in the mouth of a dead animal when the loose lips are drawn back and the teeth are discovered curving towards the ears.

'Take them, take your books, your Lordship, and come, come quickly!' said Steerpike fiercely. 'Which do you want?'

Sepulchrave turned about sharply and with a superhuman effort forced his hands stiffly to his sides and walked at once to the pine ladder. 'I am sorry to have kept you,' he said, and began to climb swiftly.

As he was lowering himself on the far side of the window they heard him repeat as though to himself: 'I am sorry to have kept you.' And then there was a thin laugh like the laugh of a ghost.

There was no longer any time for deciding who was to follow whom; no time for chivalry. The hot breath of the fire was upon them. The room was rising around them, and yet Steerpike managed to keep himself back.

Directly Flay and the Doctor had disappeared he ran up the pine-bole like a cat, and sat astride the window ledge a moment before he descended on the far side. With the black autumn night behind him he crouched there, a lurid carving, his eyes no longer black holes in his head but glittering in the blood-red light like garnets.

'Nice work,' he said to himself for the second time that night. 'Very nice work.' And then he swung his other leg over the high sill.

'There is no one left,' he shouted down into the darkness.

'Sourdust,' said Prunesquallor, his thin voice sounding singularly flat. 'Sourdust has been left.'

Steerpike slid down the pole.

'Dead ?' he queried.

'He is,' said Prunesquallor.

No one spoke.

As Steerpike's eyes became accustomed to the darkness he noticed that the earth surrounding the Countess was a dusky white, and that it was moving, and it was a few moments before he realized that white cats were interweaving about her feet.

Fuchsia, directly her mother had followed her down the ladder, began to run, stumbling and falling over the roots of trees and moaning with exhaustion as she staggered on. When after an eternity she had reached the main body of the Castle she made her way to the stables, and at last had found and ordered three grooms to saddle the horses and proceed to the library. Each groom led a horse by the side of the one he rode. On one of these, Fuchsia was seated, her body doubled forward. Broken by the shock she was weeping, her tears threading their brackish paths over the coarse mane of her mount.

By the time they had reached the library the party had covered some distance of the return journey. Flay was carrying Irma over his shoulder. Prunesquallor had Mrs Slagg in his arms and Titus was sharing the warbler's nest in the Countess's bosom. Steerpike, watching Lord Sepulchrave very closely, was guiding him in the wake of the others, deferentially holding his Lordship's elbow.

When the horses arrived the procession had practically come to a standstill. The beasts were mounted, the grooms walking at their sides holding the bridles, and staring over their shoulders with wide, startled eyes at the raw patch of light that danced in the darkness like a pulsating wound between the straight black bones of the pine trees.

During their slow progress they were met by indistinguishable crowds of servants who stood to the side of the track in horrified silence. The fire had not been visible from the

Castle, for the roof had not fallen and the only window was shielded by the trees, but the news had spread with Fuchsia's arrival. The night which had so dreadful a birth continued to heave and sweat until the slow dawn opened like an icy flower in the east, and showed the smoking shell of Sepulchrave's only home. The shelves that still stood were wrinkled charcoal, and the books were standing side by side upon them, black, grey, and ash-white, the corpses of thought. In the centre of the room the discoloured marble table still stood among a heap of charred timber and ashes, and upon the table was the skeleton of Sourdust. The flesh was gone, with all its wrinkles. The coughing had ceased for ever.

SWELTER LEAVES HIS CARD

THE winds of the drear interim that lies between the last of autumn and the first of winter had torn the few remaining leaves from even the most sheltered of the branches that swung in the Twisted Woods. Elsewhere the trees had been skeletons for many weeks. The melancholy of decay had given place to a less mournful humour. In dying, the chill season had ceased to weep, and arising from its pyre of coloured leaves had cried out with such a voice as had no hint of tears – and something fierce began to move the air and pace across the tracts of Gormenghast. From the death of the sap, of the bird-song, of the sun, this other life-in-death arose to fill the vacuum of Nature.

The whine was yet in the wind; the November whine. But as night followed night its long trailing note became less and less a part of the mounting music which among the battlements was by now an almost nightly background to those who slept or tried to sleep in the castle of the Groans. More and more in the darkness the notes of grimmer passions could be discerned. Hatred and anger and pain and the hounding voices of vengeance.

•

One evening, several weeks after the burning, at about an hour before midnight, Flay lowered himself to the ground outside Lord Sepulchrave's bedroom door. Inured though he was to the cold floor boards, for they had been his only bed for many years, yet on this November evening they struck a chill into his flinty bones and his shanks began to ache. The wind whistled and screamed about the Castle and gelid draughts skidded along the landing, and Flay heard the sound of doors opening and shutting at varying distances from him. He was able to follow the course of a draught as it approached from the northern fastnesses of the Castle, for he recognized the sound that was peculiar to each distant door as it creaked and slammed, the noises becoming louder and louder until the heavy mildewy curtains which hung at the end of the passage, forty feet away, lifted and muttered and the door which lay immediately beyond them grated and strained at its only hinge, and Flay knew that the icy spearhead of a fresh draught was close upon him.

'Getting old,' he muttered to himself, rubbing his thighs and folding himself up like a stick-insect at the foot of the door.

He had slept soundly enough last winter when the snow had lain deeply over Gormenghast. He remembered with distaste how it had coated the windows, clinging to the panes, and how when the sun sank over the Mountain the snow had appeared to bulge inwards through the window panes in a lather of blood.

This memory disturbed him, and he dimly knew that the reason why the cold was affecting him more and more during these desolate nights had nothing to do with his age. For his body was hardened to the point of being more like some inanimate substance than flesh and blood. It was true that it was a particularly bad night, rough and loud, but he remembered that four nights ago there had been no wind and yet he had shivered as he was shivering now.

'Getting old,' he muttered grittily to himself again between his long discoloured teeth; but he knew that he lied. No cold on earth could make his hairs stand up like tiny wires, stiffly, almost painfully along his thighs and forearms, and at the nape of his neck. Was he afraid? Yes, as any reasonable man would be. He was very afraid, although the sensation was rather different in him from that which would have been experienced in other men. He was not afraid of the darkness, of the opening and shutting of distant doors, of the screaming wind. He had lived all his life in a forbidding, half-lit world.

He turned over, so as to command a view of the stairhead, although it was almost too dark to see it. He cracked the five knuckles of his left hand, one by one, but he could hardly hear the reports for a new wave of the gale rattled every window and the darkness was alive with the slamming of doors. He was afraid; he had been afraid for weeks. But Flay was not a coward. There was something tenacious and hard in his centre; something obstinate which precluded panic.

All of a sudden the gale seemed to hurl itself to a climax and then to cease utterly, but the interim of dead silence was over as soon as it had started, for a few seconds later, as though from a different quarter, the storm unleashed another of its armies of solid rain and hail, pouring its broadsides against the Castle from the belly of a yet more riotous tempest.

During the few moments of what seemed to be an absolute silence between the two storms, Flay had jerked his body forward from the ground, and had sat bolt upright, every muscle frozen. He had forced a knuckle between his teeth to stop them from chattering, and with his eyes focused upon the dark stairhead he had heard, quite plainly, a sound that was both near and far away, a sound hideously distinct. In that lacuna of stillness the stray sounds of the Castle had become wayward, ungaugable. A mouse nibbling beneath floor boards might equally have been within a few feet or several halls away.

The sound that Flay heard was of a knife being deliberately whetted. How far away he had no means of telling. It was a sound in vacuo, an abstract thing, yet so enormously it sounded, it might well have been within an inch of his craning ear.

The number of times the blade moved across the hone had no relation to the actual length of time which Flay experienced as he listened. To him the mechanical forward and backward movement of steel against stone lasted the night itself. Had the dawn broken as he listened he would not have been surprised. In reality it was but a few moments, and when the second tempest flung itself roaring against the Castle walls, Flay was on his hands and knees with his head thrust forward towards the sound, his lips drawn back from his teeth.

For the rest of the night the storm was unabated. He crouched there at his master's door, hour after hour, but he heard no more of that hideous scraping.

The dawn, when it came, powdering with slow and inexorable purpose the earthy blackness with grey seeds, found the servant open-eyed, his hands hanging like dead weights over his drawn-up knees, his defiant chin between his wrists. Slowly the air cleared, and stretching his cramped limbs one by one he reared up stiffly to his feet, shrugging his shoulders to his ears. Then he took the iron key from between his teeth and dropped it into his jacket pocket.

In seven slow paces he had reached the stairhead and was staring down into a well of cold. The stairs descended as though for ever. As his eyes moved from step to step they noticed a small object in the centre of one of the landings about forty feet below. It was in the shape of a rough oval. Flay turned his head to Lord Sepulchrave's door.

The sky was drained of its fury and there was silence.

He descended, his hand on the banisters. Each step awoke echoes from below him, and fainter echoes from above him, away to the east.

As he reached the landing a ray of light ran like a slender spear through an eastern window and quivered in a little patch on the wall, a few feet from where he stood. This thread of light intensified the shadows below and above it, and it was only after some groping that Flay came across the object. In his harsh hands it felt disgustingly soft. He brought it close to his eyes and became aware of a sickly, penetrating smell; but he could not see what it was that he held. Then, lifting it into the sunbeam so that his hand cast a shadow over the lozenge of light upon the wall, he saw, as though it were something supernaturally illumined, a very small, richly and exquisitely sculpted gateau. At the perimeter of this delicacy, a frail coral-like substance had been worked into the links of a chain, leaving in the centre a minute arena of jade-green icing, across whose glacid surface the letter 'S' lay coiled like a worm of cream.

THE UN-EARTHING OF BARQUENTINE

THE Earl, tired from a day of ritual (during part of which it was required of him to ascend and descend the Tower of Flints three times by the stone staircase, leaving on each occasion a glass of wine on a box of wormwood placed there for the purpose on a blue turret) had retired to his room as soon as he was able to get away from the last performance of the day and had taken a more powerful dose of laudanum than he had previously needed. It was noticed that he now brought to his work during the day a fervour quite unprecedented. His concentration upon detail and his thoroughness in the execution and understanding of the minutiae involved in the monotonous ceremonies were evidence of a new phase in his life.

The loss of his library had been a blow so pulverizing that he had not yet begun to suffer the torment that was later to come to him. He was still dazed and bewildered, but he sensed instinctively that his only hope lay in turning his mind as often as possible from the tragedy and in applying himself unstintingly to the routine of the day. As the weeks passed by, however, he found it more and more difficult to keep the horror of that night from his mind. Books which he loved not only for their burden, but intrinsically, for varying qualities of paper and print, kept reminding him that they were no longer to be fingered and read. Not only were the books lost and the thoughts in the books, but what was to him, perhaps, the most searching loss of all, the hours of rumination which lifted him above himself and bore him upon their muffled and enormous wings. Not a day passed but he was reminded of some single volume, or of a series of works, whose very positions on the walls was so clearly indented in his mind. He had taken refuge from this raw emptiness in a superhuman effort to concentrate his mind exclusively upon the string of ceremonies which he had daily to perform. He had not tried to rescue a single volume from the shelves, for even while the flames leapt around him he knew that every sentence that escaped the fire would be unreadable and bitter as gall, something to taunt him endlessly. It was better to have the cavity in his heart yawning and completely empty than mocked by a single volume. Yet not a day passed but he knew his grip had weakened.

Shortly after the death of Sourdust in the library it was remembered that the old librarian had had a son, and a search was made at once. It was a long time before they discovered a figure asleep in the corner of a room with a very low ceiling. It was necessary to stoop, in order to enter the apartment through the filthy walnut door. After having stooped under the decaying lintel there was no relief from the cramped position and no straightening of the back, for the ceiling sagged across the room for the most part at the level of the door-head, but at the centre, like a mouldering belly, it bulged still further earthwards, black with flies. Ill lit by a long horizontal strip of window near the floor-boards, it was difficult for the servants who had been sent on this mission to see at first whether there was anyone in the room or not. A table near the centre with its legs sawn off halfway down, into which they stumbled, had, as they soon discovered, been obscuring from their view Barquentine, old Sourdust's son. He lay upon a straw-filled mattress. At first sight the servants were appalled at a similarity between the son and the dead father, but when they saw that the old man lying on his back with his eyes closed had only one leg, and that a withered one, they were relieved, and straightening themselves, were dazed by striking their heads against the ceiling.

When they had recovered they found that they were kneeling, side by side, on all fours. Barquentine was watching them. Lifting the stump of his withered leg he rapped it irritably on the mattress, sending up a cloud of dust.

'What do you want?' he said. His voice was dry like his father's, but stronger than the mere twenty years that lay between their ages could have accounted for. Barquentine was seventy-four.

The servant nearest him rose to a stooping position, rubbed his shoulder-blades on the ceiling and with his head forced down to the level of his nipples stared at Barquentine with his loose mouth hanging open. The companion, a squat, indelicate creature, replied obtusely from the shadows behind his loose-lipped friend:

'He's dead.'

'Whom are you talking of, you oaf?' said the septuagenarian irritably, levering himself on his elbow and raising another cloud of dust with his stump.

'Your father,' said the loose-mouthed man in the eager tone of one bringing good tidings.

'How?' shouted Barquentine, who was becoming more and more irritable. 'How? When? Don't stand there staring at me like stenching mules.'

'Yesterday,' they replied. 'Burned in the library. Only bones left.'

'Details!' yelled Barquentine, thrashing about with his stump and knotting his beard furiously as his father had done. 'Details, you bladder heads! Out! Out of my way! Out of the room, curse you!'

Foraging about in the darkness he found his crutch and struggled onto his withered leg. Such was the shortness of this leg that when he was on his foot it was possible for him to move grotesquely to the door without having to lower his head to avoid the ceiling. He was about half the height of the crouching servants, but he passed between their bulks like a small, savage cloud of material, ragged to the extent of being filigree, and swept them to either side.

He passed through the low door in the way that infants will walk clean under a table, head in air, and emerge triumphantly on the other side.

The servants heard his crutch striking the floor of the passage and the alternate stamp of the withered leg. Of the many things that Barquentine had to do during the next few hours, the most immediate were to take command of his father's apartments: to procure the many keys: to find, and don, the crimson sacking that had always been in readiness for him against the day of his father's death: and to acquaint the Earl that he was cognizant of his duties, for he had studied them, with and without his father, for the last fifty-four years, in between his alternative relaxations of sleep and of staring at a patch of mildew on the bulge-bellied ceiling of his room.

From the outset he proved himself to be uncompromisingly efficient. The sound of his approaching crutch became a sign for feverish activity, and trepidation. It was as though a hard, intractible letter of the Groan law were approaching – the iron letter of tradition.

This was, for the Earl, a great blessing, for with a man of so strict and unswerving a discipline it was impossible to carry through the day's work without a thorough rehearsal every morning – Barquentine insisting upon his Lordship learning by heart whatever speeches were to be made during the day and all the minutiae that pertained to the involved ceremonies.

This took up a great deal of the Earl's time, and kept his mind, to a certain degree, from introspection; nevertheless, the shock he had sustained was, as the weeks drew on, beginning to have its effect. His sleeplessness was making of each night a hell more dreadful than the last.

His narcotics were powerless to aid him, for when after a prodigious dose he sank into a grey slumber, it was filled with shapes that haunted him when he awoke, and waved enormous sickly-smelling wings above his head, and filled his room with the hot breath of rotting plumes. His habitual melancholy was changing day by day into something more sinister. There were moments when he would desecrate the crumbling and mournful mask of his face with a smile more horrible than the darkest lineaments of pain.

Across the stoniness of his eyes a strange light would pass for a moment, as though the moon were flaring on the gristle, and his lips would open and the gash of his mouth would widen in a dead, climbing, curve.

Steerpike had foreseen that madness would sooner or later come to the Earl, and it was with a shock of annoyance that he heard of Barquentine and of his ruthless efficiency. It had been part of his plan to take over the duties of old Sourdust, for he felt himself to be the only person in the Castle capable of dealing with the multifarious details that the work would involve – and he knew that, with the authority which could hardly have been denied him had there been no one already versed in the laws of the Castle, he would have been brought not only into direct and potent contact with Sepulchrave, but would have had opened up to him by degrees the innermost secrets of Gormenghast. His power would have been multiplied a hundred-fold; but he had not reckoned with the ancientry of the tenets that bound the anatomy of the place together. For every key position in the Castle there was the apprentice, either the son or the student, bound to secrecy. Centuries of experience had seen to it that there should be no gap in the steady, intricate stream of immemorial behaviour.

No one had thought or heard of Barquentine for over sixty years, but when old Sourdust died Barquentine appeared like a well-versed actor on the mouldering stage, and the slow drama of Gormenghast continued among shadows.

Despite this setback in his plans, Steerpike had managed to make even more capital out of his rescue work than he had anticipated. Flay was inclined to treat him with a kind of taciturn respect. He had never quite known what he ought to do about Steerpike. When they had coincided a month previously at the garden gate of the Prunesquallor's, Flay had retired as from a ghost, sullenly, glancing over his shoulder at the dapper enigma, losing his chance of castigating the urchin. In Mr Flay's mind the boy Steerpike was something of an apparition. Most fathomless of all, the lives of the Earl, the Countess, Titus and Fuchsia had been saved by the whelp, and there was a kind of awe, not to say admiration, mixed with his distaste.

Not that Flay unbent to the boy, for he felt it a grievance that he should in any way admit equality with someone who had come originally from Swelter's kitchen.

Barquentine, also, was a bitter pill to swallow, but Flay realized at once the traditional rightness and integrity of the old man.

Fuchsia, for whom the fine art of procedure held less lure, found in old Barquentine a creature to hide from and to hate – not for any specific reason, but with the hatred of the young for the authority vested in age.

She found that as the days went on she began to listen for the sound of his crutch striking on the floor, like the blows of a weapon.

FIRST REPERCUSSIONS

UNABLE to reconcile the heroism of Steerpike's rescue with his face as she had seen it beyond the window before she fell, Fuchsia began to treat the youth with less and less assurance. She began to admire his ingenuity, his devilry, his gift of speech which she found so difficult but which was for him so simple. She admired his cold efficiency and she hated it. She wondered at his quickness, his self-assurance. The more she saw of him the more she felt impelled to recognize in him a nature at once more astute and swift than her own. At night his pale face with its closely-set eyes would keep appearing before her. And when she awoke she would remember with a start how he had saved their lives.

Fuchsia could not make him out. She watched him carefully. Somehow he had become one of the personalities of the Castle's central life. He had been insinuating his presence on all who mattered with such subtlety, that when he leapt dramatically to the fore by rescuing the family from the burning library, it was as though that deed of valour were all that had been needed to propel him to the forefront of the picture.

He still lived at the Prunesquallor's but was making secret plans for moving into a long, spacious room with a window that let in the morning sun. It lay on the same floor as the aunts in the South Wing. There was really very little reason for him to stay with the Doctor, who did not seem sufficiently aware of the new status he had acquired and whose questions regarding the way he (Steerpike) had found the pine tree, already felled and lopped for the Rescue, and various other details, though not difficult to answer – for he had prepared his replies to any of the possible questions he might be faced with – were, nevertheless, pertinent. The Doctor had had his uses. He had proved a valuable stepping-stone, but it was time to take up a room, or a suite of rooms, in the Castle proper, where knowledge of what was going on would come more easily.

Prunesquallor, ever since the burning, had been, for him, strangely voiceless. When he spoke it was in the same high, thin, rapid way, but for a great part of each day he would lie back in his chair in the sitting-room, smiling incessantly at everyone who caught his eye, his teeth displayed as uncompromisingly as ever before, but with something more cogitative about the great magnified eyes that swam beneath the thick lenses of his spectacles. Irma, who since the fire had been strapped in her bed, and who was having about half a pint of blood removed on alternate Tuesdays, was now allowed downstairs in the afternoons, where she sat dejectedly and tore up sheets of calico which were brought to her chair-side every morning. For hours on end she would continue with this noisy, wasteful and monotonous soporific, brooding the while upon the fact that she was no lady.

Mrs Slagg was still very ill. Fuchsia did all she could for her, moving the nurse's bed into her own room, for the old woman had become very frightened of the dark, which she now associated with smoke.

Titus seemed to be the one least affected by the burning. His eyes remained bloodshot for some time afterwards, but the only other result was a severe cold, and Prunesquallor took the infant over to his own house for its duration.

Old Sourdust's bones had been removed from the marble table among the charred remains of woodwork and books.

Flay, who had been assigned the mission of collecting the dead librarian's remains and of returning with them to the servant's quadrangle, where a coffin was being constructed from old boxes, found it difficult to handle the charred skeleton. The head had become a bit loose, and Flay after scratching his own skull for a long while at last decided that the only thing to do would be to carry the rattling relics in his arms as though he were carrying a baby. This was both more respectful and lessened the danger of disarticulation or breakage.

On that particular evening as he returned through the woods the rain had fallen heavily before he reached the fringe of the trees, and by the time he was half way across the wasteland which divided the pines from Gormenghast, the rain was streaming over the bones and skull in his arms and bubbling in the eye sockets. Flay's clothes were soaking, and the water squelched in his boots. As he neared the Castle the light had become so obscured by the downpour that he could not see more than a few paces ahead. Suddenly a sound immediately behind him caused him to start, but before he was able to turn, a sharp pain at the back of his head filled him with sickness, and sinking gradually to his knees he loosed the skeleton from his arms and sank in a stupor upon the bubbling ground. How many hours or minutes he had been lying there he could not know, but when he recovered consciousness the rain was still falling heavily. He raised his great rough hand to the back of his head where he discovered a swelling the size of a duck's egg. Swift jabs of pain darted through his brain from side to side.

All at once he remembered the skeleton and got dizzily to his knees. His eyes were still misted, but he saw the wavering outline of the bones; but when a few moments later his eyes had cleared, he found that the head was missing.

SOURDUST IS BURIED

BARQUENTINE officiated at his father's funeral. To his way of thinking it was impossible for the bones to be buried without a skull. It was a pity that the skull could not be the one which belonged, but that there should be some sort of termination to the body before it was delivered to the earth was apparently imperative. Flay had recounted his story and the bruise above his left ear testified to its veracity. There seemed to be no clue to who the cowardly assailant might be, nor could any motive be imagined that could prompt so callous, so purposeless an action. Two days were spent in a fruitless search for the missing ornament, Steerpike leading a gang of stable hands on a tour of the wine vaults which according to his own theory would afford, so he argued, many an ideal niche or corner in which the criminal might hide the skull. He had always had a desire to discover the extent of the vaults. The candle-lit search through a damp labyrinth of cellars and passages, lined with dusty bottles, disproved his theory, however; and when on the same evening the search parties, one and all, reported that their quests had been abortive, it was decided that on the following evening, the bones were to be buried whether the head were found or not.

It being considered a desecration to unearth any bodies from the servants' graveyard, Barquentine decided that the skull of a small calf would prove equally effective. One was procured from Swelter, and after it had been boiled and was free of the last vestige of flesh, it was dried and varnished, and as the hour of the burial approached and there was no sign of the original skull being found, Barquentine sent Flay to Mrs Slagg's room to procure some blue ribbon. The calf's skull was all but perfect, it being on the small side and dwarfing the rest of the remains far less than might have been feared. At all events, the old man would be complete if not homogeneous. He would not be headless, and his funeral would be no slipshod, bury-as-you-please affair.

It was only when the coffin stood near the graveside in the Cemetery of the Esteemed, and only when the crowd was standing silently about the small, rectangular trench, that Barquentine motioned Sepulchrave forward, and indicated that the moment had come for the Earl to attach the calf skull to the last of old Sourdust's vertebrae with the aid of the blue ribbon which Mrs Slagg had found at the bottom of one of her shuttered baskets of material. Here was honour for the old man. Barquentine knotted his beard ruminatively and was well pleased. Whether it were some obscure tenet of the Groan lore which Barquentine was rigorously adhering to, or whether it was that he found comfort of some kind in ribbons, it is impossible to say, but whatever the reason might be, Barquentine had procured from somewhere or other several extra lengths of varying colours and his father's skeleton boasted a variety of silk bows which were neatly tied about such bones as seemed to offer themselves to this decorative treatment.

When the Earl had finished with the calf-skull, Barquentine bent over the coffin and peered at the effect. He was, on the whole, satisfied. The calf's head was rather too big, but it was adequate. The late evening light lit it admirably and the grain of the bone was particularly effective.

The Earl was standing silently a little in front of the crowd, and Barquentine, digging his crutch into the earth, hopped around it until he was facing the men who had carried the coffin. One glint of his cold eyes brought them to the graveside.

'Nail the lid on,' he shouted, and hopped around his crutch again on his withered leg, the ferrule of his support swivelling in the soft ground and raising the mud in gurgling wedges as it twisted.

Fuchsia, standing at her mother's mountainous side, loathed

him with her whole body. She was beginning to hate everything that was old. What was that word which Steerpike kept denouncing whenever he met her? He was always saying it was dreadful – 'Authority': that was it. She looked away from the one-legged man and her eyes moved absently along the line of gaping faces. They were staring at the coffin-men who were nailing down the planks. Everyone seemed horrible to Fuchsia. Her mother was gazing over the heads of the crowd with her characteristic sightlessness. Upon her father's face a smile was beginning to appear, as though it were something inevitable, uncontrollable – something Fuchsia had never seen before on his face. She covered her eyes with her hands for a moment and felt a surge of unreality rising in her. Perhaps the whole thing was a dream. Perhaps everyone was really kind and beautiful, and she had seen them only through the black net of a dream she was suffering. She lowered her hands and found herself gazing into Steerpike's eyes. He was on the other side of the grave and his arms were folded. As he stared at her, with his head a little on one side, like a bird's, he raised his eyebrows to her, quizzically, his mouth twisted up on one side. Fuchsia involuntarily made a little gesture with her hand, a motion of recognition, of friendliness, but there was about the gesture something so subtle, so tender, as to be indescribable. For herself, she did not know that her hand had moved – she only knew that the figure across the grave was young.

He was strange and unappealing, with his high shoulders and his large swollen forehead; but he was slender, and young. Oh, that was what it was! He did not belong to the old, heavy, intolerant world of Barquentine: he belonged to the lightness of life. There was nothing about him that drew her, nothing she loved except his youth and his bravery. He had saved Nannie Slagg from the fire. He had saved Dr Prune from the fire – and oh! he had saved her, too. Where was his swordstick? What had he done with it? He was so silly about it, carrying it with him wherever he went.

The earth was being shovelled into the grave for the ramshackle coffin had been lowered. When the cavity was filled, Barquentine inspected the rectangular patch of disturbed earth.

The shovelling had been messy work, the mud clinging to the spades, and Barquentine had shouted at the grave-hands irritably. Now, he scraped some of the unevenly distributed earth into the shallower patches with his foot, balancing at an angle upon his crutch. The mourners were dispersing, and Fuchsia, shambling away from her parents, found herself to the extreme right of the crowd as it moved towards the castle.

'May I walk with you?' said Steerpike, sidling up.

'Yes,' said Fuchsia. 'Oh, yes; why shouldn't you?' She had never wanted him before, and was surprised at her own words.

Steerpike shot a glance at her as he pulled out his small pipe. When he had lit it, he said:

'Not much in my line, Lady Fuchsia.'

'What isn't?'

'Earth to earth; ashes to ashes, and all that sort of excitement.'

'Not much in anyone's line, I shouldn't think,' she replied. 'I don't like the idea of dying.'

'Not when one's young, anyway,' said the youth. 'It's all right for our friend rattle-ribs: not much life left inside him, anyway.'

'I like you being disrespectful, sometimes,' said Fuchsia in a rush. 'Why must one try and be respectful to old people when they aren't considerate?'

'It's their idea,' said Steerpike. 'They like to keep this reverence business going. Without it where'd they be? Sunk. Forgotten. Over the side: for they've nothing except their age, and they're jealous of our youth.'

'Is that what it is?' said Fuchsia, her eyes widening. 'Is it because they are jealous? Do you really think it's that?'

'Undoubtedly,' said Steerpike. 'They want to imprison us and make us fit into their schemes, and taunt us, and make us work for them. All the old are like that.'

'Mrs Slagg isn't like that,' said Fuchsia.

'She is the exception,' said Steerpike, coughing in a strange way with his hand over his mouth. 'She is the exception that proves the rule.'

They walked on in silence for a few paces. The Castle was

looming overhead and they were treading into the shadow of a tower.

'Where's your swordstick?' said Fuchsia. 'How can you be without it? You don't know what to do with your hands.'

Steerpike grinned. This was a new Fuchsia. More animated — yet was it animation, or a nervous, tired excitement which gave the unusual lift to her voice?

'My swordstick,' said Steerpike, rubbing his chin, 'my dear little swordstick. I must have left it behind in the rack.'

'Why?' said Fuchsia. 'Don't you adore it any more?'

'I *do*, oh yes! I *do*,' Steerpike replied in a comically emphatic voice. 'I adore it just as much, but I felt it would be safer to leave it behind, because do you know what I should probably have *done* with it?'

'What would you have done?' said Fuchsia.

'I would have pricked Barquentine's guts with it,' said Steerpike; 'most delicately, here and there, and everywhere, until the old scarecrow was yelling like a cat; and when he had yelled all the breath from his black lungs, I'd have tied him by his one leg to a branch and set fire to his beard. So you see what a good thing it was that I didn't have my swordstick, don't you?'

But when he turned to her Fuchsia was gone from his side.

He could see her running through the misty air in a strange, bounding manner; but whether she was running for enjoyment, or in order to rid herself of him, he could not know.

THE TWINS ARE RESTIVE

ABOUT a week after Sourdust's burial, or to be precise, about a week after the burial of all that was left of what had once been Sourdust, along with the calf skull and the ribbons, Steerpike revisited the Aunts for the purpose of selecting a set of rooms on the same floor as their own apartments in the south wing. Since the burning they had become not only very vain, but troublesome. They wished to know when, now that they had carried out the task according to plan, they were to come into their own. Why was not the south wing already alive with pageantry and splendour? Why were its corridors still so dusty and deserted? Had they set fire to their brother's library for nothing? Where were the thrones they had been promised? Where were the crowns of gold? At each fresh appearance of Steerpike in their apartments these questions were renewed, and on every occasion it became more difficult to leave them mollified and convinced that their days of grievance were drawing to a close.

They were as outwardly impassive, their faces showing no sign at all of what was going on inside their identical bodies, but Steerpike had learned to descry from the almost imperceptible movements which they made with their limp fingers, roughly what was happening in their minds, or to what height their emotions were aroused. There was an uncanniness about the way their white fingers would move simultaneously, indicating that their brains were at that precise moment travelling along the same narrow strip of thought, at the same pace, with the same gait.

The glittering promises with which Steerpike had baited his cruel hook had produced an effect upon them more fundamental than he had anticipated. This concept of themselves as rulers of the south wing, was now uppermost in their minds, and in fact it filled their minds leaving no room for any other notion. Outwardly it showed itself in their conversation which harped upon nothing else. With the flush of success upon them, their fingers became looser, although their faces remained as expressionless as powdered slabs. Steerpike was now reaping the consequences of having persuaded them of their bravery and ingenuity, and of the masterly way in which they, and they alone, could set the library alight. It had been necessary at the time to blow them into tumours of conceit and self-assurance, but now, their usefulness for the moment at an end, it was becoming more and more difficult to deal with their inflation. However, with one excuse or another he managed to persuade them of the inadvisability of rushing a matter of such magnitude as that of raising them to their twin summits. Such things must be achieved with deliberation, cunning and foresight. Their position must improve progressively through a sequence of minor victories, which although each in itself attracted no notice, would build up insidiously, until before the castle was aware of it the South wing would blazon forth in rightful glory. The twins, who had expected the change in their status to be brought about overnight, were bitterly disappointed, and although Steerpike's arguments to the effect that their power when it came must be something of sure foundation convinced them as he spoke, yet no sooner were they alone than they reverted at once to a condition of chagrin, and Steerpike's every appearance was the sign for them to air their grievances anew.

On this particular afternoon, as soon as he had entered their room and their childish clamour had started, he cut them short by crying: 'We shall begin!'

He had lifted his left hand high into the air to silence them, as he shouted. In his right hand he held a scroll of paper. They were standing with their shoulders and hips touching, side by side, their heads forced a little forward. When their loud, flat voices ceased, he continued:

'I have ordered your thrones. They are being made in secret, but as I have insisted that they are to be beaten from the purest gold they will take some time to complete. I have been sent these designs by the goldsmith, a craftsman without a peer. It is for you, my Ladyships, to choose. I have no doubt which you will choose, for although they are all three the most consummate works of art, yet with your taste, your flair for proportion, your grasp of minutiae, I feel confident you will select the one which I believe has no rival among the thrones of the world.'

Steerpike had, of course, made the drawings himself, spending several hours longer on them than he had intended, for once he had started he had become interested, and had the Doctor or his sister opened his door in the small hours of this same morning they would have found the high-shouldered boy bending over a table in his room, absorbed; the compasses, protractors and set square neatly placed in a row at the side of the table, the beautifully sharpened pencil travelling along the ruler with cold precision.

Now, as he unrolled the drawings before the wide eyes of the

Aunts he handled them deftly, for it pleased him to take care of the fruits of his labours. His hands were clean, the fingers being curiously pointed, and the nails rather longer than is normal.

Cora and Clarice were at his side in an instant. There was no expression in their faces at all. All that could be found there was uncompromisingly anatomical. The thrones stared at the Aunts and the Aunts stared back at the thrones.

'I have no doubt which one you will prefer, for it is unique in the history of golden thrones. Choose, your Ladyships – choose!' said Steerpike.

Cora and Clarice pointed simultaneously at the biggest of the three drawings. It almost filled the page.

'How *right* you are!' said Steerpike. 'How *right* you are! It was the only choice. I shall be seeing the goldsmith tomorrow and shall advise him of your selection.'

'I want mine soon,' said Clarice.

'So do I,' said Cora, 'very soon.'

'I thought I had explained to you,' said Steerpike, taking them by their elbows and bringing them towards him – 'I thought I had explained to you that a throne of hammered gold is not a thing which can be wrought overnight. This man is a craftsman, an artist. Do you want your glory ruined by a makeshift and ridiculous pair of bright yellow sit-upons? Do you want to be the laughing-stock of the Castle, all over again, because you were too impatient? Or are you anxious for Gertrude and the rest of them to stare, open-mouthed with jealousy, at you as you sit aloft like the two purple queens you undoubtedly are? ... Everything must be of the best. You have entrusted me to raise you to the status that is your due and right. You must leave it to me. When the hour comes, we shall strike. In the meanwhile it is for us to make of these apartments something unknown to Gormenghast.'

'Yes,' said Cora. 'That's what I think. They must be wondrous. The rooms must be wondrous.'

'Yes,' said Clarice. 'Because *we* are. The rooms must be just like us.' Her mouth fell open, as though the lower jaw had died.

'But we are the only ones who *are* worthy. No one must forget that, must they, Cora?'

'No one,' said Cora. 'No one at all.'

'Exactly,' said Steerpike, 'and your first duty will be to recondition the Room of Roots.' He had glanced at them shrewdly. 'The roots must be repainted. Even the smallest must be repainted, because there is no other room in Gormenghast that is so wonderful as to be full of roots. Your roots. The roots of your tree.'

To his surprise the twins were not listening to him. They were holding each other about their long barrel-like chests.

'He made us do it,' they were saying. 'He made us burn dear Sepulchrave's books. Dear Sepulchrave's books.'

'HALF-LIGHT'

MEANWHILE, the Earl and Fuchsia were sitting together two hundred feet below and over a mile away from Steerpike and the Aunts. His lordship, with his back to a pine tree and his knees drawn up to his chin, was gazing at his daughter with a slithery smile upon his mouth that had once been so finely drawn. Covering his feet and heaped about his slender body on all sides was a cold, dark, undulating palliasse of pine needles, broken here and there with heavy, weary-headed ferns and grey fungi, their ashen surfaces exuding a winter sweat.

A kind of lambent darkness filled the dell. The roof was sky-proof, the branches interlacing so thickly that even the heaviest downpour was stayed from striking through; the methodical drip ... drip ... drip of the branch-captured rain only fell to the floor of needles several hours after the start of the heaviest storm. And yet a certain amount of reflected daylight filtered through into the clearing, mainly from the East, in which direction lay the shell of the library. Between the clearing and the path that ran in front of the ruin, the trees, although as thick, were not more than thirty to forty yards in depth.

'How many shelves have you built for your father?' said the Earl to his daughter with a ghastly smile.

'Seven shelves, father,' said Fuchsia. Her eyes were very wide and her hands trembled as they hung at her sides.

345

'Three more shelves, my daughter – three more shelves, and then we will put the volumes back.'

'Yes, father.'

Fuchsia, picking up a short branch, scored across the needled ground three long lines, adding them to the seven which already lay between her father and herself.

'That's it, that's it,' came the melancholy voice. 'Now we have space for the Sonian Poets. Have you the books ready – little daughter?'

Fuchsia swung her head up, and her eyes fastened upon her father. He had never spoken to her in that way – she had never before heard that tone of love in his voice. Chilled by the horror of his growing madness, she had yet been filled with a compassion she had never known, but now there was more than compassion within her, there was released, of a sudden, a warm jet of love for the huddled figure whose long pale hand rested upon his knees, whose voice sounded so quiet and so thoughtful. 'Yes, father, I've got the books ready,' she replied; 'do you want me to put them on the shelves?'

She turned to a heap of pine cones which had been gathered.

'Yes, I am ready,' he replied after a pause that was filled with the silence of the wood. 'But one by one. One by one. We shall stock three shelves tonight. Three of my long, rare shelves.'

'Yes, father.'

The silence of the high pines drugged the air.

'Fuchsia.'

'What, father?'

'You are my daughter.'

'Yes.'

'And there is Titus. He will be the Earl of Gormenghast. Is that so?'

'Yes, father.'

'When I am dead. But do I know you, Fuchsia? Do I know you?'

'I don't know – very well,' she replied; but her voice became more certain now that she perceived his weakness. 'I suppose we don't know each other very much.'

Again she was affected by an uprising of love. The mad smile making incongruous every remark which the Earl ventured, for he spoke with tenderness and moderation, had for the moment ceased to frighten her. In her short life she had been brought face to face with so many forms of weirdness that although the uncanny horror of the sliding smile distressed her, yet the sudden breaking of the barriers that had lain between them for so long as she could remember overpowered her fear. For the first time in her life she felt that she was a daughter – that she had a father – of her own. What did she care if he was going mad – saving for his own dear sake? He was hers.

'My books . . .' he said.

'I have them here, father. Shall I fill up the first long shelf for you?'

'With the Sonian Poets, Fuchsia.'

'Yes.'

She picked up a cone from the heap at her side and placed it on the end of the line she had scored in the ground. The Earl watched her very carefully.

'That is Andrema, the lyricist – the lover – he whose quill would pulse as he wrote and fill with a blush of blue, like a bruised nail. His verses, Fuchsia, his verses open out like flowers of glass, and at their centre, between the brittle petals lies a pool of indigo, translucent and as huge as doom. His voice is unmuffled – it is like a bell, clearly ringing in the night of our confusion; but the clarity is the clarity of imponderable depth – depth – so that his lines float on for evermore, Fuchsia – on and on and on, for evermore. That is Andrema . . . Andrema.'

The Earl, with his eyes on the cone which Fuchsia had placed at the end of the first line, opened his mouth more widely, and suddenly the pines vibrated with the echoes of a dreadful cry, half scream, half laughter.

Fuchsia stiffened, the blood draining from her face. Her father, his mouth still open, even after the scream had died out of the forest, was now upon his hands and knees. Fuchsia tried to force her voice from the dryness of her throat. Her father's eyes were on her as she struggled, and at last his lips came together and his eyes recovered the melancholy sweetness that she had so lately discovered in them. She was able to say, as she picked up another cone and made as if to place it at the side of 'Andrema' : 'Shall I go on with the library, father ?'

But the Earl could not hear her. His eyes had lost focus. Fuchsia dropped the cone from her hand and came to his side.

'What is it,' she said. 'Oh father! father! what is it?'

'I am not your father,' he replied. 'Have you no knowledge of me?' And as he grinned his black eyes widened and in either eye there burned a star, and as the stars grew greater his fingers curled. 'I live in the Tower of Flints,' he cried. 'I am the death-owl.'

A ROOF OF REEDS

To her left, as she moved slowly along the broken and over-grown track Keda was conscious the while of that blasphemous finger of rock which had dominated the western skyline for seven weary days. It had been like a presence, something which, however the sunlight or moonlight played upon it, was always sinister; in essence, wicked.

Between the path she walked and the range of mountains was a region of marshland which reflected the voluptuous sky in rich pools, or with a duller glow where choked swamps sucked at the colour and breathed it out again in sluggish vapour. A tract of rushes glimmered, for each long sword-shaped leaf was edged with a thread of crimson. One of the larger pools of almost unbroken surface not only reflected the burning sky, but the gruesome, pointing finger of the rock, which plunged through breathless water.

On her right the land sloped upwards and was forested with mis-shapen trees. Although their outermost branches were still lit, the violence of the sunset was failing, and the light was crumbling momently from the boughs.

Keda's shadow stretched to her right, growing, as she pro-ceeded, less and less intense as the raddled ground dulled from a reddish tint to a nondescript ochre, and then from ochre to a warm grey which moment by moment grew more chill, until she found herself moving down a track of ash-grey light.

For the last two days the great shoulder of hill with the dreadful monotony of its squat, fibrous trees which covered it, had lain on Keda's right hand, breathing, as it were, over her shoulder; groping for her with stunted arms. It seemed that for all her life the oppressive presence of trees, of stultified trees, had been with her, leering at her, breathing over her right shoulder, each one gesticulating with its hairy hands, each one with a peculiar menace of its own, and yet every one monotonously the same in the endlessness of her journey.

For the monotony began to have the quality of a dream, both uneventful and yet terrifying, and it seemed that her body and her brain were flanked by a wall of growth that would never end. But the last two days had at least opened up to her the wintry flats upon her left, where for so long her eyes had been arrested and wearied by a canyon face of herbless rock upon whose high grey surface the only sign of life had been when an occasional ledge afforded purchase for the carrion crow. But Keda, stumbling exhaustedly in the ravine, had no thought for them as they peered at her, following her with their eyes, their naked necks protruding from the level of their scraggy bellies, their shoulders hunched above their heads, their murderous claws curled about their scant supports.

Snow had lain before her like a long grey carpet, for the winter sun was never to be seen from that canyon's track, and when at last the path had veered to the right and the daylight had rushed in upon her, she had stumbled forward for a few paces and dropped upon her knees in a kind of thanksgiving. As she raised her head the blonde light had been like a benison.

But she was indescribably weary, dropping her aching feet before her as she continued on her way without knowledge of what she was doing. Her hair fell across her face raggedly; her heavy cloak was flecked with mud and matted with burrs and clinging brambles.

Her right hand clung on mechanically to a strap over her shoulder which supported a satchel, now empty of food, but weighted with a stranger cargo.

Before she had left the Mud Dwellings on the night when her lovers had killed each other beneath the all-seeing circle of that

349

never-to-be-forgotten, spawning moon, she had, as in a trance, found her way back to her dwelling, collected together what food she could find, and then, like a somnambulist, made her way first to Braigon's and then to Rantel's workshop and taken from each a small carving. Then, moving out into the emptiness of the morning, three hours before the dawn, she had walked, her brain dilated with a blank and zoneless pain, until, as the dawn like a wound in the sky welled into her consciousness, she fell among the salt grasses where the meres began, and with the carvings in her arms, slept unseen throughout a day of sunshine. That was very long ago. How long ago? Keda had lost all sense of time. She had journeyed through many regions – had received her meals from many hands in return for many kinds of labour. For a long while she tended the flocks of one whose shepherd had been taken ill with fold-fever and had died with a lamb in his arms. She had worked on a long barge with a woman who, at night, would mew like an otter as she swam among the reeds. She had woven the hazel hurdles and had made great nets for the fresh-water fish. She had moved from province to province.

But a weariness had come, and the sickness at dawn; and yet she was forced to be continually moving. But always with her were her burning trophies, her white eagle; her yellow stag.

And now it was beyond her strength to work, and a power she did not question was inexorably driving her back towards the Dwellings.

Under the high, ragged and horrible bosom of the hill, she stumbled on. All colour was stifled from the sky and the profane finger of rock was no longer visible save as a narrow hint of dark on dark. The sunset had flamed and faded – every moment seeming permanent – and yet the crumbling from crimson to ash had taken no longer than a few demoniac moments.

Keda was now walking through darkness, all but the few yards immediately in front of her feet, obscured. She knew that she must sleep: that what strength remained in her was fast ebbing, and it was not because she was unused to spending the night hours alone among unfriendly shapes that she was stayed from coiling herself at the foot of the hill. The last few nights had been pain, for there was no mercy in the air that pressed its frozen hands to her body; but it was not for this reason that her feet still fell heavily before her, one after the other, the forward tilt of her body forcing them onwards.

It was not even that the trees that sucked at her right shoulder had filled her with horror, for now she was too tired for her imagination to fill her mind with the macabre. She moved on because a voice had spoken to her that morning as she walked. She had not realized that it was her own voice crying out to her, for she was too exhausted to know that her lips were giving vent to the occult

She had turned, for the voice had seemed to be immediately beside her. 'Do not stop,' it had said; 'not tonight, for you shall have a roof of reeds.' Startled, she had continued for not more than a few paces when the voice within her said: 'The old man, Keda, the old brown man. You must not stay your feet.'

She had not been frightened, for the reality of the supernatural was taken for granted among the Dwellers. And as she staggered, ten hours later, through the night the words wavered in her mind, and when a torch flared suddenly in the road ahead of her, scattering its red embers, she moaned with exhaustion and relief to have been found, and fell forward into the arms of the brown father.

What happened to her from that moment she did not know; but when she awoke she was lying upon a mattress of pine-needles, smelling of a hot, dry sweetness, and around her were the wooden walls of a cabin. For a moment she did not lift her eyes, although the words which she had heard upon the road were in her ears: for she knew what she would see, and when she at last lifted her head to see the thatching of the river-reeds above her she remembered the old man, and her eyes turned to a door in the wall. It opened softly as she lay, half drowsed with the perfume of the pine, and she saw a figure. It was as though Autumn was standing beside her, or an oak, heavy with its crisp, tenacious leaves. He was of brown, but lambent, as of sepia-black glass held before a flame. His shaggy hair and beard were like pampas grass; his skin the colour of sand; his clothes festooned about him like foliage along a hanging branch. All was brown, a symphony of brown, a brown tree, a brown landscape, a brown man.

He came across the room to her, his naked feet making no sound upon the earth of the cabin floor, where the creepers sent green tributaries questing.

Keda raised herself upon her elbow.

The rough summit of the oak tree moved, and then one of its branches motioned her back, so that she lay still again upon the pine-needles. Peace like a cloud enveloped her as she gazed at him and she knew that she was in the presence of a strange selflessness.

He left her side and, moving across the earth floor with that slow, drifting tread, unfastened some shutters and the rayless light of the north sky poured through a square window. He left the room, and she lay quietly, her mind becoming clearer as the minutes passed. The trestle bed that she lay upon was wide and low, being raised only a foot from the ground by two logs which supported the long planks. Her tired body seemed to float with every muscle relaxed among the billowing needles. Even the pain in her feet, the bruises she had sustained in her wanderings, were floating – a kind of floating pain, impersonal, and almost pleasureable. Across her the brown father had spread three rough blankets, and her right hand moving under them, as though to test the pleasure of moving itself independently from the tired mass of her body, struck upon something hard. She was too weary to wonder what it was; but sometime later she drew it forth – the white eagle. 'Braigon', she murmured, and with the word a hundred haunting thoughts returned. Again she felt about her and found the wooden stag. She brought them against her warm sides, and after the pain of memory a new emotion, kindred to that which she had felt on the night she had lain with Rantel, suffused her, and her heart, faintly at first and then more loud, and louder still, began to sing like a wild bird; and though her body heaved suddenly with sickness, the wild bird went on singing.

'FEVER'

WHITE and cool as was the light of the north window, Keda could tell that the sun was alone in the sky and that the winter day was cloudless and temperate. She could not tell how late it was, nor whether it was morning or evening. The old man brought a bowl of soup to her bedside. She wished to speak to him, but not yet, for the spell of silence was still so richly about her and so eloquent that she knew that with him there was no need to say anything at all. Her floating body felt strangely clear and sweet, lying as though it were a lily of pain.

She lay now holding the carvings at her side, her fingers spread over their smooth wooden contours, while she experienced the slow ebbing of fatigue from her limbs. Minute after minute passed, the steady light filling the room with whiteness. Every now and again she would raise herself and dip the earthenware spoon into the pottage; and as she drank her strength came back in little thick leaps. When she had at last emptied the bowl she turned over upon her side, and a tingling of strength rose in her with every moment that passed.

Again she was conscious of the cleanness of her body. For some time the effort was too great to be made, but when at last she pulled away the blankets she found that she was washed free of all the dust of her last days of wandering. She was unstained, and there was no trace of the nightmare upon her — only the sweet bruises, the long threads where thorns had torn her.

She tried to stand, and nearly fell; but drawing in a deep breath steadied herself and moved slowly to the window. Before her was a clearing, where greyish grass grew thickly, the shadow of a tree falling across it. Half in this shadow and half out of it a white goat was standing, and moving its sensitive narrow head side to side. A little beyond, to the left, was the mouth of a well. The clearing ended where a derelict stone building, roofless and black with spreading moss, held back a grove of leafless elms, where a murmuration of starlings was gathered. Beyond this grove Keda could catch a glimpse of a stony field, and beyond this field a forest climbing to a rounded summit of boulders. She turned her eyes again. There stood the white goat. It had moved out of the shadow and was like an exquisite toy, so white it was, with such curls of hair, such a beard of snow, such horns, such great and yellow eyes.

Keda stood for a long while gazing upon the scene, and although she saw with perfect clarity – the roofless house, the pine-shadow, the hillocks, the trellis-work vine, yet these were no part of her immediate consciousness, but figments of the half-dream langour of her awakening. More real to her was the bird-song at her breast, defying the memory of her lovers and the weight of her womb.

The age that was her heritage and the inexorable fate of the Dwellers had already begun to ravage her head, a despoliation which had begun before the birth of her first little child who was buried beyond the great wall, and her face had now lost all but the shadow of her beauty.

Keda left the window and, taking a blanket, wrapped it about her, and then opened the door of the room. She found herself facing another of roughly the same size but with a great table monopolizing the centre of the floor, a table with a dark-red cloth drawn across it. Beyond the table the earth descended by three steps, and in the further and lower portion of the floor were the old man's garden tools, flower pots and pieces of painted and unpainted wood. The room was empty and Keda passed slowly through a doorway into the clearing of sunlight.

The white goat watched her as she approached and took a few slender-legged steps towards her, lifting its head high into the air. She moved onwards and became conscious of the sound of water. The sun was about halfway between the zenith and the horizon, but Keda could not at first tell whether it was morning or afternoon, for there was no way of knowing whether the sun were climbing through the high east or sinking in the high west. All was stillness; the sun seemed to be fixed for ever as though it were a disc of yellow paper pasted against the pale-blue wintry sky.

She went forward slowly through the unknown time of day towards the sound of water. She passed the long roofless building on her left and for a moment was chilled by the shadow it cast.

Descending a steep bank of ferns, she came across the brook almost immediately. It ran between dark, leafless brambles. A little to Keda's left, where she stood among the thorny bushes at the water's edge, there was a crossing of boulders – old and smooth and hollowed into shallow basins by the passage of what must have been centuries of footfall. Beyond the ford a grey mare drank from the stream. Her mane fell over her eyes and floated on the surface of the water as she drank. Beyond the grey mare stood another of dappled skin, and beyond the dappled mare, at a point where the brook changed direction and bore to the right under a wall of evergreens, was a third – a horse whose coat was like black velvet. The three were quite still and absorbed, their manes trailing the water, their legs knee-deep in the sounding stream. Keda knew that if she walked a little way along the bank to her left until she gained a view of the next reach of the river, she would see the drinking horses one after another receding across the flats, each one an echo of the one before it – echoes of changing colour, but all knee-deep in water, all with their hanging manes, their drinking throats.

Suddenly she began to feel cold. The horses all lifted their heads and stared at her. The stream seemed to stand still; and then she heard herself talking.

'Keda,' she was saying, 'your life is over. Your lovers have died. Your child and her father are buried. And you also are dead. Only your bird sings on. What is the bright bird saying? That all is complete? Beauty will die away suddenly and at any time. At any time now – from sky and earth and limb and eye and breast and the strength of men and the seed and the sap and the bud and the foam and the flower – all will crumble for you, Keda, for all is over – only the child to be born, and then you will know what to do.'

She stood upon the boulders of the ford and saw below her the image of her face in the clear water. It had become very old; the scourge of the Dwellers had descended; only the eyes, like the eyes of a gazelle, defied the bane which now gave to her face the quality of a ruin. She stared; and then she put her hands below her heart, for the bird was crying, crying with joy. 'It is over!' screamed the beaked voice. 'It is only for the child that you are waiting. All else fulfilled, and then there is no longer any need.'

Keda lifted her head, and her eyes opened to the sky where a kestrel hung. Her heart beat and beat, and the air thickened until darkness muffled her eyes, while the gay cry of the bird went on and on: *'It is over! it is over! it is over!'*

The sky cleared before her. Beside her stood the brown father. When she turned to him he raised his head and then led her back to the cabin, where she lay exhausted upon her bed.

The sun and the moon had forced themselves behind her eyes and filled her head. A crowd of images circled about them; the cactus trees of the Mud Dwellings revolved about the towers of Gormenghast, which swam about the moon. Heads ran forward towards her, starting as mere pin points on an infinitely far horizon, enlarging unbearably as they approached, they burst over her face – her dead husband's face, Mrs Slagg's and Fuchsia's, Braigon's, Flay's, the Countess's, Rantel's and the Doctor's with his devouring smile. Something was being put into her mouth. It was the lip of a cup. She was being told to drink.

'Oh, father!' she cried.

He pressed her gently back against the pillow.

'There is a bird crying,' she said.

'What does it cry?' said the old man.

'It cries with joy, for me. It is happy for me, for soon it will all be over – when I am light again – and I can do it, oh, father, when I am light again.'

'What is it you will do?'

Keda stared at the reeds above her. 'That is what shall happen,' she murmured, 'with a rope, or with deep water, or a blade . . . or with a blade.'

FAREWELL

IT was a long while before Keda was well enough to set forth on horseback for the Mud Dwellings. Her fever had raged, and but for the care with which the old man watched over her she must surely have died. For many long nights in her delirium she unburdened herself of a torrent of words, her natural reticence shattered by the power of her heightened imaginings.

The old man sat by her, his bearded chin resting on a gnarled fist, his brown eyes upon her vibrant face. He listened to her words and pieced together the story of her loves and fears from the wrack of her outpouring. Removing a great damp leaf from her forehead he would replace it with another, ice-cold and shoe-shaped, from the store he had collected for her brow. Within a few minutes it would be warm from her burning forehead. Whenever he could leave her he prepared the herbs with which he fed her and concocted the potions which eventually stilled the nightmare in her brain, and quietened her blood.

As the days passed he began to know her better, in the great, inarticulate way of guardian trees. No word was spoken. Whatever passed between them of any significance travelled in silence, and taking his hand she would lie and receive great joy from gazing at his august and heavy head, his beard and his brown eyes, and the rustic bulk of his body beside her.

Yet in spite of the peace that filled her in his presence, the feeling she should be among her own people began to grow more powerful with every day that passed.

It was a long while after her fever had abated that the old man allowed Keda to get to her feet, although he could see that she was fretting. At last she was strong enough to go for short walks in the enclosure, and he led her, supporting her with his arm to the hillocks of pale hair, or among the elms.

From the beginning, their relationship had been baptized with silence, and even now, several months after that first afternoon when she had awakened beneath his roof, whatever words they spoke were only to facilitate the domestic tasks of the day. Their communion of silence which from the first they had recognized to be a common language was with them perpetually flowering in a kind of absolute trust in the other's receptivity.

Keda knew that the brown father realized she must go, and the old man knew that Keda understood why he could not let her go, for she was still too weak, and they moved together through the spring days, Keda watching him milking his white goat, and the brown father leaning like an oak against the wall of the cabin while Keda stirred the broth above the stone range, or scraped the loam from the spade and placed it among the few crude garden tools when daylight failed.

One evening when they were returning home after the longest walk which Keda had managed, they stopped for a moment upon the brow of one of the hillocks, and turned to the west before descending into the shadows that lay about the cabin.

There was a greenish light in the sky with a surface like alabaster. As they watched, the evening star sang out in a sudden point of light.

The ragged horizon of trees brought back to Keda's mind the long and agonizing journey that had brought her to this haven, to the cabin of the hermit, to this evening walk, to this moment of light, and she remembered the clawing of the branches at her right shoulder and how, upon her left, all the while there had stood the blasphemous finger of rock. Her eyes seemed to be drawn along the line of the dark trees until they rested upon a minute area of sky framed by the black and distant foliage. This fragment of sky was so small that it could never have been pointed out or even located again by Keda had she taken her eyes from it for a second.

The skyline of trees was, near its outline, perforated with a myriad of microscopic glints of light, and it was beyond coincidence that Keda's eyes were drawn towards the particular opening in the foliage that was divided into two equal parts by a vertical splinter of green fire. Even at that distance, fringed and imprisoned with blackness, Keda recognized instantaneously the finger of rock.

'What does it mean, father, that thin and dreadful crag?'

'If it is dreadful to you, Keda, it means that your death is near; which is as you wish and what you have foreseen. For me it is not yet dreadful, although it has changed. When I was young it was for me the steeple of all love. As the days die, it alters.'

'But I am not afraid,' said Keda.

They turned and began to descend among the hillocks towards the cabin. Darkness had settled before they opened the door. When Keda had lit the lamp they sat at the table opposite one another, conversing for a long while before her lips moved and she began to speak aloud:

'No, I am not afraid,' she said. 'It is I who am choosing what I shall do.'

The old man lifted his rough head. His eyes in the lamplight appeared as wells of brown light.

'The child will come to me when she is ready,' he said. 'I will always be here.'

'It is the Dwellers,' said Keda. 'It is they.' Her left hand drew involuntarily to beneath her heart, and her fingers wavered there a moment as though lost. 'Two men have died for me; and I bring back to the Bright Carvers their blood, on my hands, and the unlawful child. They will reject me – but I shall not mind, for still ... still ... my bird is singing – and in the graveyard of the outcasts I will have my reward – oh father – my reward, the deep, deep silence which they cannot break.'

The lamp trembled and shadows moved across the room, returning stealthily as the flame steadied.

'It will not be long,' he said. 'In a few days' time you shall begin your journey.'

'Your dark-grey mare,' said Keda, 'how shall I return her to you, father?'

'She will return,' he replied, 'alone. When you are near to the Dwellings, set her free and she will turn and leave you.'

She took her hand from his arm and walked to her room. All night long the voice of a little wind among the reeds cried: 'Soon, soon, soon.'

On the fifth day he helped her to the rough blanket saddle. Upon the mare's broad back were slung two baskets of loaves and other provender. Her path lay to the north of the cabin, and she turned for a moment before the mare moved away to take a last look at the scene before her. The stony field beyond the high trees. The roofless house, and to her west, the hillocks of pale hair, and beyond the hillocks the distant woods. She looked her last upon the rough grass enclosure; the well, and the tree which cast its long shadow. She looked her last at the white goat with its head of snow. It was sitting with one frail white foreleg curled to its heart.

'No harm will come to you. You are beyond the power of harm. You will not hear their voices. You will bear your child, and when the time has come you will make an end of all things.'

Keda turned her eyes to him. 'I am happy, father. I am happy. I know what to do.'

The grey mare stepped forward into darkness beneath trees, and pacing with a strange deliberation turned eastwards along a green path between banks of fern. Keda sat very still and very upright with her hands in her lap while they drew nearer with every pace to Gormenghast and the homes of the Bright Carvers.

EARLY ONE MORNING

SPRING has come and gone, and the summer is at its height.

It is the morning of the Breakfast, of the ceremonial Breakfast. Prepared in honour of Titus, who is one year old today, it piles itself magnificently across the surface of a table at the northern end of the refectory. The servants' tables and benches have been removed so that a cold stone desert spreads southwards unbroken save by the regular pillars on either side which lead away in dwindling perspective. It is the same dining-hall in which the Earl nibbles his frail toast at eight o'clock every morning – the hall whose ceiling is riotous with flaking cherubs, trumpets and clouds, whose high walls trickle with the damp, whose flagstones sigh at every step.

At the northern extremity of this chill province the gold plate of the Groans, pranked across the shining black of the long table, smoulders as though it contains fire; the cutlery glitters with a bluish note; the napkins, twisted into the shape of doves, detach themselves from their surroundings for very whiteness, and appear to be unsupported. The great hall is empty and there is no sound save the regular dripping of rain-water from a dark patch in the cavernous ceiling. It has been raining since the early hours of the morning and by now a small lake is gathered halfway down the long stone avenue between the pillars, reflecting dimly an irregular section of the welkin where a faded cluster of cherubs lie asleep in the bosom of a mildew'd cloud. It is to this cloud, darkened with *real* rain, that the drops cling sluggishly and fall at intervals through the half-lit air to the glaze of water below.

Swelter has just retired to his clammy quarters after casting his professional eye for the last time over the breakfast table. He is pleased with his work and as he arrives at the kitchen there is a certain satisfaction in the twist of his fat lips. There are still two hours to run before the dawn.

Before he pushes open the door of the main kitchen he pauses and listens with his ear to the panels. He is hoping to hear the voice of one of his apprentices, of *any* one of his apprentices – it would not matter which – for he has ordered silence until his return. The little uniformed creatures had been lined up in two rows. Two of them are squabbling in thin, high whispers.

Swelter is in his best uniform, a habit of exceptional splen-dour, the high cap and tunic being of virgin silk. Doubling his body he opens the door the merest fraction of an inch and applies his eye to the fissure. As he bends, the shimmering folds of the silk about his belly hiss and whisper like the voice of far and sinister waters or like some vast, earthless ghost-cat sucking its own breath. His eye, moving around the panel of the door, is like something detached, self-sufficient, and having no need of the voluminous head that follows it nor for that matter of the mountainous masses undulating to the crutch, and the soft, trunk-like legs. So alive is it, this eye, quick as an adder, veined like a blood-alley. What need is there for all the cumulus of dull, surrounding clay – the slow white hinterland that weighs behind it as it swivels among the doughy, circumscribing wodges like a marble of raddled ice? As the eye rounds the corner of the door it devours the long double line of skinny apprentices as a squid might engulf and devour some long-shaped creature of the depths. As it sucks in the line of boys through the pupil, the knowledge of his power over them spreads sensuously across his trunk like a delicious gooseflesh. He has seen and heard the two shrill-whispering youths, now threatening one another with little raw fists. They have disobeyed him. He wipes his hot hands together, and his tongue travels along his lips. The eye watches them, Flycrake and Wrenpatch. They would do very nicely. So they were annoyed with one another, were they, the little dung-flies? How diverting! And how thoughtful of them! They will save him the trouble of having to invent some reason or another for punishing a brace of their ridiculous little brothers.

The chef opens the door and the double line freezes.

He approaches them, wiping his hands upon his silken buttocks as he moves forward. He impends above them like a dome of cloud.

'Flycrake,' he says, and the word issues from his lips as though it were drawn through a filter of sedge, 'there is room for you, Flycrake, in the shadow of my paunch, and bring your hairy friend with you – there is room for him as well I shouldn't wonder.'

The two boys creep forward, their eyes very wide, their teeth chattering.

'You were talking, were you not? You were talking even more garrulously than your teeth are now chattering. Am I wrong? No? Then come a little nearer; I should hate to have any trouble in reaching you. You wouldn't like to cause me any trouble, would you? Am I right in saying that you would not like to give me trouble, Master Flycrake? Master Wrenpatch?' He does not listen for an answer, but yawns, his face opening lewdly upon regions compared with which nudity becomes a milliner's invention. As the yawn ends and without a suspicion of warning, his two hands swing forward simultaneously and he catches the two little wretches by their ears and lifts them high into the air. What he would have done with them will never be known, for at the very moment when the hanging apprentices are lifted about the level of Swelter's throat, a bell begins to jangle discordantly through the steamy air. It is very seldom that this bell is heard, for the rope from which it is suspended, after disappearing through a hole in the ceiling of the Great Kitchen, moves secretly among rafters, winding to and fro in the obscure, dust-smelling regions that brood between the ceiling of the ground rooms and the floor boards of the first storey. After having been re-knotted many times, it finally emerges through a wall in Lord Sepulchrave's bedroom. It is very rarely that his Lordship has any need to interview his chef, and the bell as it swings wildly above the heads of the apprentices can be seen throwing from off its iron body the dust of four seasons.

Swelter's face changes at the first iron clang of the forgotten bell. The gloating and self-indulgent folds of face-fat redistribute themselves and a sycophantism oozes from his every pore. But only for a moment is he thus, his ears gulping at the sound of iron; for all at once he drops Flycrake and Wrenpatch to the stone slabs, surges from the room, his flat feet sucking at the stones like porridge.

Without abating the speed of his succulent paces, and sweeping with his hands whoever appears in his path as though he were doing breast-stroke, he pursues his way to Lord Sepulchrave's bedroom, the sweat beginning to stand out more and more on his cheeks and forehead as he nears the sacred door.

Before he knocks he wipes the sweat from his face with his sleeve, and then listens with his ear at the panels. He can hear nothing. He lifts his hand and strikes his folded fingers against the door with great force. He does this because he knows from experience that it is only with great difficulty that his knuckles can make any sound, the bones lying so deeply embedded within their stalls of pulp. As he half expected, all to be heard is a soft *plop*, and he resorts unwillingly to the expedient of extracting a coin from a pocket and striking it tentatively on the panel. To his horror, instead of the slow, sad, authoritative voice of his master ordering him to enter, he hears the hooting of an owl. After a few moments, during which he is forced to dab at his face, for he has been unnerved by the melancholy cry, he strikes again with the coin. This time there is no question that the high, long-drawn hoot which answers the tapping is an order for him to enter.

Swelter glances about him, turning his head this way and that, and he is on the point of making away from the door, for fear has made his body as cold as jelly, when he hears the regular crk, crk, crk, crk, of Flay's knee-joints approaching him from the shadows to his rear. And then he hears another sound. It is of someone running heavily, impetuously. As the sound approaches it drowns the regular *staccato* of Mr Flay's knee-joints. A moment later as Swelter turns his head the shadows break apart and the sultry crimson of Fuchsia's dress burns as it rushes forward. Her hand is on the handle of the door at once and she flings it open without a moment's hesitation or a glance at Swelter. The chef, a mixture of emotions competing within him as might a group of worms make battle for sovereignty in the belly of an ox, peers over Fuchsia's shoulder. Not until he has recoiled from what meets his eye can the secondary, yet impelling impulse to watch for the approach of Flay appease itself. Dragging his eyes from the spectacle before him he is in time to shift his bulk a little to the right and so to impede the thin man's progress, for Flay is now immediately behind him. Swelter's hatred of Lord Sepulchrave's servant has now ripened into a fester-patch, and his one desire is to stop the breathing for once and for all of a creature so fleshless, and of one who raised the welts upon his face on the Christening day.

Mr Flay, presented with the doming back and the splay-acred rear of the chef, is on edge to see his master who has rung his bell for him, and is in no mood to be thwarted, nor to be terrified at the white mass before him, and although for many a long stony night he has been unable to rest – for he is well aware of the chef's determination to kill him during his sleep – yet now, presented with the materialization of his nocturnal horror, he finds himself as hard as ironwood, and he jerks his dark, sour, osseous head forward out of his collar like a turtle and hisses from between his sand-coloured teeth.

Swelter's eyes meet those of his enemy, and never was there held between four globes of gristle so sinister a hell of hatred.

Had the flesh, the fibres, and the bones of the chef and those of Mr Flay been conjured away and away down that dark corridor leaving only their four eyes suspended in mid-air outside the Earl's door, then, surely, they must have reddened to the hue of Mars, reddened and smouldered, and at last broken into flame, so intense was their hatred – broken into flame and circled about one another in ever-narrowing gyres and in swifter and yet swifter flight until, merged into one sizzling globe of ire they must surely have fled, the four in one, leaving a trail of blood behind them in the cold grey air of the corridor, until, screaming as they fly beneath innumerable arches and down the endless passageways of Gormenghast, they found their eyeless bodies once again, and re-entrenched themselves in startled sockets.

For a moment the two men are quite still, for Flay has not yet drawn breath after hissing through his teeth. Then, itching to get to his master he brings his sharp, splintery knee up suddenly beneath the balloon-like overhang of the chef's abdomen. Swelter, his face contracting with pain and whitening so that his blanched uniform becomes grey against his neck, raises his great arms in a clawing motion as his body doubles involuntarily for relief. As he straightens himself, and as Flay makes an effort to get past him to the door, with a jabbing movement of his shoulder, they are both frozen to the spot with a cry more dreadful than before, the long, dolorous cry of the death-owl, and the voice of Fuchsia, a voice that seems to be fighting through tears and terror, cries loudly:

'My father! My father! Be silent and it will be better, and I will take care of you. Look at me, father! Oh, look at me! I know what you want because I *do* know, father – I *do* know, and I will take you there when it is dark and then you will be better. – But look at me, father – look at me.'

But the Earl will not look at her. He is sitting huddled in the centre of the broad carven mantelpiece, his head below the level of his shoulders. Fuchsia, standing below him with her hands shaking as they grip the marble of the mantel, tilts herself towards him. Her strong back is hollowed, her head is thrown back and her throat taut. Yet she dare not touch him.

The austerity of the many years that lay behind them – the chill of the mutual reserve they had always shown to one another, is like a wall between them even now. It seemed as though that wall were crumbling and that their frozen love was beginning to thaw and percolate through the crevices, but now, when it is most needed and most felt, the wall has closed again and Fuchsia dares not touch him. Nor dare she admit to herself that her father has become possessed.

He makes no answer, and Fuchsia, sinking to her knees, begins to cry, but there are no tears. Her body heaves as she crouches below Lord Sepulchrave as he squats on the mantelpiece, and her throat croaks, but no tears relieve her. It is dry anguish and she becomes older during these long moments, older than many a man or woman could ever understand.

Flay, clenching his hands, moves into the room, the hair standing out rigidly like little wires all over his scanty flesh. Something had crumpled up inside him. His undeviating loyalty to the House of Groan and to his Lordship is fighting with the horror of what he sees. Something of the same feeling must have been going on inside Swelter for as he and Flay gaze at the Earl there is upon their faces the same emotion translated, as it were, into two very different languages.

His Lordship is dressed in black. His knees are drawn up almost to his chin. His long, fine white hands are curled slightly inwards as they hang over his knees, between which, and his supported chin, the wrists are wedged. But it is the eyes which strike a chill to the centre of those who watch, for they have become circular. The smile which played across his lips when Fuchsia had been with him in the pine wood is gone forever. His mouth is entirely expressionless.

Suddenly a voice comes from the mouth. It is very quiet:
'Chef.'

'Your Lordship?' says Swelter trembling.

'How many traps have you in the Great Kitchen?'

Swelter's eyes shift to left and right and his mouth opens, but he can make no sound.

'Come, Chef, you must know how many traps are set every night – or have you become slovenly?'

Swelter holds his podgy hands together. They tremble before him as he works his fingers between one another.

'Sir,' says Swelter . . . 'there must be forty traps in the Great Kitchen . . . forty traps, your gracious Lordship.'

'How many were found in the traps at five o'clock today? Answer me.'

'They were all full, your Lordship – all except one, sir.'

'Have the cats had them?'

'The . . . the cats, your –'

'I said, have the cats had them?' repeats Lord Sepulchrave sadly.

'Not yet,' says the Chef. 'Not yet.'

'Then bring me one . . . bring me a plump one . . . immediately. What are you waiting for, Mr Chef? . . . What are you waiting for?'

Swelter's lips move wetly. 'A plump one,' he says. 'Yes, my Lord . . . a . . . plump . . . one.'

As soon as he has disappeared the voice goes on: 'Some twigs, Mr Flay, some twigs at once. Twigs of all sizes, do you understand? From small branches downwards in size – every kind of shape, Flay, every kind of shape, for I shall study each in turn and understand the twigs I build with, for I must be as clever as the others with my twigs, though we are careless workmen. What are you waiting for, Mr Flay? . . .'

Flay looks up. He has been unable to keep his eyes on the transformed aspect of his master, but now he lifts them again. He can recognize no expression. The mouth might as well not be there. The fine aquiline nose appears to be more forceful and the saucerlike shape of the eyes hold within either sky a vacant moon.

With a sudden awkward movement Flay plucks Fuchsia from the floor and flings her over his high shoulder and, turning, he staggers to the door and is soon among the passages.

'I must go back, I must go back to him!' Fuchsia gasps.

Flay only makes a noise in his throat and strides on.

At first Fuchsia begins to struggle, but she has no strength left for the dreadful scene has unnerved her and she subsides over his shoulder, not knowing where she is being taken. Nor does Flay know where he is taking her. They have reached the east quadrangle and have come out into the early morning when Fuchsia lifts her head.

'Flay,' she says, 'we must find Doctor Prune at once. I can walk, please, now. Thank you, Flay, but be quick. Be quick. Put me down.'

Flay eases her off his shoulder and she drops to the ground. Fuchsia has seen the Doctor's house in the corner of the quadrangle and she cannot understand why she had not thought of him before. Fuchsia begins to run, and directly she is at the Doctor's front door she beats it violently with the knocker. The sun is beginning to rise above the marshes and picks out a long gutter and a cornice of the Doctor's house, and presently, after Fuchsia has slammed at the door again, it picks out the extraordinary headpiece of Prunesquallor himself as it emerges sleepily through a high window. He cannot see what is below him in the shadows, but calls out:

'In the name of modesty and of all who slumber, go easy with that knocker! What in the world is it? ... Answer me. What is it, I repeat? ... Is it the plague that has descended on Gormenghast – or a forceps case? Is it a return of midnight-mange, or merely flesh-death? Does the patient rave? ... Is he fat or thin? ... Is he drunk or mad? ... Is he ...' The Doctor yawns and it is then that Fuchsia has her first chance to speak:

'Yes, oh yes! Come quickly, Doctor Prune! Let me tell you. Oh, please, let me tell you!'

The high voice at the sill cries: 'Fuchsia!' as though to itself. 'Fuchsia!' And the window comes down with a crash.

Flay moves to the girl and almost before he has done so the front door is flung open and Doctor Prunesquallor in his flowered pyjamas is facing them.

Taking Fuchsia by the hand and motioning Flay to follow he minces rapidly to the living room.

'Sit down, sit down, my frantic one!' cries Prunesquallor. 'What the devil is it? Tell the old Prune all about it.'

'It's father,' says Fuchsia, the tears finding release at long last. 'Father's become wrong, Doctor Prune; Father's become all wrong ... Oh, Doctor Prune, he is a black owl now ... Oh, Doctor, Help him! Help him!'

The Doctor does not speak. He turns his pink, over-sensitive, intelligent head sharply in the direction of Flay, who nods and comes forward a step, with the report of a knee-joint. Then he nods again, his jaw working. 'Owl,' he says. 'Wants mice! ... Wants twigs: on mantelpiece! Hooting! Lordship's mad.'

'No!' shouts Fuchsia. 'He's ill, Doctor Prune. That's all. His library's been burned. His beautiful library; and he's become ill. But he's not mad. He talks so quietly. Oh, Doctor Prune, what are you going to do?'

'Did you leave him in his room?' says the Doctor, and it does not seem to be the same man speaking.

Fuchsia nods her tear-wet head.

'Stay here,' says the Doctor quietly; as he speaks he is away and within a few moments has returned in a lime-green dressing gown with lime-green slippers to match, and in his hand, a bag.

'Fuchsia dear, send Steerpike to me, in your father's room. He is quick-witted and may be of help. Flay, get about your duties. The Breakfast must proceed, as you know. Now then, my gipsy-child; death or glory.' And with the highest and most irresponsible of trills he vanishes through the door.

A CHANGE OF COLOUR

THE morning light is strengthening, and the hour of the Great Breakfast approaches. Flay, utterly distraught, is wandering up and down the candle-lit stone lanes where he knows he will be alone. He had gathered the twigs and he had flung them away in disgust only to re-gather them, for the very thought of disobeying his master is almost as dreadful to him as the memory of the creature he has seen on the mantelpiece. Finally, and in despair, he has crunched the twigs between his own stick-like fingers, the simultaneous crackling of the twigs and of his knuckles creating for a moment a miniature storm of brittle thunder in the shadow of the trees. Then, striding back to the Castle he has descended uneasily to the Stone Lanes. It is very cold, yet there are great pearls upon his forehead, and in each pearl is the reflection of a candle flame.

✦

Mrs Slagg is in the bedroom of the Countess, who is piling her rust-coloured hair above her head as though she were building a castle. Every now and again Mrs Slagg peers furtively at the bulk before the mirror, but her attention is chiefly centred upon an object on the bed. It is wrapped in a length of lavender-coloured velvet, and little porcelain bells are pinned here and there all over it. One end of a golden chain is attached to the velvet near the centre of what has become, through process of winding, a small velvet cylinder, or mummy, measuring some three and a half feet in length and with a diameter of about eighteen inches. At the other end of the chain and lying on the bed beside the lavender roll is a sword with a heavy blade of blue-black steel and a hilt embossed with the letter 'G'. This sword is attached to the gold chain with a piece of string.

Mrs Slagg dabs a little powder upon something that moves in the shadow at one end of the roll, and then peers about her, for it is hard for her to see what she is doing, the shadows in the bedroom of the Countess are of so dark a breed. Between their red rims her eyes wander here and there before she bends over Titus and plucks at her underlip. Again her eyes peer up at the Countess, who seems to have grown tired of her hair, the edifice being left unfinished as though some fitful architect had died before the completion of a bizarre edifice which no one else knew how to complete. Mrs Slagg moves from the bedside in little half-running, half-walking steps, and from the table beneath the candelabra plucks a candle that is waxed to the wood among the birdseed, and, lighting it from a guttering torso of tallow that stands by, she returns to the lavender cylinder which has begun to twist and turn.

Her hand is unsteady as she lifts the wax above the head of Titus, and the wavering flame makes it leap. His eyes are very wide open. As he sees the light his mouth puckers and works, and the heart of the earth contracts with love as he totters at the wellhead of tears. His little body writhes in its dreadful bolster and one of the porcelain bells chimes sweetly.

'Slagg,' said the Countess in a voice of husk.

Nannie, who is as light as a feather, starts into the air an inch or two at the sudden sound, and comes to earth again with a painful jarring of her little arid ankles; but she does not cry out, for she is biting her lower lip while her eyes cloud over. She does not know what she has done wrong and she has done nothing wrong, but there is always a feeling of guilt about her when she shares a room with the Countess. This is partly due to the fact that she irritates the Countess, and the nurse can sense this all the while. So it is in a thin and tremulous voice that she stammers:

'Yes, oh yes, Ladyship? Yes . . . yes, your Ladyship?'

The Countess does not turn her head to speak, but stares past herself in the cracked mirror, her elbows resting on the table, her head supported in the cups of her hands.

'Is the child ready?'

'Yes, yes, just ready, just ready. Ready now, your Ladyship, bless his little smallness . . . yes . . . yes . . .'

'Is the sword fixed?'

'Yes, yes, the sword, the –'

She is about to say 'the horrid, black sword', but she checks herself nervously, for who is she to express her feeling when ritual is involved? 'But it's so *hot* for him,' she continues hurriedly, 'so hot for his little body in all this velvet – though, of course,' she adds, a stupid little smile working in and out of the wrinkles of her lips, 'it's very pretty.'

The Countess turns slowly in her chair. 'Slagg,' she says, 'come over here, Slagg.'

The old woman, her heart beating wildly, patters her way around the bed and stands by the dressing-table. She clasps her hands together on her flat chest and her eyes are wide open.

'Have you still no idea of how to answer even simple questions?' asks the Countess very slowly.

Nannie shakes her head, but suddenly a red spot appears in

either cheek. 'I *can* answer questions, I *can*!' she cries, startling herself with her own ineffectual vehemence.

The Countess does not seem to have heard her. 'Try and answer *this* one,' she murmers.

Mrs Slagg cocks her head on one side and listens like a grey bird.

'Are you attending, Slagg?'

Nannie nods her head as though suffering from palsy.

'Where did you meet that youth?' There is a moment's silence.

'That Steerpike?' the Countess adds.

'Long ago,' says Nannie, and closes her eyes as she waits for the next question. She feels pleased with herself.

'*Where* is what I said: *where*, not *when*,' booms the voice.

Mrs Slagg tries to gather her thoughts together. Where? Oh, where was it? she wondered. It was long ago ... And then she recalled how he had appeared with Fuchsia suddenly at the door of her room.

'With Fuchsia ... Oh, yis ... yis, it was with my Fuchsia, your Ladyship.'

'Where does he come from? Answer me, Slagg, and then finish my hair.'

'I never do know ... No, not ever ... I have never been told. Oh, my poor heart, no. Where *could* the boy come from?' She peers at the dark bulk above her.

Lady Gertrude wipes the palm of her hand slowly across her brow. 'You are the same Slagg,' she says, 'the same brilliant Slagg.'

Nannie begins to cry, wishing desperately that she were clever.

'No use crying,' says the Countess. 'No use. No use. My birds don't cry. Not very often. Were you at the fire?'

The word 'fire' is terrible to Mrs Slagg. She clutches her hands together. Her bleary eyes grow wild. Her lips tremble, for in her imagination she can see the great flames rising about her.

'Finish my hair, Nannie Slagg. Stand on a chair and do it.'

Nannie turns to find a chair. The room is like a shipwreck. The red walls glower in the candle-light. The old woman patters her way between stalactites of tallow, boxes and old sofas. The Countess whistles and a moment later the room is alive with wings. By the time Mrs Slagg has dragged a chair to the dressing-table and climbed upon it, the Countess is deep in conversation with a magpie. Nannie disapproves of birds altogether and cannot reconcile the habits of the Countess with the House of Groan, but she is used to such things, not being over seventy years old for nothing. Bending a little over her ladyship's locks she works with difficulty to complete the hirsute cornice, for the light is bad.

'Now then, darling, now then,' says the heavy voice below her, and her old body thrills, for she has never known the Countess speak to her in such a way before; but glancing over the mountainous shoulder she sees that the Countess is talking to a bedraggled finch and Nannie Slagg is desolate.

'So Fuchsia was the first to find him, was she?' says the Countess, rubbing her finger along the finch's throat.

Mrs Slagg, startled, as she always is when anyone speaks, fumbles with the red hank in her hand. 'Who? Oh, who do you mean ... your Ladyship? ... Oh, she's always a good girl, Fuchsia is, yis, yis, *always*.'

The Countess gets to her feet in a monumental way, brushing several objects from the dressing-table to the floor with her elbow. As she rises she hears the sound of sobbing and turns her head to the lavender roll. 'Go away, Slagg – go away, and take him with you. Is Fuchsia dressed?'

'Yis ... oh, my poor heart, yis ... Fuchsia is all ready, yis, quite ready, and waiting in her room. Oh yis, she is ...'

'His Breakfast will soon be beginning,' says the Countess, turning her eyes from a brass clock to her infant son. 'Very soon.'

Nannie, who has recovered Titus from the fastnesses of the bed, stops at the door before pattering out into the dawn-lit corridor. Her eyes stare back almost triumphantly and a little pathetic smile works at the crinkled corners of her mouth. '*His* Breakfast,' she whispers. 'Oh, my weak heart, his *first* Breakfast.'

*

Steerpike has been found at last, Fuchsia colliding with him as he rounds a corner of the staircase on his way down from the aunts. He is very sprucely dressed, his high shoulders without a speck of dust upon them, his finger-nails pared, his hair smoothed down over his pasty-coloured forehead. He is surprised to see Fuchsia, but he does not show it, merely raising his eyebrows in an expression both inquiring and deferential at the same time.

'You are up very early, Lady Fuchsia.'

Fuchsia, her breast heaving from her long run up the stairs, cannot speak for a moment or two; then she says: 'Doctor Prune wants you.'

'Why me?' says the youth to himself; but aloud he said: 'Where is he?'

'In my father's room.'

Steerpike licks his lips slowly. 'Is your father ill?'

'Yes, oh yes, very ill.'

Steerpike turns his head away from Fuchsia, for the muscles of his face cry out to relax. He gives them a free rein and then, straightening his face and turning to Fuchsia, he says: 'Everything I can do I will do.' Suddenly, with the utmost nimbleness, he skips past her, jumping the first four steps together, and races down the stone flight on his way to the Earl's bedroom.

He has not seen the Doctor for some time. Having left his service their relationship is a little strained, but this morning as he enters at the Earl's door he can see there will be neither space nor time for reminiscences in his own or the Doctor's brain.

Prunesquallor, in his lime-green dressing-gown, is pacing to and fro before the mantelpiece with the stealth of some kind of vertical cat. Not for a moment does he take his eyes off the Earl, who, still upon the mantelpiece, watches the physician with great eyes.

At the sound of Steerpike at the door the round eyes move for a moment and stare over the Doctor's shoulder. But Prunesquallor has not shifted his steady, magnified gaze. The roguish look is quite absent from his long, bizarre face.

The Doctor has been waiting for this moment. Prancing forward he reaches up with his white hands and pins the Earl's arms to his sides, dragging him from his perch. Steerpike is at the Doctor's side in a moment and together they carry the sacrosanct body to the bed and turn it over upon its face. Sepulchrave has not struggled, only emitting a short stifled cry.

Steerpike holds the dark figure down with one hand, for there is no attempt to escape, and the Doctor flicks a slim needle into his Lordship's wrist and injects a drug of such weird potency that when they turn the patient over Steerpike is startled to see that the face has changed to a kind of chalky green. But the eyes have altered also and are once more the sober, thoughtful, human eyes which the Castle knew so well. His fingers have uncurled; the claws are gone.

'Be so good as to draw the blind,' says the Doctor, raising himself to his full height beside the bed, and returning his needle to its little silver case. This done, he taps the points of his long white fingers together thoughtfully. With the blinds drawn across the sunrise the colour of his lordship's face is mercifully modified.

'That was quick work, Doctor.'

Steerpike is balancing upon his heels. 'What happens next?' He clicks his tongue ruminatively as he waits for Prunesquallor's answer. 'What was the drug you used, Doctor?'

'I am not in the mood to answer questions, dear boy,' replies Prunesquallor, showing Steerpike the whole range of his teeth, but in a mirthless way. 'Not at all in the mood.'

'What about the Breakfast?' says Steerpike, unabashed.

'His Lordship will *be* at the Breakfast.'

'Will he, though?' says the youth, peering at the face. 'What about his colour?'

'In half an hour his skin will have returned to normal. He will be there ... Now, fetch me Flay and some boiling water, a towel. He must be washed and dressed. Quickly now.'

Before Steerpike leaves the room he bends over Lord Sepulchrave, whistling tunelessly between his teeth. The Earl's eyes are closed and there is a tranquillity about his face which has been absent for many years.

A BLOODY CHEEKBONE

Steerpike has some difficulty in finding Flay, but he comes across him at last in the blue-carpeted Room of Cats, whose sunlit pile they had trodden together under very different circumstances a year ago. Flay has just reappeared from the Stone Lanes and looks very bedraggled, a long dirty hank of cobweb hanging over his shoulder. When he sees Steerpike his lips curl back like a wolf's.

'What you want?' he says.

'How's Flay?' says Steerpike.

The cats are crowded upon one enormous ottoman with its carven head and footpiece rising into the air in a tangle of gilded tracery as though two toppling waves at sunset were suspended in mid-air, the hollow between them filled with foam. There is no sound from them and they do not move.

'The Earl wants you,' continues Steerpike, enjoying Flay's discomfort. He does not know whether Flay has any knowledge of what is happening to his master.

Flay involuntarily propels his gawky body forwards as he hears that his Lordship wants him, but he pulls himself up at the end of his first long step towards the door, and peers even more suspiciously and acidly at the youth in his immaculate black cloth.

Steerpike on a sudden, without considering the consequences of his action with the same thoroughness that is typical of him, forces his eyes open with the forefinger and thumb of either hand. He wishes to see whether the thin creature before him has seen the Earl during his madness. He is really banking on the assumption that Flay will not have done so, in which case the forcing of his eyes into owlish circles will have no meaning. But he has made this early morning one of his rare mistakes.

With a hoarse, broken cry, Flay, his head reddening with wrath at this insult to his master, staggers to the divan and, shooting out a gaunt hand, plucks a cat by its head from the snowy hill and hurls it at his tormentor. As this happens a cloaked and heavy woman enters the room. The living missile, hurtling at Steerpike's face, reaches out one of its white legs and as the youth jerks his head to one side, five claws rip out a crimson wedge from his cheek immediately below the right eye.

The air is filled at once with the screaming of a hundred cats which, swarming the walls and furniture, leaping and circling the blue carpet with the speed of light, give the room the appearance of a white maelstrom. The blood, streaming down Steerpike's neck, feels as warm as tea as it slides to his belly. His hand, which he has raised automatically to his face in a vain attempt to ward off the blow, moves to his cheek as he drops back a pace, and the tips of his fingers become wet. The cat itself has ended its flight against the wall, near the door through which the third figure has just entered. As it falls in a huddle to the floor, half stunned, and with the wedge of Steerpike's sallow skin between the claws of its left forefoot, it sees the figure above it; it crawls with a moan to within a pace of the visitor, and then, with a superfeline effort, springs to the height of her great breasts where it lies coiled with its eyes like yellow moons appearing above the whiteness of its haunches.

Flay turns his eyes from Steerpike. It has done him good to watch the red blood bubbling from the upstart's cheek, but now his satisfaction is at an end, for he is gazing stupified into the hard eyes of the Countess of Groan.

Her big head has coloured to a dim and dreadful madder. Her eyes are completely remorseless. She has no interest in the cause of the quarrel between Flay and the Steerpike youth. All she knows is that one of her white cats had been dashed against the wall and has suffered pain.

Flay waits as she approaches. His bony head is quite still. His loose hands hang gawkily at his sides. He realizes the crime he has committed, and as he waits his world of Gormenghast – his security, his love, his faith in the House, his devotion – is all crumbling into fragments.

She is standing within a foot of him. The air is heavy with her presence.

Her voice is very husky when she speaks. 'I was going to

strike him down,' she says heavily. 'That is what I intended to do with him. To break him.'

He lifts his eyes. The white cat is within a few inches of him. He watches the hairs of its back; each one has become a bristle and the back is a hummock of sharp white grass.

The Countess begins to talk again in a louder voice, but it has become so choked that Flay cannot understand what she is saying. At last he can make out the words: 'You are no more, no more at all. You are ended.'

Her hand, as it moves gently over the body of the white cat, is trembling uncontrollably. 'I have finished with you,' she says. 'Gormenghast has finished with you.' It is hard for her to draw the words from her great throat. 'You are over ... over.' Suddenly she raises her voice. 'Crude fool!' she cries. 'Crude, broken fool and brute! Out! Out! The Castle throws you. Go!' she roars, her hands upon the cat's breast. 'Your long bones sicken me.'

Flay lifts his small bony head higher into the air. He cannot comprehend what has happened. All he knows is that it is more dreadful than he can feel, for a kind of numbness is closing in on his horror like a padding. There is a greenish sheen across the shoulders of his greasy black suit, for the morning light has of a sudden begun to dance through the bay window. Steerpike, with a blood-drenched handkerchief wound about his face, is staring at him and tapping the top of a table with his nails. He cannot help but feel that there is something very fine about the old creature's head. And he had been very quick. Very quick indeed. Something to remember, that: cats for missiles.

Flay moved his little eyes around the room. The floor is alive and white behind the Countess, around whose feet lies the stilled froth of a tropic tide, the azure carpet showing now here and now there. He feels he is looking at it for the last time and turns to go, but as he turns he thinks of the Breakfast. He is surprised to hear his own mirthless voice saying: 'Breakfast.'

The Countess knows that her husband's first servant must be at the Breakfast. Had he killed every white cat in the world he must still be at the Breakfast in honour of Titus, the 77th Earl of Gormenghast, to be. Such things are cardinal.

378

The Countess turns herself about and moves to the bay window after making a slow detour of the room and picking up from a rack near the fireplace a heavy iron poker. As she reaches the window her right arm swings slowly back and forward with the deliberation of a shire-mare's bearded hoof as it falls into a rainpool. There is a startling split and crash, a loud cascading of glass upon the flagstones outside the window, and then silence.

With her back to the room she stares through the star-shaped gap in the glass. Before her spreads the green lawn. She is watching the sun breaking through the distant cedars. It is the day of her son's Breakfast. She turns her head. 'You have a week,' she says, 'and then you leave these walls. A servant shall be found for the Earl.'

Steerpike lifts his head, and for a moment he ceases to drum on the woodwork with his finger-nails. As he starts tapping again, a kestrel, sweeping through the star of the shattered pane, alights on the shoulder of the Countess. She winces as its talons for a moment close, but her eyes soften.

Flay approaches a door in three slow, spidery slides. It is the door that opens into the Stone Lanes. He fumbles for his key, and turns it in the lock. He must rest in his own region before he returns to the Earl, and he lets himself into the long darkness.

The Countess, for the first time, remembers Steerpike. She moves her eyes slowly in the direction where she had last seen him, but he is no longer there nor in any part of the room.

A bell chimes from the corridor beyond the Room of Cats and she knows that there is but a short while before the Breakfast.

She feels a splash of water on her hand, and, turning, sees that the sky has become overcast with a blanket of ominous dark rose-coloured cloud, and of a sudden the light fades from the lawn and the cedars.

Steerpike, who is on his way back to the Earl's bedroom, stops a moment at a staircase window to see the first descent of the rain. It is falling from the sky in long, upright and seemingly motionless lines of rosy silver that stand rigidly upon the ground as though there were a million harp strings strung vertically

379

between the solids of earth and sky. As he leaves the window he hears the first roar of the summer thunder.

The Countess hears it as she stares through the jagged star in the bay window. Prunesquallor hears it as he balances the Earl upon his feet at the side of the bed. The Earl must have heard it, too, for he takes a step of his own volition towards the centre of the room. His own face has returned.

'Was that thunder, Doctor?' he says.

The Doctor watches him very carefully, watches his every movement, though few would have guessed how intently he was studying his patient had they seen his long ingenious mouth open with customary gaiety.

'Thunder it was, your Lordship. A most prodigious peal. I am waiting for the martial chords which must surely follow such an opening, what? Ha, ha, ha, ha, ha!'

'What has brought you to my bedroom, Doctor? I do not remember sending for you.'

'That is not unnatural, your Lordship. You did not send for me. I was summoned a few minutes ago, to find that you had fainted, an unfortunate, but by no means rare thing to happen to anyone. Now, I wonder why you should have fainted?' The Doctor stroked his chin. 'Why? Was the room very hot?'

The Earl comes across to the Doctor. 'Prunesquallor,' he says, 'I don't faint.'

'Your Lordship,' says the Doctor, 'when I arrived in this bedroom you were in a faint.'

'Why should I have fainted? I do not faint, Prunesquallor.'

'Can you remember what you were doing before you lost consciousness?'

The Earl moves his eyes from the Doctor. All at once he feels very tired and sits down on the edge of the bed.

'I can remember nothing, Prunesquallor. Absolutely nothing. I can only recall that I was hankering for something, but for what I do not know. It seems a month ago.'

'I can tell you,' says Prunesquallor. 'You are making ready to go to your son's Breakfast Gathering. You were pressed for time and were anxious not to be late. You are, in any event, overstrained, and in your anticipation of the occasion you became overwrought. Your "hankering" was to be with your one-year-old son. That is what you vaguely remember.'

'When is my son's Breakfast?'

'It is in half an hour's time, or to be precise, it is in twenty-eight minutes' time.'

'Do you mean *this morning*?' A look of alarm has appeared on Lord Sepulchrave's face.

'This morning as ever was, as ever is, and as ever will or won't be, bless its thunderous heart. No, no, my lord, do not get up yet.' (Lord Sepulchrave has made an attempt to stand.) 'In a moment or two and you will be as fit as the most expensive of fiddles. The Breakfast will not be delayed. No, no, not at all — You have twenty-seven long, sixty-second-apiece minutes, and Flay should be on his way to get your garments laid out for you — yes, indeed.'

Flay is not only on his way, but he is at the door, having been unable to remain in the Stone Lanes any longer than it took him to tear his way through them and up to his master's room by an obscure passage which he alone knew. Even so he is only a moment or two in advance of Steerpike, who slides under Flay's arm and through the bedroom door as Flay opens it.

Steerpike and the servant are amazed to find that Lord Sepulchrave is seemingly his own melancholy self again, and Flay shambles towards his master and drops upon his knees before him with a sudden, uncontrollable, clumsy movement, his knees striking the floor with a crash. The Earl's sensitive pale hand rests for a moment on the shoulders of the scarecrow, but all he says is: 'My ceremonial velvet, Flay. Be as quick as you can. My velvet and the bird-brooch of opals.'

Flay scrambles to his feet. He is his master's first servant. He is to lay out his master's clothes and to prepare him for the Great Breakfast in honour of his only son. This is no time or place for the wretched youth to be in his Lordship's bedroom. Nor for that matter need the Doctor stay.

With his hand on the wardrobe door he turns his head creak-ily. '*I* manage, Doctor,' he says. His eyes move from Prune-squallor to Steerpike, and he draws back his lips in an expression of contempt and disgust.

The Doctor notices this expression. 'Quite right. Quite, quite right! His Lordship will improve with every minute that passes, and there is no need for us any longer, most assuredly not, by all that's tactful I should definitely think not, ha, ha, ha! Oh, dear me, no. Come along, Steerpike. Come along. And, by the way, what's all that blood on your face? Are you playing at being a pirate or have you had a tiger in bed with you? Ha, ha, ha! But tell me afterwards, dear boy, tell me afterwards.' And the Doctor proceeds to shepherd Steerpike out of the room.

But Steerpike dislikes being shepherded and 'After you, Doctor,' he says, and insists on Prunesquallor's preceding him through the door. Before he closes it he turns and, speaking to the Earl in a confidential tone: 'I will see that everything is in readiness,' he says. 'Leave it to me, your Lordship. I will see you later, Flay. Now then, Doctor, let us be on our way.'

The door closes.

THE TWINS AGAIN

THE Aunts have been sitting opposite one another for well over an hour with hardly a movement. Surely only vanity could account for so long a scrutiny of a human face, and as it so happens it *is* Vanity and nothing but Vanity, for knowing that their features are identical and that they have administered the identical amount of powder and have spent the identical length of time in brushing their hair, they have no doubt at all that in scrutinizing one another they are virtually gazing at themselves. They are garbed in their best purple, a hue so violent as to give physical discomfort to any normally sensitive eye.

'Now, Clarice,' says Cora at last, 'you turn your lovely head to the right, so that I can see what I look like from the *side*.'

'Why?' says Clarice. 'Why should I?'

'Why shouldn't you? I've got a right to *know*.'

'So have I, if it comes to that.'

'Well, it will come to that, won't it? Stupid!'

'Yes, but . . .'

'You do what I say and then I'll do it for you.'

'Then I'll see what my profile's like, won't I?'

'We both will, not just you.'

'I *said* we both will.'

'Well? What's the matter, then?'

'Nothing.'

'Well?'

'Well, what?'

'Well, go on, then – turn your lovely head.'

'Shall I do it now?'

'Yes. There's nothing to wait for, is there?'

'Only the Breakfast. It won't be just yet.'

'Why not?'

'Because I heard the bell go in the corridor.'

'So did I. That means there's a lot of time.'

'I want to look at my profile, Cora. Turn it now.'

'All right. How long shall I be, Clarice?'

'Be a long time.'

'Only if I have a long time, too.'

'We can't both have a long time, silly.'

'Why not?'

'Because there isn't one.'

'Isn't one what, dear?'

'Isn't one long time, is there?'

'No, there's lots of them.'

'Yes, lots and lots of beautiful long times.'

'Ahead of us, you mean, Clarice?'

'Yes, ahead of us.'

'After we're on our thrones, isn't it?'

'How do you know?'

'Well, that's what you were thinking. Why do you try to deceive me?'

'I wasn't. I only wanted to know.'

'Well, now you *do* know.'

'Do know what?'

'You *do* know, that's all. I'm not going any deeper for you.'

383

'Why not?'

'Because you can't go as deep as I can. You never could.'

'I've never *tried*, I don't suppose. It's not worth it, I shouldn't think. I know when things are worth it.'

'Well, when *are* they, then?'

'When are they what?'

'When are they worth something?'

'When you've bought something wonderful with your wealth, then it's always worth it.'

'Unless you don't *want* it, Clarice, you always forget that. Why can't you be less forgetful?'

There is a long silence while they study each other's faces.

'They'll look at us, you know,' says Cora flatly. 'We're going to be looked at at the Breakfast.'

'Because we're of the original blood,' says Clarice. 'That's why.'

'And that's why we're important, too.'

'Two what?'

'To everyone, of course.'

'Well, we're not yet, not to everyone.'

'But we will be soon.'

'When the clever boy makes us. He can do anything.'

'Anything. Anything at all. He told me so.'

'Me, too. Don't think he only tells you, because he doesn't.'

'I didn't say he did, did I?'

'You were going to.'

'Two what?'

'To exalt yourself.'

'Oh, yes, yes. We will be exalted when the time is ripe.'

'Ripe and rich.'

'Yes, of course.'

'Of course.'

There is another silence. Their voices have been so flat and expressionless that when they cease talking the silence seems no new thing in the room, but rather a continuation of flatness in another colour.

'Turn your head now, Cora. When I'm looked at at the Breakfast I want to know how they see me from the side and what exactly they are looking at; so turn your head for me and I will for you afterwards.'

Cora twists her white neck to the left.

'More,' says Clarice.

'More what?'

'I can still see your other eye.'

Cora twists her head a fraction more, dislodging some of the powder from her neck.

'That's right, Cora. Stay like that. Just like that. Oh, Cora!' (the voice is still as flat), 'I am *perfect*.'

She claps her hands mirthlessly, and even her palms meet with a dead sound.

Almost as though this noise were a summons the door opens and Steerpike moves rapidly across the room. There is a fresh piece of plaster across his cheek. The twins rise and edge towards him, their shoulders touching as they advance.

He runs his eyes over them, takes his pipe out of his pocket and strikes a light. For a moment he holds the flame in his hand, but only for a moment, for Cora has raised her arm with the slow gesture of a somnabulist and has let it fall upon the flame, extinguishing it.

'What in plague's name are you up to?' shouts Steerpike, for once losing his control. Seeing an Earl as an owl on a mantelpiece, and having part of one's face removed by a cat, both on the same morning, can temporarily undermine the self-control of any man.

'No fire,' says Cora. 'We don't have fires any more.'

'We don't like them any more. No. Not any more.'

'Not after we –'

Steerpike breaks in, for he knows how their minds have turned, and this is no moment just before the Breakfast for them to start reminiscing. 'You are awaited! Breakfast table is agog for you. They all want to know where you are. Come along, my lovely brace of ladies. Let me escort you some of the way, at least. You are looking most alluring – but what can have been keeping you? Are you ready?'

The twins nod their heads.

'May I be so honoured as to give you my right arm,

Lady Cora? And, Lady Clarice, my dear, if you will take my left . . . ?'

Steerpike, bending his elbows, waits for the Aunts to split apart to take his either arm.

'The right's more important than the left,' says Clarice. 'Why should you have it?'

'Why shouldn't I?'

'Because I'm as good as you.'

'But not as clever, are you, dear?'

'Yes, I am, only you're favoured.'

'That's because I'm alluring, like he says I am.'

'He said we both were.'

'That was just to please you. Didn't you know?'

'Dear ladies,' says Steerpike, breaking in, 'will you please be quiet! Who is in control of your destinies? Who is it you promised you would trust and obey?'

'You.' They speak together.

'I think of you as co-equals, and I want you to think of yourselves as of similar status, for when your thrones arrive they will be of equal glory. Now, will you take my arms, if you please?'

Cora and Clarice take an arm each. The door of their room had been left open and the three of them make their exit, the youth's thin black figure walking between the stiff purple bodies of the Aunts, who are gazing over his head at each other, so that as they recede down the half-lit corridor and diminish in size as they move into the long perspective, the last that can be seen, long after Steerpike in his black and the purple of the twins has become swallowed in the depths, are the tiny, pallid patterns of the two identical profiles facing one another and floating, as it were, in the mid-air shadows, diminishing and diminishing as they drift away, until the last mote of light has crumbled from them.

THE DARK BREAKFAST

BARQUENTINE is unaware that there have been grave and sinister happenings in the Castle on this historic morning. He knows, of course, that the Earl has, since the burning of the library, been in a critical state of health, but of his dreadful transformation upon the mantelpiece he is ignorant. Since the early hours he has been studying the finer points of ritual to be observed at the Breakfast. Now, as he stumps his way to the dining-hall, his crutch clanking ominously on the flagstones, he sucks at a hank of his beard, which curls up and into his mouth through long training, and mutters irritably.

He still lives in the dusty, low-ceilinged room which he has had for over sixty years. With his new responsibilities bringing with them the necessity for interviewing numerous servants and officials has come no desire to establish himself in any of the numerous suites of rooms which are his to occupy if he so desires. The fact that those who are obliged to come either to consult him or for orders are forced to contort themselves painfully in order to negotiate a passage through his rabbit hutch doorway, and when inside to move about in a doubled-up condition, has no effect on him at all. Barquentine is not interested in the comfort of others.

Fuchsia, approaching the dining-hall in company with Mrs Slagg, who is carrying Titus, hears the rattle of Barquentine's crutch following them down the corridor. At a normal time she would have shuddered at the sound, but the horrifying and tragic minutes which she had spent with her father have filled her with so violent an alarm and so nameless a foreboding as to expel all other fears. She has on the immemorial crimson which is worn by the first daughter of the House of Groan at the christening of a brother, and around her neck are the so-called Daughter's Doves, a necklace of white sandstone doves carved by the 17th Earl of Gormenghast, strung together on a cord of plaited grass.

There is no sound from the infant, who is encased in the lilac roll. Fuchsia carries the black sword at one side, although the golden chain is still attached to Titus. Nannie Slagg, beside her-self with trepidation and excitement, peers now at her bundle and now at Fuchsia, sucking at her wrinkled lips as her little feet shuffle along below her best sepia-coloured skirt.

'We won't be late, my caution, will we? Oh no, because we mustn't, must we?' She peers into one end of the lilac roll. 'Bless him that he's so good, with all this horrible thunder; yis, he's been as good as good.'

Fuchsia does not hear; she is moving in a nightmare world of her own. Who can she turn to? Who can she ask? 'Doctor Prune, Doctor Prune,' she says to herself, '. . . he will tell me; he will know that I can make him well again. Only I can make him well again.'

Before them, as they turn a corner, the door of the dining-hall looms up and, obliterating most of it, with his hand on the brass handle, is Swelter. He swings open the door for them and they enter the Dining Hall. They are the last to arrive, and more through coincidence than design this is as it should be – Titus being the guest of honour, or perhaps the *host* of honour, for it is today that, as the Heir of Gormenghast, he Enters upon the Realms, having braved the cycle of four seasons.

Fuchsia climbs the seven wooden steps which lead up to the rostrum and the long table. Away to her right spreads the cold, echoing hall, with the pool of rain-drips spreading on the stone floor. The drumming of the thick vertical rain on the roof is a background to everything that happens. Reaching down with her right hand Fuchsia helps Mrs Slagg up the last two steps. The assemblage, perfectly silent at the long table, have turned their heads towards Nannie with her momentous bundle, and when both her feet are well established upon the level of the rostrum the company rises and there is a scraping of chair-legs on the boards. It seems to Fuchsia that high, impenetrable forests have risen before her, great half-lit forms of a nature foreign to her own – belonging to some other kingdom. But though for a moment she thinks of this, she is not feeling it, for she is subjugated beneath the weight of her fear for her father.

It is with a shock of indefinable emotion that she sees him as she lifts her head. She had never for a moment contemplated his being able to attend the Breakfast, imagining that the Doctor would be with him in his bedroom. So vivid in her mind is the picture of her father in his room as she had last seen him, that to find him in this so different atmosphere gives her for a moment a gush of hope – hope that she had been dreaming – that she had not been to his room – that he had not been upon the mantelpiece with his round, loveless eyes; for now as she stares at him he is so gentle and sad and thin and she can see that there is a weak smile of welcome upon his lips.

Swelter, who has followed them in, is now ushering Mrs Slagg into a chair on whose back-rest is painted the words: 'FOR A SERVANT'. There is a space cleared before her on the table in the shape of a half-circle, in which has been laid a long cushion. When Mrs Slagg sits down she finds that her chin is on a level with the table-edge, and it is with difficulty that she lifts the lilac bundle high enough to place it on the cushion. On her left is Gertrude Groan. Mrs Slagg glances at her apprehensively. She is gazing at an expanse of darkness, for the black clothes of the Countess seem to have no ending. She lifts her eyes a little and there is still darkness. She lifts them more, and still the darkness climbs. Raising her whole head and staring almost vertically above her she imagines that, near the zenith of her vision, she can descry a warmth of colour in the night. To think that an hour earlier she had been helping to plait those locks that now appear to be brushing the flaking cherubs of the ceiling.

On her right is the Earl. He leans back in his chair, very listless and weak, but he still smiles wanly at his daughter, who is on the opposite side of the table and facing her mother. On Fuchsia's right and left sit Irma Prunesquallor and her brother respectively. The Doctor and Fuchsia have their little fingers interlocked under the table. Cora is sitting opposite to the Earl her brother, and on the left of the Countess, and facing Irma, is Clarice. A fine, succulent ham, lit by a candle, takes up most of the space at the Earl's and Cora's end of the table, where Swelter presides and has now taken up his official duties armed with carving-knife and steel. At the other end of the table Barquentine smoulders on a high chair.

•

The eating is done spasmodically whenever a gap of time appears between the endless formalities and ornate procedures which Barquentine sets in motion at the correct time-honoured moments. Tiresome in the extreme for all those present, it would be hardly less tedious for the reader to be obliged to suffer the long catalogue of Breakfast ritual, starting with the smashing of the central Vase, whose shattered fragments are gathered together in two heaps, one at the head and the other at the feet of Titus, and ending with the extraordinary spectacle of Barquentine trampling (apparently as a symbol of the power invested in his hands as warder of the unbroken laws of Gormenghast), up and down the length of the Breakfast table seven times amidst the *débris* of the meal, his wooden leg striking at the dark oak.

Unknown to any who sit there at the long table there are not nine of them upon the daïs – but ten. All through the meal there have been ten.

The tenth is Steerpike. In the late afternoon of the previous day, when the dining-hall had swum in a warm haze of motes and every movement had bred its hollow echo through the silence, he had moved swiftly up to the platform from the doorway with a black, stumpy roll of cloth and what appeared to be a bundle of netting under his arm. After satisfying himself that he was quite alone, he half unrolled the cloth, slipped up the wooden steps of the daïs, and in a flash has slithered under the table.

For a few moments there were only some scrabbling sounds and the occasional clinking of metal, but the noise mounted, and for two minutes there was intense activity. Steerpike believed in working fast, especially in nefarious matters. When at last he emerged he dusted himself carefully and it might have been noticed, had there been anyone there to notice it, that although he still carried the lumpy roll of cloth, the netting was no longer with him. Had this same hypothetical watcher glanced under the table from any part of the room he would have noticed nothing extraordinary, for there would have been nothing to see; but had he taken the trouble to have crawled between the table legs and then gazed upwards, he would have noticed that, stretching down the centre of the low 'roof' was a very comfortable hammock.

And it is in this hammock that Steerpike is now reclining at full length, in semi-darkness, hedged in with a close-up panorama of seventeen legs and one wooden stump, or to be exact with sixteen, for Fuchsia is sitting with one of hers curled up under her. He had left the Twins hurriedly on his way down with them and had managed to be the first to slip into the hall. The oak of the table is within a few inches of his face. He has had very little satisfaction, so much of the time having been spent above him in fantastic dumb shows invisible to him. There is, in fact, no conversation and all he has heard during the seemingly interminable meal is the loveless, didactic voice of Barquentine, reeling out the time-worn, legendary phrases; the irritating, and apologetic coughing of Irma, and the slight creaking of Fuchsia's chair every time she moves. Occasionally the Countess mutters something which no one can hear, which is invariably followed by Nannie rubbing her ankles nervously together. Her feet are at least twenty inches from the floor and it is a great temptation to Steerpike to give them a twitch.

Finding he is going to gain no advantage at all by having secreted himself so cunningly, and yet seeing also that it is impossible to get away, he begins to think like a machine, overhauling in his mind his position in the Castle.

Saving Sepulchrave and Titus, whose cardinal interests are still limited to the worlds of whiteness and blackness – of milk and sleep – there is very little for the remainder of the company to do other than to brood, for there is no conversation, and there is very little chance of eating the breakfast so lavishly spread before them, for no one passes anything along the table. And so the company brood through the wasted meal. The dry, ancient voice at the end of the table has had an almost hypnotic effect, even at this early hour, and as their minds move to and fro and in and out the rain continues to beat upon the high roof overhead, and to drip, drip, drip, into the pool in the far centre of the long dining-hall.

No one is listening to Barquentine. The rain has drummed for ever. His voice is in the darkness – and the darkness in his voice, and there is no end at all.

THE REVERIES

THE REVERIE OF CORA

... and it's so cold, hands and cold feet but nice ones mine are nicer than Clarice's which she pricks with her embroidery clumsy thing but hers are also cold I hope but I want Gertrude's to be colder than the ice in dreadful places she's so fat and proud and far too big and I desire her frozen with her stupid bosom and when we're stronger in power we will tell her so Clarice and I when he lets us with his cleverness which is more clever than all the Castle and our thrones will make us regal but I'm the one to sit highest and I wonder where he is and stupid Gertrude thinks I'm frightened and I am but she doesn't know and I wish she would die and I'd see her big ugly body in a coffin because I'm of the blood and poor Sepulchrave looks different which she's done to him ugly woman with fat bosom and carrots hair the vegetable thing so cold here cold and my hands and feet which is what Clarice is feeling like I suppose she's so slow compared with me she looks so silly with her mouth open not like me my mouth isn't open yes it is I've left it open but now I've shut it and it's closed up and my face must be perfect like I'll be when I get my power and the West Wing is raging with glory why was the fire so big when I don't understand and we are made to be in darkness and one day perhaps I will banish Steerpike when he's done everything for us and perhaps I won't for it's not time to know yet and I'll wait and see because he isn't really of good stock like us and ought to be a servant but he's so clever and sometimes treats me with reverence which is due to me of course for I'm Lady Cora of Gormenghast I am and there's only me and my sister who are like that and she's not got the character I have and must take advice from me it is so cold and Barquentine is so long and he is so nasty but I will bow a little to him not too much but about an inch to show that he's done his work adequately not well but adequately with his voice and his wooden crutch which is so unnecessarily stupid to have instead of a leg and perhaps I'll look at it so that he sees me while I look just for a little moment to show him I am me and he mustn't forget my blood and what is poor Sepulchrave looking like that for with his mouth slipping down on one side and upon the other while he looks at her and she looks so frightened poor stupid Fuchsia who is still too young to understand anything yet she never comes to visit us when she could be taught but her cruel mother has turned her against us with her evil I feel hungry but nobody will pass me anything for the narrow squeaky Doctor is asleep or very nearly and Swelter never notices nor does anyone except the clever boy.

*

There is a thud on the table beyond the Doctor, to her right.

REVERIE OF ALFRED PRUNESQUALLOR

... and although it is patent that he hasn't very long I can't keep pumping hydrophondoramischromatica of ash into him every five hours or so and he'll need it even more frequently than that his mouth is slipping already devil take it which is too near the mark by all that's gruesome it is but the stuff will wipe him out unless I go easy and what will happen god knows if the owl crops up again but we or rather I must be prepared for anything and make tentative plans to meet contingencies for the others have no responsibilities except to the ritual of the place and never have had a case of this transference kind so unpleasantly actual for though the depersonalization has set in for good that is the lesser thing for the hooting is outside the range of science yet what started the whole thing was the burning undoubtedly oh yes undoubtedly for it was only melancholia up till then but thanks and praise be to all the bottle gods and powder princes that I had the drugs and that I guessed the strength well enough for the moment but he must go back to bed immediately the breakfast is over and have someone in the room with him whenever I have to go for meals but they might be brought to me in his room better idea still and perhaps Fuchsia might do it though the sight of her father might be too much for her but we cannot tell yet and must be careful bless her dear heart poor girl she looks so mournful and she is holding my finger so sadly I would rather she gripped it desperately it would be more symptomatic of an honest panic in her. I must comfort her if I can though what in the name of tact can I say to calm an intelligent and sensitive child who has seen her father hooting from a mantelpiece but care must be taken great care and perhaps Irma will get a room ready for her in the house but the next few hours will tell and I must be on the alert for the Countess is no help with her mind in the clouds, and Irma is of course Irma and nothing but undiluted Irma for now and ever and must be left where she is, and Steerpike remains who is an enigma to me and of whom I have doubts very definitely and in whose presence I find less and less amusement and more and more a sense of evil which I can base upon no power of rational reasoning save that he is obviously out for himself and himself alone but who isn't? and I will bear him in mind and dispense with him if I can but a brain is a brain and he has one and it may be necessary to borrow it at short notice but no no I will not by all that's instinctive I will not and that settles it I'll handle whatever needs to be handled myself well well I don't remember quite such a strong presentiment in my old carcase for a long time we must wait and see and the waiting won't be long and we'll hope the seeing won't be long either for there is something very unhealthy about all this by all that's bursting into flower in an April dell there most undeniably is and my languorous days seem to be over for the time being but bless me the gipsy girl is squeezing a bit harder and what on earth is she staring at his mouth is slipping and it's coming on again . . .

•

There is a thud on the table beside him. . . .

... what can I do oh what can I do he is so ill and pale like the
thin face that he has got that is broken all alone but he is better
better than he was oh no the sickness in me no I mustn't think
of eyes oh who will help me who will you must look now
Fuchsia be brave you must look Fuchsia look how he is better
now while he is here at table he is quite close to me my father
and so sad why does he smile smile oh who will save him who
will save me who will be the power to help us father who will
not let me be near and let me understand which I could and he
is better remember he is better than oh Fuchsia be brave for
the roundness of his eyes is gone gone but oh no I mustn't why
were they round round and yellow I do not understand oh tell
me my trees tell me my trees and rocks for Nannie won't know
oh doctor dear you must tell me and I will ask you when we're
alone oh quick quick this horrible breakfast quickly go and I
will take care of him for I understand because the tower was
there the tower was over his long lines of books his books and
its shadow fell across his library at morning always always
father dear the Tower of Flints that the owls live in oh no I
do not understand but I know dear father let me comfort you
and you must never be like that again never never never and I
will be your sentry for always always your sentry and will
never talk to other people never only you my dear pale man
and none will come near you only perhaps the doctor when
you want him but only when you do and I will bring you
flowers of every kind of colour and shape and speckled stones
that look like frogs and ferns and all the beautiful things I can
find and I will find books for you and will read to you all day
and all night and never let you know I'm tired and we shall go
for walks when you are better and you will become happy
happy if only you could be if only sad thin broken face so
pale and none else would be there not my mother nor anyone
not Steerpike no no not him, he is too hard and clever not like
you who are more clever but with kindness and not quick with
clever words. I can see his mouth his mouth oh Dr Prune quick

quick the blackness and he's going far away and the voice Dr Prune quick the voice is going far away of Barquentine is going far away I cannot see no no oh black my Dr Prune the black is swaying ... swaying ...

*

A darkness is closing its midnight curtains across her mind and the shapes before her of her mother, Nannie, Clarice and the Earl recede into floating fragments, while like the echo of an echo the voice of Barquentine stammers on and on. Fuchsia cannot feel the Doctor's finger any longer in her palm except as an infinitely far away sensation, as though she were holding a thin tube of air. In a final wave the blackness descends once and for all, and her dark head, falling forward, strikes the table with a thud.

REVERIE OF IRMA PRUNESQUALLOR

... and I'd very much like to know what advantage I am getting out of having spent so long a time in the bath and preparing myself for them so exquisitely for my swan-white throat is the most perfect one in Gormenghast though I wish my nose weren't quite so pointed, but it is velvet white like the rest of my skin and it's a pity I wear spectacles with black lenses too I suppose but I am positive my skin is snow white not only because I can see it dimly in the mirror when I take my spectacles off although it hurts my eyes but also because my writing paper is perfectly white when I've got my glasses on and look at my face and throat in the mirror and then hold a piece of my white writing paper next to my face I can see that my skin and the stationery are exactly the same tone of grey and everything else in the mirror all around me is darker and very often black but what's the use of writing-paper with crinkled edges to me for there's no one to write to us there used to be when I was younger not that I was more attractive then for after all I am still a virgin but there was Spogfrawne who had had so many beautiful adventures among the people he redeemed from sin and he appreciated me and wrote me three letters on tissue paper although it was a pity that his pen-nib used to go right through it so often and make it difficult for me to read the passionate parts where he told me of his love in fact I couldn't read them at all and when I wrote and asked him to try and remember them and write me a fourth letter just putting in only the passionate sentences which I couldn't read in the first three of his beautiful letters he wouldn't answer me and I think it was because I asked him in my last message to him to either write more carefully on the tissue paper or to use ordinary paper that he became shy poor silly stupid glamorous Mr Spogfrawne who I will always remember but he hasn't been heard of since and I am still a virgin and who is there to make love to me tenderly and to touch the tip of my snowy hands and perhaps just a tiny touch on my hip bone which juts out so magnificently as Steerpike mentioned that evening when Alfred was called away to get a fly out of that Slagg woman's eye for Steerpike bless the boy has always been most observant and I know how it broke my heart to see him so miserable on the day he left us and now I never see him and it is a pity that he is not a little older and taller but once he speaks to me and fastens his eye on me in that respectful way he has noticing the beauty of my skin and hair and the way my hips come out so excitingly then I do not wish him any different but feel a little queer and realize how impelling he is for what is age anyway but years and years are nothing if not silly and ridiculous man made things which do not understand the way of delicate women with the years coming so unkindly and how could they be so many in my case all forty of them that have never had their due or why I am unmarried I do not know when I take so much care over my cleanliness but who is there who is there oh my emptiness is all alone and with Alfred who can be so silly though he's really clever but doesn't listen to me and falls asleep like he is doing now and I wish he wouldn't keep looking at the Earl who after all isn't someone to be stared at although there is something very strange about him tonight and how chilly it is in this big and empty and horrible hall which is so famous but what use is it if we don't talk to each other and there are no men to watch every gracious movement of my throat and I will be glad to be back in my house again where I will go on reading my book, and it won't be so cold and perhaps I can write a note to Steerpike and ask him to supper yes I will do that Alfred said he won't be in tomorrow evening and . . .

Her thoughts are broken by a thud to her left.

THE REVERIE OF LADY CLARICE

Her thoughts have been identical with those of her sister in every way save only in one respect, and this cleavage can best be appreciated by the simple process of substituting Cora's name for her own wherever it appears in the reverie of the former.

REVERIE OF GERTRUDE THE COUNTESS OF GORMENGHAST

. . . at any rate the old Sourdust would have taken longer over this job than this one and it won't be long before I can have my white cat who is crying at my heart again may the fiends wrack the long servant's bones and I've left enough water in the basin for the ravens' bath and can see to the sandpipers' wing directly I get away from here and my white cat is comforted but the stupid man has about fourteen pages to get through yet thank heaven I don't have many of these things to attend and there won't be another child if I know anything about it but now here is a son for Gormenghast which is what the Castle needed and when he is older I will teach him how he can take care of himself and how to live his own life as far as it is possible for one who will find the grey stones across his heart from day to day and the secret is to be able to freeze the outsider off completely and then he will be able to live within himself which Sepulchrave does in the wrong way for what use are books to anyone whose days are like a rook's nest with every twig a duty and I shall teach the boy to whistle birds out of the sky to his wrist which I have never taught Fuchsia because I have kept my knowledge for the boy and if I have the time before he is twelve years old and if it's a pleasant evening I might take him to the pool that is as green as my malachite ring with the silver setting and let him watch the lesser-fly-spotted-wag-catchers building their soft grey nests out of moth-wings and dew-twine but how do I know he will be observant and careful with birds for Fuchsia disappointed me before she was five with her clumsiness for she used to ram the flowers into the glass vases and bruise the stalks although she loved them but it is my son I wish to teach for there is no use in my revealing my secrets to a girl but he will be so useless for a long time and must be kept away from my room until he is about five at least when he will be able to absorb what I tell him about the skies' birds and how he can keep his head quite clear of the duties he must perform day after day until he dies here as his fathers have done and be buried in the sepulchre of the Groans and he must learn the secret of silence and go his own way among the birds and the white cats and all the animals so that he is not aware of men but performs his legendary duties faithfully as his father has always done whose library was burned away along with old Sourdust and how it started I have very little idea except that the Steerpike youth was very quickly upon the scene and though he was the means of our escape I do not like him and never shall with his ridiculous little body and slimy manners he must be sent away for I have a feeling he will do harm and Fuchsia must not be with him for she is not to mix with so cheap and ignoble a thing as that sharp youth she converses too often with Prunesquallor with whom I saw her talking twice last month for he is not of the blood and as for the murderous and devilish Flay who has hurt my poor defenceless cat so much that all the other white glories will be uneasy through the black hours of night and feel the pains which he feels as he is curled in my arms for Flay has broken himself with his ghastly folly and shall be banished whatever Sepulchrave may say whose face has changed tonight and has been changed on the three occasions on which I have seen him since the burning of his books and I will tell the Doctor to attend him constantly for I have a presentiment of his death and it is good that Titus is born for the line of the Groans must never be broken through me and there must be no ending at all and no ending and I shall tell him of his heritage and honour and of how to keep his head above the interwoven nest and watch the seasons move by and the sounds of the feathered throats. . . .

A thud upon the table immediately opposite her causes the Countess to lift her eyes slowly from the table cloth.

REVERIE OF NANNIE SLAGG

. . . yees yees yees it's all so big and wonderful I suppose it is oh my poor heart this lovely rich breakfast which nobody eats and the little precious boy in the middle of the cutlery bless his little heart for he hasn't cried once not once the tiny morsel and with everybody around him too and thinking about him for it's his breakfast my pretty precious and Nannie will tell you all about it when you're a big boy oh my poor heart how old I'll be by then and how cold it is a good thing I wrapped the little boy in his wrap which is under all the lilac windings yees yees and he mustn't sneeze oh no but be still though I am so cold and his great heavy mother beside me so that I feel I don't matter at all and I suppose I don't matter at all for nobody takes any notice of me and nobody loves me except my darling caution but even she sometimes forgets but not the others who never think of me except when they want me to do something for them for I have to do everything and oh my poor heart I'm not young any more and strong and I get tired and even Fuchsia never remembers how tired I get even now I'm tired for having to sit so long in the cold so far beneath the huge Countess who doesn't even look at her little boy who's being so good and I don't think she could ever love him like I love him but oh my poor heart it's a good thing the Countess can't hear me thinking about her like this though sometimes I think she can tell when I think against her because she's so silent and when she looks at me I don't know what to do or where to go and I feel so little and weak and I feel like that now but how cold it is and I'd rather have my own simple kind of breakfast by the fire in my own small room than look at all this food on the table getting cold although it's all here for the little boy bless him and I will look after him as long as I have any strength in my poor bones and make him a good boy and teach Fuchsia to take care of him and she is loving him more than ever she did before though she doesn't like to hold him like I do and I am glad because she might drop him the clumsy caution and oh my poor heart if he should ever fall and be killed oh no no never she must never hold him for she is so ignorant of how to be careful of a little baby she doesn't look at him now in the middle of the table any more than her mother or any of the others do but just stares at her father with her naughty dark face so sad what can it be for she must tell me and tell me everything leaving nothing out about why she looks so mournful the silly girl who can have no trouble at her age and hasn't got all the work to do and the trials which I have on my old shoulders all the time and it is silly for her to be so sad when she is only a child and doesn't know anything bless her.

Nannie is startled by a thud upon the table nearly opposite her.

REVERIE OF SEPULCHRAVE, 76th EARL OF GORMENGHAST

. . . and there will be a darkness always and no other colour and the lights will be stifled away and the noises of my mind strangled among the thick soft plumes which deaden all my thoughts in a shroud of numberless feathers for they have been there so long and so long in the cold hollow throat of the Tower and they will be there for ever for there can be no ending to the owls whose child I am to the great owls whose infant and disciple I shall be so that I am forgetting all things and will be taken into the immemorial darkness far away among the shadows of the Groans and my heartache will be no more and my dreams and thoughts no more and even memory will be no longer so that my volumes will die away from me and the poets be gone for I know the great tower stood above my cogitations day and night through all the hours and they will all go the great writers and all that lay between the finger-ed covers all that slept or walked between the vellum lids where for the centuries they haunted and no longer are and my remorse is over now and forever for desire and dream has gone and I am complete and longing only for the talons of the tower and suddenness and clangour among the plumes and an end and a death and the sweet oblivion for the last tides are mounting momently and my throat is growing taut and round round like the Tower of Flints and my fingers curl and I crave the dusk and sharpness like a needle in the velvet and I shall be claimed by the powers and the fretting ended . . . ended . . . and in my annihilation there shall be a consummation for he has come into the long line and is moving forward and the long dead branch of the Groans has broken into the bright leaf of Titus who is the fruit of me and there shall be no ending and the grey stones will stand for always and the high towers for always where the raindrifts weave and the laws of my own people will go on for ever while among my great dusk haunters in the tower my ghost will hover and my blood-stream ebb for ever and the striding fever over who are these and these so far from me and yet so vast and so remote and vast my Fuchsia dusky daughter bring me branches and a fieldmouse from an acre of grey pastures. . .

HERE AND THERE

SWELTER'S thoughts were glued upon Flay's death at his own hand. The time was ripe. He had practised the art of silent and stealthy movement until he could no longer hear even the breath-note of his own footstep which over the stretch of the last fortnight he had striven to stifle. He now moved his bulk across the earth as silently as the passing of a cloud through the dusk. His two-handed cleaver had an edge to it which sang with the voice of a gnat when he held it to his fungus of an ear. To-night he would leave a small pink wafer at the top of the last flight of stairs, within a bare twenty feet of the thin man. It would be a dark night. He listened to the thrumming rain and his eyes turned to the lake on the cold floor, far down the dining hall. He stared at but did not see the bleared reflection of the flanking cherubs a hundred feet above the steel-grey veneer of water. His eyes were unfocused. He would do the work he had waited to do tomorrow night. Tomorrow night. As his tongue emerged from between his lips like a carrot and moved from side to side, his eyes moved from the water to Flay, and the vagueness was at once gone from them. In his stare was the whole story; and Flay, lifting his eyes from the top of his master's head, interpreted the vile expression.

He had known that the attack upon his life was imminent. The coloured cakes when he had found them on the three preceding occasions had been successively closer to him. Swelter was trying to wreck him by torturing his mind and twisting his nerves and he had not slept for many nights but he was ready. He had not forgotten the two-handed cleaver in the green light and had found in the armoury an old sword, from which he had removed the rust and had sharpened to a point and an edge in the stone lanes. Compared to the edge which Swelter had given to the cleaver the sword was blunt but it was murderous enough. In Swelter's expression he could read the nearness of the night encounter. It would be within a week. He could not tell which day. It might be this very night. It might be any night of the next seven.

He knew that Swelter could not see him until he was practically upon him at his Master's door. He knew that the Chef could not know that he had read his eyes so clearly. He also knew that he was banished from the Castle grounds. Swelter must not know this. Gertrude would see that he, Flay, was not at Lord Sepulchrave's door from now onwards, but he could return in the night and follow the monster as he crept upwards to the passageway on his lethal mission.

That is what he would do. He would wait every night in the cloisters until the huge body stole by him and up the stairs. Not till then would he decide where and when to strike. He only knew that he must lead his foe away from his sick master's door and that the death must take place in some remote part of the castle, perhaps in the room of spiders ... or under the attic arches, or even among the battlements themselves. His thoughts were broken by the thud of Fuchsia falling forward and he saw the Doctor rise to his feet and stretch across the table for a glass, his left hand moving around Fuchsia's shoulder as he did so.

On the table itself young Titus began to kick and struggle and then with a high thin cry poor Mrs Slagg watches him kick the vase of flowers over, and tear at the lilac-coloured velvet with his hands.

*

Steerpike hears the thud above him and taking his cue from the varying contortions of the legs which hem him in is able to guess pretty accurately what is happening. There are only two legs which do not move at all and they are both Gertrude's. Fuchsia's only visible leg (for her right is still curled beneath her) has slipped sideways on the boards as she slumps forward. Nannie's are struggling frantically to reach the floor. Lord Sepulchrave's are swinging idly to and fro and are close together like a single pendulum. Cora and Clarice are going through the motions of treading water. The Doctor's have straightened out into unbroken lengths and his sister's have entered upon the last stages of a suicide pact, each one strangling the other in an ivy-like embrace.

Swelter is shifting the soft, dace-like areas of his feet backwards and forwards, a deliberate and stroking motion, as of something succulent wiping itself on a mat.

Flay is rubbing the cracked toe-cap of one of his boots rapidly up and down his shin bone immediately above the ankle, and, this done, Steerpike notices that his legs begin to make their way round the long table towards Fuchsia's chair detonating as they go.

During this short space of time while the screaming of Titus is drowning the barking of Barquentine, Prunesquallor has dabbed a quantity of water over Fuchsia's face with a napkin and has then placed her head gently between her knees.

Barquentine has not ceased a moment in the administration of his duties as the occasional lulls in Titus's howling testify, for during the short intervals of what might have been rain-filled silence the dry, acid tongue of the Librarian stutters on and on.

But it is nearly over. He is laying his tomes aside. His withered stump which, since Fuchsia's faint and the howling of Titus has been scratching at the boards with an irritability such as might suggest that its ugly termination was possessed of teeth instead of toes and was doing its best to gnaw its way through the oak boarding below it – this stump is now setting about another business, that of getting itself and the rest of Barquentine upon the seat of the chair.

Once aboard the long, narrow table it is for him to march up and down it from end to end seven times regardless of the china and golden cutlery, regardless of the glassware, the wine and the repast in general, regardless of everything in fact save that he must be regardless. Mrs Slagg snatches the year-old baby from before the approaching crutch and withered leg, for Barquentine has lost no time in complying with tradition and the ferrule of his crutch strikes jarringly upon the polished oak, or cracks among the china plates or splinters the cut glass. A dull soggy note followed by a squelch betrays the fact that his withered leg has descended ankle deep in a tureen of tepid porridge, but it was not for him to turn aside in the promulgation of his duty.

Doctor Prunesquallor has staggered away with Fuchsia in his arms, having instructed Flay to escort Lord Sepulchrave to his room. The Countess strangely enough has taken Titus from Nannie Slagg and having descended from the platform to the stone slabs below is walking heavily to and fro with the little boy half over her shoulder. 'Now then, now then', she says, 'No use crying; no use at all; not when you're two; wait till you're three. Now then, now then, wait till you're bigger and I'll show you where the birds live, there's a good child, there's a . . . Slagg . . . Slagg,' she bellows suddenly, interrupting herself. 'Take it away.' The Earl and Flay have gone and so has Swelter after casting a baffled eye over the table and at the wizened Barquentine as he stamps into the exquisitely prepared and despoiled breakfast.

Cora and Clarice are left watching Barquentine with their mouths and the pupils of their eyes so wide open as to cause these caverns to monopolize their faces to the extent of giving to their countenances an appearance of darkness or of absence. They are still seated and their bodies beneath their straight dresses are perfectly rigid while their eyes follow the ancient's every movement, leaving him only momently when a louder sound than usual forces them to turn their eyes to the table to observe what the latest ornament to be broken may be.

The darkness in the great hall has deepened in defiance of the climbing of the sun. It can afford to be defiant with such a pall of inky cloud lying over the castle, over the cracked toothed mountain, over the entire and drenching regions of Gormenghast from horizon to horizon.

Barquentine and the Twins trapped in the shadows of the hall which is itself trapped within the shadows of the passing clouds are lit by one lone candle, the others having guttered away. In this vast, over-arching refectory these three – the vitriolic marionette in his crimson rags and the two stiff purple puppets, one at either end of the table – look incredibly minute, tiny fierce ribs of colour glinting on their clothes as the candle-flame moves. The broken glass on the long table darting forth a sudden diamond from time to time. From the far end of the Hall near the servants' door, and looking down the inky perspective of stone pillars, the spectacle of the three at the table would seem to be taking place in an area the size of a domino.

As Barquentine completes his seventh journey, the flame of the last candle stumbles, recovers, and then sinks suddenly into a swamp of tallow and the Hall is plunged into a complete obscurity, save where the lake in the middle of the Hall is a pattern of darkness surrounded by depths of another nature. Near the margin of this inner rain-fed darkness an ant is swimming for its life, its strength failing momently for there are a merciless two inches of water beneath it. From far away near the high table comes a scream, and then another and the sound of a chair falling to the stone slabs seven feet below the platform, and the sound of Barquentine cursing.

Steerpike, having observed the legs disappearing out of the door, and to whom they belonged, has wriggled from his hammock under the table. He is groping his way to the door. When he reaches it, and has found the handle, he slams it violently and then, as though he has just *entered* the room he shouts:

'Hello there; what's happening there! What's the trouble?'

On hearing his voice the twins begin to scream for help, while Barquentine yells 'Light! light! fetch a light you dotard. What are you waiting for?' His strident voice rises to a shriek and his crutch grinds itself on the table. 'Light! scumcat! light! curse and split you!'

Steerpike, whose last hour and a half has been a dire disappointment and boring in the extreme, hugs himself for joy at their shouts.

'Right away, sir. Right away,' he dances out of the door and down the passage. He is back in less than a minute with a lantern and helps Barquentine off the table who, once on the ground, batters his way without a word of thanks down the steps and to the door, cursing as he goes, his red rags glowing dully in the lantern light. Steerpike watches his horrid body disappear and then raising his high sharp shoulders still higher he yawns and grins at the same time. Cora and Clarice are on either side of him and are both breathing very loudly, their flat bosoms rising and falling rapidly like hatchways. Their eyes are glued upon him as he escorts them through the door, down the corridor and all the way to their apartments, which he enters. The windows are streaming with the rain. The roof is loud with it.

'My dear ladies,' says Steerpike, 'I feel that some hot coffee is indicated, but what do *you* feel?'

PRESAGE

TOWARDS evening the heavy sky began to disintegrate and a short time before sundown a wind from the west carried the clouds away in dense and shambly masses and the rain with them. Most of the day had been spent in ceremonial observance of multifarious kinds, both in the castle and in the downpour culminating in the pilgrim-like procession of the forty-three Gardeners headed by Pentecost, to Gormenghast mountain and back, during which time it was their duty to meditate upon the glory of the House of Groan and especially on the fact that its latest member was twelve months old, a subject (however momentous) they must surely have exhausted after the first mile or so of the soaking and rock-strewn paths that led them over the foothills.

Be that as it may, Barquentine, lying exhausted on his dirty mattress at eight o'clock in the evening and coughing horribly as his father had done so convincingly before him, was able to look back with sour satisfaction on a day of almost undiluted ritual. It had been an irritating thing that Lord Sepulchrave had been unable to attend the last three ceremonies, but there was a tenet in the law which exonerated his absence in the case of dire illness. He sucked his beard and his withered leg lay quite still. A few feet above his head a spider scrawled itself across the ceiling. He disliked it, but it did not anger him.

Fuchsia had regained consciousness within a short while and with Mrs Slagg had bravely taken her part in the day's observances, carrying her small brother whenever the old nurse grew weary. Prunesquallor, until late in the evening when he left Flay with his lordship, had kept a strict watch upon his patient.

An indescribable atmosphere of expectancy filled Gormenghast. Instead of Titus's birthday bringing with it a feeling of completion or climax as it should have done, there was, conversely, a sense of something beginning. Obscure forces were, through the media of the inhabitants of the castle, coming to a head. For some, this sensation was extremely acute although unrecognizable and was no doubt sharpened and conditioned by their own personal problems. Flay and Swelter were on the edge of violence. Sepulchrave was moving at the margin of climax and Fuchsia hardly less so, being consumed with fear and anguish at the parental tragedy. She also was waiting; they were all waiting. Prunesquallor was suffering no little strain and was eternally on the watch and the Countess having held interview with him and having heard as much as Prunesquallor dared tell her, and having guessed a good deal more, was remaining in her room and receiving hourly bulletins as to her husband's condition. Even Cora and Clarice could tell that the normal, monotonous life of the castle was not as heretofore and in their room they sat silently – waiting also. Irma spent most of her time in her bath and her thoughts were constantly returning to a notion new to her and shocking to her, and even terrifying. It was that the House of Groan was different. Different. Yet, how could it be different? 'Impossible! I said Impossible!' she repeated to herself, through a lather of fragrant suds, but she could not convince herself. This idea of hers was creeping about Gormenghast insidiously, remaining for the most part unrecognized save as a sensation of uneasiness.

It was only Irma who put her finger on the spot. The others were involved with counting the portentous minutes before their own particular clouds broke over them, yet at the back of their personal troubles, hopes and fears, this less immediate trepidation grew, this intangible suggestion of *change*, that most unforgivable of all heresies.

A few minutes before sunset the sky over the castle was a flood of light and the wind having dropped, and the clouds vanished, it was difficult to believe that the mild and gilded atmosphere could ever have hallowed such a day as began so darkly and continued with such consistent violence. But it was still Titus's birthday. The crags of the mountain for all their jaggedness were draped in so innocent a veil of milk and rose as to wholly belie their nature. The marshlands spread to the North in tranquil stretches of rush-pricked water. The castle had become a great pallid carving, swarmed here and there by acres of glittering ivy whose leaves dripped diamonds.

Beyond the great walls of Gormenghast the mud-huts were gradually regaining the whitish colour of their natural earth as the late sunlight drew out the moisture. The old cactus trees steamed imperceptibly and beneath the greatest of these and lit by the slanting rays of the sun was a woman on horseback.

For a long while there seemed to be no movement either in her or her mount. Her face was dark and her hair had fallen about her shoulders. The pale light was on her face, and there was a mournful triumph and an extreme loneliness. She bent forward a little and whispered to the horse who raised his forefoot on hearing her and beat it back into the soft earth. Then she began to dismount and it was not easy for her, but she lowered herself carefully down the wet grey flank. Then she took the basket from where it had been fastened to the rope bridle and stepped slowly forward to the horse's head. Running her fingers through the tangled and dripping forelock, she moved them over the hard brow beneath. 'You must go back now,' she said slowly, 'to the Brown Father, so that he may know that I am safe.' Then she pushed the long wet, grey head away from her with a slow and deliberate movement. The horse turned itself away, the rain bubbling up in the hoofmarks and forming little gold pools of sky. It turned back to her once, after a few paces. Then lifting its head very high it shook its long mane from side to side and the air became filled with a swarm of pearls. Then suddenly it began to pace along the track of its own hoofmarks and without a moment's abatement in its pace or the least deviation from its homeward course, it sped from her. She watched it as it appeared, disappeared, only to reappear again, as the undulations of the region gave cause, until it was almost too small to observe. At last she saw that it was about to reach the ridge of the last stretch of upland before its descent to the invisible plain. As she watched, it suddenly came to a dead halt, and her heart beat rapidly, for it turned about and stood for a moment motionless. Then lifting its head very high as it had done before, it began to move backwards step by step. They were facing one another over that vast distance as the grey horse was at last swallowed beneath the horizon.

She turned towards the mud-huts lying below her in a rose red light. A crowd had begun to gather and she saw that she was being pointed out.

With the warm glow of the dying light upon them, the mud dwellings for all their meanness and congestion had something ethereal about them, and her heart went out to them as a hundred re-awakened memories flew to her mind. She knew that bitterness was harboured in the narrow streets, that pride and jealousy leaned like ghosts against the posts of every carver's doorway, but for a fleeting moment she saw only the evening light falling across the scenes of her childhood, and it was with a start that she awakened from this momentary reverie to notice how the crowd had grown. She had known that this moment would be like this. She had foreseen such an evening of soft light. She had foreseen that the earth would be glassed with rain and she had the overpowering sensation of living through a scene she had already enacted. She had no fear although she knew she would be met by hostility, prejudice and perhaps violence. Whatever they did with her it would not matter. She had suffered it already. All this was far wan history and an archaism.

Her hand moved to her brow and pushed away a cold lock of hair that clung blackly to her cheek. 'I must bear my child,' she said to herself, her lips framing the soundless words, 'and then I shall be complete and only myself and all will be over.' Her pupils grew vast. 'You shall be free. From the very beginning you shall be free of me, as I shall be free of you; and I shall follow my knowledge – ah, so soon, so soon into the julip darkness.'

She folded her hands and moved slowly towards the dwellings. High on her right hand the great outer wall had become colder; its inner face was draped with shadow and in the depths of the castle Titus sending forth a great tear-filled cry began to struggle with an unnatural strength in the old nurse's arms. All at once an eyelid of the rich dusk lifted and Hesper burned over Gormenghast as under Keda's heart her burden struggled.

IN PREPARATION FOR VIOLENCE

THE twelve month cycle was ended. Titus had begun his second year – a year which, though hardly fledged, was so soon to bring forth violence. There was a sickness in the atmosphere.

Of all this suspicion and restlessness, he knew nothing, and he will have no memories of these days. Yet the aftermath of all that was happening in his infancy will soon be upon him.

Mrs Slagg watched him querulously as he tottered in his efforts to keep balance, for Titus had almost learned to walk

'Why won't he smile?' she whimpered. 'Why won't his little Lordship ever smile?'

The sound of Barquentine's crutch echoed down the hollow corridors. His withered leg padded beside it and the red sacking flapped its tatters in hot gusts. His edicts went forth like oaths.

Drear ritual turned its wheel. The ferment of the heart, within these walls, was mocked by every length of sleeping shadow. The passions, no greater than candle flames, flickered in Time's yawn, for Gormenghast, huge and adumbrate, out-crumbles all. The summer was heavy with a kind of soft grey-blue weight in the sky – yet not *in* the sky, for it was as though there were no sky, but only air, an impalpable grey-blue substance, drugged with the weight of its own heat and hue. The sun, however brilliantly the earth reflected it from stone or field or water, was never more than a rayless disc this summer – in the thick, hot air – a sick circle, unrefreshing and aloof.

The autumn and winter winds and the lashing rain storms and the very cold of those seasons, for all their barbarism, were of a spleen that voiced the heart. Their passions were allied to human passions – their cries to human cries.

But it was otherwise with this slow pulp of summer, this drag of heat, with the incurious yellow eye within it, floating monotonously, day after day.

At the river's edge the shallow water stank and mists of insects drifted over the scum, spinning their cry of far forgotten worlds, thinner than needles.

Toads in the green ooze belched. In the river's bosom the reflection of the topmost crags of Gormenghast Mountain hung like stalactites, and in the scarcely perceptible motion of the water appeared to crumble momently – yet never to diminish or to disintegrate for all their crumbling. Across the river a long field of sparse grey-green grasses and dove-grey dust lay stretched as though stunned between its low flint walls.

Little clouds of the fine dust were rising at the every footfall of a small mottled horse, on whose back sat a man in a cape.

At every fifth step forward of his mount's left leg the rider stood up in his stirrups and placed his head between the horse's ears. The river wound beside them, the fields undulating and fading in a blur of heat. The mottled horse and the caped rider moved on. They were very small. In the haze to the extreme north the tower of Flints arose like a celluloid ruler set floating upon its end, or like a water-colour drawing of a tower that has been left in the open and whose pigment has been all but washed away by a flirt of rain.

Distance was everywhere – the sense of far-away – of detachment. What might have been touched with an outstretched arm was equally removed, withdrawn in the grey-blue polliniferous body of the air, while overhead the inhuman circle swam. Summer was on the roofs of Gormenghast. It lay inert, like a sick thing. Its limbs spread. It took the shape of what it smothered. The masonry sweated and was horribly silent. The chestnuts whitened with dust and hung their myriads of great hands with every wrist broken.

What was left of the water in the moat was like soup. A rat floundered across it, part swimming, part walking. Thick sepia patches of water were left in the unhealthy scum where its legs had broken through the green surface.

The quadrangles were soft with dust. It had settled along the branches of the nearby trees. Footmarks were left deeply until the dry gusts came again. The varying lengths of stride – the Doctor's, Fuchsia's, the Countess's, Swelter's, could all be measured here, crossing and recrossing one another as though at the same time, yet hours, days and weeks divided them.

In the evening the bats, those fabulous winged mice, veered, tacked and slid through the hot gloom.

Titus was growing older.

It was four days since the Dark Breakfast. It was one year and four days since he was born in the room of wax and birdseed. The Countess would see no one. From daybreak to sunset she turned her thoughts, like boulders, over. She set them in long lines. She rearranged their order as she cogitated upon the Burning. She watched from her window as figures passed below. She turned her impressions over heavily. She was pondering all who passed by. From time to time Steerpike passed, as she sat at her window. Her husband was going mad. She had never loved him and she did not love him now, her heart being awakened to tenderness only by her birds and her white cats. But though she did not love him for himself, her unthinking and rooted respect for the heritage which he personified and her dumb pride in the line of his descent had filled her since her discovery of his illness.

Flay had gone, at her orders, to what lay beyond the great walls. He had gone, and though she would no more have thought of recalling him than of ceasing to tend the cat which he had bruised, yet she was aware of having uprooted a part of Gormenghast, as though from an accustomed skyline of towers one had been broken down. He had gone – but not altogether. Not for a little while, completely.

On the five nights following the day of his banishment – Titus's first birthday – he had returned unobserved when light had fallen.

He had moved like a stick-insect through the grey star-pricked, summer night, and knowing every bay, inlet and headland of the great stone island of the Groans, of its sheer cliffs, of its crumbling outcrops, he had pursued his way without hesitation on a zig-zag course. He had only to lean against the cliff face and he was absorbed. For the five last nights he had come, after long, sultry days of waiting among the skirting trees of the twisted woods, through a gap in the castle walls to the western wing. In his banishment he had felt the isolation of a severed hand, which realizes that it is no more part of the arm and body it was formed to serve and where the heart still beats. As yet, for him, the horror of his ostracization was too close for him to grasp – only the crater-like emptiness. The stinging-nettles had not had time to fill the yawning hollow. It was loneliness without pain.

His loyalty to the castle, too deep for him to question, was his heart's background: to all that was implied by the broken line of the towers. With his knees drawn up to his chin he pored upon that skyline as he sat at the base of an outcrop of rock among the trees. At his side lay the long sword he had sharpened. The sun was going down. In another three hours he would be on his way, for the sixth time since his banishment, to the cloisters he had known since his youth. To the cloisters in whose northern shadows was an entrance to the stairhead of the wine vaults and the Kitchens. A thousand recollections attached themselves to these cloisters alone. Sudden happenings – the awakening of ideas that had borne fruit or had withered at his touch – the memories of his youth – of his infancy even, for a brightly coloured vignette at the back of his dark skull recurred from time to time, a vignette of crimson, gold and grey. He had had no recollection of who it was who led him by the hand, but he recalled how, between two of the southerly arches, he and his guardian were stopped – how the air had been filled with sunshine – how a giant, for so he must then have appeared to the child, a giant in gold had given him an apple – the globe of crimson which he had never released from his mind's empyric grasp, nor the grey of the long hair that fell across the brow and over the shoulders of his first memory.

Few of Flay's memories were as colourful. His early years had been hard, grinding and monotonous. His recollections were associated with fears and troubles and hardships. He could remember how beneath the very cloister arches to which he was so soon to make his way he had received in grim silence, insult and even violence, no less than twinges of pleasure. He had leaned there, against the fourth pillar, on the afternoon following his unexpected summons to Lord Sepulchrave's study, where he had been told of his advancement – of his being chosen as the Earl's first servant; of how the Earl had noticed and approved of his silent and taciturn bearing, and of his reward. He had leaned there, his heart thumping; and he recalled how he had for a moment weakened, wishing he had a friend to whom he might speak of his happiness. But that was long ago. Clicking his tongue he dismissed recollections from his mind.

A gibbous moon was rising and the earth and the trees about him were dappled and striped with slowly shifting blotches of black and pearlish white. Radiance, in the shape of an oyster, moved across his head. He turned his eyes to the moon among the trees and scowled at it. This was no night for a moon. He cursed it, but in a childlike way for all the grim formation of his bones, stretching out his legs, on whose knees his chin had been supported.

He moved his thumb along the edge of his sword, and then unrolled a misshapen parcel at his side. He had not forgotten to bring some food with him from the castle, and now, five nights later, he made a meal upon all that was left of it. The bread had gone dry, but it tasted sweet to him after a day's abstinence, with the cheese and the wild blackberries he had gathered in the woods. He left nothing but a few crumbs on his black trousers. There was no rational reason why he should feel, as he finished the berries, that horror lay between his last mouthful and his next meal – whenever it might be, and however he might acquire it.

Perhaps it was the moon. On his five previous nocturnal journeys to the castle there had been no light. Thick rainless clouds had provided a perfect cover. Schooled to adversity he took it as a sign that the hour was approaching. Indeed, it seemed more natural that Nature should be his enemy.

He rose slowly, and from beneath a heap of ferns he drew forth into the moonlight great lengths of cloth – and then began a most peculiar operation. Squatting down, he began, with the concentration of a child, to bind the cloth about his knees, around and around endlessly, until they were swathed to a depth of five thick inches, loosely at the joint and more tightly as they wound below and above it and as the binding thickened. This business took him the best part of an hour, for he was very scrupulous and had several times to unwind long swathes to adjust and ease the genuflexions of his knees.

Finally, however, all was ready and he got to his feet. He took a step forward; then another, and it seemed as though he was listening for something. Was there no sound? He took three more paces, his head lowered and the muscles behind his ears working. What was that that he heard? It was like a muffled clock that ticked three times, and stopped. It sounded very far away. There were a few lengths of cloth left over and he bound his knees to another half inch of thickness. When he next stepped forward the silence was absolute.

It was still possible for him to move with comparative freedom. His legs were so long that he had become accustomed to use them as stilts, and it was only with the slightest bending of the knee that they were wont to detonate.

The moonlight lay in a gauze-like sheet of whiteness over the roof of the Twisted Woods. The air was hot and thick, and the hour was late when he began to move towards the castle. To reach the cloisters would take him an hour of rapid walking. The long sword gleamed in his hand. At the corners of his lipless mouth was the red stain of blackberries.

The trees were left behind and the long slopes where the juniper bushes crouched like animals or deformed figures in the darkness. He had skirted the river and had found a clammy mist lying like a lover along its length, taking its curves and hugging its croaking body, for the bull-frogs had made the night air loud. The moon behind the miasmic wreaths swam and bulged as though in a distorting mirror. The air was sickly with an aftermath of the day's heat, as lifeless as though it had been breathed before, thrice exhaled and stale. Only his feet felt cold as they sank ankle-deep in the dew. It was as though he trod through his own sweat.

With every step he became more conscious that he was narrowing the distance between himself and something horrible.

With every step the cloisters leapt forward to meet him and his heart pounded. The skin was puckered between his eyes. He strode on.

The outer wall of the castle was above him. It mouldered in the moon. Where colonies of lizards clung to its flaking surfaces it shone.

He passed through an arch. The unchecked growth of ivy which clung about it had almost met at the centre of the aperture, and Flay, bending his head, forced his way through a mere fissure. Once through and the grounds of Gormenghast opened balefully out with an alien intimacy as though an accustomed face should, after confining itself for years to a score of cardinal expressions, take on an aspect never known before.

Keeping as much in the shadows as he could, Flay made rapid progress over the uneven ground towards the servants' wing. He was treading on forbidden ground. Excommunicated by the Countess, each footfall was a crime committed.

During the final stages of his progress to the cloisters he moved with a kind of angular stealth. At times he would come to a halt and genuflect in rapid succession, but he could hear no sound; then he would move on again, the sword in his hand. And then, suddenly, before he realized it, he was in the servants' quadrangle and skirting the wall to the cloisters. Within a minute and he was part of the charcoaled shadow of the third pillar where he had waited so patiently for the last five moonless nights.

BLOOD AT MIDNIGHT

TONIGHT the atmosphere was alive – a kind of life made even more palpable by the torpor of the air – the ghastly summer air of Gormenghast. By day, the heat of the dead light; by darkness, the vomitings of the sick room. There was no escaping. The season had come down.

As Mr Flay waited, his shoulder-blades against the stone pillars, his thoughts flowed back to the day of the Christening when he had slashed at the great soft face – to the night when he had watched the rehearsal of his murder – to that horrible sack that had been *he* – to the day of the debauchery of the Great Kitchens – to the horrors of the hooting Earl – to a hundred memories of his tormentor, whose face in his imagination opened out before him in the darkness like something septic.

His ears were strained with listening and his muscles ached. He had not moved for over an hour, save to turn his head upon his neck. And then, suddenly, what was it that had changed? He had shut his eyes for a moment and on opening them the air had altered. Was the heat even more horrible? His torn shirt was stuck to his shoulders and belly. It was more than that – it was that the darkness was omnipresent. The quadrangle was as inky as the shadows in which he had been shrouded. Clouds had moved over the moon. Not even the bright sword in his hand could be seen as he moved it out into what had been moonlight.

And then it came. A light more brilliant than the sun's – a light like razors. It not only showed to the least minutiae the anatomy of masonry, pillars and towers, trees, grass-blades and pebbles, it conjured these things, it constructed them from nothing. They were not there before – only the void, the abactinal absences of all things – and then a creation reigned in a blinding and ghastly glory as a torrent of electric fire coursed across heaven.

To Flay it seemed an eternity of nakedness; but the hot black eyelid of the entire sky closed down again and the stifling atmosphere rocked uncontrollably to such a yell of thunder as lifted the hairs on his neck. From the belly of a mammoth it broke and regurgitated, dying finally with a long-drawn growl of spleen. And then the enormous midnight gave up all control, opening out her cumulous body from horizon to horizon, so that the air became solid with so great a weight of falling water that Flay could hear the limbs of trees breaking through a roar of foam.

There was no longer any necessity for Flay, shielded from the rain by the roof of the cloisters, to hold his body in so cramped a manner. What little sound he made would be inaudible now

419

that the falling rain hissed and drummed, beat across the massive back of Gormenghast and swarmed down its sides, bubbling and spurting in every cranny of stone, and swilling every niche where had lain for so long the white dust.

Even more so now had he to listen for the sound of approaching paces, and it is doubtful whether he would have been able to disengage the sound of the chef's feet from the drumming background. What he had never expected happened and his heart broke into an erratic hammering, for the impalpable darkness to his left was disturbed by a faint light, and, immediately after, the source of this hazy aura moved through the midnight. It was a strip of vertical light that appeared to float on end of its own volition. The invisible bearer of the octagonal lantern had closed all but one of the shutters.

As Flay edged his fingers more firmly along the butt of his sword, the glow of the lantern came abreast of him and a moment later had passed, and at this same moment, against the pale yellow glow could be distinguished the silhouette of Swelter's upper volume. It was quite simple. It curved up and over in one black dome. There seemed to be no head. It must have been thrust down and forward, an attitude that might have been imagined impossible in one whose rolls of lard-coloured fat filled in the space between the chin and the clavicles.

When Flay judged the silhouette a good twelve paces distant he began to follow, and then there began the first of the episodes – that of the stalk. If ever man stalked man, Flay stalked Swelter. It is to be doubted whether, when compared with the angular motions of Mr Flay, any man on earth could claim to stalk at all. He would have to do it with another word.

The very length and shape of his limbs and joints, the very formation of his head, and hands and feet were constructed as though for this process alone. Quite unconscious of the stick-insect action, which his frame was undergoing, he followed the creeping dome. For Mr Swelter was himself – at all events in his own opinion – on the tail of his victim. The tail did not happen to be where he supposed it, two floors above, but he was moving with all possible stealth, nevertheless. At the top of the first flight he would place his lantern carefully by the wall, for it was then that the candles began and continued at roughly equal distances, to cast their pale circles of light from niches in the walls. He began to climb.

If Mr Flay stalked, Mr Swelter *insinuated*. He insinuated himself through space. His body encroached, sleuth-like, from air-volume to air-volume, entering, filling and edging out of each in turn, the slow and vile belly preceding the horribly deliberate and potentially nimble progress of his fallen arches.

Flay could not see Swelter's feet, only the silhouetted dome, but by the way it ascended he could tell that the chef was moving one step at a time, his right foot always preceding his left, which he brought to the side of its dace-like companion. He went up in slow, silent jerks in the way of children, invalids or obese women. Flay waited until he had rounded the curve of the stairs and was on the first landing before he followed, taking five stone steps at a time.

On reaching the top of the first flight he moved his head around the corner of the wall and he no longer saw the silhouette of his enemy. He saw the whole thing glowing by the light of two candles. The passageway was narrow at this point, broadening about forty to fifty feet further down the corridor to the dimensions of a hall, whence the second flight led up to Lord Sepulchrave's corridor.

Swelter was standing quite still, but his arms were moving and he appeared to be talking to someone. It was difficult for Flay to see exactly what he was doing until, a moment after he had heard the voice saying: 'And I'll make you red and wet, my pretty thing,' he saw the dim bulk half turn with difficulty in the constricted space of the passageway and he caught the gleam of steel, and a moment later a portion of the shaft and the entire murderous head of the double-handed cleaver. Mr Swelter was nursing it in his arms as though he was suckling it.

'Oh, so red and wet,' came the moss-soft voice again, 'and then we'll wipe you dry with a nice clean handkerchief. Would you like a silk one, my pretty? Would you? Before we polish you and tuck you up? What, no answer? But you know what Papa's saying, don't you now? Of course, you do – after all that he has taught you. And why? Because you're such a quick, sharp baby – oh, such a sharp baby.'

And then Mr Flay was forced to hear the most disgusting sound – as of some kind of low animal with gastric trouble. Mr Swelter was laughing.

Flay, with a fair knowledge of low life, was, nevertheless, unable to withhold himself and, kneeling down quickly upon the great pads at his knees, he was silently sick.

Wiping the sweat from his brow as he rose to his feet he peered again about the angle of wall and saw that Swelter had reached the foot of the second staircase where the corridor widened. The sound of the rain, though less intense, was perpetually there. In the very sound of it, though distant, could be felt an unnatural weight. It was as though the castle were but the size of a skull over which a cistern of water was being rapidly emptied. Already the depressions and valley-like hollows in the castle grounds were filled with dark lakes that mounted momently, doubling and trebling their areas as their creeping edges met. The terrain was awash.

A closer degree of intimacy had been established in the castle between whatever stood, lay, knelt, was propped, shelved, hidden or exposed, or left ready for use, animate or inanimate, within the castle walls. A kind of unwilling knowledge of the nearness of one thing to another – of one human, to another, though great walls might divide them – of *nearness* to a clock, or a banister, or a pillar or a book, or a sleeve. For Flay the horrible nearness to *himself* – to his own shoulder and hand. The out-pouring of a continent of sky had incarcerated and given a weird hyper-reality of *closeness* to those who were shielded from all but the sound of the storm.

Lying awake, for none could hope to sleep, there was not one in all the dark and rattling place who had not cogitated, if only for a moment, on the fact that the entire castle was awake also. In every bed there lay, with his or her lids apart, a figure. They saw each other. This consciousness of each other's solid and individual presences had not only been engendered by the imprisoning downpour but by the general atmosphere of suspicion that had been mounting – a suspicion of they knew not exactly what – only that something was changing – changing in a world where change was crime.

It was lucky for Flay that what he had relied on, the uncommunicative character of the Countess, held true, for she had not mentioned his banishment to a soul, although its cause still smarted in her prodigious bosom.

Hence Swelter's ignorance of the fact that, as he made his first few porridge-like paces along Lord Sepulchrave's ill-lit corridor, he was approaching a Flay-less darkness, for immediately before the door there was impenetrable shadow. A high window on the left had been blown in and glass lay scattered and, at the stairhead, glittered faintly by the light of a candle.

Mr Flay, in spite of the almost unbearable tension, experienced a twinge of ironic pleasure when, having mounted the second flight, he watched the rear of his enemy wavering into the darkness, in search of his own stalker.

There was a shallow alcove across the passageway from the top of the stairs – and with two strides Mr Flay had reached it. From there he could watch the darkness to his left. It was purposeless to follow his enemy to the door of his master's room. He would wait for his return. How would the chef be able to aim his blow in the darkness? He would prod forward with the cleaver until it touched the panels of the door. He would take a soft pace backwards. Then, as he raised the great instrument above his head, a worm, wriggling its bliss through his brain, would bring the double-handed cleaver down, like a guillotine, the great blade whetted to a screaming edge. And as this picture of Mr Swelter's methods illumined the inside of Mr Flay's darkened skull, those very movements were proceeding. Concurrently with Flay's visualization of the cleaver falling – the cleaver fell.

The floorboard beneath Mr Flay's feet lifted, and a wooden ripple ran from one end of the passageway to the other, where it broke upon a cliff of plaster. Curiously enough, it was only through the movement of the boards beneath his feet that Mr Flay knew that the chef had struck, for at the same moment a peal of thunder killed all other sound.

Swelter had brought the cold edge downwards with such a

concentration of relish that the excruciating sense of consummation had dulled his wits for a moment, and it was only when he attempted to work the steel away from what gripped its edge that he realized that something was amiss. It is true that he had expected the blade to slide through the 'prostrate' beneath him as through butter, for all the thin man's osseous character – but not, surely – not with *such* ease – such *liquid* ease. Could it be that he had given to the double-handed cleaver such an edge as set up a new sensation – that of killing, as it were, without knowing it – as lazes through long grass the lethal scythe. He had not prodded forward with his toe to make doubly sure – for it had never occurred to him that he who had lain there, night after night, for over twelve years, could be elsewhere. In any event he might have wakened the long scrag by so doing. What had gone wrong? The orgasmic moment he had so long awaited was over. The cleaver was difficult to shift. Perhaps it was caught among the ribs. He began to run his hands down the shaft inch by inch, bending his knees and trunk as he did so, hot tracts of hairless clay redistributing their undulations the while. Inexorably downwards moved his fingers until they itched for contact with the corpse. Surely his hands must by now be almost at the boards themselves, yet he knew how deceptive the sense of distances can be when darkness is complete. And then he came upon the steel. Sliding his palms greedily along either edge he gave a sudden loud, murderous hiss, and loosing his fingers from the edge of the cleaver he swung his bulk about as though his foe were close behind him – and he peered back along the passage at the faint light at the stairhead. There seemed to be no one there, and after a few moments of scrutiny he wiped his hands across his thighs, and turning to the cleaver, wrenched it from the boards.

For a short while he stood fingering his misused weapon, and during this space Mr Flay had conceived and acted, moving a few yards further down the corridor where an even more favourable ambush presented itself in the shape of a sagging tapestry. As he moved out into the darkness, for he was beyond the orbit of the candles' influence, the lightning struck again and flared bluishly through the broken window so that at one and the same moment both Swelter and Flay caught sight of one another. The bluish light had flattened them out like cardboard figures which had, in the case of the chef, an extraordinary effect. Someone with an unpleasant mind had cut him out of an enormous area of electric-blue paper the size of a sheet. For the few moments that the lightning lasted his fingers and thumbs were like bright blue sausages clasped about the cleaver's handle.

Flay, presenting no less the illusion of having no bulk, struck not so much a sense of horror into Mr Swelter as a fresh surge of malice. That he should have dulled the exquisite edge of his cleaver upon Flay-less boards, and that he who should now be lying in two pieces was standing there in *one*, standing there insolently in a kind of stage lighting as a tangible criticism of his error, affected him to the extreme of control, and a horrid sweat broke from his pores.

No sooner had they seen one another than the darkness closed again. It was as though the curtain had come down on the first act. All was altered. Stealth was no longer enough. Cunning was paramount and their wits were under test. Both had felt that theirs was the initiative and the power to surprise – but now, for a few moments at least, they were equated.

Flay had, from the beginning, planned to draw the chef from Lord Sepulchrave's doorway and passage, and if possible to lure him to the storey above, where, interspaced with wooden supports, for the roof was rotten, and with many a fallen beam, mouldered the Hall of Spiders, at whose far end a window lay open to a great area of roof, terraced with stone and turreted about its sheer edges. It had occurred to him that if he were to snatch the candle from the stairhead he might lure his enemy there, and as the darkness fell he was about to put this idea into operation when the door of Lord Sepulchrave's bedroom opened and the Earl, with a lamp in his hand, moved out into the corridor. He moved as though floating. A long cloak, reaching to his ankles, gave no hint of legs beneath it. Turning his head neither to left nor right, he moved like the symbol of sorrow.

Swelter, flattening himself as much as he was able against the wall, could see that his lordship was asleep. For a moment Mr

Flay had the advantage of seeing both the Earl and the chef without being seen himself. Where was his master going? Swelter was for a few moments at a loss to know what to do and by that time the Earl was almost abreast of Mr Flay. Here was an opportunity of drawing the chef after him without the fear of being overtaken or slashed at from behind, and Flay, stepping in front of the Earl, began to precede him down the passage, walking backwards all the while so that he could see the chef over his Lordship's shoulder as the dim figure followed. Mr Flay was well aware that his own head would be lit by the Earl's lamp whereas Swelter would be in semi-darkness, but there was no great advantage to the chef in that – for the creature could not get *at* him for fear of waking the Earl of Gormenghast.

As Flay receded step by step he could not, though he tried to, keep his eyes continually upon the great cook. The proximity of his Lordship's lamp-lit face left him no option but to turn his eyes to it, rapidly, from time to time. The round, open eyes were glazed. At the corners of the mouth there was a little blood, and the skin was deadly white.

Meanwhile, Swelter had narrowed the distance between the Earl and himself. Flay and the chef were staring at one another over their master's shoulder. The three of them seemed to be moving as one piece. Individually so much at variance, they were, collectively, so compact.

Darting an eye over his shoulder, as though without reference to the head that held it, Flay could see that he was within a few feet of the stairway, and the procession began the slow ascent of the third flight. The leader, his body facing down the stairs, the while, kept his left hand on the iron banister. In his right the sword glimmered – for, as with all the stairways of Gormenghast, there were candles burning at every landing.

As Flay reached the last step he saw that the Earl had stopped and that inevitably the great volume of snail-flesh had come to a halt behind him.

It was so gentle that it seemed as though a voice were evolving from the half-light – a voice of unutterable mournfulness. The lamp in the shadowy hand was failing for lack of oil. The eyes stared through Mr Flay and through the dark wall beyond and on and on through a world of endless rain.

'Good-bye,' said the voice. 'It is all one. Why break the heart that never beat from love? We do not know, sweet girl; the arras hangs: it is so far; so far away, dark daughter. Ah no – not that long shelf – not that long shelf: it is his lifework that the fires are eating. All's one. Good-bye . . . good-bye.'

The Earl climbed a further step upwards. His eyes had become more circular.

'But they will take me in. Their home is cold; but they will take me in. And it may be their tower is lined with love – each flint a cold blue stanza of delight, each feather, terrible; quills, ink and flax, each talon, glory!' His accents were infinitely melancholy as he whispered: 'Blood, blood, and blood and blood, for you, the muffled, all, all for you and I am on my way, with broken branches. She was not mine. Her hair as red as ferns. She was not mine. Mice, mice; the towers crumble – flames are swarmers. There is no swarmer like the nimble flame; and all is over. Good-bye . . . Good-bye. It is all one, for ever, ice and fever Oh, weariest lover – it will not come again. Be quiet now. Hush, then, and do your will. The moon is always; and you will find them at the mouths of warrens. Great wings shall come, great silent, silent wings. . . . Good-bye. All's one. All's one. All's one.'

He was now on the landing, and for a moment Mr Flay imagined he was about to move across the corridor to a room opposite, where a door was swinging, but he turned to the left. It would have been possible, indeed it would have been easier and more to Flay's advantage to have turned about and sped to the Hall of Spiders, for Lord Sepulchrave, floating like a slow dream, barred Swelter's way; but at the very idea Mr Flay recoiled. To leave his sleeping master with a prowling chef at his shoulder horrified him, and he continued his fantastic retreat as before.

They were about half way to the Hall of Spiders when, to both Flay's and Swelter's surprise, the Earl moved off to the left down a narrow artery of midnight stone. He was immediately lost, for the defile wound to the left after the first few

427

paces and the guttering of the lamp was quenched. His disappearance had been so sudden and unexpected that neither party was prepared to leap into the vacuum left between them and to strike out in the faint light. It was in this region that the Grey Scrubbers slept and some distance down there was suspended from the ceiling a broken chandelier. Towards this light Mr Flay suddenly turned and ran, while Swelter, whose frustrated blood-lust was ripe as a persimmon, thinking the thin man to have panicked, pursued him with horribly nimble steps for all the archless suction of his soles.

Covering the flagstones with a raking stride, Mr Flay was for all his speed little more than nine feet in advance of Swelter as he broke his way into the Hall of Spiders. Without losing a moment, he scrambled over three fallen beams, his long limbs jerking out fantastically as he did so, and turned when he had reached the centre of the room to discover that the door he had entered by was already filled with his enemy. So intent had they been on their game of wits and death that it had not occurred to them to wonder how it was that they were able to see one another in what was normally a lightless hall. They found no time for surprise. They did not even realize that the fury had died out of the storm and that the only sound was of a heavy, lugubrious droning. A third of the sky was clear of cloud and in this third was the humpbacked moon, very close and very white. Its radiance poured through the open wall at the far end of the Hall of Spiders. Beyond the opening it danced and glittered on the hissing water that had formed great walled-in lakes among the roofs. The rain slanted its silver threads and raised spurts of quicksilver on striking water. The Hall itself had the effect of a drawing in black, dove-grey and silver ink. It had long been derelict. Fallen and half-fallen beams were leaning or lying at all angles and between these beams, joining one to another, hanging from the ceiling of the floor above (for most of the immediate welkin had fallen in), spreading in every direction taut or sagging, plunged in black shadow, glimmering in half-light, or flaming exquisitely with a kind of filigree and leprous brilliance where the moon fell unopposed upon them, the innumerable webs of the spiders filled the air.

Flay had broken through a liana of shadowy webs, and now, in the centre of the room – watching the cook in the doorway, he clawed away the misty threads from his eyes and mouth with his left hand. Even in those areas of the hall where the moonbeams could not penetrate and where great glooms brooded, the darkness was intersected here and there by glittering strands that seemed to shift their position momently. The slightest deflection of the head drew forth against the darkness a new phenomenon of glittering twine, detached from its web, disarticulated, miraculous and transient.

What eyes had they for such ephemera? Those webs to them were screens to aid or hinder. To snare with or be snared by. These were the features of Death's battleground. Swelter's shadowy moonless body at the door was intersected by the brilliant radii and jerking perimeters of a web that hung about halfway between himself and Mr Flay. The centre of the web coincided with his left nipple. The spacial depths between the glittering threads of the web and the chef seemed abysmic and prodigious. He might have belonged to another realm. The Hall of Spiders yawned and shrank, the threads deceiving the eye, the distances, shifting, surging forward or crumbling away, to the illusory reflectings of the moon.

Swelter did not stay by the door longer than it took him to gain a general impression of the kind of hovel in which the thin man chose to protect his long bones. Seeping with malice, yet the chef was not inclined to under-rate the guile of his antagonist. He had been lured here for some reason. The arena had not been of his choosing. He swivelled his eyes to left and right, his cleaver poised before him. He noted the encumbrances – the haphazard beams, dusty and half decayed, and the omnipresent awnings of the spiders. He could not see why these should be more to his disadvantage than to the man he intended to sever.

Flay had never had a concrete reason for his choice of the Hall of Spiders. Perhaps it was because he imagined that he would prove more agile among the webs and beams; but this he now doubted, having found how swiftly the chef had followed him. But that he had fulfilled his intention of inveigling his enemy to the place of his own choosing must surely infer that the initiative once again lay with him. He felt himself to be a *thought* ahead of the cook.

He held the long sword ahead of him as he watched the great creature approach. Swelter was sweeping aside the webs that impeded him with his cleaver, keeping his eyes upon Mr Flay and shifting his head on his neck from side to side in order to improve his view. He came to a halt and with his eyes perpetually fixed on Mr Flay began to drag away the clinging cobwebs from the blade and handle of his weapon.

He came forward again, sweeping the cleaver in great arcs before him and treading gingerly over the slanting timbers, and then seemed about to halt once more in order to repeat the unwebbing process when, with an obvious change of purpose, he moved forward as though no obstacles were in his path. He seemed to have decided that to be continually reconditioning himself and his weapon during the blood-encounter was ill-advised and untimely, not to say an insult to the occasion.

As pirates in the hot brine-shallows wading, make, face to face, their comber-hindered lunges, sun-blind, fly-agonied, and browed with pearls, so here the timbers leaned, moonlight misled and the rank webs impeded. It was necessary to ignore them – to ignore them as they tickled the face and fastened themselves about the mouth and eyes. To realize that although between the sword and the hand, the hand and the elbow, the elbow and the body, the silvery threads hung like tropical festoons, and although the naked steel was as though delivered in its caul, that the limbs were free to move, as free as ever before. The speed of the swung cleaver would in no way be retarded. The secret was to *ignore*.

So Swelter moved forward, growing at each soft, deft pace more and more like something from the deeps where the grey twine-weed coils the sidling sea-cow. Suddenly stepping into a shaft of moonlight he flamed in a network of threads. He peered through a shimmering mesh. He was gossamer.

He concentrated his entire sentience on the killing. He banished all irrelevancies from his canalized mind. His great ham of a face was tickling as though aswarm with insects, but there was no room left in his brain to receive the messages which his nerve endings were presumably delivering – his brain was full. It was full of death.

Flay watched his every step. His long back was inclined forwards like the bole of a sloping conifer. His head was lowered as though he was about to use it as a battering ram. His padded knees were slightly bent. The yards of cloth were now redundant, but there was no opportunity for him to unwind them. The cook was within seven feet of him. Between them lay a fallen beam. About two yards to Swelter's left its extremity had settled into the dust, but to the right, the relic of an old iron box supporting it roughly at its centre, it terminated about three feet up in the air, spilth'd with fly-choked webs.

It was towards the support of this beam that Swelter made his way, beating the filigreed moonlight to his knees where it sagged and flared. His path could be traced. He had left behind him from the door, to where he stood, the web-walled canyon of a dream. Standing now, immediately behind the broken box, he had narrowed the distance between them to just over the measure of his arm and cleaver. The air between them was a little clearer. They were closer now than they had ever been this raining night. That dreadful, palpable closeness that can only be felt when there is mutual hatred. Their separate and immediate purposes were identical. What else had they in common? Nothing but the Spider's Hall about them, the webs, the beams, the by-play of the spangling moon and the drumming of the rain in their ears.

At any other time the chef would have made play with his superior wit. He would have taunted the long, half-crouching figure before him. But now, with blood to be spilt, what did it matter whether or not he incensed his foe? His wit would fall in a more concrete way. It would flash – but in steel. And let his final insult be that Flay could no longer tell an insult from a lamb-chop – unless with his body in two pieces he were still able to differentiate.

For a moment they stood, moving a little up and down on their toes. With his sword before him Mr Flay began to move along his side of the fallen beam, to the left, in order presumably to come to closer grips. As Swelter moved his little eyes to the right following every movement of the other's body, he found that his vision was being impeded by so heavy an interfusion of ancient webbing that it would be unwise for him to remain where he was. In a flash he had both taken a sideways pace to his left and switched his eyes in the same direction. Flay at once crept in upon him, his face half shrouded by the thick webs through which he peered. His head was immediately above the lower end of the beam. Swelter's rapid glance to his left had been fruitful. He had seen the lifted end of the beam as his first true friend in a hall of hindrances, and when his eyes returned to his thin foe his fat lips twisted. Whether such a muscular obscenity could be termed a 'smile' he neither knew nor cared. Mr Flay was crouching exactly where he had hoped that he might lure him. His chin was, characteristically, jutting forwards – as though this habit had been formed for Mr Swelter's convenience alone. There was no time to lose. Swelter was three feet from the raised terminal of the long beam when he sprang. For a moment there was so much flesh and blood in the air that a star changed colour under Saturn's shoulder. He did not land on his feet. He had not intended to. To bring the entire weight of his body down upon the beam-head was all that mattered. He brought it down; and as his under-belly struck, the far end of the beam leapt like a living thing, and, striking Mr Flay beneath his outstretched jaw, lifted him to his full height before he collapsed, a dead weight, to the floor.

The chef, heaving himself grotesquely to his feet, could hardly get to the body of his victim quickly enough. There he lay, his coat rucked up at the level of his arm-pits, his lean flank exposed. Mr Swelter raised the cleaver. He had waited so long for this. Many, many months. He turned his eyes to the web-shrouded weapon in his hands, and as he did so Mr Flay's left eyelid fluttered, and a moment later he had focused the chef and was watching him through his lashes. He had not the strength to move at that horrifying moment. He could only watch. The cleaver was lifted, but he now saw that Swelter was peering quizzically at the blade, his eyebrows raised. And then he heard the sponge-like voice for the second time that night.

'Would you like to be wiped, my pretty one?' it said, as though certain that a reply would be forthcoming from the brutal head of steel. 'You would, wouldn't you – before you have your supper? Of course. And how could you ever enjoy a nice warm bath with all your clothes on, eh? But I'll soon be washing you, little blossom. And I must wipe your face, dear; wipe it blue as ink, then you can start drinking, can't you?' He held the lean metal head at his bosom. 'It's just the thing for thirsty ones, my darling. Just the very nightcap.' There followed a few moments of low gastric chuckling before he began to drag the webbing from the cleaver's blade. He was standing about two feet away from the prostrate figure of Flay, who was half in and half out of moonlight. The demarcation line lay across his bare flank. Luckily for him it was his upper half that was in shadow and his head was all but lost. As he watched the overhang above him and noted that the chef had all but cleared the blade of cobwebs, his attention became focused upon the upper segment of the face of his foe. It was veiled, as indeed was the rest of the face and body, with the ubiquitous webs, but it seemed that above the left ear there was something additional. So accustomed had Swelter become to the tickling of the webs across his face and to the hundred minor irritations of the skin, that he had not noticed that upon his right eye there sat a spider. So thickly had his head been draped that he had accepted this impediment to his vision as being part of the general nuisance. Flay could see the spider quite clearly from where he lay, but what he now saw was something fateful. It was the spider's mate. She had emerged from the grey muddle above the left ear and was taking, leg by leg, the long, thin paces. Was she in search of her husband? If so, her sense of direction was sound, for she made towards him.

Swelter was running the flat of his hand along the steel face of his weapon. It was naked for use. Putting his blubber lips to the moonlit steel he kissed it, and then, falling a short step back, he lifted the cleaver with both hands, grasping the long handle high above his lowered head. He stood upon tip-toe, and, poised for a moment thus, went suddenly blind. His left eye had become involved with a female spider. She sat upon it

433

squarely, enjoying the rolling movement of the orb she covered. It was for this precise instant that Flay had been waiting ever since he had caught sight of the insect a few seconds previously. It seemed that he had lain there stretched vulnerably beneath the murderous cleaver for an hour at least. Now was his moment, and gripping his sword which had fallen beside him when he fell, he rolled himself with great rapidity from beneath the belly of the cook and from the cleaver's range.

Swelter, sweating with irritation at being baulked for the second time in this business of climax, imagined nevertheless that Flay was still below him. Had he struck downwards in spite of the spiders on his eyes it may be that Flay could not have escaped. But Mr Swelter would have considered it a very sorry ending after all his pains to find he had made slaughter without having been able to see the effect. Outside Lord Sepulchrave's door it was different. There was no light, anyway. But here with a beautiful moon to illumine the work it was surely neither the time nor the place to be at the mercy of a spider's whim.

And so he lowered the cleaver to his bosom and, freeing his right hand, plucked the insects from his eyes, and he had started to raise the weapon again before he saw that his victim had gone. He wheeled about, and as he did so he experienced a white-hot pain in his left buttock and a searing sensation at the side of his head. Screaming like a pig, he wheeled about, raising his finger to where his ear should have been. It had gone. Flay had swiped it off, and it swung to and fro in a spider-made hammock a foot above the floor-boards at the far end of the room. And what voluptuary ever lolled with half the languour of that boneless thing!

A moonbeam, falling on the raddled lobe, withdrew itself discreetly and the ear disappeared into tactful darkness. Flay had, in rapid succession, jabbed and struck. The second blow had missed the skull, but he had drawn first blood; in fact, first and second, for Swelter's left rump bled magnificently. There was, in point of fact, an island growing gradually – a red island that had seeped through to the white vastness of his cloth rear. This island was changing its contours momentarily, but as the echo of Swelter's scream subsided, it very much resembled in its main outline the inverted wing of an angel.

The blows had no more than gored him. Of Swelter's acreage, only a perch or two here and there might, if broken, prove vulnerable loam. That he bled profusely could prove little. There was blood in him to revitalize an anaemic army, with enough left over to cool the guns. Placed end to end his blood vessels might have coiled up the Tower of Flints and half way down again like a Virginia creeper – a vampire's home from home.

Be that as it may, he was blooded, and the cold, calculating malice had given way to a convulsive hatred that had no relation to the past. It was on the boil of *now*, and heading into the webs that divided them, he let loose a long scything blow at Mr Flay. He had moved very rapidly and but for the fact that the moonlit webs deceived him as to the distance between them, so that he struck too soon, it is probable that all would have been over bar the disposal of the body. As it was, the wind of the blow and the hiss of the steel were enough to lift the hairs on Mr Flay's head and to set up a horrible vibration in his ears. Recovering almost at once from the surprise, however, Flay struck in return at the cook, who was for a moment off his balance, catching him across the bolster-like swelling of his shoulder.

And then things happened very rapidly, as though all that had gone before was a mere preamble. Recovering from the flounder of his abortive blow, and with the fresh pain at his shoulder, Swelter, knowing he had, with his cleaver extended, the longer reach, gripped the weapon at the extreme end of the handle and began to gyrate, his feet moving with horrifying rapidity beneath his belly, not only with the kind of complicated dance movement which swivels the body around and around at great speed, but in a manner which brought him nearer every moment to Mr Flay. Meanwhile, his cleaver, outstretched before him, sang on its circular path. What remained of the webs in the centre of the room fell away before this gross, moon-dappled cyclone. Flay, nonplussed for the moment, watched in fascinated horror, the rapid succession of faces which the swivelling of

435

Swelter conduced; faces of which he had hundreds; appearing and reappearing at high speed (with an equal number of rear-views of the huge head, interlarded, in all literalness). The whirr of steel was approaching rapidly. The rotation was too speedy for him to strike between the cycles, nor was his reach long enough were he to stand his ground.

Moving backwards he found that he was being forced gradually into a corner at the far end of the room. Swelter was bearing down on him with a kind of nightmare quality. His mind was working, but the physical perfection of his footwork and the revolving of the steel had something of the trance about them – something that had become through their very perfection detached and on their own. It was difficult to imagine how the great white top could stop itself.

And then Mr Flay had an idea. As though cowering from the oncoming steel, he moved back further and further into the corner until his bent backbone came into contact with the junction of the two walls. Cornered of his own choosing, for he would have had time to leap for the rain-filled opening of moonlight had he wished, he raised himself to his full height, prising his spine into the right-angle of the walls, his sword lowered to his feet – and waited.

The scything cleaver spun nearer momently. At every glimpse of the chef's rotating head he could see the little blood-shot eyes focused upon him. They were like lumps of loathing, so concentrated was his every thought and fibre upon the death of Flay that, as he whirred closer and closer, his normal wits were in abeyance, and what Flay had hoped for happened. The arc of the long weapon was of such amplitude that at its left and right extremes it became all of a sudden within a few inches of the adjacent walls and at the next revolution had nicked away the plaster before, finally, as the walls – so it seemed to Swelter – leapt forward to meet him, the chef discovered the palms of his hands and forearms stinging with the shock of having taken a great section of the mouldering wall away. Flay, with his sword still held along his leg, its point beside his toe-cap, was in no position to receive the impact of Swelter's body as it fell forward upon him. So sudden and so jarring had been the stoppage of his murderous spinning, that, like a broken engine, its rhythm and motivation lost, its body out of control, Swelter collapsed, as it were, within his own skin, as he slumped forwards. If Flay had not been so thin and had not forced himself so far into the corner, he would have been asphyxiated. As it was, the clammy, web-bedraggled pressure of Swelter's garments over his face forced him to take short, painful breaths. He could do nothing, his arms pinned at his sides, his visage crushed. But the effects of the shock were passing, and Swelter, as though suddenly regaining his memory, heaved himself partially from the corner in a tipsy way, and although Mr Flay at such close range was unable to use his sword, he edged rapidly along the left-hand wall and, turning, was within an ace of darting a thrust at Swelter's ribs when his foe staggered out of range in a series of great drunken curves. The giddiness with which his gyrations had filled him were for the moment standing him in good stead, for reeling as he did about the Hall of Spiders he was an impossible target for all but mere blood-letting.

And so Flay waited. He was acutely aware of a sickening pain at the back of his neck. It had grown as the immediate shock of the blow to his jaw had subsided. He longed desperately for all to be over. A terrible fatigue had entered him.

Swelter, once the room no longer span around him and his sense of balance was restored, moved with horrible purpose across the Hall, the cleaver trembling with frustration in his hand. The sound of his feet on the boards was quite distinct, and startled Flay into glancing over his shoulder into the moonlight. The rain had ceased and, save for the dolorous whispering of Gormenghast a-drip, there was a great hush..

Flay had felt all of a sudden that there could be no finality, no decision, no death-blow in the Hall of Spiders. Save for this conviction he would have attacked Swelter as he leaned, recovering from his giddiness, by the door at the far end of the room. But he only stood by the moon-filled opening, a gaunt silhouette, the great cloth rolls like malformations at his knees, and waited for the chef's advance, while he worked at the vertebrae of his aching neck with his long bony fingers. And then had come the onrush. Swelter was upon him, his cleaver

437

raised, the left side of his head and his left shoulder shiny with blood, and a trail of it behind him as he came. Immediately before the opening to the outer air was a six-inch step upwards which terminated the flooring. Beyond this there was normally a three-foot drop to a rectangular walled-in area of roof. Tonight there was no such drop, for a great lake of rain-water lapped at the dusty boards of the Hall. To a stranger the lake gave the appearance of profound depth as it basked in the moon. Flay, stepping backwards over the raised strip of boarding, sent up a fountain of lemon-yellow spray as his foot descended. In a moment he was spidering his legs backwards through water as warm as tea. The air, for all the downpour, was as oppressive as ever. The horrible weight of heat was undispersed.

And then the horror happened. Swelter, following at high speed, had caught his toe at the raised lip of the opening, and unable to check his momentum, had avalanched himself into warm water. The cleaver sailed from his grasp and, circling in the moonlight, fell with a fluke of flame in the far, golden silence of the lake. As Swelter, face down and floundering like a sea-monster, struggled to find his feet, Flay reached him. As he did so, with a primeval effort the cook, twisting his trunk about, found, and then lost again, a temporary foothold and, writhing, fell back again, this time upon his back, where he floated, lashing, great washes of water spreading on all sides to the furthermost reaches. For a moment he was able to breathe, but whether this advantage was outbalanced by his having to see, towering above him, the dark, upreaching body of his foe – with the hilt of the sword raised high over his head, both hands grasping it and the point directed at the base of his ribs, only he could know. The water about him was reddening and his eyes, like marbles of gristle, rolled in the moonlight as the sword plunged steeply. Flay did not trouble to withdraw it. It remained like a mast of steel whose sails had fallen to the decks where, as though with a life of their own, unconnected with wind or tide, they leapt and shook in ghastly turbulence. At the masthead, the circular sword hilt, like a crow's nest, boasted no inch-high pirate. Flay, leaning against the outer wall of the Hall of Spiders, the water up to his knees and watching with his

eyes half-closed, the last death throes, heard a sound above
him, and in a shudder of gooseflesh turned his eyes and found
them staring into a face – a face that smiled in silver light from
the depths of the Hall beyond. Its eyes were circular and its
mouth was opening, and as the lunar silence came down as
though for ever in a vast white sheet, the long-drawn screech
of a death-owl tore it, as though it had been calico, from end to
end.

GONE

IN after years Mr Flay was almost daily startled to remem-
brance of what now ensued. It returned in the way that dreams
recur, suddenly and unsolicited. The memory was always unearthly, but no less so than the hours themselves which followed upon Swelter's death – hours as it were from a monstrous
clock across whose face, like the face of a drum, was stretched
the skin of the dead chef – a clock whose hands trailed blood
across and through the long minutes as they moved in a circular trance. Mr Flay moved with them.

He would remember how the Earl at the window was awake;
how he had held his rod with the jade knob in his hand, and
how he had stepped down in the lake of rain. He had prodded
the body and it had twisted for a minute and then righted itself,
as though it were alive and had a positive wish to remain
staring at the moon. The Earl then closed the cook's eyes,
moving the two petals of pulp over their respective blood-
alleys.

'Mr Flay,' Lord Sepulchrave had said.

'Lordship?' queried his servant, hoarsely.

'You did not reply to me when I saluted you.'

Flay did not know what his master could mean. Saluted him?
He had not been spoken to. And then he remembered the cry of
the owl. He shuddered.

Lord Sepulchrave tapped the hilt of the sword-mast with his
rod. 'Do you think that they will enjoy him?' he said. He parted
his lips slowly. 'We can but proffer him. That is the least we
can do.'

439

Of the nightmare that followed it is needful to say only that the long hours of toil which followed culminated at the Tower of Flints to which they had dragged the body, after having steered it between a gap in the battlements through which the lake was emptying itself. Swelter had descended in the two-hundred-foot cascade of moon-sparkling water and they had found his body, spread to the size of a sheet and bubbling on the drenched gravel. A rope had been procured and a hook attached and the long drag had at last been effected.

The white silence was terrible. The moonlight like a hoar frost on the Tower of Flints. The shell of the library glimmered in the distance far down the long line of halls and pavilions, and of domed, forsaken structures. To their right the lit pine-woods were split with lines of midnight. About their feet a few cones, like ivory carvings, were scattered, anchored to the pale earth by their shadows.

What was once Swelter glistened.

And the Earl had said: 'This is my hour, Flay. You must go from here, Mr Flay. You must go away. This is the hour of my reincarnation. I must be alone with him. That you killed him is your glory. That I can take him to *them* is mine. Good-bye, for my life is beginning. Good-bye ... good-bye.' And he had turned away, one hand still holding the rope, and Flay half ran and half walked for a short distance towards the Castle, his head turned over his shoulder, his body shuddering. When he stopped, the Earl was dragging the glistening thing behind him and was at the time-eaten opening at the base of the Tower.

A moment later and he was gone, the flattened weight undulating as it slithered up and over the three steps that led into the corroded entrance, the form of the steps showing in blurred contour.

Everything was moving round and round – the Tower, the pines, the corpse, the moon, and even the inhuman cry of pain that leapt from the Tower's throat into the night – the cry, not of an owl, but of a man about to die. As it echoed and echoed, the lank and exhausted servant fell fainting in his tracks, while the sky about the Tower became white with the lit bodies of circling owls, and the entrance to the Tower filled with a great weight of feathers, beaks and talons as the devouring of the two incongruous remains proceeded.

THE ROSES WERE STONES

ALONE among the Twisted Woods – like a branch himself, restless among the rooted trees, he moved rapidly, the sound of his knees becoming day by day familiar to the birds, and hares.

Ribbed with the sunlight where the woodlands thinned, dark as shadows themselves where no sun came, he moved as though pursued. For so long a time had he slept in the cold, lightless corridor that waking, as it were, with no protection from the dawn, or stretching himself for sleep, defenceless before the twilight and sundown, he was at first unable to feel other than nakedness and awe. Nature, it seemed, was huge as Gormenghast. But as time went on he learned to find the shortest and most secret ways of hill and woodland, of escarpment and marshland, to trace the winding of the river and its weed-bound tributaries.

He realized that though the raw ache for the life he had lost was no less with him, yet the exertions he was obliged to make for his own preservation and the call that such a life made upon his ingenuity, had their compensations. He learned, day by day, the ways of this new world. He felt proud of the two caves which he had found in the slopes of Gormenghast mountain. He had cleared them of rocks and hanging weeds. He had built the stone ovens and the rock tables, the hurdling across their walls to discourage the foxes, and the beds of foliage. One lay to the south at the fringe of the unexplored country. It was remote and very thrilling to his bones – for the mounttain lay between him and the far Castle. The second cave was in the northern slope, smaller, but one which on rainy nights was more likely to prove accessible. In a glade of the Twisted Woods he had constructed a shack as his primary and especial home. He was proud of his growing skill at snaring rabbits: and of his successes with the net he had so patiently knotted with lengths of tough root fibre; and it was sweet to taste the fish he prepared and ate alone in the shadow of his shack. The long evenings were like blond eternities – stifling and silent save for the occasional flutter of a wing or the scream of a passing bird. A stream which had all but dried moved past his doorway and disappeared in the shadows of the undergrowth to the south. His love of this lost glade he had selected grew with the development of a woodland instinct which must have been latent in his blood, and with the feeling that he possessed something of his own – a hut he had made with his own hands. Was this rebellion? He did not know. The day over, he would sit at the door of his cabin, his knees beneath his chin, his bony hands clasping his elbows, and stare ruminatively (a stranger would have thought sullenly) before him as the shadows lengthened inch by inch. He had started to turn over in his mind the whole story of Gormenghast as it had affected him. Of Fuchsia, now that he could see her no longer, he found it painful to reminisce, for he missed her more than he could have imagined possible.

The weeks went by and his skill grew, so that he had no longer to lie in wait for half a day at a time at the mouths of warrens, a club in his hand; nor waste long hours by the river, fishing the less hopeful reaches for lack of lore. He could devote more and more of his time to conditioning his shack against the approaching autumn and inevitable winter; to exploring further afield, and to brooding in the evening sunlight. It was then that the vile, nightmare memory would most often return. The shape of a cloud in the sky – the sight of a red beetle – anything might suddenly awake the horror; and he would dig his nails into the palms of his hands as the recollection of the murder and of the subsequent death of his master discoloured his brain.

There were few days in which he did not climb the foothills of the Mountain, or pick his way to the edge of the Twisted Woods, in order to see the long broken line of Gormenghast's backbone. Hours of solitude in the woods were apt to detach him from the reality of any other life, and he would at times find that he was running gawkily through the boles in a sudden fear that there was no Gormenghast: that he had dreamed it all: that he belonged to nowhere, to nothing: that he was the only man alive in a dream of endless branches.

The sight of that broken skyline so interwoven with his earliest recollections reassured him that though he was himself ejected and abandoned, yet all that had given him purpose and pride in life was there, and was no dream or fable, but as real as the hand which shielded his eyes, a reality of immemorial stone, where lived, where died, and where was born again the lit line of the Groans.

On one such evening, after scanning the Castle for some while, and moving his eyes at last across the corruscation of the mud huts, he rose to his feet and began his return journey to the glade, when suddenly changing his mind, he retraced a hundred or so of his steps and set off to his left, penetrating with astonishing speed a seemingly impenetrable valley of thorns. These stunted trees gave way at length to sparser shrub, the leaves, which had all but fallen with drought, hanging to the brittled branches only by reason of the belated refreshment which the sudden storm had given to their roots on the night of the murder. The incline on either side could now be seen more clearly, and as Flay picked his way through the last barrier of shrubs, ash-coloured slopes lifted unbroken on his either hand, the grass as sleek and limp as hair, with not a pale blade upright. There was not a breath of wind. He rested himself, lying out upon his back on a hot slope to his right. His knees were drawn up (for angles were intrinsic to his frame in action or repose) and he gazed abstractedly over the small of his outstretched arm at the sheen on the grasses.

He did not rest for long, for he wished to arrive at his northern cave before dusk. He had not been there for some while, and it was with a kind of swart enjoyment that he surrendered to the sudden whim. The sun was already a far cry from its zenith, hanging in haze, a few degrees above the horizon.

The prospect from the northern cave was unusual. It gave Mr

443

Flay what he imagined must be pleasure. He was discovering more and more in this new and strange existence, this vastness so far removed from corridors and halls, burned libraries and humid kitchens, that gave rise in him to a new sensation, this interest in phenomena beyond ritual and obedience – something which he hoped was not heretical in him – the multiformity of the plants and the varying textures in the barks of trees, the varieties of fish and bird and stone. It was not in his temperament to react excitedly to beauty, for, as such, it had never occurred to him. It was not in him to think in terms. His pleasure was of a dour and practical breed; and yet, not altogether. When a shaft of light fell across a dark area his eyes would turn to the sky to discover the rift through which the rays had broken. Then they would return with a sense of accomplishment to the play of the beams. But he would keep his eye upon them. Not that he supposed them to be worth looking at – imagining there was something wrong in himself for wasting his time in such a fruitless way. As the days went by he had found that he was moving to and fro through the region in order to be at one place or another in time to watch the squirrels among the oaks at noon, the homecoming of the rooks, or the death of the day from some vantage point of his finding.

And so it was this night that he wished to watch the crags as they blackened against the falling sun.

It took him another hour of walking to reach the northern cave, and he was tired when he stripped himself of his ragged shirt and rested his back against the cool outer wall. He was only just in time, for the circle, like a golden plate, was balancing upon its rim on the point of the northernmost of the main crags of Gormenghast Mountain. The sky about it was old-rose, translucent as alabaster, yet sumptuous as flesh. And mature. Mature as a soft skin or heavy fruit, for this was no callow experiment in zoneless splendour – this impalpable sundown was consummate and the child of all the globe's archaic sundowns since first the red eye winked.

As the thin man's gaze travelled down the steep sides of this crag to the great heart-shaped gulch beneath it where what vegetation there was lay sunk in a sea of shade, he felt rather than saw, for his thoughts were still in the darkness, a quickening of the air about him and lifting his head he noticed how, with a deepening of the rose in the sky, all things were tinted, as though they had awaited the particular concentration of hue which the sky now held, before admitting the opinions of their separate colours to be altered or modified. As at the stroke of a warlock's wand the world was suffused – all things saving the sun, which, in contradiction to the colour of the vapours and the forms that it had raddled, remained golden.

Flay began to untie his boots. Behind him his swept cave yawned, a million prawn-coloured motes swaying against the darkness at the entrance. He noticed, as he worked his heel free of the leather, that the crag was biting its way into the sun and had all but reached its centre. He leant his bony head backwards against the stone, and his face became lit and the stubble of his first beard shone, its every hair a thread of copper wire, as he followed the course of the crag's crest in its seemingly upward and arrow-headed journey, its black barbs eating outwards as it climbed.

Inexorable as was its course, there was, that summer evening, more destiny in the progress of another moving form, so infinitesimal in the capacious mountain dusk, than in the vast sun's ample, spellbound cycle.

Through her, in microcosm, the wide earth sobbed. The starglobe sank in her; the colours faded. The death-dew rose and the wild birds in her breast climbed to her throat and gathered songless, hovering, all tumult, wing to wing, so ardent for those climes where all things end.

To Flay, it was as though the silence of his solitude had been broken, the senses invading each other's provinces, for on seeing the movement of something the size of the letter 'i', that moved in silhouette against the gigantic yellow plate, he had the sensation of waking from a dream which took hold of him. Distant as it was, he could tell it for a human form. That it was Keda it was not in his power to realize. He knew himself for witness. He could not stop himself. He knelt forward on his knees, while the moments melted, one into the next. He grew more rigid. The tiny, infinitely remote figure was moving across the sun towards the crag's black edge. Impotently, he watched, his jaw thrust forwards and a cold sweat broke across his bony brow, for he knew himself to be in the presence of Sorrow – and an interloper upon something more personal and secret than he had the right to watch. And yet impersonal. For in the figurette was the personification of all pain, taking, through sliding time, its final paces.

She moved slowly, for the climb had tired her and it had not been long since she had borne the child of clay, like alabaster, the earthless daughter who had startled all. It was as though Keda was detached from the world, exalted and magnificently alone in the rose-red haze of the upper air. At the edge of the naked drop to the shades below she came to a standstill, and, after a little while, turned her head to Gormenghast and the Dwellings, afloat in the warm haze. They were unreal. They were so far, so remote. No longer of her, they were over. Yet she turned her head for the child's sake.

Her head, turning, was dimensionless. A thong about her neck supported the proud carvings of her lovers. They hung across her breasts. At the edge of age, there was a perilous beauty in her face as of the crag's edge that she stood upon. The last of footholds; such a little space. The colour fading on the seven-foot strip. It lay behind her like a carpet of dark roses. The roses were stones. There was one fern growing. It was beside her feet. How tall? . . . A thousand feet? Then she must have her head among far stars. How far all was! Too far for Flay to see her head had turned – a speck of life against that falling sun.

Upon his knees he knew that he was witness.

About her and below lay the world. All things were ebbing. A moon that climbed suddenly above the eastern skyline, chilling the rose, waned through her as it waxed, and she was ready.

She moved her hair from her eyes and cheekbones. It hung deep and still as the shadow in a well; it hung down her straight back like midnight. Her brown hands pressed the carvings inwards to her breast, and as a smile began to grow, the eyebrows raised a little, she stepped outwards into the dim atmosphere, and falling, was most fabulously lit by the moon and the sun.

'BARQUENTINE AND STEERPIKE'

THE inexplicable disappearance of both Lord Sepulchrave and Swelter was, of course, the burden of Gormenghast – its thoughts' fibre – from the meanest of the latter's scullions to the former's mate. The enigma was absolute, for the whereabouts of Flay was equally obscure.

There was no end to the problem. The long corridors were susurrous with rumour. It was unthinkable that so ill-matched a pair should have gone together. Gone? Gone where? There was nowhere to go. It was equally unthinkable that they should have gone singly, and for the same reason.

The illness of the Earl had, of course, been uppermost in the minds of the Countess, Fuchsia and the Doctor, and an exhaustive search had been organized under the direction of Steerpike. It revealed no vestige of a clue, although from Steerpike's point of view it had been well worth while, for it gave him occasion to force an entry into rooms and halls which he had for a long while hoped to investigate with a view to his own re-establishment.

It was on the ninth day of the search that Barquentine decided to call a halt to exertions which were going not only against his grain, but the grain of every rooted denizen of the stone forest – that terraced labyrinth of broken rides.

The idea of the head of the House being away from his duties for an hour was sufficiently blasphemous: that he should have *disappeared* was beyond speech. It was beyond anger. Whatever had happened to him, whatever had been the cause of his desertion, there could be no two ways about it – his Lordship was a renegade, not only in the eyes of Barquentine, but (dimly or acutely perceived), in the eyes of all.

That a search had to be made was obvious, but it was also in everyone's thoughts that to find the Earl would cause so painful, so frantically delicate a situation that there would be advantages were his disappearance to remain a mystery.

The horror with which Barquentine had received the news had now, at the end of the ninth day, given place to a stony and intractable loathing for all that he associated with the personality of his former master, his veneration for the Earl (as a descendant of the original line) disassociating itself from his feelings about the man himself. Sepulchrave had behaved as a traitor. There could be no excuses. His illness? What was that to him? Even in illness he was of the Groans.

During those first days after the fateful news he had become a monster as he scoured the building, cursing all who crossed his path, probing into room after room, and thrashing out with his crutch at any whom he considered tardy.

That Titus should from the very beginning be under his control and tutelage was his only sop. He turned it over on his withered tongue.

He had been impressed by Steerpike's arrangements for the search, during which he had been forced to come into closer contact with the youth than formerly. There was no love lost between them, but the ancient began to have a grudging respect for the methodical and quickly moving youth. Steerpike was not slow to observe the obscurest signs of this and he played upon them. On the day when, at Barquentine's orders, the searchings ceased, the youth was ordered to the Room of Documents. There he found the ragged Barquentine seated on a high-backed chair, a variety of books and papers on a stone table before him. It was as though his knotted beard was sitting on the stone between his wrinkled hands. His chin was thrust forward, so that his stretched throat appeared to be composed of a couple of lengths of rope, several cords and a quantity of string. Like his father's, his head was wrinkled to the brink of belief, his eyes and mouth when closed disappearing altogether. Propped against the stone table was his crutch.

'You called for me?' queried Steerpike from the door.

Barquentine raised his hot-looking, irritable eyes and dropped the cross-hatched corners of his mouth.

'Come here, you,' he rasped.

Steerpike moved to the table, approaching in a curious, swift and sideways manner. There was no carpet on the floor and his footsteps sounded crisply.

When he reached the table and stood opposite the old man, he inclined his head to one side.

'Search over,' said Barquentine. 'Call the dogs off. Do you hear?'

He spat over his shoulder.

Steerpike bowed.

'No more nonsense !' barked the old voice. 'Body of me, we've seen enough of it.'

He started to scratch himself through a horrible-looking tear in his scarlet rags. There was a period of silence while this operation proceeded. Steerpike began to shift the weight of his body to his other leg.

'Where do you think you're going to? Stand still, you rat-damned misery, will you? By the lights of the mother I buried rump-end up, hold your clod, boy, hold your clod.' The hairs about his mouth were stuck with spittle as he fingered his crutch on the stone table.

Steerpike sucked at his teeth. He watched every move of the old man in front of him, and waited for a loophole in the armour.

Sitting at the table, Barquentine might have been mistaken for a normally constructed elder, but it came as a shock even to Steerpike to see him clamber off the seat of the high-backed chair, raise his arm for the crutch and strike a path of wood and leather around the circumference of the table, his chin on a level with its surface.

Steerpike, who was himself on the small side, even for his seventeen years, found that the Master of Ritual, were he to have brought his head forward for a few inches, would have buried his bristling nose a hand's breadth above the navel, that pivot for a draughtsman's eye, that relic whose potentiality appears to have been appreciated only by the dead Swelter, who saw in it a reliable salt-cellar, when that gentleman decided upon eggs for his breakfast in bed.

Be that as it irrelevantly may, Steerpike found himself staring down into an upturned patch of wrinkles. In this corrugated terrain two eyes burned. In contrast to the dry sand-coloured skin they appeared grotesquely liquid, and to watch them was ordeal by water; all innocence was drowned. They lapped at the dry rims of the infected well-heads. There were no lashes.

He had made so rapid and nimble a detour of the stone table that he surprised Steerpike, appearing with such inexpectation beneath the boy's nose. The alternate thud, and crack of sole and crutch came suddenly to silence. Into this silence a small belated sound, all upon its own, was enormous and disconnected. It was Barquentine's foot, shifting its position as the crutch remained in place. He had improved his balance. The concentration in the ancient's face was too naked to be studied for more than a moment at a time. Steerpike, after a rapid survey, could only think that either the flesh and the passion of the head below him was fused into a substance of the old man's compounding; or that all the other heads he had ever seen were masks – masks of matter *per se*, with no admixture of the incorporeal. This old tyrant's head *was* his feeling. It was modelled from it, and of it.

Steerpike was too near it – the nakedness of it. Naked and dry with those wet well-heads under the time-raked brow.

But he could not move away – not without calling down, or rather calling *up*, the wrath of this wizened god. He shut his eyes and worked his tongue into a tooth-crater. Then there was a sound, for Barquentine, having exhausted, apparently, what diversion there was to be found in the youth's face as seen from below, had spat twice and very rapidly, each expectoration finding a temporary lodging on the bulges of Steerpike's lowered lids.

'Open them!' cried the cracked voice. 'Open them up, bastard whelp of a whore-rat!'

Steerpike with wonder beheld the septuagenarian balancing upon his only leg with the crutch raised above his head. It was not directed at himself, however, but with its grasper swivelled in the direction of the table, seemed about to descend. It did, and a thick dusty mist arose from the books on which it landed. A moth flapped through the dust.

When it had settled, the youth, his head turned over his shoulder, his small dark-red eyes half closed, heard Barquentine say:

'So you can call the dogs off! Body of me, if it isn't time! Time and enough. Nine days wasted! Wasted! – by the stones, wasted! Do you hear me, stoat's lug? Do you hear me?'

Steerpike began to bow, with his eyebrows raised by way of indicating that his ear drums had proved themselves equal to the call made upon them. If the art of gesture had been more acutely developed in him he might have implied by some hyper-subtle inclination of his body that what aural inconvenience he experienced lay not so much in his having to strain his ears, as in having them strained for him.

As it was, it proved unnecessary for him to ever complete the bow he had begun, for Barquentine was delivering yet another blow to the books and papers on the table, and a fresh cloud of dust had arisen. His eyes had left the youth – and Steerpike was stranded – in one sense only – in that the flood-water of the eyes no longer engulfed him, the stone table as though it were a moon, drawing away the dangerous tide.

He wiped the spittle from his eyelids with one of Dr Prune-squallor's handkerchiefs.

'What are those books, boy?' shouted Barquentine, returning the handle of his crutch to his armpit. 'By my head of skin, boy, what are they?'

'They are the Law,' said Steerpike.

With four stumps of the crutch the old man was below him again and sluicing him with his hot wet eyes.

'By the blind powers, it's the truth,' he said. He cleared his throat. 'Don't stand there staring. What is Law? Answer me, curse you!'

Steerpike replied without a moment's consideration but with the worm of his guile like a bait on the hook of his brain: 'Destiny, sir. Destiny.'

Vacant, trite and nebulous as was the reply, it was of the right *kind*. Steerpike knew this. The old man was aware of only one virtue – Obedience to Tradition. The destiny of the Groans. The law of Gormenghast.

No individual Groan of flesh and blood could awake in him this loyalty he felt for '*Groan*' the abstraction – the symbol. That the course of this great dark family river should flow on and on, obeying the contours of hallowed ground, was his sole regard.

The seventy-sixth Earl should he ever be found, dead or alive, had forfeited his right to burial among the Tombs. Barquentine had spent the day among volumes of ritual and precedent. So exhaustive was the compilation of relevant and tabulated procedure to be adopted in unorthodox and unforeseen circumstances that a parallel to Lord Sepulchrave's disappearance was at last rooted out by the old man – the fourteenth Earl of Groan having disappeared leaving an infant heir. Nine days only had been allowed for the search, after which the child was to be proclaimed the rightful Earl, standing the while upon a raft of chestnut boughs afloat on the lake, a stone in the right hand, an ivy-branch in the left, and a necklace of snail-shells about the neck; while shrouded in foliage the next of kin and all who were invited to the 'Earling' stood, sat, crouched or lay among the branches of the marginal trees.

All this had now, once again, hundreds of years later, to be put in hand, for the nine days were over and it was in Barquentine that all power in matters of procedure was vested. It was for him to give the orders. In his little old body was Gormenghast in microcosm.

'Ferret,' he said, still staring up at Steerpike, 'your answer's good. Body of me, Destiny it is. What is your bastard name, child?'

'Steerpike, sir.'

'Age?'

'Seventeen.'

'Buds and fledglings? So they still spawn 'em so! Seventeen.' He put a withered tongue between his dry, wrinkled lips. It might have been the tongue of a boot. 'Seventeen,' he repeated in a voice of such ruminative incredulity as startled the youth, for he had never before heard any such intonation emerge from that old throat. 'Bloody wrinkles! say it again, chicken.'

'Seventeen,' said Steerpike.

Barquentine went off into a form of trance, the well-heads of his eyes appearing to cloud over and become opaque like miniature sargassos, of dull chalky-blue – the cataract veil – for it seemed that he was trying to remember the daedal days of his adolescence. The birth of the world; of spring on the rim of Time.

Suddenly he came-to, and cursed; and as though to shake off something noxious he worked his shoulder-blades to and fro, as he pad-hopped irritably around his crutch, the ferrule squeaking as it swivelled on the carpetless floor.

'See here, boy,' he said, when he had come to a halt, 'there is work to do. There is a raft to be built, body of me, a raft of chestnut boughs and no other. The procession. The bareback racing for the bagful. The barbecue in the Stone Hall. Hell slice me up, boy! call the hounds off.'

'Yes, sir,' said Steerpike. 'Shall I send them back to their quarters?'

'Eh?' muttered Barquentine, 'what's that?'

'I said shall I return them to their quarters?' said Steerpike. An affirmative noise from the throat of strings was the reply.

But as Steerpike began to move off, 'Not yet, you dotard! Not yet!' And then: 'Who's your master?'

Steerpike reflected a moment. 'I have no immediate master,' he said. 'I attempt to make myself useful – here and there.'

'You do, do you, my sprig? "Here and there," do you? I can see through you. Right the way through you, suckling, bones and brain. You can't fool me, by the stones you can't. You're a neat little rat but there'll be no more "here and there" for you. It will be only "here", do you understand?' The old man ground his crutch into the floor. '*Here*,' he added, with an access of vehemence; 'beside *me*. You may be useful. Very useful.' He scratched himself through a tear at his armpit.

'What will my salary amount to?' said Steerpike, putting his hands in his pockets.

'Your *keep*, you insolent bastard! your *keep*! What more do you want? Hell fire child! have you no pride? A roof, your food, and the honour of studying the Ritual. Your *keep*, curse you, and the secrets of the Groans. How else could you serve me but by learning the iron Trade? Body of me – I have no son. Are you ready?'

'I have never been more so,' said the high-shouldered boy.

BY GORMENGHAST LAKE

LITTLE gusts of fresh, white air blew fitfully through the high trees that surrounded the lake. In the dense heat of the season it seemed they had no part; so distinct they were from the sterile body of the air. How could such thick air open to shafts so foreign and so aqueous? The humid season was split open for their every gush. It closed as they died like a hot blanket, only to be torn again by a blue quill, only to close again; only to open.

The sickness was relieved, the sickness and the staleness of the summer day. The scorched leaves pattered one against the next, and the tares screaked thinly together, the tufted heads nodding, and upon the lake was the stippled commotion of a million pin-pricks and the sliding of gooseflesh shadows that released or shrouded momently the dancing of diamonds.

Through the trees of the southern hanger that sloped steeply to the water could be seen, through an open cradle of high branches, a portion of Gormenghast Castle, sun-blistered and pale in its dark frame of leaves; a remote façade.

A bird swept down across the water, brushing it with her breast-feathers and leaving a trail as of glow-worms across the still lake. A spilth of water fell from the bird as it climbed through the hot air to clear the lakeside trees, and a drop of lake water clung for a moment to the leaf of an ilex. And as it clung its body was titanic. It burgeoned the vast summer. Leaves, lake and sky reflected. The hanger was stretched across it and the heat swayed in the pendant. Each bough, each leaf – and as the blue quills ran, the motion of minutiae shivered, hanging. Plumply it slid and gathered, and as it lengthened, the distorted reflection of high crumbling acres of masonry beyond them, pocked with nameless windows, and of the ivy that lay across the face of that southern wing like a black hand, trembled in the long pearl as it began to lose its grip on the edge of the ilex leaf.

Yet even as it fell the leaves of the far ivy lay fluttering in the belly of the tear, and, microscopic, from a thorn-prick window a face gazed out into the summer.

In the lake the reflections of the trees wavered with a concertina motion when the waters ruffled and between the gusts slowed themselves into a crisp stillness. But there was one small area of lake to which the gusts could not penetrate, for a high crumbling wall, backed by a coppice, shielded a shallow creek where the water steamed and was blotched with swarms of tadpoles.

It lay at the opposite end of the lake to the steep hanger and the castle, from which direction the little breeze blew. It basked in the northerly corner of the lake's eastern extremity. From west to east (from the hangar to the creek) stretched the lake's attenuate length, but the north and south shores were comparatively close to one another, the southern being for the main part embattled with dark ranks of conifers, some of the cedars and pines growing out of the water itself. Along the north shore there was fine grey sand which petered out among the spinneys of birch and elder.

On the sand, at the water's edge, and roughly in the centre of the northern shore, was spread an enormous rust-coloured rug, and in the centre of the rug sat Nannie Slagg. Fuchsia lay upon her back, close by her, with her head upon one side and her forearm across her eyes to protect them from the sun. Tottering to and fro across the hot drab sand was Titus in a yellow shift. His hair had grown and darkened. It was quite straight, but made up for its lack of curls by its thickness and weight. It reached his shoulders, a dark umber, and over his forehead it hung in a heavy fringe.

Stopping for a moment (as though something very important had occurred to him) in the middle of a tiny, drunken totter, he turned his head to Mrs Slagg. His eyebrows were drawn down over the unique violet of his eyes, and there was a mixture of the pathetic, the ludicrous, and the sage in the expression of his pippin face. Even a suspicion of the pompous for a moment as he swayed and sat down suddenly having lost his balance – and then, having collapsed, a touch of the august. But, suddenly, in a sideways crawl, one leg thrusting him forward, his arms paddling wrist-deep through the sand and his other leg making no effort to play its part, content only to trail itself beneath and behind its energetic counterpart, he forsook the phlegmatic and was all impetuousness; but not a smile crossed his lips.

When he had reached the rust-coloured rug he sat quite still a few feet from Mrs Slagg and scrutinized the old lady's shoe, his elbow on his knee and his chin sunk in his hand, an attitude startlingly adult and inappropriate in a child of less than eighteen months.

'Oh, my poor heart! how he *does* look,' came Mrs Slagg's thin voice. 'As though I haven't loved him and toiled to make him joyous. Worn myself out to the marrow for his little Lordship, I have, day after day, night after night, with this after this and that after that piling ag'ny on ag'ny until you'd think he would be glad of love; but he just goes on as though he's wiser than his old Nannie, who knows all about the vacancies of babies,' ('vagaries', she must have meant), 'and all I get is naughtiness from his sister – oh, my weak heart, naughtiness and spleen.'

Fuchsia raised herself on her elbow and gazed at the brooding conifers on the far side of the lake. Her eyes were not red from crying: she had cried so much lately that she had drained herself of salt for a little. They had the look of eyes in which hosts of tears had been fought back and had triumphed.

'What did you say?'

'That's it! that's it!' Mrs Slagg became petulant. 'Never listens. Too wise now to listen, I suppose, to an old woman who hasn't long to live.'

'I didn't hear you,' said Fuchsia.

'You never *try*,' replied Nannie. 'That's what it is – you never *try*. I might as well not be here.'

Fuchsia had grown tired of the old nurse's querulous and tearful admonishments. She shifted her gaze from the pines to her brother, who had begun to struggle with the buckle of one of her shoes. 'Well, there's a lovely breeze, anyway,' she said.

The old nurse, who had forgotten she was in the middle of chastening Fuchsia, jerked her wizened face towards the girl in a startled way. 'What, my caution dear?' she said. And then re-membering that her 'caution' had been in her disfavour for some reason which she had forgotten, she pursed her face up with a ridiculous and puny haughtiness, as much as to say: 'I may have called you "my caution dear", but that doesn't mean that we're on speaking terms.'

Fuchsia gazed at her in a sullen sadness. 'I said there's a lovely breeze,' she repeated.

Mrs Slagg could never keep up her sham dignity for long, and she smacked out at Fuchsia, as a final gesture, and misjudging the distance, her blow fell short and she toppled over on her side. Fuchsia, leaning across the rug, re-established the midget as though she were setting an ornament and left her arm pur-posely within range, for she knew her old nurse. Sure enough, once Nannie Slagg had recovered and had smoothed out her skirt in front of her and reset her hat with the glass-grapes, she delivered a weak blow at Fuchsia's arm.

'What did you say about the breezes, dear? Nothing worth hearing, I expect, as usual.'

'I said they were lovely,' said Fuchsia.

'Yes, they *are*,' said Nannie, after reflection. 'Yes, they *are*, my only – but they don't make me any younger. They just go round the edge of me and make my skin feel nicer.'

'Well, that's better than nothing, I suppose,' said Fuchsia.

'But it's not *enough*, you argumentary *thing*. It's not *enough* when there's so much to do. What with your big mother being so cross with me as though I could help your poor father's dis-appearance and all the trouble of the food in the kitchen; as though *I* could help.'

At the mention of her father Fuchsia closed her eyes.

She had herself searched – searched. She had grown far older during the last few weeks – older in that her heart had been taxed by greater strains of passion than it had ever felt before. Fear of the unearthly, the ghastly – for she had been face to face with it – the fear of madness and of a violence she sus-pected. It had made her older, stiller, more apprehensive. She had known pain – the pain of desolation – of having been for-saken and of losing what little love there was. She had begun to fight back within herself and had stiffened, and she began to be conscious of a vague pride; of an awakening realization of her heritage. Her father in disappearing had completed a link in the immemorial chain. She grieved his loss, her breast heavy and aching with the pain of it; but beyond it and at her back she felt for the first time the mountain-range of the Groans, and that she was no longer free, no longer just Fuchsia, but of the blood. All this was cloud in her. Ominous, magnificent and indeterminate. Something she did not understand. Something which she recoiled from – so incomprehensible in her were its workings. Suddenly she had ceased to be a girl in all save in habits of speech and action. Her mind and heart were older and all things, once so clear, were filled with mist – all was tangled. Nannie repeated again, her dim eyes gazing over the lake: 'As though *I* could help all the troubles and the badnesses of people here and there doing what they shouldn't. Oh, my weak heart! as though it were all *my* fault.'

'No one says it's your fault,' said Fuchsia. 'You think people are thinking what they don't. It hasn't been anything to do with you.'

'It hasn't, *has* it – oh, my caution dear, it hasn't, *has* it?' Then her eyes became focused again (as far as they were able). '*What* hasn't, darling?'

'Never mind,' said Fuchsia. 'Look at Titus.'

Nannie turned her head, disapproving of Fuchsia's answer as she did so, and saw the little creature in his yellow shift rise to his feet and walk solemnly away, from the great rust-coloured rug and over the hot drab sand, his hands clasped before him.

'Don't *you* go and leave us, too!' cried Nannie Slagg. 'We can do without that horrid, fat Mr Swelter, but we can't do without our little Lordship. We can do without Mr Flay and –'

Fuchsia rose to her knees, 'we can't! we can't! Don't talk like that – so horribly. Don't talk of it – you never must. Dear Flay and – but you don't understand; it's no good. Oh, what has happened to them?' She sank back on her heels, her lower lip quivering, knowing that she must not let the old nurse's thoughtless remarks touch on her open wounds.

As Mrs Slagg stared open-eyed, both she and Fuchsia were

startled by a voice, and, turning, they saw two tall figures approaching them through the trees – a man – and, could it be? – yes, it was – a woman. It had a parasol. Not that there would have been anything masculine about this second figure, even were it to have left the parasol at home. Far from it. The swaying motion was prodigiously feminine. Her long neck was similar to her brother's, tactlessly so, as would have been her face had not a fair portion of it been mercifully obscured by her black glasses: but their major dissimilarity was manifest in their pelvic zone. The Doctor (for it was Prunesquallor) showed about as much sign of having a pair of hips as an eel set upon its end, while Irma, in white silk, had gone out of her way, it appeared, to exhibit to their worst advantage (her waist being ridiculously tight) a pair of hips capable of balancing upon their osseous shelves enough bric-a-brac to clutter up a kleptomaniac's cupboard.

'The top of the morning to you, my dears,' trilled the Doctor; 'and when I say "top" I mean the last cubic inch of it that sits, all limpid-like on a crest of ether, ha, ha, ha.'

Fuchsia was glad to see the Doctor. She liked him, for all his windy verbiage.

Irma, who had hardly been out of doors since that dreadful day when she disgraced herself at the Burning, was making every effort to re-establish herself as a lady – a lady, it is true, who had lapsed, but a lady nevertheless, and this effort at re-establishment was pathetically ostentatious. Her dresses were cut still lower across her bosom; her peerless, milky skin appearing to cover a couple of perches at least. She made even more play with her hips which swayed when she talked as though, like a great bell, they were regulated and motivated by a desire to *sound*, for they did all but chime as her sharp, unpleasant voice (so contrasted to the knell her pelvis might have uttered) dictated their figure-of-eight (bird's-eye view, cross section) patternations.

Her long, sharp nose was directed at Fuchsia.

'Dear child,' said Irma, 'are you enjoying the delicious breeze, then, dear child? I said are you enjoying the delicious breeze? Of course. Irrefutably and more so, I have no doubt whatever.'

She smiled, but there was no mirth in her smile, the muscles of her face complying only so far as to move in the directions dictated, but refusing to enter into the spirit of the thing – not that there was any.

'Tut tut!' said her brother in a tone which implied that it was unnecessary to answer his sister's conventional openings; and he sat down at Fuchsia's side and flashed her a crocodile smile with gold stoppings.

'I'm glad you've come,' said Fuchsia.

He patted her on the knee in a friendly staccato way, and then turned to Nannie.

'*Mrs* Slagg,' he said, laying great emphasis upon the 'Mrs' as though it was some unique prefix, 'and how are *you*? How's the blood-stream, my dear, invaluable little woman? How's the blood-stream? Come, come, let your doctor know.'

Nannie edged a little closer to Fuchsia, who sat between them, and peered at the Doctor around her shoulder.

'It's quite comfortable, sir ... I think, sir, thank you,' she said.

'Aha!' said Prunesquallor, stroking his smooth chin, 'a comfortable stream, is it? Aha! v-e-r-y good. V-e-r-y good. Dawdling lazily 'twixt hill and hill, no doubt. Meandering through groves of bone, threading the tissues and giving what sustenance it can to your dear old body. Mrs Slagg, I am *so* glad. But in your*self* – right deep down in your*self* – how do you feel? Carnally speaking, are you at peace – from the dear grey hairs of your head to the patter of your little feet – are you at peace?'

'What does he mean, dear?' said poor Mrs Slagg, clutching Fuchsia's arm. 'Oh, my poor heart, what does the Doctor mean?'

'He wants to know if you feel well or not,' said Fuchsia.

Nannie turned her red-rimmed eyes to the shock-headed, smooth-skinned man, whose eyes behind their magnifying spectacles swam and bulged.

'Come, come, my dear Mrs Slagg, I'm not going to eat you. Oh, dear no. Not even with some toast to pop you on, and a little pepper and salt. Not a bit of it. You have been unwell, oh dear, yes – since the conflagration. My dear woman, you have been unwell – most unwell, and most naturally. But are you *better* – that's what your doctor wants to know – are you *better?*'

Nannie opened her puckered little mouth. 'I ebbs and I flows, sir,' she said, 'and I falls away like.' Then she turned her head to Fuchsia very quickly as though to make sure she was still there, the glass grapes tinkling on her hat.

Doctor Prunesquallor brought forth a large silk handkerchief and began to dab his forehead. Irma, after a good deal of difficulty, presumably with whalebones and such like, had managed to sit down on the rug amid a good deal of creaking as of pulleys, cranks, hawsers and fish-hooks. She did not approve of sitting on the ground, but she was tired of looking down on their heads and decided to risk a brief interlude of unladyness. She was staring at Titus and saying to herself: 'If that were my child I should cut his hair, especially with his position to keep up.'

'And what does your "ebbing" consist of?' said the Doctor, returning his silk handkerchief to his pocket. 'Is it your heart that's tidal – or your nerves – or your liver, bless you – or a general weariness of the flesh?'

'I get tired,' said Mrs Slagg. 'I get so tired, sir. I have *everything* to do.' The poor old lady began to tremble.

'Fuchsia,' said the Doctor, 'come along this evening and I'll give you a tonic which you must make her take every day. By all that's amaranthine you really must. Balsam and swansdown, Fuchsia dear, cygnets and the eider bird, she must take it every day – syrup on the nerves, dear, and fingers cool as tombs for her old, old brow.'

'Nonsense,' said his sister. 'I said nonsense, Bernard.'

'And here,' continued Doctor Prunesquallor, taking no notice of his sister's interjection, 'is Titus. Apparisoned in a rag torn from the sun itself, ha, ha, ha! How vast he is getting! But how solemn.' He made clucking noises in his cheek. 'The great day draws near, doesn't it?'

'Do you mean the "Earling"?' said Fuchsia.

'No less,' said Prunesquallor, his head on one side.

'Yes,' she answered, 'it is in four days' time. They are making the raft.' Then suddenly, as though she could hold back the burden of her thoughts no longer: 'Oh, Doctor Prune, I must talk to you! May I see you soon? Soon? Don't use long words with me when we're alone, dear Doctor, like you sometimes do, because I'm so ... well ... because I've got – I've got worries. Doctor Prune.'

Prunesquallor languidly began to make marks in the sand with his long white forefinger. Fuchsia, wondering why he did not reply, dropped her eyes and saw that he had written:

'9 o'clock tonight Cool Room.'

Then the long hand brushed away the message and at the same moment they were conscious of presences behind them and, turning, they saw the twins, Fuchsia's identical aunts, standing like purple carvings in the heat.

The Doctor sprang nimbly to his feet and inclined his reedy body in their direction.

They took no notice of his gallantry, staring past him in the direction of Titus, who was sitting quietly at the lake's edge.

From the sky's zenith to where he sat upon the strip of sand it seemed that a great backcloth had been let down, for the heat had flattened out the lake, lifted it upright on its sandy rim; lifted the sloping bank where the conifers, with their shadows, made patterns in three shades of green, sun-struck and enormous; and balanced in a jig-saw way upon the ragged edge of this painted wood was a heavy, dead, blue sky, towering to the proscenium arch of the vision's limit – the curved eyelid. At the base of this staring drop-cloth of raw phenomena he sat, incredibly minute; Titus in a yellow shift, his chin once more in his hand.

Fuchsia felt uncomfortable with her aunts standing immediately behind her. She looked up sideways at them and it was hard to conceive that they would ever be able to move again. Effigies, white-faced, white-handed, and hung with imperial purple. Mrs Slagg was still unaware of their presence, and in the silence a silly impulse to chatter gripped her, and, forgetting her nervousness, she perked her head up at the standing Doctor.

'You see, excuse me, Doctor sir,' she said, startling herself by her own bravery, 'you see, I've always been of the energetic system, sir. That's how I always was since I was a little girl, doing this and that by turns. "What *will* she do next?" they always said. Always.'

'I am sure they did,' answered the Doctor, reseating himself on the rug and turning to Nannie Slagg, his eyebrows raised, and a look of incredulous absorption on his pink face.

Mrs Slagg was encouraged. No one had ever before appeared to be so interested in anything she said. Prunesquallor had decided that there was a fair chance of the twins remaining transfixed as they were, for a good half-hour yet, and that to hang around on his elegant legs was neither in his interests, physically, nor in accord with his self-respect, which, although of peculiar brand was neverthelesss deep-rooted. They had not acknowledged his gesture. It is true they had not noticed it – but that was not his fault.

'To hell with the old trouts,' he trilled to himself. 'Breastless as wallpaper. By all that's sentient, my last post-mortem had more go in it than the pair of 'em, turning somersaults.'

As he held forth, inwardly, he was paying, outwardly, the most passionate attention to Mrs Slagg's every syllable.

'And it's always been the same,' she was quavering, 'always the same. Responserverity all the time, Doctor; and I'm not a little thing any more.'

'Of course not, of course not, tut, tut; by all that's shrewd you speak nobly, Mrs Slagg – very nobly,' said Prunesquallor, considering at the same time whether there would have been enough room for her in his black bag, without removing the bottles.

'Because we're not as young as we *were*, are we, sir?'

Prunesquallor considered this point very carefully. Then he shook his head. 'What you say has the ring of truth in it,' he said. 'In fact, it has every possible kind of ring in it. Ring-ting, my heart's on the wing, as it were. But tell me, Mrs Slagg – tell me in your own concise way – of Mr Slagg – or am I being indelicate? No – no – it couldn't be. Do *you* know, Fuchsia? Do you? For myself, I am at sea over Mr Slagg. He is under my keel – utterly under. That's queer! Utterly under. Or isn't it? No matter. To put it brutally: was there a – No, no! Finesse, please.. Who was – No, no! Crude; crude. Forgive me. Of Mr Slagg, dear lady, have you any ... kind of – Good gracious me! and I've known you all this long while and then *this* teaser comes – crops up like a dove on tenderhooks. There's a "ring" in that – ha, ha, ha! And what a teaser! Don't you think so, dear?'

He turned to Fuchsia.

She could not help smiling, but held the old nurse's hand.

'When did you marry Mr Slagg, Nannie?' she asked.

Prunesquallor heaved a sigh. 'The direct approach,' he murmured. 'The apt angle. God bless my circuitous soul, we learn ... we learn.'

Mrs Slagg became very proud and rigid from the glass grapes on her hat to her little seat.

'Mr Slagg,' she said in a thin, high voice, 'married *me*.' She paused, having delivered, as it seemed to her, the main blow; and then, as an afterthought: 'He died the same night – and no wonder.'

'Good heavens – alive and dead and half way between. By all that's enigmatic, my dear, dear Mrs Slagg, what can you possibly *mean*?' cried the Doctor, in so high a treble that a bird rattled its way through the leaves of a tree behind them and sped to the west.

'He had a stroke,' said Mrs Slagg.

'We've – had – strokes – too,' said a voice.

They had forgotten the twins and all three turned their startled heads, but they were not in time to see which mouth had opened.

But as they stared Clarice intoned: 'Both of us, at the same time. It was lovely.'

'No, it wasn't,' said Cora. 'You forget what a nuisance it became.'

'Oh, *that*!' replied her sister. 'I didn't mind *that*. It's when we couldn't do things with the left side of us that I didn't like it much.'

'That's what I said, didn't I?'

'Oh no, you didn't.'

'Clarice Groan,' said Cora, 'don't be above yourself.'

'How do you mean?' said Clarice, raising her eyes nervously.

Cora turned to the Doctor for the first time. 'She's ignorant,' she said blankly. 'She doesn't understand figures of eight.'

Nannie could not resist correcting the Lady Cora, for the Doctor's attention had infected her with an eagerness to go on talking. A little nervous smile appeared on her lips, however, when she said: 'You don't mean "figures of eight", Lady Cora; you mean "figures of speech".'

Nannie was so pleased at knowing the expression that the smile remained shuddering in the wrinkles of her lips until she realized that she was being stared at by the aunts.

'Servant,' said Cora. 'Servant . . .'

'Yes, my lady. Yes, yes, my lady,' said Nannie Slagg, struggling to her feet.

'Servant,' echoed Clarice, who had rather enjoyed what had happened.

Cora turned to her sister. 'There's no need for you to say anything.'

'Why not?' said Clarice.

'Because it wasn't you that she was disobedient with, stupid.'

'But I want to give her some punishment, too,' said Clarice.

'Why?'

'Because I haven't given any for such a long time. . . . Have you?'

'You've *never* given any at all,' said Cora.

'Oh yes, I have.'

'Who to?'

'It doesn't matter *who* it was. I've given it, and that's that.'

'That's what?'

'That's the punishment.'

'Do you mean like our brother's?'

'I don't know. But we mustn't burn *her*, must we?'

Fuchsia had risen to her feet. To strike her aunts, or even to touch them, would have made her quite ill and it is difficult to know what she was about to do. Her hands were shaking at her sides.

The phrase, 'But we mustn't burn *her*, must we?' had found itself a long shelf at the back of Doctor Prunesquallor's brain that was nearly empty, and the ridiculous little phrase found squatting drowsily at one end was soon thrown out by the lanky newcomer, which stretched its body along the shelf from the 'B' of its head to the 'e' of its tail, and turning over had twenty-four winks (in defiance of the usual convention) – deciding upon one per letter and two over for luck; for there was not much time for slumber, the owner of this shelf – of the whole bone house, in fact – being liable to pluck from the most obscure of his grey-cell caves and crannies, let alone the shelves, the drowsy phrases at any odd moment. There was no real peace. Nannie Slagg, with her knuckles between her teeth, was trying to keep her tears back.

Irma was staring in the opposite direction. Ladies did not participate in 'situations'. They did not *apprehend* them. She remembered that perfectly. It was Lesson Seven. She arched her nostrils until they were positively triumphal and convinced herself that she was not listening very hard.

Dr Prunesquallor, imagining the time to be ripe, leapt to his feet and, swaying like a willow wand that had been stuck in the ground and twanged at its so exquisitely peeled head – uttered a strangely bizarre cry, followed by a series of trills, which can only be stylized by the 'Ha-ha-ha-ha-ha-ha-ha-ha-ha-ha-ha-ha-ha-ha-ha-ha-ha-ha-ha-ha-ha-ha-ha-ha, of literary convention, and wound up with:

'Titus! By all that's infinitesimal. Lord-bless-my-soul, if he hasn't been eaten by a shark!'

Which of the five heads turned itself the most rapidly would be difficult to assess. Possibly Nannie was a fraction of a second behind the others, for the double reason that the condition of her neck was far from plastic and because any ejaculation, however dramatic and however much it touched on her immediate concerns, took time to percolate to the correct area of her confused little brain.

However, the word 'Titus' was different in that it had before now discovered a short cut through the cells. Her heart had leapt more quickly than her brain and, obeying it involuntarily, before her body knew that it had received any orders through the usual channels, she was upon her feet and had begun to totter to the shore.

She did not trouble to consider whether there could possibly *be* a shark in the fresh water that stretched before her; nor whether the Doctor would have spoken so flippantly about the death of the only male heir; nor whether, if he *had* been swallowed she could do anything about it. All she knew was that she must run to where he used to be.

With her weak old eyes it was only after she had travelled half the distance that she saw him. But this in no way retarded what speed she had. He was still *about* to be eaten by a shark, if he hadn't already been; and when at last she had him in her arms, Titus was subjected to a bath of tears.

Tottering with her burden, she cast a last apprehensive glance at the glittering reach of water, her heart pounding.

Prunesquallor had begun to take a few loping, toe-pointed paces after her, not having realized how shattering his little joke would be. He had stopped, however, reflecting that since there *was* to be a shark, it would be best for Mrs Slagg to frustrate its evil plans for the sake of her future satisfaction. His only anxiety was that her heart would not be overtaxed. What he had hoped to achieve by his fanciful outcry had materialized, namely the cessation of the ridiculous quarrel and the freeing of Nannie Slagg from further mortification.

The twins were quite at a loss for some while. 'I saw it,' said Cora.

Clarice, not to be outdone, had seen it as well. Neither of them was very interested.

Fuchsia turned to the Doctor as Nannie sat down, breathless, on the rust-coloured rug, Titus sliding from her arms.

'You shouldn't have done that, Doctor Prune,' she said. 'But, oh, Lord, how funny! Did you see Miss Prunesquallor's face?' She began to giggle, without mirth in her eyes. And then: 'Oh, Doctor Prune, I shouldn't have said that – she's your sister.'

'Only just,' said the Doctor; and putting his teeth near Fuchsia's ear he whispered: 'She thinks she's a lady.' And then he grinned until the very lake seemed to be in danger of engulfment. 'Oh, dear! the poor thing. Tries so hard, and the more she tries the less she *is*. Ha! ha! ha! Take it from me, Fuchsia dear, the only ladies are those to whom the idea of whether they are or not never occurs. Her blood's all right – Irma's – same as mine, ha, ha, ha! but it doesn't go by blood. Its equipoise, my Gipsy, equipoise that does it – with a bucketful of tolerance thrown in. Why, bless my inappropriate soul, if I'm not treading on the skirts of the serious. Tut, tut, if I'm not.'

By now they were all sitting upon the rug and between them creating a monumental group of unusual grandeur. The little gusts of air were still leaping through the wood and ruffling the lake. The branches of the trees behind them chafed one another, and their leaves, like a million conspiring tongues, were husky with heresy.

Fuchsia was about to ask what 'equipoise' meant when her eye was caught by a movement among the trees on the farther side of the lake, and a moment later she was surprised to see a column of figures threading their way down to the shore, along which they began to move to the north, appearing and disappearing as the great water-growing cedars shrouded or revealed them.

Saving for the foremost figure, they carried loops of rope and the boughs of trees across their shoulders, and excepting the leader they appeared to be oldish men, for they moved heavily.

They were the Raft-makers, and were on their way by the traditional footpath, on the traditional day, to the traditional creek – that heat-hazy indentation of water backed by the crumbling wall and the coppice where the minnows and the tadpoles and the myriad microscopic small-fry of the warm, shallow water were so soon to be disturbed.

It was quite obvious who the leading figure was. There could be no mistaking that nimble, yet shuffling and edgeways-on – that horribly deliberate motivation that was neither walking nor running – both close to the ground as though on the scent, and yet loosely and nimbly above it.

Fuchsia watched him, fascinated. It was not often that Steerpike was to be seen without his knowing it. The Doctor, following Fuchsia's eyes, was equally able to recognize the youth. His pink brow clouded. He had been cogitating a great deal lately on this and that – *this* being in the main the inscrutable and somehow 'foreign' youth, and *that* centring for the most part on the mysterious Burning. There had been so strange a crop of enigmas of late. If they had not been of so serious a character Doctor Prunesquallor would have found in them nothing but diversion. The unexpected did so much to relieve the monotony of the Castle's endless rounds of unwavering procedure; but Death and Disappearance were no tit-bits for a jaded palate. They were too huge to be swallowed, and tasted like bile.

Although the Doctor, with a mind of his own, had positively heterodox opinions regarding certain aspects of the Castle's life – opinions too free to be expressed in an atmosphere where the woof and warp of the dark place and its past were synonymous with the mesh of veins in the bodies of its denizens – yet he was *of* the place and was a freak only in that his mind worked in a wide way, relating and correlating his thoughts so that his conclusions were often clear and accurate and nothing short of heresy. But this did not mean that he considered himself to be superior. Oh no. He was not. The blind faith was the pure faith, however muddy the brain. His gem-like conclusions may have been of the first water, but his essence and his spirit were warped in proportion to his disbelief in the value of even the most footling observance. He was no outsider – and the tragedies that had occurred touched him upon the raw. His airy and fatuous manner was deceptive. As he trilled, as he prattled, as he indulged in his spontaneous 'conceits', as he gestured, fop-like and grotesque, his magnified eyes skidding to and fro behind the lenses of his glasses, like soap at the bottom of a bath, his brain was often other-where, and these days it was well occupied. He was marshalling the facts at his disposal – his odds and ends of information, and peering at them with the eye of his brain, now from this direction, now from that; now from below, now from above, as he talked, or seemed to listen, by day and by night, or in the evening with his feet on the mantel-piece, a liqueur at his elbow and his sister in the opposite chair.

He glanced at Fuchsia to make sure that she had recognized

the distant boy, and was surprised to see a look of puzzled absorption on her dark face, her lips parted a little as though from a faint excitement. By now the crocodile of figures was rounding the bend of the lake away to their left. And then it stopped. Steerpike was moving away from the retainers, to the shore. He had apparently given them an order, for they all sat down among the shore-side pines and watched him as he stripped himself of his clothes and thrust his sword-stick, point down, into the muddy bank. Even from so great a distance it could be seen that his shoulders were very hunched and high.

'By all that's public,' said Prunesquallor, 'so we have a new official, have we? The lakeside augury of things to come – fresh blood in summertime with forty years to go. The curtains part – precocity advances, ha, ha, ha! And what's he doing now?'

Fuchsia had given a little gasp of surprise, for Steerpike had dived into the lake. A moment before he dived he had waved to them, although as far as they had been able to judge he had not so much as moved his eyes in their direction.

'What was *that*?' said Irma, swivelling her neck about in a most lubricated way. 'I said, "what was *that*?", Bernard. It sounded like a splash; do you hear me, Bernard? I say it sounded like a *splash*.' 'That's why,' said her brother.

'"That's why?" What do you mean, Bernard, by "that's why"? You are so tiresome. I said, you are so tiresome. That's why *what*?' '

'That's why it was like a splash, my butterfly.'

'But *why*? Oh, my conscience for a normal brother! Why, Bernard, was-it-like-a-splash?'

'Only because it happened to be one, peahen,' he said. 'It was an authentic, undiluted splash. Ha! ha! ha! An undiluted splash.'

'Oh!' cried Mrs Slagg, her fingers plucking at her nether lip, 'it wasn't the shark, was it, Doctor sir? Oh, my weak heart, sir! Was it the shark?'

'Nonsense!' said Irma. 'Nonsense, you silly woman! Sharks in Gormenghast Lake! The very idea!'

Fuchsia's eyes were on Steerpike. He was a strong swimmer

and was by now halfway across the lake, the thin white arms obtusely angled at the elbows methodically dipping and emerging.

Cora's voice said: 'I can see somebody.'

'Where?' said Clarice.

'In the water.'

'What? In the lake?'

'Yes, that's the only water there is, stupid.'

'No, it isn't.'

'Well, it's the only water there is that's near us now.'

'Oh yes, it's the only water of *that* sort.'

'Can you see him?'

'I haven't looked yet.'

'Well, look now.'

'Shall I?'

'Yes. Now.'

'Oh . . . I see a man. Do you see a man?'

'I told *you* about him. Of course I do.'

'He's swimming to me.'

'Why to you? It might as well be to me.'

'Why?'

'Because we're just the same.'

'That's our glory.'

'*And* our pride. Don't forget that.'

'No, I won't.'

They stared at the approaching swimmer. His face was most of the time either under water or lying sideways along it to draw breath, and they had no idea that it was Steerpike.

'Clarice,' said Cora.

'Yes.'

'We are the only ladies present, aren't we?'

'Yes. What about it?'

'Well, we'll go down to the shore, so that when he arrives we can unbend to him.'

'Will it hurt?' said Clarice.

'Why are you so ignorant of phrases?' Cora turned her face to her sister's profile.

'I don't know what you mean,' muttered Clarice.

'I haven't time to explain about language,' said Cora. 'It doesn't matter.'

'Doesn't it?'

'No. But this is what does.'

'Oh.'

'We are being swum to.'

'Yes.'

'So we must receive his homage on the shore.'

'Yes ... yes.'

'So we must go and patronize him now.'

'Now?'

'Yes, now. Are you ready?'

'When I get up I'll be.'

'Have you finished?'

'Nearly. Have you?'

'Yes.'

'Come on, then.'

'Where?'

'Don't bother me with ignorance. Just walk where I do.'

'Yes.'

'Look!'

'Look!'

Steerpike had found himself in his depth and was standing upright. The water lapped at the base of his ribs, the mud of the lake's floor oozing between his toes, while he waved his arms over his head to the group, the bright drops falling from them in sparkling strings.

Fuchsia was excited. She loved what he had done. To suddenly see them, to throw off his clothes, to plunge into the deep water and to strike out across the lake to them, and then finally to stand, panting, with the water curling at his narrow wiry waist – was fine; all upon the spur of the moment.

Irma Prunesquallor, who had not seen her 'admirer' for several weeks, gave a shriek as she saw his naked body rising from the lake, and covering her face with her hands she peered between her fingers.

Nannie still couldn't make out who it was, and months afterwards was still in doubt.

473

Steerpike's voice sounded over the shallow water.

'Well met!' he shouted. 'Only just saw you! Lady Fuchsia! good day. It's delightful to see you again. How is your health? Miss Irma? Excuse my skin. And, Doctor, how's yours?'

Then he gazed with his dark-red, close-together-eyes at the twins, who were paddling out to meet him, quite unconscious of the water up to their ankles.

'You're getting your legs wet, your ladyships. Be careful! Go back!' cried the youth, in mock alarm. 'You do me too much honour. For God's sake, go back!'

It was necessary for him to shout in such a manner as gave no indication that he held authority over them. Indeed, he did not care two straws whether they marched on until they were up to their necks. It was a quaint situation. In the interests of modesty he could move no farther shorewards.

As he intended, they were unable to recognize the authority in his voice which they had learned to obey. The twins moved deeper in the water, and the Doctor, Fuchsia, and Nannie Slagg were amazed to see that they were up to their hips in the lake, the voluminous skirts of their purple dresses floating out magnificently.

Steerpike stared past them for a moment and indicated by a helpless shrugging of his shoulders and a display of the palms of his hands that he was powerless to cope with the situation. They had become very near him. Near enough for him to speak to them without being heard by the group which had by now gathered at the fringe of the lake.

In a low, quick voice, and one which he knew by experience would find an immediate response, he said: 'Stand where you are. Not one more step, do you hear me? I have something to tell you. Unless you stand still and listen to me you will forfeit the golden thrones which are now complete and are on their way to your apartment. Go back now. Go back to the Castle – to your room, or there will be trouble.'

While he spoke he made signs to those on the shore; he shrugged his shoulders impotently. The while, his quick voice ran on, mesmerizing the twins, hip-deep among the sparkling ripples.

'You will not speak of the Fire – and you will keep to your-selves and not go out and meet people as you are doing today against my orders. You have disobeyed. I shall arrive at your rooms at ten o'clock tonight. I am displeased, for you have broken your promise. Yet you shall have your glory; but only if you never speak of the Fire. Sit down at once!' This peremp-tory order was one which Steerpike could not resist. Their eyes had been fixed on him as he spoke, and he wished to convince himself that they were powerless to disobey him at such mo-ments as this – that they were unable to think of anything save what he was driving into their consciousness by the pecu-liar low voice which he adopted and by the constant repetition of a few simple maxims. A twist of his lips suggested the vile, overweening satisfaction he experienced as he watched the two purple creatures sink upon their rears in the lukewarm lake. Only their long necks and saucer-like faces remained above the surface. Surrounding each of them was the wavering fringe of a purple skirt.

Directly he had seen, tasted and absorbed the delicious essence of the situation, his voice rapped out: 'Go back! Back to your rooms and wait for me. Back at once – no talking on the shore.'

As they sank into the lake, automatically, at his orders, he had, for the benefit of the watchers, clasped his head in his hands as though in desperation.

Then the aunts arose, all stuck about with purple and made their way, hand in hand, to the amazed gathering on the sands.

Steerpike's lesson had been well digested, and they walked solemnly past the Doctor, Fuchsia, Irma and Nannie Slagg and into the trees; and, turning to their left along a hazel ride, pro-ceeded, in a kind of sodden trance, in the direction of the Castle.

'It beats me, Doctor! Beats me completely!' shouted the youth in the water.

'You surprise me, dear boy!' cried the Doctor. 'By all that's amphibious, you surprise me. Have a heart, dear child, have a heart, and swim away – we're so tired of the sight of your stomach.'

'Forgive its magnetism!' replied Steerpike, who dived back

under water and was next to be seen some distance off, swimming steadily in the direction of the Raft makers.

Fuchsia, watching the sunlight flashing on the wet arms of the now distant boy, found that her heart was pounding. She mistrusted his eyes. She was repelled by his high, round forehead and the height of his shoulders. He did not belong to the Castle as she knew it. But her heart beat, for he was alive – oh, so alive! and adventurous; and no one seemed to be able to make him feel humble. As he had answered the Doctor his eyes had been on her. She did not understand. Her melancholy was like a darkness in her; but when she thought of him it seemed that through the darkness a forked lightning ran.

'I'm going back now,' she said to the Doctor. 'Tonight we will meet, thank you. Come on, Nannie. Good-bye, Miss Prunesquallor.'

Irma made a kind of curling movement with her body and smiled woodenly.

'Good day,' she said. 'It has been delightful. Most. Bernard, your arm. I said – your *arm*.'

'You did, and there's no doubt about it, snow-blossom. I heard you,' said her brother. 'Ha! ha! ha! And here it is. An arm of trembling beauty, it's every pore agog for the touch of your limp fingers. You wish to take it? You shall. You shall take it – but seriously, ha! ha! ha! Take it seriously, I pray you, sweet frog; but do let me have it back some time. Let us away. Fuchsia, for now, good-bye. We part, only to meet.'

Ostentatiously he raised his left elbow and Irma, lifting her parasol over her head, her hips gyrating and her nose like a needle pointing the way, took his arm and they moved into the shadows of the trees.

Fuchsia lifted Titus and placed him over her shoulder, while Nannie folded up the rust-coloured rug, and they in their turn began the homeward journey.

Steerpike had reached the further shore and the party of men had resumed their *détour* of the lake, the chestnut boughs across their shoulders. The youth moved jauntily ahead of them, spinning the sword-stick.

COUNTESS GERTRUDE

LONG after the drop of lake water had fallen from the ilex leaf and the myriad reflections that had floated on its surface had become a part of the abactina of what had gone for ever, the head at the thorn-prick window had remained gazing out into the summer.

It belonged to the Countess. She was standing on a ladder, for only in such a way could she obtain a view through that high, ivy-cluttered opening. Behind her the shadowy room was full of birds.

Blobs of flame on the dark crimson wallpaper smouldered, for a few sunbeams shredded their way past her head and struck the wall with silent violence. They were entirely motionless in the half light and burned without a flicker, forcing the rest of the room into still deeper shade, and into a kind of subjugated motion, a counter-play of volumes of many shades between the hues of deep ash-grey and black.

It was difficult to see the birds, for there were no candles lighted. The summer burned beyond the small high window.

At last the Countess descended the ladder, step after mammoth step, until both feet on the ground she turned about, and began to move to the shadowy bed. When she reached its head she ignited the wick of a half-melted candle and, seating herself at the base of the pillows, emitted a peculiarly sweet, low, whistling note from between her great lips.

For all her bulk it was as though she had, from a great winter tree, become a summer one. Not with leaves was she decked, but, thick as foliage, with birds. Their hundred eyes twinkled like glass beads in the candlelight.

'Listen,' she said. 'We're alone. Things are bad. Things are going wrong. There's evil afoot. I know it.'

Her eyes narrowed. 'But let 'em try. We can bide our time. We'll hold our horses. Let them rear their ugly hands, and by the Doom, we'll crack 'em chine-ways. Within four days the Earling – and then I'll take him, babe and boy – Titus the Seventy-seventh.'

She rose to her feet. 'God shrive my soul, for it'll need it!' she boomed, as the wings fluttered about her and the little claws shifted for balance. 'God shrive it when I find the evil thing! For absolution, or no absolution – there'll be *satisfaction* found.' She gathered some cake crumbs from a nearby crate, and placed them between her lips. At the trotting sound of her tongue a warbler pecked from her mouth, but her eyes had remained half closed, and what could be seen of her iris was as hard and glittering as a wet flint.

'Satisfaction,' she repeated huskily, with something purr-like in the heavy-sounding syllables. 'In Titus it's all centred. Stone and mountain – the Blood and the Observance. Let them touch him. For every hair that's hurt I'll stop a heart. If grace I have when turbulence is over – so be it; and if not – what then?'

THE APPARITION

SOMETHING in a white shroud was moving towards the door of the twins' apartment. The Castle was asleep. The silence like space. The Thing was inhumanly tall and appeared to have no arms.

In their room the aunts sat holding each other by the empty grate. They had been waiting so long for the handle of the door to turn. This is now what it began to do. The twins had their eyes on it. They had been watching it for over an hour – the room all lit – their brass clock ticking. And then, suddenly, through the gradually yawning fissure of the door the Thing entered, its head scraping the lintel – its head grinning and frozen, was the head of a skull.

They could not scream. The twins could not scream. Their throats were contracted; their limbs had stiffened. The bulging of their four identical eyes was ghastly to see, and as they stood there, paralyzed, a voice from just below the grinning skull cried:

'Terror! terror! terror! pure; naked; and bloody!'

And the nine-foot length of sheet moved into the room.

Old Sourdust's skull had come in useful. Balanced on the end of the sword-stick, and dusted with phosphorus, the sheet hanging vertically down its either side, and kept in place by a tack through the top of the cranium, Steerpike was able to hold it three feet above his own head and peer through a slit he had made in the sheet at his eye level. The white linen fell in long sculptural folds to the floor of the room.

The twins were the colour of the sheet. Their mouths were wide open and their screams tore inwards at their bowels for lack of natural vent. They had become congealed with an icy horror, their hair, disentangling from knot and coil, had risen like pampas grass that lifts in a dark light when gusts prowl shuddering and pressage storm. They could not even cling more closely together, for their limbs were weighted with cold stone. It was the end. The Thing scraped the ceiling with its head and moved forward noiselessly in one piece. Having no human possibility of height, it had *no* height. It was not a tall ghost – it was immeasurable; Death walking like an element.

Steerpike had realized that unless something was done it would be only a matter of time before the twins, through the loose meshwork of their vacant brains, divulged the secret of the Burning. However much they were in his power he could not feel sure that the obedience which had become automatic in his presence would necessarily hold when they were among others. As he now saw it, it seemed that he had been at the mercy of their tongues ever since the Fire – and he could only feel relief that he had escaped detection – for until now he had had hopes that vacuous as they were, they would be able to understand the peril in which, were any suspicion to be attached to them, they would stand. But he now realized that through terrorism and victimization alone could loose lips be sealed. And so he had lain awake and planned a little episode. Phosphorus, which along with the poisons he had concocted in Prunesquallor's dispensary, and which as yet he had found no use for – his sword-stick, as yet unsheathed, save when alone he polished the slim blade, and a sheet. These were his media for the concoction of a walking death.

And now he was in their room. He could watch them

perfectly through the slit in the sheet. If he did not speak now, before the hysterics began, then they would hear nothing, let alone grasp his meaning. He lifted his voice to a weird and horrible pitch.

'I am Death!' he cried. 'I am all who have died. I am the death of Twins. Behold! Look at my face. It is naked. It is bone. It is Revenge. *Listen*. I am the One who strangles.'

He took a further pace towards them. Their mouths were still open and their throats strained to loose the clawing cry.

'I come as Warning! Warning! Your throats are long and white and ripe for strangling. My bony hands can squeeze all breath away . . . I come as Warning! *Listen!*'

There was no alternative for them. They had no power.

'I am Death – and I will talk to you – the Burners. Upon that night you lit a crimson fire. You burned your brother's heart away! Oh, horror!'

Steerpike drew breath. The eyes of the twins were well nigh upon their cheekbones. He must speak very simply.

'But there is yet a still more bloody crime. The crime of speech. The crime of Mentioning, Mentioning. For this, I murder in a darkened room. *I* shall be watching. Each time you move your mouths *I* shall be watching. Watching. Watching with my enormous eyes of bone. I shall be listening. Listening, with my fleshless ears: and my long fingers will be itching . . . itching. Not even to each other shall you speak. Not of your crime. Oh, horror! Not of the crimson Fire.

'My cold grave calls me back, but shall I answer it? No! For I shall be beside *you* for ever. Listening, listening; with my fingers itching. You will not see me . . . but *I* shall be here . . . there . . . and wherever you go . . . for evermore. Speak not of Fire . . . or Steerpike . . . Fire – or Steerpike, your protector, for the sake of your long throats . . . Your long white throats.'

Steerpike turned majestically. The skull had tilted a little on the point of the sword-stick, but it did not matter. The twins were icebound in an arctic sea.

As he moved solemnly through the doorway, something

grotesque, terrifying, ludicrous in the slanting angle of the skull
– as though it were listening ... gave emphasis to all that had
gone before.

As soon as he had closed the door behind him he shed himself
of the sheet and, wrapping the skull in its folds, hid it from
view among some lumber that lay along the wall of the passage.

There was still no sound from the room. He knew that it
would be fruitless to appear the same evening. Whatever he
said would be lost. He waited a few moments, however, expect-
ing the hysteria to find a voice, but at length began his return
journey. As he turned the corner of a distant passageway, he
suddenly stopped dead. It had begun. Dulled as it was by the
distance and the closed doors, it was yet horrifying enough –
the remote, flat, endless screaming of naked panic.

*

When, on the evening of the next day, he visited them he
found them in bed. The old woman who smelt so badly had
brought them their meals. They lay close together and were
obviously very ill. They were so white that it was difficult to tell
where their faces ended and the long pillow began.

The room was brightly lit. Steerpike was glad to notice this.
He remembered that, as 'Death', he had mentioned his prefer-
ence for 'strangling in a *darkened* room'. The strong lights indicated that the twins were able to remember at least a part of
what he had said that night.

But even now he was taking no chances.

'Your Ladyships,' he said, 'you look seedy. Very seedy. But
believe me, you don't look as bad as I feel. I have come for your
advice and perhaps for your help. I must tell you. Be prepared.'
He coughed. 'I have had a visitor. A visitor from Beyond. Do
not be startled, ladies. But his name was Death. He came to me
and he said: "Their Ladyships have done foul murder. I shall go
to them now and squeeze the breath from their old bodies." But
I said: "No! hold back, I pray you. For they have promised
never to divulge a word." And Death said: "How can I be
sure? How can I have proof?" I answered: "I am your witness. If their Ladyships so much as mention the word FIRE

or STEERPIKE, you shall take them with you under wormy ground." '

Cora and Clarice were trying to speak, but they were very weak. At last Cora said:

'He ... came ... here ... too. He's still here. Oh, save us! save us!'

'He came here!' said Steerpike, jumping to his feet. 'Death came here, too?'

'Yes.'

'How strange that you are still alive! Did he give you orders?'

'Yes,' said Clarice.

'And you remember them all?'

'Yes ... yes!' said Cora, fingering her throat. 'We can remember everything. Oh, save us.'

'It is for you to save yourselves with silence. You wish to live?'

They nodded pathetically.

'Then never a word.'

'Never a word,' echoed Clarice in the hush of the bright room.

Steerpike bowed and retired, and returned by an alternative staircase flanked by a long, steep curve of banister, down which he slid at high speed, landing nimbly at the foot of the stairs with a kind of pounce.

He had commandeered a fresh suite of rooms whose windows gave upon the cedar lawns. It was more in keeping with the position which his present duties commanded.

Glancing along the corridor before he entered his apartments, he could see in the distance – too far for the sound of their footsteps – the figures of Fuchsia and the Doctor.

He entered his room. The window was a smoke-blue rectangle, intersected by black branches. He lit a lamp. The walls flared, and the window became black. The branches had disappeared. He drew the blinds. He kicked off his shoes and, springing on the bed, twisted himself onto his back and, for a moment, discarded his dignity and became, at least physically, a little more in keeping with his seventeen years; for he wriggled, arched his spine and stretched out his arms and legs with a terrible glee.

Then he began to laugh and laugh, the tears pouring from his dark-red eyes until, utterly exhausted and helpless, he fell back upon the pillows and slept, his thin lips twisted.

*

An hour earlier, Fuchsia had met the Doctor at their rendez-vous, the Cool Room. He had not been flippant. He had helped her with words well chosen and thoughts simple and direct that touched deftly on the areas of her sorrow. Together they had covered in their conversation, the whole range of lamentable and melancholy experiences which it had been their lot to en-counter. They had spoken of all connected with them, of Fuch-sia's brooding mother; of the uncanny disappearance of her father, and whether he was dead or alive; of the Doctor's sister and of the Twins: of the enigma of Swelter and Flay and of little Nannie Slagg; of Barquentine and of Steerpike.

'Be careful of him, Fuchsia,' said the Doctor. 'Will you re-member that?'

'I will,' said Fuchsia. 'Yes, I will, Doctor Prune.'

Dusk was beyond the bay window ... a great, crumbling dusk that wavered and descended like a fog of ashes.

Fuchsia unfastened the two top buttons of her blouse and folded the corners back. She had turned away from the Doctor as she did so. Then she held her hands cupped over her breast bone. It seemed as though she were hiding something.

'Yes, I *will* be careful, Doctor Prune,' she repeated, 'and I'll remember all you have said – and tonight I had to wear it – I had to.'

'You had to wear what, my little mushroom?' said Prune-squallor, lightening his voice for the first time, for the serious session was over and they could relax. 'Bless my dull wits if I haven't lost the thread – if there *was* one! Say it again, my Swarthy-sweet.'

'Look! – look! – for you and for me, because I wanted to.'

She dropped her hands to her side, where they hung heavily. Her eyes shone. She was a mixture of the clumsy and the mag-nificent – her head bridled up – her throat gleaming, her feet apart and the toes turned in a little. 'LOOK!'

The Doctor at her command looked very hard indeed. The ruby he had given her that night, when for the first time he had met Steerpike, burned against her breast.

And then, suddenly, unexpectedly, she had fled, her feet pounding on the stone floors, while the door of the Cool Room swung to and fro ... to and fro.

THE EARLING

THE day of the 'Earling' was a day of rain. Monotonous, sullen, grey rain with no life in it. It had not even the power to stop. There were always a hundred heads at the windows of the North wing that stared into the sky, into the rain. A hundred figures leant across the sills of the Southern wall, and stared. They would disappear back into the darkness, one by one, but others would have appeared at other windows. There would always be about a hundred starers. Rain. The slow rain. The East and the West of the Castle watched the rain. It was to be a day of rain ... There could be no stopping it.

Even before the dawn, hours before, when the Grey Scrubbers were polishing the walls of the stone kitchen, and the Raft Makers were putting the finishing touches to the raft of chestnut boughs, and the stable boys, by the light of lanterns, were grooming the horses, it was obvious that there was a change in the Castle. It was the Greatest Day. And it rained. It was obvious, this change, in many ways, most superficially of all, in the visual realm, for all wore sacking. Every mortal one. Sacking dyed in the hot blood of eagles. On this day there could be no one, no one save Titus, exempted from the immemorial decree – 'That the Castle shall wear sacking on the Earling day.'

Steerpike had officiated at the distribution of the garments under the direction of Barquentine. He was getting to know a great deal about the more obscure and legendary rites. It was in his mind to find himself on Barquentine's decease the leading, if not the sole authority in matters of ritual and observance. In any event, the subject fascinated him. It was potential.

'Curse!' he muttered, as he woke to the sound of rain. But still, what did it matter? It was the future that he had his eyes on. A year ahead. Five years ahead. In the meantime, 'all aboard for glory!'

Mrs Slagg was up early and had put her sacking garment on at once in deference to the sacrosanct convention. It was a pity that she could not wear her hat with the glass grapes, but of course, on the day of the Earling, no one wore hats. A servant had brought in, the night before, the stone which Titus was to hold in his left hand, the ivy branch which he was to carry in his right, and the necklace of snail-shells for his little neck. He was still asleep, and Nannie was ironing the white linen smock which would reach his ankles. It was blanched to a quality as of white light. Nannie fingered it as though it were gossamer.

'So it's come to this.' Nannie was talking to herself. 'So it's come to this. The tiniest thing in the world to be an Earl today. *Today!* Oh, my weak heart, how cruel they are to make a tiny thing have such responsiverity! Cruel. Cruel. It isn't righteousness! No, it isn't. But he *is*. He *is* the Earl, the naughty mite. The only one – and no one can say he isn't. Oh, my poor heart! they've never been to see him. It's only *now* they want to see him because the day has come.'

Her miniature screwed-up face was skirmishing with tears. Her mouth worked itself in and out of its own dry wrinkles between every sentence. 'They expect him to come, the new little Earl, for their homage and everything, but it's me who baths him and gets him ready, and irons out his white smock, and gives him his breakfast. But they won't think of all that – and then ... and then ...' (Nannie suddenly sat down on the edge of a chair and began to cry) 'they'll take him away from me. Oh, justlessness – and I'll be all alone – all alone to die ... and –'

'I'll be with you,' said Fuchsia from the door. 'And they won't take him away from you. Of course, they won't.'

Nannie Slagg ran up to her and clung to her arm. 'They *will*!' she cried. 'Your huge mother said she would. She *said* she would.'

'Well, they haven't taken *me* away, have they?' said Fuchsia.

'But you're only a girl!' cried Nannie Slagg louder than ever.

'You don't matter. You're not going to be anything.'

Fuchsia dislodged the old woman's hand and walked heavily to the window. The rain poured down. It poured down.

The voice behind her went on: 'As though I haven't poured my love out every day – every day. I've poured it all away until I'm hollowed out. It's always me. It always has been. Toil after toil. Moil after moil; with no one to say "God bless you". No one to understand.'

Fuchsia could stand it no longer. Much as she loved her nurse, she could not hear that melancholy, peevish voice and watch the doleful rain and keep herself calm. Unless she left the room she would break something – the nearest breakable thing. She turned and ran, and in her own room once more, fell upon her bed, the skirt of a sacking costume rucked up about her thighs.

*

Of the Castle's countless breakfasts that dark morning there were few that tasted well. The steady monotone of the pattering rain was depressing enough, but for it to descend on such a day was sheer gloom. It was as though it defied the Castle's inmost faith; taunted it with a dull, ignorant descent of blasphemy, as though the undrainable clouds were muttering: 'What is an Earling to us? It is immaterial.'

It was well that there was much to do before the hour of twelve, and there were few who were not occupied with some task or another relevant to the Day. The great kitchen was in an uproar of activity before eight o'clock had struck.

The new chef was in great contrast to the old; a bow-legged, mule-faced veteran of the ovens, with a mouthful of brass teeth and tough, dirty grey hair. His head appeared to sprout the stuff rather than grow it. There was something ferocious about it. In the kitchen it was said that he had his head cropped every other day – indeed, there were some who held that they had seen it on the move at the speed of the minute hand of a great clock.

Out of his mule face and from between the glintings of his

486

teeth a slow, resonant voice would make its way from time to time. But he was not communicative, and for the most part gave his orders by means of gesturing with his heavy hands.

The activities in the great kitchen, where everything relating to the preparation of food in all its aspects seemed to be going on at the same moment, and where the heat was beginning to make the stone hall sweat, were not, in fact, being pursued in readiness for this Day of Earling, but for the morrow; for, alongside the sartorial beggary went a mendicant's diet, the figures of sacking having only crusts to eat until the next day dawned, when, once more in their own clothes, the symbolic humility in the presence of the new Earl of Gormenghast over, they were able to indulge in a barbecue that rivalled that on the day of Titus' birth.

The kitchen staff, man and boy, and the entire servantage in all its forms and both its sexes, were to be ready at half-past eleven to troop down to Gormenghast Lake, where the trees would be in readiness for them.

The carpenters had been working at the lakeside and among the branches for the last three days. In the cedars had been erected the wooden platforms which had for twenty-two years been leaning against a midnight wall in the depths of the ale vaults. Strangely shaped areas of battened planking, like fragments from an immense jig-saw pattern. They had had to be strengthened, for twenty-two years in the unhealthy cellars had not improved them, and they had, of course, to be repainted – white. Each weirdly outlined platform was so shaped that it might fit perfectly in place among the cedar branches. The varying eccentricities of the trees had many hundreds of years ago been the subject of careful study, so that at all the future Earlings the stages, so ingeniously devised, might be slipped into place with the minimum of difficulty. On the back of each wooden stage was written the name of the tree for which it was constructed and the height of the platform from the ground, so that there would be no confusion.

There were four of these wooden inventions, and they were now in place. The four cedars to which they belonged were all thigh deep in the lake, and against the great boles of these trees

487

ladders were erected which sloped across the shallow water from the shore to a foot or so below the level of the platforms. Similar but ruder structures were wedged in among the branches of ash and beech, and where possible among the closely growing larches and pines. On the opposite side of the lake, where the aunts had paddled from the sand to the dripping Steerpike, the trees were set too far back from the water's edge to afford the necessary vantage; but in the densely wooded hangar were a thousand boughs among the convolutions of which the menials could find themselves some kind of purchase or another.

A yew tree in a clearing, rather farther back from the water than the rest of the inhabited trees, had the wedge-faced poet as its guest. A great piece had been torn from its side, and in the cleft the rain bubbled and the naked flesh of the tree was crimson. The rain fell almost vertically in the breathless air, stippling the grey lake. It was as though its white, glass texture of yesterday was now composed of a different substance – of grey sandpaper – a vast granulated sheet of it. The platforms ran with films of the rain. The leaves dripped and splashed in the films. The sand on the opposite shore was sodden. The Castle was too far to be seen through the veil of endless water. There was no individual cloud to be seen. It was a grey sky, unbroken, from which the melancholy strings descended.

The day drew on, minute after raining minute; hour after raining hour, until the trees of the steep hanger were filled with figures. They were to be found on practically every branch that was strong enough to support them. A great oak was filled with the kitchen staff. A beech, with the gardeners, Pentecost sitting majestically in the main dividing fork of the slippery trunk. The stable lads were perching themselves precariously among the branches of a dead walnut and, cat-calling and whistling, were pulling each other's hair at every opportunity or kicking out with their feet. For every tree or group of trees, its trade or status.

Only a few officials moved about at the water's edge, awaiting the arrival of the principal figures. Only a few *officials* among the trees, but on the further shore, and along the strip of dark sand, there was gathered a great congregation. It stood in complete silence. Old men, old women, and clusters of strange striplings. There was about them a complete silence. They were apart. They were the Mud Dwellers – the denizens of the Outer Wall – the forgotten people – the Bright Carvers.

There was a woman by the shore. She stood a little apart from a group. Her face was young and it was old: the structure youthful, the expression, broken by time – the bane of the Dwellers. In her arms was an infant with flesh like alabaster.

The rain came down on all. It was warm rain. Warm melancholy and perpetual. It laved the little alabaster body of the child and still it laved it. There was no ending, and the great lake swelled. In the high branches of the dead walnut tree the whistling and scuffling had ceased, for horses were moving through the conifers of the adjacent shore. They had reached the water's edge and were being tethered to the low sweeping arms of the cedars.

On the first horse, a great grey hunter by any normal standard, was seated, side-saddle, the Countess. She had been hidden among leaves, only the horse showing itself; but immediately she became exposed to view her mount became a pony.

The symbolic sacking hung about her in vast, dripping folds. Behind her, a roan bore Fuchsia, with her legs astride. She was patting its neck as she came through the trees. It was like patting soaked velvet. Its black mane was like a repetition of Fuchsia's hair. Lank with the rain, it clung to the forehead and the throat.

The aunts were in a pony trap. That they were not in purple seemed extraordinary. Their dresses had always been as indigenous and inevitable a part of them as their faces. They seemed uncomfortable in the sacking and kept plucking at it with their limp hands. The thin man who led the pony brought it to a halt at the lake side, and at the same moment another trap, of similar design but painted a dark and unpleasant orange, trundled through the pines, and there was Mrs Slagg, sitting as upright as she could, her proud attitude (as she supposed it) nullified by the terrified look of her face, which protruded like

some kind of wizened fruit from the coarse folds of the garment. She could remember the Earling of Sepulchrave. He had
been in his teens. He had swum out to the raft, and there had
been no rain. But – oh, her poor heart! – this was so different. It
would never have rained at an 'Earling' when she was a young
girl. Things were so different then.

On her lap was Titus – drenched. Even so the smock she had
been so carefully ironing looked miraculously white, as though
it gave forth light instead of receiving it. He sucked his thumb
as he stared about him. He saw the figures peering down at him
from the trees. He did not smile: he simply stared, turning his
face from one to another. Then he became interested in a golden
bangle which the Countess had sent him the same morning,
pulling it as far up his arm as he could, then down to his plump,
wrinkled wrist, studying it seriously all the while.

The Doctor and his sister had a sycamore to themselves. Irma
took some time being hoisted, and was not at all happy about
the whole business. She disliked having her hips wedged between rough branches even in the cause of symbolism. The
Doctor, seated a little above her, looked like some form of bird,
possibly a plucked crane.

Steerpike had followed Nannie Slagg in order to impress the
crowd. Although he should have been in a pine-for-four, he
now selected a small ash, where he could both be seen and could
see with equal advantage to himself and the rest of Gormenghast.

The Twins were keeping their mouths tightly shut. They repeated to themselves every thought as it occurred to them, to
find whether the word 'fire' could possibly have crept into it,
and when they found it hadn't, they decided in any event to
keep it to themselves, in order to be on the safe side. Thus it
was that they had not spoken a word since Steerpike left them
in their bedroom. They were still white, but not so horribly so.
The breath of a yellow reflection had infiltrated itself into their
skin and this was nasty enough. Nothing could have been more
truly spoke than when Steerpike (as Death) had cried that he
would be forever with them. They held each other tightly as
they waited to be helped from the trap, for Death had not left

them since that curdling night and his livid skull was before their eyes.

By well-proportioned mixtures of brute-strength and obsequious delicacy the officials had at last established the Countess Gertrude upon her stage in the enormous swarthy boughs of the cedar tree. A red carpet had been spread over the woodwork of the platform. The waders and lakeside birds of many breeds which had been disturbed by the activities of the Day, after flying distractedly hither and thither over the forest in swarms, had, as soon as the Countess was seated in the enormous wicket-work chair, flocked to her tree, in which they settled. Angling and disputing for positions at her feet and over various parts of her accommodating body were a whitethroat, a fieldfare, a willow-wren, a nuthatch, a tree-pipit, a sand martin, a red-backed shrike, a goldfinch, a yellow bunting, two jays, a greater spotted woodpecker, three moorhens (on her lap with a mallard, a woodcock, and a curlew), a wagtail, four missel thrushes, six blackbirds, a nightingale and twenty-seven sparrows.

They fluttered themselves, sending sprays of varying dimensions according to their wing-spans through the dripping air. There was more shelter beneath the cedars with their great out-stretched hands spread one above the other in dark-green, dripping terraces, than was the case for those in alternative vegetation.

At this extreme the stable boys in the top branches of the walnut might as well have been sitting in the lake, they could not have been wetter.

It was the same for the Dwellers on the shore – that proud, impoverished congregation. They cast no reflection in the water at their feet – it was too triturated by the pricking of the rain.

Getting Barquentine established on his stage was the trickiest and most unpleasant task which fell to the lot of the officials. It took place to the accompaniment of such hideous swearing as caused his withered leg to blush beneath the sacking. It must have been hardened by many years of oaths, but this morning an awakened sense of shame at what the upper part of the body could *descend* too, raddled it from hip to toe. Its only consolation was that the contaminating influence had not descended lower than the lungs, and what diseases the withered leg experienced were entirely physical.

When he was seated on the high-backed 'Earling' chair he pushed his crutch irritably beneath it and then began to wring out his beard. Fuchsia was by now in her cedar. She had one to herself and it was comparatively dry, a thick foliage spreading immediately above the stage – and she was gazing across the water at the Dwellers. What was it about them that quickened her – those people of the Outer Wall? Why did she feel ill at ease? It was as though they held a dark secret of which, one day, they would make use; something which would jeopardize the security of the Castle. But they were powerless. They depended upon the grace of Gormenghast. What could they do? Fuchsia noticed a woman standing a little apart from a group. Her feet were in the lake. In her arms she held a child. It seemed, as Fuchsia watched, that she could see for a quick moment the dark strands of rain through the limbs of the child. She rubbed her eyes and again she stared. It was so far. She could not tell.

Even the officials had climbed into the ivy-throttled elm with its broken limb that hung by a sapless tendon.

The Aunts, on the fourth of the cedar stages, shivered, their mouths tightly closed. Death sat with them and they could not concentrate on the procedure.

Barquentine had started, his old voice grating its way through the warm downpour. It could be heard everywhere, for no one noticed the sound of the rain any more. It had been so monotonous for so long that it had become inaudible. Had it stopped suddenly the silence would have been like a blow.

Steerpike was watching Fuchsia through the branches. She would be difficult, but it was only a matter of careful planning. He must not hurry it. Step by step. He knew her temperament. Simple – painfully simple; inclined to be passionate over ridiculous things; headstrong – but a girl, nevertheless, and easy to frighten or to flatter; absurdly loyal to the few friends she had; but mistrust could always be sown quite easily. Oh, so pain-

fully simple! That was the crux of it. There was Titus, of course
– but what were problems for if not to be solved. He sucked at
his hollow tooth.

Prunesquallor had wiped his glasses for the twentieth time
and was watching Steerpike watching Fuchsia. He was not
listening to Barquentine, who was rattling off the catechismic
monody as fast as he could, for he was suffering the first twinges
of rheumatism.

'... and will forever hold in sacred trust the castle of his
fathers and the domain adhering thereto. That he will in letter
and in spirit defend it in every way against the incursions of
alien worlds. That he will observe its sacred rites, honour its
crest, and in due time instil into the first male of his loins,
reverence for its every stone until among his fathers he has
added, in the tomb, his link to the unending chain of Groans.
So be it.'

Barquentine wiped the water from his face with the flat of his
hand and wrung out his beard again. Then he fumbled for his
crutch and hoisted himself on to his leg. With his free arm he
pushed aside a branch and screamed down through the branches:

'Are you skulks ready?'

The two Raftmen were ready. They had taken Titus from
Nannie Slagg and were standing on the raft of chestnut boughs
at the lake's edge. Titus was sitting at their feet in the middle of
the raft, the size of a doll. His sepia hair was stuck to his face
and neck. His violet eyes were a little startled. His white smock
clung to him so that the form of his little body was divulged.

The clinging cloth was luminous.

'Push off, curse you! Push off!' yelled Barquentine. His voice
raked the water's surface east to west.

With a long, gradual shoving of their poles the two men propelled the raft into deeper water. Moving up either side of the
raft and plunging their poles a dozen or so times brought them
near the centre of the lake. In a leather bag hung at his waist
the older of the two Raftmen had the symbolic stone, ivy branch
and necklace of snail-shells. The water was now too deep for
them to strike bottom and they dived over the side and, turning,
clasped the edge of the raft. Then, striking out, frog-like with

their legs, they had soon brought the raft to the approximate position.

'More to the west!' screamed Barquentine from the shore. 'More to the west, idiots!'

The swimmers splashed themselves around to the adjacent edge of the raft and once more began to kick out. Then they lifted their heads from the rain-prodded water and stared in the direction of Barquentine's voice.

'Hold!' yelled the unpleasant voice. 'And hide your damned selves!'

The two men worked their way around until their heads were very nearly obscured by the thick chestnut rim of the raft on the far side from the trees.

With only their faces bobbing above the surface they trod water. Titus was alone. He stared about him, bewildered. Where was everybody? The rain streamed over him. His features began to pucker and his lips to tremble, and he was about to burst into tears when he changed his mind and decided to stand up instead. The raft had become quite still and he kept his balance.

Barquentine grunted to himself. This was good. Ideally speaking, the prospective Earl should be on his feet while being named. In the case of Titus this tenet would naturally have had to be waived if the infant had decided to keep seated or to crawl about.

'Tiuts Groan,' cried the ancient voice from the shore, 'the Day has come! The Castle awaits your sovereignty. From horizon to horizon all is yours, to hold in trust – animal, vegetable and mineral, time without end, save for your single death that cannot stem a tide of such illustrious Blood.'

This was the Raftsmen's cue, and clambering over the side they placed the necklace of snails around the little wet neck, and as the voice from the shore cried, 'Now!' attempted to place in Titus's hands the stone and the ivy branch.

But he would not hold them.

'Hell's blood and gallstones!' screamed Barquentine, 'what's the matter? Rot your hides! what's the matter? Give him his stone and ivy, curse you!'

They opened his little fingers with difficulty and placed the symbols against his palms, but he snatched his hands away from them. He would not hold the things.

Barquentine was beside himself. It was as though the child had a mind of its own. He smote the stage with his crutch and spat with fury. There was not one, either, among the dripping trees or along the strip of bubbling sand – not one whose eyes were not fixed on Titus.

The men on the raft were helpless.

'Fools! fools! fools!' came the hideous voice through the rain. 'Leave them at his feet, curse your black guts! Leave them at his feet! Oh, body of me, take your damned heads away!'

The two men slipped back into the water, cursing the old man. They had left the stone and the ivy branch on the raft at the child's feet.

Barquentine knew that the Earling was to be completed by noon: it was decreed in the old tomes and was Law. There was barely a minute to go.

He swung his bearded head to left and right. 'Your Ladyship, the Countess Gertrude of Gormenghast! Your Ladyship Fuchsia of Gormenghast! Their Ladyships Cora and Clarice Groan of Gormenghast! Arise!'

Barquentine crutched himself forward on the slippery stage until he was within a few inches of the edge. There was no time to lose.

'Gormenghast will now watch! And listen! It is the Moment!'

He cleared his throat and began and could not stop, for there was no time left. But as he cried the traditional words, his finger-nails were splintering into the oakwood of his crutch and his face had become purple. The huge beads of sweat on his brow were lilac, for the colour of his congested head burned through them.

'In the sight of all! In the sight of the Castle's Southern wing, in the sight of Gormenghast mountain, and in the sacred sight of your forefathers of the Blood, I, Warden of the Immemorial Rites proclaim you, on this day of Earling, to be the Earl, the only legitimate Earl between heaven and earth, from skyline to skyline – Titus, the Seventy-seventh Lord of Gormenghast.'

A hush most terrible and unearthly had spread and settled over the lake, over the woods and towers and over the world. Stillness had come like a shock, and now that the shock was dying, only the white emptiness of silence remained. For while the concluding words were being cried in a black anger, two things had occurred. The rain had ceased and Titus had sunk to his knees and had begun to crawl to the raft's edge with a stone in one hand and an ivy branch in the other. And then, to the horror of all, had dropped the sacrosanct symbols into the depths of the lake.

In the brittle, pricking silence that followed, a section of delicate blue sky broke free from the murk of the clouds above him, and he rose to his feet and, turning to the dark multitude of the Dwellers, approached in little careful paces to the edge of the raft that faced the side of the lake where they were gathered. His back was turned to Barquentine, to the Countess his mother, and to all who stared transfixed at the only moving thing in the porcelain silence.

Had a branch broken in any one of the thousand trees that surrounded the water, or had a cone fallen from a pine, the excruciating tension would have snapped. Not a branch broke. Not a cone fell.

In the arms of the woman by the shore the strange child she held began to struggle with a strength that she could not understand. It had reached outward from her breast, outward, over the lake; and as it did so the sky began to blossom in azure and Titus, at the edge of the raft, tore at his necklace with such force that he found it loose in his hands. Then he lifted his head and his single cry froze the multitude that watched him on every side, for it was neither a cry of tears nor of joy; nor was it fear, or even pain – it was a cry that for all its shrillness was unlike the voice of a child. And as he cried he swung the necklace across the sparkling water; and as it sank a rainbow curved over Gormenghast and a voice answered him.

A tiny voice. In the absolute stillness it filled the universe – a cry like the single note of a bird. It floated over the water from the Dwellers, from where the woman stood apart from her kind; from the throat of the little child of Keda's womb – the bastard babe, and Titus' foster-sister, lambent with ghost-light.

MR ROTTCODD AGAIN

THE while, beneath the downpour and the sunbeams, the Castle hollow as a tongueless bell, its corroded shell dripping or gleaming with the ephemeral weather, arose in immemorial defiance of the changing airs, and skies. These were but films of altering light and hue: sunbeam shifting into moonbeam; the wafted leaf into the wafted snow; the musk into a tooth of icicle. These but the transient changes on its skin: each hour a pulse the more – a shade the less: a lizard basking and a robin frozen.

Stone after grey stone climbed. Windows yawned: shields, scrolls, and legendary mottoes, melancholy in their ruin, protruded in worn relief over arches or doorways; along the sills of casements, in the walls of towers or carved in buttresses. Storm-nibbled heads, their shallow faces striated with bad green and draped with creepers, stared blindly through the four quarters, from between broken eyelids.

Stone after grey stone; and a sense of the heaving skywards of great blocks, one upon another in a climbing weight, ponderous and yet alive with the labour of dead days. Yet, at the same time, *still*; while sparrows, like insects, flickered in wastes of ivy. Still, as though paralysed by its own weight, while about it the momentary motions fluttered and died: a leaf falling: a bull-frog croaking from the moat, or an owl on wings of wool floating earthwards in slow gyres.

Was there something about these vertical acres of stone that mouthed of a stillness that was more complete, a silence that lay *within*, and drummed. Small winds rustled on the castle's outer shell; leaves dropped away or were brushed by a bird's wing; the rain ceased and creepers dripped – but *within* the walls not even the light changed, save when the sun broke through and a series of dusty halls in the southern wing. Remoteness.

For *all* were at the 'Earling'. Around the lakeside was the Castle's breath. Only the old stone lung remained. Nor a footfall. Not a voice. Only wood, and stone, and doorway, bannister, corridor and alcove, room after room, hall after hall, province after province.

It was as though, at any moment some inanimate Thing must surely move; a door open upon its own, or a clock start whirling its hands: the stillness was too vast and charged to be content to remain in this titanic atrophy – the tension must surely find a vent – and burst suddenly, violently, like a reservoir of water from a smashed dam – and the shields fall from their rusty hooks, the mirrors crack, the boards lift and open and the very castle tremble, shake its walls like wings; yawn, split and crumble with a roar.

But nothing happened. Each hall a mouth that gaped and could not close. The stone jaws prised and aching. The doors like eye-teeth missing from the bone! There was no sound and nothing human happened.

What moved in these great caves? A shifting shadow? Only where sunlight through the south wing wandered. What else? No other movement?

Only the deathly padding of the cats. Only the soundlessness of the dazed cats – the line of them – the undulating line as blanched as linen, and lorn as the long gesture of a hand.

Where, in the wastes of the forsaken castle, spellbound with stone lacunas – where could they find their way? From hush to hush. All was unrooted. Life, bone and breath; echo and movement gone. . . .

They flowed. Noiselessly and deliberately they flowed. Through doors ajar they flowed on little feet. The stream of them. The cats.

Under the welkin of the flaking cherubs doming through shade, they ran. The pillars narrowing in chill perspective formed them their mammoth highway. The refectory opened up its tracts of silence. Over the stones they ran. Along a corridor of fissured plaster. Room after hollow room – hall after hall, gallery after gallery, depth after depth, until the acres of grey kitchen opened. The chopping blocks, the ovens and grills, stood motionless as altars to the dead. Far below the warped beams they flowed in a white band. There was no hesitation in their drift. The tail of the white line had disappeared, and the kitchen was as barren as a cave in a lunar hillside. They were swarming up cold stairs to other lands.

Where has she gone? Through the drear sub-light of a thousand yawns, they ran, their eyes like moons. Up winding stairs to other worlds again, threading the noonday dusk. And they could find no pulse and she was gone.

Yet there was no cessation. League after league, the swift, unhurried padding. The pewter room slid by, the bronze room and the iron. The armoury slid by on either side – the passageways slid by – on either side – and they could find no breath in Gormenghast.

The doorway of the Hall of the Bright Carvings was ajar. As they slid through the opening it was as though a long, snow-soft serpent had appeared, its rippling body sown with yellow eyes. Without a pause it streamed among the carvings lifting hundreds of little dust clouds from the floor. It reached the hammock at the shuttered end, where, like a continuation of silence and stillness in a physical form, dozed the curator, the only living thing in the castle apart from the feline snake that was flooding past him and was even now on its way back to the door. Above it, the coloured carvings smouldered. The golden mule – the storm-grey child – the wounded head with locks of chasmic purple.

Rottcodd dozed on, entirely unaware, not only that his sanctum had been invaded by her ladyship's cats, but unaware also that the castle was empty below him and that it was the day of the Earling. No one had told him of the Earl's disappearance for no one had climbed to the dusty Hall since Mr Flay's last visit.

When he awoke, he felt hungry. Hauling up the shutters of the window he noticed that the rain had stopped, and as far as he could judge from the position of the sun it was well into the afternoon. Yet nothing had been sent up for him in the miniature lift from the Kitchen, forty fathoms below. This was unheard of. It was so new an idea that his food should not be awaiting him that for the moment he could not be certain that he was awake. Perhaps he was dreaming that he had left his hammock.

He shook the cord that disappeared into the black well. Faintly he could hear the bell jangling far beneath. Remote as was the thin, metal sound, it seemed that it was much clearer today, than he ever remembered it to have been before. It was as though it were the only thing in motion. As though it had no other sound to contend with, not so much as the buzzing of a fly upon a pane – it jangled in so solitary a way, so distinct and so infinitely far. He waited, but nothing happened. He lifted the end of the cord for the second time and let it fall. Once more, as though from a city of forsaken tombs, a bell rang. Again he waited. Again nothing happened.

In deep and agitated thought he returned to the window which was so seldom open, passing beneath the glimmering chandeliers. Accustomed as he was to silence, there was something unique today about the emptiness. Something both close and insistent. And as he pondered he became aware of a sense of instability – a sensation almost of fear – as though some ethic he had never questioned, something on which whatever he believed was founded and through which his every concept filtered was now threatened. As though, somewhere, there was *treason*. Something unhallowed, menacing, and ruthless in its disregard for the fundamental premises of *loyalty* itself. What could be thought to count, or have even the meanest kind of value in action or thought if the foundations on which his house of belief was erected was found to be sinking and imperilling the sacrosanct structure it supported.

It could not be. For what *could* change. He fingered his chin and shot a hard, beady glance out of the window. Behind him the long, adumbrate Hall of the Bright Carvings glimmered beneath the suspended chandeliers. Here and there, a shoulder or a cheek bone or a fin or a hoof burned green or indigo, crimson or lemon in the gloom. His hammock swung a little.

Something had gone wrong. Even had his dinner been sent up

the shaft to him in the normal way he must still have felt that there was something wrong. This silence was of another kind. It was portentous.

He turned his thoughts over, tortuously and his eyes, losing for a moment their beady look, wandered over the scene below him. A little to his left and about fifty feet beneath his window was a table-land of drab roof around the margin of which were turrets grey with moss, set about three feet apart from one another. There were many scores of them, and as his eyes meandered over the monotonous outline he jerked his head forwards and his focus was no longer blurred, for he had suddenly realized that every turret was surmounted by a cat, and every cat had its head thrust forwards, and that every cat, as white as a plume, was peering through slit eyes at something moving – something moving far below on the narrow, sand-coloured path which led from the castle's outhouses to the northern woods.

Mr Rottcodd, gauging by the converging stares of the turreted cats, what area of distant earth to scan, for with such motionless and avid concentration in every snow-lit form and yellow eye, there must surely be a spectacle of peculiar interest below them, he was able within a few moments to discover, moving toy-like, from the woods, a cavalcade of the stone castle's core.

Toy horses led. Mr Rottcodd, who had long sight but who could hardly tell how many fingers he held up before his own face save by the apprehension of the digits themselves, removed his glasses. The blurred figures, so far below his window, threading their way through sunlight, no longer swam, but, starting into focus, startled him. What had happened? As he asked himself the question, he knew the answer. That no one had thought fit to tell him! No one! It was a bitter pill for him to swallow. He had been forgotten. Yet he had always wished to be forgotten. He could not have it both ways.

He stared: and there was no mistaking. Each figure was tiny but crystal clear in the rain-washed atmosphere. The cradle-saddled horse that led the throng: the child whom he had never glimpsed before, asleep, one arm along the cradle's rim. Asleep on the day of his 'Earling'. Rottcodd winced. It was Titus. So

Sepulchrave had died and he had never known. They had been to the lake; to the lake; and there below him on a slow grey mare was borne along the path – the Seventy-seventh.

Leading the mare by a bridle was a youth he had not seen before. His shoulders were high and the sun shone on a rounded forehead. Over the back of the mare, beneath the saddle-cradle, and hanging almost to the ground, there was hung a gold embroidered carpet riddled with moth holes.

With Titus in the cradle was tied a cardboard crown, a short sword in a sky-blue scabbard and a book, the parchment leaves of which he was creasing with his little sprawling thighs. He was fast asleep.

Behind him, riding side-saddle, came the Countess, her hair like a pin-head of fire. She made no movement as her mount paced on. Then Mr Rottcodd noticed Fuchsia. Her back very straight and her hands loose upon the rein. Then the Aunts in their trap, whom Mr Rottcodd found it difficult to recognize for all the uniqueness of their posture, shed as they were of their purple. He noticed Barquentine, whom he took for Sourdust, his dead father, jabbing his crutch into his horse's flank, and then Nannie Slagg alone in her conveyance, her hands at her mouth and a stable boy at the pony's. As vanguard to the pedestrians came the Prunesquallors, Irma's arm through her brother's followed by Pentecost and the wedge-faced poet. But who was that mule-headed and stocky man who slouched between them, and where was Swelter the chef, and where was Flay? Following Pentecost, but at a respectful distance, ambled the rank and file – the innumerable menials which the far forest momently disgorged.

To see, after so long a while, the figureheads of the castle pass below him – distant as they were – was, to Rottcodd in his hall of the Bright Carvings, a thing both of satisfaction and of pain. Satisfaction because the ritual of Gormenghast was proceeding as sacredly and deliberately as ever before, and pain because of his new sense of flux, which, inexplicable and irrational as it appeared on the surface, was, nevertheless, something which poisoned his mind and quickened his heart-beat. An intuitive sense of danger which, although in its varying forms and to varying degrees had made itself felt among those who lived below – had not, until this morning disturbed the dusty and sequestered atmosphere in which it had been Mr Rottcodd's lot to doze away his life.

Sepulchrave dead? And a new Earl – a child not two years old? Surely the very stones of the castle would have passed the message up, or the Bright Carvings have mouthed the secret to him. From the toyland of figures and horses and paths and trees and rocks and from the glimpse of a green reflection in the lake the size of a stamp, arose, of a sudden, the cry of an old voice, cruel, even in its remoteness, and then the silence of the figures moving on, broken by an occasional minutiae of sound as of a tin-tack falling on a brick, as a hoof struck a stone; a bridle creaked with the voice of a gnat, and Rottcodd stared from his eyrie as the figures moved on and on towards the base of the Castle, each with a short black shadow sewn to its heels. The terrain about them was as though freshly painted, or rather, as though like an old landscape that had grown dead and dull it had been varnished and now shone out anew, each fragment of the enormous canvas, pristine, the whole, a glory.

The leading mare with Titus on her back, still fast asleep in the wickerwork saddle, was by now approaching that vaster shadow, cast by the Castle itself, which fanned itself out prodigiously, like a lake of morose water from the base of the stone walls.

The line of figures was stretched out in an attenuate sweep, for even now with the head of the procession beneath the walls, the far copses by the lake were still being emptied. Rottcodd switched his eyes back for a moment to the white cats – each on its grey-moss turret. He could see now that they were not merely staring at the group, as before, but towards a certain section of the line, towards the head of the line, where rode the silent Countess. Their bodies were no longer motionless. They were shuddering in the sun; and as Mr Rottcodd turned his pebbly eyes away, and peered at the figurettes below (the three largest of whom might have been fitted into the paw of the most distant of the cats, who were themselves a good fifty feet below Rottcodd), he was forced to return his gaze at once to the heraldic malkins, for they had sent forth in unison from their quivering bodies a siren-like, and most unearthly cry.

The long, dusty hall behind Mr Rottcodd seemed to stretch away into the middle distance, for with its lethal silence reaffirmed by that cry from the outer world, its area appeared to expand and a desert land was at his shoulder blades; and beyond the far door, and under the boards in the halls below, and beneath them stretching on either hand where mute stairs climbed or wound, the brooding castle yawned.

The Countess had reined in her horse and lifted her head. For a moment she moved her eyes across the face of the precipice that overhung her. And then she pursed her mouth and a note like the note of a reed, shrill and forlorn, escaped her.

The turrets of grey moss were suddenly tenantless. Like white streams of water, like cascades, the cats sped earthwards down the mountainous and sickening face of stone. Rottcodd, unable to realize how they had so suddenly melted into nothing like snow in the sun, was amazed to see, when he transferred his eyes from the empty tableland of roof, to the landscape below him, a small cloud moving rapidly across a field of tares. The cloud slowed its speed and swarmed, and as the Countess jogged her slow mount forwards, it was as though it paddled in a white mist, fetlock deep, that clung about the progress of the hooves.

Titus awoke as the mare which bore him entered the Castle's shadow. He knelt in his basket, his hair black with the morning's rain and clinging snake-like about his neck and shoulders. His hands clasped the edge of the saddle-cradle before him. His drenched and glittering smock had become grey as he passed into the deep, water-like darkness where the mare was wading. One by one the tiny figures lost their toy-like brilliance and were swallowed. The hair of the Countess was quenched like an ember in that sullen bay. The feline cloud at her feet was now a smoke-grey mist. One by one, the bright shapes moved into the shadow and were drowned.

Rottcodd turned from the window. The carvings were there. The dust was there. The chandeliers threw their weak light. The carvings smouldered. But everything had changed. Was this the hall that Rottcodd had known for so long? It was ominous.

And then, as he stood quite still, his hands clasped about the handle of the feather duster, the air about him quickened, and there was *another* change, *another* presence in the atmosphere. Somewhere, something had been shattered – something heavy as a great globe and brittle like glass; and it had been shattered, for the air swam freely and the tense, aching weight of the emptiness with its insistent drumming had lifted. He had heard nothing but he knew that he was no longer alone. The castle had drawn breath.

He returned to his hammock – strangely glad and strangely perplexed. He lay down, one hand behind his head, the other trailing over the side of the hammock in the cords of which he could feel the purring of a sentient Castle. He closed his eyes. How, he wondered, had Lord Sepulchrave died? Mr Flay had said nothing about his being ill. But that was long ago. How long ago? With a start, which caused him to open his eyes he realized that it was over a year since the thin man had brought the news of Titus's birth. He could remember it all so clearly. The way his knees had clicked. His eye at the keyhole. His nervousness. For Mr Flay had been his most recent visitor. Could it be that, for more than a year he had seen no living soul?

Mr Rottcodd ran his eyes along the wooden back of a dappled otter. Anything might have happened during that year. And again he experienced an acute uneasiness. He shifted his body in the hammock. But what *could* have happened? What could have happened? He clicked his tongue.

The Castle was breathing, and far below the Hall of the Bright Carvings all that was Gormenghast revolved. After the emptiness it was like tumult through him; though he had heard no sound. And yet, by now, there would be doors flung open; there would be echoes in the passageways, and quick lights flickering along the walls.

Through honeycombs of stone would now be wandering the passions in their clay. There would be tears and there would be strange laughter. Fierce births and deaths beneath umbrageous ceilings. And dreams, and violence, and disenchantment.

And there shall be a flame-green daybreak soon. And love itself will cry for insurrection! For tomorrow is also a day – and Titus has entered his stronghold.

BY MERVYN PEAKE
ALSO AVAILABLE IN VINTAGE

☐	Gormenghast	074939482X	£7.99
☐	The Gormenghast Trilogy	0099288893	£15.00
☐	Mr Pye	0099283263	£7.99
☐	Titus Alone	0749394870	£7.99

FREE POST AND PACKING
Overseas customers allow £2.00 per paperback

BY PHONE: 01624 677237

BY POST: Random House Books
C/o Bookpost, PO Box 29, Douglas
Isle of Man, IM99 1BQ

BY FAX: 01624 670923

BY EMAIL: bookshop@enterprise.net

Cheques (payable to Bookpost) and credit cards accepted

Prices and availability subject to change without notice.
Allow 28 days for delivery.
When placing your order, please mention if you do not wish to receive
any additional information.

www.randomhouse.co.uk/vintage